Freya North

SALLY

CHLOE

This edition published in 2000 by Cresset Editions,
an imprint of The Random House Group Ltd,
20 Vauxhall Bridge Road, London SW1V 2SA

Sally first published in 1996 by William Heinemann
Chloë first published in 1997 by William Heinemann

Printed and bound in Germany

ISBN 0 0918 7202 2

FREYA NORTH

Sally

For BJP

PROLOGUE

She lay there, in a small heaven of sorts.

This is the definitive rampant fling.

She grinned widely, partly because her clitoris was being rubbed, partly because she suddenly envisaged her actions set down in type, immortalized, in a racy best-seller. *I could sell these details to Jackie Collins*, she thought, as her right nipple was being nibbled and her left was being kneaded. *This kind of thing is right up her street.*

Yes, nibbled nipples had a certain titillating ring to it (tit-illating, oh very droll), but would also look good on the printed page. In her mind's eye, she inverted the 'b' and played with the 'p':

bb
pp
ni*bb*led
ni*pp*les

and thought that Jackie C would really rather like them. So, while he left her nipples to traverse her body, she penned a few thoughts.

Dear Ms Collins, this is what happened. No, this is what's happening: I'm lying on my back with my legs wrapped around the back of a most glorious superstud, his 'throbbing manhood', *his* 'enormous dick', *his* 'stupendous cock' *is surging into me. My neck is thrown back and is being licked greedily. This man on top of me has the physique of a Rodin sculpture, Ms Collins, a Rodin sculpture with an insatiable sexual appetite.*

I am grabbing on to a pair of buttocks so firm, so exquisitely honed, that it is only their warmth and a slight fuzz of hair which persuade me they are real and not perfectly hewn marble. We've been going at it, this fast-motion super-bonking, for the best part of two hours, so you see real people really can keep it up (literally).

Hello hello, I am now being flipped over and I am on top, in the driving seat. I am grinding down on him, now I am lifting myself off. Plunge, lunge, down I go again. I think I'll sit upright and throw my head back alluringly – just in case he can see me through those eyes glazed with near-fulfilled desire. He is surging, make that 'pumping'. *He is abandoned to the sensation. And do you know what? I am doing this, I am making him feel this way. He is putty in my hands, but he is hard as a rock inside. A* 'rock-cock' – *now there's a jaunty little phrase for you, Ms C. Oh, up he sits, a moment's tenderness too. Kisses are slower, more lip, less tongue. He's actually rather nice, sweet and gentle, but tonight I want wild and rampant. So, here I go, pushing him down, covering him again. Forget in-out, I'm rotating fluidly and what a pelvis I have! Ten years of ballet had its merits after all. Our legs are so entwined, so taut, that cramp threatens in my left thigh, but a potentially mammoth orgasm is very much on the horizon. Here it comes. Here I come. More more more.*

Yes.

Jesus.

Oh!

Pure bestseller material, that'll be me. I'll give your

previous heroines a run for their money. I'm coming to your rescue, Jackie. Oh!

As the regular throbs racked her body, her brain (which was really quite a good one, having gained a First from Bristol University) was working energetically too.

On second thoughts, Ms Collins will not have this, not for a while at least. No, this will be for me, this shall become my secret, my own touchstone. When I am either a) an aged spinster (she was 25 – the official age, she'd recently read, for spinsterhood to commence) *or b) a good little housewife, cooking and breeding superlatively, then shall I derive much pleasure recounting to myself (be it in a rocking-chair or at a school play), the time I was an outrageous vamp, a shameless slapper, an utterly debauched nympho.*

She came to her conclusion as he came to his. He started to pant raspingly and called out 'Oh my God, oh goddo goddo Goh' with enormous conviction. She felt rather proud of herself.

No, Mister Man, it's 'goddess' actually, oh your goddess. For that is what I shall be. That is who I am for today, and for the times when I shall again allow you to experience such delicious sex with me.

Inadvertently, she gave out a little sigh, one of satisfaction, intellectual rather than physical. It was answered by a sucking kiss from the man whom she straddled. She smiled. He smiled. She smiled again, with ulterior motives. He smiled back, oblivious but ensnared.

Ho ho! So my secret is safe. Look at you, smugly grinning, proud as punch, purely because you think you've taken me to heaven and back. Which you have. But who was it who was in control? I shall strive hard to keep it that way, and I shall strive to keep it hard. I shall not fall in love with this man. I shall not day-dream wistfully of babies and scones baking in an Aga. Nor must you fall in love with me, only lust and long for me until you positively ache. Even if you marry and live in blissful domesticity, you will frequently think of me and surge inside on remembering the joy and liberation of sex with me.

I must, she decided, *become an enigma. Remain one. To everyone, henceforth.* A wave of absolute exhilaration coursed through her. *This is it; this is not a search for self but the creation of it. I shall play and I shall act and I shall have much fun. I shall be the conductor. The baton is in my hand and the balls are in my caught.*

She rushed to the bathroom with Handel's 'Hallelujah Chorus' careering around her head. Predictably, the orgasm had sent urgent messages to her bladder and, sitting in the silence of her bathroom, she contemplated the release of pee versus an orgasm on the pleasure scale. Today, peeing came second. She checked it was really her in the mirror.

Gracious Good Lord! It is me! Sally Lomax, what on earth have you just done?

I've just had rampant sex.

She smiled hugely, winked, said 'Go for it, girl' out loud, and flushed the toilet with triumphant force. The phone had begun to ring. Sally gave herself another beaming smile and then sauntered, positively swaggered, to answer it. It was her mother, officious as ever, voice shrill, no time for a greeting.

'Darling I've been ringing for hours, I thought you'd be busy marking essays?'

'No, I had to be elsewhere, something far more pressing,' Sally said truthfully.

'What?'

Oh, you know how it is, Mum. When there's six foot of beefcake in your bed, more handsome and brawny than in your most incorrigible dreams, great hands, a wonderful mouth and a dick to die for; obviously marking a ten-year old's 'What I did over half term' rather pales into insignificance.

Taking a sharp bite on her tongue, Sally, however, did not speak her mind. My, how she would have relished the ensuing stunned silence of matriarchal disbelief. How she would have loved to have breezed straight on with mundane enquiries about the health of the cat and the younger sisters (in that order). Today, though, decorum won. The ravaged Rodin was diplomatically replaced by an old friend who would have been quite compliant had she known the circumstances (she was, in fact, holidaying in Tunisia).

'Daph is a little low, so I've been with her.'

'Darling, you did remember Aunt Martha's seventieth?'

Sally had forgotten.

'Is blasphemy really necessary? I suggest you phone her right this minute.'

So she did. Sally, sweet Sally; the prettiest of the nieces, the dutiful, good-natured Sally, chatted to Aunt Martha for a full and enjoyable ten minutes. She was careful not to mention her late uncle, and remembered to ask if the cold was causing the dreaded arthritis.

'Arthur Ritus comes to us all in old age, it's to be expected, I'm not one to complain . . .' But she was and she did. Sally ummed, ahhed and tutted at the apposite moments and Aunt Martha, as she hung up the phone, took down the silver-framed photo of her husband and declared to it that Sally was a gem and would make a treasure of a wife.

Sally gazed at the replaced handset.

Do I feel guilty? Should I? For what? For forgetting Aunt Martha's birthday? For lying to my mother? Or for having performed a carnal act of such outrageous proportions? Guilt, show me thy face! I'll give you three seconds!

Right then, off I go, back to my boudoir, quick-change into my doppelgänger, *the temptress, the vixen, the wicked lusting girl. Woman! Hardly a lady, hardly a girl. Today I am suddenly the sort of person I thought I was not and yet today I really feel like Me. Pure and simple, this is who I am.*

She entered her room and any purity simply vanished. She flew on top of the knackered male form and kissed it outrageously with a scheming and very lively tongue.

ONE

Such a lovely girl, what an angel, isn't she wonderful, such a good girl. Sally Lomax was adorable and adored. She was extremely polite, tirelessly friendly, always amiable and genteel. She was chatty and respectful to the elderly and a much-loved teacher of youngsters. She kept herself trim, never let the ends of her hair split and always folded clothes away at the end of a day. She cooked well, cleaned well, and although she could not knit, she made enviable things on her sewing machine. When in her car, a spotless if noisy six-year-old Mini Cooper, she was courteous and never lost her temper, never overtook on the inside and slowed down well in advance of pedestrian crossings – even on a deserted Sunday. Just in case.

When Sally was a child, she was angelic in physique and character. Skin as smooth and opalescent as her prettiest Bakelite doll, features and figure doll-like too, her demeanour open and engaging. Sally at six was altogether flawless, faultless. It was as much a pleasure for her parents to invite ageing relatives for tea, as it was for them to venture out of retirement bungalows to be sung to and danced for. At tea-time, Sally never stretched over, never ate with her mouth open, and always asked if she could have some more with a 'please'. At her birthday parties she never snatched her guests' presents and was always keen for the entertainer not to show her any favouritism. But Sally was simply everyone's favourite.

At twenty-five, her skin is still flawless and, though we would be hard-pressed to call the Sally we've just met *angelic*, it took very little hard pressing for the Rodin to deem the ways and wiles of her body thoroughly heavenly.

Well, where do we find Sally today? It is the day after the Big Bonk. She is spending Sunday afternoon by herself, in the one-bedroom flat she rents in Highgate. He had stayed for breakfast-cum-lunch and had thus deprived Sally of her sacred hour with the *Observer*, so she is reading it now. Her routine is out of sync, she really should be ironing. It will wait a week. Today Sally is not flustered by such a thing, today she is enjoying aloneness. Today she enjoys the self-condoned liberation from the previously self-imposed Sunday schedule. She is very proud of herself and finds she frequently bursts into an ecstatic smile.

What does it mean, this smile, what does it mean?

Her answer is defiant.

I feel wonderful. It was good. It was a good thing to do.

She laughs at the paradox. In the clear light of a November day, and looked at objectively, she had indeed committed a wanton act of slack morals and shameful lust which, justifiably, could be categorized by most as Bad. Yet Sally feels good and can see nothing to be ashamed of. She feels elated, happy and downright proud.

My flesh might be ravaged, my mind sullied, but Gracious Good Lord do they feel the better for it!

Sally knows what she wants, and what she must do.

It'll be a swift and easy transition, and it must start,

quite simply, with a change to my wardrobe. I shall do Ms Collins proud and move with one fell swoop from Laura Ashley to Whistles, from Marks and Sparks undies to none whatsoever. Hampstead here I come, cheque book at the ready.

Should I be ironing?

No.

I should be buying clothes that are Dry Clean Only.

TWO

Sunday in Hampstead, silver winter sun making everybody look beautiful. The Barbour Brigade are out walking retrievers who have never retrieved in the countryside because the Heath suffices. The Young Trendies are here in force, hanging out, hanging about, sipping cappuccino at the pavement café, queuing for crêpes, looking around all the while to catch sight of their reflection whilst spying out anyone good-looking to look good for.

There is a young woman who weaves in and around these two species. She is smiling; it is a smile of energy and ease and it is infectious. She seems simultaneously absorbed in her own world yet aware of, and enjoying, her surroundings. And the shopping, by the looks of the two bags she swings. She is of average height, of slight build and her hair is a nothing-special brown, mid-length with a kink that is natural and nice. Her skin glows and there is a sheen to her very good cheekbones, a becoming blush to her cheeks, an endearing rosiness to the edge of her chin and the end of her nose. Her hazel eyes glint and dance. Her lips, naturally full, are soft red – Sally always uses lip balm during the winter months. And, though her legs would not see her to a Levi jeans commercial, her walk is a sexy, assertive stride. As a package, she looks very pleasingly put together. She is not stunning but she is radiant and heads turn.

Sally jigs past a boutique, one selling excessively expensive accessories. Two strides later (and unknowingly witnessed by at least three envious Hampstead Darlings), our erstwhile ballerina performs a fluid halt, heel-spin, about-turn, and floats effortlessly into the shop. Inside, the opulent aroma of fine leather envelops her, the hand of a skilled interior decorator is much in evidence and her senses are solicited at once. The rag-rolled walls in *Homes-and-Gardens* hues of ecru and taupe, and the polished wood floor covered here and there by a jaded kelim, provide a splendid setting for pieces of old furniture over which cashmere throws and finely woven woollen shawls are nonchalantly draped. Belts hang from a fabulously gnarled piece of driftwood; from leather trunks, suitcases and holdalls, a carefully spewed selection of socks and silk camisoles accost the eye. But Sally, who thinks the current fashion and hefty prices for bashed, blemished, artistically distressed leather goods somewhat daft, has made a beeline for the old Welsh dresser where the hats are displayed.

She has never worn a hat but she is trying them on with the jaunty confidence of one who would not entertain going out without one. The black felt cloche suits her well but makes her look too cutesy, the trilby is too butch and the beret too *ordinaire*. She looks stunning in the claret bowler but feels best in the black velvet. It is soft, floppy but beautifully cut. It hugs her skull and the brim, up at the front, falls gently around her face and drapes elegantly at the back. She looks at herself in the mirror and the shop assistant, usually pushy, looks on too. She makes no attempt to goad her customer; she watches, slightly jealous, from a discreet distance. Sally is intrigued to find that the shape of the hat accentuates her bone structure and appears to lengthen her neck; under the black velvet, her eyes turn from hazelnuts into freshly shelled conkers.

I look really rather good, sort of alluring, feminine and vampish all at the same time.

It takes Sally but an instant to decide the hat must be hers; costing, though it does, a day's pay.

At the Tea Pot Shoppe, Carlos was clearing the mountain of froth-stained cups from one of the outside tables, pocketing a mound of gratuitously small change left as a gratuity. It was nearing the end of his first month in England, he was tired and slightly homesick. It was a thankless job for a nuclear physics graduate, and the tips were lower than he'd been led to believe. Then he saw her, caught in profile as she started to cross the road, a pretty face framed perfectly by a sumptuous black hat. Suddenly, life in this strange country of offish Barbours and oafish Trendies had a plus to it. This, Carlos realized with a great deal of excitement, was his first glimpse of an English Rose. He gawped transfixed; watching the cars slither and toot while she danced and laughed her way between them. There is a zebra crossing a hundred yards ahead but today Sally prefers to jay-walk. *Bella, bella*! The hat, the face, the rosiness – and here she is, ordering a cappuccino and a Danish pastry.

Sally graciously accepted the compliments of the waiter. Soon she was deftly scooping up the chocolate-dusted froth and thinking of nothing in particular as it fluffed into nothingness on her tongue. The pastry was absolutely heavenly and she even closed her eyes as the first mouthful revealed to her tastebuds apple, *crème patissière* and the lightest of pastry. By the second sip and third mouthful, Sally was happily recalling the details of her decadent afternoon. A coffee-brown lambswool blazer; two silk shirts, one olive, one cream; a pair of exorbitant expensive designer jeans; and a short (was it too short?) black devoré velvet skirt.

When on earth am I going to wear that?

You will.

She had indulged in garments of the finest fabrics, and at the most exorbitant prices. The whole experience had been so pleasurable, the looking, the touching, the trying on; the decision-making so effortless. Finally, it had been a joy and well worth the money to watch her acquisitions being coddled in tissue paper and then handed to her so reverently.

As she pressed a determined fork against the last flakes of Danish, she pondered for a moment; common sense versus decadence. Sally, you must understand, had spent her rainy-day money. Frequently she put a little aside 'for a rainy day', not really knowing when that would be. But it was definitely today and common sense had a place neither in her scheme of things nor her purse.

Today, she told herself as the brisk November breeze reddened her nose and chin a little more, *today it is pouring.*

Despite the pavements being dry and no umbrella in sight, Sally decided that it was the rainiest day in ages and the spending of pounds amassed from hard-saved pennies was utterly justified. These purchases, after all, were an *investment*. She turned to look for her waiter, and in doing so felt a whisper of velvet against her cheek. Its caress felt wonderful and, as the waiter was nowhere to be seen, she kept her head still a moment longer.

Over her second cappuccino, Sally indulged in recalling, moment by moment, thrust by thrust, the athletics of the previous night, and if one can feel light-headed between the legs, then that was how Sally was feeling.

Never have I been worshipped like that, never have I been so aware of my body, what it can do, how it can feel, how it can make another feel.

Perhaps it was because she had consciously watched,

analyzed even, a man totally absorbed in her, so hungry for her, that her own physical awareness had been heightened. The sex seemed so much more fulfilling, the orgasm so exquisite. New. Sitting there, in Hampstead, with the light growing thin, a November navy replacing the afternoon silver, Sally decided to recast herself as a fly on the wall of her replay and ran the whole sequence again, this time as a series of film stills. Vivid in her mind's eye was the interlocking of two bodies, the various formations and patterns, firm flesh, the spaces in between; Rodin's marble; Henry Moore's bronze.

Carlos found himself unable to resist. The English Rose, smiling carefree out loud, was compelling, magnetic. He was helpless in the face of her. As his luck would have it, she turned to him with that very smile as he presented the bill to her. With his very best English, he let go:

'Señorita, your smile, it makes my day. Is so very beautiful. In you I see the English Rosa. If I was Shake His Speare, I write a play for you. You are foods for my 'eart and a vision for my eyes. Is so very lovely. I am breaking open for your smile of pretty innocence.'

Hand pressed with conviction against his heart, he kissed up at the sky as if imploring the gods to grant his wish. Sally was flattered to the hilt. Cocking her head, she gave him the smile to make his day, a wink too, and a tip which far exceeded her previously uniform ten per cent.

Not quite, thought Sally as she strolled away home, *but thank you anyway.* She threw back her head and grinned hugely at the near-dark sky. *Actually, the smile that has made your day is not that of an innocent English Rose, but is rather the glow of a well-laid woman.*

THREE

'Foxy Lady!'

Jimi Hendrix's chocolate voice, the aggressive twang and slice of his guitar, rings out and reverberates off the walls. The music is loud and frantic. It adds action and life to the room.

There is little furniture but what there is has, undoubtedly, the British Design Council seal of approval. The run of the floorboards, interrupted only occasionally by a piece of carefully chosen, intelligently placed furniture, leads the eye to the fireplace above which an Alexander Calder gouache explodes colour and shape on to the intensely white wall. The low coffee table is a sleek construction in burnished steel and tinted glass. It supports a matt black vase stuffed with emphatically upright tulips; white, waxy but real. On a diagonal to the table's edge is a copy of Warhol's *Diaries*. Along one wall stands an ash and glass cabinet. Understated and stunning, the carpentry is exquisite. It is filled with books meticulously organized into a personal library system. Pride of place is given to the leather-bound volumes: Shakespeare, Donne, Fielding, the *Complete Oxford Dictionary*, the *Dictionary of Quotations*. On the shelf above are art books, epic tomes and sumptuous catalogues: Mantegna, Vermeer, Cézanne and Poussin. The shelves below carry novels, all hardback, all standing proud in alphabetical order: Bellow, Heller, Kafka, Marquez, Nabokov, Pasternak, Seth.

On one side of the fireplace, a fabulous Conran standard lamp stands to attention while on the other side is the CD system, a veritable piece of sculpture in itself; wafer-thin, subtle Scandinavian lines, matt black, obviously. On custom-built shelves (oak and chrome) are enough CDs to open a shop. They are categorized, of course; the concise rock section alphabetically, the comprehensive classical section chronologically: Monteverdi, Bach, Mozart, Beethoven, Brahms, Mahler, Schoenberg, Bartok, Tippett. And yet it is Mr Hendrix who somewhat anomalously fills this unnervingly chic room in Notting Hill with sound.

Can you guess where we are? It is still the day of the Big B. and, a few miles away, Sally has just arrived home, where she is presently dancing Giselle in the devoré skirt and nothing else. Physically, she may be some distance from Jimi and the Calder and the tulips; however, the memory of her is very much here, clear and current in the mind of this flat's occupant, evoked by Mr Hendrix's beast of chase. It is time for the Rodin to assume his true identity.

Would Richard Stonehill please stand up?

Look there! Against the long sash window, framed movie-like by imperceptibly breezing muslin drapes. That's him, resting his brow against his outstretched arm against the window. Turn around – oh, just look! Six foot two and-a-bit, perfectly carved and gorgeously chiselled. Now this *is* the stuff of Levi jeans commercials. Hair the colour of the sand at Rosilli Bay where his childhood was spent, Richard's skin boasts the health, vitality and natural tan of someone who lived long in the care and goodness of Welsh sea air. His eyes are the most extraordinary dark violet, his teeth are very good, his hands could be those of a concert pianist, he is fiendishly good-looking and he smells delicious – a fine mixture of freshly laundered clothes, scrubbed skin and Calvin Klein scent.

Eyes closed, long and lithe legs stretched out, arms relaxed, Richard Stonehill slithers into his black leather recliner, and converses with Jimi.

'I'm too exhausted to get up and scream, Mr Hendrix,' he apologises, but finds ample energy to sing that he too has wasted precious time; that he has therefore made up his mind to make this foxy lady his, all his.

Bay-beh!

Jimi, it appears is singing about Sally. Or someone just like her. But Richard has never met anyone who comes remotely near her. He sincerely hopes that this vixen will have her sport with him a while longer.

A wry smile creeps from one side of his mouth to the other. He opens his eyes and shakes his head. What does he shake in it? Disbelief? But it did happen, his pleasantly tired body is proof, and so are the images which constantly assault his memory. Does he shake it in amusement? But the night with Sally was more than just fun. His gaze rests upon *Julius Caesar*, third volume into the run of Shakespeare. Richard sees its title and suddenly Sally, in her naked glory, appears before him too. Caesar. *Seize her.*

Seize who? Who on earth is this woman? This Sally Lomax? The classic friend of a friend of a friend whom he met less than twenty-four hours ago at the party of a friend of a friend. How come he had not met, even heard of her before? Fate. It must have been. At 11 o'clock the previous evening, Fate had pushed them both on to the balcony at that dull party in Barnes. Fate had allowed conversation to flow, flattery and flirtations to be accepted, and Sally to be without a ride back into London. Fate took them past an all-night bagel bakery and Fate uncovered a shared passion for the smoked salmon-cream cheese variety. Fate filled Richard's car with laughter and sexual chemistry. If Fate took him to Highgate, where he'd never even thought of going before, where was it to take him from here?

As quickly as the vision came, Sally now disappeared from the cabinet and the complete works of Shakespeare stared back at Richard in their leather-bound splendour. Hendrix was now proclaiming that an angel had come down from heaven yesterday, staying just long enough to rescue him.

Richard, who did not feel rescued so much as released, rose and sauntered to the bathroom, a tiler's delight in damson, citron and *bleu di bleu* majolica ceramic. His bladder was full and he stood expectant for the blissful moment of release. Nothing happened. Puzzled, he glanced down. It looked like it always did and felt like it should. Eyes tightly closed, he tried again. Nothing. Slight pain but nothing.

Come on, mate, syphon the python, have a slash, take a leak.

Nothing. He fiddled a bit, gave a little squeeze, a little pull, a slight twist, a gentle shake. Nothing. He turned the tap on to a drizzle.

But I'm bursting.

Bursting. Immediately his mind flashed up an image of the night before, a clear picture and a vivid sensation at the same time. There is Sally's nipple brushing the corner of his mouth; he sees himself thrusting into her, pump, spurt, release.

Stop it, I've got to piss.

Richard looked down and his penis, as erect and straining as his perfect tulips, leered up at him lasciviously. No peeing for the time being. He ached in his lower back and his groin and decided to sit awhile instead. Chin resting on a fist, elbow balanced on a knee; he is Rodin's Thinker to a 't'. Catching sight of himself in the mirror, he took a long, hard stare.

I am thirty-five and have had a mind-blowing sexual encounter. I do not know the girl, though carnally I know her inside out. And today I cannot pee. Look at me, blond, handsome – very – virile, manly, hunky, horny. Suave, debonair, sophisticated. In control – of my life, of my mind, of my work.

But not of my dick.

Who is this woman? This Sally Lomax? She is a teacher, she is twenty-five, she lives by herself in urban cottagey style amongst pine dressers, floral table cloths, Lloyd-Loom chairs and a patchwork eiderdown. Shabby chic, everything fresh, clean and bright. Objectively, she is not even that beautiful, not really my type. So what has she done to me? My tackle has never ached before, nor my gut felt so hollow, my mind so distracted. What have I done? What has been done to me? Why can't I pee? When will I see her again? Jeez, will I see her again?

The horror and accompanying adrenalin at the thought of never seeing Sally again opened the sluice gates of the Stonehill bladder. Richard had just enough time to release the Thinker's pose so that the torrent hit the bowl and not the double weave, thick-pile carpet.

FOUR

'Did you see Miss Lomax in assembly? Did you see what she was wearing? You can see her *knees*! And she has make-up on. Definitely mascara and lipstick.'

'My mum says that a woman should never go out without lipstick on.'

'But Miss Lomax is a teacher!'

'My mum says it's tarty to put make-up on unless it's a special occasion.'

'Yes, but Miss Lomax is a *teacher*.'

Gossip was always an integral part of Monday morning school but rarely were the teachers its main topic. On a Thursday or a Friday maybe, but Monday was usually dedicated to the football scores, shopping trips and birthday parties of the weekend just past. That Monday morning, in the all-too-short ten minutes between assembly and first lesson, Miss Lomax was the exclusive subject for discussion.

Class Five were stupefied, traumatized and desperately excited. Scandal, they believed, was about to shake the school. Of what it was they were as yet unsure. To an extent it was irrelevant, the truth may not be nearly so exciting as wild conjecture. Was she going somewhere after school? If so, where? To dinner? To the opera, the theatre? To court? Was she about to get engaged? Was she leading a double life as a model as well as a teacher? (To a ten-year-old, anyone taller or older, anyone in high heels or even just a trace of lipstick, was very glamorous indeed.) Maybe she was going to elope – please, no, that would mean a new teacher and Miss Lomax was irreplaceable. Miss Lomax warranted compliments usually paid to footballers, pop stars and ponies; she was the business, the bestest, brill, fab.

'Who do you think she's going to elope with?'

'Maybe they'll be catching a train to Gretna Green straight after school!'

'Quick, who passes King's Cross Station on their way home?'

Suddenly the classroom reverberated with the age-old sound of desks creaking, chairs being scraped into forward-facing position and a few nervous, last-minute giggles and whispers. Teacher had arrived. There she was, resplendent in a tight skirt and loose, silky blouse. Miss Lomax stood before them, feet slightly apart, hands on hips.

'Hi.'

Thirty champion chatterboxes were stunned into a unified hush.

Hi?

Hi?

What's 'Hi'?

Hey, maybe she's on drugs!

Miss Lomax perched herself in a perfect serpentine on the edge of her table, black Lycra-clad legs plaited around each other.

Maybe she's drunk!

'Today I thought we'd do something different. I read your "What I did over half term" stories and I'm not particularly interested in what you did this weekend. It seems that you all tend to do the same old things anyway, and your writing is rather boring. You lot don't seem to have much imagination. With the exception of Rajiv, who seems to have a little too much because every weekend he apparently saves family or friends from fire, flood or sinking ship.'

Twenty-nine children laughed. Miss Lomax smiled gently at Rajiv and cocked her head as if to say, Don't take it to heart.

'Shush. Thank you. No, today I thought we could talk about our best daydreams, our favourite fantasies. Now who will start? Rajiv? Okay. And easy on the fires, floods or drowning baby cousins. Fire away, fire away.'

Rajiv began his story. His fantasy was to be all by himself, away from his family and friends, in a spacecraft made for one, operated by one. He would leave Earth, head for the stars, alight on one and discover living aliens. He would stay and befriend this new people, introduce them to such concepts as clothing empires and hotel chains and fast-food outlets. He would become their undisputed, much-loved leader, an intergalactic Richard Branson.

Marsha, who had a soft spot for Rajiv, explained that she aimed to become a fireman-woman, so that she could help Rajiv in his brave adventures. They could be a team – firefighting heroes but also husband and wife with six children. Rajiv buried his head in his hands, wishing his spacecraft could be ready that afternoon. Miss Lomax succeeded – but only just – in suppressing potentially uncontrollable giggles. Rajiv, however, quickly succumbed to a tell-tale redness which travelled all over his face and burnt right through to his ears. A roar of 'Ugghh' and a spatter of laughter erupted. Marsha stared straight at him and at Miss Lomax alternately, imploring, 'But it's true, it's true.'

Law and order was easily re-established, the class was keen to listen and tell. Ambitions were mooted: to win the Grand National on a small Welsh pony; to become a very famous actress and appear on *This Is Your Life*; to take England to victory as the top goal scorer in the next World Cup ('Come on now, Andrew, be slightly realistic', 'Well, maybe the World Cup after next'); to be the Queen's favourite chef. The children were loose, stimulated and creative. They produced some of their best work that day without realizing it was work at all. Miss Lomax felt proud. She was having fun.

'Yes, Alice? Tell you my fantasy or daydream?' The bell for break clanged. *Saved by the bell, ho ho*, thought Sally. Yet for once none of the children moved. Pen lids were left off pens, books lay threateningly open. Thirty pairs of inquisitive eyes said that break did not matter, they wanted Miss Lomax's dreams.

'My dream?'

Yes, Miss, your dream.

'Maybe next time, it's break-time.'

We don't want our break, we want your fantasy!

There was no escape, she could not punish them for showing such enthusiasm for her lesson. She could not disappoint them by merely taking theirs and not giving them hers.

'Okay, okay. In a nutshell, I would like to live in Tuscany – that's in Italy, here on the map. In a beautiful stone villa set amidst flowers and cypress trees, with its own pool and near a perfect little village. I'd like a devilishly good-looking Italian husband who is a pasta wizard, a batch of beautiful babies and a satisfying job teaching perfectly behaved, diligent (look it up in the dictionary) pupils.'

Sally only sort-of lied. It had certainly been her fantasy right up until last week, but that was before Richard Stonehill and her current fantasies, which would most certainly earn her a dismissal and severely disturb the fresh, absorbent minds of her young charges. The Tuscan Idyll would have to suffice.

'Now scram!' Thirty pairs of androgynous legs scrammed. Out, out into the playground to munch chocolate, elaborate further on their stories and to discuss whether or not they believed Miss Lomax. The majority (all except Paula-Teacher's-Pet-Thomson) did not.

As she headed towards the staff-room, Miss Lomax talked silently to the satchels and gym shoes which lined the walls.

My fantasy? Best daydream? If it's come true, or is coming true, is it still valid? I want the memory of me, the feel of me, my taste, my smell, my touch, to stay with Richard Stonehill for the rest of his life. The knowledge that it has done so will give me the pleasure and strength never to let myself feel small and worthless. Actually, maybe that's all a little too metaphysical. Let's start again. On a physical level. My fantasy is to have the most delicious, wicked, life-enhancing affair with this Adonis, this Richard 'call me Conan' Stonehill.

'Hullo, Sal!' (*Don't call me that.*) Mr Bernard – John – (Head of Maths), greeted Miss Lomax – Sally (great at giving head).

'You certainly look radiant today. Don't tell me Class Five had done their homework? All of them? I've a double period with them after break, so help me God. Might you be free for a drink this evening? No? A shame, a great pity. Some other time, perhaps, maybe?'

Miss Lomax, who had never talked much more than shop with Bernard, was a little taken aback.

It's not the short skirt, is it? She hastily persuaded herself it must be her aura instead.

Miss Lomax made coffee in a mug bearing the school's emblem and maxim, *In Loco Parentis*, and sauntered over to where Miss Lewis – Diana – (teacher of Art and Craft) sat. They were close friends and allies in the field of staff-room politics. Diana, the dictionary definition of a wacky art teacher, was always bowled over by the small happenings and vagaries of life. Indeed, great interest and pure enthusiasm were expressed for practically everything and everyone around her. Her exaggerated inflection assisted the expression of such fascinations. To her great amusement, this rendered her a willing sitting duck for many a playground impersonation. She had an absolute field day with Sally that break-time.

'Look at you! You look *fab*-u-lous. Who is he?'

'Huh?'

'Sa-*lly*!'

But all Diana had for a reply was Sally taking a non-committal gulp at her coffee.

'Okay then, Miss Sexy Sal.' (*Don't call me that*!) 'What did you do over the weekend? Apart from *plun*-der your bank account?'

'Actually, that was about it. Just a quiet weekend, a bit of sewing, finishing a novel, generally pottering about. You know, one of *those* weekends.'

I do know 'those weekends', thought Diana, *and you most certainly did not have one! You're fibbing to me, but you have your reasons. Only tell me soon, Sally, Sexy Sal, do!*

FIVE

'He's late today, isn't he? Most unusual. Did he have a meeting? Check for me, will you? I don't think I could stand these butterflies all day!'

'No, Sandra, no meeting for him. Maybe he's sick? Or maybe he's eloped!'

'Stop it, Mary, that's not fair.'

'But you've been working here over two years and you get the same courteous "Good Morning, Good Evening, Merry Christmas" as the rest of us. You know he'll only ever be married to his work. He's probably a lousy lover anyway. No one female ever rings for him. You never know, maybe women aren't his *thing* anyway.'

'Oh, shut it. Let me have my hopes and fantasies. It's all right for you, with your mortgage and your steady Steve and your . . . oh my God, he's coming! Oh my Gordon Flipping Bennett. Keep cool and sophis, San. Hello, Mr Stonehill!'

'Good morning, Sandra. Morning, Mary.'

Morning, morning. Mourning.

Sandra's gaze followed him down the corridor. Mary watched her closely. Smitten. Sandra absorbed every detail, storing it for later, for the arduous journey that she would make, always made, seatless and depressed, back to High Barnet.

I love that navy suit, I love the way he walks. His hair lifts slightly with each stride, the trousers outline his calf muscles with every step. Why was he late? How can I find out? Please, please, please not a woman in his life. Pretty please a gas leak or something. One day, me, please. One day, me. Or, for one day, me. All I ask.

0181 348 6523. No answer. Of course not, Sally's at school. But does she have an answering machine? Richard wonders, hanging on. Obviously not. But does she go home for lunch? he wonders two hours later as he re-dials. Obviously not. Does school end at 3.30 nowadays? No, apparently it does not.

Richard has done little work. As the working day nears a close, his drawing board remains irritatingly bare. He just could not seem to settle down to concentrate on the plan for the quasi-Georgian building commissioned by the Americans. Instead, he doodles and a Play School house stares back, with a chimney, a door, and windows; one, two, three, four. You never know the Americans, they might like it. He twirls around in his swivel chair; his jacket is off, his shirt sleeves rolled up to the elbow revealing beautifully tanned forearms brushed with a down of flaxen hairs. He clasps his hands behind his head and places his left foot on his right knee. Fine ankles can be discerned beneath Ralph Lauren socks. Out of the window he sees the river, a pleasure boat, captivated tourists on board, the guide changing her microphone from hand to hand as she points to the left, to the right. On the opposite bank, a crane performs its slow-motion task. Up river, Waterloo Bridge straddles south and north banks. Matisse is showing at the Hayward Gallery, he read the review in yesterday's paper. Maybe Sally would like to go? Maybe Titian at the Royal Academy is more her thing? Something to find out. 0181

348 6523. Was that dialled correctly? 0181 348 6523. She's his first 0181 girl.

638 5454. 'Bob Woods, please . . . Bob? Hey! Fancy a *sesh* at the gym? Great. In an hour? Fine.'

Keeping at a constant 80 r.p.m., Bob and Richard tackle the simulated hill programme on the *Lifecycle*. They've broken the twenty-minute, red-face barrier and are working through into the serious sweat zone. Speech comes in staccato gasps, whole sentences interspersed with long pauses. However, having worked out together for many years, Bob and Richard have brought such conversation to a fine art, barely comprehensible to those uninitiated but utterly intelligible between these two.

'So, you and Sally Lomax left together and then what?'

'What do you know about her?'

'Not a lot. Friend of a friend of Catherine. Met her once before, about six months ago. So, you left and *then* what?'

'Does Catherine know her?'

'And then WHAT?'

'What?'

They pedalled on, then pedalled down, then stopped. Both leant forward and dropped their heads on to folded arms and huffed in unison for a few moments.

'*Stairmaster?*'

'After you, I'll work on my abs.'

Delts, quads, glutes, abs. Half an hour later, they met up over the bicep curls, heaving their limbs, exhaling and grimacing in such perfect time as to make any synchronized swimming corps envious. They were, unknowingly, the centre of attention, the brawniest there, the handsomest. Admiring women, in fluorescent, up-the-bum all-in-ones, strutted their well-toned stuff in the hope that they might be seen and even achieve a date. Less brawny blokes were suddenly inspired to work harder, to up the level on the *Lifecycle*, to increase their weights by 10 Ks. Today, like any other day past or to come, Bob and

Richard were unaware of their audience. To them, the gym was less a place to see and be seen as it was their sanctuary where they could dissolve the pressures of work or relationships and simply enjoy their easy friendship which spanned well over a decade. And keep their bodies in peak condition too, of course.

Over the gush of the shower, the waft of shampoo-conditioner and the clatter of lockers, Bob picked up where Richard had left off.

'Have you phoned her?'

'Who?'

'Who-my-arse!'

'Sort of.'

'*Sort of*! What's "sort of"? How can you *sort of* ring a person? Either you have or you have not. She was either there or she was not. She either said: "Yes, I'd love to", or she said "No" and thanked you for calling. Enough "sort of". Did you?'

'Yes.'

'Yes?'

'Yes.'

'And? And?'

'No reply.'

'Try again?'

'No reply.'

'*Will* you try again?'

'What do you know about her?'

'Ri-*chard*! She's a friend of a friend of Catherine's. I met her once before. I am sure – in fact, there can be no question about it – she'll be sitting in all evening willing the phone to ring with your dulcet tones offering dinner *chez Ricardo*. So, stop skirting the issue. You left together and then what?'

'I took her home. Fancy a drink? My shout.'

Bob watched his friend as he dressed and preened.

Good Lord, he's gone! A goner! Not that he knows it yet. Goodbye, Old Mister Pump-and-Dump, Sir Love 'Em and Leave 'Em. Or rather Lord Leave 'Em Before You Fallinlovewith 'Em. I don't believe it!

Bob felt a wave of fondness and happiness for his pal so he slapped his back and squeezed his delts.

'Your shout. Just a swift half, mind. Promised Catherine that we'd go to the flicks.'

Their swift half turned into a leisurely two-pinter. Bob decided not to pry further. This one needed nurturing. Instead, they indulged in a trip down Memory Lane, recalling wild times shared at college, remembering, try for try, every rugby game that they'd played together, remarking on how far they had both come since moving to London to make their respective marks on the world of Law and Architecture. Bob talked about Catherine, their next holiday to Northern Portugal, the extension to the house, the current discord over the baby issue – her desire, his reluctance. ('But me, a dad? I mean, I'm not old enough! I've got a dad of my own still! Catherine's broody though, very. I've even checked her Pill packets recently to make sure she's not forgetting accidentally-on-purpose.')

Richard was simultaneously envious of Bob's security, his constant and loving relationship, and yet also thankful that he had no one but himself to think of. Poor old Bob, soon to be dragged off to a schmaltzy American weepy that he'd never go to see out of choice. But there again, didn't he seem to beam with affection when, on the way to the pub, he'd made a detour to buy tissues and wine gums?

'Hey, look at the time! I've got fifteen minutes to get to Leicester Square! Great to see you, Richie.' (*Don't call me that.*) 'Still on for squash on Sunday morning? Great. You going to call her? You *are* going to call her! Must dash. Later!'

'Later! Love to Catherine. Don't sob too hard!'

Bob left the pub backwards, making a telephone

gesture as he did so. Richard raised his pint and smiled. A minute or two later he left it, half-full, and caught a cab home to Notting Hill.

0181 348 6523.

'Hullo?'

'Sally! Richard here.'

'Hu-*low*!'

'How are you?'

'Well! Yes! You?'

'Mmm!'

A pause verging on embarrassing silence.

'Sally, would you like to have dinner with me? Friday night? At mine?'

'That would be nice. Why, yes. Thank you. Address? Time? Lovely!'

'Friday, then.' *And wear those lovely little knickers.*

'Friday.' *And make sure the sheets are fresh.*

SIX

With the mock-Georgian folly taking good form on the drawing-board, Richard felt justified, for the first time in his working career, in packing up at lunch-time and taking the afternoon off.

Goodbye Sandra, goodbye Mary. Goodbye, Mr Stonehill. Goodbye navy suit and calf muscles. Sandra plunged herself into a chasm of pessimism rescued only by a chocolate éclair tactfully provided by Mary. No, Mary, he's far too fit ever to need a doctor. It can only mean a woman.

What a delight, thought Richard, *to shop at Sainsbury's on a weekday afternoon*. What a revelation it was that a supermarket could look like that. No obstacle course of trollies and baskets, plenty of everything left, no people-snake at the check-out. *No men*, realized Richard.

As he trollied his way to the cereals, he thought what a mercy it was that he was unmarried. He pondered how it was that shopping for groceries became such a trial for the married man. On your soap box, Richard, away you go.

Take any ordinary Saturday – tomorrow for instance –

they'll be here in force, frantic and bewildered, chained to The List. It says baked beans so Married Man stops by the baked beans, and regards them. Look at the list, look at the produce, look at the list. Move on a couple of paces, walk backwards knocking over a child before finally plucking two tins of said beans. Place them carefully in the trolley but manage somehow to bruise the avocados in the process. Wipe brow, unscrunch List and go in search of Free-range Eggs. Buy Farm Fresh instead – they're cheaper after all. Little does M.M. realize that they will ultimately work out twice as dear when Wife sees them, bins them and hollers: 'FREE-RANGE!' Don't they know that there's a reason for lard, crinkle cut chips, white sliced bread and bumper-pack beer not to be on The List?

Richard Stonehill, I think you will find that a packet of SuperNoodles lurks behind that box of lo-fat, lo-salt, sugar free lite-bran (organic) which you have strategically positioned in your trolley.

It is at the check-out, Richard rued whilst searching for an eco-friendly bleach, *where M.M. comes most unstuck. You can see them gaze in wonder at the well-spaced items processing along on the conveyor belt of the female shopper* (or that of Mr Stonehill). *The contents of M.M.'s trolley are in a veritable profiterole pile as they head towards the black looks of the check-out assistant. M.M. wonders how women know instinctively how to pack – is it passed down from Mother to Daughter?*

More to the point, why on earth does M.M. insist on packing eggs and pastry cases, watercress and tomatoes first; soap powder, bottles and tins last? What happens to men when they marry? Richard pondered as he sashayed past the beverages and preserves (choosing Broken Orange Pekoe and Damson Extra respectively). *Do these married men – erstwhile bachelors after all – lose all notion, every shred of common sense as to what constitutes a well-stocked larder? Why and how does this innate and irrational fear of supermarkets suddenly develop?*

Is there a cure?

Divorce?

Richard was relieved, on that decadent afternoon, that this sub-species was busy elsewhere (probably making important decisions at business, running the city, organizing the country, designing buildings, ministering law, order, justice and peace) so that he could cruise the aisles without incident or irritation. Deftly he swooped and plucked and picked as he breezed along. Under his expertise, his trolley behaved impeccably. Gone were those forever-spinning wheels; it became some kind of miniature hovercraft. Such was his skill and grace at handling corners, the elegant stops and effortless starts, the two of them became the Torvill and Dean of Sainsbury's. Packed to perfection – frozen goods in one bag, bottles, tins and tubes in a box, fresh produce in another bag – Richard headed home.

It never occurred to him that Married Man is the beast he is because he thinks not only for himself. He has responsibilities to others. Commitment. After all, Richard has had fifteen years to bring his shopping – content and technique – to a fine art for he has bought and thought only for himself. He has been his own man. And nobody else's.

The few special ingredients, those which would make his meal for Sally a veritable and memorable feast, were brought from Gambini's, the specialist Italian delicatessen that was, by a useful turn of Fate, Richard's corner shop. Now here was a place he would browse and deliberate at leisure. *Pappardelle* or *Orecchiette* or *Gigli del Gargano*? *Ciabatta* or *Focaccia*? Stuffed olives or those marinating happily in thyme-flavoured cold-pressed extra virgin olive oil? The shop was cramped, the smell almost overpowering as cheese mingled with salami and olives jostled for olfactory recognition against garlic-drenched sauces. From floor to ceiling, the Gambinis had packed the shelves tight with the necessities for maintaining Italian culinary standards in England. All the regions of Italy were represented under this one roof in Notting Hill. From Umbria, Tuscany, Sicily and Pugilia was extra virgin olive oil spanning the spectrum from pale gold to deep khaki. Small pots of *Pesto Genovese* rubbed shoulders with little jars of capers from Lipari. Jams of wild chestnut and wild fig jostled for space next to jars of chocolate hazelnut cream, and packets of *Cantucci* biscuits were balanced precariously against a tower of boxed *Panforte.*

Richard was caught, quite compliantly, in the Gambinis' web of luxury and tantalizing variety. When it came to vinegar there was Chianti, Balsamic, peach or plum to choose from. Impossibly fat olives vied for attention, gleaming up at him from their bowls of marinades. Although the *porcini secchi* seemed somewhat *ordinaire* next to dry morels from Tibet and Fairy Ring *Champignons*, Richard bought some anyway and Sardinian Saffron proved to be a must-have, despite its imaginative price tag (in fact, *because* of its price tag).

Signora Gambini, known to the select few (Richard amongst them) as Rosa, watched as he smelt, felt and tasted his way through her wares. His shopping list was at once forgotten as his eyes, nose and mouth traversed the shop. His eyes lingered over the chargrilled baby onions in olive oil, the wild mountain goat pâté and the grilled polenta but his nose pulled him away and positioned him in front of the cheeses where the *Taleggio*, with its peach rind striated with powder grey, solicited him uncompromisingly. The *Torta al Limone* proved even harder to resist, glinting up at him wickedly with its creamy golden heart dusted delightfully with icing sugar, the whole encased by crisp, caramel-coloured pastry.

'Someone special for dinner, Signor?' cooed Rosa. 'I give to you my special menu, guaranteed to win her heart. With it, I captured Germano and for forty-three years he is with me.'

Rosa was a clever lady. Her suggestions, made shyly, were each concluded with a question mark. Consequently, Richard bought exactly what she planned he should, but believed himself to have conceived the entire selection. With his wallet pleasurably empty and his bags satisfyingly full, he bade Rosa farewell and promised to tell her how the meal went. With plump arms folded triumphantly across a magnificent bosom encased by straining floral polyester, she sent him on his way with a '*Ciao*' and a conspiratorial wink.

Back at his flat, Richard took the shopping into the kitchen, simultaneously undoing his tie and unbuttoning his shirt. He draped his tie (Hermès) around the bedroom door handle, his shirt (Thomas Pink) he bundled into the washing machine from whose drum stared the crumpled faces of four other white, worn-once shirts (Turbull & Asser, Hilditch & Key, Hawes & Curtis, Lewin). His suit (Hugo Boss) was given a good shake, placed over a thick wooden hanger and hung in the far left section of the wardrobe where it joined a regiment of other finely tailored suits (David Rose, Yves Saint Laurent, Armani – Giorgio, not Emporio). Socks (Ralph Lauren – we already know that) and boxer shorts (Calvin Klein – we would have guessed) were put in the laundry basket (Richard never mixes his washes). Shoes (Church's?) (Yes) were shoe-treed and placed at the foot of the cupboard. They will of course be polished before they are next worn.

Naked, Richard was heading for the shower when he stopped and philosophized. *No, cook first, then clean, then shower.*

He jumped into jogging pants and a faded polo shirt (both Timberland) and selected the music for the afternoon's industry. He'd cook to Mendelssohn's Italian, he'd clean to the Scottish, then relax and await Sally with Brahms. *Più animato*, Richard joined the strings of the first movement and skittered around his kitchen, gathering utensils and food stuffs and placing them in rational order according to the menu.

Richard, you could have been a Michelin-starred chef. Just look at you with your Sabatiers, how fast you chop, so evenly and accurately. Why don't the onions make your eyes water, why do you not subconsciously lick a finger and find it coated with garlic? How can you cook so exquisitely without using every utensil in your kitchen? Why is there no mess on the floor? You remember to preheat the oven, you wash up as you go, you do not splash tomato juice on your shirt, no bits of parsley wedge themselves under your nails. There really is no need for you to wear an apron but you look dinky in one anyway. All is cooked to perfection, you needn't taste it but you do, with a special spoon for the very purpose because you wouldn't dream of using the spoon with which you stirred the sauce (*à la* Marco Pierre White) and with which you were compelled to conduct the fourth movement *saltarello*. Talking of salt, you even know intuitively what constitutes a definitive pinch.

Finito.

The perfect four hours left for the flavours to mellow and the pungent fumes in the kitchen to subside into provocative wafts.

On with the second task. Cleaning. No *Shake 'n' Vac* short cuts for Richard. He glides around the sitting-room, eyes constantly searching out invisible dust, ears tuned to the oboe, serene above the crowded strings of the opening of the Scottish Symphony. Dust first, plump the cushions, straighten the tulips. Hoover. Spick and span.

Bedroom. Change the sheets, open the window. Hoover. Next.

Bathroom. Clean the bath, the sink; disinfect the toilet,

change the pot pourri; wash the tiles and the mirror, rinse well. Buff up. Hoover. Done. Next?

Body. 'Go running' is next on the Stonehill Schedule. Put on Nikes, put the wine in the fridge, look once round the flat, feel pleased, proud and at ease. Off you go.

Richard's daily run took him four miles and twenty-six minutes. Usually he thought of nothing, and thinking of nothing ensured he was relaxed and psychologically out of the office by the time he returned. Today, however, his mind was running faster than his feet.

Say she doesn't turn up? Say she's a vegetarian? Say my mother rings? Say Bob and Catherine pop round? Shit, did I turn the gas off? Have I got any condoms at home? Shall I buy Beaumes de Venise *too? Yes, definitely. But I'd better buy that now so it can chill thoroughly. Wait, work this through. Get home, check condoms . . . no, check gas first. Then condoms. Shower? No, buy the pudding wine, then shower, then phone Mother. Other way round. Let's just get home.*

Sprint, Richard, sprint!

Home, James. You didn't spare the horses today: 23 minutes 34 seconds. Not bad, not bad.

The gas was, of course, off.

Half an hour later, with condoms and wine bought and placed in bedside table and fridge respectively, Mother was phoned, the table laid, the sauce checked and fresh purple basil scattered through it. At last, Richard can start the final, crucial lap. Preening.

Hands on hips, upper lip sucked in by lower, wardrobe doors thrown open, he peruses his clothes. He touches nothing, just looks and assesses. Navy cotton chinos, brown suede belt, shirt striped thickly in blue and thinly in peppermint, white boxers, navy socks and navy nubuck loafers.

Navy, navy, navy, do you think that's too conservative?

No, Richard, you look wonderful in navy. Anyway, if you want to be pedantic, there's a subtle but effective difference between the French Navy of your shoes and the true navy of your trousers. If you're not happy, why not wear the shirt striped with olive and pink?

I'll go for the olive and pink.

In the tiler's delight bathroom, Richard showers. It is his routine to take it moderately hot and to finish off with a prolonged blast of freezing cold which, he assures himself, is invigorating and good for the circulation. Old habits die hard and this one stemmed from eight not always easy years at boarding school.

With a towel wrapped effortlessly around his trunk and another draped nonchalantly over his shoulder, Richard gives himself a close shave. To a fly on the wall, or on a majolica tile, the scene has all the features of a classic after-shave advert, bar the transatlantic voice-over drawl proclaiming: '*L'Homme, one hundred per cent.*' But this is Notting Hill and our Richard, towel now slipping irretrievably, is standing with eyes watering from the healthy smart of his one-hundred-per-cent manly after-shave. A few strange and not desperately appealing physiognomic contortions aid recovery but his towel still lies, somewhat comically, about his feet. No need and no time to rescue it and save his style. There is pressing work to be done involving a comb, an agile wrist and a damp mop of light-magnetic, sand-coloured hair. Comb it this way, then that. Run through a little mousse, comb again then lightly shake through with your fingertips. Result: the perfect, tousled look.

Get dressed, Richard, Sally will arrive in the hour. No, there's another job; out with the nail clippers and emery board, ensure that fingers and toes are neat and tidy. They are, they always are. Step into your boxers, slip on your trousers, pull on your shirt and slide into your loafers. You're ready, you're gorgeous. Now just lounge about, reinstate Mr Mendelssohn where your run so rudely cut him off, relax and await the arrival of Ms Lomax.

Miss Lomax was late back from school. An emergency meeting had been held to determine whether to expel or merely suspend an eleven-year-old boy for smoking in the girls' toilets. Sally suggested doing neither but making him smoke the entire packet. In front of his friends. However, the boy was suspended and sent home directly, with his packet of cigarettes. After school the teachers gathered to formulate the Monday morning assembly on the evils of smoking. It's bad for your health, very expensive and *not clever at all.*

But she's home now and is perturbed to find that she does not have time for her customary Friday evening bath, her *luxuriate.* Instead, a quick shower must suffice.

The Lomax legs are shaved and two stray hairs are tweezed from the bridge of her nose. Sally gives her hair an energetic brush and thanks the stars that she'd washed it the previous evening. She swirls a soft brush around a pot of bronze balls of rouge and carelessly but effectively whispers it over her cheeks and eyes. And cleavage, why not! After a quick spritz of *Ysatis,* she deftly flosses her teeth. Into the bedroom she goes, humming absent-mindedly 'The Lord Is My Shepherd', that morning's hymn. It's black velvet skirt time. She teams it with the olive silk shirt and black suede pumps with just the right height of heel to give her unremarkable legs an elegant send-off. Under it all, her little white cotton broderie anglaise knickers, for good luck.

Sally, you won't need it.

Before leaving the flat, she stops for a prolonged glance in the mirror and gives herself a slightly bashful smile.

Off you go, you old slapper! Shall I seduce him in between hors d'oeuvres and main course? Or before?

That's something for you to ponder on the Highgate–Notting Hill drive. Off you go, Sally.

Adjusting the choke, smoothing non-existent wrinkles from her skirt, Sally mirrored, signalled and manoeuvred – and then reversed straight back into the space she had just vacated. She unclipped her seatbelt and walked briskly back to her flat. She stopped in the sitting-room and gazed at the telephone which was ringing pleadingly. Beaming an ecstatic smile at it, she marched assertively into the bathroom. Giving her reflection a conniving wink, Sally plucked her toothbrush from the beaker and slipped it into her bag.

SEVEN

As soon as Sally entered Richard's flat, it was she who was seduced. And not by Richard. It was the smell of cooking: a mellow base of tomato and something she couldn't put her finger on, laced with top notes of garlic and basil. She realized how ravenous she was. For food. For sex too, but for food first and foremost. She'd passed on the shepherd's pie offered for lunch that day at school and had had to make do with a floury Cox's and a rubbery chunk of cheddar.

Sally was surprised that she wasn't in the least nervous. Richard, however, was. Unseen, and feeling queasy with excitement, he had watched Sally drive up and down the street looking for a parking place. He had gone straight to the kitchen and kept his hands motionless under the cold tap – sweaty palms would not be a turn on and were most unStonehill.

And here they are now, together again less than a week since their first meeting. How do they look to each other? How do they feel? Knowing full well how memory can often play havoc with reality and turn reptiles into royalty, Sally is relieved that Richard is just as good-looking and suave as she remembered. Richard is thrilled, his flat seems instantly infused with energy and light and his palms remain cool and dry. He thinks she looks scrumptious and has to fight back an impulse to scoop her up and twirl her around.

Nonchalant 'Hi's were followed with the briefest of pecks on the cheek. Richard led Sally through and lowered the volume of the Brahms. While he fixed her the obligatory drink ('Spritzer will be lovely, thanks'), she perused his books – just as Richard had at Sally's. She was amused that many of her dog-eared paperbacks were duplicated in here in pristine hardback. She wondered if he really *enjoyed* Nietzsche and what his favourite Shakespeare was.

'Seize her,' Richard murmured.

'I like the History Plays too,' Sally agreed.

Mentally, she catalogued all she saw and it all seemed to add up to the man she thought and hoped Richard was. Tulips in November, how decadent. A gleaming kitchen, ten out of ten. Leather recliner, lose five points. Cream sofa piled high with cushions, five points restored.

'Can I use your bathroom?'

'Sure, through there.'

Full marks for hygiene, bonus marks for the thickness of the towels, an overall gold star for taste. She flushed the loo just to make it seem that her trip to the bathroom had been for a purpose other than a snoop. Coming back into the lounge she had a furtive glance into the bedroom – it seemed quiet, airy and muted. Good.

'Sally, let's eat.'

For Sally, this meal was to be a sounding board for her scheme. All week, in the privacy of her flat and with a mirror propped close as the harshest of critics, she had practised a new technique on a variety of foods. Food, she had decided, was not so much to be eaten to be digested, as eaten to seduce. Hitherto she had merely cut asparagus into spearable, bite-sized chunks, now she could devour them whole with slow, sensual appeal. Although she had never really got to grips with the taste or method of oysters, she could now sip and gulp them with the alluring grace of a film star. To her relief, neither was on the menu tonight – anyway, asparagus had a strange effect on her bladder and she simply did not like those slithering detritus feeders, full stop.

Richard had prepared a meal that was as chic and delicious as it was simple. He had laid the table with a fine white damask cloth, dark red linen napkins, and cutlery and glass that shone proud. He'd toyed with the idea of a candle and a rose but was instantly repelled at the corniness of it (they would have had minus marks from Sally anyway). Instead, he dimmed the lights just slightly and, at Sally's request, replaced Brahms with Van the Man. *'My Brown-eyed Girl' indeed*, thought Richard.

He brought out the *Prosciutto S. Daniele* which he had rolled around *grissini.*

Shall I lick at it and suck at it suggestively?

Hold off a while, Sally. You don't want to be too obvious.

Ultimately, it was far too delicious to do anything to but eat and enjoy.

Richard stared at her, held her gaze for a groin-stirring moment and then dropped his eyes to her mouth.

Just look at that crumb nestling in the corner of her lips. A peony mouth, just like Hardy's Tess. Don't realize it's there, Sally, let me linger on it a while longer. I have to have that crumb, your mouth.

He leant forward, driven by the desire to lick the crumb, but Sally's tongue beat him by a split second. He'd lost the crumb but was awarded a tantalizing taste of her tongue tip. Her eyes spoke of the wry smile her lips wore but which he could not see, so close was he to her face. Unfortunately, it was not a pose he could hold comfortably indefinitely, propped as he was on his elbows and precariously close to the jug of vinaigrette. He sat back and saw how Sally's wry smile was not confined to her lips but covered her whole face. It raised her cheekbones, it caused delicate lines around her eyes, it dimpled her chin just very slightly.

I want to suck your chin.

'Delicious.'

Giving himself a dignified minute in which to let his erection melt away, he rose to fetch the next dish. A warm salad of rocket and baby spinach with roasted red peppers and individual goat cheeses. Richard offered to dress it for Sally. She watched him whisk the vinaigrette and liked the way that such a simple task was possible only with great effort from the ligaments and tendons of his wrist – she wanted to place a finger over them lightly as they twitched and sprang. She thought how lovely Richard's wrist was, slender and tanned and sporting a most beautiful watch (Cartier). She had never paid attention to a wrist before.

Sally ate delicately, folding the leaves securely over her fork and cutting each slither of pepper into careful pieces. She could not risk splash-back tonight – for the sake of both Richard's libido and her new silk shirt.

Richard finished before Sally. He watched. She stared back, eating all the while.

The skill of it! Every forkful placed perfectly in the centre of your perfect mouth without looking! Can I kiss you yet? When?

The plate was now bare but there was still a film of vinaigrette left. It was such a beautiful dressing, why shouldn't Sally run her finger round her plate? After all, *waste not, want not.* And, after all, it stirred Richard's groin again, not that Sally was aware of it.

The main course consisted of a bed of *pappardelle* woven throughout with *porcini* and chicken, and suffused with garlic, basil, sage and the ubiquitous olive oil.

That it was extra virgin and cold pressed goes without saying, we know Richard now. Sally had never had *porcini* before and was at first baffled as to whether they were meat or vegetable, so savoury was the taste, so firm the texture.

I must buy some of these.

Sally, they cost Richard twelve pounds.

The whole was a perfect partnership and created a lovely warm aromatic cloud in the mouth.

Thank God we're both having garlic, thought Sally, anticipating post-dinner sport. The pasta, broader than *tagliatelle*, was much more fork-friendly, preventing dribbles of sauce to the chin, or stray pieces hanging regrettably from the corner of the mouth (much to the chagrin of Richard's tongue).

The olive oil gave Sally's lips a gloss, too tantalizing for Richard to sit and merely observe. The vinaigrette jug was now off the table, the bread basket was on the floor. The scene had set itself for Richard; there was space for him to lean across, there were the sides of the table to hold for stability. Assertively he swiped Sally's mouth with his tongue. Her lips tasted of dressing, her mouth of Sally. Richard's tongue tasted of passion. Sally was buzzing between her legs, her bosom was heaving cinematically. She was ready to leave the meal for a banquet of sex.

No. Wait. Not yet. Keep it going, keep him just there. Let him stay a while hovering on the brink of being crazed and senseless with desire. Pull away. Smile as sweetly as you can and take a coy sip of that lovely Bardolino.

'Cheese?' Richard croaked.

'Please,' Sally purred.

Just two cheeses, complementing each other and the food that had gone before and that was to follow; the oozing, subtle *Taleggio* and spicier *Pecorino* accompanied by further slithers of Rosa Gambini's *ciabatta*, flatter yet with so much more spring and taste than the dull supermarket counterfeits. Richard had cleverly judged the servings and though they were both thoroughly satisfied, an all-important space still existed in their stomachs.

Undoubtedly, the *pièce de résistance* was the pudding. *Tiramisù*, of course. Another first for Sally. Richard had bought a complete dish from Rosa, just under a foot square, and Sally was soon fantasizing about diving into the centre of it and eating her way to the surface. Remembering his first taste of *tiramisù*, that it was not merely a delicious flavour but a sensation, an unforgettable experience too, Richard decided to halt his spoon midway to his portion so he could observe Sally's reaction.

As she spooned into it, she thought how beautiful it looked. The dark matt brown of the cocoa powder, the soft ivory of the *marscapone*, the glistening sponge, speckled through with espresso coffee.

I think I'm probably going to enjoy this very much. It could be dangerous!

As the spoon neared her mouth, a wisp of scent seduced her nose. Coffee-booze-chocolate. She looked across at Richard, waiting in anticipation. She smiled, giving a fleeting twitch of eyebrow. Still holding his gaze, she slowly pushed the loaded spoon into her mouth. It was like a trigger, a chemical reaction: her eyes snapped shut and simultaneously Richard grinned broadly. The first thing to accost her was the bitterness of the cocoa, thick and dry against the roof of her mouth. In an instant, the cool fluff of *marscapone* filtered through, wetting the powder which metamorphosed into a subtle and heavenly chocolaty sludge. The texture and taste were heady and incomparable. Then the marsala and rum, sodden in the sponge, broke through and created a warmth that trickled down into her chest. Finally, a kick from the espresso forced her eyes open and her head to shake slowly in astonishment. It was the signal for Richard to have his spoonful. For Sally, *tiramisù* was more than a 'pick me up', she was literally stoned on the stuff.

An orgasm versus a first taste of tiramisù. *A tough choice if ever there was one! Both, please!*

Later, Sally, later. There's still one more thing for you to try.

After Sally's second helping (Richard was delighted – he could not abide the Abstemious Woman), he poured her a full and very chilled glass of Beaumes de Venise. Again he watched. First Sally cleaned her teeth with her tongue, searching for any hidden cocoa. Somewhat dismayed, she found nothing. She raised the glass, now aesthetically bloomed with condensation, and took note of the golden blush colour and the sweet, floral smell. Bouquet, Sally, bouquet. She took a sip. It was liquid silk. It was cold, clean and exquisite. If ambrosia is *tiramisù*, and she suspected it very probably was, then Beaumes de Venise was nectar. The food, the drink of the gods.

Sally's eyes wore a glazed expression. She looked across to Richard who looked soft and mellow under the wine and the dimmed lights. She was having a thoroughly good time. Never had she been so overwhelmed by such different taste sensations. Never had she simply enjoyed food so much. Now she knew for sure that aphrodisiacs existed.

Clever boy, Richard, you've seduced her with food, she's now ready, waiting and willing for part two of the evening's schedule. Physical pleasure.

Up you get, walk across and stand behind her chair. Scoop her hair up into a pony tail, tilt her head back slightly. Release her hair and let your hands fall on to her neck. It's delicate, you notice how vulnerable it feels, encircled entirely by your overlapping hands. Venture down and let your finger tips rest on her collar bone. Stroke that soft dip at her throat. Take one hand away and palm back the hair from her forehead. Gaze into those eyes, keep the gaze and move your other hand from her neck down across the silk of her shirt. You are between her breasts now. Find her left breast, cup it, press it, squeeze it. Let your hand lie soft, feeling her pip-like nipple in your palm. The touch of silk, the warmth and firmness of the flesh beneath.

Pull her to her feet and grasp her close to you. Keep the one hand holding her neck, put the other into the small of her back and pull her tightly against you. Press yourself against her; feel yourself hard, straining. Move your leg across and push her legs slightly apart. Now she too has something to push against. Lower your hand and feel her buttocks tense, you remember perfectly what they look like.

A gorgeous peach of an arse.

To feel its curve under velvet is as alluring as a breast under silk. But flesh itself is better. Her flesh is what you want.

Kiss her. Don't open your mouth, just press your lips against hers. Her tongue fleets at your lips. You respond. As the kisses become longer and deeper, you both push and grind your groins against each other. You feel like eating her. Nibbling at her lips does not suffice. Push her mouth open wide, as wide as it will go and probe as deep as you can. Feel her search back. Feel her run her tongue over the inside of your teeth. Bite her. Feel her simultaneously flinch yet move even closer and more insistently against you. Bite her again and feel her bite back. You are aware that her hand is starting to travel down. Away from your earlobe, down, down.

Lower, Sally, lower. Find me hard, rub your hand against me. Tracc the shape of me. No don't take your hand away. Don't pull away from my lips. I want you. Where have you gone?

The CD had long stopped but the silence was loaded. Richard and Sally stood there, panting, mouths reddened, feet apart, a foot apart. Sally reached out and pulled Richard towards her by grasping the front of his trousers. Again they ate-kissed. Again they separated. Again at her instigation. He stepped towards her and she stepped back. He stepped towards her and again she retreated. The two were tangoing. Then he was ready. He took two steps forward to her one back and had her again, close to him, squeezing her waist with one arm, the other enmeshed in her hair. She gasped as her hair snagged around his fingers. She tried to tug away but he simply tightened his grip. To hear her breath, rasping, sent him into a fast frenzy of desire. He held her at arms' length as she tried to approach. Now he pushed her away.

Once more they stared, like matador and bull. Slowly he came to her and slid his hand up her skirt. It was tight but she helped by standing on her tiptoes. He wriggled upwards, effortlessly, to bullseye position. Sally lowered her heels back down. He could feel how moist she was under her panties and, with his thumb and third finger, tweaked and pressed superlatively.

Spot on, Richard.

Still they stared relentlessly into each other's eyes while Richard's skilful fingers set to work.

Look at her face, glazed eyes as if she does not see me though she looks right at me. Let me rub you right there. Let me go a little further. Look at your eyelids flicker. Look at your head tilt slightly back exposing your neck which I must graze with my teeth. Let me undo your blouse.

Deftly, Richard unbuttoned just enough of Sally's blouse to expose an exquisite breast. He ceased movement with his other hand though Sally pushed herself against it eagerly.

Look at me, Richard. Never have you desired a woman so much as you yearn for me this very moment. Feel me, move your hand from my arm but don't leave my gaze. Feel the breast that you've released from its shield of olive silk. Feel it. Yes, just like that. Increase the pressure. Again. Oh.

Richard introduced his finger tips and twisted Sally's nipple gently. He felt her move against his other hand and he made his fingers there come suddenly alive. Probing, twisting, rubbing. He looked at Sally's face. Her head was now involuntarily thrown backwards and to one side; it enticed him to suck at her neck, to fondle her breast firmly, to increase the speed of his fingers below. He felt her rocking her pelvis faster and faster. A surge of moistness. She let out a noise midway between a yelp and a gasp and brought her head back straight, once again meeting his eye directly. They stared into each other as they both felt the pulsations ebb away and stop. After a moment's stillness, Richard probed again, stroking with dexterous mastery. The throbs returned, less defined but certainly there. Sally's face had begun to soften. Her eyelids closed more frequently and for longer. Her head dropped slightly. To both of them, her body seemed to be melting.

Richard drew Sally towards him and cradled her carefully, holding her still and steady and close for minutes. Her head was buried against his chest, her shoulders were slumped, her exposed breast was now blushed, the nipple soft and puffy. She stayed against him feeling safe with the smell of him; sweat and pheromones filling her nose, his taste still in her mouth. He kissed the top of her head. She looked up and kissed him on his lips while he kept them motionless. With a hand on her shoulder and another around her waist, he led her to his bedroom and, on the bed with the fresh, crisp linen, he made slow and languid love to her.

EIGHT

Was it a chip in the paintwork or was it a spider?

Sally had been staring at the small, dark mark on the ceiling, trying to make up her mind. In that state of reverie, when eyes are young and focusing is lazy, she had been sure, alternately, that it was the one and then the other. Now that her eyes were awake and functioning she decided that it must be a mark or a dent.

And then it moved.

It was a spider. The intimate peace of the situation had been disrupted. Sally was now aware of other movements and noises. The blind breezed forward every now and then. The duvet curved up and fell down peacefully with her breathing. She could hear the clock, digital but audible; phit, phit, phit. For every three phits came one long, hushed, oblivious breath from Richard. A distant thrush sang to the morning while an occasional car hummed by. Under it all she could decipher the fridge adjusting its thermostat.

She lay on her back with Richard's arm lolling on top of the quilt over her stomach. She checked for the spider and found him a little further along the ceiling, playing dents again.

If I woke now, and saw him, I'd probably presume again that he was a dent. I wonder if he times his sorties according to phits? Sally grinned at her early-morning dedication to pointless ponderings, her commitment to theorizing over nothing particular. Shyly, she looked across at Richard. Asleep and safe and soundless. She wondered what time it was and reckoned round about 7.30. But then knowing the exact time suddenly assumed great importance so she tuned into the phitting and travelled her eyes up over Richard to locate the clock. 7.45. She smiled. And then smiled again, not knowing why.

He's awfully good-looking. I have chosen well.

But over and above the surge she felt on gazing at him, was a softness and warmth inside for him.

Stop it, stop it. Sally, stop.

And yet she found herself not recalling, thrust by thrust, the athletics of the previous night, but simply looking at him in the here and now. Asleep. Lovely. She felt compelled to reach out and delicately stroke away the flop of hair meandering over his eye and the bridge of his nose. Then she lingered and, with her fingertips, traced his eyebrows and the soft dips in the corners of his eyes. A careful fingertip brushed away an endearing pip of sleepydust. Again she found herself smiling and felt that same softness and warmth within.

No, Sally, no. Stop it. No. Impossible. Not after a week. Not ever.

The spider was on the move again and scuttled across and over to where the cupboards met the ceiling. The crack was plenty big enough and it disappeared from view.

Well, if the spider can snoop then so can I.

She left the bedroom noiselessly and went through to the lounge and over to the kitchen.

You can tell a lot about a person by what he keeps in the fridge.

You can tell a lot about a person by what they eat for breakfast, and with the fridge door still open, Sally ate *tiramisù* straight from the dish. Crouching on her heels, she noted that the milk was semi-skimmed and the eggs were free-range. There were peppers of every conceivable colour, flat-leaf parsley in a small tumbler of water, live yoghurts, slices of meat in Harrod's cellophane and a punnet of raspberries.

In November!

Having had enough *tiramisù* (for now), Sally opened a limed oak cupboard and catalogued the fine oils and vinegar, the packet of *porcini* which looked withered, rather sorry and somewhat inedible in their dried state. Much to her amusement and relief, right at the back she spied a large bottle of HP Sauce. She smiled and opened the next cupboard and examined the china. Villeroy and Boch.

That'll do.

Over in the lounge, she went to the bookcase to handle those sumptuous leather volumes. She ran her hand along the ash, very smooth and surprisingly warm. With a tentative fingertip, she felt the embossed spines and read the titles to herself. She took down *Julius Caesar* and ran it over her cheek. She fanned the pages and inhaled deeply. Then she touched the spine with her tongue tip and was miles away in another small heaven of her own when peace was shattered by the post.

He gets The National Geographic, *what luxury!*

Leaving the rest of the post with the *Guardian* on the doormat, Sally curled up on the leather recliner and lost herself in the social behaviour of the humpback whale, and went on a fascinating trip through Alaska by husky.

And that was how Richard found her when he surfaced half an hour later.

'Morning, Sal.'

'Morning, Richie.'
'Breakfast?'
'Mmm.'
'In bed?'
'And why not!'

How civilized: warm croissants, freshly juiced oranges, a good pot of Earl Grey and the morning paper.

'This is my favourite part of Saturday's *Guardian*, the Questionnaire,' revealed Sally, and they laughed out loud at Alan Bennett's disclosures. Richard grabbed a spoon and turned it into a microphone.

'Sally Lomax, twenty-five, teacher, *National Geographic* reader, *tiramisù* demolisher and sex-goddess, what is your idea of perfect happiness?' He thrust the spoon at her.

Delighted, Sally sparked back: 'A beautiful stone farmhouse in Tuscany and a dark swarthy male to go with it.'

Actually, Saturday morning, breakfast in bed, the paper and you would do nicely. But you shan't know that.

'With which historical figure do you most identify?'

'Lady Godiva.'

'Which living person do you most admire?'

'Aunt Celia. She's seventy and has the strength of an ox and the courage of Samson.'

'What vehicles do you own?'

'Strong pair of legs.'

'And a Mini Cooper. What is your greatest extravagance?'

'Danish pastries.'

'And *tiramisù* for breakfast?'

Sally blushed.

'Sal, you're blushing! What objects do you always carry with you?'

'Donor card, paracetamol, rape alarm, pocket hankies, emery board, safety pins, stamps, address book.'

'Am I in it?'

'No.'

'What makes you most depressed?'

'Child abuse. Oh, and synthetic cream.'

'What do you most dislike about your appearance?'

'I rather like it!'

'Sally!' Richard chastized.

'Okay, my bikini line hair,' Sally confided.

'What is your most unappealing habit?'

'I don't have any.'

'Sally!' Richard warned again.

'Oh, God. Okay, I fart in the bath.' They fell about laughing and Richard admitted quite happily that he did too.

'What would you like for your next birthday?'

'An answerphone. No, a weekend in Boston.'

'When is your birthday?'

'Next year. May the nineteenth.'

'What is your favourite word?'

'Funicular.'

'You *what*?'

'It's a lovely word to say. Try it.'

'Fu-nic-u-lar. Hmm. What is your favourite journey?'

'The road to Oban, the boat to Mull; to Aunt Celia's.'

'Who are your favourite musicians?'

'Genesis, Van the Man, Dylan.'

'Anyone told you it's now the 1990s? Who are your favourite writers?'

'Alice Thomas Ellis and Jane Austen.' *Oh, and Ms Collins.*

'What or who is the greatest love of your life?'

She panicked momentarily and looked at him blankly. 'Myself?' she ventured. He seemed pleased with that.

'Which living person do you most despise?'

'Despise? I don't care much for Myra Hindley or Peter Sutcliffe.'

'What do you consider the most overrated virtue?'

'Chasteness. Decorum.' Richard raised his eyebrows at the intensity of her proclamation.

'What is your greatest regret?'

'Not being good enough to go to ballet school.'

'Ballet?'

'Ten years of it.'

'That explains your hyper-mobility then! When and where were you happiest?'

'Childhood holidays at Aunt Celia's in Mull.'

'What single thing would improve the quality of your life?'

'A farmhouse in Tuscany.'

'And the dark, swarthy man?'

'Him too.'

'What would your motto be?'

'Don't look before you leap.'

'How would you like to die?'

'When I'm ready.'

'How would you like to be remembered?'

'With desire and longing and a twinkle in the eye.'

'Thank you, Ms Lomax,' said Richard, pouring her another cup of Earl Grey and stirring it with the microphone, 'that was intriguing!'

And necessary, my love. 'But there's one more question,' he asked lasciviously, 'how do you like it best?'

Sally smirked. 'Milk, no sugar?' she ventured.

Richard raised his eyebrows in a that-won't-do fashion.

'I'll show you later. First, there's the small but pressing issue of your answers, Richard Stonehill.'

'And then you'll show me?'

'Then I'll show you.'

NINE

'Richard Stonehill, thirty-five, architect, new-age man and all round good-looker, what is your idea of perfect happiness?'

'Yachting in Australia.' *You, Sal.*

'Ever done it?'

'Yes, I have.'

'What is your greatest fear?'

'Multiple sclerosis.'

'With which historical figure do you most identify?'

'Byron.'

'How pretentious! Which living person do you most admire?'

'Bob.'

'Bob-and-Catherine Bob?'

'Yes.'

'What vehicles do you own?'

'An Alfa Romeo Spyder and a Cannondale mountain bike.'

'What is your greatest extravagance?'

'Silk ties and olive oil that's as expensive as the former.'

'What objects do you always carry with you?'

'Why, my little black book of course.'

'Am I in your little black book?'

'You are in my little black book.'

'What makes you most depressed?'

'Housing estates. Oh, and nylon.'

'Hear hear. What do you most dislike about your appearance?'

'My legs.'

'Your legs?'

'Too skinny.'

Richard, they're gorgeous, unquestionably masculine, you vain old thing.

'What is your most unappealing habit?'

'*Moi? Rien!*'

'Ri-*chard!*'

'Okay, I pick my nose, fart and belch.'

'Big deal.'

'Simultaneously. In the bath.'

'Gracious Good Lord. What would you most like for your next birthday present?'

'You. Wrapped up in brown paper and red ribbons.'

'When is your birthday?'

'June the second.'

'I'll see what I can do. What is your favourite word?'

'Telecommunication,' proclaimed Richard. 'Well, it *sounds* nice, doesn't it?' Sally raised an eyebrow. 'Oh, all right then – copulation.'

'Later. What or who is the greatest love of your life?'

'My mummy!'

Laughter erupted and Sally tickled Richard into saying 'Architecture' and finally admitting 'Food'.

'Oops, watch that cup! What do you consider the most overrated virtue?'

'Etiquette.'

'What is your greatest regret?'

'That my father and I did not get along.'

'It's never too late for a reconciliation.'

'He's dead.'

'Oh. Poor Richie. Mine died when I was fifteen. When and where were you happiest?'

'Finishing the London marathon three years ago.'

'What single thing would improve the quality of your life?'

'A housekeeper-cum-therapist-cum-masseuse-cum-sex-goddess. Want the job? Seven-fifty an hour?'

'Ten? Done! Which talent would you most like to have?'

'Telepathy.'

'What would your motto be?'

'*Bien faire ce que j'ai à faire.*' Sally nodded, earnestly hoping to veil the fact that she had not the faintest idea what that meant.

'How would you like to be remembered?'

'As Sally Lomax's favourite lay!' *As Sally Lomax's favourite.*

'Thank you, Richard Stonehill, for your co-operation and honesty. Would you like your reward now or after lunch?'

'What do you think?'

Richard and Sally explored each other's bodies with a new inquisitiveness and a new depth. A new tenderness, too. Richard found how Sally's personality shone through; her breasts spoke of it, her fuzzy bikini line proclaimed it. She spent a long time caressing his legs, with hands, lips and eyes, showing him that they drove her wild. She whispered 'telecommunication' as she chewed and licked his ear lobes. He hummed Genesis and sang 'Turn It On Again' after she came. She came again. She felt more fulfilled than she had with any other man, not that there had been that many. Now they both wanted to give, not merely to take. To give and to receive, to linger and to lap it up.

What is it that I am feeling? thought Sally as she

showered, alone, in Richard's bathroom. *What is it?* she wondered, as she swathed herself in Richard's thick, burgundy towelling robe. *What is it that feels so, well, nice?* she asked herself as she padded across the bedroom to gaze out of the window at nothing in particular.

They lunched and munched together, snuggled deep in Richard's voluminous sofa; *du pain, du vin, du Boursin.* Later, they browsed and tinkered at Portobello Market. He bought her two pounds of Cox's Orange Pippins, she bought him half a pound of pear drops which tasted of white paper bag, just like they had in childhood, just as they should. The weather was as crisp as the apples, their noses were reddened and noisy, their fingers chilled. They thawed out at the Gate Cinema and were warmed by coffee, carrot cake and a Louis Malle matinée.

On her way home she stopped at a chemist. And bought a new toothbrush. She had not forgotten to take hers home, nor had she planned to leave it. She did not leave it accidentally-on-purpose, nor had she connived with herself in the bathroom mirror. She had done no grinning at the toothbrush. It was in the same beaker as Richard's but they were not touching. His was an angle-poised, hard bristle; hers was small-headed and soft. She had left it merely because it had looked just fine in the beaker with Richard's. Richard was not madly excited to find it there later, but certainly he was happy that it was there. That night, alone but not lonely in their respective beds, they did not think of each other but of themselves. Friday nights and Saturday mornings were to become an institution, not that they knew it then. If waves of contentment can travel, then the vibes from Highgate and those from Notting Hill would have met, crashed and fallen to earth somewhere around Regents Park. Which is precisely where, three days later, Sally and Richard next met.

TEN

With the future of the Zoo uncertain, schools all over London chose it over Hatfield House or Madame Tussaud's for their annual school outings.

With the future of the Zoo uncertain, a team of architects was consulted over proposals for a building dedicated to research and conservation of endangered species. The idea was to promote the Zoo as a foundation, a trust dedicated to understanding and preserving and improving the future for threatened wildlife. It was to lose its image of merely housing bored tigers and sloping-shouldered eagles in cracked concrete. The hope was, that if seen as environmentally aware and ecologically sympathetic, funding from all sectors would be more readily available. In theory alone, the proposal had been met with great enthusiasm from the public and the government had given it a quiet nod or two already.

The Zoological Society, placed as it is in the outer circle of the Park, affords a sweeping vista. Especially from the wide window from which Richard gazed, plastic beaker of instant coffee in hand, waiting for the first, crucial meeting with his potential clients. He watched nostalgically as a human crocodile of ten-year-olds made its haphazard approach to the main gates, sections of its vertebrae frequently slipping out of alignment. He remembered well the joy of walking hand in hand with a best friend, the despair of having to hold hands tightly with an enemy, the humiliation of holding hands with the most unpopular boy in the class. The crocodile's nose was black and red, because those were the only colours Diana Lewis wore. Its body was a multicoloured jumble of school children in mufti. Its navy tail caught and captured Richard's attention.

The tail of the crocodile was Sally Lomax.

'Good morning, Mr Stonehill, we are sorry to have kept you waiting. Shall we start?'

But I want to see the crocodile!

'Mr Stonehill?'

I don't want to be in this stuffy building, I want to find the crocodile and watch its tail swish.

'Gentlemen, lady, this is Richard Stonehill from Mendle-Brooke Associates.'

'Good morning,' said Richard somewhat reluctantly, as he took the head of the table and began unravelling the roll of drawings, crocodiles still foremost in his mind. However, as soon as his design unfurled itself, Richard was totally focused. His personality, his gifted presentation and the skill of the design itself kept his audience rapt. An hour and a half shot by. Had they had the money there and then, they would have pressed cash into his hand and given him *carte blanche* to start immediately. Reality, however, would impose a minimum two-year wait.

'I think I'll just have a wander,' Richard informed his hosts as everybody shook hands. 'It's the crocodiles that fascinate me.'

The children were having a lovely time, especially Marsha and Rajiv who were still holding hands long after the crocodile had disintegrated. Sharp, sweet wafts of dung and straw were filtered by the chill air and were pleasing to the nose. The bellow of the camel was impersonated very well by Marcus who was offered a ride by the keeper. Squeals of delight filled the air as the dromedary lunged and lurched itself up. The children's zoo proved very popular too; little hands gently petted even littler furries and packed lunches were shared illicitly with the bleating, pleading, pocket-nuzzling deer and goats.

Around Miss Lewis, a band of keen young artists had gathered to sketch the elephants.

It was cold, cold, but clear. Everyone was in a thoroughly good mood.

'Oh, children, the light's just *per*fect! *Sim*ply perfect. I've brought charcoal and 4B pencils and some waxy crayons. Who wants what?' The waxy crayons were the first to be snapped up followed sharply by the charcoal. The pencils were the last to go because Miss Lewis forbade erasers – 'Work *through* your mistakes, make your errors a part of your de*sign*' was her oft-chanted dictum. Experience had taught Class Five that any child caught smuggling a rubber would have it ceremoniously confiscated and, worse, would have to contend with Miss Lewis's inconsolable hurt.

With not much more than an ear or tusk completed, the children began to complain of cold toes and numb fingers. Miss Lewis had overcome that problem by investing in a pair of red mittens, the tips of which could be folded back to reveal black, fingerless gloves. She sat on the bench surrounded by the hastily dumped materials of her protégés (off to see the *yeuch! spi*ders and *urgh! beet*les) and breathed in the coarse, sweet smell of elephant. Wielding a 4B as a conductor might his baton, she began to draw fervently, making any mistake a committed part of the overall design.

Sally, who had just finished a quick chat with the polar

bear (he had winked at her, slowly and wisely), contemplated the scamper and flurry of her class, released from the greyness of school and its buildings. She felt a little sad, imagining how the animals too would kick up their heels and squeal with delight if they were turned out into pastures new, let alone to their native habitats. She thought it cruel how the children teased the rhino for being so ugly, the way they grimaced and growled at the motionless lion, chattered and jumped around in front of the chimps and tapped on the glass of the aquarium to see if the fish would budge or the clam slam shut. She walked past the birds of prey and couldn't associate the moth-eaten raptors with those she remembered from her childhood holidays, soaring in majestic abandon over the hills near Aunt Celia's.

Miss Lewis had a hushed audience about her. All over her scarf (black) and her jumper (red) were chunks and furls of wood and lead: 'Never use a sharpener, gives a *gha*stly line. Scalpel. That's the answer. *Su*per edge. Absolutely not, Marcus, only I can use it. *Horribly* sharp. Trust me.' The children were wowed into silence by the skill with which Miss Lewis brandished her 4B, the verisimilitude of her drawing. The keeper recognized the sage old face immediately as Bertha. Richard Stonehill had glanced at the picture, greatly impressed. But he looked more intently at what had been the nose of the crocodile; he wondered what her name was and how well she knew Sally. Bertha, with unarguable dignity and grace, nevertheless answered the call of nature with an extremely ripe-smelling and resounding thud. The keeper didn't smell it at all any more but the children shrieked with delight and bolted away, proclaiming 'Poo! Poo!' for the uninformed. Distracted, Miss Lewis looked up momentarily, caught Richard's eyes, smiled fleetingly and returned her undivided attention to Bertha who was, she decided, the most beautiful creature she had ever seen. Richard wandered off in search of a sandwich.

Sally wandered over to Diana.

'Lunch?'

'Mmm? Nyet. Iniminit.' Sally wandered off in search of a sandwich.

Every corner Richard turned, every enclosure he went to see, he felt sure he would finally come across Sally. His adrenal glands were in overdrive and he had demolished the sandwich in seconds without tasting it. Now it sat in his throat in a stodgy lump and felt as if it further protruded his Adam's apple. Swallow as he might, he could not shift it an inch lower nor soften it at all. A drink was a possible solution.

The kiosk was a round structure with only one serving hatch. As Sally bought her cheese and pickle sandwich and carton of Ribena and walked away anticlockwise, Richard came from the other direction and exited clockwise. But there was no Chaplinesque crash and they each remained oblivious to the tantalizing proximity of the other. Sally had already disappeared behind the pandas and was wondering what bamboo tasted like.

Richard went to the reptile house to look at the crocodiles.

Are those Sally's kids?

'What time did Miss Lomax say we were to meet at the penguins?'

Yes, they are.

'Two o'clock. Ten minutes' time.'

The penguins, two o'clock, nine minutes' time. As he stared at the crocodile, it flickered its eye shut, opened it again and stared back at Richard. He found it rather disconcerting and decided to arrive early at the penguins to ensure the best possible view. As he approached he could see Sally from the back, a posse of children surrounding her. They held her hands and all hopped from foot to foot – whether this was a bid to keep warm or an imitation of the penguins was not altogether clear.

They seem to like her, she's probably their favourite

teacher. Lenient, no doubt, but commanding respect and obedience.

Richard was puzzled at just how nervous he was, hands clammy and the sandwich had reappeared to pester his Adam's apple. The contents of the butterfly house had taken residence deep in his stomach and the sawdust of the possums' cage appeared to be in his mouth. As he approached he could hear her voice.

'Ooh, wouldn't you love to take one home with you?' she cooed to her entourage. Richard was within a couple of yards of her. He could now see just how enthralled she was by her flippered friends. Up she was on tiptoes, bouncing, as she marvelled at their clumsy acrobatics.

She's quite wonderful. Enchanting.

He walked past and around the penguin pool and took position on the opposite side. He stared at Sally but Sally was rapt. And anyway, Richard was the last person she was expecting to see at London Zoo on a Tuesday lunchtime.

The penguins seemed to like their enclosure. Richard did too. A hilly maze of steps and slopes in blue and white, just like the Arctic, surrounding a generous pool of cold water. He would make few changes to it. Perhaps a bridge. Deepen the pool. A few hidey-holes in the sides. New surfacing. The penguins never seemed to tire of running up and down and around in a complicated and irrational route to the water into which they joyfully tumbled. Natural entertainers, the bigger their audience, the more comic their antics. An audience *and* feeding time was the best possible combination; clapping and laughter encouraged them to catch their fish in the most elaborate fashion. And there was a fair-sized audience at two o'clock. But Richard saw only Sally. And he soaked up what he saw.

She watched one penguin in particular, slightly smaller than the others, his tuxedo glossy, his shirt snowy, his walk pompous and assertive. A fish had been thrown into the centre of the pool and two penguins, positioned on a ridge above it, looked at the water and shifted from leg to leg. Sally's pal hurried along the ridge and barged into one who crashed into the other. Both fell in while he stood, shifting from side to side, proudly smacking himself with his flippers. He then belly-flopped into the water and surfaced almost immediately with the fish while his two comrades splashed about, thoroughly disoriented. Sally was thrilled and clapped energetically while jumping up and down on the spot, cheering. She had her hands splayed and ridged, bashing them together enthusiastically, her smile wide, her jaws well apart, her lips forced back to reveal every tooth in her mouth.

And then she saw Richard.

And she brought her hands together in one final clap. Her mouth was still open but the corners had dropped. She stood paralysed with her hands still rigid, as if in prayer. Richard beamed a broad grin in her direction. The penguins were satiated and dozed on their stomachs, heads and legs suspended. Richard waved his roll of drawings at Sally, Diana saw him and then turned to Sally who was still praying. *Ah ha!* she thought. *Here is the reason for the swagger, the new wardrobe, the infuriating evasiveness, The Glow. Introduce me, Sal – oops, Sally. Do!*

Richard had begun to stroll around the pool. Sally remained transfixed by the space he left. Though rosy and alive, her face spoke a glimmer of slow panic too. Diana saw this and acted upon it immediately.

'Okay, kids, one last look at the creepy crawlies and then back to the coach,' she more or less ordered, and though she was desperately intrigued by Sally's stunned immobility, she tore herself away and went off in search of tarantulas and stag beetles. Sally remained motionless, her pose and poise reminiscent of church sculpture. She did not, however, feel her exterior stillness within. She was lurching and churning, not knowing what to make of the situation.

I hadn't planned this. I don't quite know what to do. What shall I do? Think. He should not have seen me like this. Soft. Penguins. Clapping. That won't do. Think.

Richard was very near.

'Wait!' Sally suddenly cried after Diana. But Richard was there and Diana was not. He was unaware of Sally's sudden crisis.

'Hello, Sal!'

'Hello, Richard. I must dash.'

'Call me.'

The coach was a zoo in itself. Rubbery spiders careered through the air, jelly snakes and sugary polar bears littered the floor. The children were now chimps, charged with manic chattering, climbing all over the seats. Diana, still mittened, wasn't that bothered about enforcing order and silence. She was more concerned and extremely inquisitive about Sally's defiant silence. She nudged her with her elbow. Sally turned slowly towards her.

'Well?'

'Well what?'

'Who was that gorgeous man thing?'

'Someone I sort of know.'

The women looked at each other. Sally wanted to look away but found the pull of Diana's enquiring eyes too strong, too comforting. Still Diana searched Sally's face. Sally felt safe and she also felt strong. She broke into a broad, conspiratorial smile. The camaraderie between the two women was intense, almost tangible. Knowing full well that she could trust Diana implicitly, Sally felt euphoric and, in hushed tones, she told Diana why.

'I've been terribly naughty, Di.'

'Oh, *do* tell!' implored Diana, grasping Sally's knee with mittened zeal but trying not to sound too keen. So

Sally gave Diana an uncensored account in glorious Technicolor replete with close-ups. Though no detail of the action was neglected, she did, however, omit the underlying motive. There was no insinuation that this unbridled lust was driven by a carefully conceived plan. What Sally wanted was an approval of sorts, a 'God, I wish I'd done that'. Diana did not disappoint her there.

'This is the stuff of an airport groin-grinder! A veritable Jackie Collins bonk-buster. Wow!'

Sally was delighted. She did not expose the psychological bent of the situation, for not only did she fear the inevitable 'It'll only end in tears, someone's bound to get hurt', but fundamentally she wanted the fact that it was a calculated project kept all to herself.

Diana was quite exhausted when they arrived back at school.

When Sally arrived home she felt strangely depleted and a little anxious.

But I didn't want him to see me like that. What can he think? Surely a true femme fatale *wouldn't go potty for penguins? She wouldn't clap and squeal like a child. I don't want to break the spell. I wonder if I have. He probably thought me quite sweet. I don't want to be sweet, I want to be scandalous. He's probably contemplating my merits as child-bearer and biscuit-baker this very moment. I must remedy the situation, reassert myself as a veritable vamp, a tough cookie, a steel butterfly. But how?*

'Hello, Richard?'

'Sal! Enjoy the Zoo?'

'Very much.'

'Pop over?'

'Now? Ten-thirty?' Sally was in her red nightshirt (a present from Diana), fluffy green bed socks, an old tatty cotton scarf in her hair. 'Sure,' she purred, already scrambling out of her night clothes. She slipped on a black skirt and polo neck and declared to the African Violet that all was not lost. She hovered at her front door and then returned to her bedroom where she derobed and then dived back into her nightshirt. She drew the line at the socks and scarf, dabbed on a little perfume and slipped on her pumps. She covered up with her long trench coat, partly as protection against the drizzle, partly because what was underneath was for Richard alone.

It felt exciting to be going out when normally she would have been going to bed. But she also felt old and bemused, remembering how University nights would not yet have started. The roads were fairly empty and the traffic lights were on her side. She enjoyed hearing the fizzy whish made by wheels on the wet tarmac, seeing the sparkling orange flecks on the road cast by the street lights. It took less than twenty minutes, without breaking the speed limit or jumping amber lights, for Sally to arrive and park in Notting Hill where the bars were still throbbing and the bright young things would be enjoying *tapas* for a good while yet.

The lift in Richard's building was old and cumbersome. The door had to be opened, the grille coaxed back then cranked closed, the floor selected with an assertive press and then an infuriating delay tolerated until the instructions registered. In the chug between ground and first floors, Sally had an idea. As first floor came and went, she unbuckled and unbuttoned her coat. By the time the lift was approaching the second floor, she had her nightshirt over her head. The lift stopped and so did Sally's heart. But nothing happened and no one was there. Was the machinery trying to tell her something? It juddered on up and, for a delicious few seconds between the second and third floors, Sally stood completely naked.

The young lady who got out of the lift on the fourth floor smiled sweetly at the pizza delivery boy who got in. He watched her saunter down the hall and thought how well her long mac suited her. Sally's knickers were still in the lift but he presumed them to be a handkerchief and, having recently recovered from a cold, he kept a clear distance. (They were discovered by the porter the next morning who sincerely hoped that nothing untoward had happened. In twenty-seven years he had never once had a pair of knickers lurking in his lift. Handkerchiefs and scarves maybe. Knickers, no. Mr Stonehill from Flat C tutted with him and said it was a disgrace.)

Richard answered the door, enveloped in his towelling robe. He kissed Sally on the cheek and before he had a chance to ask her more about the school trip, about her job, her colleague the elephant lover – all of which he was keen to know – Sally had pulled him towards her and nearly suffocated him with the deepest kiss imaginable. Her carrier bag fell to the floor and Richard's penis soared skyward, pressing somewhat uncomfortably against the buckle on Sally's coat.

Let's undo that for starters.

Go on, Richard, unbelt me, unbuckle me, unbutton me, see what you can find. Richard had the belt off immediately and, still enmeshed in her kiss, he began to fumble with the buttons which were big but sat tight in their button holes.

I'm enjoying this! thought Sally.

I'm enjoying this! thought Richard.

When Richard had all the buttons undone, he slipped his hands under the lapels to push the coat away. Sally's soft shoulders greeted him. *What has she got on?* he wondered, images of black lacy basques and cream, silky camisoles assaulting his mind while he glued his mouth to Sally's and shut his eyes with the pressure of pleasure.

What has she got on? Nothing? Nothing! Goddo!

Sally felt the muscles of Richard's lips break into a smile. She pulled her head back to look at him and he looked at her, naked, glorious and right there in his apartment. She raised her eyebrows in a cheeky quiver and he tutted before grabbing her towards him and planting a scorching kiss on her right breast.

They made love, there and then, by the door which was still ajar. Sally later had to take her mac to the dry cleaners. When she left at 7 a.m. Richard pressed a little paper bag into her hand before sending her to school with a kiss on the forehead, a nip on the lips and a smack on her bottom. In her rush to race home, shower, dress appropriately for a teacher and make it to assembly, Sally forgot about the packet until morning break. Sitting on the toilet, she unscrunched the bag and saw it had *London Zoo* and a tiger design emblazoned on the front. Out of it she tipped a small keyring. In the shape of a penguin.

ELEVEN

When can love begin? And can you fight it? When does love begin and when should it? But can you fight it?

Richard fell in love with Sally that morning at the Zoo. In a moment. He was as sure as his walk that he was in love with Sally Lomax. He felt peaceful and content about it. And happy. Secure. He didn't bother to pontificate on what love is or should be, whether it was possible or realistic to feel love and know it after just a few meetings, meetings in which physical desire had, after all, played a dominant part. Sally had never stopped to think whether she might fall in love with Richard, too busy was she making sure that he didn't fall in love with her but was instead subsumed by lust for her. Richard certainly lusted after her, but now he lusted out of love. Sally was blind to that love, she judged her happiness and success solely on the rigidity, endurance and explosion of his penis. Consequently, she completely neglected any exploration of her own subconscious, devoting all energy to new and invariably more outrageous seduction situations.

But, Sally, you are so lovable, togged up in your old

Swan Lake tutu and turning up at Richard's a mere two hours after you had left one Sunday night. Who could not love a girl who pulls her man into the ladies' toilets to give him a blow job after an overlong Belgian film? Or guides his hand under her skirt beneath the table of a dinner party so he can discover she has on no panties? And Sally, your eyes are artless and provide a short cut into your soul; Richard has gazed at them, beyond them, often. Your smile is so full and real and alluring. He sees your face, Sally, in ecstatic rapture as you climax under him, on top of him, on his hand, on his mouth. He watches you and he feels he could burst with desire.

But he watches you when you do not know it. He observes you as you watch the News and he sees your face crease in anguish for war victims, for beached whales, for families of the murdered, for the women who were raped. And he gazes at you for hours while you sleep, he watches while you stare out of windows at nothing in particular. What he sees, he loves. Laughing at penguins. 'Gracious Good Lord'. He sees the tears film over your eyes at the close of a play, the end of a film, as you finish a novel. Richard watches you all the while, but you don't know it. Richard is in love with you but you don't see it. You will, you will. And then how will you feel?

Richard wanted to sing his joy from the roof-tops, to swing from the steeple and proclaim it, to climb trees and laud it. Instead, he informed Bob quite casually over their customary post-workout swift half.

'Where are you spending Christmas? Want to come for lunch? We're also having a New Year's Eve bash, can't decide whether to have a theme or not. You know, come as a painting, come as a film. I could just see you as a Degas ballerina!'

'I am in love with Sally Lomax.'

'And he just said it, no prompting?'

'He just came right out with it, I hadn't even mentioned her.'

Bob had ensured that it had indeed been a true and very swift half indeed and not the usual excuse for a two-pinter. He could not wait to tell Catherine. It really was ground-breaking news. It really was the most extraordinary occurrence.

Richard is in love. Gracious, old Richie boy in love and declaring it. No more 'she's all right's, now it's 'she's the one'. He's found her! At long bloody last, he's found her. And he seems so sure. And he seems, well, just so bloody happy! And I knew it, I knew it, didn't I? I could see it a mile and a half off and now he can see it too and he's as happy as fucking Larry.

Outwardly, Catherine was delighted. Secretly she was just a little dismayed. It had been nice to have Richard generally unattached, to know that she was perhaps the most important woman in his life. She loved it that he spent much of his time with them, being charming, good-looking – and hers, in a way. For as long as she had known him, he had never been short of female attention. He had always brought them over to Catherine and Bob's for Catherine to dissect later over a lengthy phone call. And when such liaisons inevitably came to grief, he had always enjoyed a healthy *post mortem* with her. They exchanged *Vogue* for *GQ*. They often lunched together and shopped together – Richard provided the perfect mannequin for Catherine to outfit her shop-shy husband. For Catherine, Richard was the older brother she never had, and for whom she would gladly swap her younger one (whose passions were fired almost solely by motor-bikes). Now Richard was in love and intuition told her it very well might be The One. Sally Lomax she liked though she was but a friend of a friend's. Catherine was inquisitive to see if Richard-in-Love differed in any fundamental way from the Richard she knew and adored.

'Let's have them to dinner. No, how about Sunday lunch? This Sunday. Go on, Bob, phone. Phone now!'

And so the four of them lunched together on Sunday, and on other Sundays. They all dined at Richard's too, and went to the theatre, and walked on Kenwood, and went to exhibitions at the Serpentine. They decided together that the New Year's Eve party would be a masked ball. Sally conspired with Catherine to make their outfits on her sewing machine and, with inordinate pleasure, they refused to help the men in any way with theirs. The women became more than the partners of their partners, they became friends. Catherine was delighted that Richard was just the same only more so, more animated, more charming, happier than ever she had known him. Bob liked Sally but rarely spoke to her one to one. Sally didn't really notice Bob, Richard was her project, he was not. The more time the four of them spent together, the more Richard spoke to Bob in private about Sally. But he never told Sally. He never said the 'L' word to her though he used it frequently with Bob. The word was never empty but always saturated with conviction.

Sally called him Richie, and to him Sally was Sal. Bob and Catherine never tired of shooting each other knowing smiles and conspiratorially raised eyebrows when these diminutives, forbidden to all others, were used. Catherine tried using it once with Richard but his wince was sharp. Richard would remain Richie to Sally alone.

Diana too was let into their cocoon. Or rather they into her black and red one. Evenings of macro-biotic food, ambient music and good grass became almost a weekly institution in the run-up to Christmas. Invariably it was a Monday night, serving as a boost for the architect and two teachers for the week ahead. Richard and Sally would lie sprawled on the black, sagging couch, watching Diana gesticulating vividly from the depths of the voluminous red bean-bag, listening with mirth to her many tales – some true, some surely not, who cared? They would wend a weary way home to Sally's, make love lazily and then embrace a stoned slumber, to awake amazingly refreshed and energetic to continue their working weeks.

Sally grew fonder of Diana and loved to hear her describing Richard, admiring his statuesque body, his composed but agreeable person. '*Mar*vellous teeth and *beau*tiful nails, prerequistes you know, pre*req*uisites.' Sally often granted Diana an insight into their sex life – something Richard never gave Bob. The women would sit in a corner of the drab staff-room and fill it with colourful laughter. Sally loved to see Diana reel back in awe and delight. It made her feel proud. Sometimes Sally's account was deliciously bawdy, sometimes downright scientific. Mostly, she recalled their couplings so eloquently and with such passion that Diana's eyes watered and she was rendered anomalously speechless. Occasionally, she even suggested little bed-time tricks and Sally could not wait to tell her the effect they had had. These were the machinations of Diana's increasingly warped imagination – she had not tried them out. She wouldn't dare. Anyway, on whom? The live yoghurt was completely unsuccessful, the raw cake mixture downright messy, but the carefully proportioned mix of orange juice and just a little olive oil (extra virgin, cold-pressed) was a gem of Diana's for which Sally became eternally grateful.

But Sally never mentioned the 'L' word. Sally didn't know anything about it. 'L' for what? Yet Diana, gifted with some intrinsic insight, could see it. She quietly made notes of their body language, the way that Sally so comfortably welded to Richard on the sofa. She observed how attentive Sally became when Richard was speaking, how she laughed more strongly if Richard laughed, how she watched him and not Diana when the other two spoke. And Diana saw how Sally would touch Richard somewhere, anywhere, if he got up. And how she'd slip her hand around the top of his thigh as he led her out at the end of an evening, his arm about her waist. And Diana felt Sally glower when, on one occasion, she called her Sal. Richard witnessed this and his head buzzed.

Though the pair of them now shared themselves with their trusted friends, they spent much time locked into each other. They walked and they talked, they sat together in communicative silence; they enjoyed each other's company as normal couples do. The Heath or Holland Park were favourite stamping grounds. Sometimes they visited briefly just to feed the ducks; at other times they marched round these urban swathes of green, lost and deep in intimate conversation. When Richard spoke of his late father, of his childhood, Sally brimmed with tenderness and support. When he talked of his work, she concentrated hard. Now when she was out and about she didn't restrict her sight to eye-level but conscientiously looked up and around and noted pediments and architraves, Corinthian capitals and original window glass in the most unlikely of buildings. Sally talked, too, but carefully. Richard understood her childhood to have been happy, her previous relationships to have been few, fairly short-term and unsuccessful.

'Why unsuccessful? In what way? Have you been hurt?'

'I have never been in love.'

Her love was her work, he decided, for on that subject she became animated and spoke so descriptively about her pupils, past and present, that Richard formed a clear picture of each. She spoke with great fondness of her friends, who were few but to whom she was devoted though they lived as far afield as Ireland and South Africa. She talked of her passion for ballet and what she deemed to be her failure – weak knees. She danced for him on Hampstead Heath in her wellingtons, quickly, lightly, and, he believed, perfectly.

But such walks, talks and insights always finished with

passionate love-making, more often than not at Sally's instigation. For Richard, this sealed such days, for Sally it was a necessity. Just in case.

Just in case he loses sight of what I am, the extraordinary lover I must be.

You mean, just in case this mere rampant fling should dare to transmute into something quite other.

And hasn't it?

Their love-making was as exciting and as satisfying as it had ever been. The physical peaks that they reached were a revelation, and an exquisite one. But a spiritual element crept in, silently, unannounced and uninvited. It was inevitable. And it was welcome. They looked at each other more while they were making love. They were able to penetrate deeper. And though Sally did not necessarily look at and into Richard with love, she did look at him as Sally, as herself. And he saw that. She liked to gaze at him. She wasn't entirely sure why.

Maybe my funny old shyness has gone.

Maybe, Sally, maybe. But perhaps there's something else you ought to consider. When you're ready.

TWELVE

On New Year's Eve, when Richard told Sally that he loved her, her world fell apart. It crashed about her feet in a deluge of shattered hopes and splintered desires. Ruined ambition lay smattered about her.

'Merry Christmas, Miss Lomax!'

'Merry Christmas, everyone. Now remember, the coach leaves for Paris from school at five in the morning on January the fourth. Remember too that we will be away for five days so bring enough underwear and any medication. And I want you all to prepare a piece on one figure of French History – painter, King or Emperor, whoever. Oh, and no hand-held computer games.'

'Mi-iss!'

'*Is* that understood?' she bellowed. Grudgingly, it was understood. The girls placed Miss Lomax's presents in front of her with a smile, some with a kiss, and skipped merrily out of the classroom and into their Christmas holidays. Most of the boys shuffled up to the desk and reluctantly dumped their gifts, furiously avoiding eye-contact, before swaggering to the door and defiantly beeping into life their electronic games.

'Oh, Diana!'

'My, what a pile of goodies you've amassed! Now, have yourself a *won*derful Christmas and make sure you take snaps of your outfit for the Thingies' masked ball. Call me before Paris – I must have *all* the intricacies of the Stonehill-saga before you go! Oh! I read something about cold macaroni cheese and the libido but I can't remember if you *eat* it or *use* it. I'll be sure to let you know! Merry Christmas! Mmwah! Mmwah!' With a pair of vivid scarlet lip marks on either cheek, Sally gathered her things together and left school for Christmas.

Christmas was Christmas. Sally being Sally did not overeat nor did she drink too much. She bought thoughtful presents for her family and sent charity cards to everyone she knew, including Bob and Catherine with a PS: 'Outfit-making, Highgate, 27th'. She bought Richard two truffles and a pasta dish; he gave her a vibrator. Momentarily she was taken aback but quickly asserted a knowing smirk for him.

But his doesn't look like that at all. And what an odd colour.

She tried it in private but the noise was like a shaver and its mechanical quivers reminded her of her car starting; giggles quashed any glimmer of sexual connotation and Sally's first and last vibrator was banished to the back of her socks drawer. She went to Lincoln where she was a priceless mother's help. Richard spent a dutiful Christmas Eve with his mother and then returned to London and shared Christmas and Boxing Days with Bob and Catherine.

He thought about Sally and he missed her. He was surprised that he missed her but inwardly it pleased him.

You can only miss what you know, and like.

Love.

Sally, surrounded and swamped by the mundanities and trivialities of her mother's Lincoln set, the sagas of her sisters' lives and the monotony of being good and courteous, longed for Richard.

For sex, she persuaded herself.

On Boxing Day evening, their coming together, in every sense of the word, was urgent and passionate. It was delicious, like a favourite food not tasted for many months.

Sally was pleased, Richard had exchanged his customary 'Omigod o goddos' for 'Oh Sally, oh Sal, oSallio'. But she sent him home to his own bed that night, relishing her power and his disappointment, and really quite looking forward to playing seamstress with Catherine the next morning.

'And I also found this piece with black sequins. How's Richard?'

'Oh, fine, fine.'

Fingers picked at buttons, the bobbin hurtled merrily, the needle pumped incessantly. Eyes were cast down, scrutinizing, measuring; the atmosphere was one of committed and creative labour. There was, however, space enough to chatter and to allow the occasional dip into one of the many end-of-term chocolate boxes.

'Yuk, strawberry fondant!'

'Pass it over then, I'll swap you a caramel. Bob thinks he may just don his goggles. Any idea what Richard's planning?'

'Nope.'

'Everything all right between you two?'

'Yes, why?'

'Oh, nothing really. I don't know, it's just whenever I bring him into the conversation, you never really linger.'

'That's because I'm a doer, not a talker!'

'So what do you do?'

'Bonk superlatively.'

'Good gracious! Sally Lomax, was that you?'

''Fraid so!'

But that was all that Catherine was given. She tried, she pried, but Sally smiled sweetly and kept her secrets tucked into her thimble.

'I've done something bad, Sally. Can I tell you? In confidence?' Sally laid down the feathers and tipped the diamanté bits back into their little pot. She was flattered.

'Of course you can.'

'I've stopped taking the Pill. Bob doesn't know. I take one out of the packet each night and I tip it down the sink.'

'But why?'

'Why? Because I want to have a baby, thickie.'

'Yes, yes, but why mustn't Bob know?'

'Because he feels too young to be a father and he says I'm too young to be a mother. But, you know, I feel ready . . . I don't know, *ripe*. Nougat? I think there comes a time when you just have to look inward and see how old or ready you *feel*. Not go by all this media bullshit dictating that couples ought now to breed only well into their thirties when they have a combined salary of "X". I'm not even that gooey or broody. Quite simply, I feel it is the right time to get pregnant. I looked inward, and that's what I saw.'

Sally sucked on the nougat thoughtfully. She was quite stunned by Catherine's frankness but was moved too by her wisdom. A closeness and warmth and camaraderie now existed between the two women. Sally had heard that elusive click, the bonding that ties women together as soul friends. She had it with Diana and with Daph. Not with her mother, nor Aunt Martha. But with Aunt Celia, yes. And now Catherine too. After that, they rarely talked about their menfolk but about themselves, about women they knew and others they admired, about vices they had and virtues they longed for. It made for a great working atmosphere and by the end of the afternoon, feathers and sequins and brocade and frogging had been coaxed into masks of supreme beauty and formidable workmanship. Catherine had also been afforded snippets of Sally.

'So after James at Bristol Uni, there was . . . ?'

'Jim.'

'Not one and the same?'

'No! But funnily enough, after Jim came Jamie.'

'You obviously go for Jims.'

'Actually, I prefer Dicks.'

'What was wrong with Jim?'

'Jim was okay, but boring. He used the "L" word halfway through our first date. And then frequently thereafter. He was a fair bit older than me and kept saying how I needed someone to watch over me and take care of me and pamper me. Meaning him. Thank you but no thank you. I sent him packing.'

'Ooh, you're a cruel woman! How?'

'He told me he loved me and I said "But I don't love you" and he said "But you will, you know, you will" and I said "I won't, you know, I won't". That didn't work so I told him, without beating about the metaphorical bush, that I found him physically unappetizing. But in truth, the greatest turn-off had been to declare his undying love.'

'And that worked?'

'Obviously – enter Jamie.'

'Jamie.'

'Scottish, a cab driver.'

'Is that how you met? In the back of his cab?'

'Well, yes, actually.'

'But did you ever do it in the back of his cab?'

'No.'

'Have you with Richard?'

'Yes.'

'In your car or his?'

'Mine.'

'In a *Mini*? Wait up, I've got to work this one out?'

'Well, I'll ramble on about Jamie while you do. Jamie was such fun at first, always cracking jokes in his glorious accent and bringing me little treats. He was dark and swarthy but gentle too. At first.' Sally trailed off and Catherine observed her turn to her sewing with a near-desperate application. She waited and as she waited she could see the pain.

'Sally?'

'Mmm?'

'Talk to me.' Sally laid down the feathers and bows and sighed. It was as if the memory had worn her out and aged her visibly. She looked Catherine in the eye and was comforted by a smile of sympathy and support. She focused at some point over Catherine's shoulder and her eyes glazed, her speech became dull and flat.

'Jamie had a temper. He broke my crockery and he smashed my nose. Here, feel.'

Sally guided Catherine's forefinger over the bridge of her nose. They felt the bump and dent together and Catherine allowed her finger to linger, letting it stroke Sally in a gentle whisper of comfort. Sally allowed her eyes to close under Catherine's touch while she worked hard to shut the memory back out.

On opening her eyes, the matter was closed. And would remain so. Catherine knew Sally had taken her into her confidence and that in itself had been a difficult and generous decision. She was grateful and flattered. It felt good to have a part of Sally that Bob and Richard didn't have. Catherine felt her first wave of love for Sally and was half-tempted to embrace her fully. Instinctively, however, she knew that her job was to lessen the load and lighten the atmosphere.

'James, Jim, Scumbag and now Richard. And I think you've scored at last there, Ms Lomax.'

'Yes, Richard. Richard is – ' Sally paused, fiddling with a line of red sequins before concluding ' – nice.'

*

Bob, meanwhile, plundered the impeccably dressed Christmas tree and strung his booty in glorious abandon over his old diving mask.

Richard went to the local toyshop and bought a Lone Ranger mask. And then he went to Dunn and Co. and bought an extremely expensive Stetson.

'Sal?'

'Hey, Richie!'

'So you didn't need me to thread your needles?'

'No, I just about managed.'

'Will you come?'

'I beg your pardon?'

'Over? Now?'

'But I'm in bed!'

'Hasn't stopped you in the past.'

'But I'm tired!'

'Ditto.'

'Beaumes de Venise?'

'It's in the fridge.'

'I'm there!'

''Bye.'

''Bye.'

'Sal? Sally?'

'Yes?'

'Nothing.'

THIRTEEN

Richard had his hand full of buttock.

'I'll pick you up, shall I, eightish?'

'No you shan't! We are to arrive separately!'

'Why?'

'Because, if you take me, then it won't be a surprise. And you'll recognize me which defeats the purpose of a masked ball utterly. And anyway, because I say so.'

'Ooh, but say I don't? Say I mistake another for you?'

'I'll give you a little sign.'

'A little sign, and what will that be?' Sally ran her finger tip lightly and temptingly up Richard's fly. He let go of her buttock. With one arm he pulled her towards him; with the other cinched around her waist he kept her there, and sewed a kiss deep into her mouth. Her eyes smiled lasciviously at him. He let her go and watched her dress, craning for a last look at the two tiny dimples at the base of her back before they were swallowed away by denim.

The best thing, thought Sally, *about sex in the afternoon is that it sends you on your way with a spring in your step and a euphoric energy to tide you through the rest of the day.*

She had always loved New Year's Eve day and as she sauntered along Highgate High Street the shopkeepers to whom she usually smiled were now given a big wave.

'Happy New Year, Miss Lomax!'

'Happy New Year, Joe!'

'Off dancing tonight, love?'

'Certainly am!'

'Dancing and Romancing?'

'You bet!'

'See ya next year, love!'

'It'll be a good one, Joe!'

On a whim, Sally went to the newsagent and bought a packet of ten cigarettes, low-tar and mentholated. 'Oh, yes, and a box of matches, please. Happy New Year.' She then went to the bookshop, old, musty, magnetic, and browsed the minutes away into three-quarters of an hour before selecting two recently reviewed, highly acclaimed novels. 'You'll enjoy those, Happy New Year.' Her final stop was at the French *patisserie* where she ummed, ahhed and crooned and then chose a strawberry tartlet, gloriously red and glazed to glistening perfection. '*Année!*'

Back in her flat, Sally placed the books, in the bag, on the mantelpiece. She tapped them, deciding not to peek at all until she was on French soil. She then went into her kitchen and took out a cake fork and tea plate on to which she slid the tartlet. Kettle boiled, Earl Grey brewed and poured into a matching tea-cup and saucer, she retired into the lounge and settled down to a few minutes of luxury. Such times had to be conducted in silence. No television or radio, no rustling of magazines, no pencil in one hand hovering over a crossword. It had to be just Sally, her cake and her cuppa. Too soon, though, there was not even a crumb left despite a hopeful dabbing finger searching every inch of the plate, just in case. She burped quietly under her breath and sat a while longer, looking, as always, at nothing in particular. She enjoyed the friendly silence of her own company, she liked her little flat, and was content just to sit and look around her, itemizing her possessions, checking on her paintwork and scanning her heaving bookcase, smiling and nodding at favourite volumes as they came into view.

Well, this is no good, just sitting here like a lazy lemon. There's work to be done, a party to prepare for, a man to wow! Come on, let's have a fag, Sal!

Sally smoked self-consciously as she pottered from room to room. Every now and then she darted back to the kitchen to flick ash into the sink.

Disgusting habit, but what can one do when one does not possess an ash-tray?

The cigarette gave her a slight head-rush which she thought amusing, and she giggled out loud as she went into the bathroom to check how she looked, fag in hand, fag in mouth. Could she talk like that? No. She tried blowing smoke rings but couldn't. She checked how she looked sucking on the butt in side profile and again from the front. She watched herself inhale and exhale. Inhale and exhale.

Lordy, I feel dizzy!

She exhaled and smiled, watching the smoke whisper over her teeth and veil her face.

Nope! Smoking does not suit me at all. So I shan't.

With that, she threw the butt down the toilet and retrieved the packet from the lounge, took it outside and dumped it ceremoniously in the dustbin.

Sally ran a bath. Deep. She tweezed stray eyebrows and scrutinized her face for anything to squeeze. Nothing. She soaked for a while but found she was not in a luxuriating frame of mind so she shaved her legs and her armpits, showered off freezing cold (she'd learnt it from Richard) and then swooped her bath sheet around her. Getting dry was such a bore so she took the phone into her room and called Diana. Who wasn't in. So she called Richard, who was.

'I've got nothing on.'

'Neither have I.'

'See you later.'

'Alligator.'

'Crocodile.'

Time to get ready, body is dry and silk-soft, hair likewise. What a lovely little dress you've bought, Sally.

I know, I couldn't resist it. It's from that shop that I've only ever drooled in front of. I shouldn't've. But I just had to. I want to knock him for six tonight.

But you have already done so, you know.

Mmm, I want to make sure.

It's black crêpe, isn't it? Completely straight, two little darts giving it a perfect line. It's just above your knee, just right. Sleeveless though, mightn't you be chilly?

No, not once I'm at the party. Look, do you see how cleverly the zip is hidden at the back? It feels heavenly on.

It suits you, fits beautifully.

Look, little Dupion court shoes too!

Perfect. What knickers have you chosen?

At first, I wasn't going to wear any at all. But it is December. I know Richard goes wild for those little white cottony ones but I've never had black silk panties so I bought some. I'll make sure he likes them.

Let us see your mask, Sally.

Just look at my mask! I know it's bad to brag but I'm terribly pleased with it. See how it fits snugly over the bridge of my nose? And then dips down over the tops of my cheeks? Catherine's is more elaborate but I decided against any wild flourishes. I just studded the edges alternately with silver sequins and little pearls, then I attached the soft downy black feathers over the brow. I wanted to look swan-like, or cat-like, or something. But it fits well, doesn't it? It's awful when a mask is lop-sided, or reveals more of one eye than the other.

It fits, Sally. Perfectly.

Actually, it's rather nice to wear. You can sort of hide behind it. It's as if I can see out but they can't see in.

Go on, one last check in front of the mirror, then you'd best be on your way.

I hope I arrive after Richard. I've never really been in a situation where I can make my big entrance. It is my prerogative after all!

Check your flat, Sally, the gas, the plugs, the windows. Close the curtains, the doors. Double lock. Outside lights on. Off you go, off to the Ball, Sally Lomax. Have the most wonderful night. And Happy New Year.

See the Mini chortle down the road, heading for West London and a night of festive celebration. See its precious load: a young woman, decked out in her finery. She looks almost beautiful. Not classically, not even that classy, but there is something about her that is enchanting and rather lovely. She smiles and she is excited, anticipating an evening of fun and frolics. The lights turn orange but tonight our usually pedantic driver throws caution to the wind and accelerates through, a rush of adrenalin adding to her fizzy mood. Does she not seem happy, her fine mask coddled in tissue on the seat beside her? She is happy and she tells herself so out loud. You can see her mouth it as she drums on the dash-board: *I am happy, I'm really happy.*

So one year is on its way out and the next is tangibly near. What does it hold in store? Sally has no idea. If she's at the metaphorical steering wheel, as she intends to be, she believes she'll journey through it safely and soundly.

But what if someone else takes the wheel, uninvited? Sally hasn't thought of that. And if there is someone else there, where will they take her? And will she let herself be taken?

Just now, however, it is Sally's New Year's Eve and she is looking forward to it very, very much.

FOURTEEN

'Bob! It's completely wonky. Up on the left, up on the left!'

'Stop flapping, would you? Is that better?'

'Up on the bloody left!'

'There.'

'Now the streamers, now the streamers!'

'Where?'

'Door frames, door frames!'

'Leave me to it, you old bag! Go and get yourself ready and then lie down for half an hour.'

Catherine obeyed. Their parties were always a success, but if she didn't fret and if certain things weren't left to the last minute it could surely be a bad omen.

I must try and calm down. I really must. Just in case.

Catherine's period should have come the previous morning so she was hoping and praying, silently and desperately.

If I am, then I must keep calm. Just in case.

She lay down on their bed and wondered if the faint nausea was due to pregnancy and not pre-party nerves. Bob woke her half an hour later and she had no recollection of falling asleep. Deeply too. His usual kiss on the nose had been ineffectual, a good shake was required. She clambered into her rich violet silk two-piece and gave him a twirl. He marvelled at her elegant beauty. Dark and sinuous like a willowy, giant anemone. Bob put on a loud Hawaiian shirt and a pair of garish Bermuda shorts. The ensemble clashed violently.

He looks quite revolting, marvelled Catherine, *but he looks the part!*

Catherine breezed around, placing bowls of nuts and nibbles on every available surface. Bob stuck himself at her dressing-table mirror and wrestled with his diving goggles, trying to find a way to make them fit snugly without forcing his lips and cheeks into a rubbery and uncomfortable contortion.

Well, I'll just have to suffer for my art until all the guests have seen it on, then I'll tip it up on to my head. But that bauble clonks me in the eye, so I'll just adjust it – slightly. There.

'Catherine! Where's the string?' She appeared with the errant string and a piping hot canapé, a dazzling smile beaming from a cloud of purple-blue silk. Delicious.

'You are a treasure, darling. Belle of the ball.'

'And that's a hell of a bauble clonking your eye, Bob. Here, let me help.'

The beauty of a fancy dress party, although everybody initially moans wondering where they'll find the time and inspiration to make their costume, is that enormous effort is inevitably made by all and such parties have great atmosphere before the doorbell is even sounded. Bob and Catherine's parties were talked about for years: The Bad Taste Party for Bob's big three-o, The Flowers and Flares Party on their third wedding anniversary, Catherine's Sinners and Saints Party; all went down in the annals of record-breaking party history. And now the New Year's Masked Ball. They had transformed the ground floor of their home into a magical grotto. Black net, sprinkled with glittery stars, had been draped over and across all the ceilings. The long wall of the living-room was covered entirely with silver foil, the other walls adorned with burgundy crêpe-paper bows and swathes of steel-grey shiny material (Sally knew of the shop, £2 a metre).

The hallway leading in had been turned into an avenue of six-foot weeping figs (hired for the night). In the kitchen, reams of dark red velvet swagged the doorway and masked the cupboards that were not to be opened. The long, rustic beech-wood trestle table was covered with a starched white sheet and adorned around the edges with black crêpe-paper rosettes. On it, a glutton's wildest fantasy met the eye. Bowls of new potato salad, sprigged through with wisps of dill; an enormous shallow dish heaped with leaves of ruccola, radicchio and oak-leaf lettuce, coloured exquisitely with borage flowers and dressed to perfection with Bob's famous vinaigrette. In between sat two mounds of Catherine's home-baked herbed bread but the eye was drawn compulsively to the centrepiece, a twelve-and-a-half-pound wild Scotch salmon lying pink-peach and fat on a bed of transparent-thin cucumber slithers. The fridge hid from view the two Pavlovas, one raspberry, one strawberry, both a foot high. The oven warmed the canapés, Catherine's forte. Mouthfuls of ecstasy; puff, filo and shortcrust pastries enveloping creative fillings of spinach (fresh), chicken (spiced) and mushrooms (wild), all treated to proportionately extravagant doses of cream, fresh herbs and the ubiquitous garlic.

('Bit anti-social, darling?'

'Bob! You know everyone'll eat 'em!')

The guests arrived in a flurry and whirl of cloaks, coats and good cheer. At the doorstep bursts of laughter, coos of admiration and peals of excited chatter as the masks met. Oddly, or perhaps not so oddly, the men for the most part went for the wildly eccentric and humorous, while the women opted for demurely bejewelled intricacy and opulent glamour. There were two Batmen and two stocking-headed bank robbers. Marilyn Monroe arrived with Margaret Thatcher. And while the bought masks were entertaining, those that were home-made were infinitely more impressive and deceptive. All manner of objects had been coaxed and teased into face-concealing devices. Friends with children had studied their comics, made fact-finding trips to Hamleys and plundered the dressing-up boxes. And nearly everyone admitted to having watched the odd *Blue Peter* programme hoping for ingenious ways to transform a cereal packet, a yoghurt pot and polystyrene egg cartons into the mask of their dreams (with a little help from double-sided sticky tape and that globby white glue).

Andy Dalken had taken it one step further. A partner of Bob's, at work he was famous for his waste-paper, paper-clip and used biro sculptures. For the party, he had taken a cereal packet, two sizes of yoghurt pot and a host of cardboard tubes from toilet and kitchen rolls, constructed them into a towering and intricate head-dress and sprayed them evenly with gold and silver paint. But he had also strategically added fairy lights and propellers. For the first half-hour he hardly spoke but flashed, whirred and twinkled when spoken to. Robert Tobias, an old rugby chum of Bob and Richard's, wheezed his way through the party, intimidating and unrecognizable behind a Second World War gas mask. Douglas Christian (also an old First Fifteener) arrived masked beyond recognition, delectably coiffured by a foot-high, Marie Antoinette wig, his face powdered white, his lips painted into a pert and very scarlet rosebud. Only his jeans and trade-mark tennis pumps gave him away. Alex Daniels, Catherine's errant younger brother, turned up on his motorbike in an enormous glitter-gold crash helmet and a slinky black cat-suit adorned by a Groucho Marx jock-strap.

'Masked Balls, Cath, Masked Balls.'

'*Marx*ed Balls, Alex, Marxed Balls!'

Richard arrived and looked gorgeous, like a grown-up little boy in his Lone Ranger outfit.

'Catherine, is that Richard S.? I haven't seen him for years. What a dish! I'm feeling exceptionally frivolous tonight, might just get my net out.'

'No hope, I'm afraid. He's well and truly spoken for.'

'You're joking! Richard? Never! Who by?'

'Sally Lomax. Oh, funny! Look, that's her just arrived, over there with Bob.' The women watched her, one with fondness and pride, the other with inquisitiveness laced with envy. Catherine swished over to her.

'Sally! Magnificent!'

'Happy New Year, Catherine! The mask looks brilliant – mind you, I don't think we could have dreamt up Bob's in a million years, it's a masterpiece!'

'Richard's here, or somewhere!'

'Mmm, is he?'

'Douglas, tell me about your move then. Manchester, isn't it?' Richard had found Douglas whom he had not seen for many moons.

'No, Sheffield. I'm looking forward to it. Fed up with the Old Smoke. Jane's already found a house. And a job. And she's pregnant! Bob was saying that, er, you've found yourself a, um, partner?'

'Mmm. She'll be coming later. You'll like her. She's very natural. And absolutely beautiful.'

'She the one, then?'

'The one? Where? Oh, *the one*! Ha! Oh! Hmm.' Richard fiddled with his waistcoat and fumbled with his words.

She is *the one*, thought Douglas.

'Playing any rugger?'

'No, not for years. I run a fair bit, and thrash Bob at squash.'

'Do you remember that last season at college? Invincible or what! If BJ hadn't been injured in the semis, we'd've won the lot without a doubt. Boy, could he *kick*! You and I, what a second row we made. Wow, look there!'

They looked and watched her move, catlike and languid, over to the table to swoop up a glass of champagne. Her black cocktail dress whispered against her, revealing now and again a curve or line of the body beneath. It ended just above the knee; shapely calves and dainty ankles delineated by the sheerest of stockings. Her arms were bare and slender, and every time she moved her head, her neck was kissed by locks of glossy hair. Her face was pretty – the parts which the mask did not hide. The darkness of the mask itself, the richness of its decoration, accentuated the milky softness of her skin. Her lips shone red, full and defined under the puffs of black feathers which adorned her brow. Richard oozed with pride.

'That, Douglas, is Sally.'

Douglas watched as Richard sauntered over, unnoticed, behind her. He watched as Richard encircled his arms around her waist, one hand resting gently on her stomach, the other grasping her wrist. He saw her tilt her head back and Richard make sweeping kisses from behind her ear down her neck, feathers touching his hair, his Stetson casting aesthetic shadows over their faces. Douglas watched as Sally turned her body towards Richard, so lithe and balletic so that he could keep his face buried in her neck as she turned. Douglas felt his mouth dry and his groin stir as Sally wrapped her arms around Richard's neck, held his face in her hands, slipped one hand through his hair, the other over his ear, and drew him close so she could kiss him deeply. They remained like that, glued and tongue-tied, for minutes. Then Sally laughed; Douglas could hear it above the music, melodic, excited. He saw her twang Richard's mask and then he saw Richard lift hers, place his thumbs just below her eyes, return the mask and then kiss her. Sally grasped Richard close with all the strength in her body; they were pressed against each other and folded into one another. Douglas watched, mesmerized, turned on. Envious.

'You recognized me!' Sally pouted.

'It could only have been!' Richard replied.

Had Bob and Catherine owned a chandelier, it would have been swung from. But the party was swinging regardless. The dancing was lively, the chatter was animated. The food was excellent and plentiful, the drink flowed extravagantly. Everybody mixed and mingled. Sally was enjoying herself thoroughly. She was charming and she was charmed by Bob and Catherine's friends. It was wonderful to catch sight of Richard in earnest conversation over the other side of the room. To catch his eye. To watch him unnoticed. To brush against him, accidentally on purpose. They found each other in the corridor, they shared a mound of Pavlova. He sucked the cream from her chin, she held her glass for him to sip from. She was happy, she was high.

Later, in the loo queue, Sally nattered with Alex.

'What on earth is Catherine doing in there?' questioned Batman. And then it became clear just what she was doing. Catherine was being violently and vociferously sick. It did not take long for most of the queue to disperse, for most to decide that they did not need the toilet all that urgently after all. Alex and Sally stayed.

'Crikey, do you think she's all right? Cath? Catherine?' Alex implored. They heard her moan and then retch again.

'Should I get Bob? I think I will. Sally, would you, could you stay? I'll just find him.' Of course Sally would stay.

'Catherine,' she cooed gently, 'I'm here if you need me.'

Catherine chucked up her reply. It went on and on and on. She really was being desperately ill. Finally the toilet flushed and Catherine emerged, frighteningly pale, her eyes bloodshot. And an enormous grin on her face. Sally stared, puzzled. Catherine took her hand and squeezed it, giving her an odd, indecipherable smile. Bob had arrived.

'Sweetness, are you okay?'

'I'm fine, darling, just fine.' With that, she waltzed down the corridor and back into the midst of her party. Bob shrugged at Sally and jogged after Catherine, baubles and wooden figurines dancing out the Nativity on his head. Sally went into the bathroom but despite what Catherine's racket had suggested, there was absolutely no indication of it at all. She found some air freshener and gave a liberal spritz anyway. *Is she, isn't she?* she wondered as she looked at the plughole and envisaged a stack of redundant contraceptive pills beneath it. She washed her hands and looked up to see the Lone Ranger standing silent and strong behind her.

'Evening, Cowboy. Is that a gun in your pocket, or are you just happy to see me?' Sally chuckled at her clichéd corniness. The cowboy remained silent, locked the door, closed the toilet seat, sat on it and pulled her towards him.

It wasn't a gun.

FIFTEEN

'Come on, everyone, fill up your glasses, it's almost time! Bob? Bob! Switch the telly on. Shit, where's my glass?' Catherine had made a remarkable recovery.

The music was turned off, the television on. People stood, excited and to attention. Big Ben was in close-up, the camera and all the eyes in the room fixed to the clock face, the minute hand just two notches away from New Year. Richard stood behind Sally and could see and feel her quivering with anticipation and delight. Andy Dalken's mask flashed and buzzed, Douglas cooled himself camply with a lacy fan. Almost there, almost. Any minute. Any second. *Doyng*! Cheer! One! *Doyng*! Hurray! Two! Richard squeezed Sally as she bounced on her tiptoes as she had at the penguins. *Doyng*! Eleven! And then the whole room shouted in unison: '*Doyng*! Twelve! Happy New Year!' Champagne corks hit the roof and spirits soared. Hugging was liberal and kisses were free. Douglas was quite keen to embrace Sally but Richard was hogging her to himself. 'Auld Lang Syne' was briefly launched but when tra-la-la-ing replaced unknown words, it was abandoned in favour of more hugging, kissing and champagne guzzling. Richard and Sally were still on last year's kiss, their celebratory drinks untouched and spilling.

The point of the party had come and gone but the festive air remained and the party rampaged along. Sally danced with Douglas. Lucky Douglas. And Richard helped Catherine to mop up a bottle's worth of spilt red wine. Bob had his goggles back on and danced a merry jig with Robert who suddenly had to throw off the gas mask, puce-faced and spluttering for breath. Margaret Thatcher and Marie Antoinette were in earnest conversation in one corner while Andy wrestled to release himself from his mask so he could taste the lips that Minnie Mouse was offering to him. Douglas had spun Sally off her feet. She was hot and ruffled and disappeared to reorganize her dress and mask and recompose her being.

In Catherine and Bob's bedroom, she sat on the bed and listened to her quickened breathing. She caught sight of herself in the mirror and smiled. She lay back on the bed in between the two piles of coats, listening to the thud and boom of the merry-making downstairs. She felt cosy on the soft bed with the silent mounds of other people's coats surrounding her.

I could quite happily either doze off right here and now, or I could party through the night and well into the morning.

She stared at a mark on the ceiling and soon lost the focus to gaze on at nothing in particular. Her body relaxed and her mind wandered. She made plans to service her car before she went to France. She mentally packed her suitcase and tried out a few sentences in French. She wondered just what that warm, cloudy herb was in the vinaigrette. Sage? Tarragon! She thought of the film *Jules et Jim* and was frustrated at being unable to remember the theme tune.

No, not like that, that's not it, that's the tune that Moreau sings. The theme is softer and sadder. Damn.

Now, what was Moreau's character called? Catherine! How is Catherine? When will she know for sure? Will she tell Bob? Tonight? I've got it! I've got the tune. Yes, yes! Da da Da da Da da, mmm mmm mmm. Lovely.

Sally closed her eyes and let a head full of violins take over the bare notes she'd remembered.

Richard found her, shoeless and maskless, half-asleep, humming brokenly. He leant over and kissed her. Her eyes opened slowly and looked at him with a sleepy loveliness.

'I love you, Sally Lomax.'

The silence was startling. Richard waited for her smile to break. But watched instead the shine in her eyes evaporate and felt her whole body stiffen. Her eyes stuck to him but he no longer knew them. She said nothing.

'I love you, Sal.'

It was a pleasure to hear his own voice, to hear himself saying Those Words out loud. Slowly Sally pulled herself up and sat. Still staring flatly. Still silent.

'Sally, I . . .'

'I heard, I heard,' she said in a horribly quiet voice. Something else now laced her eyes. Richard brought his face closer to hers for a better look. It was terror. He made to kiss her. With her whole hand she pushed him away. One finger caught and scratched the side of his nostril, the other pressed into his left eye.

'Sally!'

'Don't you dare!'

'Sally!'

She leapt from the bed and fumbled into her shoes, her ankles twisting. She was shaking, she was racking her brains visibly, almost audibly. Richard, though, could not tell what she was thinking. He grasped her tightly, to steady them both.

'Sally!' She turned her face away. He brought it back in his hands. He felt like a vet examining a reluctant pup as he scanned her face and sought her eyes. Probing.

Needing a clue. Needing to know. He managed to bring her eyes into line and focus with his. The terror he had seen previously had subsided. Now there just seemed to be unbridled sadness.

'Sally,' he murmured. Good, she held his gaze. 'Sally, I have never felt before what I've felt with you. I have never felt for anyone what I feel for you. I love you and I want to share life with you. You mean more to me than anything. Sally.' He held her, silent and broken. He felt her tear, warm, fat and oily, splash on to the side of his finger and then course its way down his hand. He looked at her face. Her left eye was hazed and fuzzed by the tear that welled, impossibly large for the lower lid to contain. It fell, fast, smooth and horribly wet on to her neck and down through her cleavage. He kissed it away, tasting Sally's sad salt. He looked up and again into the face of the woman he loved and saw her eyes replenished with fresh, devastated, ready-to-fall tears.

'Sal?'

'No!' she said hoarsely, removing his hands from her face. She glanced distractedly around the room. 'Impossible,' she whimpered, refusing to meet his gaze. 'Absolutely not!' she said quite quietly as she found her mask and rummaged for her coat.

'Sally.'

She had found her coat and made for the door. Richard lunged forward and caught her. She wrestled back momentarily and then let her body go still. Still but rigid. Richard held her firmly and lovingly. He bent his head low and found unresisting lips which he kissed but which did not respond. He looked at her; she looked dejected, messy and small. Still he loved her.

'You can't love me,' she said. 'You mustn't. You've got it all wrong. It's all gone wrong.'

She looked lifeless and incredibly tired. Like a rag doll with all the stuffing beaten flat, Richard recalled later. He let her go.

I can't let her go.

Let me go.

He let her go and watched her head for the door.

'Sally?' he implored.

She shook a tear-stained face, caught his eye and held it deeply for a desperate, gorgeous, doomed moment. Then dropped her gaze and shook her head. She was gone.

Bob passed Sally in the corridor, he was searching for his elusive Catherine.

'Sally! What on earth . . .'

Her face was wet but set. She walked past him with as much dignity as she could muster, straight out of the house like Cinderella. Bob looked after her and then, on hearing the door slam, turned back and saw Richard standing motionless in the doorway to his bedroom. As Bob walked towards him, Richard leant the weight of his heavy and tired body against the door post. Bob led him into the room and shut the door. And waited, patiently and sensitively. Richard went over to the window and lifted the curtains to look distractedly down the street. He let the curtains go and they fell back into position, obediently, silently. Without turning around, he spoke, flatly, quietly and devastated.

'I told her I loved her.'

Without turning around, Richard could feel Bob's puzzled expression and hear his silent question.

'I told her I loved her and she's left me.' Richard turned to face his friend who was looking at him in shocked, disbelieving sympathy. Bob shook his head and raised his eyebrows and shoulders.

'I told her I love her more than anything, and as I've never loved before. And she left. She's gone. She cried, Bob. Cried and she said "No".'

Bob racked his brains for advice, anything constructive, comforting, both preferably.

'Richie, maybe she just needs time. God, women! You know, "been hurt before" and all that?' Richard turned away and looked through the curtains again. He shook his head and Bob watched his shoulders slump.

'But why say "No"? Why weep from the very soul? Why not say "I'm flattered, but I'm sorry"? Why not ask for time? Why the anger, the fear? It was as if she loathed me, Bob.'

Catherine burst in, sobbing hysterically. The men looked at her in wide-eyed disbelief. She looked at them wildly.

'Out! Get out! Leave me! Alone! Now!' They didn't need to be told twice. The men went next door into the spare room but Catherine's weeping was too disconcerting so they left for Bob's study at the end of the hallway. The men sat on different chairs, away from each other but very much with one another. The strength of their friendship and the deepness of their understanding saturated the room as supportive and nourishing silence. They were unaware of time passing. A feeble little patter at the door roused them from their sanctuary and Catherine popped a bedraggled face around the door.

'Bob?' she implored. Bob went to her. Richard remained motionless, statuesque, Rodin's Thinker once again. But try as he might, he could not think why his declaration of love had been met by anything other than the reciprocation he had anticipated. Could he be that wrong? Could he have read her all wrong? Could proclaiming his love for her be wrong? He thought not. So why?

Catherine pulled Bob into their bedroom and pointed to the waste-paper basket as explanation. In it he found her panties. Blood-stained.

'Poor darling, no wonder you were feeling ropy. Did you spoil your trousers?'

Catherine shook her head and gulped, holding out her arms for him. He came to her and held her.

The last of the die-hard guests were making a lethargic and drunken effort to leave.

''Bye, Andy. You're not driving, are you? Oh, Alex, you off too? Right then, 'bye. Happy New Year!'

'Bob, what time did Richard go?'

'Has he gone?'

'He has gone. Sally too, of course. Strange that they should just disappear like that.' Bob sighed and, taking his wife's hand, locked up, switched lights on or off and led her up to their room where he revealed the precious little that he knew. Not such a happy New Year after all.

SIXTEEN

Sally walked slowly to her car, a measured step to keep her bewilderment from running amok. Her hands, though, shook so much that the key missed its target again and again. Hardly surprising; she was using the ignition key. She fumbled with the key ring and was suddenly overwhelmed with hatred for the penguin dangling off the end. She pulled it and twisted it, she tugged at it, she even bit it. She grasped it and gave a determined yank. Off it came, the jag of metal tearing at the palm of her hand. Cutting deep, drawing blood. With venom, she hurled the penguin away from her and into the gutter. It stared back at her, an inane smile etched on its plastic face. Finally, she opened her car door and collapsed on to the seat. She pushed all the breath out of her in one long moan. She was involuntarily silent for a moment before a stuttering intake of air was released easily into racking sobs.

What have I done?

She beat her hands against the steering wheel. Her head dropped against her hands and she wept, tears of bitterness, wails of disappointment. *Bitch, bitch, bitch.*

Suddenly she stopped and sat bolt upright. She was alert, her head was clear.

Get out, get out, get away. Go.

She kicked her car into life and it roared at her indignantly. She turned it on a sixpence and vroomed off and away, seat-beltless and silent. Sally, you're doing sixty, slow down. Sally, that was a red light, watch out. Dodging the occasional pedestrian, she weaved in and out of what little traffic was there, like a pony in a gymkhana game.

Get me North, get me North. Get away from West London, away.

By the time she was at Hampstead, the roads were deserted and the pavements scattered sparsely with the odd reveller making a weary way homeward. Whitestone Pond shimmered in the new moon of a New Year but Sally gave it only a cursory glance. Hampstead Lane, and home was frustratingly near. With the Heath flanking her, dark and watchful, she belted along like a latterday Dick Turpin, fleeing to the safety of her stamping ground. Dick and Sally, fugitives in Highgate. Dick, Richard . . . no, no, not the same.

Come on, Mini, don't groan, carry Sally up the hill. She pulled her car around the corner into her road with a screech of tyres that was very Hollywood, most un-Highgate and very un-Sally.

Darling flat, I can see you. Oh, I'm home. I'm home.

Sally leapt from the car and left it unlocked, the steering wheel sticky with blood, headlights on. She didn't notice and even if she had, she was too desperate for the sure solitude and safety of her flat to care.

Sally is really quite beside herself. In fact, she is downright manic. She runs into the flat and greets everything that she sees. All is blissfully familiar.

Hello, flowers. Hello, comfy chair! Little teapot! Hello, my lovely, darling bed!

As she scampers from room to room, she sheds her clothes. She has ended up in the kitchen in her underwear, breathless, holding on to the ironing board, smiling at the crockery on the draining board, the dainty, matching teacup, saucer and plate from that afternoon which seemed a dream away and was indeed last year. Enough, Sally, go to bed, dissolve into sleep, empty your head, close your eyes and shut out your distress.

And Sally slept. She fell immediately into a fathomless and comatose world of soft dark numbness, a dreamless state in which Richard did not exist. And nor did Sally. Motionless and silent, sleep rescues her, she looks innocent and child-like. The weight on her shoulders, the burden she bears, now gone and forgotten until reverie will return it to the forefront of her being. Outside, her Mini stares down the street, its happy headlamps blaring away. Dejected, the battery withers and is completely flat by morning. On the seat inside, Sally's mask stares vacantly up at the rear-view mirror. Unseeing.

The first thing Sally noticed on waking was that the curtains were not drawn. Sunlight streamed in and momentarily she felt peaceful before memories assaulted her sleepy head and turned her stomach. She closed her eyes in a futile attempt to block them out. But she could neither do that nor fall back to sleep. Heart pounding, she lay staring out of the window at the linear patterns of the winter bare branches. She rewound the tape in her mind and played back Richard's every word again and again. And again. And still she hated them. And hated him. And really rather hated herself too. Sighing a hopeless sigh of failure, she rose and looked about her. One shoe, a crumpled mound of black crêpe, a little clump of streamers – where had they been? In her hair?

Bath. Let's have a bath. That's what they do in the

films, in books. Wounded heroines soak long and contemplatively in hot tubs, soothed by billows of bubbles.

Sally is shocked. Her stomach is swiped with blood, dried now and therefore brownish, but blood, definitely blood. And it's on her left thigh. She ventures over to the mirror and finds it smudged on her left cheek. She looks at her left hand and sees that her nails are dirty with it, the cracks of her fingers are trailed with it. She turns her palm uppermost and sees the gash, quite nasty, scabbed over with a very dark brown, crusty, shiny slug of it. What would a palmist say, the lines and troughs picked out in blood? Sally bravely holds her hand steady under a hot tap. The water stings, the scab is but temporary and is washed away. She looks deep into the cut, intrigued.

This is what God must see, looking down and into an earthquake, she reasons.

The phone rings. Sally is frightened and sits awkwardly in the bath willing it to stop. It does. She cries. Her face is sweaty. Her nose runs. The bath concept isn't working at all.

'Diana?'

'Ho, Sally! Don't *you* sound fragile today!'

'Diana?'

'Sally? Sal?' (*Don't call me that.*) Diana heard a faint, strangled yelp. 'I'll be right there, Sally. Just hold on a short mo'.'

0181 348 6523.

Sally, Sally, I'm sure you're there. Answer it, answer the bloody phone, talk to me. Sal, talk to me.

Sally stared at the phone. It rang pleadingly. She did not answer it. Richard hung up, his head hung low. He went for a run. His head ached, but he went for a run. Five miles, fifty minutes, shit time, *shit* time. What a shit time.

Diana caught a cab to Sally's. The walk would have taken only twenty minutes but she felt a strong pull to be there as soon as possible. She walked the short path to Sally's door and noted that the curtains in the front room were ominously closed.

But it's one in the afternoon.

She pressed the bell. And pressed it again.

I'm here, Sally, it's me.

Sally heard the bell and backed into her bedroom. It sounded again. She had forgotten that Diana was coming. She heard the letter box flip up. She stood stock still.

'Sally? It's *me*! It's Diana.' Sally was released. It's Diana. She bolted to the front door, checked the peep-hole just to make sure and flung open the door and threw herself at her black and red confidante. And there she clung, Diana having to steady herself.

'Hey hey, Sally, let's go inside.' Diana sat Sally down in the Comfy Chair, the Lloyd-Loom with the tear and the faded, lumpy, patchwork cushion. She drew up a low stool and took Sally's hand, looking into her face, a wide-eyed and sorrowful world. Diana waited. She held Sally's hand and she waited. Suddenly Sally looked her straight in the eye, directly and unflinchingly. It was disconcerting. And so was her voice. Flat, toneless but strong.

'Richard,' she paused, 'is in love. With me.'

Diana broke into a spontaneous and genuine smile. She squeezed Sally's hand. Sally glowered.

'Richard is in love with me. The man has gone and fallen in love with me!' she cried indignantly. Diana was baffled. Sally leapt up and marched, irritated, over to the mantelpiece.

'Don't you see? It's all gone wrong. This wasn't meant to happen. He was *not* to fall in love with me. But he has. It's spoiled everything. It's all ruined.' Diana was amazed.

'But Sally, it's, it's *lovely*. Surely. Isn't it?'

The women looked at each other. Sally suddenly felt let down in some sort of way. Defensive. Confused.

'No, I don't think it's lovely at all.'

'But why not?'

Sally had to think. Suddenly she didn't feel like talking, she had neither the energy nor inclination to explain.

'Just *because*, Diana. Because actually I did not want him to. He wasn't meant to. But he's gone and done so.' Diana bit the bullet and shot her the fundamental question.

'Do you mean to say that you are *not* in love with Richard?' Sally stared at her blankly and then shook her head vigorously. 'Really?' said Diana, cocking her head, 'Are you sure? Not just the tiniest bit? A little hint of it somewhere in the deepest recesses of your heart?'

'My heart,' Sally declared, avoiding Diana's eyes, 'is not in this.'

Liar, thought Diana.

SEVENTEEN

*0*181 348 6523

Come on, come on, come on!

January the second, the second time that day that Richard has called for Sally. January the first he spent listless and low. Today he feels determined and motivated, like someone with a big project to get under way. He lets the phone ring until an electronic voice suggests that he try later. Actually, Sally *isn't* in, she's walking on the Heath, trying to soul-search but failing. The space and the trees and the chill wind and the sharp bursts of sunlight are too distracting. She just walks and gazes and, in her aloneness, she feels safe and in control. Thank God. At last. Richard? Richard who?

That evening Mozart failed to soothe Richard. It was quiet and dark outside. *Enough* he thought, *enough*. He left his flat with music and lights still on and marched to his car in shirt sleeves not noticing the cold.

Highgate, I'm going to Highgate.

And off he went.

Blissfully unaware, Sally sat curled and comfortable in a chair, transferring her itinerary for Paris from mind to notepad. Antiseptic cream, plasters, underwear, two jumpers, one thick, one lightweight, alarm clock; she was engrossed in mundanity when she heard the car pull up. The engine was unmistakable, the Alfa Romeo purred and then whispered to a standstill.

Hide. Hide.

She ran into the darkness of her bedroom and waited. Not with dread actually, but with excitement. Footsteps; Richard's. A pattern of knocks; Richard's. A gentle voice; Richard's.

'Sally? It's me. Can we at least talk?'

Silence; Sally's.

Richard tried again. He rang the bell too. Still no response but he knew she was there. And she knew that he knew. And he knew that she knew that he knew. Game playing, with a winner and a loser; Sally was both. He knocked, he called for her. And then all was silent. *He's gone, he's gone.* But she was perturbed and not relieved. She found herself walking to the door. Why? To run after him? Why?

I don't know.

She was halfway to the door when Richard knocked again and called her name; his name for her: 'Sal, Sal, let me in. Please?' She stood frozen to the spot. She saw the letter box flip open. As it shut she darted back to her room. A watched mouse scurrying back into its hole. The cheese can wait.

I don't want it anyway.

You do, Sally. Oh, but you do.

Richard stood outside. Now he was cold. But he guarded the door. He stood patiently, occasionally looking through the letter box, trying to detect signs of life through the drawn curtains, attempting to knock and call as imploringly and attractively as possible. Lure her out, lure her back. But how? It wasn't going to work. Not tonight at any rate. Like a cat whose dignity had been compromised by a cocksure mouse, Richard quickly composed himself. He raised his hand and hovered over the bell. Then thought better of it. He sauntered away.

I don't really want the mouse. I only wanted to play. I'll come back another time. She will be mine. She has my name written all over her.

From her bedroom, Sally knew that he was going. She rushed to the window and pinched the curtains just enough to admit one eye. She watched him go. Excited. Disappointed. She watched the headlamps blaze into life, temporarily obscuring the car from sight. She heard the engine. She watched the swift, effortless three-point turn, and she watched the car slink away, rejected but graceful. Turning to the silent brightness of her room, she felt lonely.

Why didn't you knock some more?

Richard absent-mindedly took a left, a right, he crossed some lights and took another left. He had no idea where he was going or where he was.

Come on, mate. Stop a minute. Get a grip. Let's think this one through.

He thought it through and decided that Diana might have an answer of some sort. A bit late, past midnight, but then she was a night owl. He noted with a smile the gangly holly bush outside her house, its leaves inked black by the night, its berries still defiantly red. How very Diana. She was in and she was delighted and relieved to see him. They hugged and held on to each other like people mourning a lost friend.

'What is she playing at? Is she playing? Has the whole thing been some long, perverted game?'

Diana looked at Richard. He sat stiff and forward on the sagging couch and looked decidedly wrong there without Sally. He clasped his hands, his arms on his knees, his hair tousled, his eyes tired. She felt enormous tenderness for him, but she felt singularly ill-equipped to offer him any truly worthwhile advice.

'I honestly don't know. I've tried to talk. She's incredibly distressed.'

'But,' panicked Richard, 'but what *has* she said? Now? In the past? Think, Diana, help me here.' Diana thought and could offer only a sympathetic shrug.

'Richard,' she shook her head and Richard watched her homemade holly berry earrings (were they real?) swing haphazardly in support, 'Sally kept saying that you shouldn't have fallen in love with her. That it had spoiled things. Not that I know what "things" mean. She didn't tell me. I asked, I tried. But actually, I don't think that even *she* knows what "things" mean.'

Richard sat silent and pensive for a while. And then started with another needy 'but'.

'But, in the past, Diana. In the past?'

'In the past, she's spoken of you, of you and her, with – well, with passion. With relish. I don't know, with a sort of *greed.* To tell you the truth, Richard, I've never seen her like this. She's so, well, *sassy*! But . . .'

'But?'

'I don't know. There was also an element of naïveté . . .'

'Explain? Please?'

'That would be impossible, Richard. It's just, well, just so *Sally*, I suppose.'

'But I'm in love with her, with her sassiness *and* her naiveté. What on earth is so terrible about that?' Diana shrugged again, feeling hopeless. What indeed *was* so terrible about someone like Richard falling in love with someone like Sally?

'Richard, Richard, give her time. I'm *sure* she'll come round, come to her senses and realize just what she has. What she is jeopardizing.'

'Diana, has she ever told you that she loves me?'

'No.'

'Implied it?'

'Richard, Sally has never used the "L" word. About anyone.'

'Nor had I.'

We'll leave Richard with Diana. He finds in her a tangible if indirect link with Sally, he finds her bohemian boudoir comforting and suddenly preferable to his comparably stark flat and his own, bad company. Diana will talk, she'll tell him the precious little she knows about the florid proclamations of love and the horrid tales of violence that Sally endured with the Jims and Jamies of her past. Richard will confide in Diana, he will use the 'L' word with such conviction and sincerity that she will feel moved to the verge of tears. Richard will compare Sally with the women he has known, and will declare her incomparable. But though Diana will comfort him, and will bolster him with her own belief that he could be the best thing to happen to Sally only Sally doesn't yet see it, she will also rightly tell Richard that it is Sally who has to come back to him. He must discipline himself to steer clear until then. Because if, or when, she returns, it will be off her own bat. And if she comes back it will be for good and for real. But for now, leave her be. Disappear. It will be difficult, Richard, but it can be done, it must be done. Listen to Diana, heed her advice – she has both your and Sally's best interests at heart. Do as you're told. Sally is off to Paris. No, you can't follow her there.

So we'll leave Richard, floundering in his anxiety, desperate in his longing, sorrowful in his thwarted love. We'll go instead to Sally, we'll cross a lurching English Channel with her and accompany her through Paris. We'll watch what she does and we'll see where she goes; unseen witnesses to her most private world.

EIGHTEEN

It could have been England. The weather was so English, rain and a lot of it; the countryside looked like England – a lush landscape divided and organized into patchwork fields. But it wasn't England. England was over the sea and far away. This was France and you knew it every time the train hurtled past a station or through a village. It was France because the rural architecture said so. It was France because the men and women that the train passed were so, well, rustic. Where does British Rail pass through that affords the passenger a glimpse of a farm-worker in partisan clothes and a battered cloth cap, astride an ancient tractor held together with twine and with time? How many rural stations in Britain are bedecked with ceramic tiles and festooned with flowers?

The children were quiet; the ferry crossing had been rough, quite a few had been sick and no one escaped feeling peaky. This, combined with the early start and the soothing movement of the train churring along, lulled the class into a dozy, hushed state. Sally sat with two seats to herself. She bagged the window seat while her bags sat grandly next to her. Across the aisle, Madame Pelisou

(Head of French, Cleo to the staff) read *Paris Match*. Every now and then she pushed her glasses back on to her short nose. Everything about her was short: her stature, her hair, her fingers and their neat, square nails, her vowels, and of course her temper. She disliked children who did not try almost as much as she detested English bread. She was old but did not seem elderly, her true age being anywhere from mid-fifties to early seventies. Sally liked her. All the staff liked her. The children dreaded her. Madame Pelisou was one of a dying breed of French teachers who commanded respect and achieved consistent top grades through a style of teaching that was unashamedly dictatorial, tyrannical and tough. She was most generous at handing out humiliation and punishment. Many a child had left her lessons covered in chalk dust or doused with water (how else would they learn what *un seau d'eau* was?). Many a child had been reduced to tears. Many a child had a week of break-times confiscated. Many a child had been on the receiving end of a menacing, icy stare and a venomously spat 'Fool!' And yet not one child ever failed French and, deep into adulthood, the memory of Madame Pelisou remained vivid. With hindsight she was remembered fondly as a colourful and brilliant teacher. Sally watched her reading, saw her nod and frown and smile and tut. She looked up and caught Sally's eye and offered her a barley sugar. *Merci*.

By the time they reached Paris the rain had stopped and the city welcomed them, glistening grey and marvellously grand. It looked beautiful, enhanced by the post-downpour sunlight filtering between the buildings. A minibus awaited them and they travelled up the Champs Elysée and over the Pont Neuf heading for the Sorbonne where, down a snaking, overcrowded side street they found the pension that was to provide beds and breakfasts for the duration of their stay. For the children, this compared most favourably to their previous school trip under canvas in a waterlogged Welsh field. Now they were in France, in Gay (snigger snigger) Paris. Oh, la la!

Madame Pelisou suggested that she took the room on the floor where the children were, so Sally had a little room without a view but pretty anyway on the floor below. Diana had been considered for the trip but had requested Florence the following year. Sally thought about this as she unpacked. Uncharitably, she felt relieved that Diana was not in Paris.

I'm not having anyone telling me I ought to reciprocate Richard's love, that Richard's love is good and desirable. I don't want it and I do not want him either.

The bed invited one to snuggle down deep and Sally fell asleep, cosy and exhausted, staring distractedly at a corner of the room where the wallpaper was coming away in a perfect furl.

'Marcus, come here *now! Venez ici*! Rajiv, stop it. Class Five, settle down. Thank you. This is Notre Dame. This is a Gothic cathedral and we're standing in front of the west portal that dates to the 1220s. Marcus, you are really pushing it. Thank you. This is the main entrance so the sculpture is *didactic* – there are lessons to be learned by reading the stories depicted by the sculpture. Also, way back then, everything would have been painted in vivid colours. So, before people came to pray they would be confronted by all these tales in the sculpture. Now, why do you think that was so important? Alice?'

'Because most people couldn't read?'

'Absolutely! Marsha?'

'Also because they might learn from the scenes and then go inside and pray extra hard and properly.'

'Absolutely. Look up there, that's the Gallery of Kings. If you look above that, the sculpture depicts the Last Judgment and the Resurrection. Now those are the archivolts and if you look hard, you can see that the scenes up there are of the Damned and the Blessed. Look, there are the blind riders of the Apocalypse, and here are the Damned being shovelled into the mouth of Hell. It's so fantastic! Now, these are called the socles and in the socles are carved *per-son-if-i-cations* of the Virtues and Vices. These were to show the people the ways of life of which God either approved or disapproved. Look (*Marcus*!), see over here, this man is hitting a Bishop so this is a warning against sins against the Church. But this vice was the worst – it's a monk running away and deserting the Church altogether. And here are the goodies: Faith over here, and then Hope and over there Charity. So in the olden days, you'd come along to church and you'd see all these terrible sins and above them, sinners being thrown to Hell – as Marsha says, you'd go into the Cathedral and pray pretty hard!'

The children stood, necks craning, heads back, mesmerized (apart from Marcus who was more interested in the donkey with the straw hat and sun-glasses). Madame Pelisou winked at Miss Lomax.

Bien, let's go inside.

The class stood stock still in hushed reverence. From the impossibly large nave windows, light hung silent in dusty, gossamer walls. From the east end, the rose window burst forth glorious colours and ethereal light. Wide-eyed and open-mouthed, children and teachers alike were cast under the Cathedral's enduring spell. Marcus was held motionless by the stare of the stone-weary face of a saint; Marsha closed her eyes as light from the stained glass blessed her face in a mosaic of colour and warmth; Rajiv looked up and up and up and still did not reach the vaulting; Alice stood against a column and hugged it tight, her outstretched arms covering a mere fraction of its circumference. Sally was thrilled, thrilled to be back in Paris and charmed by the response of the children. It was a job persuading them to leave after a good hour.

Just wait until they see Sainte Chapelle tomorrow!

In stark contrast, the Pompidou Centre that afternoon provided endless and irreverent fun for Class Five. They stared and they frowned and they sniggered their way through. Shrieks of 'Call that Art?' and 'I could do that' and 'That's crap!' assaulted Sally's ears. She was now genuinely relieved that Diana was not with them.

She'd have wept.

'I know it's just one colour blue, Alice, but don't you feel a sense of space? That the colour describes the space around it? That shape and colour represent movement and space?' Miss Lomax tried to reason.

'No,' came a defiant answer.

'But,' Miss Lomax pressed, 'why does painting need to represent *something*? These modern painters believe that painting need represent nothing but itself. The very act of putting colour on canvas justifies its existence.'

'Still think it's crap,' fidgeted Alice, who was actually starting to see Miss Lomax's point, but was too galled to admit it.

'Language!' warned Miss Lomax.

'Sorry,' murmured Alice.

'Is there anything here you like?'

'I like Pick Arso.'

Sally sighed in dismay and went off to buy postcards. She had a headache threatening and expounding the merits of Modernism had not helped. Could Madame Pelisou possibly manage without her for a few hours? Could she cope with all thirty on the *bateau mouche*?

Cope? Manage?

Bien sûr!

So Sally left them and wandered back to the Left Bank.

Meandering through the Latin Quarter, charmed by its quaintness, energized by its off-beat vitality, the headache never materialized. Sally felt fine and Sally felt happy. Up the Boulevard St Michel, window-shopping, she turned left on to the Boulevard St Germain. Opposite sat the Musée Cluny; it was tempting but Sally decided not to be victim to Gallery Guilt and boldly strolled past with Catherine's song from *Jules et Jim* matching her footfalls as she went.

Wait! That's the Café de Flore, that's where Picasso et al *whiled away their hours. And there's a free table! I'm there, I'm there.*

'*Café au lait, s'il vous plaît!*'

Sally sits and sips and watches Parisian life bustle by. The day is beautiful, crisp and bright. Her eyes are slightly watery, her nose a little numb. She feels someone staring. She glances to her left and catches the eye of an impeccably suave, quintessentially French and devilishly good-looking man. Feeling reckless, she stares back. He leans with his arm on the bar, a very small, thick glass of Pernod nearby, an unfiltered cigarette resting idly between his fingers. Sally holds his gaze, intensely and unrelenting, until the man gives in and beams a salacious smile of perfect teeth. They talk with their eyebrows. May he join her? He may.

His name is Jean-Claude and he is a designer. This is his favourite café and usually he likes to sit alone. But he saw an English Rose and his own company was suddenly not enough. Another *café*? Please? *Garçon!*

As he ordered, Sally stared into her empty cup and took stock.

No one knows where I am! At this very moment, no one knows what I'm doing, that I am here, right here. This is all mine! I can be who I want and I can do as I please!

Sally felt a stream of warmth and satisfaction trace through her body at this realization.

He doesn't know who I am, and nobody I know knows that I am here. I am totally free; to be.

It felt illicit, it felt wonderful. And now his attention is back with Sally, she must talk and not think.

Talk? Flirt!

'Your English is excellent!' Thank you, he studied at Oxford and what is she doing in Paris?

'I'm a teacher, I have a class of thirty children. We are here for another two days.' Thirty children? But where are they? With much Gallic shrugging, Jean-Claude searches for them under the table and behind Sally's jacket. She shrieks with laughter, perhaps a little too enthusiastically, but what the hell? She will never see him again and no one will know anyway. They make small talk for a long time and Sally is won over by the way that simple English words and phrases ('Good Lord, you don't say?' *par example*) are transformed by a throaty French accent which oozes sensuality and Gauloises. Would she like to meet him later, right here, for a decent drink? Ooh, she would, that would be lovely. Only she can't promise; she may have teacherly duties to attend to. No matter, no matter, he is here most nights. If it is not tonight, maybe it is tomorrow night? Maybe. But Sally must go now, images of Cleo and Marcus have filtered across her mind's eye. She gathers her things about her and feels Jean-Claude looking openly at her breasts as they jut while she twists her body into her jacket. Again they stare. This time it is Sally who smiles first. See you. Yes, I hope so.

When Sally reaches the corner she looks back. He is still looking.

Longing, I do believe.

He raises his glass, she smiles widely and then sets off with a jaunty little stride and a discernible wiggle.

Sally has an idea.

She feels exhilarated, it is such fun mooting it.

Richard's loss with be J-C's gain; Richard's mistake will be J-C's triumph.

Wishing to define it further and in privacy, she walks straight past the turning for the pension and jigs along, head down, smiling distractedly, meandering in her walk and in her mind.

He won't fall in love with me. There simply isn't the time! I'll strip bare the trimmings and trappings of Jackie Collins.

Sally is scheming, Sally's spunk has returned. Sally has an idea, a plan, another project.

This time it'll be Erica Jong who's proud of me. I am going to pursue the Zipless Fuck.

NINETEEN

Sally did not make it back to the café that night. Cleo had suggested they take their entourage to Montmartre. Sally was temporarily disappointed, but reasoned that there was always tomorrow.

Mustn't appear too keen, remember, and he's there most nights.

An evening of potential lust was exchanged for a few hours of fun with the class but to her delight, Sally found that she could quite easily mind her charges while summoning up assorted images of wild love-making. Although she could not remember J-C's face his voice remained vivid and enabled her expertly to conjure up a body that could very well be his. While she walked, while she talked to the children or organized with Cleo, she was confronted by images of a firm and muscle-bound torso, of her own body being fondled dexterously. As she listened to Marcus's theory on French footballers, she dreamt up various positions for the next night; most of them were decidedly off-side. When Alice wanted to hear more about Modernism, Sally could say '*Art pour l'art*' while undressing Jean-Claude very slowly with her mind's eye. It was like being in two places at once. It was fabulous.

But Montmartre was fun too. They were rewarded, after a steep climb, by a floodlit Sacré-Coeur soaring transparent-gold and beautiful. Montmartre was buzzing and Sally's tales of Toulouse Lautrec and Dance Hall Days put a spring in the step and a sparkle in the eyes of Class Five. Marcus and Rajiv performed a boisterous can-can which won applause all around. Crêpes were scoffed and caricatures sat for. Madame Pelisou was on hand to barter down the exorbitant prices so that the children could purchase the masterpieces.

'Miss Lomax, have yours done. Go on! And you too, Madame Pelisou.' So they sat for a double portrait. Watching Miss Lomax and Madame Pelisou being fashioned into bulbous-nosed, bug-eyed, buck-toothed caricatures provided the class with much hilarity. The likeness was tenuous but that was hardly the point.

'Look! The Eiffel Tower. Tomorrow we're going up, up, up! Can't we go there *before* the Loo?'

'Blaspheme like that, Marcus, and I'll have you in the Louvre until closing time and beyond. The plan for tomorrow, Class Five, is to visit Sainte Chapelle and then spend two hours at the Louvre – and not in the café; I want a page of writing or a drawing of something you see there. After that we'll go up the Eiffel Tower and then on to Forum Les Halles in the afternoon where you can spend your pennies – francs rather. Everybody happy? Good!' Madame Pelisou regaled the group with an embellished biography of Toulouse Lautrec, complete with dialogue and songs. They were back at the pension before they knew it. Tired but happy, Class Five were unanimously obedient and went straight to bed and to sleep.

It is the evening of the next day. Fun was had by all. Marcus loved the Louvre and was late to meet the group.

Géricault and Delacroix had become his new heroes. Climbing the Eiffel Tower seemed dull in comparison to entering a painting and becoming a fighter for *Liberté, Egalité* and *Fraternité.* He spent most of his money on a book on nineteenth-century French art. It was in French but the pictures were fabulous, and anyway, Madame Pelisou promised she would help him translate.

Now it is the evening. The children are packing. Cleo and Sally are chatting. Sally asks Cleo if she would like to go for a stroll, for a drink? She knows that she will decline. Cleo declines. She will keep watch on the third floor, should the young proletariat build barricades or find imaginary Bastilles to storm.

'Well, I think I'll go for a walk. I don't know when next I'll be in Paris.'

'Have a good time, Sally. When the children are asleep, I shall tuck down for an early night. I'll see you at breakfast, eight-thirty.'

'*À demain!*'

Sally strolled to the Boulevard St Germain. There was the Café de Flore and it was heaving. Will he be there? Is this a good idea? She weaved to the bar and ordered a Kir. She looked about, trying hard not to look like she was looking for someone.

He's there.

Sally spied J-C talking animatedly with two friends.

Catch my eye, catch it! I'm over here. Over here, J-C.

Jean-Claude looked up and saw Sally. She smiled, he looked momentarily blank, then registered and swiftly tilted his head up. Sally jumped at the response and made her way over. The jostle of people knocked her sideways, her wine spilled over the sleeve of her shirt but she recovered her poise by the time she reached her target. Her smile flashed sheepish for a second.

'Hello, Jean-Claude.'

'Hello, Susan.'

'Sally!'

'Sally. Hello, Sally.' If it is possible for an embarrassing silence to pervade in a noisy and frantic bar, then the café reverberated with it.

'These are my friends, Michel and Luigi.'

'Hello, hello! Luigi, are you Italian?'

'They speak no English. Luigi is French also.'

'Oh.'

Sally felt awkward and Sally felt shy. Suddenly she wished she had never come. She wanted to go.

Go, Sal. Just up and leave. You'll never see him again. No one knows you are here.

She was tempted but two words crept through her brain, across her eyes and down her body.

Zipless Fuck.

So Sally stays and is heartened when J-C replenishes her drink. She tells him what she's been doing. She asks him about his job, about living in Paris. Has he been to London? Yes. Did he like it? Yes. Will he come again? Maybe. In between one-word answers, Jean-Claude natters to his friends. They laugh a lot, raucous and guttural. Sally cannot join in. She shifts uncomfortably from foot to foot and runs her finger over the rim of her glass again and again, trying to keep a sassy smile in place. Once more she feels she ought to go. Yet again, Jean-Claude buys her another Kir so she stays. She is not having fun. It is trying and it is tiring.

But I must pursue the Z.F. I have to. And anyway, I'll never see him again. No one who knows me knows that I am here.

Sally feels a pearl of sweat trickle down her back. She knows her cheeks are flushed and she feels slightly self-conscious. How long has she been here? She takes a furtive look at her watch. Two hours. They're talking in French and they're talking fast. Sally takes a good look at J-C. Dishy is the most appropriate adjective. He is tall. Taller than Richard? Yes, a little. His hair is dark, glossy and straight, cut into a classic bob. He has broad shoulders and slender hands. Beautiful fingers, long and elegant with well-shaped nails. There is hair on the sides of his hands and just above each knuckle. Richard's hands are smooth. He is wearing a pink shirt unbuttoned at the neck, dark blue jeans, penny loafer slip-on shoes and a navy jacket fashionably crumpled. She glances at his face and notes deep-set and dark brown eyes, a longish but aristocratic nose, a strong jaw line and an attractive smattering of stubble.

I like what I see. He'll do. He'll do nicely, thank you very much. 'Sally and the Zipless Fuck'; where are Ms Collins, Ms Jong? A book depends on this. Follow me!

And what does Jean-Claude see? A pretty enough English girl. Not really his type, not quite chic enough. Her dress sense could be greatly improved, the skirt is terrible, the length is all wrong. If she wants it short, then it must be knickers-skimming; just above the knee is so *passé*. But she's keen. She'll do. Beatrice is away in Lyons and Michel and Luigi have been goading him on. She'll do. For the night. Anyway, he'll never see her again. And it's been ages since he slept with an English girl. And Luigi says rumour has it that English Roses are tigers in bed. We'll see. She'll do.

Sally feels more relaxed. Luigi and Michel have gone. They said something to Jean-Claude and she understood it to be along the lines of 'give her one from me', 'and me'.

Bloody cheek! It's me that's calling the shots tonight.

Jean-Claude has switched on the charm that he gushed the day before and Sally has allowed herself to be swept along with it. He claims that he was talking business with the other two. Would Sally like a Gauloise? And another drink? Sally sucks the cigarette and is overcome by its strength, she lurches for her wine and gulps twice before she has exhaled. Yuk! And a head-rush too. Suddenly, everything seems terribly loud and she feels slightly dizzy.

Fool! Don't you remember, smoking doesn't suit you? Just make the cigarette last two more drags. And easy on the wine, that's the fourth. No, fifth. Damn.

Unaware, Jean-Claude saves her.

'Let's take a walk.'

Outside it has been raining and the pavement is dressed in glistening pools cast gold under the street lights. They don't walk, they saunter. The pavement cafés are emptier now, just the die-hard bar-proppers sipping Pernod and philosophizing. Jean-Claude suggests they head for the Luxembourg Gardens but when they arrive all the benches are wet; it has started to drizzle and Sally feels chilled. Her head has cleared and she has sobered up. She and Jean-Claude do not really have that much to talk about. They both know what they want to happen. And they both know that it *will* happen. And they both know that the other is willing and waiting.

Sally cannot really be bothered to play out a whole seduction scene. Just a means to an end. An abbreviation will suffice. She wants her Z.F., and she just wants her Z.F., that's all. She and J-C are walking heads down against the rain, hands in pocket to keep warm; silent. Sally's footfalls provide her with thinking time. She remembers back to the party where she met Richard. She recalls with a smile the flirting and the eye contact and the euphoric energy she felt. She remembers the teasing mini-kiss she planted on his lips before spinning on her heels to mix and mingle. And she sees again the erotic kissing that they launched into uncontrollably once the front door of the party had closed behind them. 'Come to Highgate,' she had suggested. Progress had been slow, with every red light an excuse to grope and kiss each other greedily. 'Pull over! Pull over!' Sally had cried when they were but a mile from base. Richard had swerved recklessly to the side of the road; Hampstead Heath, silent and conspiring, flanking them. Sally had dived for him. Richard, in ecstatic disbelief, remained defenceless while she sucked and licked her way down to his groin into which she buried her head for a tantalizing and all too short moment. For both, it was a taste of what was to come. And come.

Sally remembers the desperation to shed clothes as soon as her front door shut. Initially, they had tried to undress each other but it had proven cumbersome and too time-consuming. So, while they kissed, they wriggled and ripped their way out of their clothes. Burning naked, they made it to Sally's bed, the kiss which had started on the doorstep never stopped and Richard was forced to walk backwards, eyes shut, body raw, as Sally grappled and guided him into her bedroom. There, they melted into the bed and fell fast and deep into the pleasures and needs of scorching flesh.

Sally has no inclination to seduce Jean-Claude. There's no thrill to this chase. She doesn't care if he is bowled over by what a sassy vamp she is. She just wants to see what pure sex is like, no emotions attached. After all, she will never see him again. They walk and make small talk. The drizzle has stopped and a brisk wind taken its place.

'I live quite close to where we are now. Would you like to come up? For coffee?'

Coffee, etchings! Here we go!

'Yes, I'll come.'

TWENTY

Sally was sorely disappointed by Jean-Claude's apartment. As soon as she set foot inside, warning bells rang out but she chose to remain deaf to them. In her fantasy on the way to Montmartre the day before, he had taken her to an old tenement building where the high-ceilinged rooms breathed faded grandeur. She had envisaged tall windows with billowing muslin, mismatched colour-washed cupboards in a tiny kichenette, and a balcony with a seen-in-a-dream view. And, of course, a bidet in the bathroom. She had imagined his bed as old and high, enclosed by sinuous brass bedsteads and banked with white linen; crumpled and voluminous. She had imagined herself sinking into it while he deftly undressed her. No fumbling. No zips.

But reality usually lets a day-dream down and the details of Sally's were deflated in an instant. J-C's flat turned out to be on the fourth floor of a modern block. The lift was out of order so they had traipsed up the stairs and wandered down a faceless corridor. On entering the apartment, the first thing that Sally thought was: *The man has no taste. He is a designer and yet he has no taste.*

Each item of furniture was obviously expensive but nothing went with anything. Each piece was merely and clearly some status symbol. Sally's prime dismay, however, occurred in the bathroom.

Yuk, look at the state of that bath! And where's the bidet? There is no bidet. Woe.

Toothpaste oozed, solid and dry, from a topless tube; razor clippings scummed the sink. Sally recalled Jean-Claude's attractive stubble and calculated that he could not have shaved for at least two days.

Sally, if he has a grungy bathroom and no bidet for you, why are you staying? Why not go? It is not too late. You need never see him again. Think of Richard's bathroom; tasteful majolica, spick and span.

Sally refuses to think of Richard. But he's there, oh, he's there all right. Unwittingly, he's the very reason for Sally being in this sorry bathroom. She glances at herself in the mirror and is taken aback by the puzzled expression that meets her gaze. Defiantly, she smiles back. Obstinately, she won't let go of the Z.F. concept. She *has* to try it. No one will know but she. Looking at and not into the mirror, she absent-mindedly cups her hands over her breasts.

'Sally, you are okay?' the husky French voice enquires.

How very considerate.

'Yes, I'm fine. Give me a minute.' A minute later she emerges and Jean-Claude is hovering outside the door. He approaches and she allows herself to be kissed.

Mmm, he's a good kisser. Yes, this is fine. A good idea. I'm going to have fun.

No you're not.

Jean-Claude pulls Sally closer towards him. He grabs her arm with one hand and grabs her breast with the other. He *is* taller than Richard, her aching neck confirms it.

Ow, my arm.

Sally tries to free herself but it serves only to excite him and he grips tighter and kisses harder. He pulls away and, with a chuck of his head, he motions to a room Sally has not yet seen but presumes to be his bedroom.

The bed is unmade, the linen is striped brown and beige. J-C is undressing himself. Sally's hands are behind her back, finding the zip of her skirt which snags and catches as she pulls it down. It affords an ogling J-C a good look at her breasts doing their famous jut and he lunges for them.

He is naked while she is merely skirtless and he lounges on the bed, his erection arrogantly leering at her. Sally doesn't take her eyes off Jean-Claude; he keeps his eyes on her body, soaking up what every shed piece of clothing reveals. Sally lies down next to him and rests her arms on his chest, her leg folded around his. They kiss and she looks at him; his eyes are closed and she hears him give a throaty murmur under his breath. She smiles.

It's working.

Now his hands are everywhere, at least they're everywhere he wants them to be but they're not quite where Sally would like. She tries to guide his hand to her secret erogenous zones but he takes them away too soon. Sally wouldn't say that her breasts were being fondled; mauled rather. He's found her clitoris but is hardly sensitive to its sensitivity. He has no idea. She flinches but he reads it as pleasure and increases the pressure. Firmly, she pulls his hand. He looks up, puzzled.

'Not like that, *comme ci*,' she guides. He looks sulky but obeys. Sally is enjoying the sensation, she is close, she is very close. But though her breathing quickens and her body writhes, he stops.

'Don't stop.'

'I just find Mister Condom.'

Already?

Jean-Claude seems to think so.

She strokes his back while he rolls and snaps the condom into place and as he turns towards her, she reaches to kiss him. Jean-Claude can't be bothered with that just now, there's work to be done. He spreads her legs very wide and then puts his arms under the base of her back and hauls her up high. He barges into her. Sally moans. It feels good though. They hump and grind and Sally feels her neck being bitten. It hurts, but it feels exciting. He is thrusting harder and faster and Sally uses both hands to pull his head up and into line with hers. It's heavy, but she has his eyes. They kiss.

He's devouring me.

Sally wants to go on top. She tries to shift him but he's a leaden lump of pumping flesh.

'Jean-Claude, wait. Stop for a minute.'

'Why, what's wrong?'

'Nothing's wrong! Just stop so I can go on top.'

'Okay, okay.' That's better, Sally feels she has more control. She sets a slower pace and rotates her pelvis in the way she enjoys, the way that drove Richard wild. But Jean-Claude has stopped moving. She looks at him, he is looking at the ceiling. She stops too.

'Enough?' he delicately enquires.

'No!' Sally retorts.

'Later,' he suggests as he flips her on to her stomach. As he takes her from behind she feels a surge of excitement in her abdomen. But it disappears once he's settled himself into his own pattern of bumps. It does nothing for Sally but she reasons that it is his 'go' so that's okay. He lifts her on to her knees and after a moment's thrill for Sally, he finds his favoured pace again. He grabs her breasts and just keeps them grabbed. Sally decides it is time for a change but she cannot shift him. He is hurling himself into her, her arms are aching, her knees are getting chafed and her breasts hurt under his grip. She arches her back in an effort to free herself but his arms clasp her around her stomach and he squeezes her as he thrusts into her. Her breathing is distorted, it is not comfortable, it is not sexy at all. She imagines they must look like dogs mating.

This is not my mate.

She feels sore. She gives up. Faster he goes.

Come on, J-C, you must be close. Come on. Come.

She is bashed and she is bumped against. His pace is frenetic and he starts to moan.

Bébé, bébé. Mon Dieu, mon Dieu. Monde.

She can feel every spurt and every surge.

Mon Dieu.

He's finished.

Thank God.

Staring at the hideous linen, Sally bemoans that *hors d'oeuvres* was fundamentally *ordinaire*, that she had been deprived main course and there had been no suggestion of pudding. Now he flops down on top of her and her sore knees grate against the sheets. Her face is smothered by pillow and sweaty brute of a man. She wants to go.

'You want to stay?'

'No.'

So, Sally Lomax, you've had your Zipless Fuck. And how do you feel? You're walking back, through deserted Paris streets, it is almost two in the morning. How do you feel! Was it worth it? Was it as you expected? Did you like it? Do you want more? Has it made you feel good – in your body, your self? Are you now happy?

Was that it? What have I done? And why have I done it? So that was a Zipless Fuck. Erica J., you've got it all wrong. It can't have been. No, no, but it was. It wasn't like in the books, it was not like in the films. It's me – I've let Ms Jong down. I've let myself down. I feel down. I'm alone in Paris. And I feel lonely, full stop. I'm sore. Where am I? Oh, yes, first left then right.

What did I do that for? It wasn't like Ms Jong made out. I'm obviously not heroine material for her books. Richar. . . no, no, no, what am I saying? I don't want him. Jean-Claude, J-C, vous êtes un grand cochon. *But if he's a pig, then I can only be a dog. I don't know what I'll think of myself in the morning, in the clear light of day. Well, I'll never see him again. I'll never do this again. But where do I go from here? Put it down to experience? It's an experience I wish I'd never had. There's the pension. I'm home and dry.*

But it's not home and I'm soaking wet.

Sally crept up the stairs and into her room. She had a scorching shower and did not finish off with a blast of cold. Hot water felt more cleansing and she felt filthy. She scrubbed and rubbed and soaped her fingers, cleaning as far up as she could reach. Condom or no condom, she could feel and smell him still. He did not smell like Richard yet she was neither comforted nor pleased by this. She dried herself, pulling the towel over her body harshly. She looked at her knees, they were red. She looked at her neck and was reviled by the dark raspberry blotch she saw. A love bite was a contradiction in terms, this was a selfish lust suck and she wished it was not there.

Sally fell into bed. Her heart was pounding and her mind was rattling with a jumble of hazed thoughts.

No, no. Sleep.

She shut off and slept, dreamless but safe again.

TWENTY-ONE

Sally could not quite manage breakfast even though she knew that the croissants and hot chocolate would be as delicious as they had been throughout their stay. She retired, still tired, to her room to pack. The suitcase ready and by the door, she lay on the crumpled bed hoping she could find comfort in closed eyes. But her eyes were held open and fixed on the furl of wallpaper which, today, looked yellowing and sorry. A very hot, oily tear eased its way from her tear-duct, over her eyeball, to dribble lethargically from the corner of her eye down her cheek. Sally wondered what it was there for. She did not think she felt like crying. It evaporated, leaving a slight tightness to the cheek. She splashed her face with water from the tap and called 'I'm coming!' to Cleo's knock.

* * *

'Come in!' called Richard, over the sea and far away.

'It's *Mzzz* Filey, from Marlborough Ward *Ink*,' Sandra announced with a wide-eyed smile.

'Of course. Do show her in,' Richard motioned whilst sorting through the mock-Georgian folly plans.

A long pair of legs walked in, the longest that Richard had seen or thought could exist. He followed them upwards, travelling yards of sheer Lycra before arriving at a bright blue and very short skirt, teamed with matching and flatteringly cut jacket. Crowning the ensemble was a chiselled face with manicured eyebrows, perfect lips and a glossy, jet black head of hair organized into a sharp, clean, hundred-dollar crop. Sophistication personified. And in his office.

'Carlotta Filey.'

'Richard Stonehill.'

They grasped hands; hers were cool and strong, garnished with perfectly shaped and polished nails.

Stop gawping, Richard.

Rich-ard, *get a hold of yourself, man! What on earth!*

As she concentrated on the drawings before her, Richard absorbed the picture in front of him.

Quite frankly, I've never seen anything like her – like this!

Though hidden, he was aware and ashamed of his sudden erection.

Think Sally, think Sally.

But Sally is in Paris and she hates you and it's over.

Richard heard himself making small talk, asking after her flight, the hotel.

'How long are you staying?'

'I leave late Saturday.' Tomorrow.

Carlotta liked what she saw. She was delighted with the plans and was pleased with their creator.

A flying visit. A flying fuck? Perhaps. Gee, why the heck not?

'Listen, Richard, could I take these with me? I don't want to take up too much of your time right now.'

'No, no! But you're not. Please!'

She held his eyes and saw what an easy catch he was going to be.

'Really, I'd like to spend the afternoon going over them. Say, why not continue this over dinner?' His eyes lit up.

Richard, you're so transparent.

'Yes, let's!'

'You know some place nice?'

'Oh, yes!'

'You want to pick me up from the hotel? I've gotten so lost in London before. Eight, eight-thirty?'

'Yes! Fine, fine. I'll be at the Savoy at eightish.' He watched the legs slink away and saw his tube of drawings encircled by exquisitely manicured hands. His penis, enthusiastic and with a mind of its own, imagined vividly where those hands could be much better clasped. Richard's eyes admired the rear view as she breezed out of his room. His mouth was dry, his ears full of her slow, deep drawl, and her suggestion of dinner, eight, eight-thirty, replayed itself like a scratched record.

Well, Richard, we have seen what your eyes saw, we heard what she said, we know how your body has reacted but what, exactly, is going on in your mind?

Wow! he thought, while Sandra, dowdy and depressed, brought him a cheese sandwich.

Wow! he thought as he fingered the bread and tipped the food, untouched, into the bin.

What on earth! he thought as he swivelled in his chair and fixed his hands behind his head watching the cranes and the river being busy beneath him.

That was some woman, he mused as he dropped a hand to loll over his subsiding erection.

Some woman! he concluded as he twirled back to his desk to answer the phone.

'Richard? Bob! Squash?'

'No!'

'No? Why?'

'Busy.'

'Where?'

'Business.'

Odd, thought Bob as he hung up.

* * *

Sally brought up the rear of the crocodile as it trooped to the Orangerie. Today Paris was noisy and threatening to her. Suddenly it seemed to be a place she neither liked nor knew. Highgate seemed rosy and very far away. The children were impatient to run amok in the Tuileries gardens so they raced around the gallery, bought postcards under Madame Pelisou's approving supervision and then followed her outside until she reached her chosen bench near the fountains and released them. They scampered away on their final burst of holiday energy. Sally remained inside. She wandered down the stairs and found Monet's *Water Lilies*, silent and serene, just as she had left them three years previously. She had them all to herself. She was alone with them and they enveloped and soothed her like a grandfather. She sat herself down, shoulders drooping, her neck and head poking lazily upwards. She looked like a shabby zoo vulture but she felt like a mouse. She gave little attention to the paintings which surrounded her, she knew them well and they required little effort for their spell to be woven. The vast, encircling canvasses of muted hazed colours granted Sally the hush and peace she desperately needed, that her own company for once could not provide. She became lost in the privacy and calm of Giverny. Her head drooped and dropped lower than her shoulders. Noiselessly, she wept.

Unseen, Marcus, who had returned to search for his clipboard, watched Miss Lomax's hunched back heave with wracking silent sobs.

Miss Lomax is crying. Why is Miss Lomax crying?

Marcus realized in an instant that this was not the stuff

of playground gossip. He saw her take her hands to her face and heard her sniff and gasp, strangled and private. He wanted to sit on her lap and cuddle her as he had his mother when his grandfather had died. But he knew he couldn't and shouldn't and mustn't. He felt compelled to watch over her; he felt he should, just until she stopped. The water lilies seemed to smile benevolently over her but it was not enough. Marcus felt he should remain there, out of sight, just until she stopped crying. Eventually she did. Marcus saw her body slump exhausted and crumple a little bit more now that the sobbing had subsided. Silently he backed away and out of sight to the stairwell. A Rodin bust met him eye to eye. The bronze and battered face, alternately shiny and dull, black and silver under the spotlight, carried the sorrow and pain that Marcus recognized as Miss Lomax's. He left her there, being looked after by her water lilies, watched over and understood by Rodin.

When she emerged twenty minutes later, Marcus nonchalantly took time out from a game of tag and ventured over to the bench where she and Madame Pelisou sat. He offered her a piece of apricot-flavoured chewing gum, Madame Pelisou too. Miss Lomax took it gratefully and smiled weakly at him. The tears were gone and no redness around the eyes suggested they had ever been there. But behind the smile and behind the eyes, Marcus could see that her sorrow had not abated. He took it upon himself to sit by her on the train and to stand near her on the deck of the ferry, offering her a crisp, a sip of Ribena, another piece of chewing gum; peach melba-favoured this time.

The party arrived back at the school at 7 that evening. The children stampeded to their parents with garbled tales of the time of their lives they had just had. Most hurried away to the family Volvos without a backward glance. Marcus, who had already re-enacted David's *Death of Marat* and had told his father about the donkey with the hat and the sun-glasses, was just beginning a discourse on Delacroix when he stopped and caught Madame Pelisou's eyes. Beaming at her, he then looked for Miss Lomax and waved expansively. She raised her hand and held it there. Suddenly a wave was not enough. He charged back into the playground, shouting: '*Merci! Merci!*' to Madame Pelisou as he ran to Miss Lomax and told her that she was the best teacher in the whole wide world and that he'd see her in class on Monday morning.

'Home! Hello, little flat. Hello, chairs. Hello, dead flowers. I'm home.'

Leaving her suitcase by the door, Sally went through to the kitchen, thumbing through the mail as she filled the kettle and found her favourite mug. Disappointed that there were no handwritten letters, she set aside the bills and bank statement for the next day and dumped the circulars in the bin. It was nearly 8 o'clock and she dialled for Diana though she wondered if she really felt like talking. The line rang and rang, and rang redundant; Diana obviously was not in. What did Sally want to say anyway? Would she confide? Did part of her want to run to Diana, let go and reveal how ghastly it had been and how wretched she felt? Would she just say she was feeling low and hide the reason? But who is the reason, Sally? Richard or Jean-Claude?

Well, Diana was not in so Sally was saved the decision. She sipped her tea in the bath and considered the noise she made; a whistling intake of breath, the slurp of liquid travelling past her lips into her mouth, the hollow echo of the gulp as she swallowed. She acknowledged how the flavour and warmth of this humble beverage brought comfort to her tastebuds, her stomach and her mind. She acknowledged too that she was absorbed in such menial thoughts because she did not want to think about that which she knew she should.

At 8.30, Sally was in bed, her teeth brushed, a clean

pair of pyjamas on, and a cassette of *Woman's Hour* short stories filling the room and providing a welcome diversion from the knot of thoughts and emotions pressing on her mind.

When Sally fell asleep half an hour later with the tape still running, Richard wiped his mouth with a linen napkin and stared at Carlotta's lips, awaiting the main course.

TWENTY-TWO

'Are you married?'

'Good Lord, no!' Richard exclaimed. He scanned her left hand, saw no band of gold and decided against asking her the same. The remains of the main course, delicious and rich, had been cleared away. They were eating at the Savoy: 'So we can spread your plans out on the floor afterwards,' Carlotta had told him. *And I can spread my legs after that*, she had mused. Richard was dumbstruck by her beauty and elegance, but not so mesmerized that he could not assess, with slight dismay, that she was fashionably abstemious with her food. He remembered Sally gorging herself and swooning with pleasure at the meals they had enjoyed together.

Forget Sally.

The pudding trolley was wheeled before them for their delectation. *Don't*, prayed Richard, *please don't choose tiramisù*. Carlotta chose fresh strawberries and Richard was relieved, and silently bewildered that he was indeed relieved. But the chocolate-Cointreau parfait distracted him from the naggings of his subconscious.

This woman is a thoroughbred racehorse to Sally's half-breed filly.

'Let's have coffee over the plans in my room,' suggested Carlotta.

In the lift, Richard and Carlotta held each other's gazes unrelenting. Her eyes were an astonishing deep emerald accentuated by careful, precise make-up. Her lips were full and constantly pouting and Richard marvelled how they could keep their glossy red coating throughout an entire meal, many glasses of wine, and frequent dainty dabs on a napkin. She was wearing a startling dress; red, sleeveless, tight and short. In her high black patent heels, she was almost as tall as Richard who had changed into casual shirt and blazer. He followed two steps behind as she sashayed to her door and he watched, excited, as she calmly slid the key into the lock and flicked her wrist to open it. She used the side of her body to press the door open and Richard observed her calf muscle flex temptingly as she did so.

The suite was palatial if anonymous and they went through to the lounge area where, true to her word, the plans lay unravelled on the floor. Richard had no plans, he was happy to be led. Stepping out of her shoes, Carlotta laid a hand on Richard's shoulder to steady herself and left it there a suggestive moment longer once she was shoeless and a few inches shorter than him.

'Screw the coffee, let's have port!' Carlotta broke the silence uncompromisingly. Richard was dying for coffee, but if Carlotta said port, then so be it. He and his penis watched in awe and anticipation as she grasped the neck of the bottle and slid her thumb up to the mushroom cork and eased it off. She snaked over to him, two glasses in her hands, and came up close, very close, before handing him the fuller glass and coiling herself to the ground. Richard closed his mouth and sat down opposite her, the plans in between them.

'I like this,' Carlotta said as she leant across, affording Richard a front seat view of her fabulous cleavage. 'And this is cool,' she cooed, gesturing to the elegant portico.

'But couldn't we have bay windows with that neat leaded glass effect?' she asked, sitting back on her knees and placing her impossibly long hands on her beautifully dipped waist.

'No,' Richard murmured, and then cleared his throat, delivering the first few words of his reason in an unnaturally loud voice. 'No, I really don't think so. This is mock-*Georgian*, not mock-*Tudor*. It would be a travesty and the overall elegance would be compromised – decimated, actually. Awfully sorry. No can do.' *God, can I kiss you?*

'Okay,' Carlotta conceded. Richard looked at her, waiting for her next query. Architecture, architecture. A stunning woman across from him; think architecture. Richard dropped his gaze to his plans, beautifully orchestrated even if he did think so himself. He was pleased with his work and Carlotta Filey, on behalf of Marlborough Ward Inc., gave it their seal of approval.

'It's great. I just love it. We'll have it,' Carlotta concluded. 'Let's fuck,' she said.

Richard's head jerked up.

What did she just say? I beg your pardon?

Come on, Richard, why so startled? You knew from the moment she suggested dinner earlier this morning that you would have some kind of sex.

Indeed, he had known, from the way they caught each other's eyes and held them, smouldering, over dinner, that they would end up in bed. He knew, by the way they had stood so close and brushed against each other intentionally and unnecessarily in the lift, that desire was mutual and strong. He could tell by her body language, obvious and seductive, here in the room, that she wanted him. And he knew, by the messages relayed from his brain to his groin and back again, that he wanted her. And yet he was taken aback. It seemed so sudden, so aloof, so unsexual. Hands still on her waist, she looked at him, stonily, lips parted.

'You *do* wanna, doncha?' she asked him, a patronizing edge lacing her question.

Do I want to go to bed with this woman? Just look at her, man. Just look at what you can have. Sod Sally. Screw her. Screw Carlotta.

'Yup,' Richard declared, rising to his feet to follow her into the bedroom.

Carlotta breezed over to him and spun around so that he might unzip her dress. It caught halfway down and snatched at the material. She pushed his hands away and eased the dress off. She was trussed up in black lace lingerie, the whole works; half-cup boned bra, suspenders, minuscule knickers, lacy-topped stockings. *Like a billboard ad for Triumph or Playtex or whatever*, Richard thought later. He wanted to touch her but was not sure where. His palms were clammy too.

'Wait,' he said, 'I'm just popping to the bathroom.' Locking himself in as quietly as he could (*Don't want her to think I'm a prude or something*), he ran the tap on full until it gushed soothingly cold water. He held his wrists still, shifting his body so that the water no longer splashed back at him. He lessened the flow and cupped water to his face, keeping his eyes open all the time. He shook his head and looked at himself straight, in the mirror. He felt rather bewildered.

Richard, what are you going to do? Are you sure you want to? Is it to spite Sally? Is it to persuade yourself that you're over her, that she never meant that much anyway? Is it to reinstate your macho pride which she inadvertently damaged? What do you see as you look at your wet face? As you watch the drops fall from your nose and from your chin?

Richard Stonehill, do you want it? Is she worth it? Was Sally worth it? I thought so, didn't I? Sal, who were *you? Were you trying to be a Carlotta, all vampish and sophisticated and alluring? Carlotta is a vamp but I can see her for what she is. That is all she is. I do want her. I want to screw and be screwed. Illicit. No deep, meaningful looks. Just sex, raw and uninhibited. Yes, I want it and I'll go and get it. Sorry, Sally, but you lost your chance, so play your games with someone else. Come on, Richie, dry your face and let's get laid.*

Richard lunged for the door to take him to the pleasures of the body and, noisily, found it locked. He fumbled with the bolt and, with a final clatter, burst into the room where Carlotta stood pretty much where he had left her. She began to unbutton his shirt and he slid his hands to her waist.

Is it slimmer than Sally's?

Carlotta eased the shirt away from his chest and traced a long, pointed and polished nail down his neck and around and over his nipples. Down she went in a straight line, dipping into and out of his navel until she arrived at his trousers. She undid the button with an assertive pop and then tugged the zip down. Richard pushed his trousers away as Charlotta pulled at his boxer shorts. He caught sight of himself in the mirror on the wall in front of him yet, somehow, the image of a stunning woman giving head was more of a turn-on than the sensation itself. As blow jobs went, it was good. But it was familiar. Richard shut his eyes from the mirror and saw Sally and felt again the astonishing newness of their couplings.

Don't think Sally.

Richard opened his eyes and there again, in the mirror, was the man, him, being sucked and licked by this gorgeous woman. And once again, the physical pleasure of the here and now subsided a little.

Don't look at the mirror!

Why, Richard? Afraid of what you see there? What does the mirror reflect? Only the truth.

Shut up.

Richard pulls Carlotta to her feet and pushes his tongue into her mouth. He can taste himself on her. He finds her breasts and fondles them but there's too much itchy lace. Get it off. He fiddles with the clasp but Carlotta rescues him and now she is naked. That's better.

They're big, more than a handful. They're different. They're not as firm or smooth as – stop it! These nipples are much longer, sort of rubbery. Nice, though.

Carlotta pushes Richard's head down to them and he decides they taste pretty much the same. He also decides to concentrate more on the job in hand and to concentrate on not thinking or comparing size, look and texture to Sally.

Sally's in France. And Sally hates me.

They fall to the bed and Richard feels Carlotta up and down. There is plenty of bare flesh *up*, but only a lot of interfering material *down*. Get it off, get it off. It seems to be desperately complicated. As Richard fumbles and follows ribbons and cords to cul de sacs, Carlotta lies still, bored; eyes looking at the plaster flourishes on the cornice. She smiles sweetly at Richard as she pushes him away and sits up to unsnap her suspenders and wriggle free from her panties.

Perhaps he can manage to roll down a pair of stockings?

He can, and expertly runs his soft, warm hands over the cool, firm flesh of her legs and follows his touch with kisses that she finds touching.

Get to it, baby, get to it, cut the crap and lick me!

Carlotta pulls Richard's head from her thighs, spreads her legs and pushes his face to where she wants him.

Am I doing something wrong? Richard wonders. *Why won't she writhe?* It occurs to Carlotta that the concept of oral sex is far sexier than the reality itself so she is quite content when Richard leaves off to travel his tongue up and over her body.

He's got a great body, she assesses. *Good, broad shoulders, a strong, muscular back tapering to a tight, firm butt. Let me look at your chest. You could be hairier for my liking but I like to see your stomach. I just love those little boxes of muscles on either side. Oh, so you like it when I run my fingers feather-light over them? You do, do you? Well, I fancy feeling your dick, which I know you'll like too. About average, I'd say, neat little balls. Uncircumcized! Shit, cut the crap, I want you in me sooner rather than later.*

Richard flips her off and under him, which excites her. He pins her arms above her head and lowers his face to hers, eyes closed. His flop of hair tickles her nose but ceases to do so once the kiss has been planted.

She doesn't do much work in the kissing department.

He lifts himself away and looks at what is beneath him. Glorious and picture perfect. Every curve and dip just where supermodels dictate they should be. Her skin is taut and smooth and evenly bronzed. Long legs, neat knees, pancake flat stomach. Almost too perfect to be real.

Let's do it.

Richard spreads her legs and lowers himself slowly, slowly, over her; masterful control thanks to his extremely strong arms.

'Hold on, Mister!' Carlotta interjects. With one hand on Richard's chest, he is held in mid press-up position while her other arm slides over to the bedside table, from the top drawer of which she brings back her hand, condom between her first and second fingers. Richard looks at her face as she unrolls it and fits it adeptly. She's categorically beautiful.

Very.

But?

Bland.

Carlotta lies on her back and lets Richard take control. He pushes into her and she moans which turns him on. He holds himself up on his arms and she grasps his straining biceps.

'Hard, hard,' she cries, so he grinds into her and she

arches her back and asks for it harder and faster. To accommodate her request, Richard lets himself down and lies on her, scooping her up slightly and folding his arms under her, around her waist, thus finding good leverage to hump her hard and fast. She moans and gasps and calls out, 'Yes, baby!' Richard smiles and then decides a little variety might be nice. He rolls Carlotta on top and tries to push her up so that she might sit and straddle him. No, no. She flops on to his chest and humps against him, hard and fast.

'Harder! Faster! Jesus, what's up with you?'

'I can't go any faster and I'm as hard as I'll ever be!' Carlotta does not see the joke and stops still to look at him, exasperated. Richard smiles at her, she scowls back.

Oh, so you want to play it mean, do you?

He rolls back on top and gives a most almighty plunge as hard and deep as is anatomically possible. She groans and says *yes, yes*. He plunges again. *Yes, yes*. And again. *Oh, baby*. And again. He looks at the clock – half-past midnight. *Faster, faster!* Okay, okay. The small of his back begins to ache as Richard plunges and surges as fast as he can. He looks at her face, flushed and strewn with wisps of jet black hair. Her eyes are closed, her lips mouth *faster, harder, baby, yes*. He tries to grant her request, consequently neglecting his own physical preferences. Suddenly her eyes are open and they both cry out; Carlotta as the orgasm assaults her at last, Richard as her pointed nails dig deep into his flesh, one set lynched on to his left buttock, the other ripping into his right shoulder. She's finished, she's still, her hold has dropped away. Richard finds his pace and moves into her. She remains motionless.

'Carlotta?'

'I'm pooped, hon. You take it how you wish. That's fine by me.'

Richard looks at the slumbering American beauty in disbelief and anger. He moves into her and still she just lies there. He stops looking at her face and drops his gaze to her breasts, jutting sky-high and still unbelievably pert.

Must be silicone.

They are.

He looks up at her, checking if she's asleep; alive even. He finds her analyzing the plaster work on the ceiling rose. Richard withdraws.

'What's wrong?'

'No, no, nothing.'

'I don't mind, carry on!'

'No, no, it's okay, I'm tired anyway.'

'Maybe in the morning, babe.'

'Maybe.'

Richard went across to the bathroom with the ulterior motive of masturbation. But once he had pulled off the condom and put a towel on the too-cold toilet seat, he lost the inclination, the desire and the erection itself. He crept back to the bed from where the audible sound of Carlotta sleeping rose. Sliding silently in between the sheets, he sidled over to the very edge of the bed, turning away from the foreign body next to him.

What on earth was all that? he wondered as he fixed tired eyes on the gap in the curtains.

Go to sleep, Richard.

TWENTY-THREE

Well, Sally and Richard have both pursued what they thought they wanted. And both have been left dry and dismayed by their discoveries. What do they want now? They wonder. I think we know. I think we know that somewhere they must know too. How will they get there, though? Will they fight? Resist? Will pride prevent a happy ever after?

'Di!'

'Sal-*lee*! Whenjoogeback? How was it? How are you? When are you coming round?' Diana gabbled away and Sally surprised herself by doing something she thought impossible: she laughed out loud. Diana had the gift, given by God or genetics, of cheering up the saddest of souls quite inadvertently. She had no idea that Sally was caught in a chasm of gloom, that she had woken helpless and alone. Diana's happy self, coupled with her devotion to her friend, dribbled forth uncontrollably, travelling supersonic through the telephone wire, out of the receiver and slap into the very heart of Sally's being.

'Oh, Diana, it's good to be home. Please, come over to mine? I'll cook.'

'Yum. When?'

'How about a late lunch?'

'Sounds heavenly. Tell me, Sally, tell me everything! At once! No, no, no! Not now! Can't wait to see you, Sugar Pop. I'll come at one-ish?'

'Two-ish, please?'

'Oh. Shame. Okay. 'Bye-bye, 'bye-bye!' Sally was exhausted but her head felt lighter and a smile surreptitiously crept across her lips.

I'd better pop out and buy some food then. What shall I do? What does Diana like? I know, something nice with pasta. I'll zip over to Hampstead and go to that fresh pasta shop. Damn! What am I going to wear? I've been slacking, just look at that mound of washing, and that pile of ironing. Sally Lomax, you should be ashamed of yourself!

Scramble into anything, Sally, it's only ten o'clock on a Saturday morning. And anyway, who is going to see you? There must be something at the back of your cupboard. Come on, get your skates on.

Wearing an old floral frock whose hem hung low at the back, a shabby Aran-knit cardigan for warmth, trainers with ankle socks for comfort and her hat for good measure, Sally set out for Hampstead, greeting her car like a long-lost friend. She was temporarily set back by the gaze of her mask lying on the passenger seat but, after a moment's rueful contemplation, tossed it into the back where it nestled next to the de-icer on a tartan rug. The Mini groaned and wheezed. Sally cooed and coaxed, took the key out and blew on it; she urged, she goaded, she bit her tongue. Her car was lifeless, she was bemused. Sitting still and wondering what to do, she focused on a piece of paper held by the wind-screen wiper. Winding down the window she retrieved it, a handwritten note. She read it out loud: ' "*Dear owner, it is New Year's Day and I notice that your headlights are on. I do hope you make it to your car before the battery runs flat! Best wishes for a happy year, Bill.*" ' Who's Bill? Sally moaned. She moaned for her poor car and blamed herself for its current death. She moaned for herself as she remembered New Year's Eve. She moaned as she gathered her bag, her list and her wits about her and decided what to do.

Walk; that was the solution and not a bad one either. It was a precious sunny January day, cold but invigorating. Sally's route took her via Kenwood and over the Heath to Whitestone pond and the reaches of Hampstead. Once she had traded pavement for path, her mien was restored. The ground felt good underfoot, it was soft but not muddy so she could put a spring in her step without collecting clods on her shoes. The sun, trying hard to break through the thick haze created by the chill air, hung as a luminous and distant pinky puff. Sally thought it most poetic and proclaimed, ' "Glory be to God for Dappled Things" ' to a robin who cocked his head in agreement as she passed by.

I feel really okay, she thought as she patted the bark of a particularly gnarled oak.

I think it won't be too bad a year, she decided as she stooped to pocket a perfect pine cone.

I have my health, I have my Self, I don't need another; I am full, she thought as she sat on a bench near the magnolia tree at Kenwood and regarded the great swathe of lawn to the mirror-flat lake.

Quite happy to stop awhile with her contemplations, Sally turned her gaze about her and felt cheered by the day. Energy and sound surrounded her; the shrieks of children, the hearty laughter of adults and the merry yapping of dogs. The residue of Christmas, its mood and paraphernalia, clothed the park. Small children rode shiny tricycles, not-so-small children tottered on sparkling bicycles with stabilizers and thoroughly big children terrorized all asunder on already muddy mountain bikes. Christmas was in the beautiful micro-fibre macs worn with pride and aplomb, in the small puppies trotting skittishly on leads, the stunt-kites and dolls' prams, the Timberland accessories and the excited voices which passed by Sally. The happy atmosphere was infectious and Sally smiled broadly to all who caught her eye. More often than not, a nod and a 'morning' were returned. Feeling buoyant, she continued her trek to Hampstead, chatting to the flora and fauna on the way.

* * *

In his reverie, Richard wondered, quite calmly, where on earth he was. His eyes were half-closed, his left eye focused only on a bloom of whiteness which he discerned to be a pillow. His right eye made out a gap in heavily tasselled curtains. He was comfortable in the bed, warm and safe. But where was he?

'Morning, Dick.'

Who?

Richard raised his head in a relaxed movement and scanned for the owner of the voice. He found her, sitting statuesque at the other side of the room.

Of course, Carlotta. Damn!

Richard let his head drop back to the pillow and tried to lull himself back into that just-woken state of blankness. But could not. He heard her padding towards him and she sat herself down on the edge of the bed next to him. A long, strong nail traced patterns on his bare shoulder. It felt nice.

'Say, get yourself up. My plane goes this evening and I fancy taking breakfast some place nice.' Her voice, so deep and sensual the previous day, now grated on his ears as he detected a slight whine behind the transatlantic drawl. He looked at her and only half-recognized her. Something was different. What?

'Morning, Carlotta.'

'Why are you looking at me like that?' Richard looked perplexed and furrowed his brow in contemplation.

'Something's different. What?' She laughed and batted her eyelids at him. 'This London water made my eyes change colour!'

He looked at them. They were the most incredible violet, more violet than Elizabeth Taylor's. It came back to him. The woman he had slept with had lured him with strong emerald eyes. Beautiful eyes. Now they were violet. More violent than violet. Suddenly they didn't seem quite so beautiful. In fact, Richard thought the concept decidedly suspect.

'What colour are they naturally?'

'Heck, any colour I want them to be!'

Baffled, Richard made his naked way to the bathroom. On the side of the basin was a container, inside which two green contact lenses were held in suspension. Richard held them to the light.

How very bizarre.

He furtively peeped into the glitzy world of her vast wash-bag. Potions, lotions, brushes, slabs of colour, tubes of lipstick, cream for Thrush.

God! Please, no.

He rummaged as silently as he could and came across another container with 'Sultry Mahogany' written on the side. Two deep brown contact lenses glared back at him. He had a quick look at his own eyes and found he was quite content with the colour they naturally were. He glanced at his hands and thought his well-cared-for nails vastly preferable to the plastic talons in umpteen shades of red which Carlotta kept in little boxes.

Richard gave his reflection a chastising shake of the head. He drew his fingers across his eyes, dragging the skin down and around in a bid to shed their bleariness and reactivate. His hands may be elegant but his fingers smelt of sex. He was keen to have a thorough shower and did so, freezing cold of course. He felt depleted and sullen, his stomach felt hollow but not with hunger. The shower helped physically, but emotionally he felt drained and desperate for solitary peace and quiet.

But the lady must be breakfasted. And not at my place, no siree!

He emerged, wrapped up in a luxurious towelling robe, his hair still damp and delectably tousled. Naturally.

Carlotta came over to him and slid her hands through his hair. He let himself be kissed and was surprised that his only reaction was wondering if any of her lipstick had transferred itself to his mouth or cheeks. He glanced at the mirror and was relieved to see that it had not. Still she held him. He didn't really want to be held, not just now, not this morning. Not by her. He took her wrists and smiled genially.

'I'll take you to Hampstead. We'll have breakfast there and you'll find it rather, um, *quaint*.'

Can you guess?

Ill-fated lovers who cross paths in the most ghastly and cruel of circumstances cannot be restricted to the novels of Hardy and Dickens. I apologize but there is little I can do. Sally is already in Hampstead and Richard's Alfa Romeo is now nearing Swiss Cottage. Must they bump into each other? Can it not be that we alone know that they're both there? Alas, such a meeting, unfair as it may seem, is now sadly inevitable.

Unbeknown to Richard, he chose Sally's Tea Pot Shoppe, which she had left twenty minutes before, having been revived by an incomparable cappuccino and Carlos's reverent compliments. 'My Engel Eesh Rosa, I know zat 'at anywhere. Please, please. Sit!' he had crooned, trying hard to disregard the rest of her appearance.

En route to the pasta shop, Sally was diverted by the antiques corridor and was caressing an old engraved pewter tankard that would make a fabulous vase but was expensive at thirty pounds while, a few yards away,

Richard tucked into a decadent cooked breakfast and Carlotta sipped orange juice.

'I like those green waxy coats,' she enthused.

'Barbour. Very popular. Very practical. Quintessentially English. Rather expensive,' ventured Richard.

'Well, I'd like a take-home present before I go, so I think I'll treat myself to one.'

'We could stop off at Austin Reed on the way back to your hotel,' suggested Richard, sorting through his wallet to pay the bill. Carlos scurried off for change; lots of small change to encourage a generous tip. But Richard did not know who Carlos was.

'I tell you what else I love, not my style though, and that's those pretty little flowery dresses that your English girls like to wear. They're so sweet, so countrified and old fashioned. So *Tess of the D'Urbervilles.* So oldy worldy. Look, like that one there,' she motioned.

Richard looked.

My God, it's Sally.

There she was, over the road and up a bit, window shopping. Richard watched as she scratched the back of one leg with the foot of her other, her arms out to either side steadying herself. His heart soared and raced and plummeted.

She can't see me here. Not with this woman. My God, but look at her! That dress? Those shoes! That cardie? Carlotta's right; so sweet, so pretty, so domestic and cosy. Well, this is a revelation. But a welcome one. She's lovely. So lovely. But she can't see me here. Not now. Shit, Sal, what have I done? And what have you done to me? It's no good, I've got to get out of here. Now. Quickly.

'Come on, let's go and get your Barbour.' Richard urged Carlotta to her feet and left without waiting for his change. Lucky Carlos, a tip twice the cost of the breakfast. Richard looked again but Sally was gone. He felt simultaneously greatly relieved and yet terribly disappointed.

Was it her? Just an apparition? It was her, of course it

was. I want her and I don't want her. I want her like that – gorgeous in rags and colour clashes – but not yet. Not now. Not today. Not 'till I've rid myself of this American affliction; not until she wants me. God, where is she? Just another peep to tide me along. Let me see her unseen.

Simultaneously desperate for another glimpse but dreading being seen, Richard tried to set the pace, brisk and assertive. Carlotta resisted, drawn compulsively to the tempting shop windows. Richard's heart was heaving and his breakfast sat defiantly at the base of his throat; his stomach too tight to allow access. His palms were clammy, his feet were cold and his knee joints stiff, though he needed them now more than ever to carry him away.

His car was around the next corner at the top of Fitzjohn's Avenue; close, frustratingly close, and yet horribly far away. He grasped Carlotta around the waist and pleaded that they really should get going if she wanted to shop for a Barbour. As he pulled her away and made her walk, he saw Sally.

And she saw him.

And they were just a few feet apart, hopelessly headed for each other.

Sally stood stock still. Richard was so overcome with horror that he could neither prevent his legs from moving nor remove his arm from Carlotta's waist. Fortunately Carlotta, unaware of the tragedy of the situation, freed herself to scrutinize a pair of boots and was soon inside the shop, leaving Sally and Richard less than a yard away from each other. Richard felt sick but not half as sick as Sally. They stood there, defying Newtonian time; their mouths open, their minds whirring, their eyes disbelieving and searching, their hearts in overdrive. He wanted to push the lock of hair away from her mouth. He wanted to fall on his knees at her feet. He wanted to swoop her up, into his arms and take her a million miles away from this place and this moment. He just wanted to touch her. But all he could do was remain frozen and desperately remorseful.

Sally wanted to dissolve. She wanted to be back in childhood, away from all this. She wanted to cry, to be sick, to fall asleep and wake up yesterday. She wanted to be anywhere but here. She wanted Richard to cradle her in his arms and kiss her forehead.

No, I don't.

Yes, you do.

'Hon, I'm through, let's go.'

Carlotta, oblivious and brash, broke through their tragic barrier and destroyed the frozen moment. Richard heard Sally give a sharp and involuntary intake of breath and watched, helpless, as she fled across the road, the back of her dress dragging in a puddle as she went. He wanted to go after her; to catch her, to shake her, to explain to her, to kiss her. But he was rendered immobile. He had no strength to move, his body felt heavy, his eyes were fixed to the loaded space Sally had left, his heart was grinding to a halt. Carlotta, bored and still brash, hauled him to his car.

'C'mon, hon. Take me to Dustin Reeves or wherever it is I can buy an oily Barburry.'

Austin Reed, you stupid cow, Richard thought witheringly as he crunched his gears and sped recklessly away.

TWENTY-FOUR

Our poor heroine, sad old Sal. Poor Sally of the shabby dress, she of the comfy cardie, of the tatty trainers; Sal of the dirge and frills.

How do you feel, scurrying to nowhere in particular just to get away? You can feel the gritty wet of your dress slap against the back of your calves. You can feel the chill in the air whistle its way through the holes in your cardigan, through the buttons in your frock. You're chilled, aren't you, chilled to the bone? Numb too. Poor old girl, what a nasty shock, what a beastly thing to have happened. What are you thinking, Sally Lomax? And how do you feel?

How do I feel? What do I think? I think I feel sick. I feel like I've swallowed a lump of lead. There is something in my head, a noise, it's thudding around. Every time I move my head it crashes against a side of my skull.

But what are you thinking?

What am I thinking? I'm thinking that I'm frightened, she frightened me. I can't get her out of my mind's eye. Did you see her?

Yes, we saw her, Sally, we've seen quite a lot of her, not that you'd know. But yes, we saw her.

Who is she? Who is *she? Has he slept with her? Why were they in Hampstead? Does she live near me? When did it start between them? But did you* see *her? All high heels and couture clothes, cheek bones to die for and lips to pray for. Did you see her? I did. And I saw Richard's hand around her waist and he didn't even drop it when he saw me. He couldn't keep his hands off her. He had his hand glued to her gorgeous horrid tiny waist. It seems bizarre but I feel rather like Hamlet. Remember his distress and disgust with his mother for exchanging the love for a husband not two months dead, for the bed of another?*

A *husband*, Sal? Oh, girl! If only you knew. Think not of Hamlet, but only of yourself. What do you make of it all?

He said he loved me.

And you hated him for it.

I never hated him. I just didn't like the idea of it. In retrospect, I loathed myself more, I think. Richard, Richie, who is she? Was she good? In bed? Did you think of me? Did you compare us? Well, I compared J-Bloody-C to you. And he was lacking. I bet I was far from your mind, from your soul, from the desires of your body. Get me away from all this. Get me to a nunnery!

Sally!

Where is Richard right now? What is he thinking just this very second?

If you want to know, he has dumped *that woman* at Austin Reed with a cursory farewell to her, and 'good riddance' racketing through his mind. He has just zoomed over a zebra crossing forcing innocent and indignant pedestrians to stand motionless and precarious in the middle of a road. He is on his way home. He does not feel very well. Like you, he's wondering about you.

'But you don't understand. He was with a *woman*,' Sally pleaded as Diana helped herself to the untouched pasta on Sally's plate. Diana chewed thoughtfully, gazing at the swirled irises patterning Sally's laminated Liberty tablecloth.

What does she want me to say? What can I say? I'm not likely to say: 'Well, it's all your fault, Sal.' Until she says it, says the 'L' word that she abhors so much, then I really can't say much, can I? After all, if the love-factor didn't exist, then I doubt whether she'd be this devastated.

Diana looked across at Sally, sitting shabby and collapsed in her funny old clothes that actually only seemed funny in the wake of her recent sassy wardrobe. Sally sat still, her lower lip jutting out; in a sulk, in anger, in sadness? It was difficult to decipher its provenance. But her eyes told her tale, downcast but constantly on the move, an eyebrow furrowing, pupils darting, eyelids beating fast to prevent ready tears. Diana had finished Sally's plate and was full. She'd had enough and she had had enough.

'Sally?' she ventured. Sally remained slumped but looked up with her eyes and scanned Diana's face desperately. 'What is it that you want?'

Sally's eyes dropped under the weight of such a question. She sat silent and let it go unanswered. Suddenly she spurted forth a torrent of uncontrolled woe.

'Diana! He saw me like that, like *this*!' She brushed violently at the bodice of her dress, pulled at her cardie and kicked her legs out to the side of the table to emphasize the socks and trainers. 'And Diana! You should have seen *her*! She was, she was horrible, she was stunning and slick, and such a . . . such a . . . She was a *vamp*,' she spat, 'a *femme fatale*,' she wailed, 'a *vixen*,' she moaned. 'She wasn't like *me*, you see.'

Sally trailed off, her voice now a defeated whisper. Diana waited, breath baited like an expectant fisherman's fly. All was silent and still and loaded. Bite it! Then movement. Sally turned her head and Diana glanced at the tear which had fallen with a sonorous splash on to the stamen of a printed iris. More movement. Sally rose, arms folded, hugging the Aran knit about herself. Passing Diana, she crossed over to the window. Diana swivelled in her chair and saw her as a silhouette, pressed two-dimensional and opaque against the cold, white January light. Immediately, she had an idea for a painting but tactfully put the creative inspiration on hold and returned in spirit and sight to Sally. And she waited. Finally, she was rewarded. In a voice that was broken and frail, Sally at last uttered the truth.

'She wasn't like me, you see,' she started, 'she wasn't like me because I'm not like her. You see. But, I wanted to be a sort of "her". That's what I wanted to be. And that's what I tried hard to be, for Richie, for me. It was hard work, but I did it, I got there, and I enjoyed it. I believed in it and I really enjoyed it. But I know now that it's just not me. I don't have the guts, I don't have the strength. I don't even have the style. Nor the money, nor the easy sophistication. And I don't have the body. At the end of the day, I don't really have the personality. It's not in my nature, it's not natural, it's just not me.'

Slowly, Sally turned to Diana. She shrugged her shoulders and dropped her head. Her shoulders drooped and shook twice before she checked the sobs with all her might and braced her body upright. Diana was drawn to her, drawn to her plight and drawn to her damaged, battered state. She went to her and placed her hands on Sally's shoulders. She shook her gently. And then she shook her more forcefully and spoke in rhythm and in time with her shakes.

'But, Sally, you're *there*!' she proclaimed. 'You know who you are *not*. You know who you *are*! Look what you've learnt, look what you've found out!' It all seemed very clear-cut and simple to Diana. Diana was smiling. But she was soon perplexed that Sally remained so unhappy. She shook Sally again. And again, almost irritated by the limp and feeble body in her hands. In fake submission and an effort to free herself from being shaken, Sally nodded her head reluctantly and Diana eased her grip but let her hands rest gently on the weary shoulders.

'But don't you see, Di? *She* wasn't like *me*. I'm not like *her*.' Sally nodded her head energetically, a frown cutting deep into her brow. Diana did not understand. In fact, Sally hadn't understood either, not until just then. The effort and discipline of organizing her thoughts and woe into coherent, spoken form had rewarded her with clear insight. She could see now what it really was that she felt, why she felt it, and what she wanted. Sally cleared her throat.

'Diana.' Diana tipped her head to one side inviting Sally to continue, unhurried, unjudged.

'Diana. I'm not like *her*. But Richard is with her. She's not like *me*. But Richard was with her. Richard,' she declared, 'wants that kind of woman.' The room resounded with the noisy silence of the wracking of brains.

Go on, Sally.

'But,' she faltered, 'I want Richard.'

'You want Richard?'

'Yes.'

'But, Sally, Richard told *you* that he loved you!' Problem solved, solution easy, happy ending in sight, rejoiced Diana to herself. 'He loves you. Go get him, girl!'

'Yes, Diana. No, no, Di. Richard wasn't in love with *me*. He was in love with the *me-type*. I mean the her-type. The wrong me – I'm not her! I am not like that. So that makes a nonsense, somewhat, of his words.' Now it is Sally who can see the clarity of the unfortunate truth, or what she believes it to be, and Diana's mind is in a muddle as she tries to decipher Sally's theory, assess the facts and present a helpful solution to still-suffering Sal.

Think, Diana, think.

Ah, but of course! Go easy here, tread softly.

'But you want Richard?'

'Yes.'

'Why?'

'Why?'

'Why do you *want* him?'

Sally looked at Diana with incredulity, as if she was dim and dippy.

'You know!'

No. Diana does not know, or at least makes it seem that way. She does, of course, know. But, until Sally says it out loud, umprompted, Diana will remain supposedly in the dark. Sally must remain untouched and have no prompting. Take your hands away from her just now, let her stand tall. Say it, Sally, say it.

'Dian-arr!' Sally looks at her, encouraging her to say it for her. Diana merely shrugs though it is excruciating to have to do so. A whisper of bewilderment flickers across Sally's face. Diana sees it. No, Diana, don't help her! Not now! Not for this! As much as you love her, leave her alone, you know it must come from her, you said as much to Richard. Let her say it.

Come on, Sally, feel the solidarity urge you on.

Diana, bite it, bite your tongue, bide your time.

'Sally. Are you in love with him?'

Oh, hush, Diana. Damn! Bad move, big mistake; huge. See how the Lomax barrier has come down, the shield raised? See Sally lower her veil? It may be as thin as gossamer, as transparent as muslin but it is as strong as steel.

An infuriating shrug with a twitch of the lips is all Sally's giving out today. Time to go, Di.

'Am I in love with him?' Sally later asked the African Violet as she watered it and tweaked off two dead leaves.

'Do I love Richard?' she asked the kettle as she waited for it to boil.

'Is it *love* that I feel?' she enquired of the tea towel as she turned her back on the kettle in the hope that, if unwatched, it might come to the boil faster. Sally could not find the answer in the flora or domestic appliances in her flat, so she sipped her tea and looked at the mismatched laces holding her trainers together.

'*Is* it love?' she asked the rain as it drizzled its haphazard way down the window pane.

'Is he the *one*?' she quizzed the tea leaves which had gathered conspiringly in the base of her cup.

If the tea leaves don't hold the answer, who does?

Sally continued to search for the answer as she made an inroad into the ironing. Needless to say, shirts, skirts and hankies did not have it.

'Am I in love with Richard Stonehill?' she asked her knees as she sat on the toilet, her legs suspended and stretched out in front of her.

But Sally knew where she could find the answer, where hitherto she had avoided looking. Sally knew she'd find it once she pulled the chain. She had only to turn around and confront it. Turn, Sally. Ask.

And there was the answer, staring her straight in the face. The mirror, of course. There was Sally and there was the mirror, and there, in the mirror, was Sally. There was no need to ask out loud.

Do I love him?

Yes, I love him.

TWENTY-FIVE

So Sally is in love. Are we surprised? No, not really. But how will she show it? How will she deal with the inherent responsibility of such knowledge? And is she happy? Would she have acknowledged how she felt had she not seen Richard with the Other Woman? Miss Tiny Waist, Madam Long Legs, Lady Luscious Lips. (*Damn them and their perfect Cupid's Bow shape!*) And if Sally puts down her shield and throws back her veil, will she be lost mercilessly to day-dreams of babies, of scones baking in an Aga and all the other things she previously deemed reprehensible? Who might she be letting down if she lets her heart rule her head? Ms Collins? Ms Jong? Herself?

Sally had chased fun – fun that was not chaste – through playing and creating a whole new persona, a very different woman. She had wanted The Richard Thing to be a delicious secret that she could recall with enduring pleasure at her leisure. She had orchestrated The Richard Thing to be something she could carry with her through her life, a sort of magic rune that she could take out at times when things might not be going well.

Tedious dinner parties – *oh! remember how he would kiss me!*

Trying Christmases – *and there was that time when he hired a box at the Opera and we made love while Violetta sang.*

Tiring school functions – *remember his eyes travelling my body, glazed with desire that burned unheeded.*

The Richard Thing would enable her to take a mind-flight away from being boring wifey with brood and Aga, back to the time when she was an outrageous vamp, desired madly by a living Rodin. The Richard Thing was to be fun, it was to be slightly reckless, somewhat irresponsible, rather naughty, thoroughly liberating – all the things Sally presumed adulthood and marriage to forfeit. She had envisaged standing in front of her mirror in her forties, fifties, sixties, even seventies, smiling gleefully at the memory of a man totally ensnared in her seductive web, one she had spun all by herself, following no known pattern. Maybe Sally, sweet Sally, good girl Sally, wanted to know that she had the ability and independence to be as she wished and to be whom she probably knew all along she was not.

But what is wrong with the real you, Sal? After all, it did not take our Richard long to see what was behind the veil, to be lost in the spell of you! Maybe you wanted merely to have a good time and great sex without suffering the consequences and catches of a rampant fling dampening down into a relationship. But why the fear of a relationship, Sal? Why the trepidation of going through life conventionally – marriage, children, dinner parties, school events? Is fun confined merely to an illicit fling? Are men who are the stuff of rampant affairs a different species from those who have the substance for a relationship? More to the point, are women?

Sally had neither envisaged Fling Thing falling in love with her, nor had she foreseen Fling Thing assuming his true identity as Richard Stonehill so quickly. She had been thoroughly unprepared for her reaction and for the consequences; she desired the person under the muscle, she respected the brain beneath the brawn, she felt the heart behind the hands, she saw the soul through the (beautiful) eyes. Fling Thing was fabulous but Richard Stonehill was far better. Sally had naively presumed that utter lust and deep love were poles apart. Now she must reconcile the two.

When Richard phoned her almost a fortnight later in the staff-room, Sally was relieved, and just a little thrilled too. Twice since that fateful morning in Hampstead she had ventured out to see him. Once, dressed in heels and black Lycra, she had made it as far as pulling the choke on her Mini but slunk home to eat chocolate instead. Two days later she tried again, this time making it right to his flat. She drove appallingly and her wits were truly frazzled by the time she approached Notting Hill. On spying Richard's Spyder, the surge of adrenalin made her head so light and her hands so heavy that she nearly veered straight into it. She drove straight past, round the block and then back again, juddering to a halt outside the building she so wanted to enter but just could not quite. She counted up the floors and took note of the lights that were on. *He must be in.*

Obviously.

I'll just wait until it turns 9 on the dot.

The clock read 8.57. As it turned 9, fear and timidity subsumed her and, with shaking hand and defeated soul, she made a lurching and not terribly swift getaway.

Unbeknown to her, Richard had seen her and had been dumbstruck. There was he, bored on a Tuesday night, thinking of Sally, fantasizing that she might come to him. In his mind he acted out the scenario in such vivid and believable detail that he had, in reality, gone to the window to see if maybe her car was indeed there and that perhaps she was on her way up.

My God, omigod, omigod. She is *here!*

The shock was so great that Richard whipped away out of sight of the window, pressing himself flat against the wall, like a movie-star dodging the bullets of the bad guy. With his heart in his mouth and no gun in his holster he remained paralysed, released only by the unwanted sound of a familiar engine starting up. Keeping his body still but craning his neck to its limit, he witnessed the sorry sight of the little Mini clumping and chugging its way away.

Away. She's gone. But she was *here.*

Richard was very blue. Feeling uncomfortably numb, he sought solace in Pink Floyd. Wishing with all his might that Sally was here, he was wailing: 'We're just two lost souls swimming in a fish bowl' somewhat histrionically when the doorbell sounded.

He jumped.

Sally. Sally?

A patter of knocks followed.

'Hello?' implored a muffled voice through the letter box. 'Is there anybody in there? Is there anyone at home?' Richard opened the door.

'Come on now, I hear you're feeling down.' Waters and Gilmour had become Bob and Catherine.

'It was all my wife's idea,' explained Bob. 'She thought you'd probably not be eating, not looking after yourself,' he justified as he unpacked carton after carton from the excellent Mandarin Duck Takeaway. In between grateful mouthfuls (Richard had *not* eaten all day) Richard told all.

'It's all turning into a veritable nightmare, I tell you. Sally: I'm sure you've guessed. Pass the seaweed, please. You know she wouldn't open the door to me on New Year's Day? Oh yes of course, you counselled me that evening. Sweet and Sour, please. Well, on Saturday morning I was in Hampstead. I bumped into her. Into Sally. It was absolutely horrendous. Crispy Duck, anyone? Mind if I finish it?'

'Finish the story, Richard!' squealed Catherine as she licked her fingers but then plumped for another dumpling. 'What happened?' she said, noticing with some horror that Jimi Hendrix rubbed shoulders with Bach (*'B' should be before 'H', and surely Jimi should be on the shelf below?*)

'She ran away.'

Do I really want to relive this? To share it? No amount of halving this problem is going to solve it.

'Did you talk to her?'

'No.'

'Whyever not?'

Richard raised his eyebrows.

'Are you *sure* it was her?' Bob quizzed, making neat piles with shrivelled tulip petals which lay forlornly on the floor.

Richard raised his eyebrows further and grabbed the dumplings off Catherine. 'Of course it was her.'

'Couldn't you've?'

'No.'

'*Shouldn't* you've?'

'Not possible.'

'Why?'

'I wasn't alone. I was with someone else. A woman. It's all a complete nightmare.'

Bob and Catherine sat gawping; Catherine had a trail of seaweed hanging on to the corner of her mouth, Bob's chin was smeared with Sweet and Sour sauce. Suddenly, Richard felt like bursting out laughing but, reading their true concern and bewilderment, resisted and continued unprompted.

'This woman is a client. Nothing happened. Well, I mean it did, but it is of absolutely no importance to me.

You know, just a dose of good old sex – only it wasn't very good. It wasn't a casting couch job – the contract was already in the bag. I just wined and dined her.'

'And sixty-nined her?' Catherine couldn't resist it, as if she needed to make light of it to contain the deep dismay she felt.

Richard, Richard – maybe you haven't changed all that much.

'*She* seduced *me*,' spelled out Richard, determined that the Woodses would not think him the perpetrator. 'Okay, I let myself be seduced. Only it wasn't very seductive. I'd given up on Sally. Well, what I mean is, I'd given up on her ever coming back to me. God, I want her back! Anyway, I'm in Hampstead, reluctantly breakfasting this *fling thing* when she points over the road to a "quaint li'le English gal" which just happens to be Sally. My, she did look quaint! In fact, she looked absolutely gorgeous. She was wearing this extraordinary amalgam of flowery frock, Aran knit, floppy hat – and trainers would you believe! It was a revelation to me and yet so very Sally too. Well, I was horrified and thought a hasty retreat should be beat – I knew it would be too awful if we saw each other. But it happened. We just stood and stared and then Sally was gone.'

'Did she see the other woman?' Catherine felt quite sick.

'That's the cruellest part. Desperate to get away, I was trying to drag her physically. That's when I caught Sally's eye. I was turned to stone. I couldn't do a thing. My hand was stuck to this woman's awful skinny waist.'

'Nightmare,' Catherine groaned.

'Nightmare,' agreed Bob.

'Nightmare,' confirmed Richard. 'Only something strange happened this evening. She was here!' Again the Woodses' mouths fell and again Richard swiftly diverted his gaze from the debris still adorning them. 'Well, she was and she wasn't. It was so spooky – I had been thinking about her, about her doing a real "Sally" and just suddenly turning up in a tutu or something. Anyway, I was so engrossed in the fantasy that I went over to the window just to check. Chrise-Orlmighty if her car wasn't double-parked right outside! It gave me one hell of a shock – I quickly hid! What a berk!'

'What a *berk*!' confirmed Catherine, racking her mind for a solution – or a good idea at the least.

'*What* a berk!' chastized Bob.

'And then it was all too late. I heard the car start up and I just watched her drive away.' Richard shook his head and the Woodses' heads' shook in sympathy. 'What am I going to do, guys?'

Catherine looked from Richard to his CD collection. With its former thematic, alphabetic splendour gone, it served to accentuate Richard's malady.

All really is not well. Schubert is as out of his depth next to Van Halen as Richard is without Sally. Think. We have to get through to him, raise and restore him.

'Well,' she said breezily, hoping she sounded reassuring, 'for a start, I think the very fact that she was here tonight should raise your hopes. You are obviously in her thoughts but I reckon Hampstead must have knocked her for six. I mean, you can't undo what happened – you did sleep with this woman and you did bump into Sally with her. That's a nightmare. You can't undo what happened but you could *reinvent* the past you know. And you *can* salvage Sally – I think that's probably what she wants but I think it's up to you.'

'Rein*vent* the past?' Richard probed. Catherine cocked her head and Bob finished her theory, utterly in tune with her drive.

'No sex. Business breakfast in Hampstead. Plane to catch. Contract won. White lie – smallish one. That's all.'

'Bloody brilliant!' exclaimed Richard. Though his problem was neither halved nor solved, it now seemed more manageable.

'Call her. You *must* call her,' insisted Catherine with very intense eye contact.

'You bet,' Richard nodded vigorously, 'bloody brilliant.'

'Tummies full. Problems solved. Time we were off,' announced Bob, handing Richard the tulip debris. 'We're trying for a baby, you know,' he beamed, 'every night! It's wonderful! Only if we don't wend our way home now, I'll be too shagged to . . .'

'Shag?' ventured Richard, absent-mindedly compacting the petals before dumping them in a take-away carton. Catherine gave Richard's arm a supportive stroke.

'Precisely!' she giggled. 'Only you'll have to wash all that goop off your face first, Bob.'

'And you, dear wife, must extricate that fine piece of seaweed too.'

So there was a phone call for Sally in the staff-room. Had she not seen Catherine the night before, quite possibly she would have refused the call.

'Sally? Catherine! I'm taking you out for dinner tonight. It's top secret. Bob's been told I'm cooking for my brother. I shall pick you up at eight sharp. Okay? 'Bye! Oh, Sally?'

'Yes?'

'Okay?'

'Yes.'

''Bye for now.'

They had gone to a particularly nice brasserie in West Hampstead, safe territory for both. They sat opposite each other, elbows defiantly on the table, heads together in enthusiastic conspiracy. Sally spoke first.

'Are you pregnant, Catherine?'

'No.'

'I'm sorry. Are you still trying?'

'But of course.'

'In secret?'

'No.'

'Oh! How's Bob then?'

'Frightened but happy – he's rather enjoying all the practice it requires! In fact, I'm six days late but trying not to think about it. You know, be nonchalant, cool and collected,' Catherine said, nibbling her lip and fidgeting with her hair, eyes bright and dancing.

Sally assessed this happy turn-about. So if pregnancy was no longer the problem, why the illicit dinner? Catherine's go.

'Sally?'

'Yes?'

'Are you in love?' The rocket and roast pepper salad had arrived.

'Yes.'

'With Richard?' Catherine ventured with her mouth full.

'Yes, with Richard,' Sally confirmed, licking her lips. 'Who else?' she grinned.

And so began a luxuriously long meal. Sally felt thoroughly safe with Catherine and was desperate for news of Richard. She was moved by what she learnt. Catherine told her about the end of the party. She thought hard for a moment and then decided to tell Sally all that Richard had said to Bob that night. And how he had said it. Sally felt wretched. She could have left the restaurant and gone straight to him, holding him in her arms and saying sorry. But she stayed because she wanted to listen and she wanted to talk.

'But I don't hate him, I never hated him. I just didn't want him to fall in love with me.'

'But whyever not?'

'Because I didn't want to fall in love with him.'

'Whyever not?'

'Because it would complicate things.'

'What things?'

'Life!'

'Oh, Sally, how pretentious and how silly. What do you mean, "life"?'

'Well, if you give yourself away, you leave yourself open to hurt.'

'True, but if you keep yourself to yourself, think how much life would lack. You can enjoy your own company, but if there are two of you, it is logical and it goes without saying that there is twice as much of everything – happiness, fun, sex, normality – they are all so much more *colourful*, they're all *bigger*, they are all so much more *worthwhile*.'

Sally smiled meekly at Catherine, timid at the thought of this colourful, big, worthwhile life lying tantalizingly close and potentially there for the taking. Catherine told her of their recent visit to Richard, to feed him and listen to him. Waiting for Sally to probe deeper, she spoke of the dead tulips and the fact that Jimi and Johann Sebastian now shared the same shelf. Unalphabetically.

'But, Catherine, what about Richard? That woman?'

'Woman? Who?' Catherine feigned ignorance so Sally told her of Saturday bloody Saturday. Catherine felt the tiny white lie was in order and Sally felt stronger for hearing that the vamp was merely one of the Americans for whom Richard had designed the Georgian folly. A client. Just business. Just a business breakfast. That's all.

'And Richard said what was so ghastly,' concluded Catherine, 'was that it was his own mercenary greed that led to his come-uppance in bumping into you like that. Now what did he call her? Something along the lines of an infuriating, attention-seeking transatlantic tramp. She was being evasive as to whether the company would take the work so he had to wine and dine and give her a breakfast-time tour of London before she caught her plane.'

'Did it work?'

'Yup!'

'Good for Richard. But you should have *seen* her.'

'She can't have been that great because we all know that Richard's *hobby* is to have and hold the most beautiful and perfect of things. He *loves* beauty – in anything, I mean look at his bloody hi-fi, his Sabatier knives, his Alfa flipping Romeo! (By the way, his Alfa's *filthy* at the mo'!) He loves beauty and appreciates it in a very objective way. Well, he didn't once mention this woman in terms of any of her physical attributes. But you! My, how he waxes Lomax lyrical! We could never shut him up. It was quite possibly the most boring Christmas I've ever had, listening him drone on about Sal-this and Sal-that, and Sal's eyes and Sal's smile. He even relates your tales of the classroom. I feel I know Rajiv and Marcus personally. What an old bore Richard has become. He's yours, Sally, just go to him with honesty – and a pretty please.'

Sally blushed and said nothing. Deep inside she was brimming with song and laughter. Catherine continued, unprompted.

'You know, in the past, Richard's women have all been rather, um, I don't know. He always had one, but I never warmed to them, and nor did Bob. Probably because Richard was so obviously not taken with them himself. He had a reputation, you know.' No, Sally did not know.

'I remember Bob pointing him out at a University Ball and calling him "Herr Heart-breaker". He didn't break hearts willingly,' she continued, 'it's just he never fell for any of the people who fell for him. And anyone who ever dated him fell hopelessly for him of course. So he became known as "Pump and Dump" and a whole host of other names.'

Sally hooted with laughter and Catherine thought how pretty she was. 'There was never anyone special, Sally, not till you. You wouldn't believe what being with you has done to him. Done *for* him. He's dropped that outer reserve, he's not so aloof, he's more open and he seems so much more at ease. He's happy – that's it. Really happy, true happiness. I mean,' corrected Catherine with dramatic emphasis, 'he *was*.'

Catherine trailed off and Sally felt sad. They sat still in silence awhile, Catherine gazing at the flickering candle and Sally looking at nothing in particular. Any awkwardness dissipated with the arrival of the dessert-trolley to which the women turned their attention with an expert eye and wicked delight. Sally felt simultaneously exhausted and high. Her head was zipping with the insights Catherine had so sweetly given her.

'Call him,' Catherine suggested, laying a warm and comforting hand on Sally's leg as she pulled up alongside her flat.

'Hey, Cathers, it's been the most wonderful evening. I really mean it, and I want to thank you for being so supportive and such a good listener.'

Catherine, who'd never been called Cathers and actually rather liked it, brushed away the effusive compliments and patted Sally again on the same leg.

'Call him.'

It wasn't a suggestion, it was an order. Sally always did what she was told.

Sally had summoned the courage and decided that it would indeed be this day, now, and not the infamous tomorrow, when she'd lift the receiver and make amends. Richard, however, beat her to it. He feared her driving away right out of his life as she had driven away, out of his street. Anyway, Bob and Catherine had urged him to call her, Diana too.

'Richardrichardrichard. You must *must* call her. I saw her and she's totally devastated. If you are with this other woman then call Sally so that she doesn't suffer much longer. If you're not, then call her and try and work things out.'

'Diana, is Sally suffering?'

'Yes.'

'Why?'
'I'm not spelling it out, dolt!'
'So why don't you tell her to call me?'
'I did. She won't.'
'Why not?'
'I'm not spelling it out! Please call her? Soon?'

As Richard contemplated the handset and smiled at Diana's kooky sincerity, he wondered how soon was 'soon'. It was too soon, just that day. Maybe tomorrow.

But when Catherine phoned him at work that Friday morning, he knew that 'soon' was now.

'I had supper with Sally while you and Bob played squash or whatever it is that you do!'

'Catherine!' cautioned Richard. 'I thought you were cooking for Alex?'

'I lied.'

'Catherine!' he reprimanded. 'How is she?' he asked. 'What did she say?' he implored.

'She's okay. All the better for hearing that the mystery woman was a client.'

Richard thanked her for her tact. Catherine continued, 'I think you should call her, right away. You really ought. I've realized something, Richard. You are both really quite similar. If you don't talk and get together soon, you'll both pull your "self-defence" blankets over your heads and that,' she declared, 'will be that.'

'Catherine, thank you. I appreciate it. But what did she *say*?'

'Call her.'

'That's what she said? Through you?'

'No. Just call her. You owe it to yourself. And to her. Call her – now. Here's the number for the staff-room at school. First Break is at 10.15. 'Bye-bye Richard.'

'Sal?'

Sally whizzed around, spiralling with phone cord around her body like a helter-skelter. No one could hear her and no one was particularly interested anyway. First Break was a very precious twenty minutes. There were cups of tea by which to be relaxed and weary eyes to rub. Had Diana been there, her eyes and ears would have been perked to straining point, but she was in the studio, making preparatory sketches for a screen-print of a solitary silhouette against a window.

'Hullo,' Sally replied in a hushed and gentle voice.

'Can I see you? Tonight at eight? Go for a walk. Talk?'

'Yes.'

'Somewhere different. Let's meet somewhere like Covent Garden. No, the river, let's meet on the South Bank, outside the Hayward Gallery. By that sculpture.'

'Yes.'

'Goodbye, Sally.'

''Bye-bye Richie.'

Richie, she called me Richie. Maybe all is not lost.

Hope tided Richard along for the rest of the day and the chairman's metaphorical pat on the back for the Georgian folly put a spring in his stride as he left the office for the weekend. Hope in his heart, his eyes longed for the sight of her.

'Good night Sandra, Mary.'

Sally felt quiet and timid, not nervous, not particularly excited. Just quiet and private. She looked hard in the mirror before she left for town. She scanned that familiar face, scouring for external proof of what she felt inwardly. She smiled benevolently at the furrowed brow and winked at the startled eyes.

'Hey hey, Sal,' she murmured comfortingly. She looked at her face so hard and for so long, staring relentlessly, until it assumed strange contortions and was her face no longer. She remembered doing the same as a child, staring and staring so her face would metamorphose into a completely strange visage: *the face of your husband*, the playground legend had said. But as she stared no man's face replaced her own, she was but a privileged fly on the bare wall of her mind's eye. She saw not merely into herself, but she saw herself. She liked her. She was standing on the threshold of something huge and daunting. But she had trust and she had faith. At that moment she loved Sally Lomax and she knew her very well.

No acting, she promised, *no acting*.

TWENTY-SIX

Our girl from Highgate felt like a mole above ground, a timid creature thrust into the glare and not-quite-glamour of Friday Night In Town. Sally felt like a stranger in a very different and rather extraordinary country. Normal people sit safe at home, or celebrate the end of the week and welcome the weekend with a trip to their local locals, don't they? So who were these people littering the pavement and wearing down the concrete five yards either side of each and every aesthetically grimy pub? Men and women, and all in suits. Navy is the order of the day! Pints all round! I'll have a half. Mine's a double.

Ah-ha! It's the work-force that keeps the town ticking. *They seem like normal people*, Sally thought, *but what are they all doing here? In the centre of town? They're not tourists. Maybe they don't have local locals. Maybe they even live in Zone 1 of the Underground network. Surely not?*

Sally thought them a happy race. As she weaved her way through Covent Garden, she observed how the scenarios she passed by were repeated with alarming regularity and subscribed religiously to unadventurous conventions. She witnessed the casting of wanton glances, she picked up on the licentious edge to the voices, she took note of the obvious-over-risqué *double-entendres.* Chit chat, chatter, chatter. Ah-ha! It's a chat-up! They're not talking shop; they've forgotten about the exchange rates, the press releases, and they've put the computers to bed until Monday morning. They are here to try and unravel the person behind the job, see if there's an inkling, a chance of post-work extra-curricular activities. Suggestions fly of 'this nice little restaurant I know'. It's Friday night! It's cliché time!

'I've had too much to drink.'

'Let me take you home.'

Travelcards open the gates to the tackily upholstered world of the tube train which will carry their loads weekendward and away from the safety of their weekday workaday personae.

'Want to come in for a coffee?' *What will they say at work?*

'I'm married, you know, but it's all over.' *Well, it is, isn't it?*

A hasty reinterpretation will always augur the faintest but sincerest hope that indeed 'it might be different this time'.

Who are they? Each and every one has a life, a home, a chest of drawers full of undies and shirts, a fridge with shopping and a front door that is opened and then shut tight and private for the night. I don't know any of them, not one! But they all clean their teeth, these people; they've all been ill at some point, cried, flown into a temper. They all fart! And all are naked beneath the navy. They have families, they're someone's little boys and little girls. They have secrets and sacred late-night last thoughts. And I'll never know. But they'll still be living! Every day they'll be waking up and doing things, saying things, thinking things – just like I do! I don't know them, nor they me. I'll go on with my life but they'll still Be. I'll never know them, these living people, and there are so many and they're all real! Do they see me? Might they wonder about me?

As she scurried her way through the throngs of these strange yet native folk, Sally occupied her racing mind with her usual intoxicating meanderings. It was far too scary to think of Richard. She was less than a mile, less than twenty minutes away from him. Her nerves coursed through her body with gay abandon, her mind raced faster than her legs and walking was further impeded by her quivering knees. Come on, Sally, do get a grip. It's only Richard. Nothing to be afraid of. Enjoy!

Funny, Sally thought, *how one can wander and wonder and be all absorbed in a world of funny old thoughts and yet still have your legs carry you to where you must be at 8 o'clock; negotiating traffic, dodging pedestrians and mastering all heights of curb, seemingly without the aid of eyes or ears or mind. From A to B as easy as ABC. And see, here is the Hayward sculpture, winking and humming its semi-broken neon welcome.*

It is 8, just gone; late, a little – a woman's prerogative indeed but still her tardiness, insubstantial as it is, irritates her. Is he there? Is he there?

Richard, where are you?

He is there. Here he is, coming towards the girl who has taken his whole being and turned it upside-down, thrown his machismo and reserve away and far, rid him of his vices and banished his negativity. Richard had watched Sally as she looked everywhere but at him. Now the two of them are tantalizingly close, within reach. Sally can see the legs of his trousers, even if she closes her eyes his smell tells her he is almost upon her, yet still she cannot look at him. So close now, almost there, almost together again. Sally's mouth seems full of something that is not anything at all, Richard has a lump of nothing stuck in his throat. Where are the cameras?

Where are the violins? A drum-roll at the very least. But there is nothing but silence thumping around the heads of these two people. Both wish they were a million miles away and alone, yet both would not be anywhere else than the here and now, together. They are reeling with relief. Their combined euphoria is tangible after so long, too silly long apart. See how Sally brushes past Richard and he catches her around the waist and draws her tight and close and quick. Watch him kiss her cheek. She kisses him back hurriedly, awkwardly, her teeth grazing the side of his chin. Happiness and hope are encapsulated in their silence, in the very fabric of their quaking bodies.

'Hullo, Sal!' Richard coos, but Sally doesn't reply. He looks at her face and sees her eyes shine and glisten in the chill and darkness of the night around them. He shakes her gently and she looks at him with such menacing intensity that it is Richard who darts his eyes away and rests them on the couple strolling huddled under an umbrella even though it is not raining. Sally takes stock of his profile; so clean and sculptured, his cheek-bones high, his cheeks hollowing slightly under them, his strong and defined jaw line. She is looking at him objectively and sees how quintessentially good-looking he is, yet she finds that she has the ability to see behind too, and there she finds his soul and his being and she likes what she sees, she loves what she sees.

'Hey, Richie,' she replies eventually. They look and they smile, sincere and open. Their eyes talk and say what they cannot utter with their mouths because those words are too clumsy and their voices are still too delicate. Very, very, intoxicatingly slowly, Richard cups Sally's face in his hands. Her cheeks feel so cold and soft and they look like porcelain under the romantic glow of the South Bank lights. Sally knows she is about to be kissed and she knows that this kiss will probably hold more import and be more loaded than any kiss she has had or will ever have. As Richard plants the gentle press of his mouth against hers, he sows into her heart and his a message that would seem inevitably trite if spoken with words.

They went and sat with Bailey's in plastic cups at one of the incongruously rustic picnic tables by the river outside the Royal Festival Hall. There was a chill in the air but they were snug in each other and glad to be gone from the brightness and the noise and the ladies-and-gentlemen-please-take-your-seats. As they fidgeted into relaxed positions, a young Waterloo boy jerked his cold and homeless way towards them. He only wanted 10p but Richard pressed a nugget of a pound coin into his twitching fingers. The smile on the boy's face was quite extraordinary as he graciously thanked him and bowed his way away from them and into the Festival Hall.

'Makes me sad,' Sally said gently. Richard raised his glass and they drank to him. Richard had planned what he wanted and needed to say, but the imminence with which he could instigate it was daunting and had rendered him verbally impotent. He was about to tell her that he had missed her, *a lot, you know*, when the young beggar emerged from the lights and warmth and made a bee-line for them. In his hand, he held on tight to a helium balloon, silver and blue. It had broadened his smile into a near-manic contortion.

'Look! Look what they gave me! It's a balloon!' His naiveté and happiness were at once charming and saddening. So much pleasure and thanks for merely a pound, for just a balloon. Who said that money could not buy love and joy?

'It's a fine balloon,' confirmed Sally.

'They gave it to me. There are plenty in there, maybe you could get one too. I think it's brill!' he concluded as he broke into a twitching trot away from them, looking back every other stride to check his balloon was there. It was his, his own, it had been given to him. It was his metaphorical friend, his substitute dog on the end of a piece of string. Pleasure had been brought into his life. Richard scanned Sally's face unseen. She was watching the boy and his balloon disappear into the labyrinthine concrete. She was watching after him, she was saying a prayer for him, futile she knew, but she had to. Richard saw the prayer and the care in her face and knew he was in love with what he saw. Her pretty face, her funny face, her familiar and Sally-face. She was transparent and he was warmed by what he could read there. The beauty of it.

'Sal?'

The boy was gone from sight. She turned to Richard and looked at him in anticipation with eyes that were large and soft and just a little timid.

'Talk?' she implored him tentatively. He held her eyes and though she wanted to look away from the enormity of what she prophesied was about to be said, his eyes and their deep and dark sincerity caught her in a magnetic hold.

'Sally, I love you. It's a word and not a very good one. But it's a word that we are brought up to understand, to trust and believe in. Believe me. I want you to know that falling in love with you has been an utter revelation. I realize that whatever I felt before for anyone else was not love at all. I'm desperate for you. I want you so much. You excite me, you calm me, you make me so frighteningly happy. I didn't think it could be like this, I wasn't expecting to find this in my life. I'd always sort of thought that I'd walk on through in my life, having fuck-flings, meaningless dalliances with women I could categorize as beautiful or fun – but never did I think that another person could so enhance the quality of my life. It's not as if I felt life was lacking before you came along, I never thought that something was missing, that life would be better *if only dot dot dot*. But now that I've had you, that I've felt you and loved you and discovered how you can make me feel, in my mind, in my body – now I know that I don't want not to have you here with me. Now I know that without you there will be a void, an emptiness which no one else can possibly fill. I want you to fill my life and I want to be there for you. Only you. There is no one else for me. I want *you*.'

There was silence, stunned silence. Sally mulled over Richard's words and replayed them to herself. She acknowledged the solemnity of the occasion, she was struck by his courage and volition. There was still a part of her that wanted to run, but there was a stronger impulse now to stay and for the first time it neither scared nor repulsed her.

But it did tie her tongue. She wanted to say to him, 'Yes, I feel it too.' She wanted to confirm that love was the last thing she had been looking for when she met him, that she had previously deemed love overrated, somewhat pointless and inherently dangerous. But Sally could not say a word, she certainly could not manage the 'L' word though it no longer terrified her so. All she could do was to reach out a cold and fragile hand and place it against Richard's cheek. She turned it over and stroked his face with the back of her hand, then she switched it back and laid her palm still, her thumb just resting on the corner of his mouth, her fingertips touching his ear-lobe, his neck, and the start of his hair.

'Quite frankly, Sal,' launched Richard in a businesslike and decided way but let her hand stay as it was, 'I want to do something about it.' Sally took her hand away from him and waited, head cocked and eyes soft. Richard glanced at his cup and saw that it was empty though he could find no trace of Bailey's in his mouth or his memory. He asked Sally if she wanted another; her cup was practically full but she nodded anyway. Richard disappeared and left Sally wondering what his breath had been bated to say. She looked out across the river and thought how beautiful London looked for once. The lights from the Embankment fell into golden shards across the water and the buildings loomed elegant and proud behind. Staring at St Paul's, ghostly and emotive in the floodlit night, she was thinking about nothing in particular when Richard returned.

She greeted his approach with a soft little smile. But who is that walking beside him? Richard was accompanied by the crustiest, dirtiest person Sally had ever seen. 'Godforsaken' was the word she thought of later that night. He was Richard's height but half his build and wore the filthiest clothes, baggy and torn, shiny in parts with grease, dull in others with grime. His hair was hacked to an uneven, precarious mohican, tinged in green and peroxide. Little of his face was visible under the scraggly beard and tattoos which webbed over his cheeks and throat. The earrings, of which there were many, were not confined to his ears but were in both nostrils, on his right eyebrow and on his lower lip. As Sally recoiled she chanced upon his hands.

He had the most beautiful hands, she noticed, as he placed them flat on a table near her. Very much like Richard's; long, shapely and manicured. She was transfixed. Intrigued by her captivation, Richard curled her fingers around the cup for her and sat down astride the bench, cowboy style, just like Sally. Was *it*, that person, upsetting her? Would she rather they move? No, not at all. She was compelled by the man. The figure was immediately pathetic, even menacing, and yet he exuded a composure and elegance which were mesmerizing. Richard could see that she was neither frightened nor repulsed so they sat and sipped and looked at each other while casting frequent furtive glances to their neighbour.

With a slug of Bailey's to bolster him, Richard decided to bite his bullet and drew a deep breath accordingly.

'Sally,' he started, taking her hand and turning her face towards him. He cleared his throat but she kept her eyes trained on the other man. Richard took another deep breath but Sally pipped him to it with a whisper fringed with awe.

'Look, Richie, look!' she implored. Richard followed her eyes and they sat and watched in amazement and pity the man with Richard's hands. From every pocket in his old combat trousers and jacket, he retrieved a seemingly unending supply of the little free cartons of UHT milk and coffee whitener. Food; free.

Methodically he placed them to form a line. And another. And still they came. Another line, and another. He paused and looked steadily at the four even rows in front of him. Sally scanned them, ten in each, forty altogether – a glass-worth?

With concentrated and pedantic dedication, he systematically peeled the lids back from each pot. Again he stopped still and just regarded.

Like a teacher, thought Sally, *presiding over a class.*

Carefully he lifted each pot to his mouth and drank his way, daintily, scrupulously, up and down the rows. Sally saw his tongue dart to salvage every last smear. With maddening precision, each pot was conscientiously returned to its place in the row. Empty. Soon they were finished and the meal was over. He stood still a moment longer and then took his beautiful hands away from the table, out of Sally's sight, and buried them deep into his jacket. He rumbled off, oblivious to his audience. In silence, they hoped he had had enough, that he was satiated, that he might have a square meal tomorrow, though they doubted it.

Richard looked at Sally and saw how her eyes were smarting with tears. With his fingertips he gently eased her face away from the pregnant space left in front of the empty cartons. He felt no need to draw a brave breath.

'Sally.'

She looked at him. She was open and there, ready and committed to listen.

'I can't be bothered with game-playing and acting and waiting. I propose that we move in together. I want to live with you, I want to have you beside me every morning and night. Quite frankly, I can't be having the two or three times a week. I think we should move in together. Soon. Now. With a view to the Big "M". We have enormous potential. I've never wanted anything more and I don't want to settle for anything less.'

Like an eavesdropper, Richard clearly heard the words as they were uttered. Premeditated and planned for days and weeks, they had been proclaimed previously in the safety of his head, during the privacy of a run, in a lunch-time day-dream, in late-night, sleep-greeting sanctuary. And yet he took himself by surprise as the words tumbled away, out into the open unchecked by any better judgment. He recognized the sound of his own voice and heard the words he was saying; they were familiar, he knew them well, yet they induced a surge of adrenalin to course through his body and reach his stomach in a wave of nausea that was at once awful and pleasant. Though his head was high, his heart was full, his eyes were alight and his body trembled, Richard was racked with anxiety at the portent of his words. The very meaning of them engulfed him, the consequences they would have on his life, the effect they would have on Sally.

The very effect they will have on Sally is something Richard cannot foresee. Why should his words, spoken after all with honesty and great depth of emotion possibly bring her anything but great happiness and security? Why indeed? Because, poor man, they are the wrong words for someone who is only just feeling comfortable with the trimmings, trappings and whole idea of being in love.

The ensuing silence was unbearable. Richard was perturbed by the absence of the smile he was so desperate to see. Sally gulped, both with her eyes and her throat. Fear flickered across her face; it was manifest in the twitching and creasing of her brow, the purse and pucker of her lips.

'Talk to me,' Richard demanded, his voice breaking. Sally didn't trust her voice at all but the tears that she was desperate to vanquish threatened to choke her instead. Richard cradled her head in his hands, wove his fingers through her hair, pressed her face against his chest where she could feel his heart pounding and it frightened her.

'Talk to me, talk to me, talk to me,' he murmured over and over again, rocking her in rhythm to his words. Sally's mind raced and ran so fast that it was impossible to pin down her thoughts, to analyze her churning emotions, to organize them into sentences coherent enough to be said out loud. Richard was patient, his soliloquy had now a soothing effect on him, he felt light; a weight had been shifted.

Little did he realize how it had fallen twice as heavy on to Sally's half as broad shoulders.

'Sal?' he implored after what he considered to be a reasonable length of loaded time. She raised her face and slowly shook her head. Richard looked unbearably sad and Sally was surprised at how swiftly his pain restored her voice.

'Don't know, Richie, just don't know. Too soon, perhaps, I think.'

For some reason, she found it impossible to form a grammatically correct sentence. 'Can't think just right now. Can I think, go away and have time to think?' Her eyes were wide. 'Richard? Can I? Seems too big, scary and I don't know. Too much, don't know. Frightened. Need time and space. Can't answer you, it's too big. Richie?'

Richard looked at her and decided that he would grant her all the time in the world in the hope that she would find her answer quickly. As long as it was the answer he wanted to hear. He nodded at her and was rewarded with her smile. Sally's smile said 'thank you'. It said something else too, Richard could see it quite clearly but refused to believe it until she said it.

But Sally did not, she just could not quite say it to him that night.

In bed, warm and alone two hours later, she said 'I love you, Richard' out loud. She spoke the four words with conviction, a veritable proclamation. She heard her voice, she knew it was hers. She heard the words and knew they came from her head as much as from her heart.

As Richard and Sally had strolled across Waterloo bridge, they had passed the balloon boy. Minus his balloon.

'Where's your balloon gone?' Sally asked.

'It just flew away, I let it go – just to see – and it just flew up and away. It went over there somewhere.'

'That's a pity. But I think there are plenty more back inside, I'm sure they wouldn't mind you taking another.'

He smiled at Sally and she saw how young he was, his dirty face fresh and just pubescent. He looked a little like Marcus. 'There are plenty more,' she reiterated.

'No,' he said wisely, 'I don't want another one. I would just want to let that one go too.'

TWENTY-SEVEN

It is a quiet, fresh Saturday morning. Sally has woken, thankfully alone, and is staring at nothing in particular through the gap in the curtains. Feeling small, tearful and sorry for herself, she is reluctant to rise and wants to start the day with a good old cry in the comfort of her little bed (a double bed, in fact, but so cosy and safe that Sally always thinks of it as her little bed). We'll leave her be awhile and travel south-westwards to Notting Hill where Catherine has just popped by, accidentally on purpose, to see how her husband's (soon to be father of her first child) best friend is faring today.

'Hey, Catherine!'

Richard, resplendent in grey marl jogging bottoms and a dark red sweatshirt, greeted her with a kiss on both cheeks. 'I was just off out for a run but it can wait. Come in, come in! Coffee? Tea? Juice? Juice coming up! Grapefruit? Orange? Both freshly squeezed in the groovy juicer-whatsit. What a great Christmas present. I did thank you, didn't I? Profusely, I seem to remember.'

Catherine was swept through into Richard's sitting-room, borne along on the stream of his cheerful bearing.

I have before me a happy boy. Thank goodness! she thought. *Come on Richie-ard, tell me do! Reveal to me the provenance of your smile, the reason for the spring in your step, the song in your voice!*

Richard, however, was whistling too sonorously to tune into Catherine's attempted telepathy.

She slid into his leather recliner and wriggled off her shoes. Daffodils caught her eye. Wherever she turned, their golden fanfare greeted her. The flowers were shoved into vases, crammed into jugs; haphazard and glorious.

Much much better than those de rigueur *hothouse tulips*, she thought, and smiled. With relief, she saw that Bach came before Bizet and, on the shelf below, Hendrix came after Genesis. Through the archway, she could see Richard slicing the grapefruit with fell swoops, nonchalantly tossing the halves into the juicer gadget. Watching him from behind, seeing his broad shoulders, tapered waist and neat bottom, she was happily transported back to memories of college days. Those evenings, what fun! Food and wine, on a budget but heavenly, lounging around, smoking joints and travelling to the dark side of the moon and back with Pink Floyd. Bob and Richard; fit as fiddles, keen chefs and devoted flatmates. Catherine had felt special to 'the boys', madly and deeply in love with Bob but treasuring too the platonic closeness and openness of her friendship with Richard. She had loved to watch dinner for four, a familiar occurrence, take shape. She enjoyed seeing Bob and Richard vie for space in their small, cramped but outrageously well-equipped kitchenette. She thrilled to their fondness for each other, manifest in every half-finished but intuitively understood silence, in their easy laughter, their incessant teasing, in their generous pats, slaps and nudges. She remembered how she would marvel at the flexing in Bob's forearms as he whizzed his knife through an innocent cucumber, how he would look up, hold her gaze and smile his dashing, winning smile, before setting to work on the carrots. Always Bob-and-Richard-and-Catherine. And X.

X was invariably long-legged and luscious but on the scene for so short a time that her name was a foregone forgotten inevitability.

Bob had proposed to Catherine a year or so later in a kitchen, a different kitchen but a kitchen all the same. He had cut his finger, she had laughed at his ever-so-injured face and had kissed the droplet of blood away. As she wrapped a wadge of paper towel tenderly around his finger (having caused him to squeal at the undiluted disinfectant) Bob had asked her to marry him nevertheless. Dumbstruck, she could only squeeze his wounded digit so hard in acceptance that he very nearly reneged his proposal. Here she was, a decade later, the very Mrs Woods, watching Richard, the self-same Richard, still King of the Kitchen.

Something's missing, something's changed.

Sally was most noticeable by her absence. Catherine was struck by how alone Richard looked tinkering in his kitchen. He looked wrong, awkward somehow, minus his shadow, his Sally; getting in his way, sticking her finger in this and that, sniffing and fiddling and tasting, her eyes never leaving him. Catherine had watched her well; she had recognized something, a vestige of herself in Sally. She had seen her gaze at Richard's forearms, she had seen the smile spread as Richard wielded his Sabatier with gay abandon along the length of an unsuspecting cucumber. Catherine had watched Richard too, observing how he gently guided Sally away from his path with a tender push at her waist, his hand, inevitably, lingering.

It won't be long, Catherine had thought, *before he's proposing to her.* Whether it would happen in the kitchen she could not know, but she hoped that it might. A good omen, a good beginning.

But of course. Sally's not here.

Catherine returned, somewhat reluctantly, to the day at hand and wondered instead just what it was about a man expertly slicing cucumber that solicits utter admiration from a woman, inspiring a flutter both to heart and groin. Here she was, Catherine Woods-née-Daniels, married and pregnant and blissfully happy, being handed juice in an elegant wine glass by Richard Stonehill who drew up a chair and sat astride, cowboy style, opposite her.

'How's the morning sickness?' he enquired, matter-of-factly.

'It's evening sickness and it's terrible and I love it!' she hooted, consequently snorting into her grapefuit juice and finding much mirth in the mess.

'Want a bib, Catherine?' Richard laughed, handing her a piece of patterned kitchen paper. 'I'm so chuffed for you both. I hope it goes without saying that I'll be godfather. I mean, who else could you trust to show your child *the way*? I'll teach him/her the Stonehill Statutes; I'll ensure that my morals are engraved at the very centre of their being. What better start in life, hey?'

'Lord help the little thing!'

'Seriously, Catherine, Bob's utterly thrilled. Thrilled to the extent that's he's becoming a domestic bore. *I'm going to be a dad! I'm going to be a dad!*' Richard mimicked, then took a contemplative sip and continued, nodding earnestly, 'Seriously, though, it's great news. What names have you decided? When is it due? Do godfathers have to be at the birth? Phew! Can you start thinking about names now? Or does one buy the pram and nappies and decide when the thing arrives?' Richard was manic and Catherine laughed. He carried on in two voices:

'*Mmm, looks red and wrinkly to me, must be a Roger.*'

'*Nonsense, his name's Bert, it's written all over his face!*'

'*Have you got a pram?*'

'No, but I have a baby in my womb called Janet-if-it's-a-girl and John-if-it's-a-boy.'

'Stop, stop!' Catherine pleaded. 'If you split my sides there won't *be* a baby! But to answer your question, we'll call *her* Sally, or we'll call *him* Richard.'

Richard jerked. His face was startled and the sparkle in Catherine's eyes eluded him. She reached forward and placed a hand on his arm. 'Joke, it was a joke,' she assured him, 'but I'm sitting here with curiosity enough to kill a pride of bloody lions let alone a humble cat, wondering when on earth you're going to tell me how it went!'

'It?'

'Rich-*ard*!' The silence was excruciating but Catherine held her ground as she held Richard's gaze. She felt well within her rights to expect a not-too-ambiguous response and she was rewarded as Richard began to smile and cast his eyes downwards, coyly even. Chuffed, to be sure.

'Sally?' she prompted.

'I think,' he faltered, 'that the definitive happy-ever-after is on the horizon.'

He raised his head and looked at Catherine directly; the light of the still relatively new year streamed through the elegant sash windows and struck his eyes with an aesthetic ferocity to add drama and impact to his words.

'She needs some Time with a capital "T". But the signs are there. In her eyes, in her confusion, in her willingness to listen, in her need and request to think. I never thought that I'd want someone, actually really *want* someone. I don't need her, I just want her, plain and simple. And I've told her what I want. You see, Cath, I can see through her veil and behind her outer reserve. I know they're there for her protection and self-preservation and I understand, I respect that.

'I don't know what it's been like for her in the past, the way she's felt, other men. It's always been nothingy for me, as you know only too well. There's something private and guarded with Sal, yet I have no desire to pry. I want her to realize that that's her past and it's passed. And that my only request is that she unwind herself and lay herself bare, that she accept me and my true desire to make her happy. She's a steel butterfly, my Sal, a steel butterfly. Beautiful and strong, fragile yet determined. Awesome! I think, Catherine, no, I *know* . . . I know she's going to come around. She just has to shake off her fears and greet herself with honesty and courage. Like I have. And I feel happy. I'm a happy man. I'm in love and it's the best thing in the world. Funny how I ridiculed Bob all those years ago when he talked about you, and him and you. He said to me once, "The time comes when you know, *you just know.*" And the funny thing is, you *do*, you just do!'

Richard knocked three and a half minutes off his best time on his run half an hour later.

Catherine returned to Bob, threw up the grapefruit juice, thought, *Shit, morning sickness*, and told him that she thought she could hear bells. Bob didn't understand, he thought perhaps it was a vagary of pregnancy and made her a cup of tea. But two days later, when he saw Richard who slaughtered him at squash, he understood. He could hear bells too. Faint. Distant. But there.

Diana heard bells, phone bells. *Sally!* she thought intuitively.

'Of course I'll come over, of course it's not a problem. No, it's not inconvenient. Will you *hush*, dear girl, I don't have anything planned. And even if I did, you silly old thing, nothing takes precedence over my Sally! You'd be the same for me, wouldn't you? 'Xactly! 'Bye-bye, I'm there already.'

Sally had been morose all morning. She had dithered and shilly-shallied and had been thoroughly incapable of pulling herself together. In fact, subconsciously and somewhat perversely, she had made a concerted effort to keep herself entrenched in her low ebb. There was something rather cathartic about being maudlin; Samuel Barber's 'Adagio for Strings' filled the flat and she even read the closing pages of *Black Beauty.*

'*My troubles are all over, and I am at home,*' she wailed out loud with a good sniff.

Well, they've only just started and I wish I was far away.

Sally bumbled her way through Saturday morning half-doing only half the jobs she'd earmarked. She was continually, uncharacteristically, distracted. With half a shirt badly ironed she hurried to her bedroom to change the bed-linen but did not manage the pillowcases because the bath implored her to scrub it instead. She even heard herself calling 'Mummy, Mummy' out loud yet her mother was the last person but one that she wanted and she had never called for her before. So why now? Sally heard her voice. It was worryingly quiet and feeble.

Sal! Get a grip!

Phone Diana.

I'll phone Diana.

Lifted a little by the anticipation of her friend's imminent knock on the door, Sally charged about her flat collecting debris and retrieved a piece of crockery from every room. On each, the remains of some food or other lay forlornly: a piece of toast, a boiled egg, a portion of corn flakes. Spasmodically half-eaten, the egg was now cold, the toast bendy, the cereal soggy. No time to feel guilty chucking them all away, there was so much to do: the ironing, the cleaning, the thinking . . .

What thinking?

The Richard-Thing thinking. He wants you, remember – the whole shebang? Remember?

Gracious Good Lord, I can't even think straight, let alone have the time to think at all.

Of course you do. You may have relegated it to the furthest reaches of your mind, but it is still there.

Well, I'll take down the net curtains to wash instead. Yes. No, no! I must empty the Hoover and oil the wok. Diana will be here in a mo'.

Knowing she was soon to be saved by the bell, Sally continued her chores humming the theme to *Love Story.*

As Diana wriggled her arms through her red duffel coat and jostled with the mittens (black) attached playground-style to elastic, she thought how fragile Sally sounded. Not desperate as she had done on Other Woman Day, just frail and feeble. Half an hour later, Little Voice Lomax welcomed Diana in to the warmth of her relatively tidy Highgate home and the knots of her troubled soul. Initially, Sally was still falling over her grammar and sentence construction but Diana tried her best to sift and make sense of the bits and drabs offered. Soon Sally was pouring out the details of the previous evening, in a veritable torrent. Out came Richard's proclamation, the balloon boy, the milk man with the beautiful hands. Diana had an idea for a painting, no, maybe a lino cut, so much more emotive.

Hush now! Listen to Sally, help her through.

'So, have you thought about it?'

'Di-*anarr*! It's only the next day. But I have thought about it quickly, and quite frankly I don't know what I think. It's like I'm trying to think of so much but there isn't the space. I feel so *bewildered*, like I don't know what's going on. Like I have no control. What is happening to me? Why don't I feel overjoyed, over the moon, high as a kite? I don't know, Di, I just feel sort of low and overawed and overwhelmed and not very happy. I thought, if and when I fell in you-know-what, that I'd be singing from the roof-tops and floating and smiling and feeling invincible. Instead I feel rather vulnerable and utterly confused.'

'What about? That you're not sure of your feelings?'

'No!' Sally retorted. 'Yes?' she furthered. 'I don't bloody know!' she wailed.

'*Are* you in you-know-what?' Diana ventured.

'I am deeply and irrevocably very much in love,' proclaimed a sad Sally, 'with Richard,' she sighed, 'who is everything I thought no man could possibly be. I love him totally, with my body and with my Self. The point of no return is way back there somewhere,' she continued, gesticulating wildly at nowhere in particular. 'It's gone from the safety of my view,' she concluded, down, dejected, diminutive. There was silence, an initially awkward soundlessness which eerily metamorphosed into a graceful and welcome peace. Only Sally broke it. Giving Diana an almighty shock, she shrieked an urgent and most un-Sally-like: 'Fuck!' Slapping her hands flat, smack, against her soft cheeks, 'Shit!' she fulminated, her eyes wide and darting, her hands scratching and pulling her face. 'Bugger, bugger, what am I doing! Get me away. I don't want *this*! I'm not nearly ready. I can't, I won't!'

Everything fell; tears, her hands away from her red cheeks, her shoulders, her head, everything tumbled down.

'Cope,' she whimpered, 'I can't cope. I want to be like before, by myself. It's just too much.' Sally crumpled to the floor of her sitting-room and sobbed.

She was broken yet it was she who had broken herself, and though Diana rushed to her side and crouched beside her and laid a hand of comfort and support upon her shoulders, she knew and Sally knew that only one person could help. She lay broken and smashed about herself yet it was she who had wielded the metaphorical hammer. So she would have literally to pick herself up. Of all the King's horses and all the King's men, none would be able to help her; she was the only one who could put herself together again.

'What should I do, Diana?' But Diana couldn't find her own voice, let alone offer Sally constructive advice of any merit. Still Sally sobbed, on the floor in an embryonic hunch, her face contorted with the frustration of it all, the salt of her tears reddening her eyes and stinging her cheeks. Diana looked on and saw for the first time that Sally was noticeably thinner; her face had a new gauntness that threatened to overpower its former prettiness. Her shoulders looked a little bony, making her head seem a little too large. With a degree of horror, Diana conceded to herself that she looked quite pathetic.

'Why not go away for a little while?' she ventured. 'To your Mum's, to Lincoln?'

Sally gave her a don't-be-so-stupid look.

'Paris?' Diana suggested. But suddenly J-C, his bedroom, his bathroom, his smell, his taste, rushed uninvited into Sally's mind and she shuddered until she had quite shaken him away.

'I can't. School, silly,' Sally whimpered.

'But you seem awfully poorly to me,' Diana cooed, stroking her hair. The maternal connotations of the word 'poorly' coupled with the action of hair-stroking caused Sally to crumple down again. This time she let Diana soothe her, huddled in a muddle on the floor.

Sally made it through Saturday, Sunday too, on the steel of her butterfly wings. Just. She avoided thinking about that which she knew she had to; she just looked after herself and made sure all was neat and tidy, spick and span, safe and sound, comfy and cosy. Her voice remained silent. It was unwanted, untrusted. Her self-constructed mute world was a safe one. She mooched around in her snuggly socks and her tatty dress and her Aran-knit cardie, she darned four pairs of socks and finished off the skirt she had been making. The clacketting of the sewing-machine lulled her into a settled state and she was pleased with the finished item.

Sally made soup. Two batches subdivided into eight Tupperware containers, six to freeze, two for the fridge. Leek and potato. Pea.

Nice and hearty. Thick slush.

Tupperware containers, six to freeze, two for the fridge. Leek and potato. Pea.

Nice and hearty. Thick slush.

TWENTY-EIGHT

Sally sprinted with the speed of a cheetah and the grace of a gazelle. The warm wind buffeted her ears as she ran with it. She sprung a gravity-defying *jeté* over the irrigation dykes which loomed, with east-coast regularity, every forty strides. She thought of Hopkins:

The hurl and the gliding rebuffed the big wind.

Whoosh! Sally was master of the wind, a part of the air; the ground beneath her feet spring-boarding her upwards so she could greet the sky. Boundless energy, freedom and delight. Sally felt exhilarated. On and on she pelted, lungs and legs going strong and keen for more. The land looked lovely and felt soft, welcoming her back after every leap. The ditches glinted shards of crystal as she flew over them.

Plotted and pieced . . . Hopkins again. All her senses were alight; she could hear the soft thuds of her footfalls, her fast breath, the wind; she could smell the grass, the earth; she could taste the very freshness of the day. The day was divine and she felt so alive.

She could make out something strangely vertical in the

distance silhouetted against the sun, defiantly upright against the uncompromising horizontality of the Lincolnshire landscape. On she ran. There was a lovely rousing tune in her head, what was it? Smetna. It was like being in a film. Oh, yes! Most certainly a film because as she neared the distant post, it assumed the irregularities that told her it was a figure. A man. And as her feet raced closer, her heart hurtled to her head that maybe, just maybe . . .

Yes, it was!

Two ditches separated her and Richard.

Joy of joys! Praise be!

'Richie!' she shrieked and the breeze swept her call to his ears. His outstretched arms carried his reply. Sally's smile was so wide it could have fallen off her face but the wind held it there, forcing rivulets to run from her eyes instead.

But I'm not crying!

She leapt the last dyke and was sure that she flew; oh, the ease of it! the softness, the power, the hush and rush of the abetting wind. A final graceful leap delivered Sally into the arms of Richard. His face was kissed by the sun so she kissed it too. His eyes swallowed her and, with his strong, lovely arms about her waist, she melted into him, her head cradled close to his heart. She was breathless with excitement, speechless with joy. She could feel herself slipping out of her body into his. Oh, RichardRichardRichard.

'Darling, darling Richard. I so love you. Oh, my Richardrichardrichard.'

You're not Richard. You are not *Richard.*

Sally opened her eyes and stared drunkenly at the blurred face in front of hers. The fuzziness slowly lifted and the features asserted themselves. Familiar yes, Richard no.

'Marcus!'

'It's okay, it's okay, Miss Lomax. Are you all right? Stay still, we've gone to fetch someone. Relax. Don't worry.'

Miss Lomax did as she was told and kept her arms fixed about Marcus's straining uncomplaining neck. She closed her eyes. Nothing. Richard was gone. Gone too was the landscape and the flying and the wind and the water and the big sky and the thrill and delight of it all. All that was there was a murky brown nothingness and an infuriating thrumming.

'It's all going to be fine, Miss Lomax,' comforted Marcus. 'You just sort of tumbled. You banged your head. But you'll be right as rain. Right as rain, Miss Lomax. Promise.'

Thank God. The grown-ups were here. Phew!

'God, Sally!'

'Good Lord! Miss Lomax!'

Miss Lewis and Mr Tomlin, Diana and Geoff, Art teacher and Headmaster, friend and employer.

'Marcus, what on earth happened?' Mr Tomlin crouched beside Marcus, voice gentle, his panic hidden well.

'We were doing Alfred the Great. She – I mean Miss Lomax – stopped talking. She just kept looking out of the window. Only there wasn't anything there. She sort of came to a halt – you know, like a car? We didn't know what to do. It seemed like ages. Then she made this horrible funny noise in her throat and she just crumpled. Didn't she?'

Young voices murmured confirmation. Marcus continued: 'She just went crash. Like a tree falling. It was like in slow motion. But she clonked her head on the corner of the desk.'

'How long has she been like this? After she crumpled? Since she clonked her head?'

'Well, that's my desk there, you see, so I could get to her immediately. I leapt up as soon as she started to fall, didn't I?' Class Five said 'Yes' in unison. 'I was with her practically straight away and told Rajiv to fetch someone. I shouted, actually – I didn't mean to. I was scared, we all were. Are. Anyway, then you came. Only about three or four minutes, I suppose. I – ' Marcus faltered ' – is . . . ?' He could not do it. There was a loaded pause while little Marcus, our brave boy and Sally's saviour, bit his lip and scrunched his eyes in a futile attempt to keep tears at bay. 'Is Miss Lomax dead?' he sobbed. 'Please don't let her be,' he begged his headmaster.

'Darling Marcus,' cooed Miss Lewis, 'no, she's not dead and she's not going to die either. It seems Miss Lomax fainted. Banging her head has probably made her unconscious. You did wonderfully, all of you. Brave, darling children.'

They managed to pry Miss Lomax's arms away from Marcus's now bowed-down neck and put her feet up on a bench, crossing her arms over her chest.

'Are you hurting anywhere?' Mr Tomlin asked quietly, bending down right next to Miss Lomax's ear. She could hear him asking, somewhere in the distance, but she had forgotten how to open her eyes.

'Sally, are you hurt?' trembled Miss Lewis.

Yes, in my heart.

With enormous effort she gave a slow small shake of her head. A trickle of blood coursing down her cheek said otherwise.

'Can you sit up?' Mr Tomlin implored. He turned away from Sally and spoke in hushed, urgent tones. 'Rajiv, run to my office – *run.* Ask Mrs Gates to call an *amb-ul-ance.*' He mouthed the word, not wanting Miss Lomax to hear, not wanting to alarm the children. Rajiv bolted. Mr Tomlin turned to Miss Lewis who sat stroking Miss Lomax's hair. The tips of her fingers were wet with blood; Sally's hair was dark with it.

'Sally sweetie, can you sit up?' Diana urged.

Sally blinked twice to say, *I'll try*, and with the help of Mr Tomlin and the gallant Marcus, up she sat, Diana's hand-holding and neck-cradling supporting her all the way.

'I'm okay,' she croaked. 'Just fine,' she stammered. 'Dizzy,' she whispered. 'Want to lie down.' Marcus was out of his blazer in a flash and proffered it as a cushion. Where was Rajiv? Where was the ambulance? The class were silent. Golden children. A siren came and went, and with it their hopes. Rajiv arrived with an anxious, tearful Mrs Gates. Mr Tomlin suggested she wait by the main doors. They waited on. Another siren, louder, louder still. Here.

The stillness was gone, their job was done. Marcus, Miss Lewis and Mr Tomlin stood by, feeling sheepish even, as the paramedics swung into action. They eased Sally on to a stretcher and put orange blocks around her head and neck, placed a mask over her nose and mouth, and wrapped a blanket around her body. She no longer looked like Miss Lomax, nor did she look like Sally. Swiftly, she was stretchered away, out of their sight. Gone. Then sirens. Gone. Silent prayers, intense wishes of get-better-come-back, followed the ambulance right into Casualty.

Miss Lewis presided over shell-shocked Class Five for the rest of the afternoon. She was delighted with the way they had all pulled together, there was a great feeling of solidarity, hugs were liberal, chocolates were shared and patience was abundant. Mr Tomlin had been thoroughly impressed and was planning a special trip to the Planetarium as a reward – once Miss Lomax was back, of course. Class Five remained impeccably behaved and an air of utter concentration imbued the room as get-well-soon cards were lovingly designed. Crayons, pastels, charcoal, even pencils were set to task. No erasers, of course. Any mistakes – and there were few – were triumphantly incorporated into the overall design. Diana gathered a clutch of thirty cards, and took them, along with thirty special messages and thirty kisses, to the Whittington hospital after school that afternoon.

'Sally?'

'Di?'

'You okay? Know where you are? How are you feeling? Don't talk if it hurts. Just wink or squeeze my hand or something.'

'Why are you talking like that?'

'Huh?'

'All nasal. Funny?'

'I hate hospitals, I hate the smell! That's why I'm talking through my nose. Don't laugh, shush! Are you ready to go home? Please say you are or else I'll expire then I'll land up here and that really isn't the point so why don't we get you to your feet and go homeward Highgate-bound!' Saying a sentence with no pause for breath took its toll on Diana who flopped into a plastic chair and breathed heavily, deep into the sleeve of her jumper. Sally stared at her and tried to make her brain work.

'I feel fine. I keep telling everyone here that I'm fine. Just had a funny turn. Funny. Never happened before. Yes, Di, yes. Take me home.'

Diana bustled. She marched Sally out of the hospital holding her in a most matronly manner. She bundled her into a taxi and kept her arms locked about her for the entire journey home. She insisted on Sally staying put while she paid the driver, and then insisted that he help her walk Sally to the front door.

'You earn your tip, my man!'

Once inside, she sat Sally on the edge of the bed and eased her out of her clothing, tutting sympathetically whenever she neared her head. She put Sally into her pyjamas and added bedsocks and an old cardigan for good measure.

'Warmth, my girl. Must keep you warm. You've had a shock. You mustn't catch cold.' She tucked her in tightly, bunching the duvet around her like a cocoon. Looking quite the sorry caterpillar, Sally muffled, 'Sorry to put you to all of this,' before welcoming the comfort of her familiar pillow and drifting effortlessly to sleep. Leaving the cards by her bed, Diana kissed her carefully on the forehead, tutting some more. She watched her awhile, sleepy and childlike, and then left.

'Richard, listen! No, calm down. Richard, shut it, I can't talk if you don't shut up a bit. It isn't serious, she's okay. She fainted in class and banged her head on the desk as she went down. No, you can't visit. Certainly not you and certainly not now. She really is very woozy. She needs a quiet, long night. It's what the doctor ordered. And I'm ordering you too, so listen up! Do not worry, young man. You have a good night. Promise me? Promise! Good! Night night, ducks.'

Richard felt sick.

My poor darling baby.

After ten minutes pacing up and down, hugging himself and murmuring 'Sal, Sal', he grabbed his car keys and left the flat, lights blaring and CD still on.

Grapes, I must stop to buy grapes. No, chocolates. No, no flowers. She may not feel like eating. Flowers it is. Damn, it's nearly eleven. Quick.

He hovered outside Sally's front door with a bunch of rather vulgar gladioli, not knowing quite what to do and dreading Diana suddenly appearing and giving him what for. He flipped the lid of the letter box and peered inside. A dim light edged its way out from the bathroom, casting soft shadows.

Night light. Good idea.

He peeled his ears and sought out any sound. He thought perhaps he heard a rustle from the bedroom and cooed, 'Sally! Sal?' He thought he heard something. He couldn't be sure so he gave himself the benefit of the doubt. 'Poor bunny, don't say a thing.'

Oh God, talk to me!

Richard eased himself up from the crouch he had almost frozen into. He chewed his thumb thoughtfully and studied the grain of the front door.

I want her to know that I'm here. But I don't want to disturb her.

The flowers, Richard.

The bunch would not fit through the letter box. He toyed with propping them against the front door but knew they would have the life and colour frozen out of them before morning. There was only one thing for it. One by one he posted the stems through the letter box. He blew a kiss through it and then left, hoping sincerely that Sally found the flowers before Diana.

She did. And she knew who they were from. She thought she'd heard him last night, but there again, she also thought she'd had a chat with Queen Victoria sitting on the edge of her bed.

We hate gladioli. She smiled as she trimmed the stems.

He likes tulips. I like cornflowers. We both like love-in-a-mist. But we hate gladioli!

She stroked the knobbled stems and placed the vase surreptitiously on the mantelpiece in the sitting-room so that she could see them from her bed but would be spared any explanation to Sister Lewis.

'Darling, darling girl! How are you! Have you eaten? Toast! Well *done*!' Sister Lewis had arrived in a bustle of good cheer and nurse-knows-best. 'Is it all awfully fuzzy? Do you remember anything?'

'I've tried and I've tried and I can't. I thought I was in Lincolnshire, near home, the place I've told you about. I was running and dancing and Richard was there. Then all of a sudden I had this cracking headache and woke up in hospital.'

'Well, it appears you fainted in class and whacked your head on the desk. You were absolutely out of it when we arrived. You were hanging on to Marcus like he was your knight in shining armour.'

'I thought he was.'

'Huh?'

'Oh, nothing. Go on.'

'Well, an ambulance came and whisked you away. Luckily you didn't need stitches but they had to chop off a little of your hair to bathe the wound and put on that dinky butterfly plaster. Here.' Diana handed Sally a tiny round mirror from her bag. First Sally looked at the wound and was less distressed at the hair loss than she anticipated. She then angled the mirror downwards slightly and snuck a little look at her face. She looked rather grey and her lips were very pale.

Silly old Sal.

TWENTY-NINE

Diana tucked her tight in bed with a cup of tea, a gossipy magazine and the radio, and made it to school just after First Break. She gave a running bulletin to anyone who came into the art room and phoned Richard with an update.

'I took flowers last night. I was quiet as a mouse – promise. Does she know?'

'How very disobedient you are, Mr Stonehill. She didn't mention anything. But, come to think of it, she did keep shooting her gaze over to a vase of pretty vulgar gladdies lurking on the mantelpiece. And I thought you had taste!'

'It was late at night!' protested Richard, somewhat relieved. 'Next time I'll run along to Covent Garden.'

'*Next* time?'

'God forbid. Di, can I call her? Pop round tonight?'

Diana paused and pondered the merits of tact against truth. She plumped for a diplomatic blend of both.

'Richard, we don't even know *why* she passed out. But I would hazard a little guess that it had something to do with the state she's been in of late. Of course it's not your fault, you daft old bugger! I just think, for Sally's sake, that she'll probably recover and be back to her good old self if left to her own devices. *Compris*?'

'*Oui.*'

'*Bien.*'

Diana found Sally asleep with the radio on when she called in during lunch break. She noticed with fabricated disdain that the gladioli were now on Sally's dressing table. She warmed the pea soup and put a note by Sally's bed saying she had done so. Sally woke at three, ravenous, and sung Diana's praises as she sipped soup and listened to the afternoon play. It was riveting and she was held a happy captive by the incomparable voices of Judi Dench and Martin Jarvis. A short nap was broken by Diana calling in after school. Sitting on the edge of the bed, she chattered away while Sally tried to look fit and fine.

'First, how are you, my poppet blossom? Did you eat? Sleep? Good girl. Next, I come with strict instructions from the powers that be: no school for Sally – you're to take the rest of the week off. Hush it! I won't hear any of it, girl. You clonked your head and knocked yourself clean out, remember? Do you know how many brain cells you destroyed? Can you really *afford* not to replenish them, ho ho? You have to be one hundred per cent, Lomax. Doctor's note 'n' all. Understand?'

Sally felt tired and groggy and, though she did not want to admit it, Diana was exhausting her. A strange transformation had occurred in the face of crisis; daffy scattiness had been replaced by an unwonted bossiness – a conversion enhanced by a crisp white shirt (spattered though it was with red paint) and a pair of well-pressed trousers. Sally thought it best to remain a malleable patient. Diana thought it wise not to mention Richard. Sally did not dare. She was quietly relieved when Diana bade her farewell with kisses to the cheek and strict instructions not to move from her bed until the next morning.

She lay in stillness and in silence for a little while and, when she was quite sure all was safe, clambered out of bed for a shaky walk around. She settled in the sitting-room, curled cosily in her old Lloyd-Loom with the thirty handmade cards on her lap. Most of the children had chosen to draw a down-mouthed Miss Lomax in hospital, swathed in bandages like a mummy. Rajiv, however, had created a comic strip featuring Miss Lomax as a lump lying in the lower left corner of each frame while another figure (Rajiv, who else?) saved the day with sword, with shield, with astonishing ambulance-driving skills and with superhero powers too.

Marcus's card brought tears to her eyes.

He's my real superhero.

With glitter, crêpe paper and lusciously thick paint, Marcus had made her the most exquisite bunch of flowers, the blooms themselves filling the entire page. The intensity of the colour and the overall richness of the surface seemed to symbolize Marcus's devotion and twanged the strings of Sally's heart. Inside he had written:

Dear Miss Lomax, you're the best
Please get better, have a good rest!
We hope your head doesn't hurt or ache
Come back to school soon, for Goodness Sake!
I'm sure you'll soon be as right as rain
So you can be our fave teacher again!

Marcus (x)

Sally kissed the card back and decided she would keep it for ever. She remembered Marcus on the last day in Paris, looking after her with Ribena and apricot-flavoured chewing gum; she could see him again racing back across the playground to tell her she was the best. Had he somehow known? Had he had caught drift of her sorry soul? How discreet he had been.

Children are the most intuitive of creatures. He'll go far, Sally thought. *Somewhere out there is a very lucky ten-year-old girl! I'll be an old bag when they're ready to court. There'll just be me and my bloody memories. Just me, rocking away in the Lloyd-Loom, wizened and grey, reliving my antics over and over. Might I cringe? Might I shudder if J-C pops into mind? And Richard . . . how will I feel? Remorse? Guilt? Joy?*

Dread swept over Sally and engulfed her.

But I don't want him to be just a memory.

She sat, silent and horrified. Turning to the hat stand, she furrowed her brow and declared in a small voice: 'I don't want merely to *remember* him; I want him to be there. I want to reminisce *with* him. Gracious Good Lord, what does that imply?'

She cocked her head and contemplated the carriage clock on the mantelpiece. She had found it in a jumble sale at the Students' Union in Bristol and, despite her dwindling grant and the fact that the clock was irreparably broken, had bought it all the same. A walnut case enclosed a very pretty face with beautifully scrolled numbers, the filigree arms outstretched at ten to three for ever more. There was something vaguely comforting about it; the caught moment, time standing still, no tick-tocking the days away. There was a sense of stability about a timeless clock; the years might pass and a whole host of events befall but it would always be ten to three between Sally and the clock.

She fell asleep, waking in the small hours of the new day – perhaps it was indeed ten to three – and was distressed to see she had crushed Marcus's card. She felt hot and bothered and realized she was wringing wet; the back of her neck was clammy and her hair stuck to it in rat's tails, her forehead bristled with sweat, her eyes felt puffy and hot. Feeling very unstable, she made a slow passage to bed aided along the way by furniture, door frames and determination. She was freezing by the time she made it there but had neither the wits nor the energy to fetch a jumper. Shivering, she cocooned herself as best she could and was compliant when dreamless sleep fetched her away.

The next morning, Sally saw spots before her eyes.

There was a large one slap bang in the middle of her forehead and, on further exploration, two on her chest and one on her right wrist. She stood stock still in front of the mirror and wondered what on earth to do. She noticed that her whole body was tingling; she was hot, feverish and bemused. Resigned to the fact that something was most certainly amiss, she called for the doctor.

The cold stethoscope felt blissful against her raging skin and the doctor's umming and poke-out-your-tongue-please comforted her. Two more spots had sprung up on the top of her left thigh and a rather large one was forming below her ribs before their very eyes. Dutifully, she told him about the fainting, and he did not seem in the least surprised.

'Well, Miss Lomax,' he announced after he had taken her blood pressure, explored her ears and beamed light into her eyes, 'it's not the Lurgy, it's chicken pox!' Sally was stunned.

Chicken pox! It can't possibly be, I'm a grown up! I don't know anyone with chicken pox! Do you mean to say it's not the Richard Thing that's making me poorly? That I am no damsel in distress? Just plain old chicken pox? Damn!

A very quiet part of her felt disappointed. A greater part of her felt embarrassed and irritated. The greatest part of her was just plain hot and tingly.

'What does that mean?' she asked at length.

'Well,' came the bedside manner reply, 'expect the spots to continue for another day or so. And then be prepared for the itching. DO NOT SCRATCH or YOU WILL SCAR. Calamine should soothe but DO NOT SCRATCH or YOU WILL SCAR. What do you do?'

'Do not scratch or I will scar,' Sally said miserably.

'No, no,' tutted the doctor. 'What do you *do*, for a living?'

'I'm a teacher,' Sally replied, somewhat indignantly.

'That probably explains how you caught it. You are highly contagious,' he warned. 'Bed rest for at least three days,' he ordered, 'and no school for at least two weeks.'

'Two *weeks*?' Sally exclaimed.

'You are highly con-ta-gious,' he reiterated. 'You don't want to inflict this on your pupils, now do you?'

Sally felt thoroughly ostracized. Snapping shut his Gladstone, the doctor smiled at her, propped up by pillows and pouting.

'The spots'll go in a couple of weeks and should have faded by the end of the month,' he assured her. 'That is, if you don't scratch. You will scar otherwise,' he concluded sternly. Laying a caring-profession hand on her shoulder, he said, 'Don't worry yourself. Get some rest. I'll see myself out. Cheerio!'

Just like on the bloody television, Sally later thought, feeling utterly sorry for herself.

'Sally? Sally! Open the door. Are you all right? Heavens, girl, where are you?' Diana rang the bell again and snapped the letter box open and shut, open and shut.

'I'm coming,' came a muffled reply.

Sally opened the front door a fraction of an inch and saw Diana standing there, all but obscured by a large brown bag of groceries.

'I thought I'd made spag bol!' she announced triumphantly, brandishing a packet of spaghetti and poking herself in the eye in the process.

'You can't!' cried Sally through the crack.

''Course I can! It'll have to be veggie of course – I've bought that dried soya stuff. Open up, old thing!'

'No, you *can't*,' stressed Sally. Diana was flummoxed and pulled an appropriate expression.

'I've got bloody chicken pox,' wailed Sally, 'I'm in isolation. In quarantine. I'm VERY CON-TA-GIOUS. I can't come out for two weeks.'

After a moment's silence, Diana laughed and laughed and kept asking: 'Really?' Sally was bemused.

'Let me see! Let me see!' hooted Diana so Sally poked out her pocked wrist. 'Heavens above! It's true.' Nurse Lewis vanished at once and Diana stood there, quite horrified and starting to itch. 'Poor duck – I'm off! Look, I'll leave this bag right here on the doorstep. You watch through the spy-hole and when you're quite sure that I am a safe distance away, you can open the door and retrieve them. DON'T SCRATCH or YOU WILL HAVE FRIGHTFUL SCARS!' With that, Diana ceremoniously dumped the groceries and made off. Sally, who did not have the energy to point out that Diana would have caught it by now, waited before opening the door to take in the bag. Suddenly Diana reappeared from behind the hedge, waving and jumping up and down.

'Let's see some more!' she squealed.

Smiling now, Sally took a surreptitious look around and then lifted up her pyjama top, the cold air providing instant relief and giving Diana a good eyeful.

'Blimey! You're *covered*! I'm out of here! I'll give you a ring as soon as I'm home – you can't catch it down the phone, can you?'

When Diana phoned her an hour later, Sally did not want to talk. She had discovered a spot inside her mouth and could feel that they were in her throat too. Silent and unfed, she shuffled to bed hoping it was all an unfortunate dream.

THIRTY

'Oh, hi, Bob, hi.' Finding it impossible to hide the disappointment in his voice, Richard decided not to beat about the bush. 'Sorry, mate, not a good time. I need to keep the line free – I'm waiting for a call. About Sally. She's been in hospital. Concussed.'

Inevitably, Bob's concern (and by now Catherine was glued to the other phone too) impeded Richard's speedy getaway so he divulged all and said, 'Yes, flowers would be nice.' He was desperate to go for a run but incapacitated by the lack of news. He had rung Diana twice but there had been no answer. He was dying to ring Sally but knew he should not. The phone rang.

Pleasepleaseplease.

'Diana. Thank God. Talk to me!' Richard gasped. 'She's got *what*?' His hand shot up to his brow. 'Chicken pox?' It dropped down to his hips. '*Chicken* pox! Good Lord!' He threw his hand up to the heavens. 'Does that account for the fainting? Chicken pox. Is she covered? Is she in pain? Discomfort? Poor lamb. Has she any calamine? What can I take her?' He was out of breath. 'What!' he exclaimed. 'Two *weeks*?' he cried. 'Can I phone her? Can't catch it down the phone. What?' he whispered. 'In her *mouth*? Her *throat*? Poor darling girl.'

Richard felt hoarse and strangely excited. He ran very fast over to the Woods's and panted out Sally's ailment.

'Two weeks,' gasped a horrified Catherine. 'Whatever'll she do?'

Sally wondered the same thing on waking the next day. With trepidation, she went to greet herself in the mirror. She was rooted to the spot (sorry, Sally, bad pun) and could not manage even a groan of displeasure. Wriggling out of her pyjamas, she stood and stared. Poor Sal.

There are too many to count. They are everywhere. They are even on my scalp and in my ears. My trunk is the worst, they are so blotchy and puffed up there. They are neat and small on my arms, larger on my legs, and I can't even see my face for them. I look sort of roasted. I look awful. Christ, they're even between my toes. And on my buttocks. And – Gracious Good Lord – not there too?

She still felt feverish and could bear no more clothing next to her skin than a pure cotton vest, knickers and Aunt Celia's hand-knitted cashmere shawl. She teetered around the flat chanting 'Feed a cold and starve a fever' but thought perhaps it was 'Starve a cold and feed a fever' and was at once in a dither, convinced that if she put into practice the wrong permutation, the spots would surely wreak vengeance. What was she to do? The solution lay in the cashmere shawl.

'Hello?'

'Aunty Celia? Guess who!'

'Sally? Gracious, what a treat, how are you, my wee one? Everything okey-dokey?'

'Yes, yes. No, actually. I have *chicken* pox.'

'Poor bairn. You must be feeling rotten. Have you a fever?'

'Yes.'

'Starve it!'

It seemed trite to delineate the coincidence so Sally received the advice graciously and said, yes, she was strong enough for a little chat.

'I'm wearing your lovely shawl.'

'Ach, it must be threadbare! I made it moons ago, for your sixteenth birthday, no? I shall start a new one for you, if you like. It will be finished by May the nineteenth. How old this year? Twenty-four, is it?'

'Sorry, Aunty, twenty-six actually.'

'Eeh, tish! You're a well and truly grown-up lassie. Maybe another shawl won't suit your fashion taste?'

'I'd love another shawl, but this one's just fine.'

'A woman can never have too many hand-knitted shawls, she should have one draped on the back of every chair in her house!' Celia declared with aplomb. 'I have some lovely yarn, there was a craft fair at the Town Hall in Tobermory. It's a linen-silk mix, so soft. A lovely sort of mauve. Does that sound nice? Does that tickle your fancy?'

'Yes, Aunt Celia, I think I should love it. I love mauve,' Sally lied kindly.

They bade each other farewell with a promise to lessen the gap between calls. Feeling hungry but keen to starve her fever, Sally took a nap instead. She dreamt that Celia came to see her in her lunch-break at school. She had bustled into the staff-room and called over to her, 'Sal, my lassie,' for Aunt Celia was the only other person from whom Sally welcomed the abbreviation. She had brought the shawl, it was vast and very mauve. She wrapped it around Sally's shoulders and then went to teach Class Five rounders. Sally watched from the window, breathing in deeply (in the dream and out) the unmistakable aroma of an Aunt Celia hand-knit.

It is now tea-time. Reluctantly, Sally has gone to the mirror to check the spot situation. The pox has shown no mercy and has rooted out the last patches of clear skin to inhabit; behind her left ear, above her right eyelid and under her armpits where they are particularly painful. Feeling ravenous, fed up and not so feverish, Sally has retrieved a bumper block of milk chocolate from the fridge, taken the phone off the hook, put a Genesis tape on low and clambered into bed armed with a clutch of old diaries and photo albums. She is soon lost in adventures of old; painted in retrospect with a tint of rose and a hint of sepia.

Where's the chocolate?

It is under your pillow.

Ah, Scotland. Mull. Heather and dampness, the light, the water, the clarity. Tobermory: those pretty, brave little harbour-side houses, candy colours yet not at all twee. Look, you and Aunt Celia throwing the frisbee on the sweep of soft sand at Calgary Bay. Whose is that shadow, who is taking the picture? Must be Uncle Angus, the late Uncle Angus, gruff with whisky but always on for a reel.

Does she miss Angus, whom one only ever heard her call 'LoveLove'? It was so lovely to speak to her today. It's been so long. It must be a good two years since I last saw her.

Sally feels like having a day-dream, she wants to transport herself to Mull. Trying hard to look at nothing in particular, she finds her eyes continually stray to her mottled limbs. Mull remains far away. Take another album, Sally, another piece of chocolate. Let Phil Collins's night-time voice be a certain calamine.

Oh, look! Sally aged nine and in a tutu. And here! Sally aged thirteen, in a tutu and on points. And here is Sally aged sixteen, tutu, pointes and taking a graceful curtsey. Look at the make-up, the impeccable bun, those sinewy arms! Remember how elated you felt? Do you really miss the bleeding toes, the straining tendons, the pulled muscles, the damaged joints?

No, but I miss the poise and energy.

Don't dwell, Sal. Turn the page. Giggle at your brown and beige childhood wardrobe from the seventies, cringe at the ra-ra skirts and stretch jeans you wore with pride during your teenage years. Lose yourself again in University days. Here, a batch of photographs of friends and cohorts at Bristol: living it up at faculty balls, looking tired but cool in shabby student houses, looking dapper in mortar-boards and fur-trimmed gowns at graduation.

Where's my diary? Where's the corresponding text? Oh, this is fun! I'm right back there – chicken pox? What chicken pox! The present is unpleasant, the future is a burden, but the past is safe so back I go!

Oh, yes! Remember that first week at University? How timid I was! Every one seemed so worldly and bright, they all seemed to play so hard and work so hard too! Look here!

> *15 October: I bet I don't make any friends. I went to the Freshers' Fair and joined nearly all the clubs, even the Winnie the Pooh Club, whatever that might be. No one seems quite my type but I'm willing to talk to anyone really, at this stage. We were given our timetable. Not very full, really, lots of free time in which we are to read, because we are 'reading' for our degrees, as Professor Wratchett said, rolling his 'r's. I've got three years ahead of me and Bristol seems pleasant enough. Haven't spied any talent yet but I'm not looking for love of course. The Rambling Society are going on a weekend to North Devon, I wonder if I should go? I'm a paid-up member after all.*

You did go, remember? And twisted your ankle but were too embarrassed to mention it so you grimaced your way through the rambles and tried to blot it out with a good sup of ale, which tasted foul but was the thing to do in the evenings.

Flipping in and out of the years, Sally dips in and out of the events in her life, as if she is chattering with someone she knows well and has not seen for years. She reminisces about drunken weekends in Devon, she rereads about hectic holidays on Greek islands, she remembers flatmates she would rather forget, she ponders on the whereabouts of friends not seen for years. The memories are fond and fun. Fun until one word assaults her eyes: Jamie.

Shuddering involuntarily, Sally has snapped shut the book and sits very still, eating chocolate distractedly. Come, come, Sally, the past is safe, the past has passed. Open the book, face the pages, face the past. Read out loud if it helps. A small voice filters through the room, reading flatly from pages written three years previously.

' "I have to get out of this relationship, if you can call it that. Jamie frightens me but what frightens me more is my inability to say: 'Stop. Go away.' He hit me again and I apologized. *I* actually apologized. Why on earth did I do that? He accepted my apology – ungraciously of course – and sulked all evening. Predictably, we had sex later. Or at least he did. I didn't want to but I didn't dare say so. And my arm hurt throughout; it's still bruised today. When he climaxes he's like an animal, really base and vulgar. I can't wait to get to the loo; we use condoms but I have to pee him away.

' "He broke my little teapot, the one James bought for me before my finals. I said to him, 'Be careful.' He said, 'Why?' I said, 'Because it's precious to me.' He said, 'Why?' I told him and he slowly lifted it above his head and let it topple. It fell at my feet. The spout scuttled across the floor, a chip of china from the lid fell through the side of my shoe. I felt sure I was about to cry but I bit it back. Jamie laughed at me. I hated him for it. I hate him. Then he went all soft and said that it shouldn't mean anything to me now, I am with him now. I wish I wasn't. How do I get out of it? Where's my strength?" '

I got out of it when he broke my nose. I covered him with blood. I was unconscious and woke and was sick and he thought I was seriously damaged so he called an ambulance and told them I'd fallen down the stairs even though I was living in a ground-floor flat.

It was that lovely nurse . . . what was her name?

'Sister Watts. I'll never forget.

She sat on your bed. He had visited with flowers and charm: there had not been a peep from you.

Sister Watts sat with me and just said, 'You owe him nothing. You don't have to stay. You're far too precious. You owe it to yourself. Leave him.'

So you left! Brave girl!'

I severed all contact. I moved to Highgate. I have no idea where he is. It's been a good three years. I don't live in fear. It's as if it happened to someone else. I rarely think of him.

Time has softened his blows, healed the wounds and faded the scars.

They are still there, you know.

We know.

I want Richard

Call him.

'Richie?'

'My dotty spotty angel! My darling dalmatian! How *are* you?'

'Don't ask. I'm very contagious. I can't go to school for two weeks. Oh, and I fainted too and wound up in hospital. But I think you know that.'

'Do you have any calamine?'

'No. But I'm not itchy.'

'Yet – that is. You will be. And you MUSTN'T SCRATCH.'

'I know, I know, or I WILL SCAR.'

'What say you that I pop to an all-night chemist and buy you some calamine?'

'But I'm CON-TA-GIOUS.'

'You are certainly that! I caught the Sally bug long ago and I just can't shake it off.'

The definitive pregnant pause filled the room and broke the flow.

'Sal?' Richard enquired quietly.

'I'm sorry I called,' she faltered. 'I shouldn't've – called, that is. I . . . er. You see, I haven't really thought about, you know, *It*,' she mumbled.

'Hush! Of course you haven't,' Richard chided gently. 'You've hardly been *compos mentis*! Listen to me, Sal, I'm offering calamine. No strings attached – promise. I'll just slip it through the letter box. You can even pay me, if it makes you feel easier.'

Half an hour later Sally hovers by the letter box. She is starting to itch. Itchy feet, itchy everything. She hears the purr of the Alfa Romeo, Richard's assertive footsteps. Should she hide, open the door, peep through the curtain – what? The adrenalin is churning and her heart is heavy. She watches as the lid of the letter box flips up. She can hear Richard clearing his throat.

'Richie?' she whispers quickly. Crouching down, they can look eye to eye. They are shadows and the encounter has a dreamlike quality. They are latter-day Pyramus and Thisbe and the letter box serves as the chink in the wall. However, this is no midwinter night's dream, this is the here and now. Sally has chicken pox and Richard is sitting on his heels outside her front door, trying to keep his balance.

'You don't look too bad at all!' His voice is as lovely as the cool night air whispering through to her. 'Not too bad at all.'

So Sally puts the light on and crouches down again. Richard now has spots before his eyes. Desperate to think of something diplomatic to say, he decides on, 'Oh.'

Sally hastily switches the light off, buttons her spots

away and slips back into the safe shadows. A bulky paper bag is jostled through the letter box. Richard's knees ache like mad, cramp threatens in his calves but he daren't tell her. Spots and all, he just wants to be near for as long as he can.

'Thank you,' she whispers.

'Don't worry about anything, Sal. Just get yourself better.'

In the ease of his voice, the kindness of his words, she can see his smile and it fills her head with a delicious lightness.

'Thank you,' she says again.

There is silence among the shadows. Neither he nor she wants to go, yet they do not know how best to stay. Richard pokes his index finger through the letter box as far as he can, grazing his knuckles though he neither feels it nor cares. Tentatively, Sally meets his finger with the very tip of one of hers.

For a sweet but all too short moment, they touch.

THIRTY-ONE

The itching set in and took hold with such force as to render Sally utterly at its mercy. She had never known anything like it. It was infuriating, it was excruciating, it frequently took her to the verge of tears. It was unbearable. In her exasperation, expletives spewed forth and she spat with venom words she had spent her adult life trying to avoid. Calamine soothed but only in the cool cloud of the initial application. Once dry, and it dried all too quickly, its flakiness merely added to the overall itchiness. Sally's bed-linen and clothes were peppered with salmon pink blotches, and great clods of the dried lotion were welded to her hair. During the day, only enormous self-discipline and sheer determination, coupled with viciously clenched teeth and unbridled execration, prevented her scratching for England. Night, however, was different; even going to bed wearing mittens was little guard against the dreaded sleep-scratching. Though she detested the itching and hated the spots, she loathed herself more for having scratched – albeit in her sleep. Her chest and arms suffered the most, the tops of the pocks scratched off and a stinging pus released which dried a hundred times more itchy.

I'm going to scar, I'm going to scar, Sally thought wearily. Short of tying her hands behind her back on going to bed, there seemed to be no solution.

Sally was in a foul mood. Well-wishers would phone throughout the day to say *there, there* and to warn DON'T SCRATCH or YOU WILL SCAR. Lacking the humour to accept such advice graciously, she decided to leave the phone off the hook. Even a batch of another thirty cards from Class Five failed to lift her spirits. The children had found prodigious artistic outlet in Miss Lomax's predicament and by the end of the week, red crayons were a rare commodity in the art room. The figure of Miss Lomax was treated to a liberal and energetic dousing of red dots. The noise of thirty crayons rapping down to create them caused Mr Bernard, who was trying to teach Maths next door, to pull Miss Lewis to one side, begging her to change to collage instead. Ultimately, the cards were of little comfort; even Marcus's card, with another classic rhyme and signed *Marcus (xx)*, could not coax a smile from Miss Lomax.

Poor Miss Lomax is not well
Itchy spots are making life hell.
Get well soon, for our fave teacher you are –
But DO NOT SCRATCH or YOU WILL SCAR.

By the end of the week, the itching had abated but those spots Sally had unwittingly scratched were sore and scabby. Her mood was made even more foul after a phone call to Mr Tomlin. Sally used her brightest voice and breezed on about feeling 'one hundred per cent' even if she did not look it. She begged, she pleaded, she even flirted to be allowed to return on Monday morning. Mr Tomlin, however, who liked to do things by the book – as is the wont of a headmaster – would hear none of it.

'I believe the doctor suggested two weeks?'

'Well . . .' started Sally.

'Well then!' he declared in his most headmasterful voice. 'And, Miss Lomax,' he warned, 'considering that the chicken pox did not take hold first thing on Monday morning, we won't be counting this as a full week. We shall look forward to seeing you bright and early a fortnight on Monday – not a moment before.'

'But that'll be nigh on three weeks!' Sally squealed.

With his most qualified stern-but-fair voice, Mr Tomlin delivered his *coup de grâce:* 'Miss Lomax,' he said, 'I've had calls from anxious parents. *Anxious parents,*' he reiterated gravely. 'We simply cannot afford to have you back a minute too soon. I know you understand. Bright and early, a fortnight on Monday. Take care.'

In the face of such autocracy, Sally was as helpless as any pupil. Fearing that further begging would result in a metaphorical Detention and arguing would warrant something far worse, she let it be and sulked all afternoon, occasionally sucking in her pouting lower lip to swear at nothing in particular. There was no more 'Gracious Good Lord' in Sally's pock-marked vocabulary; her atypical effing and blinding now rhymed Him with banker.

For perhaps the first time in her life, Sally felt thoroughly anti-social and was quite content to do nothing about it. She did not even feel like chatting to her plants, the kettle or to anything in particular – let alone to Diana or Richard who were both keeping a wise and generous distance. Sally found comfort and relief only in chocolate and soap operas (preferably those of Antipodean origin, made in the mid-seventies and screened in the early afternoon). She had neither the manners nor the goodwill to respond even to the Woodses' sumptuous flower arrangement.

Yet this is the girl who took such pride in her little cards of effusive thanks for even the humblest cup of tea; this is the girl for whom *Ps* and *Qs* had hitherto been the prerequisite for honourable living. This is the girl with manners and grace constituting the very essence of her being. But see her now, stomping and slouching and swearing indiscriminately. Look in the waste-paper basket and find a batch of 'get well soon' cards barely out of their envelopes tossed nonchalantly away. See how the Woodses' bouquet could do with some water. Sally is feeling sorry for herself – and why shouldn't she? She is wallowing in a formidable sulk, seething at the cruel irony that the doctor has said she is probably contagious no longer. Even the mirror holds little solace, reflecting back a glowering, bespotted creature with a clump of spiky hair above her left temple.

There must be a solution. Someone must hold the key to unlock Sally from this unbecoming petulance. Indeed there *is* a key. It is nearly five hundred miles north and it is lying invisible in the lap of the treasured Aunt Celia.

As Sally flounces down into her Lloyd-Loom with a mug of cocoa and a sullen sigh, Aunt Celia has just come in from her small garden, ruddy-cheeked and eyes glistening. It is a glorious day on the Isle of Mull; crisp, clear and sunny with a fortifying breeze. If truth be known, it is also a lovely day in Highgate – but sulky Sal remains defiantly unconcerned.

THIRTY-TWO

Arranging a fat bunch of daffodils from her lush crop in an old earthenware jug, Celia thinks of Sally. Admiring their sunny, joyous faces, she decides if Sally were to be a flower, she would most certainly be a daffodil.

And if I were to be a flower, I would be heather. Tough, not much to look at, but clinging on, year after year after year!

Celia Lomax, sister-in-law to Sally's late father, is now seventy but looks a good decade younger, a blessing she accredits to Mull's vitalizing air. She loves her western isle passionately. It has been her home for almost fifty years and every day she is thankful that she has the good fortune to live in such a wonderful place. The first twenty years of her life were spent, anaemic and entrenched, in Glasgow. Now every morning Celia still races to her doorstep to take greedy gulps of the clean, incomparable air, and she sleeps with the window open throughout the year.

Mull cannot cease to enthrall her. She finds she still stops in her tracks to listen and look about her in awe. She never tires of the sounds of the island – it might be an uncomfortable silence to a city-dweller, but for Celia there is a veritable din and her head is filled and thankful for it. Beneath it all, she tunes into the eternal sound of the ocean. Whistling in from the sea, she can listen to the dance of the thin wind slipping its way between the hills and shaking the Scots pine with regular rattles. Under the wind, she can pick out the shimmy of the heather and the rustle of the bracken; above it, the plaintive mew of buzzards, the caw-cawing of hooded crows, the calling of the gulls. Every day, for half a century, Celia Lomax has taken grateful stock of all that is on her doorstep. She can look about her panoramically, for no tenement buildings and no grimy haze deny her a horizon. There is so much sky for the gazing! Under it, the majestic hills are swathed in hues of blue and brown from the tracts of heather and cloaks of bracken. The single-track road winds out of sight, linking the humble white cottages that pepper its way. Pattern and colour, shape and light – the beauty of Mull is a revelation to Celia each day of her life.

Angus Lomax had brought his young Glaswegian wife to Mull soon after their honeymoon in the Cairngorms. Having worked for ten years as doctor in his childhood town of Oban, he leapt at the chance to take over the General Practice for North Mull. He had never wondered or worried whether his city-bred wife would adapt and be happy out on the isle. From the moment he met her, he knew at once that her eyes were those of Mull; they were the colour of heather and as glassy, private and deep as Loch na Keal. His intuition was proved right and Celia adapted to rural life with passion and with pleasure.

While Angus busied himself with the practice and the patients, Celia made home. She limewashed the exterior of the old cottage and painted the interior. She treated the wood, she cleared the chimney, she smoothed down and buffed up the old stone floors. She made curtains for the deep windows and cushions for every chair; the kitchen she filled with local pottery. Hand-made shawls adorned the furniture and a painstakingly pieced quilt bedecked their great iron bed.

If her house was her castle, her small garden was her kingdom. She furrowed and she dug and she turned the land. The native peat was a godsend, the Gulf Stream a blessing. Tomatoes, marrow, potatoes, cabbage, beans, thyme, rosemary, alpine strawberries and fat blackberries – they all grew sweet and plentiful. Bulbs and shrubs vied for space amongst the liberally strewn wild flowers, and small alpines grew bravely in the picturesque rockery. Through every season, Celia's garden sang with colour.

At the moment, it is carpeted in yellow and blue as daffodils and crocuses run amok. The daffodils have called Sally, her favourite niece, to mind. A treasured rapport exists between them. Their bond is certainly stronger than that enforced between Sally and her mother and, secretly, they both glean a somewhat perverse satisfaction from it.

Mildred Lomax never liked Celia. ('Your strange aunt up North.') Mildred Lomax was not in tune with the sky, the wind or the sea; she found little to wax lyrical about in heather, and growing your own vegetables seemed a downright tedious pastime. ('Rather unnecessary and *affected* in this day and age, don't you think?') Mildred Lomax was a Home Counties, Women's Institute, Bridge Club and afternoon tea sort of woman. Her 1930s semi had been delectably interior designed and she had a cleaner ('my daily') to administer its upkeep. A gardener tended a very neat garden where the lawn did not look real and hybrid roses were pruned to perfection. She had never had the inclination to bake bread nor to lift a needle and thread – after all, there was a most useful little lady down the road for all of that.

What really set Mildred against Celia was her late husband's fondness for the woman and her daughter's devotion to her. Family holidays on Mull, an annual occurrence until Sally was fifteen and her father dead, had been the bane of Mildred's life. She found Mull a forsaken and bleak place, invariably swamped by mist and midges. She did not like trudging across hillocky heather wearing wellington boots, and found all that sea air rather tiring. There was nothing for her to *do* on Mull, and Mildred Lomax was not very good at doing nothing. Of course, there were walks to go on, wild flowers to seek out and wildlife to watch, but such pursuits left her cold in every sense of the word.

Her disaffection for Mull, however, stretched far beyond its terrain and was deeper seated than a mere antipathy towards outdoor pursuits. It was seeing her husband so relaxed and rustic, her daughter so free and so *muddy*, that struck a dissonant chord within. It shamed her that their unbridled laughter, an integral and unforced part of such holidays, never rang out in Lincoln. Celia irritated her; she was so wholesome with her naturally tanned, attractively weathered skin, her lithe frame, her meals (*delicious, damn them*) thrown together effortlessly from fat, flavoursome, homegrown ingredients. Celia was unswervingly generous and accommodating towards Mildred; which of course made matters far worse. There really was nothing to dislike about Celia, yet Mildred's thoughts were wholly uncharitable. She did not envy Celia her life-style nor her skills, but she bitterly envied the adoration and respect she commanded from all who knew her.

As Sally finishes her cocoa and sighs again, Celia settles down with a nice cup of tea. Mildred meanwhile has just come in from arranging the flowers at the church. Sally's ears are burning but she puts it down to a vagary of her affliction; after all, she is not to know that both aunt and mother are dialling her number simultaneously. Anyway, the phone is still off the hook. Sally regards the telephone and replaces the handset with a despondent clatter. Almost immediately, it rings and Sally finds she is pleased.

'Hullo?' she croaks in her finest 'I'm-so-poorly' voice.

'Hullo, my poppet,' soothes the familiar lilting accent. Celia has pipped Mildred to the post. Mildred has just slammed the receiver down on finding Sally's number still engaged. ('*On her death-bed, I don't think!*')

Sally is delighted that it is Aunt Celia and she talks at length about the state of each spot. Forty years married to a General Practioner has left Celia a legacy of surprisingly detailed medical knowledge.

'You'll not be contagious any more, you know.'

'Well, that's the daft thing, Aunt C. I've been literally quarantined,' Sally proclaims. 'Banished,' she declares, 'from school. I'm not allowed back until a fortnight on Monday!'

'Tush tush!' sympathizes Aunt Celia.

'I'm beside myself with boredom and ashamed of it. I feel so cooped up! I daren't go out because I look such a freak and if people stare and point, I'm sure to feel like one too!'

'What you need is to convalesce,' says Aunt Celia.

'I know, I know,' sighs a dejected Sally.

'You need rest,' her wise aunt stresses. 'You need rest, fresh air and good food.'

Sally agrees with her.

'Well!' exclaims Aunt Celia. 'When shall I expect you?'

Sally is stunned. The penny drops and a smile creeps across her face. She is at once galvanized and speechless; better already, to be sure.

'You *mean* it?' Sally squeals. 'Are you *sure*? Are you sure you've *had* chicken pox, that I'm not con-*ta*-gious? Can I really come up and stay? It won't be too much trouble for you?'

'My wee bairn,' laughs Aunt Celia, 'it's what the doctor ordered!' she declares, winking at a photograph of Angus.

*

'Darling?'

'Oh, hello, Mother.'

'I've been trying you for ages. You've been perpetually engaged. Per-*pet*-ually.'

'Sorry. The phone's been off the hook. I needed to rest.'

'Well, darling, I've been speaking to Dr Peabody. He doubts very much whether you are still con-ta-gious. I thought it would be a good idea for you to recuperate here; you know, let me look after you. Nothing that a bit of TLC and your old bedroom can't cure!'

'Oh, Mum! That's very kind – truly. And I'm not contagious any more. And I do need to recuperate . . .'

'Well then!'

'. . . so I'm going up to Mull. To stay with Aunt Celia. All that lovely air. I'm leaving tomorrow.'

'But it's *Feb*ruary! You'll catch your *death*! I'm not sure that your strange aunt up North has the *nous* to nurse you back to health. Darling, reconsider!'

'Mother,' Sally took her time, 'firstly, Aunt Celia is *not* strange. Secondly, I'll wrap up warm. Thirdly, I can't think of anywhere else where convalescence is a foregone conclusion. And fourthly,' she faltered, 'fourthly, I can't think of any place I'd rather be. I can't *wait* to go.'

My heart is in the Highlands, my heart is not here.

THIRTY-THREE

Whatever possessed Sally Lomax to pack her bag and take the high road to Scotland without telling a soul?

As the M1 unfurled ahead of her, she felt no pang of guilt, not even the slightest twinge. She was too busy singing 'Bridge Over Troubled Water', the choice of that week's castaway on Radio 4's *Desert Island Discs*. As she neared Milton Keynes, Sally was revising her eight discs for the second time but just could not choose less than nine. By the time she joined the M6, she decided that, along with Shakespeare and the Bible, her book would be a Robert Burns anthology and, as she passed Birmingham, she chose ballet shoes as her luxury. As Lancashire slipped into Cumbria, Sally decided she would have rather a good time on her desert island, dancing away to Beethoven, Stravinsky and Genesis, and would not feel a 'wee sleekit, cowrin, tim'rous beastie' in the slightest. Switching the radio off, she motored at a steady seventy and smiled at the hills as they loomed. It was a fine day, the sky seemed very high and the early-spring sun hung large and low, like a luminous pink sweet; Sally could have licked it. She felt an exhilaration she had not felt for a long while, an intoxicating mix of solitude and freedom. Glasgow lay three hours away, Oban an hour or so after that, then there was just the Firth of Lorn to cross to Aunt Celia. She was at last taking a journey whose destination was known and desired. She could not wait to arrive.

Diana was livid, Richard was not amused, Catherine was nonplussed.

'Richard?'

'Hullo, Diana.'

'I think something's wrong.'

'Whajoomean?'

'Have you spoken to Sally?'

'Well, er, no. I'm er, letting her call the tune – you know, at her own pace. I took some calamine round a few days ago but I haven't heard from her since. What is it, for heaven's sake?'

'I think she's gone. I've been ringing her, on and off, for the last two days – nothing. So I popped round half an hour ago and looked through the letter box.'

Our letter box, thought Richard. 'And?' he enquired.

'Well, it was all eerily silent. I couldn't really see anthing at all because the curtains are drawn. Thing is, I have her spare keys but I'm a bit nervy about going in by myself.'

'I'll be right there.'

With a quick call to Catherine and Bob to say he'd be late for dinner, Richard drove to Diana's with a strangely empty head. Parking at the end of Sally's street, they walked slowly to her flat, noting as they walked that her Mini was nowhere to be seen. Diana unlocked the door and Richard went in first and rushed back the curtains. All was predictably spick and span and a faint smell of polish hung in the air. The bed was without linen, its mattress turned on to one side; there was nothing perishable in the fridge; all the plants were well-watered and the bathroom and kitchen smelled of bleach.

Well, these were the clues, but where was the proof?

'Bingo!' muttered Richard. Diana swung from the window where she had been looking at nothing in particular in the hope of infiltrating Sally's psyche. From Richard's fingers a small piece of paper dangled. She took it from him and read in a voice soon tinged with tears and threaded with anger: *'Gone to Scotland. Back soon. S.L.'*

Unable to speak, she looked at Richard but saw his face blank and stony. She tossed the note aside and Richard retrieved it, carefully placing it back on the mantelpiece where he had found it.

'S*cot*land?' Diana's exasperation, though barely audible, filled the room.

'That's what it says,' replied Richard flatly. There was a loaded silence as they wondered how best to react. Diana went for spontaneity.

'Stupid, ungrateful, insensitive cow!' she spat.

Richard chose silent contemplation.

Bitch, he thought. *Why? When? Stupid cow indeed.* There was silence again as each wondered what to say to the other.

'Diana,' Richard soothed at last, 'there must be an explanation. Maybe something cropped up.'

Diana was aghast.

'Cropped up? Like what? The only person she knows in Scotland is her old aunt who lives on Skye or Shetland or somewhere.'

'Mull,' mulled Richard.

'That's *not* the point,' Diana growled, 'she can go to Timbuk-bloody-tu for all I care.' The force of her anger quite took Richard aback. Her mood was as black as her jumper, her face the same furious red as her leggings. 'But the fact is I *do* care,' she yelled. 'Am I worth so little to her that she can just up and leave without a backward glance?' Without even the tiniest phone call? Without even a scribbled note posted with a second-class stamp?' Diana stood scowling with her hands clenched to her hips. She stamped her foot and grabbed her hair. 'Who does she think she is? She's needed me and I've been there – unswervingly,' she fulminated. 'Even a "piss off" to my face wouldn't be as hurtful as this couldn't-care-less disappearance.'

Fearing that Diana was on the verge of tears, Richard eased towards her and put his arm around her shoulders. She looked up at him, wide-eyed and wounded.

'But, Richard, what about you? How on earth can this make *you* feel? Can you bear it? Will you tolerate it?'

He shrugged in a non-committal way.

'It can't possibly *not* have crossed her tiny mind that we would worry, that we would be hurt,' Diana concluded. Richard remained silent and pensive – it seemed safer that way. The hurt he felt was so deep it was nauseating. How *could* she indeed? Why Scotland? Why the secrecy?

There was no need for it – it's not as if I would have been in the position to say 'Hold on, Sal, I'm coming too'. What can have filled her head? What did she think as she locked the door? As she hit the M1?

The horrible thing is, I'm almost certain she did not think at all, let alone twice. Thoughtless. Ungrateful. Tedious. This is the last straw, the short one, and Sally has just pulled it.

Not knowing what to do with his thoughts, much less how to express them, he gave Diana a squeeze and then ushered her out, taking a last look around before he closed the door on Sally's silence. Though the flat was clean and fresh, its cosiness had disappeared with her and he now felt an intruder, a stranger. Knowing that its inhabitant did not want him there – or anywhere – cut straight to his heart. He closed the door and double-locked it dejectedly. Driving Diana home, they said of course they would keep in touch, with or without the slightest news. Yet as they parted, it dawned on both with some displeasure that Sally, the very cause of their suffering, was holding them captive, that they were at her mercy, at her beck and call. Their worlds, at which she had seemingly stuck two fingers, were still revolving around her.

Was that it?

Did she want the world to turn because of her?

Sally? Manipulative?

Surely not!

Both Richard and Diana felt beholden, and the very realization was thoroughly repugnant. At last, they hated her for it and felt fine about it.

But ask Sally why she did it.

Did what?

Ask her what went through her head as she shut the door on all around her and headed carefree for Scotland.

This time tomorrow I'll be with Aunt Cee!

Do you believe her? Mention Richard and Diana to her. Why did she not call either? Ask her if it really did not occur to her that they would be hurt, worried, confused.

See. She cannot answer.

She may falter: *I'm a burden. They've done so much. I don't want to bother them, to trouble them.*

She may limp: *I've been so unbearable, spotty and sorry for myself, I just want to creep away and return restored.*

But you will not hear her say: *I'm sure they won't mind. I know they'll understand. I would too, you know.*

Nor will you hear: *I know it'll probably land me in trouble, but I've got to do it; there's something fun about it, jetting off in secret! I wonder what they'll think when they find me gone! Will they worry? Might they be angry? What'll go through their minds? Will they care?*

You will not hear this from Sally because she cannot

yet hear it herself. Banished to the back of her subconscious is the nub of the matter: *God, I shouldn't be doing this. I should at least call, leave a note. But I want to do it – just to see.*

We certainly will not hear Sally say it out aloud for a while longer. Not until she has played this, her last hand in the game. It is a game to her, and though no one else is playing, she does not seem to realize that just yet.

So, Sally must lose if she is to have a chance to win.

To Catherine, Sally was an open book. A mere glance at the pages was enough; she had read it before and it was all very familiar. She knew well the form, the semantics, the beginning and the middle. Did she know the end? She thought so. Should she divulge it?

What – and spoil it for everyone? Tell them the punchline before the joke?

Only this is not very amusing.

Read them the last line when they're but half-way through? Tell them what'll happen in the end? I have no right to do such a thing!

Catherine's dilemma was threefold. She was torn between her concern for and loyalty to Richard, her solidarity and understanding for Sally, and her soreness that she too had been rejected. However, she did feel equipped to shed light on the syndrome and believed it was her responsibility to all concerned to do so.

Bob had alleviated a portion of Richard's melancholy with a particularly frenzied game of squash. Catherine, who had spied a bumper but half-empty bottle of HP Sauce next to a jumble of takeaway cartons in Richard's kitchen, was now trying to reason the remainder away.

'Richie – er, sorry, Rich*ard*. Please believe me, please trust me – I know women.'

'Catherine, how pretentious,' Richard retorted. '*You know women*,' he mocked. 'What on earth does that mean?' Catherine took her time.

'What I mean is, I've *been* there' she declared with gentle confidence. 'You know the saying – seen it, done it, bought the T-shirt?' Richard grimaced at her. She took no offence and clarified, 'But Sally, I think, is right *in* there, She's *seeing* it, *doing* it, she's *wearing* the T-shirt. She's just got to throw it away.'

'I do *not* understand,' Richard said tersely, his voice brittle and pinched, 'what on *earth* you are talking about.'

'I know you don't,' eased Catherine, 'that's why *you're* hurting so much, while *I'm* merely nonplussd. I *know* what's happening to Sally, it happened to me too. I've done it before – most women have, or will. I *know* the book she's reading, I *know* the game she's playing.'

'That,' declared Richard, 'is precisely it. I am thirty-five years old. I have grown out of playing games.'

'Richard,' pleaded Catherine, 'if you can just hear me. It's not malicious, it's not vindictive. It's like she's testing the water before she leaps on in.'

Still his face was pale, his brow furrowed, his eyes hollow.

'Richard,' she cooed, 'Sally is doing this to reassure herself. You know: "will he love me if": "could he love me if".'

She could see she had made no inroad into Richard's melancholy, so she pulled out her trump card.

'Look, don't you remember how I was with Bob? How I'd sometimes flirt at parties? That I'd often be late? Sometimes I'd be aloof, sometimes downright moody? Remember when I jetted off to Corfu with two girlfriends giving Bob just a day's notice *and* expecting him to drive us to the airport to boot?'

A glimmer of a smile crept into Richard's face. 'You were a prime cow, Catherine. I remember saying to Bob, "bin her".'

'And?'

'I remember how he'd just shrug it off and smile. I couldn't work him out. I thought he'd gone soft.'

'See!'

'But *why*, Catherine? I don't feel soft at all. I feel livid, absolutely livid.'

Catherine could now wrap it up.

'Look,' she said kindly, taking Richard's hand, 'Sally is teetering on that diving board. *Teetering*! I bet every time she motions to leap something leers up at her: be it that awful bloke, the one who hit her; be it wedding dresses and "*I do*"*s*'; be it saying sorry to you, to Diana – to me! After all, what is it that she'll dive into?'

Catherine's question hung in the air as the light began to break for Richard. She answered methodically: 'She must forsake all for a responsible, grown-up, death-do-us-part existence.'

Richard nodded. 'Normality!' Catherine exclaimed. 'Mundanity!' she declared. 'Gone will be her little flat, her total privacy, talking to herself, eating a tub of ice-cream in bed – she'll have to trade all that in.' Richard's face was softening and he continued to nod.

'Richard, the girl's got to find herself by losing herself,' Catherine announced with conviction, 'and what better place than Scotland – all those lochs, all that heather! I'm not belittling the situation and you might not like what she might find. This is the make or break. Whatever the outcome, it will be for the better; for both of your futures. Sally may be playing a game of sorts, Richard. But the prize she's pursuing is Truth.'

THIRTY-FOUR

'It's at times like this,' said Sally out loud, drumming her thumbs on the steering wheel, 'that I wish you were a Jaguar and not a Mini.'

Though she had completed well over half the journey, it was already afternoon and she knew she would miss the last ferry from Oban. Moreover, she wanted to enjoy the journey; she wanted to stand on the shores of Loch Lomond with bagpipes playing in her head and have a browse around Oban.

Having long thought the Lakes to be a mediocre imitation of the Highlands, Sally decided to turn right, and not left, off the motorway at Penrith, and chose a farm bed-and-breakfast near Lazonby Fell. The room was just as she hoped, with very little floor space due to a profusion of family heirlooms. The mahogany bed was high in itself but had been further banked up with feather mattresses. It reminded Sally of her favourite childhood tale, 'The Princess and the Pea', and she could hardly wait for bedtime. (Later, though she felt daft, she did check under the mattresses for an errant pea, and though she felt dafter, she was disappointed at finding none.) There was a Lloyd-Loom chair, very similar to her own, in which she sat and smiled. She admired a beautiful walnut chest of drawers and a very pretty dressing-table with filigree sconces for candles at the mirror. She creaked open the cavernous wardrobe which took up almost an entire wall and thought of C. S. Lewis; it was big enough for her to walk into so she did, but Narnia did not open up for her.

Not this time, not here.

Looking out, the Pennines rolled away, cut and crossed by dry-stone walls and thickets, and blessed by the late-afternoon sun. Venturing downstairs, Sally talked silently to the grandfather clock before pulling on her walking boots and greeting the fresh air – the first she'd had in days.

'Would you like to see the lambs?' She presumed him to be Mr Barker. ('I do Been Bee, he do farm, see,' Mrs Barker had trilled.)

'I've had chicken pox,' Sally offered by way of an explanation. Mr Baker sucked on his pipe, and cocked his head.

'The lambs'll not catch it!' he mused after awhile.

'No! I know!' stammered Sally. 'I just wanted you to know. I'm not con-ta-gious any more. But I know these spots are a fright.'

'To tell the truth, Missy, I thought it just a bad case of adilessent acme.'

Sally bit her tongue until the pain drove away any inkling of laughter.

'I'd love to see the lambs.'

Having had a very good night and a hearty breakfast of duck eggs and home-cured bacon, Sally said a last goodbye to the lambs and continued on her way. Carlisle was soon upon her and she picked up the A74 to take her into the Borders. She switched off the radio, wanting no distractions.

Here it is! Scotland!

She could have wept but motored on, shaking her head and marvelling at how distinct from England the landscape was already; laughing as she passed Gretna Green; moved to reverential silence as she saw the signs for Lockerbie. Glasgow loomed and, with some dexterity, Sally made sense of the proliferation of roads and was, at last, on the road to Oban. As always, she was struck by the vicinity of Loch Lomond to Glasgow though the hubbub of the city seemed a million miles from these lovely shores. Though she was now itching to be on the ferry, she had promised herself a few moments at the great loch and no journey to Aunt Celia's would be complete without it. Sally clambered her way through a thatch of Scots pine and crouched by the edge of the water. She thought of all the times she had done so. She thought of her father. She touched upon all the times she and he had made their pilgrimage to the shores of the loch while Mildred sat in the car eating boiled sweets. She dipped her whole hand into the water until her joints froze, then she swiped her fingers through her hair and felt anointed. *Now* she could continue to Oban.

There was one small hurdle – was she to take the magnificent road via Crianlarich, or the slightly longer route around Loch Fyne to the coast road? Showing enormous restraint, she opted for the latter. It suited her mood. It was important that this journey to Mull should be as symbolic and as Romantic as possible.

Anyway, I'll take the high road home.

Sally wound her way down into Oban. The town was bustling and she made slow progress to the dock. She bought a ferry ticket for herself and her car and then went in search of scones. Sitting over a cup of tea, she dabbed at the last crumbs and tuned into snippets of the conversation that surrounded her. She loved the accents and tried hers out in the mountaineering shop where she bought a small rucksack. No one batted an eyelid, either at her spots or at her Scottish lilt.

Och aye! I can be who I like, they'll have me for me!

Time to set sail, Sal. Caledonian MacBrayne will take you across Lorn to Craignure. All aboard the CalMac!

Herring gulls swoop and call and hover at eye-level with Sally, effortlessly defying the sharp gusts of sea breeze which take the breath away from her. Her eyes are smarting but she knows they would be so, even if there was no breeze. With a lump in her throat and a quivering smile on her lips, she hangs as far over the railings as she can, tasting the oily salt spray on her lips. The sea is wearing diamonds. Oban looks like toy town. Duart Castle is looming, standing dark and proud at its commanding position on the first point of the island. Sally can hear her father's voice. He is whispering in hushed, excited tones as he always does at this point on the journey.

'Sal, my bird. Look! Duart! "Dark Headland". Walls fourteen feet thick, my girl!' Sally sings softly with him:

> *'The Isle of Mull is of isles the fairest*
> *Of Ocean's gems 'tis the first and rarest*
> *Green grassy island of sparkling fountains*
> *Of waving woods and high tow'ring mountains.'*

They sing together again. Sally is home.

THIRTY-FIVE

So, Sally is now on the last leg of her journey. We have a feeling it is the last leg of her other journey too. She is but half an hour from Aunt Celia. Mull spreads its beauty before her and she marvels at its mystery. I could tell you of the colours put out by the heather, I could describe the incomparable beauty of the hills and of the light that the lochs contain and reveal, the sound of the sea; but Sally is now bursting to arrive and we are keen that she should reach her destination without further ado. Suffice it to say, the day is perfect, the scenery is spectacular, the colours could make you cry: Mull, in all its splendour, welcomes Sally back.

Though it has been at least two years since Sally's last visit, all seems comfortingly familiar. Tobermory looks radiant but she does not stop. She comes across the village of Dervaig, as picturesque as when she last left it, and pays a brief visit to the eccentric little shop selling just coffee and books. She buys a packet of freshly ground Costa Rican, and a small book on local walks. The proprietor cocks his head to one side in semi-recollection but Sally flinches away from his eyes, her pock marks and the vicinity of Aunt Celia preventing a 'hello' just now.

Celia stands at the end of her pathway and can see the Mini from far off. As the distance between the two diminishes, the driver can be seen bouncing up and down at the wheel, the car's horn ringing out, parp parp! Celia waves expansively, Sally parps some more before screeching to a halt and pelting to her, the engine still running, door open.

There are squeals, liberal hugs, wide smiles and much hair-stroking, but we shall let them enjoy their reunion in private.

Sally went from room to room, routinely closing her eyes to soak up remembered smells then opening them wide to take stock of all the familiar furniture, the bits and pieces, the nooks and crannies. A lick of paint had changed nothing, all was intact and her memory had served her well. She stood awhile in the kitchen, Celia quiet behind her, a hand on Sally's shoulder. The smell of baking led her eye to the scrubbed table on which a batch of perfectly risen scones cooled on racks. The smell of flowers led her eye to the deep window sills where a bowl of hyacinths took pride of place. Pretty china greeted her when she looked upon the dresser; the glint and sheen of polished copper rang out from the hanging rack above her head. Slung over the back of an old Windsor chair, a shawl felt soft to her touch; under foot the stone floor was smooth and satisfyingly uneven, all the dints and chips at once familiar.

'Want a cuppa?'

'Mmm! I'll just take my stuff up to my room.'

My room! It is my room, and it is just as I left it! Darling bed, how are you! Hello, little etching of Iona! Curtains! Oh, such lovely flowers, bet they're from the garden.

Mmm, wardrobe smells just as it should – polish with a distant whiff of mothballs. Pink padded hangers, just for me! I'll hang everything up, I'll put everything away, I'll brush my hair and have a quick wash, but first I just want to sit here on the bed and look out of the window.

For once, Sally did not gaze at nothing in particular, but ranged her eyes as far as she could to the horizon and then slowly travelled them back over the hills, through the forest, over the shaggy flanks of the cattle, across the road and back into the garden. No detail was left unobserved and, though she knew the view off by heart, she gazed out with virgin eyes and hailed all she saw.

With hair brushed, face washed and revived with ice-cold peaty water, she made a slow passage downstairs, peeking into Aunt Celia's bedroom and the sewing room as she went. Silently, Sally stood in the sitting-room, smiling at the sound of the table being laid next door. In the range, embers of the morning fire glowed and crackled, the surrounding bricks sooty, the grate spilling with ash and charred wood. The mantelpiece heaved with photographs and Sally worked her way from left to right, pleased that she was in most, her father too, her sisters in few, her mother in but one. She dwelled upon a lovely sepia photograph of her Uncle Angus, so handsome, hair waxed and waved. She looked into Angus's eyes and wondered how well she really remembered him. With a certain dismay, she supposed true memory counted for only a part, assisted recollection for most.

After all, Sally had only been ten years old when he died. His voice was unforgettable and memories of dancing merrily with him on the sand were still clear, but she wondered if she really knew the man he was, the man her aunt adored, the man her father so mourned? She did remember one night vividly, a late summer evening, the Highland dusk just drawing in, an eerie light pervading. She had dozed off into a troubled dream and had woken in a panic. Going downstairs in search of reassurance and a cuddle she had seen, unseen, Aunt Celia and Uncle Angus whiling away the evening; Aunt Cee knitting and looking over to him, Uncle Ang drawing on a pipe and gazing at her through half-closed eyes. The knitting needles provided the only sound in the room, the smell of sweet tobacco whispering through. A sense of peace pervaded and, no longer needing to go right in, Sally crept back to bed, safe and warm. She had fallen asleep hoping that, when she was all grown up, she too could be like Aunt Cee and have an Uncle Ang.

How old can I have been?

You were seven.

By the telephone was a photograph of Angus and his brother Robbie, Sally's father. She considered how similar they had looked, Angus six years older and slightly greyer, her father more portly. Their smiles were so similar, somewhat lopsided, their identical eyes crowned with neat, long eyebrows. She recalled how both shared the same gait, and remembered Aunt Celia finding much hilarity in walking behind them, trying to impersonate their loping, swinging stride. The photograph, in technicolour, showed the brothers standing on the sands at Calgary, Angus bare-chested, hands on hips, Robbie with shirt sleeves and trouser legs rolled up, his hand on Angus's shoulder, a football at their feet. Both squint at the sun with out-of-breath smiles etched wide and skewiff. Sally grinned back at them and traced her little finger around their faces.

She had loved to see them together, so comfortable in each other's company; talking earnestly, laughing privately, standing side by side thigh-deep in the sea, casting their fishing rods in unison in pursuit of elusive salmon. She recalled vividly how they would sit together in silence, always absorbed and at ease in each other's company. Scanning the bookshelves, Sally smiled at memories of bedtime fireside stories being read to her while she snuggled deep into her uncle's or her father's laps on alternate nights throughout her holiday. Their voices were almost indistinguishable and once again they filled her head as she touched the spines of the books and took down *The Just-So Stories* and buried her nose, Best Beloved, within.

'Yoo hoo! Lunchie!'

Celia's call brought Sally back to the day in hand. The Camel got his Hump, the Rhinoceros his Skin and the Leopard his Spots. Angus and Robbie finished the Sing-Song of Old Man Kangaroo and returned once more to the frozen time of the photograph, happy and strong. Much missed.

I wish they were here.

The women feasted on barley soup and cracked rolls plastered with chunks of hard, cold butter which oozed into the soup as they dunked. Dunking was an institution for the Lomaxes and Sally smiled at Celia as they plunged their bread into the soup and then swiped away the predictable dribbles from their chins. Sally remembered the annual look of disdain on her mother's face at such meal-times; she remembered too her father's furtive winks as he plopped his bread in and out of the soup – a pastime absolutely forbidden in Lincolnshire. There was nothing slovenly about such table manners, the soup tasted fundamentally the better for it. Dunking went without saying at every meal; at breakfast it was toast in and out of egg yolk (fried or boiled), at lunch it was bread into soup, at tea-time it was home-made digestive biscuits into mugs of tea, at supper it was bread into anything that could be mopped up, lastly it was shortbread into bedtime cocoa.

Today, Sally dunks with aplomb and Celia dunks as she always does.

'Well, my duck, I must say you are spotty! Do they itch still? Did you manage not to scratch? Do you feel terribly self-conscious? And that poor patch of hair – it'll grow! Well, no need to worry – you'll hardly pass by two people while you're here! I thought you might like a blow-through on the beach this afternoon.'

'Absolutely!'

'You brought muddy clothes with you, I hope?'

'Wellies, walking boots, windcheater, thermal undies, woolly hat – I'm a dab hand, remember!'

'Oh I do remember! Ach, this is fun, is it not? I have missed you, my lass. I say, "Hurray for the chicken pox"!'

'It's not just the chicken pox,' Sally said quietly.

Celia decided not to pry.

Calgary Bay was deserted and the sweep of white sand implored Sally to run as fast as she could to the sea. Celia's laughter was carried on the wind to and from Sally's ears as she ran; it was eerie. Jumping back from the waves, Sally flung her arms above her head, singing, 'It's so beautiful, so beautiful!' A grey seal bobbed his head above the swell as if to see what the commotion was about. They looked eye to eye for a caught moment and then, as if to say, 'Oh, it's you again,' he disappeared leaving Sally motionless and open-mouthed, arms still suspended, until Celia arrived by her side. The women stood and gulped the invigorating air, occasionally turning their heads to follow the swoop of a gull. They scoured the water but the seal had gone.

'You were blessed,' said Celia.

'Oh, I do believe so,' agreed Sally and, linking her arm through Celia's they strolled along the water's edge and chatted awhile about wildlife. Stooping to pick a smooth pebble, Sally skimmed it across the water – four, five, six, seven – a skill painstakingly learnt from her father. Celia clapped.

'Ach, Sal, it's so nice to have you here. You remind me so much of Robbie, and thereby of my own LoveLove too.'

'Am I like Daddy? How?'

'Well, it's not just your stone-skimming! Let me see – it's your zest for life, my duck. And that expression of wonder your face often wears – pure Robbie. Also, the way you talk to inanimate objects. He would talk at length to anything made of wood! Most of all, I see him when I see you gaze and gaze at I do not know what!'

'At nothing in particular,' confided Sally.

'Ah,' nodded Aunt Celia.

'Aunt Cee,' Sally ventured because it seemed timely to do so, 'Uncle Angus . . .' She paused. 'Do you miss him still?' Celia looked at Sally and a momentary wave of angst swept across her face.

'Every day!' she said aghast.

'No, no!' cried Sally. 'Of course you do! I mean, the *missing* him – how *is* it?' Celia looked into her niece's eyes and saw a comforting naiveté, a white page waiting to be filled with the advice, the experiences – perhaps the reassurance – of one who knew. She looked at her open face and saw an ingenuous young woman with the desire to know, to be informed, to learn, to listen. She felt touched and heartened.

'Well, girl, I miss my man. During my waking hours and in my sleep too, do I miss him! Something will happen each day that makes me turn for him – and each time I find him gone.'

Sally watched her looking out to sea as if searching for her lost husband amongst the waves. Celia saw the grey seal but was too far into her thoughts to point it out to Sally.

I think her face is so beautiful, thought Sally. *I love all those lines – they're not wrinkles, see how tight and firm the skin is, no baggy neck like Mother. These lines trace the paths of her life. She's walked with conviction through it and her lovely, brown healthy face is both her story and her reward.*

With the grey seal gone again, Angus too, Celia turned

back to Sally and took her face in her gloved hands. 'Your uncle died fifteen years too soon,' she told her, 'and next year, it was be sixteen years too soon.' Sally took Celia's hands from her face and held them in hers.

'But isn't it just too painful?' she asked, a furrow of worry knotting her brow. 'How can you bear it?'

'It is painful,' explained Celia, 'but that very pain tells me I'm alive. I can bear it because I would rather have had just six months with him than never to have had him at all. And I had thirty-five wonderful years with him. He was my light, you see, but my life is my own.'

Sally looked puzzled. Celia chortled. 'It's a bit daft when people say someone was their whole life, don't you think? Angus died but I still live. He was the light in my life and that light shines on, my duck, shines away.'

They continued in silence for a few strides. Sally stopped, closed her eyes and held her head.

'But Aunt Cee, would you have had it any other way? Fifteen years of unhappiness, loneliness – doesn't the pain you feel vanquish the pleasure of the love you had?'

'Sal, my funny thing.' She hugged Sally very close and when she spoke again, Sally heard her voice through her ribcage; magnified, unhindered. 'I am not lonely,' Celia said, 'I am just alone now. It hasn't been fifteen years just of unhappiness. Yes, I have grieved and I wish with all that I am that he was with me now. But had I not loved him so, I should not miss him, hey? And I rather *like* that feeling. It is a comfort for it can but remind me of what we had together. The pain can only be as great as the love we had, my girl. The love we had was limitless, the pain is indescribable, but the strength that love gave me allows me to sail on. *Amor vincit omnia,* my girl, *vincit omnia.'*

They looked at each other and Sally wondered how Aunt Celia could smile so benignly when she felt like crying at the injustice.

'Do you see?' Celia continued. 'Had I not loved so, had I not been so loved, then sure enough, I may not hurt. But then what would my life be like? It would be black and white. Silent. I like colour and song. Our life was full of both.'

'But he's not *here*,' stressed Sally. Celia nodded but smiled on.

'Would I that he is not here now, but was then, than he never was here at all.' Sally regarded her aunt. Her eyes shone back at her and the confusion on Sally's face slowly lifted. Now she understood and her gratitude rendered her temporarily mute. However, her smile, as it unfurled, spoke volumes to Celia.

They continued their walk, both serene now, and were blessed by the magnificent aeronautics of two golden eagles who seemed to be flying just for the sheer sake of it.

'Would I that he is not here now, but was then, than he never was here at all.' Celia's sentence had been so perfect, so full; the domain of a true poet, of one who knew. It had stuck in Sally's mind instantly.

It is 9.30 and Sally is tucked into bed; the crisp sheets, heavy blankets and a beautiful, hand-quilted eiderdown. Celia's words reverberate around her head and images from the walk assault her mind's eye. She is held a happy captive and falls asleep blanketed by the hills and accompanied by the seal. The rhythmic sound of the waves lulls her deeper and the eagles soar to keep watch overhead.

She wakes in the small hours and lies in velvet darkness for a pleasant moment. Drawing back the curtains and throwing open the window, she marvels at the true blackness of the night, no street lights invading, only a tiny patch of orange glinting from a distant cottage. If she listens well enough, she can hear the sea.

'Would I that he is not here now, but was then, than he never was here at all.'

Well, would I? Would it have been better never to have

met Richard? Would my life have been black and white and without song?

Well?

THIRTY-SIX

As the days passed, Celia watched the colour bloom back to Sally's cheeks – the spots were no less prominent, but the sparkle in her eyes and the glow of her face detracted attention away from them. Though Sally slept until lunchtime the first morning, she was soon down in the kitchen with the break of day, making porridge with a pinch of salt the Lomax way. She was very happy tinkering about with Celia and their days had a loose but welcome routine.

After breakfast, they took a tour of the garden to check that frost had been kept at bay, and to admire new faces amongst the flowers.

'Wood anemones,' Celia cooed as she and Sally crouched in awe over the low little mauve flowers.

'Wood anemones,' Sally repeated to herself, trying to commit leaf shape and petal formation to memory.

Celia's garden was a font of nostalgia for Sally. Despite the brisk air, she could travel with ease back to those heady summers of her childhood. Though it was midwinter, if she closed her eyes she could even fill her nostrils with the scent of fragile dog rose and wild honeysuckle. Gazing at the rockery for long enough turned it back into the harsh mountain her dolls had struggled to climb. Feeling the springy, peaty land beneath her feet, she remembered well the secrets of the garden that not even Aunt Celia knew. Here was the place, the space, in which she had been absorbed in play, absorbed in herself.

The garden seemed so much smaller now, but though Sally's years had altered its scale, its charm had not been compromised.

'Wild violets?' she enquired.

'Next month.' Celia informed.

And I'll miss them, rued Sally.

Having ensured that all was well in the garden for another twenty-four hours, Aunt Celia's timetable read elevenses time, and chocolate brownies were dunked into cups of coffee. After that, the infinite bits and pieces to do around the cottage took them to lunch-time. Sally implored her aunt to load her with chores. Somewhat begrudgingly, Celia obliged and Sally set about waxing the tables, scrubbing out the hearth, polishing the copper, dusting the books and giving all the window-sills a fresh lick of gloss paint. Seeing Sally beavering about her work, so thorough and attentive to her task, struck Celia.

She's me!

Where's her Angus then, Celia?

Has she an Angus?

Why not ask.

Och, no! That's for her to tell – not for me to pry.

Lunch-time was invariably followed by an excursion.

'The beauty of being retired, so to speak,' Celia had told Sally, 'is that you can turn a trip of necessity into a little outing for the afternoon! I may need a loaf of bread, but why go to Dervaig to buy it when I could have a jaunt to Salen, to Bunessan even!' Therefore, each day Celia made sure there was something to buy and whether it was a couple of apples or a fresh salmon, a pint of milk or a pound of potatoes, she ensured the route took them to far-flung corners of the island and passed outstanding viewpoints. They even took the ferry to Iona to buy soap, because Celia justified that the soap in the Abbey gift shop was not tested on animals and smelt heavenly too. Similarly, the journey back from Tobermory took them around two sides of a triangle so that they could enjoy a stroll to Loch Frisa. Invariably, they were home for tea-time dunking. One afternoon, they forsook a jaunt altogether – the film of *Greyfriars Bobby* was on the television and, armed with handkerchiefs and a bowl of home-made fudge, they munched and wept the afternoon away.

In the mellow hours between tea and dinner, a fire would be lit and the two women snuggled deep into armchairs to read, sharing their space and often snippets from their books too. Celia sang old Gaelic songs while Sally shut her eyes and let the warmth of the fire and the sweetness of her aunt's voice course through her body. Sally read passages of Scott and verses of Burns out aloud, Celia assisting her accent.

'Make it rounder, my duck, rounder. Smile while you speak. Use all the muscles of your lips. Hear the words *sing* in your mind first.'

Ye banks and braes o' bonnie Doon
How can ye bloom sae fresh and fair?
How can ye chant, ye little birds,
And I sae weary fu' o' care?

'Magical, Sal. You've got it! Robbie would be proud – both of them, Burns *and* Lomax!'

Sally drifted along, content that each day should come and go like the tide. Mull enchanted her so much that she exclusively devoted her sight and her soul to its gifts. Richard and Diana and Highgate and School were way down South, metaphorical miles from her mind too. After nearly a week, she had slipped easily into Celia's way of life, and Mull and its ways became the norm. This then freed Sally's thoughts and they began to wander. As she dug in the garden, or worked a hard-bristled brush over the flagstones, her mind travelled. Sometimes to nowhere in particular, often to her recent past, rarely to the present and never to the future.

The future will of course become apparent when the past is analyzed and the present confronted. For the time being, however, it was enough for Sally to think back over her time with Richard. Mostly she called upon specific events, blissful evenings, thrilling love-making; allowing herself a private smile, a guarded giggle, a stifled sigh. She realized with some surprise that the last time she had had sex was nearly two months ago. And in Paris. And with J-bloody-C.

I haven't made love with Richard since last year.

Occasionally, she contemplated just what it was that she had with him. She understood what had been intended as a dalliance had drifted into the Richard Thing which had in turn established itself, unasked, as a relationship.

What is it now? Is it anything? Does it exist at all?

She could not quite ask herself if she missed it.

As Sally started to mull and consider, cogs of recognition and springs of curiosity began to turn in Celia's mind.

She had been silent witness to Sally standing stock still, duster redundant in her limp hand, staring intently with a peculiar smile at the tall standard lamp.

Gazing so deep, Celia considered, *as if caught by the eyes of someone. So who?*

Moreover, at breakfast one morning, she saw Sally's shoulders give a little shake as she washed up at the sink and a mute reflection from the window pane revealed that same quirky smile. Furthermore, browsing around a bric-à-brac afternoon at Tobermory Town Hall, she was choosing notelets when she caught sight of Sally at another stall. Oblivious to the vendor's expression – oblivious to all around – she was holding a jar of honey aloft while staring distractedly, mouth half-open, at nothing in particular.

Or is it at something very particular? Celia had wondered.

'Can't I stay here? For ever?'

'Sally Lomax, Scotland may be in your blood but you've never felt your blood chill, your kidneys ache in the full grasp of a Mull winter! How would you fare then?'

'I'd wear lots of layers!'

'When the generator grinds to a halt weekly?'

'I'd fix it!'

'I think not. And the rain and the mist?'

'But it's so wonderfully sombre! Romantic! To just make out the shrouded hills, but the distinction between land, sea and air all blurred!'

'It's sombre all right!' Celia said, looking Sally straight in the eye. 'And after week upon week it's no longer wonderful. You cease to look at the mountains as ethereal, romantic. You just want to be able to see them clearly. You long to see where the land meets the sea. You crave to see the sky again. It can pull a man down, Sal. Folk this way often *hibernate* – as a precaution against depression.'

'I still think it's preferable to Highgate and all that stuff,' Sally said grudgingly.

'Well, *I* think you'd miss it,' said Celia quite sternly over the top of Sally's pout. 'I don't think you're giving enough credit to the freedom, to the very predictability it affords you.'

Sally looked hurt.

'Things seem easier here,' she said quietly, raising doleful eyes.

'It is not an easy life,' said Celia calmly. 'It suits me because I am old and set in my ways. I have few expectations. You, my lass, should be bombarding yourself with expectations, standing as you are on the threshold of your adult life.' Sally made a half-nod. Celia continued gently, 'If Things seem easier here, maybe you're saying Things are not easy in England. In Highgate? To forsake Highgate for Mull is hardly the answer. Merely geography.'

Sally remained silent and stared fixedly at the embers.

'Though Mull won't solve your problems for you,' said Celia gazing at the photograph of the two brothers, 'it might very well help *you* to do so.'

Sally let it lie. After a subtle silence she changed the subject and they chatted the afternoon away. Easier that way.

Sally has lived on Mull for a week. Last night they had fish and chips at Tobermory, eschewing a table and crockery for a harbourside bench and vinegary newpaper.

'The only way to eat fishy chips!' praised Celia.

'I'll say "aye" to that!' hailed Sally.

To Celia's delight, Sally has offered to cook tonight. Earlier, they had driven twenty miles in one direction for a bottle of Chardonnay, and fifteen miles in another for a head of garlic, the trek home readily interrupted by tea and scones (dunkable) at a small café near the shores of Loch Ba.

Celia is now helping Sally prepare – she is chopping what she is told, slicing as she is instructed, dicing as she is asked. Mendelssohn's Hebridrean Overture has been chosen to accompany their labour and the women sway and *la la* in harmony as they work.

'OK, Aunt Cee!' chirps Sally, 'off you go now. Away! Put your feet up, have a Scotch – ooh, pour me one too! I'll cast my top secret magic over this lot and a feast for two will be on the table in precisely half an hour's time!'

They dined on cheese soufflés, followed by grilled trout lashed with butter and smothered with toasted almonds, and finally a breathtaking bread and butter pudding. For the most part they were silent, occasionally catching each other's eyes to hum with appreciation.

'Mmm, can you *cook*, my lassie!'

'Mmm, thank you! More potatoes?'

Because the trout had been small and so light, seconds and thirds of pudding were justified. As one of the penultimate spoonfuls from Celia's bowl neared her lips, she bit the bullet instead and let the spoon hover as she spoke:

'Well, Sal! Seems a shame not to lavish such culinary expertise on someone more special!'

'Aunt Cee! Who could be more special than you?'

'Who indeed?' smiled Celia, letting her question hang in the air for a moment or two before she leant towards Sally and probed further.

'Who indeed? You know they say the way to a man's heart is through his stomach?' Sally cocked her head. Celia continued, 'Is there a man, Sal, whose stomach you seduce, hey?'

'Gracious, Aunt Cee!' said Sally, trying to look taken aback rather than downright taken off guard.

'Tish!' announced Celia, scraping the last of the pudding from the bowl. 'What am I saying? I shouldn't be prying, Sal. Apologies, apologies. I just remember how terrible it was for you with that insufferable chap – you know, the one who . . . I was just hoping that perhaps there was someone making you happy?'

Still Sally looked non-committal and Celia tried to look nonchalantly everywhere but at her face. She heard a stifled sniffle and glanced round to see that it had its roots in a smile. Sally tipped her head and ran her finger around her bowl. Sucking it clean, she then wrapped her napkin around it and decided to welcome her aunt into her private world.

'Well, there is *someone*, Aunt Cee.'

Silence hung like dark velvet curtains, heavy and

containing. Celia wondered whether that was all from Sally and was just about to change the conversation to the merits of trout over salmon, when Sally spoke again.

'His name is Richard Stonehill. He is thirty-five years old and drop-dead handsome!'

Celia decided there were plenty of fish in the sea so she let the trout and salmon go and turned, all ears, to her niece. With a smile that she hoped was persuasive, she put her elbows on the table and cupped her chin in her hands.

'Ooh, do tell me more, Sal!' she cooed, eyes sparkling in what she hoped was a conducive way.

'Richard is an architect. A very brilliant one, I think. He believes buildings are the backbone of our environment and must be sympathetic to, and reflective of, our lifestyle and our needs.'

Celia nodded approvingly, believing it was what Sally wished to see. It worked; Sally continued.

'He's very manly and has a lovely flat in Notting Hill – always clean; fresh flowers; good food. He's fit and healthy – and a wonderful cook!'

Celia continued to nod and felt a little prompt or two would not go amiss. 'And how long have you two known each other?'

'Since the autumn,' said Sally.

'Going steady, then?' Celia asked rhetorically. Almost instantly, she sensed Sally pull back.

'Well, I don't know if you could call it *that*,' she said somewhat flippantly. Celia mouthed 'Oh' in reply. They sat awhile contemplating their empty bowls. Sally refilled their glasses with the last of the wine.

'I call him Richie and he calls me Sal – you and he alone, an honour indeed!'

'I'll say!' said Celia, raising her glass. Taking a thoughtful sip, she steered the conversation back. 'Well, if you've been with him since the autumn but are not going steady, what is it that you have? Please, dear God, not one of those "open" relationships?'

Sally giggled. 'No, not very open at all,' she mused under her breath.

'Go on,' encouraged Celia.

'It's difficult to explain. It started as a bit of a rampant fling – you know, Jackie Collins bodice-ripping and all that?'

Celia had never read Jackie Collins.

'Erica Jong?' ventured Sally.

Celia shook her head.

'Xaviera Hollander?' she suggested.

Still Celia drew a blank.

'Anyway, Sal, I'm sure my reading matter isn't relevant. After all, we're not *talking* fiction or fantasy, are we? Just life – yours.' Celia's swift overview of the reality of the situation made Sally feel vulnerable and somewhat belittled. She felt defensive.

'Aunt Cee,' she corrected sternly, 'you'd be surprised what I can get up to in my little life in Highgate. It may not be Los Angeles or Paris or wherever, but my small flat can be a hot-bed of passion, a boudoir of sins of the flesh! What goes on in there can compete with the best of them – the very stuff that books are made of!'

Sally's eyes glinted, Celia's soul winced.

'I – I'm not sure I quite follow, duck.'

Sally was on a roll. 'I set myself up as a true *femme fatale* to trap a man,' she explained triumphantly. 'And did I ensnare a prime catch! It was fabulous and all so naughty!'

'But what about Richard?'

'I'm *talking* about Richard!' Sally laughed. '*He's* the man.'

'But *he's* the architect,' reasoned Celia, 'sensitive, mature – upright. The one who calls you Sal?'

Sally nodded vigorously, missing the point utterly. 'I thought it would be fun to be a bit of a vamp. And it was certainly the most liberating thing I've done. Only it all went horribly wrong.'

'How?'

'Love.'

Sally uttered the word in much the same tone she used for 'chicken pox'. It quite shocked Celia.

'And that was *wrong*?' she gasped, aghast.

'Oh, yes.'

'Why?'

'I suppose it made it all seem too dangerous.'

'I don't understand, Sally. How can *love* be dangerous? I'd have thought playing the tart would be much more so.'

'I wasn't a tart,' faltered Sally. Celia raised her eyebrows almost imperceptibly but enough to hit Sally in the chest. 'I just wanted to have fun,' she chirped, somewhat unconvincingly.

'And was it fun for Richard?'

'Oh, yes,' Sally answered rather too swiftly, and paused for a moment, trying not to fidget. 'At first,' she clarifed, 'then he fell in love with me so the fun stopped.'

'Why?' probed Aunt Celia sternly. 'Surely, with more substance to it, the fun would have increased, the pleasure deepened?'

'Theoretically,' stumbled Sally.

'I'm lost again, Sal,' Celia said, her voice quiet, almost flat.

'Aunt Cee, it's all such a headache. I'm sure it's part of the reason I've been run down. You see, it was wonderful when it started. I felt so strong, so high, when it was carefree and just pure passion.

'When love came into the equation, it complicated the purity.' Celia raised her eyebrows high. 'I know purity is a funny word to use,' Sally conceded, 'but when Richard told me he was in love with me, I felt absolutely swamped and smothered. Let down.'

'But, Sal, how could that be? He fell in love with you

because he finds you lov*able*, surely nothing could make one feel stronger?' As hard as she was trying, Celia could see little merit in Sally's theory. 'Is he not lovable?'

'Oh!' Sally assurd her. 'On the contrary.'

'Do you love him?' Celia suggested, watching pain scurry across Sally's brow.

'Yes,' she sighed, shaking her head forlornly, 'I do.'

Sally could see that Celia looked even more confused than she herself was feeling.

'Aunt Cee, I needed time,' she explained as gently as she could, 'time to recuperate – and not just from the chicken pox. Time to think, to consider. To make up my mind, if truth be told.'

Celia's frown slowly lifted. 'So you came to Mull? What better place! I think I see now, Sal my duck. What started as a bit of fun became serious and you wanted some space to take it all on board? Might this be *it*, then – the Big One? Might Richard be your Angus?'

Sally cast her eyes downward and smiled coyly but remained silent.

'Well, I think that's very sensible of you both and I'm sure Richard is behind you one hundred per cent, am I right?'

Suddenly the enormity of what Sally had done hit her with such force that, though she wanted to push Celia aside and run, she sat stock still and silent; winded.

'Sal?'

Slowly Sally raised her head, darting her eyes to and from Celia's face. Still she could not find her voice but a small whisper filled the room.

'He doesn't know.'

'What?' Celia's gasp was edged with horror and suffused with disbelief.

'I didn't tell him. Or anyone. Just Mother.'

Celia was flabbergasted. 'Whyever, *ever*, not?'

'I thought it would be a test?' ventured Sally feebly,

flinching away from Celia's expression. 'You know, just to see?'

'See *what*?' Celia barked, standing up. She looked down on Sally, a remoteness tinged with disgust etched on her face. 'No, Sally Lomax, I do *not* know. What on earth do you mean "a test"? Don't you think you've played with the poor man's emotions enough? Using him as some unsuspecting pawn in your stupid little game?'

'But – ' Sally pleaded.

'Hush it!' chided Celia sternly. 'I cannot believe that you, your father's daughter, just *left* without having the courtesy, let alone the conscience, to inform him. You'll be a lucky girl if he still wants you after all this. I wouldn't be in the least surprised if he passes you off. I think it's preposterous, really I do.'

'Aunt Cee!' protested Sally.

'No!' Celia scolded back. 'Here is a man who loves you. Do you know how difficult that is to come by? It takes courage and maturity to recognize and proclaim it. He loves you and you string him along – I can't believe it's you, Sal. Not you!'

Sally fiddled with her napkin, twisting it this way, then that. There was so much she wanted to say, to explain, to apologize for, yet she was struck dumb with shame and could give no voice to her tumbling thoughts.

It isn't me. It wasn't me, was it? It was the idea of who I could be.

Ultimately, someone not preferable to who I really am.

But how was I to know, without this hindsight?

You are right, Aunt Celia, I've been a callous bitch and I must make amends, if it's not too late. But do I have the courage and maturity you speak of?

Regarding her downcast expression, Celia shook her head sadly.

'Sal, my lass, God only knows what got into you. I suggest a long, solitary walk tomorrow, a good ten-miler.

Do some thorough soul-searching. And then you make a phone call. I'm going to bed now, thank you for supper.'

Sally sat alone in the kitchen for a while longer. She then washed up as quietly as she could.

I will walk tomorrow. I will walk and walk and look to the sea, to the sky, to the heather for my answers. I'll strip myself bare and I'll find the answers. I'll call Richard. I'll restore Aunt Celia's faith in me. Courage and maturity: I'll find them. They are there – somewhere.

THIRTY-SEVEN

Sally went to bed. Her sleep was troubled, deep in parts but broken. She was impatient for the next day to arrive so that she could find the answers she sought. She kept the curtains open and scoured the sky for the first hint of morning and dressed before dawn had broken. She breakfasted in careful silence, not wanting to wake Celia. In fact, she did not want to see her at all – not until she had found the answers. To help in her quest, she prepared sandwiches and took a compass, a thermos flask and the book of walks she had bought. She wrapped up warm and put plasters on her heels as a precaution. Before she left, she propped a small note against the kettle for her aunt:

'Gone walking. Love, Sal, x'.

As she closed the door silently on the cottage and stepped out into the early morning, the mystical low silvery light that suffused the island quite took her breath away. It was beautiful and sombre and matched her mood, for it seemed to veil and distort all she'd previously thought she had known. Watched approvingly by two impossibly shaggy Highland cattle, she eased her car into life and headed for the coast.

Her destination was the Treshnish headland. She remembered her father and Angus setting off for day-long walks there but, at nine years old, she had not been allowed to join them.

'But I want to see the Magic Beach,' she had protested.

'It'll still be here when you're big enough to find it,' her father had soothed. Now Sally was going to find the beach and felt sure it would proffer answers for her.

She parked at a small quarry and although it was a beautiful morning, leaving the car was oddly difficult. She stood contemplating it awhile with her hand on the bonnet, wondering whether to go for a long drive instead. As she locked it and then double-checked all the doors, she felt tearful and nervous, but of what she was unsure. Adrenalin was coursing through her veins and a host of other emotions ranging from fear to sadness flowed through her body and wrapped themselves around her mind.

Come on, Sally, it's only a walk and you half-know the answers you are walking to find. The waves and the heather and the sky and the cliffs do not really hold them and you know that. However, being alone with the land might help you unlock them from your private core. So, on your way.

'Bye-bye little Mini, I won't be long. My, the island seems so big today. Look at all that sky. Come, come, read the guide. See, it's a logical circular route and I needn't do the whole lot if I don't feel like it. It will be lovely, just what I need. There's the old Whisky Cave to find – remember all those daft stories of Uncle Angus's? Oh, and I'll see the Treshnish Isles. Maybe I'll be lucky enough to see the grey seals too. Best of all, I'll find the magic beach at long last. I'll be all on my own and it will be good for me. And, most importantly, for the others too.

She set off with a purposeful stride, interrupted every

now and then by a few haphazard steps when certain thoughts or emotions swept over her. The walk from the quarry to the cliffs was longer than she'd expected but it helped her pace herself into a comfortable stride. To assist, she conjured up a good walking chant. Her father had impressed upon her their importance: 'They focus your mind away from your feet. You can walk for hours and miles with a good 'un in your head.'

A childhood favourite had been: *'Left! Left! I had-a-good-job-and-I-left, left'*. Sally tried it for a while and lulled herself into believing her father was right there by her side. They were striding along in harmony muttering 'Left! Left!' when a squabble between two crows overhead brought her back with a jolt to the day in hand; she was twenty-five and her father was ten years dead. Though perplexed and tearful, on she went.

Walking in silence, however, seemed too noisy so she decided to create her own chant in honour of her father. It came to her quite quickly, and she winked at the sky as *'Courage! Maturity! The-answers-I-will-find! Courage! Maturity! The-answers-I-will-find'* gave purpose once again to her step. She passed through a farm to pick up the ancient track to the cliffs. The objective of the walk was already working, for her rhyme had changed. Under her breath and in her mind *'Strength! Truth! The-questions-I-must-ask! Strength! Truth! The-questions-I-must-ask'* now rang out with her footfalls.

Sally reached the cliffs. The still-distant sea stretched before her, marvellously flat and metallic; it looked like a surface one could walk on, even run on. Occasionally, patches shimmered grey, even black, before the wind restored the silver. She was smiling out loud.

I'm here!

The cliff path, though narrow, was not precarious and she felt some resentment that she had been deemed unable to tackle it at nine years of age. Down she walked, liking the way the earth was crumbly underfoot, making her steps into a dance of sorts, *The-questions-I-must-ask! The-questions-I-must-ask!*

She wound her way downwards, allowing her eye to stray out to sea once her feet had found their ground. At the base of the cliff, there was no sand, no sea, just a broad, smooth flat swathe of land. And then nothing.

The Magic Beach! I'm here!

Sally contemplated the geography, or was it the geology? She was not sure.

Having just walked down the cliff, she was standing on the hundred-foot ancient raised beach, covered not by sand but by a downy, very fine grass. The edge of this beach formed the top of further cliffs, dropping this time to the true beach below which finally met the sea. She looked behind her and in front of her.

It's like a giant pair of steps!

Delighted with the find, she stood still with arms outstretched and welcomed the sea breeze which came in whispers and gusts but with no clue as to which would be next. The crisp air forced out oily tears which dried almost immediately on her cheeks. Her face felt tight but rosy, and despite the chill in the air, she felt warm and supple.

Sally spent a happy hour on the raised beach, going right to the edge to gaze way down, and then back to the base of the first cliffs to ogle upwards

It was as if she were caught between the two.

The sky was in layers; above the first cliff a buzzard circled and climbed, beneath the second cliff gulls swooped and skittered. Sally stood buffeted amidst it all. She imagined the air falling from the first cliffs, rising from the second and fusing just where she stood.

Feeling that she was invested with the very power of the wind itself, she spontaneously sprang a loop of cartwheels, four, five, six. Could she pirouette in her walking boots? Yes, she could. She wanted to travel through the air again so, after springing three pliant *jetés*, she returned to cartwheeling. Four, five, six to the left; three, four, five to the right; three, four, five towards the sea; four, five six, back to the base of the first cliffs. She then ran as fast as she could across the entire length of the beach, stumbling slightly as she went; a smile plastering itself, along with her hair, to her face. She cartwheeled back to her rucksack (eight, nine, ten, eleven) and sank to the soft earth, breathless and elated.

Curling up embryonically, she discovered that it was warm and windless lying so close to the earth. She could hear the wind but could not feel it and decided to tune into her heartbeat instead. It was easy to believe the land itself had a heart. The earth had a warmth of its own and, coupled with that of the hazy sun, Sally was extremely snug. Feeling suddenly sleepy, she struggled to keep her eyes alert and contemplated the merits of her thermos, hidden away as it was in her rucksack. But she had no need for tea and soon dozed off and dreamt of nothing at all.

Sally slept only a short while but was revived sufficiently to continue cartwheeling. This way she went, then that; nine, ten, eleven, twelve. Soon her hands were tingling and itchy and striated with the pattern of grass. Time to stop and walk on.

Strength! Truth! The-questions-I-must-ask. Strength! Truth! The-questions-I-must-ask!

Go on then! Ask away!

In a minute.

She really could not bear to leave the raised beach and would have been quite happy to cartwheel the hours away in between a nap or two. But the decision to walk on was made for her; to her horror there were other people approaching the Magic Beach.

What are they doing here? At this time!

It is 10.30.

So? What are they doing here? Gracious Good Lord, they're wearing skirts! This is my beach. Damn. Better find somewhere else unpolluted, *as it were.*

Sally continued on the trail and covered the land as swiftly as she could, catching her breath now and then as she went over her ankle or felt her knee give way. The views were so compelling that her eyes were often seduced away from the path she was tracing until a stumble restored her concentration. Descending to the true beach, she gazed in wonder at the rock stacks and natural arches carved by the sea into the strangest of shapes. She was constantly aware of the changing formation of the Treshnish Isles, six small islands of intriguing silhouette. Now they formed a perfect line astern and she thought of them as a flotilla, sailing and sailing, yet never sailing away. She scrambled about for the Whisky Cave and found it, cleverly hidden behind a large grassy mound.

Grass on the real beach – and a grass beach that's not the real beach? Wonderful!

Although she poked her head into the cave, she ventured no further – caves were not her thing and she had no desire to vanquish such fears now. Instead, she dawdled along the water's edge and picked a selection of pebbles that begged her to do so. All the while she kept her eyes and ears peeled for wildlife. Apart from the gulls and cormorants, she was alone.

Sally decided that she would make a detour back up the cliff to a deserted village described in the book. Angus's tales of the Highland clearances had long struck a chord in her conscience and she wanted to pay homage to such a village, to Angus. After all, it would also afford her another visit to the Magic Beach.

*

Fate accompanied Sally on her upward grapple and dealt her a harsh blow.

The fall happened so quickly and yet in slow motion too. Her rucksack snagged, her foothold crumbled, her pockets full of pebbles unbalanced her, her ballet-weakened right knee gave way and she tumbled. She had not been on a very steep part of the cliff and she did not fall far, but she fell awkwardly and as she landed she heard a snap that she knew was not her thermos cracking. She needed no doctor to tell her she had broken her leg.

She sat very still while she tried to make sense of the situation. Her heart was racing too fast for her to grab any of the thoughts that were scurrying through her mind. She felt sick but she felt high and she did not feel any pain. She heard voices and wondered if they were in her head. No, they were too Scottish.

'Och, 'tis a very beautiful day, hey?'

Of course! The beskirted walkers who dared interrupt her solitude on the Magic Beach.

'Aye, I'll say. Just look there at the islands! See the Dutchman's Cap? The High One? The Flat One?'

'And that's the Little Lump!'

There's a little lump down here who needs your help.

Shout, Sally.

I can't.

Try.

She can't.

Feeling sicker and not so high, Sally was resigned to the walkers passing her by. She had no voice with which to alert them and a hang of rock obscured her from their view. Snippets of their conversation were carried to her on the wind. One was called Mary. They were talking about shags but Sally could not even manage a smile at her Freudian reinterpretation. The voices were becoming softer and she caught only drifts. They were walking away.

Please let them come back. Even if it's not for a few hours.

But, Sally, is it not a circular walk?

Fate will extend a gentle hand but Sally does not know that yet. Straining her ears and closing her eyes to assist, now only the faintest of voices reach her.

'I say we walk just over the next brow, Isla, and then have a nice cuppa.'

Sally thought perhaps she should have a cuppa too. Trying to locate her rucksack, she caught sight of her leg. It was all wrong; twisted anticlockwise with her foot pointing to her body. Whether it was the sight of her leg, or the effort of turning her head to find her rucksack Sally was unsure; whichever it was, she felt very unwell and was slowly and painfully sick.

God, where am I? How long have I been asleep? The walkers, the skirts, have they come and gone? Oh God, I've been sick. I want to move. Can I move? Let me try. Christ, my leg! I can't move. I can, I can. I'll pull myself away; away from the mess. I'll drag myself over to that clearing. Come on, Sal, come on, girl. You can do it. I can do it. I have to.

The pain was almost overwhelming but the need to be found, to be rescued, was stronger. It took forty minutes to haul her broken body less than twenty yards to a low, bunker-like clearing; the scar of a small land slip.

Sally was a good girl, a sensible girl, and though she did not really feel like it, she sipped at the tea which tasted nostalgically plasticky.

When was the last time I used a thermos? Was it the trip to the Zoo? I think it was. Richard and the penguins, how could I ever forget? That darling key-ring he bought me – that I threw away when he told me he loved me. What I'd do for it now. What I'd do for it now.

Every time she moved, be it a fraction of an inch, a sharp stab of pain ran through her body. It seemed that breaking a bone of one limb had taken its toll on her whole body. The leg itself felt simultaneously heavy yet not there at all. The base of her neck and the small of her back seemed to ache the most, though thankfully the sickness had gone. She was perspiring yet she was cold. Tears threatened as she took stock of her recent run of medical dramas. It really did seem most unfair.

In a mess. Focus your mind. Focus it.

On what? One, two, three, four, five, six Treshnish Isles. The Dutchman's Cap? I suppose it does look like one. But I want to be on the walk. The guide says I can view the islands in a line abreast later on.

The realization hit Sally: she would be going nowhere and, unless she was found, she would be staying put for goodness knows how long.

'If that is the case,' she reasoned out loud, partly to keep the tears at bay, 'I'd better keep calm, concentrate on being warm, concentrate the pain away. Just concentrate.'

Time to start, Sal.

I know.

See the young woman, propped up awkwardly on her elbow, her head resting on her shoulder, one leg stretched out, the other twisted as it should not be. See how she is looking out, way over the cliffs, seawards. She is looking far beyond the sea, beyond the horizon even. Nothing in particular meets her gaze and yet she sees everything. The panorama is exclusively hers for it does not really exist. It is not the Isle of Mull which captures her gaze for, though her eyes are directed ahead, they see only within.

The breeze and the purity of the sea air clear the tangle of her thoughts.

If she were not here, she would not be able to see, and yet it is not 'here' that she sees at all.

Mull itself does not hold the key to unlock her door nor

does she hold the key herself. The key is in her lap – dropped there by the situation.

Sally is truly alone and for the first time in her life, lonely too.

She is in pain, she is frightened. She is sitting, disabled and vulnerable, in a landscape that is at once beautiful and mean, majestic and cruel, seemingly hospitable yet wholly unforgiving.

She sits askew, asking questions and answering them too.

Why did I come to Mull? Was it really to recuperate from the chicken pox? Was it really to have some 'thinking' time?

No, it was neither. I came to Mull to continue my adventure. I came here so that I could leave with no explanation; I left with no explanation to see the effect it would have. On Richard, of course.

And yet how could I monitor that effect if I am here and have made no contact?

How do I really think he would have reacted?

I wanted him to contemplate my actions and think, 'Wow, the woman is certainly an enigma and has me bound by her spell. Oh, Sally, Sal, come back to me.'

In truth, I think he was probably immensely hurt and subsequently very angry too. Justifiably so. I must remedy that. I must abate his anger with an apology and I must soothe his hurt with honesty.

And yet if I restore him, his feelings for me to how they were, then what? And why? Do I want him to regard me as he did? Do I want to undo the knot I have pulled tight?

I was, as Aunt Celia said, a stupid, immature girl playing a heartless game with the goodness of my man's soul.

There's my answer.

He is my man.

Will he still want to be? If I can help it, yes. I hope that I will not live to regret my appalling actions of late. I am here in Scotland, lost and yet found, but Richard – so far away and for so long – does not yet know. All may be in vain indeed.

So, am I ready? To share? To compromise? What will I gain and what will I lose? I will lose my name. But I don't have to.

I will lose my flat – but I will gain a new home.

I will forsake my independence – yet Richard has made me feel stronger and more liberated than ever I felt when alone.

My late-night last thoughts – who says they have to be given up?

Talking to my plants, my things? But Richard loves me for that. Who says a Mrs Stonehill can't gaze at nothing in particular like a Miss Lomax can? Really, there is little that I will lose, much that will change, and so much more to be gained.

Why did it take me so long to see? Did I have to break my leg to break my block? Who set this block anyway?

Jackie bloody Collins, that's who, J Bloody C indeed. Erica Jong – it's her fault too. Xaviera Hollander, she has to answer for this.

No.

You ladies are in the clear. My apologies to you all.

The person at fault was the Sally Lomax who never was.

'Mary, what's that?'

'Gracious! It's the cartwheel girl.'

Through a haze of semi-consciousness, Sally saw disembodied tartan skirts run into and out of her view. Then she saw nothing.

It was time to open her eyes again and, as she did so, two pairs of tan leather, sensible lace-up shoes with hefty crêpe soles came into focus. She forced her glance upwards, over two pairs of sturdy ankles, up two sets of well-stockinged calves to the tartan skirts. One she recognized as McKenzie, the other she knew to be classic Black Watch. Her eyes travelled on and arrived at two good, weather-beating anoraks. Both were zipped against the wind, one enclosing a wiry figure, the other a more portly frame. Sally completed her tour, alighting on the faces that belonged to the skirts which had been at the back of her mind since she fell. Glinting eyes, kindly smiles and worried brows met her gaze benevolently.

'My dear lassie, look at you! Hush, hush, fear not, all is well. My name is Mary McKenzie,' spoke the wiry one in the predictable kilt.

'Poor duck, what happened?' cooed the portly one in Black Watch who Sally deduced to be Isla. 'We were admiring your cartwheels earlier and now you're all fall doon. How did it happen? Can you talk?'

With all her might, Sally spoke, choosing the most salient information, knowing she could not manage much. The two ladies crouched down beside her; Isla took her hand, Mary stroked her forehead.

'My name is Sally Lomax. I am twenty-five. I think I have broken my leg. I have had chicken pox but I am not contagious. Celia Lomax is my aunt. I'm sorry to spoil your walk.'

'Celia! Well, *we* know Celia very well and have heard her speak of you often – you are the one she says all her hopes are invested in! Isla, I'll nip back, you stay here with Sal and keep her comfy.'

Without further ado, Mary was off, heading for Sally's beloved Magic Beach, heading for help.

'We'd better prepare ourselves for an hour or so,' said Isla kindly, plumping herself down on the grass next to Sally. 'Would you care for some tea? I have some in my thermos.' Sally shook her head and murmured, 'I had some too, in my thermos. I've been sick.'

'Well!' announced Isla, and it sounded like 'wheel' in her tender, jovial voice, 'I have just the medicine for you, my lass!' From her anorak pocket, she pulled a small, pewter flask. 'Ten-year malt!' she confided triumphantly.

'No, thanks,' said Sally meekly.

'Come, come. 'Tis not an offer, 'tis an order! It'll do ye good. Just try – for Celia.' Sally did as she was told and, after a dicey moment when she felt the liquor burning its way to her stomach, it worked wonders and she felt stronger.

'There!' declared Isla. 'More?'

'Please!'

'Have as much as you like. In fact, finish it off.'

'I'm not contagious.'

'That's not the point at all.' Isla laughed. 'Mary and I have had a fair few swigs – we don't want folk to think we're drunk!'

Sally sipped the whisky slowly, gazing at the Treshnish Isles which seemed darker and more distant. She asked what was the time and was surprised to hear that it was nearing four o'clock.

'I thought perhaps you had done the circular walk and would not find me. You see, I saw you this morning – while I was cartwheeling. I wanted the Magic Beach to myself. Later, when I fell, I could hear you and Mary talking about shags and the brow of the hill and having a cuppa. But I couldn't call for you, my voice broke down with my leg. I was over there,' Sally pointed precisely, 'on a ledge. I hauled myself here because I thought I'd be safer, more visible. I prayed that you'd come back. And I assessed my life while I waited.'

'Gracious!' exclaimed Isla. 'Thank heavens we came back, hey! Mind you, we always walk A,B,A, here. Never A,A.' Sally looked puzzled. Isla clarified: 'No point doing a circular walk at Treshnish – who cares for miles of bracken and the silly old road when you can have all this twice!' She waved expansively. 'Did you call it the Magic Beach?' she asked. Sally nodded. 'May I ask why?' Sally nodded again and answered.

'Because my Uncle Angus and my dad said it was so. I wasn't allowed to come as a kid. I had to wait till now to find it. It is so magical, isn't it?'

'I'll say "aye" to that. Is that why you were cartwheeling?'

'Yes, I think it must have been.'

They sat quietly, Sally trying hard to be polite and cheery and to keep her mind from straying to the pain now focused in her leg. She looked at Isla and thought her plump, glowing face very pretty indeed. Isla returned her gaze and smiled.

'Cartwheeling and assessing life, hey! Well, you could find no better place to do either.'

The whisky had lubricated Sally well and she replied with gusto.

'The cartwheeling came first. Although I had come to walk by myself, to think a few things over. I had questions to ask and answers to find.'

Isla nodded and cocked her head. Sally continued.

'I've never broken anything before although I had my nose broken for me. And, if truth be told, I've gone and broken someone's heart.'

Isla tutted sympathetically and Sally was compelled to elaborate – for her own sake as much as for her companion's.

'While I was waiting here, I suddenly saw my mistakes so clearly. Yet I didn't flinch from them; I believe I really confronted them. You see, there is a man whom I love as I have never loved another and yet I have never told him so. In fact, I have spurned him.'

'And now you want to set things right, to ensure the happy ending?' interjected Isla. Sally nodded.

'I'm so impatient to do just that – but I'm stuck here with a broken leg. Do you think it might be too late?' she asked timidly.

'Och, no! If he is a good man, and if he is worth loving,

with all that you are, he will understand, I'm sure. Mine did.'

Sally laid her head in Isla's lap and closed her eyes, listening intently to Isla's story and hoping that history might repeat itself.

THIRTY-EIGHT

'Morning, Mr Stonehill.'

'Morning, Sandra. Please call me Richard. You make me feel so old, "Mistering" me!'

Mary winked at Sandra who blushed vigorously.

'What time are Ben Shaw's lot coming in?'

'Ten o'clock, Richard.'

'Right ho! Hold all calls until then, could you?'

'Course I can, Richard.'

'I'm sorry, Mr Stonehill is in a meeting. Could I take a message? Celia Lomax, 016884 156. Lovely, I'll ask him to call you as soon as he's free. 'Bye-bye.

'Who's Celia Lomax, Mary?'

'Never heard her.'

'Richard did say hold all his calls, didn't he?'

'Richard did, Sandra. Oh, it looks like his ten o'clock has arrived. Hello, gentlemen, Mr Stonehill is expecting you. This way, please.'

'I'm telling you Sandra, that assistant of Ben Shaw's couldn't take his eyes off you!'

'Leave it out!'

'I'm *telling* you!'

'Nah!'

'Yeah!'

'Really?'

'Sure!'

'He *was* pretty gorgeous! Do you know his name? It just says "et al" here!'

'Just one moment, I'll see if he's available, please hold the line . . . Damn! It's that Cecily Lomax – from this morning. I forgot to pass her message to Richard.'

'You did have a lot on your mind!'

'Can you believe he asked me out? I think Mr Shaw even gave me an approving wink. Martin Blakely . . . I've never been out with a Martin. Oh, Mary, what do you think? Sandra Blakely, Mrs S. Blakely – has a ring to it!'

'Sand*ra*! The phone! Buzz Richard, for heaven's sake.'

'Richard, there's a call for you on line one. A Cynthia Lomax.'

'Hello?'

'Richard Stonehill?'

'Aunt Celia?'

Celia filled Richard in on the bare bones of Sally's fall; she knew he was a busy man and did not want to swamp him with the minutiae. Richard, however, wanted to be deluged so Celia told him all she had gleaned from the doctor, from Isla and Mary, and from Sally herself.

'Could I speak to her?'

'I've put her to bed. In fact, I've had to rummage through her address book to find your phone number. I presumed that the "R" contained within the heart was you!' Richard laughed and wanted to weep.

'What can I do for you, Mrs Lomax?'

'Celia, please. Well, Sally was going to head home at the weekend but of course she cannot now drive. I wondered perhaps if you would fetch her? Maybe you would like to make a weekend of it?'

Richard thought for a moment.

'Does she know?'

Celia thought for a moment.

'No.'

Richard was silent. She spoke again.

'I do know that she has done a fair bit of thinking, and that she is not very proud of the way she has behaved. But I can see the impact you have had on my girl, and if at my old age I can assist in a bit of enforced match-making, then I'll jolly well do so!' Richard swallowed hard as a sudden burst of sunlight streamed through and struck his face.

'What's tomorrow? Friday, Friday . . .' He thought aloud. 'I may as well take the sleeper tonight. So, Aunt Celia, we'll meet at long last tomorrow morning. No, no, please . . . I'll take a cab from the ferry. Thank you so much for calling. For understanding.'

'Richard,' Celia faltered, anxious to hold him a moment longer, 'you sound – well – as lovely as you sounded.'

Richard regarded the replaced handset and then asked Sandra to book a one-way ticket to Oban. For once, Sandra did not mind that he gave no explanation. In fact, she was not remotely interested.

'Hi, Di!'

'Hullo, Stonehill!'

'I'm off to bonny Scotland.'

'Sally! When did she call? What did she have to say for herself?'

'Actually, it was the venerable Aunt Celia who called. The girl's gone and broken her leg in two places while soul-searching in the heather.'

'Serves her bloody well right!'

'She doesn't know that Celia called me. She doesn't know that I'm going up.'

'Ha! Serves her even more bloody well right!'

'Any messages?'

'Tell her she's a stupid old cow and I hate her. Tell her I'll break her other leg when I see her.'

'Right ho.'

'Oh, and Richard?'

'Yes?'

'Send her my love. All of it.'

Richard packed a small bag with a host of emotions crammed into his head. He had been so relieved to have had the contact, albeit indirect, with Sally. Yet he felt somewhat peeved that once again he was at her beck and call. And yet Celia's lovely voice, her words, had created a hope he had not felt for a long while. Though he was concerned to hear of Sally's new plight, a part of him was really rather satisfied.

'After all,' he mused to his toothbrush as he packed it, 'there is no come-uppance more severe than that dished out by oneself.'

Catherine had clapped for joy on hearing the news. 'See, Richard,' she had said, 'the time is coming. One way or the other; for better, for worse. It's what you need. Whatever happens, it will be for the best. And we love you lots.'

Richard was simultaneously excited and yet filled with dread; he brimmed with sympathy yet boiled with anger. Only the one emotion lay intact, and that was his love for Sally. It was unconditional and that irritated him supremely.

The journey passed without mishap. He had a surprisingly good sleep and an even more surprisingly good British Rail breakfast. Catching the Oban train at Glasgow, he felt relaxed and fresh and sat back to enjoy the immense scenery of the West Coast. With time to kill in Oban, he browsed through the town and visited the porcelain factory, buying a small seal for Celia, and a penguin for Sally.

If she's lucky.

As the CalMac took him across the water, he hummed 'Speed Bonny Boat' and made up his own verses replacing *'Skye'* with *'Mull'* and *'carry the Lad who's born to be King'* with *'give me the girl who's born to be mine'.*

Richard, who had never had sea legs, silently thanked the boat as he left it at Craignure. Filling his lungs with the salt-tinged air, he was swept with a sense of well-being and a feeling that his trip was indeed positive. As he turned to find a taxi, a figure amongst the busying throng caught his eye. Instinctively, he knew she was Aunt Celia and by the smile on her face, she'd recognized him too. She lifted her hand and he responded, sauntering over to her. They contemplated each other quietly for a moment or two before he tipped his head and kissed her cheek, saying it was his true pleasure. Celia said she was delighted.

As they strolled to her car they scanned each other's faces, for here in the flesh, at long last, was the other about whom so much was known already. Both felt immediately at ease in each other's company and both felt a certain sense of relief that their expectations had been met.

This is Sally's aunt.

This is Sally's man.

Waves of approval accompanied their conversation about vernacular architecture, whisky without an 'e', and Sally.

'She hadn't even woken when I set off. And her morning bath now takes her a long time. Of course, she won't have me help. But hearing her thumping and thudding, wincing and cursing – I tell you, it is all I can do to stop myself from rushing in to bathe the bairn myself!'

Privately, Richard thought how long it had been since he had bathed her.

Not since last year.

From the corner of her eye, Celia observed him looking far out of the window, scanning the landscape and smiling widely at the lochs and hills. She sensed he was itching for news of Sally but could see he was too well-mannered to pry. Feeling it was her duty and debt to Angus and Robbie, she broke the proverbial ice for him.

'I'll think you'll find that breaking her leg is a blessing of sorts.'

Richard looked puzzled but his eyes implored her to elaborate so she did. 'We had words the night before, you see. When I discovered she was here *illicitly*, so to speak, I gave her my mind. I suggested a good, long walk and a long look within. She set off at dawn the next day. Well, she didn't make the long walk but sitting alone in the open with a broken leg afforded her plenty of time for reflection – and plenty of space, in every sense of the word!' Celia laughed.

'Has she come to any conclusions?' Richard broached delicately. Celia felt that a kindly wink would suffice. Feeling bolstered, he decided to leave it there and judge for himself on seeing her.

'She's a funny old thing,' he mused, 'never known anyone quite like her.'

'I'll say "aye" to that,' agreed Celia. 'She says you've been together since the autumn?'

'Mmm. It was quite fortuitous that we met – it was a party that I decided to go to only at the last minute. And there she was.'

'There she was,' echoed Celia with a distant look in her eyes.

'She had this magnetism – I couldn't quite put my finger on what it was specifically. Still can't! I mean, our Sal's a pretty girl and has a nice figure but not really, well, eye-catching. I think it's the whole package. There's so much to her, like a huge box of treats – each time you dip in, you find something new.'

Celia laughed. 'Well, the lass certainly has a treat in store today. Are you ready?'

Richard clapped his hands together and whispered, 'I've been ready for quite some time.'

When they arrived at the cottage, the kitchen was empty with Sally's breakfast things still laid. Celia motioned Richard to sit down and mouthed, 'Tea?' Feeling quite nervous now, he shook his head and flicked through a copy of *Rob Roy* distractedly. From upstairs drifted Sally's dulcet tones singing Simon and Garfunkel most melodiously, totally unaware of the surprise awaiting her. Relaxed now, Celia and Richard giggled together and settled in at the kitchen table, nibbling digestive biscuits with half an ear on the staircase.

Sally began her clumping descent, singing 'Bridge Over Troubled Water' to steady herself.

'Aunty Cee? Crikey, I'm pooped!' she called from halfway down the stairs. 'Is the kettle on? I'll certainly need reviving, it seems to be getting harder and more tiring each day!'

'Just boiled!' Celia encouraged. Richard forced his eyes away from the door and fixed them to the spine of *Rob Roy* instead. His stomach churned with adrenalin, his palms were clammy and his mouth was dry.

Clonk, clump, here she comes.

'Mor – ' she cried, shunting open the door with a crutch, '– ning!' she croaked, flabbergasted and rooted to the spot, eyes enormous, mouth gaping.

'Morning, Sally,' Richard replied, in a voice that gave nothing away.

Sally was speechless, Celia was silent, Richard was defiant. Eventually, Sally remembered to close her mouth. She shut her eyes and opened them again, shaking her head to ensure she was not dreaming. He was still there.

'Richard?' she mouthed, aghast.

He nodded his reply, still holding on to *Rob Roy* for moral support.

'I, er, better check on the, um, daffs!' stumbled Celia as she backed away, tactfully if noisily, into the garden.

Richard took in all he saw. There she was, that wretched girl who'd played havoc with his heart, hair still spiky in the one patch, face still spotty but neater now. She was standing before him, a vision on crutches, swamped in a dirndl skirt of Celia's for she had brought only trousers, not having expected a plaster cast to hinder their wear during her stay.

He noticed how her eyes glinted and her face had a fresh bloom. He observed her wrists and saw how the tendons and veins were visible from the strain of the crutches. Her good leg was coddled in a thick sock, the broken one was obliterated by a very large, very white plaster cast – only the tips of her toes were visible and they were slightly blue.

Their eyes were fixed to one another. Quietly, he walked over to her and took away her left crutch, propping it against the door frame. Holding her left hand firmly, he took the right crutch away too and, holding that hand, steadied her. He cocked his head and looked at her; she gazed back, open and ready.

'Hey, Richie,' she said meekly.

Their embrace, after so long, too long apart, contained neither passion nor desire. It was infused wholly with tenderness, and they stood still, locked and close in each other's arms. Richard rested his face against the top of her head, Sally buried hers deep into his chest, lost in his heartbeat.

Celia found them thus when she ventured back from the garden, her arms laden with daffodils. These she promptly thrust between them while hastily brushing a tear from her eye as if it was not there at all.

THIRTY-NINE

Richard eased a sock over Sally's plaster cast.

'Richard,' she said softly, 'I cannot believe you're here.'

'I can,' he replied.

Taking her arm over his shoulder, he helped her hobble out to the Mini. Celia waved expansively from the doorstep. 'Have fun, my lovelies. Looks like the day will be fine.'

True, thought Sally.

I hope so, thought Richard.

Fine indeed, thought Celia. Watching them drive away, she turned back to her cottage and chatted to the photograph of Robbie and Angus.

I'm sure all will be fine. When two inherently good people come together, there is so much room for happiness and unity. Our Sal may have been a silly girl but she's worked very hard to redeem herself and though I feel she is restored to me, all that's left for her is to do the same to Richard. Now, there's a man who breathes courage and maturity. It can't have been easy for him, this journey into unknown territory of every kind, but he is here and I love him. I see you in him, my Angus. And

Robbie, you're living on in your daughter – she is so very full a person. I do believe a happy ending may be in sight.

'So, which way now, Sal?' Richard asks, looking as settled behind the wheel of her Mini as he does behind that of his Alfa Romeo.

'Which way now, Richie?' smiles Sally, ridiculously pleased that she's Sal once again. 'Why, forward, forward, forward!'

They take the coast road and tootle along at a relaxed pace to take full advantage of the magnificent views. At Loch na Keal, they stop but the rain starts, soon to swallow the view. Sally tries not to take this to heart. As the engine dies away, she takes a deep breath and holds it.

I've got to do it. I must tell him now. Say 'sorry'. Tell him 'yes'.

Do it, Sal.

In a minute, but I can't hold my breath any longer.

'My, that's a big sigh,' teases Richard. Sally looks shyly at her hands.

Why is he here? Did he want to come? Did Aunt Celia ask him to, to taxi me back to Highgate?

'Richard,' she asks, making a tangential start, 'did you ever read Rudyard Kipling?'

'Avidly,' he replies, batting not an eyelid at her incongruous enquiry.

'*The Just-So-Stories*?' she furthers.

'Cover to cover,' he declares. They sit in silence which is neither awkward nor heavy. Frowning a little, Sally ventures her hand to his.

'Do you remember the Leopard?' she says softly, her eyes downcast.

''Course I do,' he replies.

What is the girl getting at? Is this some big build-up to a let-down? Is she still toying with my emotions?

'It was one of my favourite stories, as a child. My dad

and Uncle Angus used to read it to me over and over. We'd chat about it afterwards, reasoning away – I can only have been eight or nine.'

Richard nods as she curls her fingers around his. He tips his head and his eyes say, Go on, Sal, go on.

Come on, Sal, come on. It's time.

Yes, it's time.

'Remember how the story starts, how the leopard has no spots and how the stripy zebra and patchy giraffe have one up on him?' Richard's nod encourages her to continue. 'Well, I suppose I felt a little like the naked leopard. You know, somewhat powerless in the face of Mother, of Jamie.' She looks at Richard with large open eyes. 'When you came along, I decided I'd create my *own* spots – moreover, that I'd be a spotless vixen rather than a leopard!' She laughs sadly. 'But I should've known.' Her voice trails away. 'We all have our spots, it's just that sometimes we can't see them.' They sit quietly and watch the light rain drizzle disjointed snakes down the windscreen.

'What I am saying is, spots have been my downfall and my salvation.'

She sees that Richard looks just a fraction confused and can feel him working hard to keep abreast of her drift.

Quick, quick! Restore him.

She looks him boldly in the eye. 'You see Richie, I thought I had none, so I painted some myself and I wore them with aplomb. Or so I thought. And then, of course, I woke to find myself covered by others uninvited.' Richard's eyebrows twitch and cross.

'Chicken?' hints Sally, gesturing at her face.

'Ah ha!' Richard says triumphantly. She nods and beams at him.

'You see, these awful itchy spots proved to me how superficial my painted ones were. I have realized that beneath them both – the chicken and the painted – are my true spots; those I was born with, those I had spurned, those that define me as, well, Me.'

Clasping Richard's hand with both of hers, she summons her will and confides: 'A leopard can't change her spots, we all know that, yet I tried to change mine. I wanted to obscure them from view beneath a veil of contrived subterfuge. But now, I should like to show you them. If you would like? If I may?'

They gaze out over the loch. The rain has caused an eerie vapour to whisper along its surface and the hills are shrouded by the mist. Richard turns slowly towards her and summons her eyes away from the water. She raises them to meet his. She is crystal clear.

'Sal,' he starts with an affectionate tap to her nose, 'at first, I was utterly blinded by your so-called painted spots. But, if truth be told, it didn't take long before I was utterly blind *to* them and could see way beneath them – that veil was pretty transparent and what was beneath was infinitely more beautiful.' He pauses. Her gaze has been unflinching and he is heartened.

'Remember how, once the leopard was accustomed to his spots, his life was good?'

Sally nods, a little forlornly. Richard takes his time, treading carefully, rather enjoying it.

'Well then!' he declares.

'Well *what*?' she worries, scouring his face.

Richard lets it lie for a moment.

And why not, Richard? The girl's led you a merry dance.

'Well then,' he says with a big grin, 'spots and all, you'll do for me!'

If Sally could have said 'sorry' in all the languages of the world, she would have done so, again and again.

Richard settled for just the one which was delivered with conviction and honesty before she kissed him.

'I'll never do it again, Best Beloved. I am quite content as I am.'

Richard returned Sally to Celia a different woman. Only her leg was broken, her spirit was whole again. While Sally slept in the next room by the fire, he declared Celia had restored his girl to him and thanked her. Celia was quite taken aback.

'It wasn't me, but you!' she gasped.

Richard shook his head gravely. 'If she hadn't come here, if you hadn't scolded her, if she hadn't walked and broken her leg, we would still be at an impasse.'

Celia refused to agree and they stood deadlocked, both too well-mannered to take any personal credit for Sally's salvation. Both felt indebted to the impact the other had on Sally. And yet both had been integral to her redemption: Celia with her directness, Richard his tact; both for their strength, support and patience.

'Let us put it down to this old isle, hey? Mull has treated Sally well – in breaking her leg, it has repaired her soul,' Celia concluded.

'I raise my glass to the Isle of Mull!' proclaimed Richard.

Celia turned to the Aga, hiding a private smile from him.

Taking a glass of whisky to the living-room, they padded around Sally. Swathed in dirndl and enveloped in an old Aran knit of Angus's, she was snuggled deep into the sofa. Her lips were slightly parted and her cheeks were rosy; one hand rested under her chin, the other was pressed between her knees. She was fast asleep, as much a part of the fabric of the sofa as the woollen shawls and hillocks of cushions. Richard and Celia sat down in the armchairs either side of the fire and sipped contemplatively. Every now and then they looked to the sleeping almost-beauty, but before long, the warmth and glow of the embers seduced them away and held them captive. Indeed, only a particularly loud crackle from a spliced branch roused them some time later and they saw it was now quite dark outside.

Still Sally slept.

On the occasional table at Richard's side teetered a pile of books. He browsed over their spines, smiled at *The Just-So Stories* but forsook Kipling, Hardy and Scott, for Burns. Celia beamed at his choice.

Closing his eyes, he caressed its worn leather cover and traced his finger over the embossed lettering. Taking the volume to his nose he breathed deeply, savouring the evocative aroma of well-thumbed pages. He laid the book in his lap, closed. Looking first at Sally, he then regarded Celia and grinned:

To see her is to love her,
And love but her forever;
For nature made her what she is,
And never made anither!

Celia clapped her hands and clasped them to her heart, exclaiming, 'A Burns boy! What joy!'

Sally woke, bleary-eyed and blotched, mumbling, 'Huh? Hey? What?'

Richard merely shrugged his shoulders at her while directing a conniving wink at Celia.

It is time for Richard and Sally to head home. Into the proverbial sunset? Would you really have wanted it any other way?

Celia will miss them both enormously but sends them on their way with a tin of home-made shortbread and a silent wish.

Sally and Richard receive it unconsciously and bid her farewell with a firm promise to return in the summer. Sally feels quite tearful to be going but both Richard and

Celia remind her that it is Sunday and there is school tomorrow. She senses she is leaving Mull to embark on the rest of her life and feels a little timid. But Mull will stay as it is, hugging the coastline of western Scotland, its treasures guaranteed. It is time for Sally to take home all she has discovered there. She knows now that mundanity and romance can happily co-exist but to put it into practice she must return home, to Highgate and school and the patch of rising damp in the bathroom.

With a chorus of parps and their hands reaching high out of the windows, Richard and Sal tootle away from the cottage and Celia soon becomes just another vague shape in the rear-view mirror.

Part of the heather, part of the cottage. Part of the land, thinks Sally.

They take a worthwhile detour to Glencoe and then follow the road to the Grampian mountains.

'It's going too quickly!' Sally rues when the shores of Loch Lomond arrive so soon after Crianlarich.

'Want to stop?' asks Richard.

'Would you mind?'

Richard parks as near to the shore as he can and helps Sally hobble to the water's edge. In she dips her hand and waits until her joints ache. She holds her fingers aloft and sees how the hazy sun is caught in the droplets the moment before they fall. Richard allows her the ritual, the space, but she gives him her wet hand and touches his lips so that they glisten.

They are now but a mile or two further down the road because the promise of a warming Scotch at a pretty pub was too hard to resist. The room is quite empty, wonderfully cosy but bright. They sip away beside the fire.

'Anything else I can get you people?' asks the landlord.

Richard and Sally shake their heads with a smile. The landlord excuses himself. Richard and Sally chat away happily. He asks her if she feels ready for school. Yes, she says, she does. She asks him if they will make it home in time for an early night. Oh, yes, he assures her, they will. Briefly excusing her actions, Sally reaches over to a neighbouring table for a clean knife. She pokes it down the side of her plaster cast and her eyes close in bliss at the sudden coolness of the steel.

'Gracious, Sal,' says Richard, 'it's quite bare!'

They regard the pristine plaster of Paris, mostly smooth but dented a little, here and there. 'We can't have that!' he cries as he searches his jacket pockets for a pen. 'Damn!' he says.

'Hold on, I may have one,' says Sally as she rummages through her bag. 'Damm,' she says.

Richard goes over to the bar, but despite his strong 'Hello?' there is no sign of the landlord. Undeterred, he leans right over in his quest until his feet are quite off the ground. Sally giggles behind her hand. With a glance to his left and to his right, he nips under the counter and searches furtively among the pint pots and peanuts.

'Aha!' he exclaims, holding his trophy aloft. 'It won't be an oil painting,' he explains, brandishing a very thick marker pen, 'but it'll do.'

Here is Richard, sitting on a stool opposite Sally. He lifts her leg on to his lap and looks at her face which glows and glints. He thinks her quite perfect. Pen poised, he ponders awhile.

Sally waits.

Richard is ready.

He writes.

Two words. Thick black. Permanent marker. Permanent.

WILL YOU?

As she looks at the shape of the letters which she read

in an instant but has now forgotten, she sees a cine film of her life flash across the white screen of her plaster cast. Childhood, youth, adolescence, young womanhood, now. Here she is and the present tells her all about her future. Here she is and she twists her head this way and that, reading it from every angle though it was quite legible, as it was, upside down.

WILL YOU?

She looks at Richard gravely and eases her leg off his lap, unwittingly clonking his shin but he neither winces nor does she even notice. Leaning forward, she puts her hand on his face. Her fingers lie on his cheek, her thumb rests over the dimple in his chin. His day-old stubble feels rather nice under her skin, like a coarse velvet. There is no need to clear her throat for it is as clear as her mind and as strong as her soul.

'Oh, yes,' she says, 'I will.'

FORTY

'She's back! She's back.'

'Have you seen her?'

'She's broken her *leg*!'

'Wow! Is it in plaster?'

'Of course, stupid.'

'Has she got crutches?'

'Yup.'

'Poor old Miss Lomax.'

'Yeah, but at least she's back.'

'Too right! No more killer lessons with that Mrs Westford.'

'Dragon!'

'Broomstick rider!'

'Hurray for Miss Lomax!'

'Shush! She's coming!'

'Hullo, Class Five. It's lovely to see you all, at long last.'

'Not half as nice as it is for us to see you!'

'Oh, Marcus, what are you after? Late with your homework?'

Snigger, chuckle. She's back.

Miss Lomax launched into her lessons with gusto and

ease. The children were delighted to have her back again. She instigated a post-mortem of sorts and Marcus and Rajiv filled her in on the missing details of her fall.

'We were so worried,' frowned Marcus.

'Some of us even cried,' confided Alice.

'I had to summon the ambulance,' Rajiv informed her.

Miss Lomax thanked each member of her class and answered their probing questions about chicken pox and breaking a leg.

'I mean, did you actually hear it go *snap*?' gawped Marsha who had chicken pox last summer but had never broken a bone.

'Oh, yes!'

Thirty gasps of approval filled the room. 'Well,' Miss Lomax clarified, 'it wasn't so much a snap as a hollow crack. Very loud.'

The children went: 'Ooh!'

Miss Lomax told them how she waited and waited and was careful not to panic, to keep warm and to sip tea.

'Why the tea?' asked Marcus.

'I'm not really sure, because I wasn't thirsty. It just seemed a sensible thing to do – and I knew I had to keep my wits about me. Anyway, how often have you heard your mummies or grandmas say "have a nice cuppa tea" when you're upset?'

'How did they get the ambulance to you?' asked Rajiv with a head full of helicopters, mountain rescue teams and St Bernard dogs with brandy barrels on their collars.

'Two wonderful women happened to come across me, Mary and Isla – I'd seen them earlier in the day – walking in the wilds wearing skirts, I ask you! Well, Isla sat with me and Mary went for help. There was a farm nearby and a big, burly chap – rather like you Sam! – called Fraser drove a tractor and trailer as near as he could. He then gave me a fireman's lift over to it and they trundled me back to the farm on the back of the trailer. An ambulance picked me up from there and I was plastered up and back at my aunt's two hours later. Here, would you like to see my X-rays?'

What a question! The children could not leave their desks fast enough.

X-rays! A broken leg! Wow!

'Cor!' said Marcus.

'Blimey!' said Rajiv.

Miss Lomax held the X-rays up to the light and thirty pairs of eager eyes admired the spliced bone. Some were secretly quite envious and made sure that they fell as dramatically as they dared when playing football at break-time.

'Now, children, back to your seats. We really should do some work, for heaven's sake!'

They groaned and moaned and slouched back to their places.

Miss Lomax felt even less like doing any work than her class, so, with a furtive smile, she told them to close their books and take out their atlases instead.

'See, here's Mull.'

'But it looks tiny!'

'Well, it is, comparatively. But turn to page ninety-four.'

'It looks huge!'

'My aunt lives right – here! And this is where I broke my leg.'

'Why is everything called "nish"?' enquired Marcus, and the children pored over the map, finding as many as possible. Quinish. Fishnish. Mornish. Mishnish. Treshnish. Miss Lomax told them of the Magic Beach, only she called it the raised beach and the children were utterly rapt. They talked about the sea, the tides and time. Only the entrance of Miss Lewis crying, 'Sal! You're back!' brought them back down to Highgate again. Blimey! Break-time already! Twenty-nine children scampered out. Marcus hung back. Miss Lomax and Miss Lewis questioned him with their eyebrows.

'Miss Lomax,' ventured Marcus. Miss Lomax raised her eyebrows and cocked her head. 'It's just that – well do you think I could sign your plaster?'

Miss Lewis and Miss Lomax smiled.

''Course you can!' said his favourite teacher as she heaved herself on to her desk, stretching out her leg and raising her skirt to her knee. With his red felt pen held aloft, Marcus sucked his lower lip contemplatively.

Miss Lewis's mouth had dropped open.

'What's "*Will you?*" ' Marcus asked.

Miss Lomax smiled at him fondly and avoided catching Miss Lewis's bulging eyes.

'Why, Marcus,' she said, 'it means will-you-sign-my-plaster?'

* * *

'What's "*Will you?*" ' whispers Diana, desperate not to squeal.

'Why, Di,' Sally says, 'it means, will you forgive me for being such a thoughtless and ungrateful old trout!'

'What's "*Will you?*" ' threatens Diana, hands on hips.

Sally catches Diana's face in her hands and kisses her firmly on the lips.

'And I said yes!' she laughs.

FORTY-ONE

O181 348 6523.

Richard stretched out his wrist to check Cartier time. *She must be home by now, it's* Blue Peter.

He rang off and played Solitaire on the computer. Sandra popped her head around the door to enquire whether 'taking an early' would be all right.

'Of course. Away with you! Somewhere nice?'

Sandra really did not have the time – nor now the inclination – for a chat with Mr Stonehill so she said, 'Theatre. Yes. Really should go,' and offered a quick wave in farewell.

Good for Sandra. I think she had eyes for me once. Wasted!

0181 348 6523.

Richard mimicked the ringing tone and, with the receiver hooked under his chin, started another hand of Solitaire.

Come on! Where are you, girl! Oh, Christ. Diana – quick!

'Di?'

'Stonehill!'

'Where's Sally? Did you take her home? I can't seem to get a reply – I tried during *Newsround* and before and after *Blue Peter*. Dear God let things be fine? Di?' Diana cleared her throat.

'I dropped that Lomax woman back at her flat just in time for *Jackanory*.'

Richard's sigh of relief whistled down the phone line into Diana's room.

'You're right – I'm an old hen. I just worry, you know? After everything – after all.' He laughed. 'See you soon, Di. And thanks.'

'Don't you dare hang up, young man!' Her bellow hit Richard in the solar plexus and rendered him incapable of speech, let alone manoeuvres with telephone receivers. 'Richard? You there?'

'Here,' he answered in a small voice.

'Would you please,' said Diana, 'per-*lease*, explain the precise meaning of "*Will you*?" '

Richard's face broke out into a smile so infectious that Diana caught it at once. They sat in silence, grinning inanely for a moment or two.

'Whaddayathink!' Richard laughed.

0181 348 6523.

Last chance before I call the police.

Let it ring, Richard. Ring right through.

'Hello?'

'Sal?'

'Hey!'

'I've been ringing for ages – you had me worried.'

'So it *was* you, was it? Have you forgotton a small matter of an enormous, unwieldy plaster cast preventing swift access to phone – or anywhere else for that matter?'

'Oh, Sal, say "unwieldy" again.'

'Unwieldy.'

'God, I love it when you say "unwieldy".'

'Richie Stonehill, you've rung three times in half an

hour, haven't you? And I'm bashed and bruised because of it. I've knocked over a lamp, dropped a dictionary on my good leg, whacked my arm on the door and bashed my good ankle with my bloody plaster cast.'

'Bashed and bruised?'

'*All* over.'

'Kiss it better?'

'That,' said Sally, covering her joy with a douse of teacher's sternness, 'is the very least you can do, Stonehill.'

Sally hobbles across to her Lloyd-Loom and eases her leg on to the upturned wastepaper bin which she has taken to carrying around with her.

Let's see, I reckon about an hour. And then he'll be here. It seems so long since he was here, in my little flat, with me. When was the last time? Was it calamine night? Was it really then? I think it was.

It was indeed.

Seems a world away. My spots have practically gone now, apart from these faint ones on my arms. Shame about my hair, I know it'll grow but it's taking an age.

It's been less than a month, Sal. Since the faint, the pox and the fall.

Tell me Jean-Claude wasn't the last person I slept with?

Sorry.

But never again. Just Richie now.

If you say.

I say so because I now know so. Because it's all that I want. I think, actually, it's all that I've ever wanted. Gracious Good Lord, there! Out in the open. At last.

At last.

Richard thought of very little as he negotiated an infuriating belated rush hour. He listened to *The Archers* for the first time in his life and made a mental note to catch the omnibus on Sunday.

It's not bad!

Richard Stonehill!

Sally listens to it avidly.

Oh, well then!

He hummed the theme tune with gusto as he sat in traffic on Hampstead High Street.

Nearly there. At last. Nearly there. Poor Sal, bashed and bruised and all my fault. My God I feel horny. I wonder if we could?

She's no longer contagious.

But logistically – with that unwieldy plaster cast. Oh, God, just five more minutes and she can whisper 'unwieldy' to me!

Red light, Richard. You've gone through a red light.

The doorbell rings. Sally positioned herself nearby five minutes ago so that she can answer it as elegantly as possible without causing herself further injury.

I'll let it ring, though. Woman's prerogative and all that!

Richard dutifully rings it again. He flips up the letter-box lid. He can see one leg bare to the knee, the other incarcerated by the now much-grafittied plaster cast. He watches their careful procession towards him.

Sally opens the door and finds Richard crouched, looking up at her with those impossibly alluring eyes.

'That's what I like to see!' she coos. 'On your knees, boy!'

With a slight creak, he pulls himself upright and plants a kiss passionately, deep into her mouth.

'I think you'd better come in,' says Sally whose neck has reddened and whose voice is hoarse.

Richard's lust is momentarily subsumed by intense relief that he is at last back in her flat and that, finally, she is by his side. She is holding his hand, she is pulling him right into the room. Welcoming him back.

Stay. Stay.

I'm not going anywhere.

Neither am I.

'Tea?'

'Please!'

He gazes after her, his head faintly bobbing in sync with her hobble. A quick recce tells him that everything is in its place. Nothing has changed though everything has changed. He hears her singing softly, tra-la-la-ing as she coaxes the kettle to come to the boil. He cannot see her for she is tucked out of sight around the corner but he knows exactly what she is doing. She is singing the theme from *The Archers*, tweaking leaves off the poinsettia, her back turned away from the kettle so that it will come to the boil.

Tea for two. Sally hands Richard cup and saucer and perches herself on the edge of the settee in which he is so comfortably ensconced.

He looks so right.

This feels so comfortable.

Tea for two but not a drop passes their lips. Sally has hovered out her leg and rotates it slowly through 180 degrees. Simple physiotherapy really, but its effect is quite astounding.

'Do you like my plaster?'

'Most artistic!'

'But somewhat *unwieldy* . . .'

'Oh, Sal!'

Tea for two can wait. Richard lunges for Sally and pulls her on to his lap. A look of hunger etches its way across his face; slightly, ever so slightly, demented. She wants to giggle and to say something witty but the urgency of Richard's kissing distracts her at once. She lets her body melt and sinks herself deep into the crook of his arm. Her eyes are closed but she is wide open.

He can have me all. Every little bit of me. There's nothing to hide. It's all for him.

She kisses him hard and bites him squarely on the

lower lip. He drops his mouth to her chin and sucks it. And bites her sharply. She winces in delight and cradles his whole head between her outstretched hands. His breathing is fast and her heart is racing. His eyes are on line with her breasts so she gives a little heave or two which drive him wild. As he fondles and kisses them, he appears to be unaware of the Aran-knit jumper which hides them from view.

'Off,' Sally whispers. 'Take it off!'

They wriggle her free and pull at his shirt. It's toasty in the flat and the curtains are drawn. Sally looks in awe at his chest. She deems it spectacular and gazes on as if she is seeing it for the first time. And yet she knows it so well: she knows that if she places her hand just here, and strokes just there, his pulse will go into overdrive. She does both and Richard moans. He is wearing button-fly jeans but the strength of his erection makes unpopping them an easy task. In fact, the one in the middle has popped all by itself already. Sally looks triumphant, Richard looks glazed. He feasts his eyes on her pretty breasts and realizes he had forgotten just how alluring her nut-brown nipples are.

They have to be kissed. Eaten.

'Skirt,' says Sally huskily. 'Take it off!'

They pull it over her head not wishing to disturb their lower limbs, now so comfortably entwined. They press against each other, rub and twist into each other. They are getting hot and are now quite wet around their faces.

I want to taste her eyelashes again.

I want to lick his sideburns.

Give me your nose.

I'm going to chew your earlobe.

Richard is wriggling out of his jeans but Sally is keeping her thighs clamped around him.

Ten years of ballet had its uses, you know.

He forgot that he still had his shoes on. Laced neatly, of course. Socks from Dunhill. Of course. He has kicked his jeans down to his shins which is far enough for his purpose. Sally grabs at his legs and wriggles herself ecstatically over their muscular form.

My Rodin.

Hands travel everywhere, all over each other's bodies as well as over their own. Richard finds her hand inside her knickers and covers her fingers to discover what they're up to.

Let me try.

'Off,' gasps Sally, 'take them off.'

They discover that, in the height of passion, removing a pair of knickers is not as easy as it should be. Especially when a plaster cast is involved. The elastic wraps itself taut around Richard's hand and threatens to cut off the blood to his little finger.

'Off!' shrieks Sally. 'Rip 'em off. Like in the films! Quick!'

How do they do it? In the films? It doesn't work. In real life.

Sally's knickers are now at her knees but Richard is loath to stop kissing her and yet his right arm will not stretch to her ankles and beyond. Sally crooks her good knee up and between them they manage to wrestle the fabric free. It has, however, caught over the top edge of the plaster cast and pull as he does, Richard cannot budge it. Sally has arms clamped about his neck and refuses to let go.

Never, never again.

She is chanting: 'Off! Off! Off!' With an almighty tug, the fabric tears free and Sally's plaster cast springs across and thwacks Richard on the funny bone.

'It's not funny!' he hollers.

'Yes it is!' laughs Sally, tears streaming and breasts wobbling.

Richard concedes that it is exceptionally funny and they collapse into each other, shaking and giggling. Sharing the mirth and the moment.

'May I say,' Richard starts, most politely, 'that this settee is giving me backache, that these cushions will make me sneeze very loudly very soon, and that cramp now threatens in my right buttock?'

Sally looks at him adoringly. 'You may.'

'Come then.' He beckons with his head in the vague direction of her bedroom. Sally nods and kisses him twice with the gentlest of kisses; one for the tip of his nose, one for the innermost corner of his eye.

Tea for two remains untouched. Tea for two has spilt all over the carpet and the settee. To the bedroom they shuffle, Richard with his jeans around his ankles, Sally limping along at his side. Hand in hand. Still laughing. Richard sneezes.

There we shall leave them. They go to greet the climax of something started long ago. Last year in fact, Gracious Good Lord.

EPILOGUE

19 June
Highgate,

Dear Ms Collins,

After careful consideration, I am afraid I really cannot take up the post as heroine in one of your stories.

Being the vampish vixen was such fun, but though I found the whole deportment so enjoyable, I must decline the role.

I did love the clothes, and I wear them still – with or without knickers, depending on my mood and the weather.

Seducing and being seduced is still, you might say, my chief leisure pursuit. Indeed, I find that I am now even more imaginative and abandoned. Please find enclosed a page of scenarios that I have enacted and can vouch for. You may use them if you wish but I would appreciate anonymity.

I have thought about this long and hard, I do assure you. (You may use 'long and hard' if you like.) The opportunity was so tempting for a while, but I have decided to pass it up.

Please do remember me to Ms Jong and Ms Hollander.

Though I am still a leopard of sorts, I must concede that Rudyard Kipling is much more my thing.

With best wishes,

Sally Lomax

Freya North

CHLOË

For Daniel

PROLOGUE

Chloë dearest,

How very strange to write in life that which will be read on death!

I hope sincerely that there will not have been too many tears – and that my funeral wishes were carried out to a 't' (especially the jazz and champagne).

Over the last few years I was haunted regularly by images of my nearest and not so dearest swooping down and picking at the bones of my just dead self; fighting over the fleshiest morsels and leaving nothing but offal for the rest and best of you. I decided therefore – quite some time ago, I might add – to cut myself up into sizeable portions and divide my spoils amongst those deep and constant in my affections.

For you, C, my dearest indeed, I leave anything of velvet in my cupboard. I leave you The Brooch which I know you have coveted since you were tiny. It goes to you because I want you to have a little part of me – and it is my eternal hope that you will carry something of me deep within, as much as on your lapel.

And for you, dear C, I leave this map. There are four

more and you will find them all. Wales first, then Ireland, Scotland and finally England. Trust me.

There is also a sum of money which will see you on your way and pay for train tickets and postcards. It will enable you to give up that lousy job and hopefully give you the independence to rid yourself of that awful boyfriend – you are much too good for the former and far too precious for the latter.

I am sending you on a voyage, dearest one, in the hope that, once you are quite travelled out, you might find a small patch that you can at last call Home.

I have great hopes for you.

Keep me in mind, my duck.

Jocelyn.

ONE

'Heavens,' Chloë Cadwallader declares for the third time. Concentrating very hard on the red wine stain on the carpet, she twiddles with a lively lock of auburn hair which springs back over her right eye just as soon as she tucks it behind her ear.

'Heavens,' she says, heaving out the 'h', 'I can't do that.'

Fingering The Brooch, she looks solemnly from letter to map and back again. Jocelyn's handwriting and the map of the United Kingdom are at once familiar and yet somehow foreign and suddenly illegible. Chloë is aware that she knows the shapes but their meaning is now strangely elusive and forgotten.

'I can*not* do it.'

An envelope marked 'Wales' lies unopened and alluring on her knees. She takes it to her nose and inhales with eyes closed tight, hoping that she might detect Jocelyn's trademark Mitsuko scent. Though the faintest whisper would suffice, the envelope, alas, smells of nothing.

'Can I?'

Chloë crosses her living-room and flicks on the light, for the ready-to-break storm outside has plunged the December lunch-time into premature darkness. Venturing cautiously over to the window, she pins the brooch to her jumper. Though the shadowy reflection offered by the pane blurs her own features, it captures the glint of the brooch. Chloë knows its intricate course of serpentines and twists off by heart. A tear smudges her sight but she squeezes her finger into the corner of her eye and pushes the tear to the back of her mind.

'Heavens,' she mutters, 'what on *earth* am I meant to do?'

The United Kingdom looms from the page; beautiful and conspiring. Wales first. Ireland next. Then Scotland. Finally, England. Clockwise and magnetic. What to do? What to do. What are you going to do? What would *you* do?

After quite some time, in which Chloë continued to consult heaven and earth to no avail (Jocelyn *must* be up there somewhere!), she kissed the brooch quickly and glanced at the envelope marked 'Wales'; still unopened. Taking it to her nose once more but again in vain, she decided to give it to Mr and Mrs Andrews for safe keeping until she felt braver, until she knew what to do with it. And with her job (lousy), and with her boyfriend (awful). Chloë knew that Jocelyn would have approved for it was she who had introduced her to Gainsborough's charming couple. Locked as they were within the fabric of a rather good framed facsimile, they had been good friends to Chloë for many years and now, with Jocelyn gone, they were her confidantes and advisers too. Immeasurably important for a timid girl, currently a little lonely and low, whose friends are few and whose family are far and distant anyway. Slotting the envelope in the gap which had appeared over the years between frame and print, Chloë was amused that it rested between the Andrews's feet, with Mr A's gun and dog protecting it further. She gazed at Mrs Andrews's pale blue frock and regarded two concert tickets nestling by the corn stooks in the bottom right corner.

'What would *you* do,' she implored of the couple, 'if you were me? What should *I* do?'

'Sink me, girl!' Mr Andrews chastised melodiously. 'You have to *ask*?'

'Of *course* I have to ask,' Chloë said somewhat incredulously.

'Go,' laughed Mrs Andrews, 'away!'

'A*way*?' Chloë gasped. 'Do you really think so?'

'To – The – Concert,' spelt Mrs Andrews kindly and to Chloë's relief.

'I do so love Beethoven,' Chloë reasoned, 'but Brett can't make it. Working late. Or something.'

'Even better!' exclaimed Mr Andrews. 'He'd only fidget.'

'Awful!' Mrs Andrews declared, with deference to Jocelyn.

'Rid yourself,' agreed Mr Andrews likewise. 'After all, if you can make it across London, you can certainly make it across country.'

With a glance at her watch and a slight bow to her intimates, who sent her on her way with their blessing, Chloë finally grabbed her coat, thrust both tickets into her pocket and locked the door on Islington. She'd open the envelope marked 'Wales' later. She'd decide what to do. Later. Hopefully.

A lovely man, of chiselled jaw and open smile, saved Chloë from an ignominious tumble down the escalator. He allowed her to hang on to his arm and swamp him with mumbled gratitude as she caught her breath and searched hard for composure. He swept away her apologies and said 'Not at all' to her profuse thanks. His was the other platform but Chloë found herself catching her breath again as he laid a hand on each shoulder and steadied her in the direction of hers. He was rather lovely. And he was so not Brett.

As the tube trundled south, Chloë thought back to first meeting Brett on the underground. Stuck in a tunnel. She had watched him twist and tut after five minutes, and heard him swear impressively after ten. As quarter of an hour approached, he had elicited her name and a giggle and, after much hastily heartfelt pleading, a dinner date for the next night too. *I must be mad!* Chloë had thought with just a little pride too and hardly able to wait to tell Jocelyn. Jocelyn, who of course had not yet met Brett, clapped her hands and thought it sounded marvellous. She and Chloë then sat down once again to watch *Brief Encounter*.

Oh, that the encounter *had* been brief; just the fancy dinner and perhaps one or two other non-committal dates. But Chloë had never met anyone like Brett, this busy man who worked in the City and who pinched the bridge of his nose while exclaiming he was so stressed out. He was an impressive decade older. He was joined at the hip to a mobile phone. He had a loft apartment in the Docklands and a 'mega pressure' job with late nights and great perks.

'You're not my usual type,' he had warned Chloë as if she should be grateful. And, for a while, she was. So busy and big and yet he'd chosen her. Without, it seemed, the need to know much about her; but a desire, it soon transpired, for her to know everything about him.

She was a captive audience then.

She was deaf ears now. Brett's ego had increased with his girth and his manners had collapsed with the stock market.

What on earth are you doing, Chloë? You seem ingenuous and good and inherently incompatible with this man!

I suppose.

So?

Habit?

They're there to be broken.

But what if? Just give Brett up? What if there's never anyone else?

Stuck in a tunnel.

Chloë gave the extra ticket to a bespectacled young man clutching a violin case like a lover. He was rendered speechless but grasped her hand in sublime appreciation, despite such a gesture causing him to rescue the slipping case with a grimace and a curiously raised knee.

As she strolled to peruse the craft exhibits in the foyer, the map of the United Kingdom loomed ever larger in her mind's eye. Such a map had superimposed itself on to whatever Chloë's eyes fell on during the journey to the South Bank. Wales was now magnified, aerially almost; the contours of imagined hills and valleys smiling up at her while a choir of rugby players and miners filled her ears and her heart momentarily. Squinting at some particularly delicate titanium jewellery, she held a pair of luminescent earrings to her ears.

'A voyage!' She tested the word to herself and found it astonishingly tasty. She crossed over to inspect some batik waistcoats but was utterly distracted by the fact that she could not remember when Christopher Columbus had embarked on his travels. She forsook enamel brooches for a browse around the bookshop, said 'Ah! fourteen *ninety-two!*' out loud and found herself buying a copy of *On the Black Hill* against her better judgement.

'Never read any Chatwin,' she explained to a totally disinterested sales assistant, 'and I *might* be going to Wales, you see. Soon. Ish.' Before she left the shop, however, she spied an illustrated copy of *Gulliver's Travels* and paid for it at a different till.

Feeling somewhat bolstered that she had made some preparation, however rudimentary, for her possible voyage, Chloë devoted the last ten minutes before the concert to a stand of the most beautiful ceramics she had ever seen. Glazed on the outside in a lustrous charcoal pewter; within, they sang out in vivid cerulean swirled into eddies and streams of shimmering turquoise. The pots trumpeted rhythm and energy, calling out to be touched and listened to. Though Chloë had an eye for craft and the like, hitherto it had never stopped her in her tracks. Somewhere in the recesses of her rational self, she could half hear the final bell, and yet she was compelled to visit each urn in turn, to place her face as close as possible. To experience and to remember.

And that was William Coombes's first sight of Chloë; her tresses of burnished copper whispering over the surface of his pots in her bid to get as near as she could to their very fabric. He saw her face fleetingly and her spattering of freckles reminded him at once of a glaze he had favoured some years before.

Lusty Red.

Watching her hurry to the stalls he caught a drift of her perfume, a glance of her neck, a shot of light from her brooch, a snippet of the orchestra tuning to an 'e'. His senses were accosted and he stood still, in silence, appreciating it, absorbed.

'Who was she, sniffing my pots?' he asked the invigilator with a quick shake of his head to return him to the present.

'She wasn't just sniffing, she was humming right down into them – with eyes closed and all!'

Intrigued, William ventured over to his largest urn and, with a fleeting but self-conscious recce, hummed into its opening.

It hummed with him. The softest of echoes. He hadn't realized.

TWO

As British Rail whisked him away from the capital, westward ho, William thought of the humming girl with the freckles set against a porcelain complexion. Gazing through the window at the monochrome winter landscape rushing past, he sipped absent-mindedly at tasteless brown liquid that could be tea or there again coffee and remembered again her russet curls vivid against the grey of his glaze. At once he had an idea for a vessel and sketched it quickly on a scrap of paper spied on the neighbouring seat. Something fairly slender but subtly curving, smothered with *terra sigillata*, the rich slip he would then burnish until it shone almost wet. And oh! how the vessel would resonate when hummed into.

Damn. He scrunched the polystyrene cup viciously, digging his nails in deep, satisfyingly. Damn, damn it. Should he have waited until the concert had ended? He unwrapped a Mars bar. And if he had? What if she didn't want to be spoken to?

What if she did?

Was his interest fired merely because his pots had kindled hers? Or did it have nothing to do with ceramics at all?

The chocolate was more sickly than childhood memory suggested so he wedged it, half eaten, in between the crushed polystyrene.

It may have been but a fleeting glance yet he burned now for what he had seen. As Dorset became Devon, he sat back and allowed a day-dream to take off. It was good for it both confronted and satisfied long dormant lust and hunger. However, as Devon became Cornwall, reality hindered its development and, resigned, William forced himself to unravel the fantasy, to work through and quash it in the harsh, prosaic winter light that streamed in through the windows from the sea.

And yet the freckles that were a shade lighter than the hair, and the eyes of mahogany that were two shades darker, swept in and out of his reasoning and accosted his groin, stirring it into an embarrassing but pleasurable stiffness concealed only by yesterday's newspaper laid conspiringly over his lap.

As the train juddered to a standstill at Penzance, he ground a halt to his dreaming, banished the lust and persuaded his cock to quieten down and soften up. The humming girl was spurned; for there on the platform, plain in the plain light of the December day, stood the reason for such meanderings to remain infeasible, for such desires to be exiled: Morwenna.

The fantasy was over at once.

There had been a time, thought William as he dropped his holdall into the boot of her Fiat, when Morwenna Saxby had been his fantasy incarnate. Fifteen years his senior, her age and experience had made her a compelling and attractive proposition when they had met five years earlier. He was then a twenty-four-year-old potter with his first studio; she was a divorcee, seductive and smouldering, set on rectifying the limitations previously imposed by her puritan and lacklustre ex-spouse. She had appointed herself at once teacher and agent. She secured William commissions and took thirty per cent of the proceeds. She also explained to him, painstakingly, the ins and outs of the G-spot and the female orgasm until he knew the route off by heart.

William stole a look at her now as she settled herself into the driving seat and hated himself for wishing that her ear met her neck in the way the humming girl's did. Morwenna was undoubtedly attractive but this was diluted by the regular reassurance that she now required.

'Bags and wrinkles,' she would sigh.

'But I like wrinkly old bags!' he would gently chide back, his irritation masked. She loathed her body generally succumbing to gravity, but he did not mind all that much.

I'm a potter. Surface beauty is defined by the underlying anchor of structure.

Exactly.

For all the small talk that was wrung out in the car on the journey north from Penzance to Zennor, they may as well have driven in silence. As they were friendly and polite, so too were they distant and withdrawn; their differences as marked as those between the south and north coasts of Cornwall. Their words, for the most part, were empty, the silences in between loaded.

William looked out over the brittle gorse to the sea, today grey and flat. He often judged his mood by the ocean and found they usually corresponded.

His cottage was now in sight and he was hopeful of making it there before a dinner invitation was offered. There would be little in his fridge but he would much rather go hungry. Lurching and rolling up the pocked and rutted track to William's cottage, Morwenna spoke to him via the rear-view mirror and he answered her eyes accordingly.

'Supper? Later? Eightish? Knowing you, your fridge'll be bare.'

'Probably. But d'you mind if I don't?' he said carefully. 'You know what London does to me!'

'Mind! Me!' she started. 'Suit yourself, my boy!'

William placed a hand on her leg because it seemed he ought to, and kissed her cheek likewise, lightly and without looking. He gathered his gear and walked towards his cottage. Without turning around he raised his hand in a motionless, emotionless wave. Morwenna read it as a halt.

She drove back to Penzance, stopping at the cliffs near Wicca to gaze at the horizon and gulp down the fortifying air.

'Damn it!' she said aloud, her voice swallowed by the wind. 'I forgot to tell him that the Bay Tree Bistro want to commission a whole service. A hundred and eighty pieces. Nice little earner. And for William, too, of course. God forbid it will be too late. Keep him sweet a while longer. Just until it's finished.'

She flexed her fingers which had started to ache in the chill of the air. She rued the fact that her knuckles looked bony, large, and she wondered why the nail beds were so purple. The sea looked ominous and dark. She shuddered and returned to her car, driving to Penzance with the radio on loud so that she could not hear herself think about William.

* * *

Well Chloë? Have you gone yet?

It's raining, has been for days.

You're still in Islington.

I'm still here.

Chloë munched a mince pie thoughtfully in front of Mr and Mrs Andrews. 'Wales' nestled unopened at Mr Andrews's feet, remaining but a daunting concept in a forsaken corner of Chloë's mind. She felt tempted to open the envelope but sticky fingers were today's good excuse not to. Good King Wenceslas looked out from the small transistor radio on Chloë's bedside table. She hummed with him, distractedly. Her first Christmas without Jocelyn was looming.

Is she at peace? she wondered as she sponged crumbs from a chest of drawers with her finger.

Couldn't she have waited a while longer? she rued as she wiped her finger along the picture frame and winced at the streak of dust that confronted her.

Just one more Christmas? she lamented, sinking down on to her lumpy mattress and tracing a new route across the cracks on the ceiling.

Oh the joys of renting! she cursed, desperate for Jocelyn to advise her to move, dear girl.

Where to?

Ha! Knowing Jocelyn, bloody Wales or Ireland, Scotland even.

What to do. Where to go.

And when.

Why should Chloë procrastinate so? Shouldn't she leap at such an opportunity? Not only is this the chance to rid herself of lousy job *and* awful boyfriend in one fell swoop, she is also being given the means to find her feet, her future and her fate. But the envelope marked 'Wales' remains unopened; Chloë has returned from another depleting day at work and Brett's arrival is imminent.

If her treasured godmother's death less than a month before had fractured Chloë's life, then her last will and testament had thrown her world into quandary. In Chloë's twenty-six years, there had been few decisions to make yet here she was being guided and goaded by a dead woman to make two that were potentially momentous. Retrieving a framed photograph of Brett, Chloë tapped his chest sternly.

'Jocelyn never liked you much,' she told him while he grinned back at her, suave and vain. She pushed her thumb over his face until it was covered completely. 'And I never actively sought her approval because deep down I think I knew there was little that warranted it.'

Chloë kept her thumb over the photograph and drummed the fingers of her free hand against the armrest of the chair. Though now headless, Brett's stance, with hands on hips and one knee cocked, spoke reams of his arrogance and vanity. She smacked her hand flat over the photograph so that only a palm tree and an innocuous tuft of hair peeped through. She ceased her finger thrumming and stared straight ahead at nothing at all and thereby deep into the very nub of the matter. Chloë placed the photograph frame face down on top of the television and flicked aimlessly through the channels. Santa Claus met her on every one and Chloë was thankful that she did not have satellite.

Knowing that Brett could swagger in at any moment, brandishing his infuriating trademark 'Ciao', produced little spurts of adrenalin which made her pace about and fiddle with things that could well have been left just so.

The curtains are hanging fine, Chloë; there is no fluff on that cushion. The pictures are dead straight.

Poor girl, she's tried twice before to sever her dealings with Brett. The first time, she located him on his mobile phone but fumbled over her words so badly that she ended up apologizing: 'Oh nothing, it's nothing, I'm just being daft.' The second time, Brett beat her to it, yet while he was flourishing his final 'ciao's, Chloë found herself pleading for another go.

'The thing to do,' Chloë said to Mrs Andrews, 'is not to mince my words.'

'Precisely,' her confidante encouraged, 'straight to the point. Plain English. No beating about the bush. And no metaphors!'

Brett has arrived and he fills the doorway with his frame, his bulky silhouette backlit from the light in the communal hall.

'Ciao!'

'Quick, close the door – it's bitter!' says Chloë a little too cheerily.

'What a day, I'm so stressed out,' he growls, slumping into the chair and up-ending the photograph frame so that he can admire himself, tanned and in Jamaica, in December and in Islington. 'What a frig of a day.'

He kicks off his shoes, stretching his legs out, imposing on Chloë's space, spouting a soliloquy peppered, as usual, with 'I' and 'me'.

'What's cookin'? I'm starvin'.' Chloë hates the way he drops his 'g's. She fiddles with picture frames and finds fluff on cushions. He checks the messages on his mobile phone. Something inside Chloë is burning and welling. It's Jocelyn. It's Mrs Andrews. 'Look at him,' they seem to be spurring Chloë, 'the repugnant lump!'

'Brett,' Chloë hears her voice suddenly escape the safety of things left unsaid, 'I have something to tell you. There's something I need to say.'

'Yeah?' he twists his toes and burps under his breath.

'You know bread?' Chloë starts, shaking down a few locks of her hair to hide behind.

'Huh?' He regards her suspiciously, curling his lip. 'Bread?'

'Mm!' she agrees, tucking the curls temporarily behind her ears. 'Once it's stale, it can never truly be revived. Not even if it was once quite tasty.'

'I'm bloody *star*-vin',' Brett snaps, caressing his belly which rumbles like the thunder slowly etching its way across his brow. 'Are you tellin' me that's all there is? Bread that's gone off?'

'That's what it is. Was,' Chloë reasons, suddenly radiant, 'and well past its sell-by date.'

It was only when Chloë heard the communal door bang downstairs that she allowed herself to sink into the chair and shake uncontrollably. After a while she picked up the photograph frame and chuckled; laughing out loud until tears of mirth oozed from the corners of her eyes and her ribs creaked for mercy.

I did it!

'Mrs A, I did it! I really, actually, did.'

'You did indeed, dear. Metaphors and all.'

Carefully, Chloë removed the photograph and tore it methodically into strips which she then twisted and coaxed into an origami star – a skill she learnt many years before not knowing quite when it would have its use. She contemplated the spiky form and rotated it, catching a little bit of Brett's hand here, a nose and half a mouth there; an elbow, part of a tennis shoe, a palm frond. Capped teeth. *In the ball of my hand, let alone under my thumb!*

'Bye-bye,' she sang, tipping the origami from hand to hand. 'The first time I ever stood up to you was ultimately the last too!' She listens to the silence and loves the peace it promises. 'Were you that "awful"?' she whispers at Brett's faceted face. 'Yes, I suppose you were.' Chloë went over to the window, peering intensely up at the ink-navy sky wishing for a star. 'Bossy,' she clarified, holding the origami star aloft and catching a glance of Brett's mouth; 'tactless,' she shuddered, 'chauvinistic, too.' She crossed to the mirror and sprung ringlets of her hair through her fingers, remembering how Brett had referred to it, when wet, as 'positively pubic'. Well Chloë, he's losing his!

She settled snugly into the armchair and contemplated the fractured photograph once more. 'You were but a cheap processed oaf,' she said, proud of the pun, 'and I think, actually, I'd rather *enjoy* something more wholesome and nourishing now.' With that, she tossed the splintered, diminished image of Brett deftly into the waste-paper basket.

Just the 'lousy' job now, Chloë; time to free yourself from the self-obsessed shackles of the lowly paid and not very good inner London Polyversity where you've shouldered the role of student-communication-liaison-welfare-officer for four thankless years. Think of it! No more students-in-need, the Sins that frequently run amok in the already cramped Islington studio you've been renting.

Chloë's flat was presently overrun by an eighteen-year-old first-year anorexic, a second-year suicidal with girlfriend trouble and a third-year in the throes of a pre-finals breakdown. They littered her flat and demanded round-the-clock counselling and unrestricted access to fridge (apart from the anorexic) and telephone (often simultaneously). Demanding indeed, with pay and praise as paltry as they were.

Finally, on a turbulent December afternoon just a day away from the end of term, bolstered by Jocelyn's legacy and inspired by the map of the United Kingdom, Chloë has decided to resign. She has her eye on a moment to savour and worries that if she procrastinates, or changes into something more becoming, the moment would be lost. Then Lent term would be mercilessly upon her. And Wales would remain unopened. Wales would be forgotten. Closed.

She could not possibly insult Jocelyn so.

And there is no law against handing in one's notice wearing jeans and trainers that should be restricted to solitary evenings safely inside.

'But Chloë, the students *need* you – you're their *life*line. If it's a rise you want, we could, at a stretch, offer you one per cent over three years?'

Chloë is surrounded by lino and melamine, strip lighting and orange plastic chairs. They are chipped and unsteady. Rain courses relentlessly down the steel-framed windows. A small puddle is forming on the flaking grey window-sill. It is unbelievably drab and depressing and Chloë feels all the more resolute for it. She rejects the pay rise and leaves guilt firmly in the room when she closes the door quietly behind her.

Well, if Chloë Cadwallader is not to be a student-communication-liaison-welfare-officer, with a boyfriend called Brett and a rented studio in Islington, what is she to be?

On Christmas Eve, she has absolutely no idea. And now there is no Jocelyn to turn to for advice. And yet, was not her godmother still overseeing Chloë's education and welfare with as much concern and motivation during her death as she had during her life? Was not her legacy precisely that there was no better place for Chloë to start in the worldwide scheme of things than in the great British Isles?

'Europe,' Jocelyn had once said to Chloë, 'is enthralling, the United States vast. Africa is captivating, Asia a jewel. Australasia is glorious and fiendishly far away but Britain, *Britain* is the garden of the world with secrets of joy lurking in every tiny nook.'

Jocelyn's bequest was that her god-daughter should discover and share those secrets. Who knows what she might find. And where. How exciting and what an opportunity. Grab it! Go! Have you gone yet?

Christmas Eve in Islington. Chloë has pinned Jocelyn's map above her bed and as she gazes at the four countries, she decides that now is the time to greet Wales. With Mr Andrews's encouragement, she extends a tentative hand out towards the envelope. But she stops midway and wonders if it is all a little too far-fetched. So Jocelyn had deemed Chloë's job deplorable and had thought Brett loathsome, but was a voyage to the distant corners of the United Kingdom really the answer? Was it a logical solution? Was it necessary?

Was it even *sensible*?

('People who are forever sensible are interminably dull, Chloë sweet. As drab as a black brolly in Islington.')

Was it a good idea? Realistically?

'I've quit job and jilted the boyf – won't that do?' Chloë says aloud with just a touch of a whine to her voice. 'What if I just move away from Islington – say, try Putney? How about I look for a job in a nice private firm – market research or something? Mr Andrews, please advise!'

Mr Andrews, however, remains silent, his grin stony and

fixed. And Chloë suspects that there is little point consulting Mrs Andrews who appears, on Christmas Eve, the sort of lady who would not speak unless spoken to but might, with a giggle and a glance, sing a little ditty if cajoled and flattered.

Chloë does not want entertaining, she wants someone to tell her what to do. She can no longer reach out to Jocelyn and seek her advice.

And yet it is Jocelyn's advice that is in dispute today.

Wales, still enveloped beyond reach, is yet tantalizingly close.

'I'll start packing tomorrow,' Chloë says decisively.

Mr Andrews cocks his rifle approvingly, Mrs Andrews giggles.

THREE

William bundled the contents of the holdall into his washing-machine, retrieving his toothbrush and razor at the last minute. He waited patiently for the whir and clicks to commence and then watched the water trickle shyly over the laundry. Satisfied that the cycle was under way (it only ever seemed to start under paternal encouragement) he confirmed that there was indeed nothing in the fridge and left the kitchen for his studio.

The studio was a stone's throw from the kitchen, which was itself a pebble's roll from everywhere else; there being neither corridors nor landings at William's cottage. Incongruously called Peregrine's Gully, the cottage was compact and thickset. It reminded William of an Exmoor pony; essentially native, ruggedly pretty and inherently suited to its environment. It sat, small and brave, in a gentle acre meadow of its own, flanked on one side by a scar of gorse, on the other by the poor land petering out to the cliff edge. Local sheep often gazed longingly at the grass on the inside of William's fence and while he was not averse to a visit and a polite nibble, a bellow from Barbara invariably saw them off.

Barbara was a goat who had sauntered in through a gap in the fence soon after William had arrived at Peregrine's Gully. He had shooed her and chased her and smacked her rump with a slipper but she had stood her ground, twitched her beard and fixed her yellow eyes on him, lovingly and unrelentingly. He had growled at her, he had waved wooden implements at her and he had ignored her, but still she stayed, nibbling the edges of the grass in a dainty and ingenuous manner. None of the farmers claimed her and a notice in the local paper brought no one. So she was invited, begrudgingly at first, to stay. William called her Barbara after her bleat.

Barbara adored him; following at his heels whilst he pottered around the garden, standing for hours with her forelegs just inside the studio door while he worked, looking up at him conversationally when he sat to eat in the kitchen, staring alongside him at the washing machine as he coaxed it to work. Barbara gave the postman short shrift and frequently chased cars down the drive or stood defiant, stamping, right in the middle as they approached. She loathed Morwenna. In the early days, she trod on her, chewed her clothing and defecated as close to her as she could. Now, she just glowered at her witheringly or ignored her entirely whilst making eyes at William. Invariably, Morwenna brought carrot butts and lettuce ends as a peace offering, sometimes even ginger-nuts as a bribe, but these placated Barbara only temporarily.

It was the windows at Peregrine's Gully that had decided William to rent the property. They had good deep sills affording place and space to his ceramics, and provided some respite from the invasive winter chill. Of the two small bedrooms upstairs, he slept in the one which looked out to the cliffs and onward to the sea. It contained only a bed, a tea chest for a bedside table and the incongruous chintzy curtains that had come with the cottage. The other room, however, was stuffed with the stuff of bedrooms: guitars, books, an enormous mirror framed by driftwood for which he had exchanged a nicely glazed set of mugs, an oversize whisky bottle half full of small change, two chests of deep drawers stuffed full of thick jumpers, and a Victorian oak cupboard he had bought for a song wherein the rest of his clothes were housed. Such items, essentials or paraphernalia, were banned from his bedroom for it was the bare white walls, the uninterrupted run of floorboards, which provided him with the empty canvas, the armature, for new works to take root in the fertile hours of daybreak.

Downstairs, the front door opened directly into the sitting-room but William only ever used the craftsmen's entrance at the rear of the cottage. Consequently a thick Turkish rug bought at great expense and inconvenience whilst backpacking some years ago, hung down from door frame to floor. The back wall was papered with books which sat crammed on bookshelves William had built by hand, leaving a gap of just an inch between tallest book and ceiling, and between bottom shelf and floor. He was not bothered about any alphabetical or thematic ordering but arranged the volumes according to height and the spines' aesthetic appeal. Viewed from the other end of the room, the books rose and fell in a sinuous sequence, rather like organ pipes or ordnance survey contours. Between the rug-door and the book-wall, a large hand-built terracotta pot four foot tall sat fat, proud and burnished to perfection. To the side of it, a selection of umbrellas and walking sticks, whose provenances were long forgotten, were propped precariously. The rest of the room was taken up by two incredibly easy chairs bought at auction and in serious need of reupholstering, and a stout Scandinavian wood-burning stove. Still warm, despite William's three-day absence. It ought to be – it cost William almost as much as he made last year.

His studio was his haven and his true home; the fact that the cottage was included in the rent was merely an added bonus. Built by a contemporary of Bernard Leach, it had been designed with no other purpose than to be a room conducive to the making of pottery. There were two anterooms, one for glazes and one being the damp room where ongoing pots could rest. The main room housed William's wheel at one end, an immensely long trestle table and a high, plaster-topped console on which clay could be kneaded and wedged in preparation. Shelves ran around two walls carrying finished pieces, experiments, failures, stimulus material such as skulls and pebbles, and a wealth of books on ceramics. The building was designed to allow its craftsman unparalleled access to the views outside, thus the other two walls were predominantly windows. Facing the trestle table at which William usually stood and worked, the windows reached from ceiling to floor and provided an inspiring panorama across the garden to the moors; the windows in the wall by the wheel were lower so that a potter throwing could still see where land became air and the great sea started. The roof itself was essentially one big skylight. The studio was never cold for the kiln at the far corner kept it cosy.

That afternoon, as the veiled December sun fizzled out over the sea to drop down beyond the horizon and hide until noon the next day, William prepared some vivid blue slip and checked on his pieces in the damp room. His mind was elsewhere and yet nowhere at all. Momentarily it flitted across Morwenna before going on a little excursion to London and the humming girl, where it stayed a rueful while to be brought back to the present by Barbara's insistent bleat. William found it was quite dark and he sat on the steps of the studio tugging the goat's ear and asking her what he should do. Her eyes glinted luminous, unnerving even, so he smacked her rump and scratched her beard before heading off for Morwenna's, driven as he was purely by his groin. Driving guilt to a far-flung corner of his conscience.

'Hungry, were you?' Morwenna fought to contain her

delight. A hundred and eighty pieces for the Bay Tree Bistro looked promising, as did an orgasm or two.

'Not really – well, not hungry for food,' qualified William with an overdone lascivious wink. He had always mixed up her money-look with her lust-look and she was so obviously wearing one of them now. Unfortunately, he could not decipher which for both incorporated moistened, parted lips and a slight glaze to the eye. He strode over and kissed her deeply, allowing his hand to travel expertly if routinely over her torso. He ran her pony-tail through his hands and looked at her face. Behind her smile he saw that her eyes were quite flat. Or were those £-signs, superimposed cartoon-like over them?

'Morwenna,' he said in as much of a drawl as he could muster convincingly, stepping towards her and kissing her as persuasively as he could.

And so they made rather unsatisfactory love. William's eyes were slammed shut throughout while Morwenna's were fixed on the lampshade, waiting for a climax that never came and was not worth simulating. Afterwards, they thanked each other politely, assuring that it had been good for them, how was it for you.

You shouldn't have to ask, thought Morwenna as she rose and went for her dressing-gown.

You shouldn't have to pull your stomach in like that, thought William as he watched her.

'Stay?' she asked, hugging her dressing-gown about her, quite keen for him to go.

'Not tonight,' William replied, as lightly as he could.

As Morwenna sipped at very sweet cocoa, she beckoned her cat to her lap. William, William. She gazed at the wallpaper without seeing its pattern. William Coombes was her lover and her livelihood; thirty per cent was thirty per cent after all, and his burgeoning reputation had seen his prices rise healthily. As much as she loved him, and love him she did, she loved the idea of him more.

She had held the reins and guided William through an exhilarating run of discovery from which she had benefited too. Multiple orgasms *and* thirty per cent. Now they were on a downward slalom heading nowhere fast. The reins were gone from her hands and yet she could not remember letting them slip. Who held them now? Not William, for sure. The shift of power was now squarely with him and yet he was using it quietly to ride away from her.

It was the creeping indifference she could not abide. His proclamations of affection were dwindling and empty and, as she confronted the truth with only her cat on her lap for comfort, she knew that he made them because he knew it was what she wanted to hear. Tracing a large vein threatening at her calf, Morwenna admitted silently with forlorn resignation that William was no longer in love with her. Her cat fixed his yellow eyes on her, his pupils expanding as he swallowed her in to his unnerving gaze. What could she do but acknowledge out loud that William simply no longer loved her? They had grown apart because he had grown up and she had grown old. She had also witnessed his growing disaffection with Saxby Ceramics.

'But Morn,' he had said under his breath once or twice, 'I actually want to make the pots I want to make. Not made to order, made to measure, made to be dishwasher safe and microwave proof.'

'You will, you will. Once you're up and running,' she had said lightly. But she could not deny that his career as a potter was now establishing itself and that his preferred frugal lifestyle could most certainly be maintained by the sale of a one-off studio piece every now and then.

'Oh well,' she said out loud in the plaguing silence of her room, 'I still have you and you love me unconditionally, don't you puss? You give me a hundred per cent, never mind thirty!' The tabby kneaded her lap in enthusiastic camaraderie before absent-mindedly springing his claws, driving them deep into Morwenna's thigh. She gasped with the shock and the hurt of it, hurling the animal off her lap, rubbing her thigh hard. The cat slunk reproachfully to the window-sill where he knocked over a photograph of William and gazed defiantly away from her.

'You and him both.'

William arrived back at Peregrine's Gully at midnight. He felt wretched because he knew he had used Morwenna, and thereby abused her. He cursed his conscience for having returned only when his testosterone had levelled. He cursed testosterone. The humming girl was far from his mind, as was the echoing urn in a river of red. Going to the side of the cottage, he went directly to the studio. Barbara, a little bleary, was none the less delighted to see him and chewed her cud thoughtfully as he fetched a block of terracotta clay and began to knead and wedge it. Pulling it towards him and then thrusting it away, he worked the clay until the wetness had gone and a cross section revealed no air pockets, just a smooth dark red-brown slab. Good enough to eat. My, he was starving. It was gone one in the morning and he was cold; the hunger that he had used as a pretext to Morwenna now gnawed at his stomach and his soul.

FOUR

Though Chloë's entire effects would have taken but a couple of hours to pack, it really did not seem an appropriate activity for Christmas Day. It could wait. Tomorrow, perhaps; Boxing Day after all. The easiest way for Chloë to block out the lack of Jocelyn was to travel backwards and pore over memories of Christmases past. Yuletide celebrations at her godmother's had been peppered with good cheer and sumptuous refreshments, and peopled by the most colourful of souls. Chloë customarily took a place in the background, happily overshadowed by the mosaic of eccentricities that surrounded her. She was oddly comfortable with her shyness when at Jocelyn's, surrounded by a host of fantastic characters scattered liberally through the house. There was the white witch, the man with the panama and the macaw, the Russian with the balalaika, the ageing French actress. But best of all, the septuagenarians, Peregrine and Jasper; made up to the nines and immaculately coiffured. ('We're the *real* Queens of England, *we* should be on the telly at three, don't you think?') Some called her Cadwallader, the white witch absent-mindedly called her Cleo, Peregrine and Jasper called her 'Clodders' as they had since she was small. She did not mind at all.

Chloë would watch with awe as Jocelyn swirled around her guests, distributing drink and food, compliments and witticisms with grace laced with abandon. Eyes dark with kohl bought in Petra, enviable cheekbones dusted with rouge from Paris and nut-brown skin bathed in Mitsuko, Jocelyn breezed about enveloped in velvet or swathed in chiffon, bejewelled extravagantly, bestowing on all her immense gift of effortless hospitality. Everyone was swept along on the tide of her countenance. Every so often and without making a scene, she would swoop down beside Chloë, usually squeezing next to her on the armchair to lavish kisses and furtive winks and nudges; 'I'm Jocelyn jostling!' she would pip in her ear. Chloë felt treasured indeed.

Mr and Mrs Andrews had been there too, ensconced in Notting Hill, in Jocelyn's glorious house. With pride of place over a *faux*-Elizabethan fireplace, they looked benevolently down on all from the gilt-edged confines of their elegant world. Of course, it was not the *original* – yet nor was it a standard print such as Chloë's. Jocelyn had commissioned hers from a young Chilean painter whom she had befriended on a coffee appreciation trip to South America in the seventies. She had brought Carlos back to London, sat him in the Tate and National Galleries, the Courtauld Institute and the Wallace Collection until he had quite mastered the Masters before sending him to Paris where she had an old friend who had known Matisse. Two years later, he enjoyed the first of many sell-out one-man shows. Now New York had him and he dressed in Gaultier and had a boyfriend called Claude whom he called 'Clode'.

But he came to Jocelyn's funeral, and wept alone and at length before disappearing.

As Chloë gazed at her own Mr and Mrs Andrews, she wondered what would happen to Jocelyn's. There, Señora Andrews sometimes appeared to be winking and wasn't there just a drift of something positively libertine about Señor Andrews?

Chloë decided if she visited the house, she would see if she could take the painting home. But where was home to be? Wales? Ireland? Scotland, perhaps? Wasn't home just a concept? Was it attainable? Really?

Because it would not have crossed their minds to call her, Chloë rang her parents just before the Queen's Speech to thank them for their perfunctory cheque. Two time zones away, they were just on their way out to cocktails with the Withrington-Smiths before a bash at Bunty and Jimbo's so could it be brief? Yes, yes, Merry Christmas to you too, Chloë. Mother sends fondest! Must fly, bye!

Owen and Torica Cadwallader: definitive ex-pats. Dictionary perfect and, as such, worthy of lengthy description or dissection in book, film or anthropological study. They whooped it up overseas, ricocheting around their vapid colonial existence; loving every minute, every year of it. Chloë had been born to them in Hong Kong and was to be their only child (a daughter – shame) who, at six years old and with a relocation to Saudi pending, had been shipped back to England to fumble her way through boarding school and other rites of passage. Had it not been for Jocelyn, she would have been quite alone. 'Far too far to fly' being her parents' dictum and excuse, Chloë rarely saw them. Perhaps once every three years or so, for a day or so. If that. This year they had flown in for the state opening of Parliament but Jocelyn's funeral two months later was 'far too far to fly – we'll send flowers' – which they did, only on the wrong day.

And yet Jocelyn remained forever discreet; she never judged them, never spoke badly about them and never colluded with Chloë who had expressed a brave indifference from a tender age anyway. Jocelyn's sympathy and support, though unspoken and unasked for, were abundant and comforting. The unequivocal, unconditional love and respect that she lavished on Chloë made her want for nothing. Why pine for parents she did not know when she had a godparent the calibre of Jocelyn? For her part, Jocelyn had a daughter without the trials of pregnancy, labour or a husband. She had this wonderful god-daughter merely because her brother had captained Owen's rugger team at Oxford.

Chloë thought herself very lucky. While other parents came up to school *en masse* and took their daughters out for cream teas in Marlborough, Jocelyn descended by Aston Martin twice a term to whisk away Chloë, and any friends she chose, for magical interludes and picnics on the Downs replete with champagne, smoked salmon and chocolate liqueurs. She helped smuggle plenty of the latter back to school: the very stuff of midnight feasts, bribery and blackmail. Once, when the weather had not been kind, the picnic was taken indoors at Badborough Court, a meandering country seat near Devizes owned by an old friend of Jocelyn's (didn't Lord Badborough kiss her for ages!).

Jocelyn wrote weekly, came to parents' evenings, sports days and school plays. When Chloë's maths teacher chastised Jocelyn over Chloë's general apathy and incompetence, the visits and the picnics and the chocolate truffles became more frequent. Not as a bribe, but as support.

'I'm not surprised your mind wanders off in maths, it's insufferably boring,' Jocelyn had said over shandy at a pub near Avebury. 'But just think, if you pass your O level you'll never, *ever*, have to do maths again! And just think, if you pass your O level you can turn your back on mental arithmetic and formulae and daft equations, to add things up on your fingers forever more! That's why we've got ten of them after all!'

Chloë gained a 'B' for her maths O level and has used her fingers to count ever since.

It was watching the Queen's Speech on the television (Chloë remained upstanding with sherry and a mince pie) that decided her what to do.

'Velvet, Your Majesty!' she cooed with reverence and gratitude. 'Jocelyn said I may have "anything of velvet" so I shall go directly and have my pick. First, though,' she announced, 'I shall pack!'

Chloë, her belongings and Mr and Mrs Andrews crossed London for Notting Hill by taxi and her sudden Christmas cheer ensured an extravagant tip on top of the seasonally quadrupled fare. Chloë grinned and waved at the familiar front door; darkly glossed hunter green, brass fittings gleaming. Hullo, hullo, hullo, she chanted, skipping up the wide steps two at a time. She had her own set of keys, of course she did. But the locks had been changed, of course they had. Feeling tearful and bewildered, she sat down on the front steps, surrounded by bags that were suddenly too heavy and bulky, wondering what to do. She thought of all the velvet items inside that were now rightfully hers, she wondered about the Chilean Mr and Mrs Andrews hoping they were still where they should be, presiding over matters in the drawing-room. Her own Mr and Mrs Andrews were too cold and cross to talk. Or was that her? She hoped nothing had been removed or even moved inside the house and yet how could she check? With her bottom numbing against the cold stone, and her lower lip jutting in bewilderment tinged with self-pity, she felt at once trapped and yet barred. Christmas Day was closing around her. It was cold.

Wales, suddenly, did not seem a good idea at all.

* * *

'Wales,' declared Peregrine, flinging his arm out in a roughly westerly direction, 'is an absolutely splendid idea!'

'Good old Jocelyn Jo!' agreed Jasper, thrusting a mug of mulled wine into Chloë's chilled hands.

Jasper and Peregrine had found her, huddled and sleepy, on their return from a promenade along the Serpentine. Their keys fitted the locks on Jocelyn's door perfectly for it was they who had had them changed. Jocelyn had left the house to them on that very condition: 'To prevent my nearest and not so dearest trespassing and traipsing through.' So Chloë had been rescued and was once again ensconced in a familiar armchair, looked down upon by the benevolent, if surreptitiously Latin, smiles of Mr and Mrs Andrews.

'Your phone,' said Jasper, 'is perpetually engaged. We've been trying you for yonks.'

'If the Sins weren't using it,' Chloë explained, 'I left it off the hook. Knowing that it would never again be Jocelyn, I can't bear to hear it ring.'

Chloë cradled a chipped cup that she knew well and nibbled biscuits from the lucky dip of Jocelyn's old Foxes' tin. Wardrobes full of velvet were just up the stairs and off the landing, and there would undoubtedly be a bottle of Mitsuko in the bathroom, one in the bedroom. And yet it seemed strange to be there, half asleep, freezing cold, sitting amongst all the familiar accoutrements and smells but with no Jocelyn.

'They say that people inhabit their places, their things, long after they're gone – but I can't find Jocelyn anywhere here,' Chloë mumbled, her nose running on to Peregrine's Hermès scarf. Jasper topped up the mulled wine and laid a slender, perfectly manicured hand on the top of her head.

'We couldn't find her either, poppet, not at first. But in drifts and droves she returned and now we chat away to her frequently, don't we, P? I hated it here at first, didn't I, dear? I found it so empty – and yet everything was in its place; all should have been comfortingly familiar, but it was alien and cold. And then, a few days on, I opened a kitchen drawer and found a shopping list scrawled by Jocelyn on the back of an envelope. It matched entirely the items currently in the larder. Suddenly I was quite warm and Jocelyn was here once more.'

'And for me,' said Peregrine, coaxing the Hermès scarf

from Chloë's clutches to replace it with a damask handkerchief from Dunhill, 'for me it was when I spied one slipper under the Lloyd Loom chair in her bedroom – you remember those pointy, turn-up-toe Indian things she had? It caught me quite unawares – it was only when, a day or so later, I found the other one lurking behind the laundry basket that I could smile. In fact, I had a right old chuckle – it was as if she had just that moment kicked them off prior to springing into bed with a magazine, a brandy and the telephone!'

'But,' sighed Chloë who had begun to thaw, 'I *miss* her. And it hurts, it *pulls* – here,' she explained, pressing both hands above her breasts. Peregrine and Jasper cocked their heads and donned gentle half-smiles.

'She'll never really be gone, you know,' said Peregrine, cuddling up to her comfortingly in the armchair.

'You'll see her again, Clodders old thing. I bet you anything she'll be in Wales!'

'Ooh! And Ireland!' cooed Peregrine, rolling his 'r's and jigging his head.

'Scotland,' philosophized Jasper, looking vaguely northwards.

'And good old Blighty!' declared Peregrine, gesticulating expansively and inadvertently clonking Chloë's nose in the process.

'In fact,' said Jasper standing up and lolling with a certain swagger against the fireplace; one knee cocked, one hand in a pocket, the other draped aesthetically over the mantel, 'you'll see her quite often – in you!'

Chloë looked at Jasper gratefully. And then she looked at him in quite a different light. She stifled giggles.

'You're Mr Andrews!' she exclaimed, looking from him to the painting above his head.

'Gracious duck!' whooped Peregrine. 'You *are*! To a 't'! What is it, Clodders? Is it the pose or the poise?'

'It's both,' she declared, delighted.

Jasper moved not one inch, if anything he lifted his chin a little higher and dropped his eyelids fractionally.

'Then I suggest, my dearest Peregrine, that you don a divine sky-blue frock and sit demurely at my side! For if I am indeed Mr A, you can be no other than my devoted Mrs A!'

'Velvet!' proclaimed a suddenly lucid Chloë having picked herself up from a fit of giggles on the Persian rug.

'Blue satin!' sang Peregrine, tears of mirth streaming down his face. He looked at Chloë slyly. 'Race you!' he hollered before diving for the door and the stairs beyond.

Because she was at least forty-five years younger than him, Chloë reached Jocelyn's bedroom first and flung open the cupboard doors with the grandest of gestures that would have done her late godmother proud. Peregrine and Chloë, and a wheezing Jasper just behind, looked in awe at the sparkle and drape of the cupboard's contents. There were yards of silk, watered, raw and crushed; swathes of satin, duchesse, brocaded and ruched; there was velvet and devoré velvet; plain taffeta and moiré; there was suede that was butter soft and cashmere that was softer than air. A superior collection of handmade shoes was hidden from view in their soft fabric sacks.

The three of them stood in silent reverence and gazed on. Jocelyn was amongst them once more. Chloë slithered into a dark green velvet dress that was far too long but it didn't matter. Jasper zipped her up and placed a lattice of jet around her neck while she scooped up her hair and he fixed it with a bejewelled pin.

'Divine,' he whispered, 'so Rossetti! So Burne-Jones!'

'Do you think I could have it altered to fit? Do you think I *should*?'

'I think you should! Jocelyn decreed it in her will, girl. No use just *having* "anything of velvet" – what good is velvet if it is not to be worn? I'll do it for you, being the accomplished seamstress that I am. Gracious, Peregrine!'

Peregrine stood before them, resplendent in washed blue

silk, one hand on his hips, the other raised affectedly above his head.

'It fits like a glove!' he declared, his voice saturated with pride heavily laced with outrage. Though it was decidedly odd seeing a man of grandfathering age wearing her godmother's dress, Chloë had to concede that it fitted perfectly, suiting him and complementing his demeanour utterly.

'I like it!' she enthused after a momentary assessment.

'I *love* it!' boomed Jasper, twirling Peregrine around. 'Shall we take more mulled wine and then play rummy?'

Jasper insisted on hanging Chloë's Mr and Mrs Andrews at the opposite end of the room to their Chilean doppelgängers.

'We could play Spot the Difference,' he declared, balanced on a Chippendale chair with a hammer between his knees and a picture hook pursed between his lips.

'Her shoes for starters,' said Peregrine, still befrocked, his nose inches from the frame, squinting through Jocelyn's reading glasses. Then he whipped them off and stared at Chloë in alarm.

'Gracious, Clodders! You haven't even opened it! Look, Jaspot – it's pristine. Not even the teeniest peek!' He removed the envelope marked 'Wales' from the frame and handed it to Jasper who held it aloft as if about to light the Olympic flame – or Jocelyn's chandelier at any rate. He looked at Chloë sternly and his left eyebrow left his forehead.

'Why ever not, girl?'

Chloë shuffled. Though she felt uncomfortable at being challenged, she felt more uneasy with the envelope suddenly out of reach. Jasper's eyebrow remained aloft.

'There just didn't seem to be a right time, ladies,' she said. 'I held it often; I sniffed at it and held it up to the light. Its contents just seem so, I don't know – *portentous*.'

Approving Chloë's vocabulary, Jasper allowed his eyebrow back down to earth.

'I was,' furthered Chloë, 'all on my own. In *Islington*, after all.'

This secured a bow from Jasper and a long nod from Peregrine who said 'Islington. Why, of *course*' very softly.

'What say you,' said Jasper cautiously, proffering Chloë the letter like a ring on a velvet cushion, 'that we open it now? You're in Notting Hill after all. With us. And the Andrewsiz. Looked over by You-know-who. Safe hands all.'

Chloë took the envelope and held it to her nose, her eyes on Jasper but seeing far beyond him.

Is it there? Is it Mitsuko? Do you know, I think so.

'Mitsuko?' asks Peregrine. Chloë nods. She turns the envelope over and wriggles her little finger into one corner. The rip, though a mere centimetre or so, is deafening. She takes her little finger to the other corner and winces as the tearing of paper screeches out.

'Bugger,' she mutters under her breath but unmistakably. 'Would *you*? For me?'

Jasper takes the envelope and slits it open with one deft movement. He passes it to Peregrine who slides the contents out with deliberation and grace. He offers them to Chloë but she must come forward to accept.

'Go on,' he whispers, 'for us.'

'For Jocelyn,' says Jasper.

'OK,' says Chloë.

There are two pages. A letter, and a map of Wales that appears to have been filched from a road atlas. In black ball-point pen, an arrow shoots inland and south, to a red asterisk marked 'Here!' Handing the map to Jasper, Chloë skims through the letter seeing the words without reading them, reading names without knowing where or who – or indeed whether a who or a where.

Peregrine's chin is tucked over her shoulder. He smells faintly of chocolate gingers and Christmas.

'Jasp!' he says once he has read it right through. 'Three guesses where she's going!' Jasper hands the map back to

Chloë and closes his eyes with a measured twitch of his aquiline nose.

'Three guesses,' says Peregrine again, nudging Chloë with a wink.

'And if I am correct in just one?' Jasper asks, eyes still closed, nostrils slightly flared.

'Oh Gracious Lordy, always a deal to be struck. Nothing's ever unconditional with the old tart!' Peregrine is pleasantly exasperated. 'If you're right in one, I'll make it worth your while. There!'

Jasper opens his eyes and smiles – benevolently at Chloë, somewhat lasciviously at Peregrine.

'Gin Trap. I bet my bottom dollar. It'll be the Gin Trap.'

FIVE

Chloë Darling,

Well done! No doubt it took simply ages for you to open the envelope. I wonder whether you had help with it in the end? Well, here we are, setting off for Wales – perhaps we've already arrived. Is it still winter? It should be, I've envisaged it that way.

Wales is a heady contradiction of rustic simplicity and rural grandeur, and 'little lines of sportive wood run wild' (Wordsworth's succinct description for hedgerows, darling). Virginia Trapper will make your stay memorable indeed.

You met Gin a couple of times when you were younger – perhaps you remember? She rarely leaves the farm now so I decreed special dispensation for her to miss my funeral. She did want to come, but I was happier for her not to be there. No doubt she'll want to know all about it so paint a technicolor picture for me, would you? Don't stint on detail and add a little flurry of brush strokes here and there, they'll go down a treat.

For all four countries that you will visit, you will see but a tiny corner of each. They are so vastly different – both from each other as well as within each itself. However, though I say so myself, I have picked rather well and assure you that each place will exude the essence of that country.

I so wish I could be there with you.

Really there.

In life, in the flesh.

Alas.

Instead, you must carry me along.

Promise me.

Of course, as I write, I have absolutely no idea whether I will indeed be able to 'look down', to watch over you once my number's up. Just now, I'd love an angel or agent to pop down and give me a clue or two but I shan't hold my breath. Ha! The consequences if I were to!!

If I find that I can, I will. If I can't, just keep me close.

Enjoy Wales and chin-wagging with the Gin Trap.

Ireland next, remember.

Fondest, as ever,

Jocelyn.

SIX

The lane was slim. It was like a gorge between the hedges which rose up over six feet to either side. Though it was January and the bare trees were pressed as inky silhouettes sharp against the sky, the hedges sprouted shoots and leaves and even boasted berries and foliage that clung on from last summer. The hedge was an ecosystem of its own and the seasons were obviously its slave. Rabbit and robin cohabited and eyed Chloë amiably *en route*. The lane was single track and poorly surfaced but Chloë appeared to be the only traffic that day. There *had* been a road – a quick phone call to Skirrid End Farm the day before, to someone who wasn't the Gin Trap, had informed Chloë that a bus would take her 'inches from the lane'. It had indeed, but Skirrid End Farm was not 'a few yards up on the left'. Chloë had walked the few yards and seen nothing but hedge. To the left or right. Estimating that she walked a mile in around fifteen minutes, she calculated that she had covered just over two of them; the run of hedgerow interrupted only every now and then by rickety gates leading to pasture.

Something's not right.

Yes, it is. Keep going.

Trudging along, half halting every few strides to hump her rucksack back into position, Chloë tried to envisage what Skirrid End Farm would look like. No clear picture entered her mind's eye and if she tried to design the farm herself, she got no further than a vast front door more suited to a church. She considered the voice on the other end of the telephone. Australian? New Zealand? South African? No, it was antipodean for sure. Male. Not bowled over with joy and excitement to hear from her but welcoming none the less.

'Ah yih! *Ker-Low-E.* Sure! Take the bus – it stops inches from the lane, we're just up on the left. Few yahds, you know. Be seein' ya. Travel safe.'

Lunch-time had obviously been and gone and Chloë did not need the rumbles from her stomach to tell her so. After all, it had been nearing noon on the train but, despite protestations from her stomach even then, Chloë had rejected sandwiches of rubber in favour of fantasy: doorstep slabs of Aga-baked bread slathered with furls of hand-churned butter and crested with wedges of crumbling cheddar gouged by blunt knife from a wax-clothed round.

There'd better be. There'd bloody well better be.

Inches from the lane. Just a few yards up on the left.

The lane was not getting any shorter and the hedges seemed to be higher now and appeared to converge ever so slightly. Any more than a few yards and they might very well close in on her. Chloë looked at her watch. Two fifty-three. Thirty-eight minutes. Seven minutes to three miles.

'Three miles is not a few "yahds",' declared Chloë out loud. 'Three miles is not funny. I'm starving hungry and have no idea where I am.'

Walking past a driveway to her right, Chloë read the sign, 'Skirrid End Farm', and trudged wearily along.

Skirrid End Farm! On the right? Back there?

She came to a standstill and, still facing forwards, craned her neck around to reread the sign. Skirrid End Farm. Definitely.

'A "few yards up"?' she shouted. 'On the *left*!'

Who's counting!

'On the *right*?' she declared to a robin. '*Must* be antipodean, that bloke. Everything topsy turvy!'

It was, however, with good humour and an easily found spring in her step, that Chloë retraced a few yards and turned left up the drive to meet whatever was to greet her. The drive was long enough to wonder. Church-type door? A smoking chimney? A rusty old Taff astride a tractor? Border collies? Straight into the kitchen to a scrubbed table with gingham cloth and the bread and the cheese and the hand-churned butter? And 'Chloë Cadwallader, there's pri-tti now!' sung in welcome?

In the event, two large rumps met her view and, as she called 'Hullo', the tail of one was raised and a steaming mound of admittedly sweet-smelling manure was dumped sonorously at her feet in welcome.

'Hullo?' she called again, somewhat nasally.

'Chloë? Is it you?' The voice was pukka and strong and came from somewhere quite close. 'Chloë?' It belonged to a rotund woman who emerged from behind a wall with a saddle under each arm and a bridle over each shoulder. 'Chloë? Cad*wall*ader?' Her hair was grey and plaited, Indian-squaw style, halfway down her back. 'Jocelyn Jo's God-Daughter Girl?' Her cheeks bloomed cerise and a pair of button-black eyes glistened a delighted welcome at Chloë.

'Yes, it's me. I'm Chloë Cadwallader.'

The other tail was lifted and a further greeting deposited with a rumble and a splat.

'Am I *glad* to see you!' The woman was very close, dumping the saddles on a low wall, offering her hand. No she wasn't, she was offering to take Chloë's rucksack. She tugged while Chloë wriggled free.

'Thank heavens it *was* you!' she was saying as she wrestled with straps and fought with buckles. 'Thank heavens it was you whom Jocelyn sent. Though who else it could have been I do not know!' Her laugh was deep and jovial. A Santa Claus chuckle. 'But thank heavens that it is you and that you are here now.' She slipped the bridles on to the two horses and rattled away without pause for breath. '*I'll* take your worldly possessions. *You* jump up on Percy here and take Rosie and Kerry around the paddock. At the far end is the wood: one gate, one track, com*plete*ly circular. About – An – Hour. Can't possibly go anywhere else, nor get lost. Bugger! The bread! An hour. Ta-ra!'

Very, very slowly, Chloë closed her mouth as she watched the Gin Trap scurry back to the farmhouse carrying her rucksack like a babe in arms. Even more slowly, she shifted her gaze downwards until it rested upon two piercing blue eyes belonging to a small girl in jodhpurs; blond hair in pigtails bedecked with meticulous red bows. With great circumspection, Chloë searched for her voice. Not knowing whether or not it would appear, what it would sound like if it did; nor, indeed, what it was she was to say, Chloë did not bother to clear it. It eventually crackled out, two tones deeper than usual.

'Are you Rosie, or are you Kerry?'

'I'm Kerry, silly. *That's* Rosie.'

Rosie turned out to be the first tail-lifter. She turned her doleful eyes on Chloë on hearing her name mentioned and misplaced.

'So *that* must be Percy?'

' 'Course!'

Rhymed with horse.

And Chloë had not ridden one for some five years.

As Kerry scurried off for hard hats, Chloë worked hard at keeping her mouth closed, her head on straight and her wits about her. Both Percy and Rosie were eyeing her quizzically. She picked her way carefully around their two pungent offerings and introduced herself self-consciously. They welcomed her unconditionally with a nuzzle and a huff apiece and then went back to chewing on their bits.

Instinctively, she checked the throat lash and noseband

on each bridle and tightened the girths on the saddles with a 'Whoa there!' to ward off any inclinations the horses had of nipping her. Chloë Cadwallader was back in the saddle.

Kerry turned out to be a very nice girl of eight years old. She put Chloë at her ease at once for she did not want to know anything about her. She saw no need for an explanation of how an apparent stranger had dumped her rucksack for Percy and was now taking her out on a hack. Such an explanation would only eat into time precious for more important topics such as snaffle bits, jute rugs and ponies with people's names.

'You'll love Jemima, she's a Cleveland Bay cross, sixteen hands with a sock on her off hind. Desmond's a bit of a pain, tends to put in a *big one* if you use your stick. Which you have to, *all the time*. He's the roan over there with the wall-eye. Harry's that big bay hunter type under the apple tree, he's started going disunited in left canter. So I'm told. He's too big for me. Might suit you, though.'

What could Chloë do but say 'I see'?

'Boris, that grey Section B over there by the brook, his show name is Boris the Bold Mark Two. Which is daft really because he's the biggest wimp out. He won't even go over a cavaletti. But Basil, he'll jump anything. I've jumped two foot six with a two-foot spread on him. And that was when I was just seven and three-quarters!'

'I see.'

While Kerry wittered on about running martingales and French gags, Chloë allowed Percy's sway to relax her. A gentle canter fixed a smile to her face and sharpened her senses to her new surroundings. The farm was set in a dimple amongst the hills and, from a viewpoint at the top of the wood, she could see that there was indeed a chimney smoking and a tractor crawling along the side of one field. The hills were soft and amiable, not nearly as bleak nor as black as she had anticipated.

'Too much Bruce Chatwin,' she murmured distractedly.

'Isn't he that showjumper?' Kerry asked.

The wood crept part way up a slope, rather like a beard. The floor of it was covered with pine needles and mulch – rather like bristles. It was soft underfoot and smelt heavenly. From the top, Chloë could see that the farm was relatively isolated. She could make out buildings way over the other side of the lane but these were so far away that it was impossible to tell whether they were merely barns and byres or a dwelling. No smoke from there. Rising in jagged steps beyond was the Skirrid mountain, most onomatopoeic.

I'll climb that one day. Maybe I'll ride up. Would you like that, Percy?

Gin Trap's directions brought Chloë and Kerry back into the yard on the dot of four – she could pick out the chimes of a grandfather clock. It wasn't coming from the house which was directly in front, but somewhere to her left. It was on entering the tack room that she discovered it, tocking patiently, brass pendulum swinging in a most leisurely fashion. Though she had been at Skirrid End for just over an hour, already the tack room seemed as good a place as any for a grandfather clock. Chloë bade goodbye to Kerry and said she could see no reason why she shouldn't take her out on another hack on Sunday.

'Brilliant. Ask if you can ride Barnaby – he's smashing. Liver chestnut, fourteen three, three-quarter Arab. Needs a kimblewick though.'

'I see.'

The small of Chloë's back nags ever so slightly. It tells her that five years has been an inordinate absence from the saddle. She rubs it tenderly and picks out the piece of chaff nestling in the corner of her mouth. She inhales deeply and closes her eyes. What is it?

I think that's bread.

And?

Something else. Everywhere. Fresh, clean air. Hang on, tractor diesel, just faintly, over there.

And?

Sheep? No, horse. Of course. And? Wet earth.

Wales.

Wales.

She opens her eyes and takes a broad look around her. A smile breaks over her face and brings light into the darkening yard. Wales. As Peregrine said, a splendid idea. An hour and a half was all it had taken to feel settled, content and at home. And yet she had never been to Wales before. With the relaxed swagger of one who spends all day in the saddle down on the farm, Chloë saunters off towards the farmhouse, in search of hot bread and gingham tablecloths and this curious woman called Gin Trap. As she nears the porch, she sees a figure propped leisurely against it. It's shadowy but it is most certainly a he. It must be the antipode.

'Yo, Chlo! I'm Carl.'

Carl is possibly the best-looking man Chloë has ever set eyes on.

SEVEN

Forty-five bowls.
Forty-five side plates.
Forty-five dinner plates.
Forty-five dessert plates.
Pale white glaze rimmed in blue, please.
By Valentine's Day.
Many thanks. Thirty per cent
deposit paid to Saxby Ceramics.
Balance on delivery.

The list had been pinned up for almost a month. William read it cursorily each time he set foot in the studio. Today, he swiped it off the wall, the drawing-pin holding on fast to a snag of the page with 'five' written on it.

'Only forty bowls, eh?' he muttered under his breath before spying Barbara's forelegs clipping their way up the two steps to the threshold of the studio.

'Well, I've done the bowls and dessert plates which gives me a month to complete the order. Nigh on impossible. What joy.' Barbara bleated and pursed her lips around the edge of the list. They tugged in a playful push-me-pull-you sort of way before Barbara fixed her yellow eyes on William accusingly, seeming to say 'Your heart's not in it, Billy Boy'. William gave her the list to chew on while he took to a corner of his thumbnail on which to ruminate.

'*Pale white glaze rimmed in blue.* They mean, of course, dolomite with cobalt oxide. Philistines!'

'Philistines!' bleated Barbara who decided that grass was more tasty than paper and wandered off to nibble the new shoots sweet in the shadow of the holly bush. William retrieved the sodden mash that the list had become and smirked to see that it was still quite legible, no smudges, no runs. Clearly, Morwenna had sent him a photocopy, keeping the original for herself.

'Very cute,' William conceded, 'keeping proof of the original order should I have any ideas for improvement. Or change.'

She had also kept the deposit as her cut, which was unusual.

'Shrewd,' said William, 'just in case I don't complete the order. Or if things change.'

But because he was still paying off the washing-machine in monthly instalments, he wedged, kneaded and weighed out five equal balls of stoneware without grumbling and effortlessly threw five side plates. Debussy crackled forth from an aged transistor which was caked in clay, chipped and cracked with neglect. William wedged, kneaded and weighed another five balls. Another five plates soon stood in monotony on a wooden plank.

'I'm bored, Babs,' said William, thumping the transistor to silence Cliff Richard (for many years, and due most probably to an inordinate amount of clay in the workings, Radio 2 was the only station transmitted). He began to knead and wedge once more.

'I'm bored to the very core.'

Barbara, who was wholly intolerant of melancholia, sneered and sauntered away. William wiped the backs of his hands across his brow, and the fronts of them down his smock, before tiptoeing into the kitchen to retrieve the telephone. Refusing to break his self-imposed law of no-clay-in-the-house, he perched precariously on the freezing cold step and dialled a cottage three miles away. The phone rang and rang but, knowing a similar clay ban was in force, William hung on patiently and gouged clay from under his nails. Finally, the telephone was answered and William leapt to his feet with the receiver tucked under his chin so he could gesticulate wildly.

'I have ninety pieces to go and am dangerously close to smashing forty-five bowls and throwing ten side plates into the reclaim,' he exclaimed, a certain glee peppering his rapidly delivered woe. There was a brief silence in which William held the phone aloft and whispered 'Ninety' into it for dramatic impact.

'You'd better come over at once, dear boy!'

It was precisely the advice William was expecting.

'I was hoping you'd say that.'

'At *once*!'

Barbara accompanied a whistling William to the end of the drive at Peregrine's Gully before turning back in the hope that Morwenna might turn up on the off chance and provide her with some sport for the afternoon. As was his way, William neither acknowledged the goat's presence nor bade her farewell – the latter would suppose the former, hence the resolute whistling.

The New Year had been one of the wettest on record and the ground ran beneath his feet like the slurry in the basin of his wheel after a day's work. As he strode the well-known route he rued the fact that it had been months – last autumn at least – since he had visited Mac. He knew his phone call was unnecessary, that he was always welcome; but he knew too that a phone call more than once in a while, a visit for a visit alone and not for advice, would not go amiss. Mac was well into his seventies after all. And after all, Mac was Mac.

Michael Mount, commonly known as Mac, was William's mentor. He had taught him everything he knew about clay but, most importantly, he had instilled in him the intrinsic magic of the stuff and had inspired him more than any teacher at college, more than any studio potter studied and lauded. More, therefore, than Bernard or David Leach, more than Lucy Rie, more than Thomas Naethe even. For it had been Mac who had wrapped William's hands around a ball of terracotta clay when he was nine years old. With his own hands covering, and uttering not a word, he had squeezed hard over William's until the clay was quite warm and had compacted under his fingernails, colouring every line and gulley in his palm.

'It's like the earth,' William had gasped in awe, scrutinizing his hand.

'Well, it *is* called *terra*cotta, dear boy!' Mac had said gruffly, having always felt awkward about conversing with children.

'No,' insisted William, '*the* earth – look, in the palm of my hand. Rivers of clay, Mac. See how it's dried here? That's an earthquake. And see this,' he explained, holding the terracotta ball aloft, 'this is like the world too – see? From my nails and your squeezing? The Himalayas. The sea. Here's England, this patch here.'

Mac hadn't the heart to tell the boy that Ireland was usually seen on the left, not the right, of mainland Britain so he patted William on the head.

'Along with diamonds, clay is the most precious thing the earth gives us,' he said sternly, tweaking William's ear and motioning him to sit. 'Man himself was fashioned out of the stuff.'

While Mac and William's father shared a pipe and a memory or two, William perched on a stool in a corner and, like Little Jack Horner, stuck his thumb deep and with relish into the clay. Instinctively, he squeezed against it with his first three fingers and began to pinch a slow, clockwise path around his thumb with deliberation and reverence. The ball had become a bowl.

That afternoon he made two more. The next week he was coiling. Bowls, urns, pots; vessels all for they both contained and revealed space. Intuitively, William made shapes where the space inside determined the form, and he built forms which described the space they occupied. At nine years old, he had no idea he was doing either. Mac was convinced that first afternoon that the child was a prodigy and, as a consequence, saw no need for any specialized child-conversing technique. With this boy he could talk unguardedly about clay; a feat rarely possible with contemporaries. The boy, too, lost all awkwardness and stilted politeness. They could, in fact, just chat. They could also be sound and secure in each other's silence. The clay had wedged shut the generation gap and had fired impermeable a friendship between them. Far more precious than diamonds.

For ten years, until he went to college, William arrived at Mac's at nine every Saturday and Sunday morning and most afternoons during school holidays. That he forfeited a coveted place in the school football team and sacrificed initiation into the intricacies of adolescent sex, bothered him not at all. A vessel, growing and undulating under his hands, damp and silky to the touch, was far more sensual a proposition than a hasty grope in a musty smelling cloakroom. Though he had yielded to the latter on a few occasions, the forms over which he ran his hands invariably felt too bony to ever pose a preoccupation, or even much of a distraction. So, William forsook teenage sport in all its guises and probably saved himself a great deal of injury. He worked harmoniously alongside Mac who produced his renowned stoneware tableware which the local cafés bought in bulk and which he sold at inflated prices to tourists. Dry glazed in trademark earth colours which Mac called 'home-made Cornish sludge', his pieces were coveted as quintessential souvenirs of the county, just like Cornish fudge and clotted cream. With the onset of arthritis, his time at the wheel was limited to a precious hour or so a day but his prices had risen accordingly and the last laugh was still all his.

Mac lived on the outskirts of a classic Cornish harbour village and the smell of fish, diesel and sea solicited

William from half a mile off. As he wound his way down into the village and up through the other side, the gulls yelled and wheeled with a scavenging greed absent from those which seemed to circle just for the hell of it over the cliffs beyond Peregrine's Gully. Alongside the gulls, jovial voices bantered out from the harbour and every now and then a rusty local van stalled and beeped its way through the narrow main street headed for the fishmongers of Falmouth and Penzance. For William, who had uttered hardly a word all week, let alone held a conversation, the noise was deafening and it was with some relief that he let himself in to Mac's cottage.

'Don't tell me you have a *car*?' were Mac's first words, his face aghast.

'Gracious no!' exclaimed William once he had his breath back. 'Whatever made you think that?'

'That look! On your face. That's the look people with cars wear when they arrive. That's what traffic jams and petrol fumes and three-point turns do! Cars distort the physiognomy, dear boy. A facial expression exclusive to the late twentieth century. Like this,' he scrunched his face tight shut, 'and like this,' he said, opening his features but fixing them askew in apparent angst.

'I see,' mulled William who would have quite liked to laugh.

'So,' said Mac, with a clap of his hands ushering William firmly inside. 'She's still got you making dinner services for the bourgeoisie?'

'Well, for a trumped-up bistro in Crickhowell, at any rate,' William laughed lightly, unwinding his scarf and settling deep into an old Windsor chair.

'Crick-who'll? Where's that then?'

'South-west Wales, I believe.'

'A hundred and eighty pieces?'

'Indeed – with an option on serving platters and small table vases at a later date. I drew the line at ashtrays.'

'As I would damn well hope! Mind you, nice little earner, my boy!'

'Less thirty per cent.'

'Ah!'

'And, of course, the subjugation of my own creativity.'

'Which, I'd confidently say, is worth *far* more than thirty per cent. But there we are. And here we are! Welcome, dear dear boy!'

After two cups each of strong tea, they sat and said not much over a pipe. William was not a smoker and yet with Mac he would gladly puff away an afternoon. He was not sure why, maybe it was to capture any remaining shred of his father, maybe it was to keep Mac company. Perhaps it was just to be polite. Maybe it was because it was downright pleasant. Just as William never had to introduce himself when he phoned, so he was relaxed enough in Mac's company to sit in affable silence. William noticed, even through the blue haze of tobacco smoke, that Mac was now quite white. And yet his thick head of hair and extravagant eyebrows, his neat moustache and tanned skin gave not the impression of age but of vitality. As if there had been no pollution or stress during his life to colour him any different. William had always known Mac as fair, hirsute and lively. He was merely two shades lighter now, that was all.

Mac observed that William was leaner than when he had last seen him, and that it suited him. His mid-brown hair flopped becomingly here and there making his dark brown eyes all the more elusive and attractive. He noticed too that William's complexion was showing the indelible signs of living amidst the tawny moorland and the lash of the sea air. Ruddy, translucent and awash with health and hardiness. Only his hands belied his habitat for they were elegant, clean and pale. A concert pianist, perhaps; a surgeon, maybe. A ceramicist, of course.

Once the pipes were cool and the fire needed stoking, Mac eased conversation in.

'My boy,' he started, poking methodically at the embers, 'I know you don't need me to tell you to give up the wholesale business and make a go of things as a *potter*.' He raised an eyebrow at William and lifted the corner of his mouth to say 'Well then?' silently but quite undeniably.

'*You're* in the wholesale business of sorts too,' protested William gently, 'with your chunky mugs and squat teapots and home-made Cornish sludge.'

'Ah,' said Mac, tapping his pipe and absent-mindedly putting it back between his teeth, 'but I do not have your skill. You're the master craftsman. I just churn out – stuff. We both work with clay, but we're worlds apart in terms of *quality*, of vocation.'

'You know clay better than anyone,' said William fixedly.

Mac chuckled and sucked on the pipe. 'Hell, I've even started putting the odd piskie here and there – peeping behind a mug handle; lounging on a plate rim; peering up from the depths of a jug!'

'Pixie,' said William.

'Piskie,' agreed Mac, retrieving a mug with a small figurine clambering over the rim, for proof. 'See! Positively Walt Disney!' he basked.

'But you're the one who inspired me! Who still does,' William protested. 'You showed me just what clay is. What it can do. What it can be. That it is organic, alive. As precious a commodity as diamonds. You are the sole reason that I am where I am and that I work with clay at all. That I love the stuff and that it is my very life-force.'

'Dear boy! You flatter! What I am trying to say is, I know where I'm at – surely that must be the goal of every artist? My limitations as a potter are also my achievements,' said Mac, giving the clay elf a ping with his thumb and forefinger. 'I feel neither restricted nor frustrated for I am content to make what I make, glaze as I do,' he declared, suddenly on his feet, twirling the fire-iron as if he were Gene Kelly. William held the mug and looked at the figurine; the ensemble was unashamedly kitsch and yet a second look revealed remarkable, secret little details that quite took him aback.

'And I know what I want to do.' He raised his face to Mac and looked most forlorn. 'But how *can* I when another depends on me?'

Mac pursed his lips and leant against the fire-iron, rocking on his heels.

'That Saxby woman has more than one young potter churning out pot-boilers to keep her warm. Toasting more like – she must be making a mint out of you.' He enjoyed his 'pot-boilers' pun but could see it was quite lost on William.

'But Mac, if I don't – for her . . . Then I can't – with her.'

Mac cocked his head and regarded William until the penny dropped.

'And how great a loss is that?'

'She's taught me, er, everything I know in that department. I just feel I *ought*, you know, to stick around? She's having a hard time – convinced that her youth and looks are passing her by.'

'Aren't they just!' chuckled Mac just within earshot. 'You mean she's giving *you* a hard time. Well,' he said, '*I've* taught you everything you need to know about clay and I would hope to goodness that you don't carry soppy guilt around about that! Though,' he furthered, tracing a semicircle across the flagstone floor in his slippered feet, 'a visit a little more *now* than *then* would be nice.'

'I was thinking that myself, as I walked here. Made a Not-So-New-Year's resolution of sorts,' William admitted apologetically.

'Dear boy, I'm jesting! Can't you tell? Every day as I sit at my wheel I know exactly where you are, that we both have slurry on our hands and an image of the finished piece in our heads!'

'Morwenna –' started William tangentially. And closed the sentence at just the one word. His discomfort was tangible and though Mac was tempted to jest further to lighten the load, he knew that William required more. It was the advice of a father that William sought. Or father figure. One, indeed, who knew.

'There's the rub!' Mac thought to himself but said out loud, unwittingly.

'Pardon?' said William, who was miles away – he had spied a bowl he had made some years before. Glazed in Lusty Red.

The humming girl's freckles.

Mac was speaking.

'I'm not one really to advise on the love element in life, never having had a wife, having only ever *had* women and never really loved any of them,' Mac trailed off with a lascivious twink in his eye. 'But, I do know what people in love look like, how they behave. I saw it in your father, many many years ago.'

'With *Mother*?' said William with certain incredulity.

'No, no. Before your mother.' Mac swept the subject away quickly. 'Anyway, I've seen how a love-struck man looks and behaves. You, William, I am sorry to say, are not one of them. Therefore I prescribe an analysis of the common cliché.' Mac was stalking the room with his fire-iron, pointing it here and there, doffing his head and playing with an eyebrow. William thought he resembled a slightly mad professor giving a lecture. Ever the attentive student, he waited. With a tilt of the head to gaze momentarily at the ceiling and yet not at the ceiling at all, Mac continued.

'The common cliché, my boy. That's what we need to consider here. After all, clichés only evolve if their sentiment is tried, tested and true. *Cruel to be kind.*' He let the phrase hang in the air a moment. 'Finish the contract – the Welsh bistro can be the last. Give her forty per cent if it makes you feel easier. And then give that Saxby woman the heave-ho. There's no contract there to be finished but there *is* a psychological tie that is fast becoming a knot. It'll soon strangle you entirely. The deed itself may well be seen as cruel, but you can execute it kindly.'

William accepted the advice and felt a certain resolve flow through his body. He gathered his coat with an effusive show of gratitude and genuine affection. A date was set for a morning's throwing the next week.

'If she protests, or if she whines, sling the old If-you-love-someone-set-them-free at her. Usually works.' Mac laid a hand on William's shoulder-blade and gave a friendly shove. As they hovered by the door prolonging their parting, William could see that he had something else to say. When it had reached the tip of Mac's tongue, William knew instantly what it was. And it was that instant that Mac knew he had been rumbled. And yet, though he could have made rapid excuses about the encroaching darkness, William remained. So Mac cleared his throat.

'And Dad?'

'Dad's gone, Mac.'

'You make it sound like he's quite dead!'

'Well, isn't he?'

'No, he is not. And, though I'd forgotten that Crick-howl is in south-west Wales, I *do* know that your father is. And you know that too.'

EIGHT

It was not just the look of Carl that had dropped Chloë's jaw and cranked long dormant cogs of concupiscence back into motion; more it was his manner, his voice especially. It was his twangy 'Yo Chlo!' that had hit her G-spot first, for he was still hidden in shadow when her ears were solicited. On closer inspection, a tall, lithe figure, blond of hair and blue of eye, was revealed. A generous smile presented a perfect set of ski-white teeth surrounded by lips like crimson velvet cushions. The smile was just slightly, but ever so alluringly, skew-whiff; causing a slight closing of the left eye, a deep dimple to the left cheek. There was a dimple in the right cheek too, but shallower. Chloë had an unbridled urge there and then to dab at the dimples with her tongue tip. It quite alarmed her but Carl's outstretched hand brought her back to her senses which were, admittedly and rather awkwardly, on fire. She grabbed at his hand and shook it heartily, noting that it was warm, dry and smooth and that his wrists were gorgeous. She really ought not to look.

I don't even know where to look. Or how.

'I'm Chloë,' she said, unintentionally huskily, 'and your directions were absolutely appalling.'

‘Ah yih!’ He threw back his head and roared a quick laugh – but long enough for Chloë to gaze at his masculine throat, his Adam’s apple vibrating most seductively.

‘Never could tell my left from my right. Back home, no probs. Sea’s on the left, mountains are on the right.’

‘And the “few yards”?’

‘Hell, distances back home are so vast, you know? Here it’s all so cramped I just presume anywhere’s a few yards from everywhere!’

‘Well, it looks like I’m here!’ Chloë acquiesced, privately thanking the heavens that she was.

‘And I’m most pleased to meet you, ma’am,’ quipped Carl, ushering her into the farmhouse with a flourishing bow.

After the gloom of the porch, and the hallway lit only by shards of light slipping through a door at the far end, the bright kitchen quite dazzled her. Though Chloë could feel the scorch of many pairs of eyes, momentarily she could not place any of them. With a strong blink, the kitchen and its inhabitants came into focus. It transpired that most of the eyes belonged to animals and, as she took in her surroundings, she spied creatures lurking in the most unpredictable of places. But the first thing that captured her eye and settled her soul was the vast Aga stretching across one side of the kitchen, bellowing forth warmth and the smell of baking bread in welcome. Above it, towels and jodhpurs were slung over the sheila-maid like bunting. The sparkle of all the eyes, and the beam from Gin Trap’s cheeks, made Chloë feel a festal welcome had been laid on in honour of her arrival.

In time, she found the kitchen always to be so. It was the heart of Skirrid End and exuded warmth and company for the Aga never went out and the room was never empty. It could lift her spirit and warm her right through on the darkest of mornings or the coldest of evenings. But she was never complacent about its gifts.

On that first day, eyes from every corner and level

assessed and greeted her. One pair were Gin's. Another, set deep into a face furrowed by years of furrowing the land, belonged to an amiable, stone-deaf Welshman called Dai the Hand, who drove the tractor and 'mendsiz things'. The others belonged to an assortment of cats and dogs of varying shapes, colours and degrees of mental stability. Though out on the yard they formed an allied force to patrol the environs, the kitchen they had subdivided into a set of incontrovertible territories.

A dopey-looking labrador sprawled under the huge, scrubbed kitchen table and mumbled in his sleep.

(*No gingham tablecloth. Never mind.*)

Another acted as a draught excluder by the doorway and had to be shoved forcibly when entry or exit was required. At either end of the Aga, two identical black cats sat motionless. It soon transpired that they were ever waiting for the emergence of Jip, the Jack Russell, from his lair in the small warming shelf of the Aga. Yap, another Jack Russell but three-legged, sat in the old Windsor chair at the head of the table and woe betide anyone who fancied sitting there themselves. JR, the final Jack Russell, sat at the foot of Yap's chair looking up imploringly with right foreleg cocked. Whether this was as a gesture of subservience or a snide reminder to Yap of his lack of right foreleg was unclear. A heap of interchangeable kittens snoozed aboard a stack of newspapers near the larder door. A greyhound, long since seen her day, lay in her dead-and-gone pose in the middle of the room, the bones of her hocks and elbows threatening to push right through the meagre pale fawn coat stretched taut over them. A small tabby cat with a shredded ear sat at the greyhound's head and counted the dog's vertebrae. Presiding in judgement over all, an immense shabby tortoiseshell with permanently half-closed eyes sat on top of the cookery books.

Though she had initially believed that all had gathered in a unified welcome, Chloë soon realized that her arrival had made negligible impact on the established ecosystem of The

Kitchen. Before long, she bore witness to a bi-daily syndrome whose cause she would never discover. This consisted of a sudden and violent bout of musical chairs (most atonal) in which fur and fury flew around the kitchen. As quickly as it started, it finished and everyone returned to their positions as if nothing had happened. The kittens were asleep, the greyhound dead, JR's leg was cocked and the tortoiseshell sat irreverently on Delia Smith perusing the scene. Without fail, Gin would look to each of the animals in turn and bellow 'A hapless reshuffle of very little point.'

She was pointedly ignored.

The farmhouse was neither old nor particularly picturesque. It was a sensible structure well suited to its purpose. Its large covered porch provided ample storage for many a pair of muddied or manured boots; the larder was more of a walk-in chamber with wall-to-wall shelving deep enough to carry stock bought in bulk (Chloë gave up the count on reaching the fourteenth bottle of Vimto). Next to the larder was a cold room where the overflow from the fridge could reside quite happily and hygienically (provided the labradors could not gain entry). The kitchen, as we have seen, was vast enough to provide abundant space for all Skirrid End inhabitants other than equine, as well as to house the huge Aga which was the source of all heat and hot water at the farm. The hapless reshuffle of very little point often caused spillage of any liquid foolish enough to be on the kitchen table, and the breakage of any crockery not tucked into the wooden plate rack above the sink. The grand flagstone floor therefore, eminently moppable, was extremely practical too. The bedrooms upstairs were spacious but with windows proportionally small to keep the wind at bay. There was a drawing-room downstairs, bedecked by a regiment of family portraits of questionable lineage, but the room was used only once a year for the Skirrid End Farm Christmas Drinks Extravaganza. Anyone who knew Gin or any of her workforce (two- or four-legged) was invited to leave their boots in the porch and to partake of home-made hot spiced cider and mince pies in the drawing-room. In their socks.

Gin gave Chloë a guided tour after heartily plying her with home-made bread, slabs of farm butter and wedges of quite pugilistic cheese. Chloë would have been quite happy to remain for evermore in the kitchen, with the unparalleled gifts of the Aga and Carl. He was smiling, you see. Without interruption.

(*At me?*

At you!)

He'll be there still, Chloë; his open face, his broad smile creating those dimples that have quite unnerved you. That are because of you.

Stop it! I'm going with Gin.

'It's clicked, my girl! We *have* met before and I do now remember you,' said Gin as she showed Chloë a fine Chippendale chair in the corner of the bathroom.

'I don't think so,' started Chloë, visibly racking her memory.

'Did too!' announced Gin, ushering her to an incongruous dressing-room bedecked with chintz and dainty china trinkets. 'Though I must say, I'd've passed you in the street – not that we were likely to ever be on the same street had Jocelyn not brought us together now.'

Gin motioned Chloë to sit beside her on a fanciful *chaise longue*. Chloë, who could not think of anything to say, did the same as Mrs Andrews and laid her hands daintily in her lap, as befitting the room.

'Oscar!' beamed Gin, leaping to her feet and folding her arms triumphantly across her breast. She led the way to her bedroom. With arms still folded, she heaved herself on to the edge of an impossibly high mahogany bed in a perverted reworking of a Cossack dance. Finally aboard and legs swinging, she said 'Oscar' again, with apparent delight.

'Oscar?' gawped Chloë, who was now about the same height as the Cossack.

'Gracious girl! Your horse!'

'Pardon?'

'Your *horse*, of course. Fifteen hands, bay thoroughbreddy thing with a white blaze, sock on the off fore, I seem to remember. Ridden in a grackle. Lovely paces, jumped like a bean. Oscar!'

Chloë was stunned and only the sight of her flabbergasted reflection in a pretty Queen Anne mirror brought her back to the present.

'My first one-day event?' she squeezed out in a whisper.

'Indeed!'

'When I was fif*teen*?'

'If you say.'

'Did you have jet-black hair?'

'I did indeed! Went grey overnight when I learnt I'd inherited this place from my brother. Actually, rather when I heard he'd shot himself in the barns the other side of the lane.'

Now Chloë folded her arms too and then stood stock-still awhile, rapidly playing a cine-film of her youth on the wall of her mind's eye.

'I *do* remember you, Gin!' she said eventually, uncrossing her arms and clambering aboard Gin's bed. 'Jocelyn brought you along and we all had whisky in the horsebox!'

'Including Oscar!'

'Including Oscar.'

It seemed that the upstairs was exclusively Gin's and the downstairs exclusively the animals'. It was therefore some surprise to Chloë that none of the extravagantly furnished rooms upstairs at the farmhouse appeared to be allocated to her. Before, that was, Chloë learnt of The Rafters.

'I've put you in The Rafters!' boomed Gin as she slung down the ruffle blinds in her bedroom.

'I thought you'd like it up there,' she continued, pushing

Chloë back along the corridor towards the bathroom. 'You *could* have the spare room next to mine but as I *ronfle comme un cochon*, I thought you'd be safer and sounder in The Rafters.'

'As you *what*?' asked Chloë as politely as possible, thinking that it must be French but not as she knew it.

'I snore like a pig!' explained Gin quite soberly. '*Comme un cochon*,' she stressed as she introduced Chloë to a steep staircase hidden by what she had previously presumed to be the airing cupboard door at the back of the bathroom.

'Just remember,' said Gin, with a sparkle in her eye, 'to give a hearty three knocks when you're coming down – I'm not a pretty sight in the bath, and even less so on the loo!'

Left by herself at last, Chloë contemplated a bottle of mane-and-tail conditioner by the bath before opening the door to The Rafters. The stairs leading there were not carpeted and she trod the boards forever upwards in a symphony of creaks and groans.

The Rafters were vast, half the house at least though the furniture had been arranged to subdivide the space further and create some vestige of cosiness. Thus, in the furnished half of the area, the beams had been painted dark green, the panels in between pale primrose. There was a skylight and a dormer window with small fussy curtains of pastel floral persuasion. They rose and fell conversationally with the breeze. (In March, she would learn they rarely touched the sill, the gales causing them to hover constantly at a ninety-degree angle to the window-pane.)

She looked over to an old iron bed in the corner with a faded kilim at the foot. Next to it was a Regency dressing-table and a stool covered and further frilled in the curtain fabric. In the centre of the floor space, a sheep fleece lay like a martyr. A grand old cupboard of the C. S. Lewis type stood sagely in the middle of the room and in line with the first painted beam. Chloë opened it and stepped inside, clacketing the wooden hangers and smelling mothballs. Between the wardrobe and the stairwell was an old, battered armchair over which a tartan travel blanket was slung. It looked conspiring and inviting and was immensely comfortable when she sat deep into it to peruse her lair.

That night, Chloë excused herself after supper and washing-up duty, and before a session of Monopoly was to start. She had caught Carl's eye many times over the meal and because her stomach leapt into her mouth each time, she found she could eat very little. He had dried while she had washed and though he chattered away most amiably, to her horror one-word answers were all that she could contribute. Each time she felt a longer sentence brewing she would catch sight of his lovely wrists, or his chiselled jaw smattered with fair bristles, and find herself confined to 'Really?' or 'Oh?' or, worse, a chirrup of a giggle. So she used the excuse of the long rides by train and horse, and the excitement of it all, to gain an early night, and hiked up to The Rafters and into bed with her writing pad instead.

Halfway through a letter to Peregrine and Jasper (in which she mentioned Carl more than once or twice in passing) she felt a certain itchiness which could not be attributed to the fine cotton sheets nor the antique patchwork eiderdown on top. There was something in between. Something heavy and coarse. She rolled back the eiderdown. Of course. There, staring Chloë uncompromisingly in the face, an old New Zealand rug lay spread-eagled. Built for the coldest, wettest weather. Designed for horses living out in the fields in winter. Its green canvas waterproof shell was uppermost leaving the woollen lining to prickle its way through the cotton sheets. For a while, Chloë stood quite still, wearing her now perfected Skirrid End Jaw Drop. Slowly, a smile spread over her face. She sniffed at the rug and found it to be quite clean, the faintest smell of its long-gone wearer pleasant in the distance. She heaved it over so the woollen side was uppermost, rolled the eiderdown back and slipped deep down into the warmth.

'Really rather sensible,' she reasoned to The Rafters, 'so warm and snug. As a bug in a New Zealand rug!'

She would finish the letter tomorrow. She was feeling pleasantly tired and pondered on a wistful innuendo about something from New Zealand keeping her warm at night, until slumber led her away and she slept, deep, dreamless and warm until dawn poured through the skylight the next day.

Mr and Mrs Andrews watched over her, this time in the form of a postcard reproduction from the National Gallery. It *was* them but they were very little and the closer Chloë looked at them, the more they disintegrated into dots which she found a little alarming. She had slipped the card into the corner of the mirror frame on the dressing-table, just so they could keep her in check first thing in the morning and last thing at night. Just so they were there.

NINE

Barbara stamped her hind hoof and positioned her forelegs squarely. She blew through her nostrils and curled her lips ever so slightly so that a noise midway between bellow and screech could hit Morwenna as soon as she shut the car door. When it reached her ears, a feeling of sinking dread coursed through and settled in the pit of her stomach. She looked over at Barbara who stared back icily with a glint most evil to her eyes. Though she opened the boot to double-check, she knew that her car was regrettably biscuit- and vegetable-free. Not a crumb. Not a shred. Not a bean.

Morwenna decided on polite conversation but it merely served to irritate the goat further. Flattery was the only option left.

'Ho! Barbara! There's a good little goaty. My, you're looking pretty, aren't you?'

Barbara stamped.

'Listen, I don't have a thing in these pockets. Very remiss of me. How about I make it up to you? Next time.'

Barbara intended to ensure that there would not be a next time.

As Morwenna approached, slightly stooped and with her

right hand outstretched making strange tickling movements with her fingers, Barbara began to bob and weave like a boxer at the ringside. With just a few yards between them, Morwenna straightened up and put her hands on her hips.

'You,' she said, striding assertively towards Barbara, 'are only a goat.'

However, she had not reckoned on a goat with a grudge and, when it came to the simultaneous butt–bite–kick, Morwenna was viciously winded. Searching desperately for breath, she sat down with a thump on the damp ground, the meagre winter grass providing little cushioning. Barbara, who had turned her back on her and was defecating triumphantly, bleated with pride. Morwenna pressed her hand lightly to her thigh and winced. Once her breathing had calmed, she picked herself up with care and caution and walked to the car slowly. With as much dignity as she could muster, without looking back.

'It was a goat,' she mumbled into the neck of her thick jumper. She had rolled down her tights and hitched up her skirt to reveal a whorl of dark crimson and French navy. A splice of dry blood. Her leg trembled slightly but she told herself that this was due to her aversion to disinfectant, to infection, to Trust-me-I'm-a-doctor. It was, in part, also due to this doctor being extremely handsome.

'A *goat* did this to you, Mrs Saxby?' he asked quietly as he held her knee and crooked her leg up. His hands were warm, strong and hairless.

'Ms,' she replied taking her face out of the cavity of her polo-neck, 'you know, with a zed. And yes, it was a goat.'

'A billy-goat?'

Ha! Billy's goat indeed.

'No. A pet goat.'

'Gracious.'

'Not mine.'

'I'm not surprised!' He laid her leg down gently and pondered into the crook of his index finger. 'I see from your records that there is no record of tetanus jabs. In fact, we have no record of you at all for the last seven years.' He looked at her face and saw anxiety sown deep behind defensive eyes. He also noticed their sparkle and felt a long forgotten butterfly take wing in his stomach. He smiled. 'Either you've been as fit as a fiddle or you have an inherent mistrust of the medical profession!'

Morwenna gave a nervous laugh and then retreated down into the mouth of her jumper.

'We'll give you a tetanus jab. And the once-over, too.'

Morwenna sank visibly.

'If it makes you feel any easier, I myself had the once-over just last week,' the doctor assured her.

Morwenna wondered why. He looked perfectly fit. He looked, actually, perfectly gorgeous.

'At our age,' he continued, scanning her notes, 'it's as important as servicing the car.'

I don't think I've ever had the Fiat serviced.

'Pardon?'

'I can't remember when I last had my car serviced,' mumbled Morwenna.

'Well then,' he said grinning, 'let's hope we don't find in you what undoubtedly lurks beneath your bonnet!'

Morwenna looked at him sternly. 'But the car's been running fine. It splutters a bit, creaks here and there and can't cope with cold mornings. Oh my God' she declared as the metaphor dawned, 'just like me!'

'And me,' he rued quite happily.

'But why meddle if there's no muddle?'

He tipped back on his chair and observed her thoughtfully, tapping his fingertips together, wondering how to prolong her welcome presence in his surgery.

'Wouldn't you prefer to know if there's a muddle before you're in the middle of it?'

Morwenna contemplated the doctor through the safety of her jumper which she had kept pulled up to just beneath her nose.

'What's involved in the once-over anyway?' she said quickly, through her visor of wool.

'Heart, blood, weight, lungs, breasts – nothing to it really. We'll do it before we do the jab if you like.'

I can't let her go – I must just see if there's a smile in there.

Morwenna gazed through the surgery window to the beach. An elderly couple walked a pair of dachshunds and two children were playing energetically; she could hear their delighted laughter through their abandoned movement. Her thigh throbbed and her mind whirled.

'OK,' she said tentatively, keeping her gaze fixed where it was, 'but I'll just go for the jab today. And quick! Before I run away.' She took her face quite out of her jumper and fixed a not-so-ambiguous smile on the doctor.

* * *

Chloë has been at Skirrid End a month now, and has the saddle sores to prove it. She has also been nipped twice and trodden on often, but not by goats. She has newly defined biceps and firmer thighs as further proof of her new life, for every morning she is mucking out by seven-thirty, and twelve hours later she has bedded down eight horses and replenished twice as many water buckets twice a day. She rather likes the changes that country living has made to her body; her face has lost its pasty Islington tinge and her lungs are glad of the crystal air. Her hands are slightly thicker, her nails stubbier but she keeps them clean and trim and they are not unattractive at all. She has a healthy glow to her cheeks due in part to the crisp weather, and in part to the certain lust she has developed for Carl. Her lips, though, are a little chapped and she has convinced herself that they will be no good for kissing. Carl grows more handsome to her every day and it seems preposterous to Chloë that a man of such beauty,

(*and humour and kindness!*)

could ever want
(*and intelligence and manners!*)
to kiss her chapped lips.

She feels a vitality each day on waking and wholesome fatigue on retiring each night. A general sense of well-being. She is healthier and happier than she can remember and often wonders whether she should even bother with the rest of the United Kingdom. She would be quite content with life ever after here in Wales. Hardly surprising, for she is cosseted and secure – an integral part of a household – and her resultant happiness defines that the household must therefore be Home. Or as near to one as she has hitherto come, remember.

Conversation is on a very different plane to that to which Chloë had become accustomed over the preceding London-bound years. No one at Skirrid End knows Anna Recksick or whether there is much difference between a Gentleman's Third and a First, and isn't a 2:2 worn by ballerinas? Concerts on the South Bank could be fun, but at fifteen pounds per ticket, ludicrous! The tube sounds most uncivilized and Islington in dire need of greenery and more sky. In its collective voice, Skirrid End denounces the levels of noise, dirt and decay of the capital as intolerable, unthinkable and not worthy of further discussion.

Instead, and to Chloë's delight, talk at Skirrid is devoted to the land, the weather and animals, interspersed readily with bawdy jokes and heated discussion as to whose turn it is to be banker in Monopoly. Chloë has even started roaring with relish 'A hapless reshuffle of very little point' at the opportune moment.

The days have a loose routine to them which provides a framework of security for Chloë. After mucking out, she gathers with Carl and Gin in the kitchen to discuss the day's schedule. Lunch is self-service, as and when. Tea is an institution with bread and butter and fruitcake shared by all in the kitchen apart from the greyhound who is faddy about her food. Supper is delicious and invariably raucous, followed by life-and-death Monopoly sessions. (There is no television at Skirrid End and many of the letters from the Scrabble set have been eaten over the years by the greyhound, though this does not preclude occasional marathons of the game.) Dai, who proves to be a spendthrift with no notion of investment, usually bows out by nine and Gin, who mostly gambles everything for a hotel on Park Lane, retires soon after.

Chloë and Carl are invariably left with a delicious hour or so together in which they make hot chocolate and light conversation and Monopoly does not matter. He tells her he is travelling and will move on in the spring. She tells him she is travelling too. Really. In a way. Ditto the spring. He whets her appetite for New Zealand and she tells him where not to go in London. He thinks he may miss London out altogether.

'Anyways, I'll be seeing Paris and Edin-burrow.'

They learn each other's favourite film ('Really? Me too!'). And food. And favourite colour. And book ('You must read it!'). They speak loosely of 'back home' but both feel compelled to live for the day and enjoy the present. Because of the Brett Years, Chloë has quite forgotten how to flirt and, deeming her lips unkissable anyway, she begins to find herself utterly relaxed in Carl's easy company and chatters away freely. He adores her for it and also finds her rather alluring. He thinks she has the most beautiful hair he has ever seen and her freckles soon become the stuff of his last, late-night thoughts. But he doesn't tell her so. Oh no. For while he is desperate to kiss her, he reads no sign of a come-on and presumes he must settle for just-good-friends. After all, not much point anyway with spring only a couple of months away to herald their separate ways.

There have been times when, to kiss her, has been quite literally on the tip of his tongue. Once, he came across Chloë cleaning bridles in the tack room, humming softly in time with the grandfather clock; he had hummed in harmony and sincerity before a fit of giggles overtook them and Chloë stuffed the saddle-soap sponge down the back of his shirt. Then there was the time when Desmond threw her off with his spectacular, trademark 'big one' and she returned to the yard muddied, bruised and cross. Carl thought she looked fabulous, all wild and windswept ('Like that chick Cathy from *Wondering Heights*') and would have kissed her right through the mud had Gin not interrupted with cotton wool and 'Is *Desmond* all right though?' Most recently, Chloë made biscuits that were so melt-in-the-mouth and sweet that Carl was convinced her lips must taste likewise and was about to make a lunge for them when a very sudden and hapless reshuffle of absolutely no point took place.

The problem, rued Carl to himself on a daily basis, was that he could rarely get Chloë on her own. And when he did, it was never for long enough for giggles and wrestling to subside and kissing to start in earnest.

Lights are usually out by ten. Carl heads for his pad above the tack room and Chloë creeps and creaks her way up to The Rafters. Sometimes, accidentally on purpose, she catches sight of him from the dormer window. If he hasn't seen her, she whips herself out of view to return for another peek when her heart has slowed up. If he has seen her, she waves nonchalantly and swings the curtains across with a blasé flourish. Each night, she stares at the green rafters and pouts and puckers her lips in readiness for the time when the Vaseline has worked its magic and her mouth is in a fit state for osculation.

At this stage, neither of them has thought much beyond a mutual exchange of lips. For both, this first home run seems momentarily so beyond reach that anything it could possibly lead to remains an unattainable and somewhat unreal notion tucked to the very backs of their minds. A kiss, for the moment, would quite suffice. But when? And how, damn it!

TEN

Chloë's day revolves around the horses and their needs. She is in the saddle for a couple of hours before and after lunch, interspersed with grooming, tack cleaning, rug mending and water-bucket replenishing. Mostly, she takes small, appreciative, pony-mad children out for a generally civilized hack (Desmond permitting). Sometimes, Gin sends her off for a ride to the woods, or down to the stream, or halfway up the hill.

'Just to check,' she tells Chloë, 'on Things.'

When she returns from such outings, Gin asks 'How's Things?' to which Chloë has learnt to reply 'Things is fine.'

Initially, she tried a more detailed report about river-banks and saplings but Gin's glazed look told her quite clearly that she had missed the point.

Today, with the loose-boxes mucked out and Chloë and Carl not quite recovered from a dung-slinging session on the muck heap (after which neither was remotely kissable), Gin has brought them a mug of tea apiece in the tack room and is telling them about the day ahead.

'Do you mind popping into Abergavenny? It's market day and a good opportunity for you, Carl, to see if there are any viable propositions in the camper-van trade, or in whatever wagon it is that you intend to traverse Europe. Chloë, I thought I might leave you to buy a few things from the tack shop for the gymkhana tomorrow. Bugger, tomorrow *is* Saturday, isn't it? Must be, if today's market day.'

'You not going to join us?' asks Carl.

'No, it appears I'm going to have my headache today. I'm even going to banish Dai to the top field for the duration so I can truly have it in peace. Take the Land Rover. And for heaven's sake, take JR too!'

Dai is in the top field. Gin has exiled herself with her biannual headache. Carl and Chloë have been banished to Abergavenny. Just the two of them. Well, and JR but they are bribing him successfully with chocolate.

Together, alone, at last.

A trip to Abergavenny was not really a treat. To Monmouth maybe; to Aber, it was more of a chore. Today, though, Chloë and Carl were thankful for the usual traffic jams and bottlenecks and the unpredictable nature of the Land Rover, as it threw them together in close proximity for longer.

'Yo! Looks like we're going to stall again! Wait for it!'

'Ready! Two, three – now!'

'Way to go, JR! Take him off the dashboard, Chlo. Can't see a thing!'

Since the moment they left Skirrid End, they have been coaxing obedience out of JR with various brands of chocolate. The Jack Russell is now looking rather green and is refusing the final offering. It enables Chloë and Carl to discover that they both share a predilection for the common Mars bar. They are excessively thrilled at the coincidence.

'I can't believe that Mars bars are your favourite too! I'm not even a chocolatey person!' chips Chloë.

'Yih!' drawls Carl, sucking glucose and goop from around his teeth. 'I'm not really a choco fan either. But once in a while, a craving for a Mars bar hits me and I'm a gonner.'

'Say it again,' says Chloë, wriggling in her seat.

'Huh?' asks Carl, taking his eyes from the road.

'*It*,' stresses Chloë, grabbing the steering wheel to avoid the ditch, 'the chocolate bar we both like!'

'Mars bar?'

'Yes, Mahz bah!' mimics Chloë delighted.

'Mars bar?'

'Mahz bah!'

'Shit Chlo,' Carl smiled, 'you're kind of spooky but – Christ! the Land Rover's going to stall again. Hold on to JR this time!'

After they had circumnavigated Abergavenny twice looking for a free parking place, they fought their way into the Pay and Display, did both, and then split up to accomplish their individual tasks. Carl went in search of 'combies', as he called the camper-vans, inadvertently driving Chloë delirious; Chloë took JR and went to buy hoof picks, mane combs and other equine accoutrements suitable for gymkhana prizes.

Needless to say, neither could keep their mind on the task in hand. After a lengthy discussion with a salesman who could have been promoting Brylcreem as much as second-hand cars, Carl made a decision.

'I'm interested, mate. I'll have a think about it. But first I'm going to kiss Chloë.'

Humming away, Chloë was studying a vulcanite D-ring snaffle while filling her nostrils with the heavenly scent of a dressage saddle when she was suddenly grasped from behind and pirouetted. She did not notice the running martingales fall from their hook and bind themselves around JR, nor did she hear the clang of ten hoof picks as they hit the floor. She was oblivious to bridles slithering off the wall and was unaware that the dressage saddle was slowly slipping off its stand. All she knew was that Carl was kissing her and the world could wait. Heaven sent him, thank you, God. With her favourite smell of leather ('Shit Chlo! Mine too!') surrounding her, she was being expertly kissed by her chosen Adonis, surrounded by merchandise devoted to equitation. Heaven now had no mystique, for it could only be such a place.

Pressed against the wall, dislodging an entire selection of clincher brow bands, Chloë gladly welcomes Carl's leg between hers and rides him gently and subconsciously as she kisses him. She can feel his erection poking through his jeans, through hers, and just above her appendix and she says to herself that it can give her peritonitis for all she cares. Slipping her hand through his hair to the back of his neck, she can feel his skin prickle and dampen under her touch. It thrills her. She feels rather proud. Carl is making noises that Chloë has never heard a man make. Spontaneous gulps and groans stifled by the intensity of lip work. She can hear similar sounds an octave higher.

It's me!

It's involuntary.

This girl can't have been kissed for a good long while, thinks Carl as he thrusts his tongue up between Chloë's cheek and teeth, *but man, can she kiss good!*

This *is kissing*, thinks Chloë, sipping Carl's tongue deep into her mouth. *Brett must have been doing something completely different all those years, something horribly lizard-like.*

Jones the Tack, as he was known, would have been quite content for the lady and her young man to kiss all day were it not for a giggle of girls imploring him to let them in to marvel at his wares. He cleared his throat and Carl kissed Chloë deeper. He said 'Hem hem' in as nonchalant a way as he could. Chloë nipped Carl sharply on his bottom lip and then pulled him tight against her, kissing and teasing it better. Jones the Tack put his index finger up to the girls to say 'A minute, will you?' and gave out a cheery whistle. JR waddled towards him under a knot of reins but Carl's hands merely wriggled through Chloë's hair to stroke their way down her back and rest at the base of her spine.

Or the top of her ass, thought Carl, ever the optimist. It was when his hands ventured gamely over Chloë's bottom, which gave an inadvertent thrust, that Jones the Tack felt things were just a little too steamy. For a tack shop. For lunch-time. For Abergavenny, my goodness!

'Ten hoof picks, was it?' he bellowed under the sweetest of smiles. Chloë and Carl leapt apart and found themselves in a tack shop in Abergavenny at lunch-time. Jones the Tack grinned away. Carl whisked himself around to bury his erection in a mountain of sweat rugs stacked conveniently behind him. Chloë stooped down to hide her blush and pick ten hoof picks from the muddle of bridles.

'And ten mane combs too, please,' she said huskily, not daring to catch the man's eye.

'Ten mane combs it is!' sang Jones the Tack. 'Anything else?'

'Hoof oil and plaiting bands, please. Thank you. Very much.'

'It's my pleasure, lady!'

'Yes,' mumbled Chloë looking at JR intensely, doubting whether she was now much of a lady. She scurried away saying 'Yup, thanks, bye'.

'Lady!' called Jones the Tack as she reached the door. 'Aren't you forgetting something?'

Chloë looked aghast. Hoof combs. Mane picks. Plaiting oil. Hoof bands. Nothing missing. She shook her head with eyebrows askew. Jones the Tack nodded in the approximate direction of the sweat rugs without actually looking, and without his smile diminishing.

Carl!

Fortuitously, it was now safe for Carl to emerge. He and Chloë left the shop with a barrage of effusive gratitude and as elegant and honest a walk as they could muster. This they retained quite impressively until the corner of the street, when they fell about laughing until the tears squeezed from their eyes and their sides and faces ached quite unpleasantly.

The journey back to Skirrid End was beset by the all the usual afflictions of a day out in Abergavenny. But now, each traffic jam was a wonderful opportunity for another kiss. And why *won't* the Land Rover stall? They have skipped lunch because they were too busy using their mouths for other things. Carl gladly forsook his research on combies because a stroll to the Linda Vista Gardens was far more attractive a proposition. There, on a picturesquely placed bench looking out over the castle meadows to the River Usk, they practised their kissing some more. Chloë declared it a far better cure for chapped lips than Vaseline.

'But I'll need a daily dose,' she implored.

'Morning and night?'

'And noon!'

'Noon too.'

It was bitterly cold. February after all. Late afternoon. A feeble effort by the sun now swallowed whole by a flat grey sky. Their noses ran and the chill ate into the muscles on their faces causing frequent twitching of the chins and the occasional physiognomic spasm that only served to make the kiss more interesting.

Skirrid End was anomalously quiet when they returned. The tractor was put to bed and all snoozed peacefully in the kitchen. Tiptoeing to the top of the stairs, they could hear the faint rumbles of Gin's porcine snoring and knew all to be well. They fed and watered the horses, bedded down and rugged up. They sneaked into the tack room for a gentle, good-night kiss and parted company for the night. Both felt simultaneously exhausted and yet still on fire. Their lips felt large. Carl soothed himself by masturbating vigorously in front of the mirror in honour of Chloë. Chloë unwound by writing in minute detail to Peregrine and Jasper.

Just before she put her light out, she inched back the curtains. Carl, gloriously bare-chested, was waiting for her. She ran her tongue over her lips and could detect no roughness. Miracle. She whirled her tongue around her mouth and tasted something unfamiliar. Somebody else's mouth. Somebody else's desire. Desire. Unfamiliar. Delicious.

Carl blew her a kiss; chaste laced with amorous intent. She cocked her head and smiled broadly. Closing the curtains as slowly as she could, she clambered into bed with a daft grin on her face. With a sigh, she closed her eyes immediately and welcomed the cushion of silence that preceded sleep. She had neither the time nor inclination to brush her hair and talk to the Andrews. In fact, she didn't dare.

ELEVEN

'Peregrine, my true love, where *are* you?' Jasper cupped his ear at the foot of the stairs and waited.

'Up here!' came a faint reply.

'Up *where* exactly?' yelled Jasper as patiently as he could.

'Up up up!' sang Peregrine, 'right at the top.'

'Oh God,' said Jasper to himself, climbing the stairs with a heavy hand on the banister and a lighter one supporting his gammy hip, 'not the damn frocks again.'

To his relief, he found Peregrine safe in his corduroys handling a Coalport tea service with reverence. He brandished a dainty milk jug in welcome.

'Look what I found! Isn't it divine! Wouldn't First Flush Darjeeling taste incomparable in these darling cups?'

'First Flush Darjeeling,' said Jasper as sternly as he could, 'is indeed incomparable. It's almost thirty pounds a pound!'

Peregrine pouted most becomingly. 'If we can't have a little luxury – us, at our age and stage in life – then what! I may as well give up the ghost right now as face Typhoo *bags* in my dwindling days.'

'Don't be such a drama queen,' Jasper said. 'You know I would rather drink no tea at all than drink anything other than FFD! Look here, look what we have!' He waved an envelope in a gracious arc high above his head.

'Postmark?' squealed Peregrine, clasping both hands tight around the sugar bowl.

'Guess!'

'Gwent?'

'Abso-blooming-lutely!'

Sitting with perfect posture and an empty cup and saucer each, Jasper and Peregrine enjoyed Chloë's letter. It seemed appropriate that as she had written from The Rafters, so they should be ensconced in Jocelyn's attic aboard an old but deceptively supportive two-seater sofa covered with a dust-sheet. Envisaging Chloë huddled beneath her New Zealand rug, they pulled an old tartan blanket tightly about their knees and placed the china cups daintily on their laps.

'*Hullo you both,*' Jasper trilled in falsetto. Peregrine took the letter from him and, placing pince-nez exactly where they should be, started to read.

'*Hope you're happy and healthy*, bla bla, *weather cold but clear*, der der der, horse, bla bla. La la, up in The Rafters, cosy, private etcetera. Early nights ditto mornings. Bla bla. Work hard but have lots of fun. Don't miss London, der der. No regrets, etcetera. *Miss you both* – us both – *madly*. Good! Etcetera. *Gin Trap a hoot*. Good Gracious Me!' Peregrine fell silent while his eyes rampaged along the remaining paragraphs which ran to two pages.

'What?' Jasper nudged him, alarmed that his eyes were so wide and that his jaw had dropped. It was either something utterly horrendous or gloriously disgraceful. 'What what what?' he piped, craning for a glimpse at the page and cursing his appalling eyesight.

Peregrine folded the letter, put it back in the envelope before taking it out again and unfolding it slowly.

'Little Hussy!' he proclaimed with unbridled pride.

'Ch*lo*ë?'

'The little tramp!' Peregrine continued, delighted.

'What *has* she done?' begged Jasper.

'What a filly!'

'Pear-rare-grin!' bellowed Jasper. 'Word for word! Go!'

Peregrine cleared his voice. 'He's called Carl, apparently. A big, strapping bushman from New Zealand! Blond, bronzed and brawny. Oh, that we were thirty years younger!'

'Speak for yourself, old crock,' said Jasper. 'Twenty would be fine for me! Is that how she describes him? A hunky thing from the bush down under?'

Peregrine reread the letter swiftly. 'No, actually, she says, *I've met a really nice bloke from New Zealand. His name is Carl and I know you'd love him,* bla bla.'

'Stop it with the bla blas,' Jasper demanded.

'OK,' conceded Peregrine, 'this is what she says: *His name is Carl and I know you'd,* bla bla. Sorry! *He lives above the tack room – I know the thought of a strapping young man amongst all that leather will probably drive you two wild, but calm down so I can tell you all!* Writes a good letter, our Chloë.'

'I never went in for leather much, but carry on, dear.'

'*We're the only youngsters here. Mind you, by your standards, Gin and Dai are spring chooks!*'

'Sprung whats?' asked Jasper.

'Ah, she explains, *as the Kiwis say for "chicken"! You know, just as soon as I set eyes on Carl, I felt strange murmurings for him which quickly transpired to be Lust, loud and clear! You see, he's big and blond and sensitive and sexy and perfect. And he kisses divinely.* She must know not to start a sentence with "and", surely Jocelyn would have drilled her?'

'Let's make an allowance – the girl's obviously quite beside herself with excitement.'

'Dormant lust, I'd say!'

'Whatever! Continue.'

'Ah, sweet Chloë, listen to this: *As you know, Things were never good with Brett* – I don't know why the capital "T" but never mind – *I realize now that I have never really been kissed before. Before Carl, that is. Can you believe that after a month of near-kisses near-misses, we finally found ourselves mouth to mouth in a tack shop in Abergavenny at lunch-time!* I'm sure she needs a comma or two, but I'll let it lie.'

'Gracious,' said Jasper proudly, 'in a tack shop in Aberwhatsit at noon!'

'All that leather!'

'So public!'

'So exciting!'

'Wild! Please continue, do.'

For some reason, on which Jasper thought it best not to comment, Peregrine took a sip from the empty cup before reading more. '*The kiss lasted an age and beyond. And then some! In fact, was it one kiss or many? Heavens, it was so exciting I could hardly breathe, mind you I could hardly breathe because there were two tongues in my mouth and our faces were pressed as close together as was physiognomically possible! I could feel how excited he was, if you know what I mean – in the trouser region, if you like.*'

'We know what you mean! And yes, we like!'

'*And I don't mind telling you that I felt positively glued to my trouser region!*'

'*Do* we mind her telling us?' Jasper interrupted.

'I don't think so,' pondered Peregrine. '*Do* we?'

'No, no, I think that will be acceptable, Perers. Go on.'

'She continues – ha! *Do I mind telling you? I wonder? But who else is there to tell with Jocelyn gone? Do you mind me telling you, though? I hope not. If I know you two, you'll find it riveting! Well, there we were, snogging for England. I mean for Wales, of course. Light-headed and tongue-tied. I was in paradise. I was on another, higher plane and begged the moment to last forever. As I said, we had been kissing for hours – ages, at least – and if it were not for Jones the Tack (honest!) hollering "Hoof picks!" at us, we'd still be at it now! (Who knows, by the time you're reading this, maybe we are, once again!) After we beat a hasty retreat and the fire in our loins had subsided* – what has the girl been reading?'

'I rather like that – fire in the loins!'

'You would, you incorrigible old codger. I think it's downright Mills & Boon. Where were we? Fire in loins – ah yes: '*had subsided, we sat on a bench and, while I'd love to tell you of the view out over the dingle, I really can't – I didn't even get a glimpse. Mostly I kept my eyes tight shut so I could just feel and taste Carl, soak it all up. Savour the moment. Remember it for eternity. Occasionally, I opened them a peep and caught the dip of his cheek or a snatch of his ear lobe, or a glint of his eye.*

'I'm not falling in love or whatever, I don't think, – oh yes she is! – *it just feels so, I don't know, fresh? Fun? That's it – fun. Just what the doctor ordered after those gloomy, sterile Brett years. Strange how, at the time I thought them neither gloomy nor sterile, yet nor was I having fun and feeling adored – as I am now. Having traded boys for horses during my teenage years and enduring only Brett since then, it now feels so liberating. Finally I can snog and grope and do all those other fun, naughty, wholesome things!*

'Believe me when I tell you his eyelashes are like pitchforks! Pitchforks, I declare! Oh, the beauty of the boy! Adonis is a Kiwi called Carl – and happiness is a gal called Cadwallader. Trust me, you two! I'll keep you posted. With love and passion, bla bla bla.'

They sat in silence for a while. Chloë was miles away, a different country indeed. There she was having the time of her life. Here they were, Jasper and Peregrine, feeling the winter in their joints, sitting in silence in Jocelyn's house. And yet *silence* in Jocelyn's house was surely anathema.

'Well?' said Jasper. 'What do we think?'

'*I* don't know *what* to think!' answered Peregrine.

'Well,' continued Jasper methodically, 'the girl is safe, cosy and having fun. She sounds happy, animated – like when she was a youngster. Now, what would Jocelyn say, do you think? What would be her view? What would she think? And, ought we to go by it?'

They sat quiet a moment longer, Jasper running the envelope through his fingers, Peregrine tapping the pages of the letter against his chin.

'Jocelyn,' said Peregrine mistily, 'dear darling Jo Jo. She, I'm sure, would be delighted. She may not approve of the sentences beginning with "and", nor, perhaps, of the very public site of this first clinch; but she, more than anyone, wished entirely for Chloë's happiness.'

'Remember how she loathed Brett?' reminisced Jasper. 'How she longed for Chloë to find the elation and bliss that she had experienced?'

'Oh so fleetingly.'

'Just the once.'

'So long ago,' rued Peregrine. They sat in silence save for a sigh apiece.

'Hush now, we're becoming maudlin,' said Jasper tapping Peregrine's knee. 'Jocelyn moved on. So must we. The past is indeed a different country, in which one no longer has a home.'

'Indeed,' pondered Peregrine.

'Alas,' concluded Jasper.

'Come now! Back to matter in hand – our Clodders swept into the clutches of lust! I know damn well what Jocelyn would think – after all, was it not she who placed map and wherewithal into Chloë's fair hands?'

Jasper raised his eyebrows high, a lascivious twinkle to his eye. Peregrine kissed him lightly on the cheek and linked arms with him lovingly beneath the tartan blanket.

'Good Lord, *Jocelyn*!' exclaimed Jasper, looking up to the eaves and beyond. 'It *is* you! You're orchestrating all of this, aren't you, old girl!'

* * *

'I've come to see Dr Noakes,' announced Morwenna breezily, shivering slightly beneath her inappropriate silk shirt. 'For my *once-over*,' she explained, content that the phrase was sufficiently medical.

The receptionist, who was old, grey, unmarried and bitter, noticed Morwenna's erect nipples with flagrant distaste before consulting the time sheet with eyebrows still raised.

It's because I'm cold, stupid, thought Morwenna, crossing her arms over her breasts defensively. *And just a little excited too*, she conceded to herself with a clipped laugh out loud. The receptionist gave her a withering look and hissed 'Dr Grey' at her, with a jerk of her head to indicate the waiting room. As she flipped through a laughably out-of-date fishing magazine, Morwenna chanted 'Why Dr Grey, why *not* Dr Noakes?' to herself incessantly. After an anguished ten minutes, she forced her attention to the magazine and tried to learn something new.

Plenty more fish in the sea? For an old trout like me?

Later, with her personal MOT renewed, Morwenna was slicing onions, wondering if William would remember their dinner date. She realized with some satisfaction, and a little sadness too, that she was not all that bothered if he had forgotten. The doorbell rang out energetically.

'Don't tell me he's early,' she muttered.

Swiping the back of her hand across her forehead to brush aside a wisp of hair, Morwenna immediately wished she'd wiped her hands first. As the sting of the onions made her eyes smart, the doorbell rang again.

'Coming,' she called, 'hold on a mo'.'

She opened the door, squinting hard through the blur of salt-water clinging to her right eye. Her left eye opened wide, startled but sparkling.

'Dr Noakes!'

'Merz Saxby!'

'Gracious!' said Morwenna, wiping an onioned hand over

her good eye and suffering the consequences immediately. Blinking fast, she cried with some dread, 'It's my *once-over*! I was too late, wasn't I? I haven't passed my MOT!' She sounded glib but was actually quite frightened. Why else would a doctor be at her door? After hours. Why else indeed?

Dr Noakes hopped lightly from foot to foot and slung his hands deep into the pockets of his well-cut navy blue coat. The collar was turned up against the chill evening and framed his face attractively.

'It's chilly, Merz Saxby!'

'Er, yes! Dr Noakes,' responded Morwenna easily, seeing through her salt-water haze that navy blue suited him very well. 'Would you like to come in?' she said, blinking hard, oily fat tears squeezing themselves out but managing to creep only to the start of her cheeks.

'Yes. Would you like to call me Robert?'

'Yes. Would you like to call me Morwenna?'

Morwenna offered tea or whisky and Robert plumped for the latter. Blotting her eyes carefully with kitchen roll, she waited for an explanation.

'You were booked in with me,' Robert explained, 'for your *once-over*, but it was my decision to pass you on to Dr Grey. She's a most excellent physician.' Morwenna raised her eyebrows as if to say 'And you're not?'

'But that wasn't the reason for the referral – I'm a pretty dab doc myself!' Morwenna's smile of agreement put Robert at his ease, so the bush was not beaten about for a moment longer.

'See, it would have been *un-pro-fessional* for me to have given you the *once-over* and, er, then to have asked you if you might like to have dinner with me.'

There!

Morwenna's soul surged. 'Oh?' was all she could manage.

'Would you?'

'Yes!' she said, a little too enthusiastically. 'Would you?'

'Would I what?' asked Robert.

'Why! Give me the once-over before dinner!'

When William remembered about dinner at Morwenna's it was already eleven at night and he had finished two rounds of stilton-and-marmalade sandwiches. First he thought how it was too late to phone. Then he thought that Morwenna would have phoned to reprimand him anyway by now. He thought it strange that she hadn't. Next he thought maybe she had forgotten as well. But he thought that odd as well. He thought for a while longer. But not about Morwenna – he thought no more of it. He went to bed, straight to sleep. Dreamless. He thought no more.

TWELVE

'Shit Chlo!' said Carl under his breath, 'what an ass!'

Chloë spun on her heels and scrutinized her reflection in the glass-fronted mahogany sideboard which sat easily in the tack room next to the grandfather clock.

'Woe!' she wailed. 'Is it the riding? All that squidging by jodhpur and squashing by saddle?'

Carl looked puzzled.

'Is it *very* noticeable?' pleaded Chloë, craning her neck and tucking up her pelvis. '*How* huge?' She bit her lip. 'Well-padded or downright unacceptable?'

'You what?' said Carl, none the wiser.

Chloë gave herself a hard pinch on the left buttock and batted doleful eyes at him. He broke into a wide smile and walked over to her. Turning her sideways on, he crouched until he was eye-level with her bottom. With a light but skilled hand, he glided over her buttocks; eyes half closed to assist his expert analysis. He stood up and turned her towards him. Putting his hands gently on her shoulders and not letting her eyes venture from his for a moment, he slid his hands down over her back to the base of her spine. Exerting a little more pressure, he traversed his hands over her buttocks and down to the tops of her thighs. To do so, he had to bend his knees slightly. To do so, he had to part his legs a little. This forced him to buck gently into her and, as a consequence, his groin was glued to hers. Keenly, he held on to the tops of her thighs, revelling in the base of her bottom resting lightly on top of his hands.

'Shit Chlo,' he said hoarsely, 'all I said was that you have a *great* ass!'

Chloë laid her hands over his pectorals which she could feel and define well beneath the ample layers of wool that the Welsh February decreed. She could feel his erection pressing into her appendix, as was its wont. Having lowered her eyes demurely, she raised them again to his. And smiled.

'I thought you meant –' she faltered.

'Daft cow!' said Carl gently. Carl's greatest compliments were his softly drawled insults.

'You *do* know that my name is Chloë?' said Chloë. 'Klo-*wee*?'

Carl pulled his puzzled expression back down over his face, knowing the effect it would have on her. Chloë clenched her buttocks with delight, tapped him on the nose and gave his chin a quick pinch. Wilfully, she ran her tongue tip over her teeth, finishing with a flourish of a smile.

'For some reason,' she said, squeezing Carl's buttocks which were firm and fitted her grasp very well, 'you've taken to *pre*fixing an ab*bre*viation – a true perversion of its virgin state.'

Carl twisted his top lip and dipped his eyebrows simultaneously, shaking his head slowly, trying to fathom her out.

'Shit Chlo, what are you on?'

'See!' laughed Chloë triumphantly. 'Shiklo!'

She grabbed a pair of bridles and, humming gaily, turned to leave the tack room.

'Chloë Cadwallader,' enunciated Carl with care and

conviction after her. Still humming, she turned towards him, the brave sun of a frosty February morning alighting on her face and throwing fire into her hair.

'Yes?'

'Chloë Cadwallader,' he said even more slowly, chewing the vowels, sucking the consonants; rolling the syllables around his mouth and booming them over to her, 'you're one crazy bitch!'

As Chloë tacked up, she smiled to herself with Carl's words stroking her psyche. Fancy such affection lacing such seeming insults! To be called a 'crazy bitch' by Carl was something to be savoured and played, again and again. And 'daft cow' – well! When Brett had called her 'darling' it had meant so little that it had grated her ears savagely. When he ended his calls with 'Love you!' she would often hold the receiver away from her ear. And hold it even more distant when he closed the conversation with his trademark 'ciao!' Now, with Carl's love-laden calumnies chiming in her ears and a small child tugging eagerly at her jacket, Chloë looked around her and beamed gratitude at the hills and the sheep and the hazy boundless sky.

Wales, as Peregrine had said, was an absolutely splendid idea. Wales, as Jocelyn had said, was a heady contradiction of rustic simplicity and rural grandeur. Wales, as Gin often trilled, was wild, wet and Welsh! Wales, as Carl said once, was a cool country, pretty and awesome in equal measures.

'Wales,' said Chloë quietly to herself as she gave the small child a leg up and checked the pony's girth straps, 'Wales is the best thing that's happened to me.'

Just you wait!

'MissChloëCadwalladerEsquire,' called Carl as Chloë and her young charge ambled out of the yard, 'you've forgotten your badge! *Agin.*'

Chloë brought Desmond to a square halt and checked. It

was quite true, once again, or agin (she now heard certain words exclusively in New Zealandish dialect).

'Where *would* I be without you!' she called with fondness, carefully unpinning Jocelyn's brooch from her breast.

'You'd be on your hands and knees scouring the grass for it, like last week!' laughed Carl, hands on hips, divine forearms on display. 'Or rummaging about on the muck heap like the week before, you dim wench!' He sauntered over, his clumping boots scumbling leisurely over the cobblestones.

'Thanks a million, young man,' said Chloë, entrusting her heirloom to the man with the perfect wrists, 'and please,' she grinned, 'call me Shiklo!'

'It's pretty,' said Carl, holding the brooch in the approximate direction of the suddenly swallowed sun. Chloë loved the way his 't's were unclipped, more a roll of the tongue inside his smile.

'It's perhaps the most precious thing I have,' she said seriously.

'Apart from your sanity? And that's on its way out!' said Carl, slapping his thighs in mirth.

Oh! His thighs!

'Oh ha bloody ha!' retorted Chloë, desperate to keep a straight and severe face.

'Well, I'd be right honoured to be Guardian of the Badge till your return, milady!' said Carl with an extravagant bow.

'Thank *you*, kind sir!' chirped Chloë, allowing him a fleeting smile and a lascivious wink. The small child regarded them with a certain incredulity, and a maturity that exceeded both theirs.

'Come!' said Chloë to the horses.

'Shit Chlo,' called Carl after her, 'wouldn't mind!'

Maybe soon.

You mean?

Yes. Well. Wanted to take it slowly. You know, have fun with the infamous bases. Base three's next you see. Got to feel ready for the home run. Heavens, this is a first for me, remember.

* * *

William felt uncomfortable. His neck felt stiff and his legs were begging for a stretch. His bladder was full. Again. He was thirsty and felt tension spread across his forehead. He looked pale. And a little panicked. But he felt uncomfortable more because he was driving. He was nearing the Severn Bridge and was bang on schedule but still he felt ill at ease. He hated driving because he trusted a bicycle more, and his legs the most. Most of all, he hated the fact that the car he was driving belonged to Morwenna.

'William!' she had chastised most unbecomingly, putting an affected whistle to the 'w', 'Well!' (she did the same there too) 'I really *do* think it's time you bought yourself a motor. A little run-around at least.' She paused. 'Hmm! A little *run-around* would suit you very well.' The barb missed William completely and fell flat on the carpet in her house.

'Morn,' he had protested in a voice he wished sounded stronger, 'it *is* for the Bay Tree Bistro! Business, not pleasure – usually it's you who takes my wares to their patrons. *I'm* offering to do this run.'

'And why?' whistled Morwenna, suddenly and quite inexplicably suspicious.

'I'm not sure really,' faltered William, 'just fancied a change of scene?'

'You!' Morwenna barked sarcastically. 'Leave Cornwall! Out of *choice*?'

William tilted his head and looked at her, loathing her. *What the hell.*

'There's someone I have to see,' he said quietly and with relish. Morwenna raised her eyebrows as disinterestedly as such a gesture allowed. William went for the kill. Why not?

'Someone I *want* to see.'

He left it at that.

And left.

She phoned Robert: 'Bloody ceramicists. So precious!'

'Not that young chap you told me about? The one who thinks dinner services are beneath him?'

'The very one. The most noisome of all my clients,' spat Morwenna, using the word 'client' like a pin in a voodoo doll.

'Sounds precious indeed,' colluded Robert. 'Fancy baulking at making things people want, in favour of making things that people won't necessarily want to buy. Not what you'd call business acumen!'

'No. Crazy! These artist types,' agreed Morwenna breezily, trying desperately to banish images of William's one-off pots from her mind's eye.

Go away.

They are sublime!

I know. But dinner services bring in the pennies.

Is that the point? Pot-boilers?

Isn't it?

Isn't it?

'The point,' said Morwenna to the replaced handset, 'is that whatever William makes from clay, people will want to buy. Whether they need them or not. Just to see them is to want them. And to want never to be without them.'

William is on the Monmouth Road. A weight has been lifted with entry into Wales. While he was still in England, this neighbouring country seemed so foreign and distant. While he was in England, he could have turned around and ditched the project. The Royal Mail could do a Special Delivery. And he had made no appointment at that other port of call in Wales. Now, he was in Wales. Just. But already its features as a distinct country were plain to the eye. The roads. What was it? Different tarmac? Better? And the fields – a slightly more verdant green? Tinged with blue in contrast to the yellow undertones in Cornwall? And, of course, the road signs. The language. As he drove, he tasted out loud the strange configurations of double 'l's and 'f's, the odd 'y', the abundance of consonants.

Tintern Abbey roused him to pull over and stop suddenly, without a thought for the motorists behind him, with no thought other than to see for himself. Serene yet melancholy, the abbey stood skeletal pewter against the dark lush valley; a torn doily of stone, defying both weather and time, infinitely more Romantic in its ruinous state than it could ever have been when standing complete. William winced at the garish tea-and-souvenir shop and gave himself instead to the abbey's bony grasp for quite some time. Drizzle brought him back to the day in hand and he made tracks for his destination and his salary.

The Bay Tree Bistro was thrilled with the crockery.

'Lovely!' bellowed the highly English proprietor.

'There's pretty,' sang the Welsh waitresses.

'Is it heat resistant?' asked the black chef with a West Midlands accent.

'Dishwasher proof?' quizzed the commie-chef.

'Yup. Yup. *And* microwave safe too!' announced William, pride in his wares unleashing the latent salesman from within.

'*We*,' said the chef clearly and with a sneer, 'do not use microwaves at the Bay Tree Bistro.'

'Of course not!' faltered William, back again to his retiring self.

'I thought perhaps some dinky salt and pepper whatsits,' said the proprietor who William thought would be far better suited to a Devonshire tearooms.

'Perhaps tiny bowls?' suggested William, biting his lip and the urge to denounce the proprietor a philistine. 'Allowing just a flick of salt, a pinch of pepper? After all,' he said with a generous and beseeching smile at the chef, 'I would say there is little practical use for condiment sets here. I'll bet the food is seasoned to perfection before it reaches the diner!'

'Soup?' said the chef, still smileless but doffing his head just almost imperceptibly at William's compliment. 'Spinach and nutmeg.'

'Please!' said William, convinced that this man was more affable than his exterior suggested. The chef stirred and took a sip. He smacked his lips with satisfaction. Reaching above for a bowl, he glanced at William whose face was open, his pose relaxed. The chef replaced the bowl with a nonchalant clatter and swooped on one of William's.

'Does it need a wash?' he asked. William shook his head. 'It'll taste far better in this,' said the chef, brandishing the most perfect and white set of teeth William had ever seen.

'Bloody pony-trekkers!' said William, digging his nails into the steering wheel and, remembering it was Morwenna's, driving them deeper for good measure. It was nearing three in the afternoon and he had wanted to make The Visit today so that he could make an early start tomorrow and be back in Cornwall by mid-afternoon. Once William had earned the chef's approval, he had been fed and watered splendidly. He thought perhaps a touch of salt would not have insulted the soup. But he did not mention it. In fact, he did not say much at all. The chef brought soup, onion tart and a heavenly rhubarb crumble in quick succession, allowing William time enough only to scrape his plate and coo appreciatively between courses. Now, with belly full and strings of rhubarb caught between his teeth, he bemoaned his appetite and his desire to please and befriend, for it meant that The Visit must be postponed until the morning and Cornwall would not see him until the evening.

The pony-trekkers ambled ahead at the neck of the lane which was single tracked and not for the overtaking. He watched one of the horses, a small pony, lift its tail and dollop generously on to the road, splaying its legs and waddling just slightly as it did so. Hoping that they might turn off into a field before he caught up with them, and thinking of Morwenna's tyres, William slowed his pace right down. He could hear the hollow clop of horse and saw billows of steam seeping rhythmically from unseen nostrils. There were only two horses but it still gave him no room to pass. It had started to drizzle and the riders pushed the horses on into trot. Up down up down. One two one two. A small girl and a young woman. Black hatted and hair bunched. Hair flapping. Up down. One two.

The hair.

The *hair*.

William did a double take. Suddenly he remembered London. Pre-Christmas. Last year, already. Busy. Bustling. Lights and music on the South Bank. Money ringing alongside praise and adulation in his ear. Seeing her hum without hearing her. Catching her hair, glimpsing her freckles, her mahogany eyes, a glance of her porcelain neck. And the urn she had inspired that was not yet started but called to William from the back of his mind each day he sat down to work on other projects. It was quite possible, of course, that the sumptuous auburn tresses of the humming girl were hers not exclusively, that somewhere in the United Kingdom at least, never mind the world at large, another girl might be similarly endowed.

'But still,' said William aloud, shifting in the seat in the hope of a glimpse of her face. He was back in Wales on a drizzly afternoon, juddering in second gear on a single-track lane.

'Shall I toot?' he asked the rear-view mirror, wondering if that would afford a good look at the rider as well as a way through. Better not, said his conscience, knowing horses to be flighty creatures, and annoyed riders a belligerent race. As luck would have it, the girl with the beautiful hair outstretched her arm and waved him on in a most policemanly fashion while she and her charge moved neatly over into a passing place. William wanted to honk his appreciation but resisted. Instead, he raised his hand as he passed, preventing though it did a look at her face. The rear-view mirror provided no further details as the drizzle had swallowed the riders and their mounts into timeless silhouettes.

William drove on. He was sure that, behind the hedges, a gorgeous landscape lay. Normally he would have explored further, but today he drove on. It was not just the rain, but his uncertainty of his destination. Could he make The Visit today? No. Was he sure of the directions to the B&B? No. He turned left into a lane which was signposted to places near where he was supposed to be going. The hedges grew higher, the sky greyer and William's mood worsened. He longed for gorse and the sea. And the space that the two afforded the sky.

'Damn it,' he said, punching the centre of the steering wheel and quite forgetting that the horn was there, 'I really haven't the foggiest.'

Up there. Look. A driveway. A few yards on the right.

The Fiat lurched and heaved over the cobbles before William brought it to a long-deserved standstill. Pulling his jacket over his head and quite resembling the hunchback of somewhere or other, he scoured the apparently deserted yard for some sign of life. He heard faint barking and lumbered off in search of it, cursing his aged suede brogues whose soles were sieve-like. Skirting around the side of the house, guided by sporadic barking and a growing light, William came across a window and peered in. A kitchen. A young man reading. Dogs and cats snoozing harmoniously. Bingo!

Giving the back door a positive rat-a-tat-tat, William entered before waiting for an answer and immediately wished he had, for at once he found himself centre stage in a broiling mass of cat hair and dog fur, claws and incisors, howling and hissing. Something bit his leg sharply and it hurt. And then suddenly, all was still. The young man reading had not seemed to notice. Slowly, he took his eyes from the page and contemplated William benignly.

'Hullo mate!'

Who?

'Er, hello?' asked William. The young man put down his book and widened his eyes in readiness to assist.

'Er, I think I'm lost. A little,' explained William. 'Might you tell me where Fforest is?'

'Ah sure mate! Go further along the lane, right? And then hang a left, swing a right, right? Is it the Blue Boar you're after?'

William nodded, trying hard to decipher the rights from the lefts and the rights.

'Right!' the young man said. 'Well, it'll be a few yards further on the right, no left. Hang on.' He rose and came into the centre of the room, miming as if driving, shutting his eyes and concentrating. 'Yih! That's it for sure. Few yards on the right! Mate!' He was triumphant and glad to be of service. He held out his hand for a shake which William accepted and returned a little reservedly.

'Okey doke,' said William, 'I go back out and then turn –'

He stopped. The young man cocked his head, urging the stranger's memory to crank back into action. After a good moment, he realized the stranger had forgotten all about directions and destinations, he was somewhere quite else. Miles away. In the fruit bowl. The young man followed his gaze and found it to rest upon the old tin badge he had tucked between the oranges and pears for safe keeping. The stranger gave a quick shake of his head to bring him back to the present, though a trace of a frown continued to hover over his brow.

'Many thanks,' he said, 'I'd better make tracks.'

'Sure thing, mate.'

'Cheers,' said William as colloquially as he could. The young man saw him to the car and William said, 'Straight, then left, right and it's a few yards on the right, right?' He offered his hand for a shake and received a pat on the shoulder too. A little lost for words, he grinned distractedly and made off.

The Blue Boar was quite a distance away. And it was on the left, not the right. William picked at rabbit pie for an early supper and then retired to a small cosy room with a single bed and mauve velveteen headboard, punched into a pointless padded pattern by matching velveteen buttons. As he waited for sleep to descend, his mind played games with the tracery of Tintern Abbey, the sinewy auburn tresses of the pony-trekker and the art-nouveau serpentines of the I'm-sure-I've-seen-it-before brooch. Their patterning intermingled until they were no longer distinct and, try as he might, he could not tell them apart.

THIRTEEN

'Mr Coombes look! A visitor! Your son! *Will-i-am.*' Mr Coombes, well over six foot but wizened and crooked down to five and a half, leapt to his feet and burst into a cacophony of wheezing and coughing.

'My son!' He looked at the care attendant as if she were mad while she nodded slowly, as one might to a child.

'Hello, Dad,' said William with care, stepping forward to take his father's hand. It was lukewarm, dry and papery, so papery. While waiting for him to respond, William looked down on it. The skin had a greenish grey tinge and stood up in crinkled peaks over the veins, the knuckles and the tendons. Coursed with blue, highly deoxygenated blood, and riddled with liver spots, the skeletal framework beneath threatened to break right through. And yet the nails were beautiful, well tended and strong. They were familiar to William for they had changed little since his childhood. Oval, smooth and even. Quality.

'Dad, hello. It's me. William. Your *son.*'

'My son?' bellowed Mr Coombes with inflection worthy of a Shakespearian actor. 'My *son*?' He looked at the care attendant. 'Have *I* a son?' She nodded keenly and flicked her head in the direction of William. It pleased him that his father should be wearing a tie, albeit with a Fair Isle tank top. William tilted his head to the nurse to say all was fine, she could go. She went. He was alone with his father. And twenty other aged men whose twilight years had been savagely forced into a ramble of darkness and indignity. Perhaps, though, the gloom was cast by those who visited, those who knew them. Before. For these elderly gentlemen knew not who they were nor much about anything at all. But they all seemed perfectly happy, despite memory failing to serve them with a credible past.

'Dad?'

'Benedict!' Mr Coombes bawled looking William straight in the eye and clasping him rigidly between his two sharp hands. 'Benedict, my dear boy! So good of you to come.'

'It's William, Dad. Remember? Your son, *Will-i-am*.'

Mr Coombes cocked his head but refused to look blankly, as if it were he who was waiting for Benedict to come to his senses. And stop larking about. He broke into a broad smile: 'Benedict!' he jested with love and mirth, raising his fists as if to spar jovially.

Come, William. He is happier for you to be Benedict. And his happiness should be your primary concern. After all, it's been years.

William obliged and, as Benedict, raised the palms of his hands allowing his father to spring a surprisingly nimble one-two-two.

'Let's sit,' he suggested, scouring the room.

'Jolly good!' wheezed Mr Coombes. He led William by the elbow; past a table on which dominoes was being played in slow motion and to rules most elaborate and lenient; past a long line of blanket-kneed veterans who sat gazing out of the window at nothing at all. Patiently. Passing time. Life passing them by. Quite content.

How do you know?

Look at their faces.

They're off their rockers.

But they don't know that.

Mr Coombes's velveteen chair was covered with yellowing antimacassars over the arms and at the head. A pile of newspapers dated some months previously lay to one side. A small wooden boat and a mug that William recognized instantly as one of Mac's lay to the other. He helped his father creak and fold his body down into the chair and pulled up a footstool on which he perched.

'So!' said William.

'Ah, Benedict,' replied his father kindly, 'so good to see you. They told me I might find you here. Long journey, I might add, but worth it. So sorry to hear of your troubles – losing a leg *and* a love, gracious me!'

William fell silent. What on earth could he say. As his father rambled about France and the Gerries and wasn't it all bloody awful, old man, he scoured his face for memories and their incumbent emotions.

I do remember your eyebrows, though they are now quite white. Hey! You should see Mac's! But those aren't your teeth, are they? They're not teeth at all – just clever prosthetics which help you speak without whistling, eat without dribbling, and give your face some semblance of dignity. But they're not yours, they're not you. Yours were idiosyncratically crooked on the bottom, and there was one missing on the top left. Do you remember? I do. Do you remember how you could fit a pea into the gap? How you could whistle through it? I do.

'Gracious me, down on the Place de la Whatjumicall, sipping pastis and smoking those frightful tabs!'

Poor man, poor human being – that it should come to this. You with your papery skin hanging in folds. Jowls like a bloodhound. Only bloodless. Witless. And insane.

'Heavens, we'll be late for the reconnoitre if we don't watch it. Ages since I've played cricket, mind.'

Allowing his father to banter on (something about steel in Sheffield and the Queen Mother), William traced his finger slowly over the condensation on the window-pane whose misty bloomed surface begged to be drawn upon. First he drew a quatrefoil at Tintern then, continuing the line, doodled an approximation of the brooch he had seen in the fruit basket. While signing his initials over and over, he realized his father had become silent. His mouth had dropped and he was staring intently straight ahead. William followed his gaze. Maybe cutting into the condensation had afforded him a snippet of the view outside. It was a glorious morning and the setting of the home was magnificent; a great arboretum festooned with snowdrops, premature daffodils breaking through the downy grass. William gazed alongside him a while.

'So, Dad,' he said merrily.

'Jer,' he replied weakly. William's shoulders slumped involuntarily and he failed to suppress a sigh of frustration.

Here we go.

He turned towards his father. Still he stared fixedly at something but probably, thought William, at nothing at all. He forced himself to stroke his hand. The action was easy but to infuse it with genuine tenderness was not. Mr Coombes seemed unaware of the gesture but his hand was still, so William continued to stroke it.

'Jer,' Mr Coombes said in a soft wail, 'je, je, je.'

He had started to drool slightly from the corner of his mouth. His breath was sweet–sour. William tried not to notice it, certainly not to be repulsed by it, so he regarded his jeans instead and admired his muscular thighs ending at neat knees. He compared them with his father's. Only there were no knees. William wondered whether, if the pale grey flannels were raised, there would be no legs. Just broom handles.

'Jer.' He turned immensely sad eyes to William. They were ice blue, but so pale that William was sure the last residue of pigment was slowly evaporating before him. The corners of his father's eyes hung in red pips pressed close to the yellowing eyeball. There was sleepy dust unattended to in the corner of the left eye. Gently, William pressed his finger against it and then flicked it away against his jeans. His father did not flinch. He did not notice. He was staring at the window, through the window and way beyond the window altogether. He was motionless.

'Jer, je, je, je,' he chanted distractedly.

William felt his fist clench.

Shut up!

I want to hit him.

He drove it instead hard into his thigh and sprang to his feet.

'Bye-bye, Dad,' he said quickly, bruising a hard kiss against the old man's forehead. He could still hear his stuttering when he reached the doorway. Somebody else's father came scurrying up to him, using battered old carpet slippers as ice-skates on the lino floor.

'Son!'

'Sorry?'

'Thomas! What a lovely surprise. Is it today or tomorrow that we're going?'

'Sorry?'

'To *Por*tugal, dear boy! Oh, or is it Spain? Damn and blast! Never mind, let's go and see if Mother has the kettle on, I know she's baked a cake. Come, Tom!'

As William was led nowhere, he turned for a final glance at Mr Coombes. Still sitting. And staring. He listened hard. Nothing. He looked intently; his father's lips were still moving.

'Je, je, je,' William said to himself before handing the old man to a nurse whom he greeted quite happily as 'Mummy'.

FOURTEEN

'Yo Chlo!' Carl nuzzled up to her as she took the screeching kettle off the Aga and poured water over instant coffee granules.

'Good morning, Carlos!' she sang.

'Who? Eh?'

Chloë pressed her mug into his hands, took another for herself and started the process again. The kettle whistled obligingly almost immediately.

'Morning youngsters!' Gin yawned leisurely and growled back at Yap: 'Hapless!' she roared in warning, her eyes narrowed and her voice deep.

'Morning Gin,' said Chloë, 'coffee?'

'Poetry to my ears – and a necessity for my brain. Please!'

Chloë gave her the second mug and ran the process one final time for her own ends.

'Morn!' sang Carl, putting great sincerity into his abbreviation.

'Now, are the horses done? Good. I'll run you into Monmouth so you can buy your tank, or whatever you intend to bulldoze Europe in! I need soap anyway and nowhere in Abergavenny stocks my *par-tic-u-lar* Christian Dior. Peasants! Chloë, do you want to come too?'

Are you matchmaking?

I might be.

'To Monmouth?' asked Chloë.

'Well, I haven't enough petrol for Timbuk-bloody-Tu! Yes, to Monmouth.' Chloë shot a glance at Carl; he was submerging spoonfuls of sugar into his coffee, hoisting them back up before they dissolved and then sucking on them sonorously. She thought of something else he could suck and then perished the thought.

How could I!

How indeed?

How easily I could.

'No, I'll stay. I might take Jemima over the cross-country course.'

'Very well,' said Gin, somewhat surprised. She slid open the drawer in the kitchen table and retrieved a fifty-pound-note from the pile of old shopping lists, sweet wrappers and odd gloves. 'Gracious,' she said, 'look here!' It was the 'x' from the Scrabble set. 'I do believe Dai has been cheating!' She asked if they thought it a sackable offence. She fed the piece to the grateful greyhound. And asked them not to inform the RSPCA.

'The thing about sex,' said Chloë to Mr and Mrs Andrews once the grumble of the Land Rover had faded, 'is that it always seems such a big deal. That one-night stand I had, just before Brett – I was so determined that it should be flippant, fun and forgettable. What happened? I spent a week fretting and regretting! It *was* a big deal. And sex with Brett; Heavens, banish the memory or let me redo the past! It was when I watched that nature programme about pigs tracking truffles that I realized where and when I'd heard such noises!'

Mrs Andrews stifled a giggle. Chloë shuddered and left the dressing-table, crossing over to the wardrobe. Cranking open the door, she inhaled deeply and then closed it again. She sat in the old chair and looked over to the dressing-table. Funny how swiftly Mr and Mrs Andrews became just a postcard. Made of paper. Not real at all. She returned to the dressing-table and brushed her hair again. It needed it. The Andrews sprang back into life. She needed them.

'You see, I don't think I've ever really *made* love. There hasn't been anyone who's made me love them for me to want to do anything but lie there and oblige. But,' she said, glancing at Mr Andrews's breeches, 'I think I'd rather like to make love with Carl.'

The Andrews seemed to think that this was a reasonable idea.

'Only, well, he's never *actually* asked.'

Mrs Andrews pointed out that Chloë was lucky to live in an age of sexual equality whereas she was pretty much restricted to waiting demurely in her boudoir, to say nothing of the confines of canvas. Chloë gazed at her frock and wondered if the lacy bits itched. For all she knew, Mrs A was very probably not wearing knickers, horny as hell, waiting for Gainsborough to finish for the day so she could hoick up her skirt and grant her husband swift entry. Right there. On the bench. Out of doors. In the estate.

'Go on,' she seemed to be saying to Chloë, 'give him one from me!'

She couldn't possibly!

Chloë looked again and glanced away quickly.

She couldn't possibly.

'But, wouldn't that be a little *wanton*? Shouldn't I wait for him to do the asking?'

Mrs Andrews raised her eyebrow mockingly. 'We're not talking marriage here, only sex, dear girl!'

'What do I do then?' Chloë retorted. 'Come straight out with it and say "I say Carl, fancy a shag"? I think not.' She pranged the bristles on her hairbrush and pressed them gently against her cheek. 'Perhaps a little note: "Carl, Carl, come to me and take me to the stars and back"? No, no.

We're never alone for long enough. And when we are, we seem to enjoy kissing and foraging for its own sake, not as a preamble to some greater sexual plane. I'm having fun as it is – but I *would* like to go further. I'd like to try. I think. Before we part, just so I know, just so I won't regret.'

Mr Andrews was not listening, he was arguing with Gainsborough who had painted out the pheasant he had shot for his wife and which currently lay in her lap.

'Look at the bird!' he exclaimed to the artist. 'What a specimen!'

'Indeed,' agreed Gainsborough, doffing a raised eyebrow to Mrs Andrews who, in turn, winked long and slow at Chloë.

A letter arrived second post from Jasper and Peregrine. Their advice was sound and welcome.

Chloë ducks, thrilled to hear your news, you saucy hussy you! Jocelyn would *be proud. Remember, condoms are a must but operatics are a turn-off! The same goes for weeping. And farmyard impersonations.*

That night, Chloë climbed into bed without a peep through the curtains. Too much of a distraction. She wanted to think on what to do, a plan of action, which course to take.

'The thing is,' she said to the Andrews though she looked up at the rafters, 'what with his lovely orange Volkswagen combie-thingy that he bought today, Carl is now leaving in a couple of weeks. Half of me wonders if I'll feel a flop if he goes and we haven't. The other half of me thinks what a perfect opportunity it would be to do It. No strings attached, no relationship to go horribly wrong. The other half – damn! I can't have three! Another part of me says perhaps it will spoil things if we *do* do It. Maybe it won't be earth-moving. And then what would be the point? I like the kissing and the rummaging. It's so furtive and exciting. Safe, too. And nice.'

Mr Andrews asked his wife what the girl was wittering on about. Mrs Andrews merely tutted, said 'you wouldn't understand,' took the pheasant from her lap and flung it over her shoulder behind the oak tree.

'Right,' Chloë said defiantly, 'I shall leave it to him. And that,' she said, turning the light off, 'is my last word on the matter.'

Quietly, she thought to herself how nice it would be to make love to someone whose accent was genuine. Brett had employed a phoney American twang once his humping exceeded a certain speed, grunting, 'Oh bay-beh, bay-beh.' Whether this was an involuntary preamble to his orgasm, or a misguided attempt to facilitate Chloë's, remained unfathomable. It hadn't worked, that was for sure.

* * *

'I like things like this,' says Chloë, running her finger along the blue rim of the soup bowl, 'don't you?'

Carl regards the crockery and realizes he does not really have an opinion on it but he wants to please Chloë so he elaborates.

'Ah yih! Dinky, I'll say. Proper English country style.'

'I agree!' says Chloë heartily, pausing before continuing crestfallen: 'I can't believe you're going tomorrow.'

Carl fiddles with a sprig of parsley and reaches across for her hand. He transfers the parsley to her and she munches it distractedly.

'Chlo,' he says gently.

'I know,' she says.

He has taken her to the Bay Tree Bistro. She adores him for it, and more so when he referred to it as the Bay Leaf Café. They have just finished a wondrous soup of field mushrooms and tarragon and are awaiting their main courses. There is a single carnation on the table and Chloë makes small tears at its petals forlornly.

Carl watches her dipping her little finger in and out of the hot candle wax. He sees that she is anxious and knows that it transcends her unhappiness that the morning will part them. It is palpable unease. At what, he wonders? The main course arrives and they eat for the most part in silence, the quality of the food warrants it. Carl sends his compliments to the chef which Chloë finds endearing. They cajole each other into ordering puddings they are too full for but too greedy to decline. Chloë teaches Carl how to pronounce zabaglione correctly. He insists on adding an 'l' in front of the 'b'; it is easier to pronounce that way and, more importantly, it sends Chloë off into fits of giggles which he finds so seductive. They dither over coffee; Carl collects the bill and they loiter for a while longer, long after the change has come and a tip been left. They play with each other's fingers and fiddle with their napkins. The waitress eyes the tip from a discreet distance and wishes they would go before they absent-mindedly pocket it. They murmur half-sentences and giggle away the rest. It is late and the proprietor is clearing her throat and looking at her watch as obviously as she can without being impolite. From the kitchen, an abusive chef can be heard ranting in an accent Carl cannot place.

'Brummy,' explains Chloë.

'Right,' says Carl. He knits her fingers together and then cups his hands over them. Through the candle's flame he catches her eyes and smiles at her without using his mouth. He stands and holds out his hand.

'Come, Cadwallader,' he says.

'How I wish,' she replies.

Back at Skirrid End the kitchen light is still on so they skirt around the stables and creep into the tack room. The grandfather clock stands guard and tocks reassuringly. The moonlight turns Chloë's skin to porcelain and sends shards of light into Carl's eyes.

Make love to me, oh, make love to me.

'Shit Chlo, I'm going to miss you.'

Take me. I want to have sex with you.

'Never met no one like you, girl.'

Let's make love. Here.

Chloë presses her lips silently and softly against his. She does not pucker them into a kiss, just pushes them into his. She can feel him breathing on her cheek. He smells garlicky and faintly of alcohol and to her, just now, right here, he smells good enough to eat. To bottle and keep.

Carl wants her lips to move. To kiss him firmly – their speciality. He kisses her slowly, drawling it out in much the same way as his sentences. Measured and calm. Chloë kisses him back, scrunching her eyes tight to absorb every minute of the here and now to take with her to the hereafter. Their faces part and they regard one another in the glorious March moonlight. Chloë realizes that she feels too sad to feel sexy and, because she can detect no probing against her appendix, she knows Carl must feel likewise.

'We haven't –' she says.

'No,' he half laughs, 'we never did.'

'And now we won't. Ever,' Chloë says forlornly, rubbing her hand up and down his stomach and keeping her eyes fixed on his belt buckle.

'We didn't need to,' says Carl. Chloë is puzzled so she punches him gently, square on the navel. He rocks her in his arms and presses his lips on the top of her head.

'Making love isn't the whole shebang, Chlo. And sometimes the whole shebang becomes just plain old boring sex. A disappointment. I'll never forget you, girl. And I'll ache for you at times when I'll least expect to.'

His words are strung as a line of pearls and she lays her head against his chest and listens to his heart beat away.

FIFTEEN

William brought the bowl through to the wheel from the damp cupboard. He had thrown it soon after his return from Wales and now, having left it awhile for the moisture to lessen, it was ideal for turning. He held the bowl aloft, like some mystical chalice, for this piece both contained his emotions and expressed them too. He was pleased with the shape; the subtle ogee curve, the furl of the perfectly proportioned lip, the precision of the tapering. Now all that was left was to turn it; to trim the uneven clay off the bottom portion, to develop a foot ring. He looked inside the vessel and then out, judging the amount of clay to be removed so that the exterior would reflect the interior and the weight of the bowl would be even. Then he decided on the positioning of the foot ring. Satisfied, he inverted the bowl and placed it down carefully on the wheel. Slowly, he set the wheel in motion, tapping at the pot until it was precisely centred. Placing three nubs of clay to hold the bowl in place, he positioned himself over the wheel and set it running high.

William enjoyed turning for it was both science and art to judge how much clay to remove to ensure that the vessel appeared to be of one skin. And there was something immensely satisfying in pressing the loop of a turning tool against the skin of a spinning pot while furls of clay twirled away to reveal fresh contours beneath. Today, it was the deep auburn coiled slithers themselves which solicited William, more than the revealing form of the vessel. As they amassed around the head of the wheel, he pushed his fingers lightly into them, drawing his hand up slowly so they trickled and tickled away. Beautiful and soft curls and coils; sinuous and sensuous in delicious burnt sienna.

When he was satisfied with the shape, that the form stood complete, he smothered it entirely with the deliciously goopy *terra sigillata* slip and began to burnish the surface. The Cornish March was mild and William spent the next few days working over the surface of the pot alternately with the back of a small silver teaspoon and a smooth piece of quartz to compact the slip and bring a dazzling sheen to the surface. Finally, the pot shone as if wet, both reflecting and giving off light. From a distance it appeared to have been dipped deep into a clear varnish but close to, it revealed the contours and minute dints of William's burnishing marks. They were his signature and were as idiosyncratic as his thumbprint.

This was the vessel that had been inspired by the humming girl just before Christmas. The recent trip to Wales, however, had woven its way silently into its fabric. William had thus decided to smoke-fire it. The finished pot blended contradiction seamlessly. Its form was open and positive, feminine even; but the decoration presented blushes of vivid red against vague areas of sootiness. And scorchings of utter blackness.

SIXTEEN

This is the life! I feel so at ease. So at home. Could it be? Could it be here?

Riding out by herself each day has afforded Chloë the quiet and the time to feel peaceful and in control. After all, the very fabric of Skirrid End and the framework of her existence there have made her feel safe and sound.

'I like to be given a timetable for my days,' she explained at length to Desmond; partly because she was working through the concept in her mind, partly because she hoped that a conversational tone would distract the horse from his customary bucking. Desmond, of course, did not answer. But neither did he buck. 'See,' Chloë continued, 'it provides me with *structure* – I have a function for each day. I am useful. I am needed.'

And you are looked after and guided. But might you not want to define the structure for your life yourself? At some point? If it wasn't for Jocelyn, for her death, would you be here? Jocelyn has sent you, Chloë, to her firm old friend Gin. Gin has welcomed you into her home for and because of her late friend. That is not to say that you would not have been given board and lodgings and a room in The Rafters if you had chanced upon Skirrid End as Carl had. But you would never have found yourself here. You never would have taken yourself away. Not unless someone told you to.

They did. And you are here. Soon you must leave and go on. But you will leave only because it is decreed. And you will travel to where you are told. There is nothing wrong in that, Chloë. But true security is that which you wrap around yourself, by yourself. And home is a place that reveals itself only once you have sought it out. Would you not like to find both? All by yourself?

Though not warm, the weather is milder and buds crack out over the horse chestnut trees as she rides by. The grass underfoot is vivid green, the snowdrops have gone and the daffodils and crocuses are browning slightly. Robins are still going about their business but now the curlews hold top note in the symphony that fills the valley. Islington might never have existed. Chloë knows now that she will never return. Brett is a name which causes her only a slight shudder. No nausea. Not any more.

'Brett?' asked Mrs Andrews, creasing her brow to aid recollection. 'Who he?'

'Who indeed!' declared Chloë triumphant.

* * *

Chloë started to pack; very slowly and without much enthusiasm. She knew that Gin had an envelope marked 'Ireland', whose contents would provide the canvas on which she would colour the next season. She half wished that the greyhound might eat it but she wondered too if it might smell of Mitsuko and she would just like to see if it did. And then perhaps feed it to the greyhound. Up in The Rafters, she has started to make neat piles, a futile activity where a rucksack is involved, but it calmed her to do so. She has not thought about Carl very much the last few days, certainly not to the extent to which she longed for him soon after his departure almost three weeks previously. Having

Gin to herself has been a source of comfort as well as entertainment; she was Jocelyn's great friend after all and Chloë has always felt safe and at ease in the company of Jocelyn's close circle.

Frequently, the two of them 'talk Jocelyn': if the mood catches the one, the other is sure to be infected. They do not so much reminisce, for such an activity requires both parties to have been present in the past, so to speak. More, they mull over memories of Jocelyn, describing her colours and remembering her traits.

'Remember sherry at five?'

'An institution!'

'With its own terminology!'

'*Time for a Tipple!*'

'It seems funny with good old Carl gone!' chipped Gin merrily, placing 'waltz' on a triple word score, 'don't you think? Chloë?'

'Hmm,' hummed Chloë, using the 'z' for 'quiz' with the 'q' on a double letter.

She smiled lightly. *She's itching to know but too awkward to ask!*

Gin was becoming somewhat predictable in her ready deployment of Carl's name during conversation with, or in front of, Chloë. Whether Chloë was in her sight or merely in earshot, Gin ensured Carl's name came to the fore. To Gin's thinly masked frustration (ample eyebrow-lifting and measured sighs), Chloë remained commendably discreet.

'My letters have me beat,' said Dai who was ignorant of his dyslexia and thus profoundly embarrassed by what he presumed to be an innate intelligence deficiency. Calling 'Nos da' over his shoulder, he grumbled out of the kitchen somewhere into the night. Chloë and Gin played on until Gin won by twenty points.

'Most unusual,' she said, 'but your mind wasn't really on it, was it?'

Chloë conceded with a shrug and a meek smile. Gin sighed and raised her eyebrows.

'I'll bet you're thinking of Ireland!' said Gin triumphantly, knowing full well that she was not and hoping therefore for denial and explanation.

'Ish,' admitted Chloë without qualifying.

'When do you want to set sail?' asked Gin, changing the subject with you-know-you-can-confide-in-me merriness. 'Jocelyn told me that you should pack your bags when the first daffs were up.'

'They've been up a while!' said Chloë with some consternation.

'Yes,' agreed Gin, 'but *most* premature.'

'I've sort of set the end of the month for my departure – if you can bear me. Perhaps the first week of April?'

'Wise,' said Gin, 'wise. But don't make it April Fool's Day – you'll find the Irish batty enough without a calendric excuse to go raving do-lally!'

Chloë arranged the Scrabble counters into increasingly complex tessellations, and jumped at Gin's suggestion to 'talk Jocelyn'.

'Funny that Jocelyn never married,' she pondered.

Gin did not respond but busied herself making a 'g' out of the counters. Chloë continued: 'For my part, selfishly, I suppose I'm quite glad – perhaps I would not have felt so special if she had had children of her own?' Gin cocked her head and lifted an eyebrow in a 'maybe'.

'Do you know Lord Badborough? In Wiltshire?' Chloë asked. 'We used to picnic in his grounds – and often in his drawing-room if it rained!'

'Yes,' said Gin quite freely, 'met the chap once or twice.'

'Was he, you know, Jocelyn's b–' Chloë paused, prophesying at once how daft 'boyfriend' would sound, '– beau?'

'For a little while,' said Gin openly. She had finished with the Scrabble pieces and was now counting the loose change in the kitchen table drawer, not to mention a number of twenty-pound notes.

'He used to kiss her most greedily!' said Chloë, thinking of Carl without being able to remember what he looked like.

'Bet she never blushed!' mused Gin, as she replaced the coins and notes in the drawer.

'No,' remembered Chloë, estimating that there must have been nearly seventy pounds, 'she received him most graciously – without humouring him or pandering to his desires.'

'That,' said Gin, 'was probably easy for her – Badders was really just one of a long line of suitors who waited patiently and fruitlessly.'

Now it was Chloë's turn to fall silent. She cleaned her nails with an obliging fork. 'Therein lay Jocelyn's skill,' decided Gin, 'that she *never* toyed with any of them. They all knew that they stood not a cat's chance in a kennels, but her company was such a delight that they were happy with whatever level she set.'

'Poor things,' rued Chloë, imagining a hundred of the finest landed gentry fetching pheasant and a good Rothschild bought at auction, laying on the silver and the Elgar to woo Jocelyn by. Expectant and forever optimistic, lavishing attention and hope on her.

'Poor Jocelyn!' exclaimed Gin with very real woe, shaking her head and looking as though she might weep. Chloë cocked her head and asked 'Why' with her eyebrows. Gin did not meet her gaze but looked far beyond it and straight back into the past. 'The poor duck,' she said mistily, 'she loved, she lost and she never found another for she refused even to look.'

'Was it not reciprocated?' Chloë asked, mulling over this, imagining a man who never knew he was The One; another who spurned her; or another who died, perhaps.

'Oh yes, Chloë,' said Gin, 'he was as deeply in love with her as she was with him.'

This puzzled Chloë. Man meets woman. Love is mutual and deep. Love, surely, is happy ever after. No compromise.

No alternative. No procrastination. *Amor vincit omnia.* Simple.

'Who *was* he?' Chloë asked, suddenly appalled that there was an aspect to Jocelyn completely new to her, that she had not known, that she had not been invited to see. She racked her memory but was unable to locate anyone who might fit this role.

'Did Jocelyn never talk of him to you?' Gin obviously felt compromised and her cheeks bristled red accordingly. Chloë continued to rack, squinting hard at the centre of the table in doing so.

'No, I don't think so.'

Gin shared Chloë's focus on a whorl in the pine.

'You'd know so if she had.'

'I don't recall,' said Chloë slowly, hoping that she was masking the hurt from her voice.

'You would, I assure you, you would,' said Gin kindly.

'Might you tell me, Gin?' asked Chloë, wondering if a light tone might encourage Gin by dampening the strangely grave significance of the situation.

'Gracious girl!' Gin declared, reddening again until her chin was the only part of her face not burgundy. 'Couldn't possibly. It would be like going behind Jocelyn's back.'

Initially it hurt Chloë that there was a fundamental part of Jocelyn that had been kept private from her. But, predictably, she accepted and respected quite quickly. Jocelyn would have had her reasons and Chloë's best interests at heart. Surely. And her privacy was her prerogative after all.

I've had my own secrets after all.

Yes?

Goodness, of course! From acquiring trinkets from the corner shop without paying, to the infamous one-night stand.

Ah.

Just the once, though. For both.

Chloë and Gin continued to talk Jocelyn at least once a day, but steered a respectful curve away from anything that compromised her privacy too deeply. Chloë granted Jocelyn's wish that Gin should be spared no detail of her funeral. Gin clapped with glee on hearing that there had been champagne, and she wept when told that the sound of Louis Armstrong accompanied the coffin.

'I should have gone!' she cried.

'But Jocelyn gave you special dispensation,' said Chloë gently.

'Bugger that! I could have pulled myself together and made it. If I can manage Monmouth – which is a good forty minutes – then London really should not pose a problem.'

'Three and a half hours?'

'I could have taken breaks. And Valium.'

'Hyde Park Corner?'

'I'd have taken the train!'

'Changing lines? And then Paddington Station?'

'I'd have hired a driver!'

'And trusted *his* driving?'

'Chloë Cadwallader,' sighed Gin, placing her hand over Chloë's, 'you know me very well.'

'I tell you, Gin,' said Chloë kindly, sandwiching Gin's hand between both of hers, 'when I first learned I was coming here, that you were a friend but one I had no recollection of, well I was a little concerned. But having been here three months, I can understand why you are loath to leave the farm. You are needed here because you are the very bones of the place. It couldn't function without you and,' she broke, hoping it would not sound patronizing as it was meant only as a compliment, 'I doubt whether you could function without the farm.'

Gin chewed over Chloë's insight and was not offended in the least. As she contemplated how soundly Chloë thought, and how this quality was indeed Jocelyn's legacy, she smiled and nodded and mouthed 'I know'.

'I would have liked to have been there. To have paid my

last respects in a dignified way. To have heard Satchmo. To have become drunk on good Krug. Though I love Jocelyn the more for insisting that I was not there, I still wish that I could have been. Said a proper, fitting farewell.'

'No one judged you, Gin. Least of all, Jocelyn. She'd have shuddered in her shroud if you had turned up on Valium and with a chauffeur – you'd have quite stolen her show! And say, just say, a hapless reshuffle of very little point had occurred in your absence? Can you imagine the consequences?'

'Dear girl, you're quite right of course. So terribly young – and yet furnished with such wisdom! How can that be?'

'It's having Jocelyn for a godmother,' said Chloë. 'Had,' she rued. Gin squeezed her hand and winked largely.

'Chloë,' she declared, 'I think it's Time for a Tipple! To the drawing-room! We'll have sherry in our socks. We'll drink to Jocelyn and then play Monopoly.'

SEVENTEEN

With two days to go, Chloë tucked down for an early night. She now has the envelope marked 'Ireland' and Mr and Mrs Andrews are looking after it. She remembers how 'Wales' was dwarfed by them for weeks, nestling in a corner of the cornfield, but now, with the Andrews superimposed in miniature on to card, they teeter on top of this new envelope; the 'I' of 'Ireland' being quite as tall as Mr Andrews. Unfortunately, there was no trace of Mitsuko; Gin took a great sniff too but could detect nothing. Chloë has peeped at the contents. Another map, apparently culled from the same road atlas. Another letter, as yet unread.

During a particularly good dream, a loud crack woke Chloë. Initially she thought it part of the dream so she lay quiet and tried to remember what the noise might have been. Satisfied that it was probably the burly woodman in the smock chopping logs (the muscles in his forearms were delightful), she decided to go back to sleep and see if she couldn't get a little closer to him. Before she made it to the start of the forest, another noise intercepted. She sat up in bed and wondered who or what was playing games with her mind or her sleep. *Had* she heard something? She'd just have to sit tight and wait awhile. Before long, another noise. It could have been an owl for the uninitiated, but Chloë knew well the call of the local owls. And Chloë knew Carl better.

Thud. Something hit the window. Chloë had neither the wits nor the inclination to suppress her squeal. Without checking her hair, or buttoning her nightdress, she whipped back the curtains and flung open the window. It was pitch-black and starless.

'Psst!'

'Hey Chlo!' He sounded wonderfully throaty in his best whisper. Because he had been gone for shorter than the span of an animal's memory, none of the farmyard four-leggeds reacted adversely to his voice. Desmond gave a low whicker but he did so frequently during the night anyway. In the kitchen, the dogs and cats cocked ears but once they had detected no stranger they settled back into sleep.

'What on earth are you doing here?' Chloë tried hard to whisper but was unable to prevent the involuntary edges of her voice coming through. She could make him out now, a break in the clouds allowing the new moon to send a soft light down to him. He was breathtaking. Chloë waved. He saluted.

'Hey Chlo!'

'Carl!'

'You want to mate?'

'What?'

'Mate!'

'Pardon?'

'For-nic-ate!'

'I'm coming!'

'Yih? You bet you will be, girl!'

Chloë has no idea what she is doing, what she should be doing and what she most certainly should not be doing.

What should I wear?

Does it matter? Will you be in it for long?

It's still pretty cold! There! Jumper. Thermal socks. I may as well keep my nightie on.

She shakes slightly as she struggles with a back-to-front jumper that will do for now. She pads across the room as quietly as the boards will let her. Holding her breath, she eases the door to The Rafters and treads the steep staircase as balletically as she knows how. She hovers by the bathroom door, grasps the handle firmly and inches it clockwise.

Please don't creak, Mr Door.

It's silent. She thanks it.

Closing the bathroom door to within an inch, Chloë stands still and peels her ears while her eyes grow accustomed to the gloom. Along the corridor, Gin is snoring for Wales and Chloë blows a silent kiss in her approximate direction. Luckily, a large groan from the top stair is accompanied at that moment by a sonorous gruffle from Gin. The rest of the stairs are obliging accomplices and soon she is thrusting her legs into the first pair of gum boots she can find. They are not a pair. The right fits perfectly but the left is twice the size. It really does not matter. From the kitchen, she can hear JR murmur in his sleep. She kisses the front door and it heaves open without a murmur.

Chloë stands still, the silence and chill of the night catches her. She can hear the distant grandfather clock but momentarily she can see nothing. A blink and a deep breath afford her greater vision and she starts to see with her ears and her nose. A faint thread of diesel. A slight scuffle on the cobbles.

'Carl?' she whispers.

'Right here.'

Carl and Chloë collapse into one another, burying faces in each other's jumpers, stifling giggles while merry snorts keep full-blown laughter at bay. Chloë wriggles against Carl because she is ecstatic and because the March night is so cold. It has just gone two in the morning, Carl's ferry leaves from Dover in eight hours. He has come from Scotland via Derbyshire and considers Skirrid End a minor detour to the south coast. For Chloë, the detour is major, she is immensely flattered and quite high; adrenalin and pheromones course through her, overriding instantly her calmness during the recent Carl-free weeks. He tells her she smells fantastic, she cannot think of a reply so she kisses him daintily on the nose instead. Something hard presses against her appendix and she allows herself a wry smile into the depths of Carl's thick jumper. Carl tells her that he has parked in a lay-by a few yards up on the right. Chloë rejoices in his words and her ears buzz with the substitution of 'ah' for 'ar'.

'Come!' he says with a lascivious twinkle in his eye. He holds out his hand and Chloë knits her fingers deep into it. They scurry across the cobbles and into the night like schoolchildren playing hookey.

Despite the darkness, Carl's combie glares out from the lay-by.

'Heavens,' exclaims Chloë, still whispering, 'isn't it orange!' Her inane statement washes over both of them.

'Yih!' nods Carl, showing her his newly acquired stickers. From Sherwood Forest to Gretna Green, from the bridge over the sea to Skye to the ferry across the Mersey, Carl has seen it and done it and now he's back with Chloë *en route* for France and who knows where.

'You've made it very homey!' whispers Chloë, taking a good look around the van. Carl plumps cushions proudly and opens a small cupboard to reveal neatly stacked tins of soup and beans and the smallest saucepan Chloë has ever seen. Carl has already flipped the table over into a bed so there is no embarrassment and also no alternative place to sit. They snuggle up and stretch their legs out in front of them, wiggling their socks and performing a synchronized dance of sorts with their feet. They both know what is coming, literally and metaphorically, and yet they wonder how to start. They catch each other's gaze and smirk and giggle. They nudge each other tenderly.

'Sgood to see yous!'

'It's lovely to see you too, Carl!'

Chloë sighs melodiously. Carl chuckles through his nose.

Come on!

Carl takes Chloë's hand to his mouth and kisses each knuckle in turn; he keeps his eyes on her while she looks demurely away and, subconsciously, straight to his crotch. She observes, there, a little tremble and then a definite lurch. She looks at him, wide-eyed and impressed. He grins expansively, his tongue tip working against the corner of his mouth. Chloë twitches her nose and raises her eyebrows, she is so excited that she can no longer giggle, let alone speak.

'Say Chlo,' says Carl, 'now I've got you here, can I have my wicked way? Hey?'

Chloë nods.

'Can I give you a good seeing to? Please?' he asks.

Chloë nods vigorously.

'Can I make your eyes water and set your pussy on fire?'

Chloë bounces up and down on the bed with enthusiasm.

'Till you beg for more and holler for mercy?'

Chloë squeals from the back of her throat.

'Can I take your top off?'

Chloë shakes her head while her eyes dance, and leaps off the bed, regarding Carl slyly, hands on her hips. Pursing her lips into a new smile that is both awkward and elated, she flings away her jumper and casts off her nightie. And so she stands before him, proud and confident, gloriously naked but for her knee-length chunky socks.

'Shit Chlo,' drools Carl, 'what a bod!'

Still Chloë cannot speak so she sidles over to him, smiling all the while. He perches on the end of the bed and she wades in between his legs. He places his hands on her waist and kisses the dip between her breasts which would have been a cleavage had nature been more generous. Carl does not clock any shortcomings, he thinks her nipples the rosiest and prettiest he has ever seen. He traces a line of kisses straight down to her navel into which he flicks his tongue lightly. Chloë's stomach muscles tense and twitch in delight so Carl does it again and hears her give a little gasp. Her arms have sprung goose-pimples and the downy hairs stand on end. She speaks.

'I'm f-f-freezing!'

'You daft cow! And I thought it was all me, the pert nipples and goose-bumps. Pah!'

'Believe me, you can take all the glory for the former but this drafty old van is the sole cause of the latter!'

'Do you mind! She has a name – Bertha.'

'You have given the van both name and gender?'

'Sure thing – I'm going to be sleeping with her for the next few months after all. Thought it was polite. Thought it was humane.'

'Er, yes!' says Chloë, seeing that Carl is utterly serious. She snuggles deep into the quilt and watches Carl strip. He is now down to polka-dot boxer shorts and odd socks; Chloë flings the duvet right over her head, giggling uncontrollably. Carl says not a word. Slowly, she peeks over the top. He pounces on top of the duvet and straddles her while making strange roaring noises and pummelling where he approximates her buttocks to lie. Chloë shrieks and laughs until it is positively painful.

'Stop! Stop! Please!'

'Already?'

'Come in, come in! Quick!'

She holds open a corner of the duvet and he sidles in, affording her a peek of his pubic hair and a glimpse of his socks.

Writhing and snuggling to keep warm, they knock heads and rub noses affectionately. Carl's hands are everywhere but Chloë is happy for them to go anywhere they like. He rubs her thighs and buttocks because they are cold; he strokes her stomach because he loves the way it twitches beneath his touch; he runs his hand over her knees because she coos when he does so; he walks his fingers right up her inner thigh because it makes her gasp and writhe and this turns him on.

Chloë kisses Carl. All over his face. She licks his neck and chews his ear lobe. Lightly, she brushes the back of her hand over his smooth chest, her fingers tripping over his pronounced stomach muscles. She weaves her fingers through a gentle fuzz of stomach hair and lets her hand travel lower.

Oh! Crikey! Heavens!

Well, what did you expect down there?

She traces the shape of his cock gingerly at first, but hearing his breathing quicken instils confidence in her hands so she explores further with a firmer touch.

'Shit Chlo!'

Chloë says nothing. She is lying across his chest listening to his heart and her own thoughts. Carl has a foreskin while Brett was circumcised but, though new, it seems to aid her manipulation and Carl is obviously enjoying it.

'Give us a suck, girl!'

Chloë whips her hand away and stares at him squarely. He looks glazed, his lips are parted and she can feel his breath on her face.

'Excuse me,' she cries, 'but ladies first, if you please!'

This delights Carl who scurries down between her legs and licks at her thighs like an excited puppy. Chloë wriggles and giggles and clamps her legs around his neck. He makes a strange noise in his throat which turns into a laugh when she releases the pressure slightly.

'Here, puss puss,' he muffles from the depths, making little kissing noises and tickling the very tip of Chloë's pubis, 'come here, you sweet little pussy!' Chloë laughs uncontrollably and her thighs clamp together.

'Come come, my cute little furry pussy wussy.' The more Carl tickles and twitters, the tighter the grasp of her thighs. He smacks Chloë lightly on the stomach and lies heavily on top of her.

'Come on girl,' he groans, batting doleful eyes at her, 'show us your snatch!'

For Chloë, this is cunnilingus really for the first time – Brett's occasional half-hearted dry dabs most certainly do not count. With her eyes closed, she rocks herself slowly against Carl's mouth, gyrating slightly so that his tongue meets the precise point intended. He has one hand grasping her thigh tight, the other is dancing over her left nipple like a feather. Her mouth is dry but she is vocal none the less and gasps and moans spontaneously. She moves faster but Carl's tongue has the edge and moves into and away from where he knows she wants him, before she can hump her pelvis towards him. Carl knows she is close to orgasm but Chloë is living only for the moment. It feels so idyllic, whatever could better it?

She yells. She bucks her body up from the bed and yells some more. Her body momentarily loses all its structure before it is racked into spasm once more. She sits bolt upright, clonking Carl on the chin. Her eyes roll, her mouth is agape. She can feel the blood pumping. Her heart seems to be beating right there in the centre of her sex.

'Oh – my – God!' she chants hoarsely, 'what on earth! Heavens God Jesus! What the bloody hell!'

Carl grins.

'That, Chlo, was your orgasm! And by the way,' he says, pinching her nipple and winking at her, 'it was all *my* own doing – nothing to do with those guys from the Bible!'

It does not bother Chloë to share with Carl that it was indeed her first orgasm. She tries to express the feeling but gets only as far as 'It's like, it's like' before Carl plugs her mouth with a deep kiss. The fact that it was her first orgasm, and he was, undoubtedly, the perpetrator, excites him. He has sustained his erection for a good half-hour and quite rightly feels it is his turn.

'Wannanather?' he asks, making a fan of a selection of condoms for Chloë to choose from.

'Hey?' says a woozy Chloë, fingering the packets and pressing her buttocks against Carl's cock. 'Come again?'

'Ah! You *do*!' He smiles as she points to *luxury light-weight rippled*. 'Well then, hold on for the ride of your life, girl!'

It had been months since Chloë last had sex but her new-found orgasmic facility left her well lubricated and Carl slipped inside her with ease and an ecstatic gasp apiece. It had been quite some time for him too, not since that au pair at his cousin's house in the Bay of Islands. Or was it that student with the tattoo? Whichever, both were pretty nondescript. For sure, neither had fired his hunger in the way Chloë had. And the fact that he was so firing hers made his appetite all the more acute. Keeping the rhythm slow at first, he continued to explore her body with his mouth and hands. As he twisted and humped to reach all parts of her, Chloë slipped her hands into the spaces he made between their bodies so she could feel, touch and hold both him and herself. And yet she felt it deep within her when she traced his lovely broad shoulders, her breasts quivered as she slipped her hands over the smooth mound of his buttocks, her sex tightened as she reached for his balls. He gasped as she held her breath. He tasted her neck as she smelled his forehead. It was the first time for her that sex had been an act to share, that the pleasure increased with the give and take, that her enjoyment was as important to him as his own. The purpose of it all was not the release of sperm into a handy vessel, but the cerebral and physical happiness that two bodies could create. The communication.

Chloë smiled throughout. And when Carl took his face from her neck, or away from her breasts or the depths of her delicious-smelling armpits, he grinned back at her. Laughter followed naturally. The squelching and slipperiness. The threat of cramp. Sometimes, though, they paused for silence just to appreciate fully the bliss of it all.

Chloë realized that she had never felt a man's orgasm

before. When Carl came, his cock leapt about so enthusiastically that Chloë found herself coming alongside him simultaneously. ('Synchro!' marvelled Carl. 'Cool!') Previously, she knew Brett was coming only because of his Americanized grunting, the wetness oozing out down her thigh, his repugnantly repeated 'Bay-beh'.

Now, for the first time, she felt a man dance with delight within her and because of her. And, for the first time, no pseudo accent was used. For the first time, it was her own name that she heard honoured. As Carl came, he panted her name while blaspheming joyously. Once his blood pressure and heart rate relaxed a little, and a doze on her breasts had resuscitated him, he lifted himself up on his elbows and regarded her with wonder and with gratitude.

'Shiklo!' he murmured, kissing her nose tenderly. 'Shagama life!'

EIGHTEEN

Well my duck,

That was Wales and this is Ireland!

You'll miss the Gin Trap but, I assure you, Gus will not disappoint. Nor will County Antrim. I know folk wax lyrical about the South but, as you are on a trip of the United Kingdom, Eire is logistically out of bounds! Suffice it to say, Northern Ireland is a very special place and I hold it dear in my heart – me and Seamus Heaney! (Read S H before or during, please.)

As I write, a cautious ceasefire has been in place for a while. I hope sincerely that it still remains so. I wonder, quietly, if we cannot accredit the unspoilt beauty of Northern Ireland in some part to the Troubles; certainly they have preserved the landscape against the unpalatable consequences of over-tourism. And yet, there are parts of the landscape that no sensitive holiday-maker, let alone traveller, would want to forgo. Once you have seen them, you will feel for those who never will.

Go to the Giant's Causeway, find a suitable stack and sit awhile. I'll be there with you, Chloë, for part of me will always be at the Causeway – in the air, deep in the sea, amongst the basalt columns, down in the mayweed. The fulmars and the pipits will speak of me. We shall fill our noses with the sweet coconut scent of the gorse.

You and I will share the space and look over the sea towards Scotland. And beyond.

J

NINETEEN

Fergus Halloran was portly and of a cheerful demeanour expressed at once by the red blooms to his cheeks and the wheezing smile permanently worn. His walk was distinctive; whether striding over his farm or strolling through town he would hoick and twist his trousers every seven strides. His medicine-ball belly, which dictated this gait, spoke too of the fat of his land; the sweet waxy potatoes, the soda farls baked fresh each day, the buttermilk. Gus's hands were thick and rosy, with white wiry hairs curling around the sides and sprouting in thatches along the fingers. Not unlike a good joint of pork. Around the trunk of his neck, St Christopher dangled in gold from a large belcher chain. Gus also wore a gold ring set with jet which acted as a corset to his little finger and gave it the appearance of an hourglass waist. His eyes glinted and shone, catching the light and colour from his dense, bristly pale hair. His voice sang when he spoke though what he spoke was, for the most part, a foreign language whose meaning could be insinuated from the accompanying facial gesticulation.

'Dear knows don't bother yer barney! Come, have a drap of scald and some tattie oaten.'

Sentences were invariably prefixed with 'Jayz!' and finished off with a triumphant 'Hey nye?'

The Halloran homestead was a fat little cottage, whitewashed and with green doors and frames. It was dark inside but not gloomy for an abundance of ornaments ('dornamints') offered glints of colour from every direction. Flagstone floors were barely covered by threadbare rugs but the curves and dents of the slabs were pleasing to the stockinged foot. The *Irish Times* and *Racing Post* gathered in piles beside every chair and a stack of them waited bravely by the vast wood-burning stove. Photographs of Gus's beloved late wife Maebh crowded the window-sills and smiled out from the walls. Chloë's bedroom was small and reminded her of one in a convent; a plain, wooden single bed with sheets and a grey blanket, stained canvas curtains at the small, deep-silled window, a faded and buckled print in a glassless frame of a landscape that could be Ireland or could be anywhere else, a photograph of Maebh grinning away in the fifties, an old mahogany cupboard slightly askew whose door hung ajar permanently.

Life on the farm was gentle and rosy and would have suited Chloë well had it been more than merely conjectural day-dreams on the plane over to Belfast. Reality rendered them obsolete.

* * *

Ballygorm Manor is an imposing neoclassical residence concealed from the road by a long, forested drive and ringed from the world by an old stone wall mottled with moss and fringed with flops of ivy. It sits in a peaceful valley of its own just up and outside of Glenarm and off the Ballymena road. The sea is near but you cannot see it; its proximity, however, is evident from the light bursting from over the hill. Chloë's bedroom is furnished liberally with antiques and has an *en suite* bathroom. The bed is queen-size with scrolled walnut ends and is laid with fine linen, covered by an imposing dark grey and maroon silk eiderdown. There is no New Zealand rug beneath it; Chloë checked. The curtains are from Liberty's and the window offers views out over the parkland to the woods: ash, hazel and ancient oak. The carpet is flaxen and luxurious and a small rectangular kilim lies to the left-hand side of the bed. There isn't one to the right so Chloë has obediently got into and out of bed from the left.

And the left, she fears, is the wrong side, for she has not been very happy during her first weeks here.

Not happy at all, really.

Rather lonely, actually.

Gus Halloran is an easy six foot tall with a lithe physique defying his seventieth year. His hair is slicked back meticulously and waxed with precision; yellowing, rather like the whites of his eyes. His full moustache is off-white too, but the odd dark whisker whispers out and tells of its former jet-black glory. Gus does not wear any jewellery and his finely tailored corduroys remain pristine throughout the day. He wears dark lambswool V-neck sweaters, lightly checked shirts and sober ties. When he goes out into the estate he adds a tweed jacket and long waxed coat; when he goes into town, he leaves the waxed coat behind.

His accent belies any trace of his heritage. When Chloë confided her anticipation of abundant 'begorra's and 'b'jayz's, Gus said 'Eton' at her rather witheringly. There are no photographs of Maebh for there has never been a Maebh and, at the moment, Chloë, who is a little troubled, is hardly surprised. Gus's manners are indeed impeccable and he has ensured that Chloë has everything she might need for her comfort (there is a small transistor radio in her room, a sewing kit, a run of Dickens and a cut-glass jar filled with cotton-wool balls). He accepts Chloë's gratitude graciously and they dine together every evening at seven. Mostly, they eat in silence. Between courses, Chloë might offer an opening into gentle conversation. Gus answers her directly, succinctly and politely, but invites no repartee. It is not that he is *unfriendly* nor does he seem to mind her presence; he just does not seem that bothered by her at all. Chloë, who has always judged herself on the response by others, feels hurt and unsteady.

There is no Maebh but there is Mary who has kept Chloë's pecker up at times when it has started to droop. Mary is housekeeper and calls Gus 'Mr Halloran'; not so much from courtesy, for he is happy for first-name terms, but from habit: she has been at Ballygorm for twenty-five years. Now, Mary *is* portly with a becoming blush to her cheek and an exemplary grasp of Ulster vernacular.

'Bout ye!' she said to Chloë on first seeing her. 'I'm taking a wee skite to the veggy patch – preys for the champ – come for a dander witmee?' Chloë jumped at the opportunity for, after showing her to her room, Gus had disappeared and a timid call of his name had hung unanswered in the silence of the spacious hall.

Presuming the champ to be a disease that praying and skiting might cure, Chloë turned her thoughts to whatever a *dander witmee* was. As they left the kitchen by the split door, she wondered if it was a vegetable peculiar to Ireland, or, perhaps, the tool used to dig one up. As Mary led her leisurely to the kitchen garden, stopping now and then to put her hands on her hips or to nod at the trees or acknowledge a sparrow, Chloë translated dander as a stroll and deduced that a skite must be one too. The champ turned out to be the mashed potato they were to have for dinner; the preys, blushing pinky-orange beneath their earthy vests, were of course the raw ingredients. That merely left 'witmee'. Chloë wondered if it described the sort of stroll – perhaps a short one for culinary end? She felt, however, a little bashful to ask and it was two days before she learnt the meaning.

'Have a bistik witmee!' Mary had said, offering a tin laid neatly with flapjacks.

'Mmm!' Chloë said as she munched, thinking 'Aha! biscuit!' to herself. '*With me*!' she said triumphantly, through a muffle of crumbs.

'Hey?' said Mary. 'Getalang-widger!'

Chloë knew instinctively what a long widger was.

'I'll get along with me!' she said gratefully.

Far from being rosy and fun, life at Ballygorm Manor is hard work. But the most demanding task for Chloë so far has been to fathom why Jocelyn has sent her here. And why to Gus.

'A very special place and I hold it dear in my heart.'

Some mistake, surely. Not here. Not him.

'You'll be wanting to earn your keep, Miss Cadwallader?' said Gus on the first night over the fruit compote and a glass of port. 'Yes?'

'Yes, oh yes,' stammered Chloë, hoping that effusive enthusiasm and obedience might endear her to him a little more and thereby entice the 'real' Gus to step forward. The one that Jocelyn assured Chloë 'will not disappoint'. 'But of course!' she enthused. 'Indeed! Just tell me how!'

Gus had not answered, merely nodded whilst spearing a hunk of stilton.

When Chloë had bidden him a very good-night and had praised the champ to the hilt, he had not taken his eyes from his brandy; merely held it to the light, twirled it expertly and then said, 'Nine o'clock, then. In the study. Breakfasted, if you please.' With that, Gus closed the conversation and closed the door on the early evening. Chloë went to bed forlornly without even a glance at the Andrews who seemed very much at home at Ballygorm. Much more so than Chloë.

The next morning, Gus's demeanour had changed completely. After some analysing, Chloë attributed this not to the kippers which Gus obviously loved but whose oily, pungent, bony bodies had quite unnerved her, nor to the strong black coffee, nor even to the very fine morning; but wholly to the study. She soon discovered that the grounds at Ballygorm had the same effect on Gus; not nature itself, not the landscape in general, not just being out of doors, but specifically the land lying within the estate boundary.

'Sculpture, Chloë, sculpture!'

Chloë widened her eyes and parted her lips and nodded faintly.

'Well, look at this place!' he exclaimed, moving his arms expansively. Chloë slung a careful look around the study, noting an oak table strewn with papers and shelves of books whose titles her glance did not register. She saw that Gus was gazing intently out of the window. On a sweep of grass curved off by trees, a fat wood-pigeon plumped his breast leisurely while a squabble of crows made merry in the neighbouring branches.

'It's – oh! Truly magnificent!' said Chloë helpfully. 'And I do like sculpture!'

'The point,' said Gus sternly, tapping the window-pane only to be stared at vacantly by the pigeon, 'is that Ballygorm is an easy half-hour from Belfast.'

'Ah,' said Chloë, trying not to add a question mark. Gus gave the window-pane a hard rap but whether this was an expression of his irritation with her or the pigeon, she was unsure.

'Thirty minutes from the capital city of a country for the time being no longer Troubled, as it were. Come!'

Chloë followed him out of the study, across the hallway and out through the vast double doors on to the gravel drive. There was silence save for the pleasant crunch of the stones underfoot and the cawing of the crows. April was apparently not a cruel month in the Irish calendar, but a most affable one. Though dew still swept over the grass, the air was dry and fresh and the sun shone gently, taking the edge off the constant breeze.

Gus led her to where the gravel met the grass. Carefully, she positioned her feet just like him, an inch or so away from the start of the lawn. She heard him fill his nostrils and exhale gladly. She closed her eyes momentarily and wondered whether to comment on the gifts of the morning.

'The Ballygorm Sculpture Trail!' Gus announced quietly, but with aplomb. They stood in silence; slowly Chloë began to superimpose sculptures on to the land before her. The genius of Gus's project was at once evident for, against the backdrop of Ballygorm, works of art would be assured a remarkable habitat.

'You see,' said Gus, 'you take away the hessian-clad confines of a gallery wall and suddenly the classical can coexist quite happily with the abstract.'

Chloë followed his drift and his gaze, and placed against the landscape imaginary pieces of solid marble and others of filigree metal; figurative bronzes and abstract constructions in timber.

'Fantastic!' she said genuinely.

'A money spinner,' qualified Gus, 'by appointment only. Schoolchildren permitted only when I am *not* here.'

He clapped his hands before his sentence was finished, which startled Chloë and extricated the pigeon from the long grass. The crows were shocked into silence for Gus's clap sounded remarkably like his air rifle.

'Right then! To work!'

Chloë soon found herself working a full day under Gus. Her typing speed has doubled out of necessity because the workload is heavy and her boss is easily displeased. Apart from the occasional rushed morning in Ballymena and an afternoon on the beach at Ballygally, where she gazed wistfully over to the Mull of Kintyre slumbering in mauve across the water, Chloë has rarely left the estate. She does not protest, for the work is stimulating and Gus's praise is something she craves. However, a tiny voice deep inside sometimes asks whether Jocelyn knew of this, whether it is as she intended. It goes unanswered because Jocelyn herself has been pointedly left out of their discussions. Very early on, Chloë tried to draw Jocelyn into the conversation. Over the *crème brûlée,* she remembered fondly how this was her godmother's favourite dessert – did you know that? do you remember? She had no idea whether Gus knew or remembered for he laid his spoon carefully beside the dish, fixed her with a stare which said 'Don't!' and ate no more.

Chloë does not protest or object for she has neither the pluck nor the knowledge to do either.

'I wonder though,' she pondered while dangling her legs off the bed and trying to appreciate the merits of yet another early night. She posed it to the Andrews: 'Is this the atmosphere, the reaction, Jocelyn anticipated?' she asked. 'Did she know it would be like this? That *he* would be like that? What do *you* think?'

'Unfortunately, my girl,' Mr Andrews replied gravely, 'we cannot now ask her.' But in the moment that Chloë then mourned her godmother, she questioned her too.

'If all of this *was* known to her,' she began, 'Why – Send – Me?'

The couple puzzled over this until Gainsborough protested that their furrowed brows were about to be indelibly added to the portrait.

'To see how you'd cope?' suggested Mrs Andrews limply but kindly.

'How you'd make a "go" of the situation?' furthered her husband.

'What! "Character-building stuff"?' Chloë wailed. 'Well, that'd be downright mean of her – she knows, *knew*, me! She wouldn't subject me to this wilfully. It would be too out of character. Too unkind.'

'No, no,' rushed Mr Andrews. 'I mean, yes, yes.'

'There'll be an answer,' encouraged his wife. 'It just might take a little questioning to uncover it.'

'But,' Chloë faltered, 'if Jocelyn did *not* expect it to be as it is, she'll be turning in her grave, surely. And then what should I do about it *now*? Ultimately,' she sighed, 'how on earth am I meant to ascertain if the Ballygorm and Gus that have me now are those she intended, envisaged?'

Mrs Andrews seemed suddenly to find her shoes rather absorbing, while Mr Andrews nodded at the encroaching clouds and suggested to Gainsborough that they call it a day.

Why here? Chloë wondered a little later, consulting her warped reflection in the tiles around the bath. She loomed her face close until the nose touched her nose and left a bloom of condensation on to which she then inscribed a question mark.

Did Jocelyn know it would be like this? Had she any idea?

She lay back in the water and listened hard for an answer. The ensuing silence was not what she wanted to hear so she reached for the welcome diversion of a book. Flicking around for her place in *Great Expectations*, Chloë realized Jocelyn could not have known about the sculpture garden for her death preceded it. And yet oh! how immensely grateful she was all of a sudden for Gus's project. Contemplating the consequences of her stay at Ballygorm without it made her shiver and add more hot water until she was up to her neck.

* * *

'Jasp? Ho, Jasper!' Peregrine leaned on the banister, craning his neck and peeling his ears for clues as to where his lover was and what he was doing.

'Jaz-*pah*!'

'In the tub!' came the burbled reply. 'Soaking wet! What on earth is it? Tell 'em I'll call back later!'

Peregrine smiled to himself as he trod his way measuredly upwards to the bathroom; his joints were no tighter and yet the stairs were certainly steeper.

'Knock, knock!' he said, outside the bathroom door.

'Enter!' Jasper replied.

'Are you decent?' asked Peregrine, hand hovering above the doorknob.

'That,' said Jasper amidst sonorous splashing, 'is totally

subjective. But you may avert your gaze should anything offend!'

Peregrine found Jasper swamped by bubble bath, wearing Jocelyn's floral shower cap and brandishing the loofah.

'Gracious boy!' exclaimed Peregrine. 'Put it away!'

Jasper, of course, merely wielded the loofah more furiously in lewd thrusting movements, from which he derived much hilarity. Peregrine raised an eyebrow witheringly.

'Submerge that Thing or else!'

'Else what!' pouted Jasper.

'Or I shan't be reading you the missive just arrived from Ireland.'

Jasper laid the loofah neatly on the side of the bath in between a plastic hippo and a glass jar of dark mauve bath salts.

'Read!' he said, settling back down into the bubbles and concentrating on the reflection of his bony toes at the far end of the bath.

'*Hullo Boys!* bla bla . . .'

'Perers, per-*lease*! No bla bla-ing!'

Peregrine settled himself, fully clothed, on to the bidet, stuffing a towel against the taps and another behind his head. Clearing his throat, he swiftly scanned the letter, smiling at some parts, looking perplexed at others.

'Gracious, damn!'

'What?'

'Gus Halloran, that's what – remember how we prophesied that he'd be one way or the other?'

'Don't tell me it's *the other*?'

'I don't need to – Chloë's done that. Bugger him!'

Jasper raised his eyebrows.

'I think you'd better just read it, actually.'

'Righty-ho. Well, I've done the Dear-boys-health-and-weather bit.

'*Ireland is a funny place, I think it's probably very beautiful but to tell the truth, I've seen very little. If I had my own way, I'd have seen a great deal more but here at*

Ballygorm I must do as I'm told for there are consequences if I don't. Doing as I'm told amounts to working hard all day, each day, apart from Sundays. Sundays I am restricted to places within walking distance because the cars are washed and pampered and out of bounds. Usually I'm too tired to do much other than read beneath one of the great oaks; at least it affords me peace and quiet and a chance to transport myself some place else.

'Gus is setting up a sculpture trail in his estate and I am typing things and calling people for him. I think his idea is wonderful but unfortunately I will be long gone by the time it opens. Or should I say fortunately?'

'Here we go.'

'Indeed, poor Clodders. '*Darling Jasper and dearest Peregrine. Damn, damn it. I'm feeling tearful as I write. I'm beneath an old oak and have no tissues – the view is so pretty and yet I feel so isolated. I don't dare phone you as the sound of your voices would be too far away. But I'm not very happy here at all. I can't say that it's specifically Ireland I don't like, for I've seen so little of it to judge. And I can't say that the people are unfriendly for I have Mary the housekeeper who is lovely to me, and Pat the gardener who has few teeth but a great sense of (mostly unintelligible) humour. However, I cannot find solace in these two for long enough, for Gus is demanding on my presence. The work is interesting enough – and I do like sculpture – but, well, Gus, you know.*'

'Gus *what*, Chloë?'

'Give her a mo' – can't you tell that she feels somewhat humiliated? '*It's not that he's hostile or inhospitable – I mean, you should see my room, all the lovely suppers – and he is most polite. It's just that he isn't particularly friendly and I feel a little insecure. I am trying hard but I can't engage him. Was I just spoilt with the Gin Trap? I don't know – you know when you love someone, you automatically want to love the people special to them? Well, Gus must've meant something to Jocelyn or else she would not have sent me here. And yet, I find it difficult to like him for I feel he is tolerating me merely as a favour to Jocelyn. Or to her memory. And that's the nub of it, boys – I have no idea who he is in that respect because he hasn't mentioned her since I arrived. He shot me a look saying "don't!" when I tried to talk about her. He even asked that I don't wear my brooch – he says "It'll catch on things". And I suppose that's why I feel lonely – there's no point of contact here. Gin and I would "talk Jocelyn" for hours on end – often repeating ourselves quite happily. Gin was immediately fond of me simply because I was Jocelyn's god-daughter and I trusted and liked her from the start because she was my godmother's pal.*

'Who is Gus Halloran? Do you know? Did Jocelyn? Really know him? Why has she sent me here – do you know?

'Can you help?

'Shall I come back?

'I'm wondering whether I might venture to Scotland earlier – from the Antrim coast you can see the Mull of Kintyre and Ailsa Craig clearly. At Torr Head, Scotland is only twelve miles away and, though I've never been there, it does appear to have this magnetic pull.

'Wales seems a dream away.

'Islington no longer exists.

'You two seem so far.

'I miss you and send you all my love, hoping that you'll write to me very, very soon. Please don't phone me, it would make me cry and I mustn't.'

'Poor duck,' said Jasper.

'Poor lamb,' said Peregrine.

'Poor Gus.'

'Poor man.'

'We ought really to tell her no more than Jocelyn has,' reasoned Jasper, scrutinizing his wrinkled skin and trying to distinguish between the furrows caused by his excessively leisurely baths and those attributable solely to age.

'Indeed. As much as my heart bleeds for Chloë, it is her

heart that Jocelyn believed was in need of a little toughening.'

* * *

'Ronan will be arriving tomorrow morning – I'll be in Belfast. Make sure you're around from eightish.'

'Course!' said Chloë in between mouthfuls of mushroom tart. 'Please – excuse my ignorance – but could you remind me who Ronan is?'

'I cannot remind you of that which previously I have not informed you,' said Gus somewhat irritated, chewing quickly on the quiche and congratulating Mary on it with his eyebrows. The three of them continued their lunch in uneasy silence. Chloë tried to eat as noiselessly as possible and became acutely aware of the clink of cutlery and Gus's breathing. It was fairly fast and slightly whistling. It sounded angry. Certainly it annoyed her.

Dabbing the corners of his mouth and taking careful sips at his apple juice, Gus took an orange and rolled it vigorously between his hands before peeling it.

'Ronan Brady is to be our sculptor in residence. You'll show him to the cottage at the end of the south field. You will tell him that his order of Kilkenny limestone has arrived and you'll take him to the small barn where it is awaiting him.'

'OK,' said Chloë, refusing fruit and looking at her lap. 'What's his work like?' she asked though she would have preferred to remain silent.

'Sublime,' answered Gus, pressing his thumbs down into the centre of the orange to part it. A jet of juice speared out and caught Chloë sharply in the eye.

'Ouch!' she said.

'Excuse me,' said Gus.

TWENTY

'Look, *Morwenna,*' said William to the dirty dishes, '*I'm just not ready for commitment.* Damn no, that's too clichéd.' He turned his attention to unloading the washing-machine and spoke to his socks as he hung them over the radiator to dry. '*Morwenna, I love you but I'm no longer in love with you* – no – *I don't feel in love with you.* No, no, no! Far too corny.' William spoke no more to his crockery or apparel but went about the housework half-heartedly until his muttering irritated him so much that he left his cottage for his studio.

'*Morwenna, I just feel we've grown apart.* Je-*sus*! Are there no original sayings for terminating relationships?'

He kneaded and wedged a batch of raku clay with another of fine white, slicing the clay into sections and then slamming them against each other, blending the bodies together and removing any air pockets. He continued his soliloquy, sometimes out loud, sometimes to himself.

'Damn it, Morwenna' he cried at a spoutless teapot, 'I no longer love you and doubt whether I ever did. I don't want you to be a part of my life and I don't want to make cups and saucers for you to sell either.'

He turned his attention back to the prepared clay and

stared at it for a while. He broke into a smile and chuckled as he divided it into fist-size balls.

I'll make cups and saucers for my own bloody use!

'Look, Morwenna, this isn't working. I feel stifled and I am unhappy. Please understand that I do this not to hurt you. I want to be by myself for a while. I do not want a relationship with you.'

He hurled a ball of clay on to the wheel and started it running high. Dripping water over the clay, he cupped his hands around it and, thrusting his elbow into his hip, sustained the pressure as he began to centre it and commence a good day's work. There was no room for Morwenna in his thoughts. No room for her at all.

* * *

'He called me Benedict, talked about the War, about Sheffield, and then blabbered for ten minutes solid,' said William to Mac as they puffed away an afternoon on their pipes, 'jer, je, je, je!'

'Dear oh dear,' brooded Mac, looking with admiration at the cup and saucer William had brought him, 'what caused the jer je-ing?'

'Lunacy!' declared William, his voice breaking.

Mac let it lie.

* * *

Morwenna closed her car door, wrapped her coat and her arms around herself and took a deep breath. Barbara hovered with delight at the side entrance to Peregrine's Gully, her yellow eyes flickering menace, her stubby tail quivering in anticipation. Morwenna refused to establish eye contact and sustained an assertive march to within inches of the goat. Barbara gave an odd gurgle in her throat and pawed the ground, lowering her head and brandishing her stubby horns. Morwenna was about to stand stock-still but suddenly thought better of it.

'Oh fuck off, Barbara,' she hissed witheringly, thrusting her knee into the unsuspecting flank of the flabbergasted creature, 'as if it's *you* I've come to see.'

He looks up from the wheel knowing the footfalls are not Barbara's. Acid rises in his stomach and he racks his brains for his little speech. He's rehearsed it well. And now forgotten it totally. Her presence is unexpected and throws him off his guard so he waits until he sees her from the corner of his eye and she is right inside the studio.

'Morwenna!'

'William!' she says cordially. She is wearing a navy blue woollen coat and dark leather gloves. She looks smart. A grown-up. Intimidating. A little. 'Am I disturbing you?'

'Well,' he falters, glancing at the perfect cylinder begging to be moved into a vase.

'I'll not be long.' Her tone is businesslike and unnerves William further.

'Everything OK?' He wipes his hands on his apron but stays astride his wheel. Morwenna twitches her face and gives a strange half-smile.

'I've come with your birthday present,' she says brightly, thrusting her hands into her pockets and perching on a small corner of the table. William looks perplexed.

'But my birthday's not until August!'

'I do know that – but I thought you'd like it early.'

'Oh!'

What else could he say? What was it he was going to say?

'I thought you ought to start your thirties as you mean them to continue,' says Morwenna with a generous smile. William looks quietly for the present but, apart from her hands, there is obviously nothing in her pockets.

'Thirty!' he exclaims. 'Don't remind me!'

'It reminds me how long ago it was for me,' says Morwenna morosely, silently chastising herself for doing so. William looks at the clay awkwardly, anticipating the you-think-I'm-old-and-ugly tirade.

'Very nice,' he says instead.

'What is?' Morwenna demands.

'A birthday present four months early!'

An awkward silence descends for a moment-hour. Eventually, Morwenna rises and walks to the door before turning to face William, tinged by hazy sunlight, at the other end of the studio.

'For your birthday, William, for your thirtieth, I am giving you your freedom. I want you to turn thirty unencumbered. I want you to be able to look back on all this as something that happened in your twenties – something that was fun at first though it soured inevitably.'

Now that is some soliloquy! She's taken the words from the jumble inside his mouth and placed them squarely, clearly, in the open. Out in the open, they've closed the regrettable situation. William parts his lips in the effort to make sense of all she is saying. Morwenna is tempted to cross over and kiss them one last time. William's lips are full and sensuous and he used them divinely. And most definitely in the past tense.

A split second hangs awkwardly in the heavy air between them. Morwenna is tempted to back up all she had said with 'If that's what you want'. Similarly William, who hates confrontation on things emotional, fights from saying 'Morwenna, don't worry, it will all be fine. I just need time'.

But neither speaks.

Waves of gratitude pass from one to the other. Though it hurts, Morwenna is relieved that William has made it easy for her by not contesting. He is enormously thankful that she has spared him the task he was dreading. And he is grateful to her, for he craves freedom.

'OK,' he says gently, shrugging his shoulders and nodding slowly with respect.

'OK, then!' Morwenna says cheerfully and with dignity.

'So,' says William, 'no more dinner services?'

Morwenna laughs lightly but with an edge. 'Oh no!' she says. 'Neither dinner services nor dinners themselves. You need have no more relations, let alone contact, with either Saxby Ceramics or its proprietor.'

For a good ten minutes after she left, William sat askew at his wheel and regarded the space she had left behind. A space indeed, but not a hole in his life, not something gaping that would need filling – just space. He felt a breeze travel over to him from the open door. He could taste the spring and smell the promise of summer.

At last. And it had been so easy. He laughed briefly. Barbara appeared at the door. He turned away from her and back to the clay cylinder: plain, precise and with potential. He smiled broadly and shook his head in amazement, sharing another moment when he and the clay were inextricable. You could use no ornithological analogies with William; Morwenna had not clipped his wings, nor was she now setting him free to fly on his own. Nor had he left the nest. Or mated for life.

Morwenna Saxby, he realized, had got her hands on him when he was in his malleable early twenties. She had formed him into this straight-sided cylinder; upright but featureless, strong but somewhat dull.

William set the wheel spinning. He slowed the speed. Twisting, he dipped one hand down within the vessel and made a knuckle with the finger of the other which he placed against the outside of the form. In harmony, instinctively, he drew both hands upwards and outwards. The clay travelled and grew and stretched, and the form opened out under his hands. Its body curved before widening beautifully; like the mouth of a trumpet, like speeded footage of a flower opening. William hummed cheerfully. The work was good and it was pleasing. The form: strong and individual.

The cylinder was gone. But it was still the backbone of this new form in front of him.

* * *

'Robert?'

'Darling!'

'You busy?'

'Heavens no, it's dead this afternoon, quite dead – like most of my patients, ha! It's a typical A and P Wednesday.'

'A and P – arthritis and piles?'

'No, no! Nothing nearly as exciting, merely the Aches and Pains brigade – they invariably turn up mid-week in the hope of taking a legitimate sicky from school or work for the rest of the week.'

'And I bet you're as attentive to Mr Hypochondriac as you are to all your patients.'

'My bedside manner, you mean?'

'Ho! I for one can't get enough of your bedside manner, Dr Noakes. Actually, there are a few A's and P's of my own that need closer inspection!'

'Merz Saxby! Sounds like an emergency! I'll be round to make you say "Ahh" just as soon as I can.'

'I'm positively bedridden.'

'Good. Stay there. I'm on call this evening but I'd rather be called out from the wrong side of your bed than from the right side of mine.'

'Dr Noakes, it'll be a pleasure to have you, regardless of interruptions. Oh! By the way, I did it – I sacked William Coombes!'

'Oh well bloody done! You can do without these prima donnas – how did he take it?'

'Quite well, it must be said. Sulked a little and said he didn't want to do any more dinner services anyway.'

'No grip on reality! Whether this is down to the artistic temperament or just general immaturity I've yet to decide. Mind you, what's the odds that he'll come to you with his tail between his legs and an armful of crockery when he's feeling the pinch?'

'He won't.'

'Just wait till he has a hole in his pocket – he'll be begging you to sell his ashtrays!'

'He most certainly won't.'

'You sound very sure.'

'Oh I am. I'll not be hearing from William Coombes again. Though I may hear *of* him – he is a talented potter after all.'

TWENTY-ONE

'Oh!' Chloë exclaimed, mouth agape and eyes very wide. Ronan Brady was startled and looked swiftly about him.

'No, no!' said Chloë loudly. 'I'm sorry – you surprised me, that's all.'

'Were you not expecting me?' he said, the lilting softness of his southern accent soliciting Chloë's ears at once.

'Not at all,' she responded. 'I mean, yes I was – but not *you*.'

'I don't catch you?' Ronan looked justifiably perplexed but refused to drop eye contact with her.

Chloë gave a quick laugh through her nose and looked down at her feet, suddenly acutely aware that she had odd socks on.

'I'm sorry,' she said, 'I just didn't expect Ronan Brady to *look* like you.'

'Oh?'

'I presumed – ignoramus that I am – that somehow all sculptors were very old.'

Ronan did not respond but kept peering at Chloë as if she were a whole new species to him, perhaps a subject he was about to sketch. Chloë twisted herself into her embarrassment.

'You know – a shock of grey hair, aquiline features, long bony hands.'

'Like Rodin?'

'Not exactly,' said Chloë who had no idea what Rodin looked like, 'there again, perhaps short and balding with a kindly, furrowed face and eyebrows of character; hands calloused but strong.'

'Moore?' said Ronan, tucking his own hands into his pockets.

'No,' said Chloë, 'that's as far as my imagination took me.'

'I meant Henry,' he explained patiently, 'but don't bother your barney.'

'Hey?'

'And who are *you*?' asked Ronan.

'Oh, me! I'm just Chloë, Chloë Cadwallader. I'm staying here for a while. Helping out. Till the summer. A couple more months. I must show you to your cottage.'

'In your socks?'

Chloë scurried into the depths of the house leaving Ronan on the doorstep to breathe in the thin, precise air of the late April morning while considering Chloë Cadwallader. Nice legs, naïvety attractive. While Chloë laced up her trainers, she pondered how she had indeed presumed all men of art to be old and worldly, of weathered physiognomies peculiar to their vocation. Certainly, she had never expected this sculptor to have piercing blue eyes set deep into a finely chiselled face crowned by a shock of black hair, all of which sat atop a body that, despite clothing, was obviously honed from a single block of smooth marble.

'What are your sculptures like?' asked Chloë as she led Ronan across the great lawn to a gate in a far corner.

'What do you mean?' asked Ronan as he vaulted over the gate and waited for Chloë to climb it.

'Well, I hear they're *sublime*,' she said, as if it were common opinion and not just Gus's, 'but what do they look like?'

'You've not seen any?' Ronan looked a little anxious.

'No. I'm afraid not,' said Chloë with a shrug of her shoulders and an apologetic smile.

'I'm fairly well represented north *and* south,' he said, quite intentionally embarrassing Chloë.

'Well, I'm English,' she said by way of an excuse as she led him across south field towards a small building nestling against a stretch of beech and rowan.

'Aye,' said Ronan, sympathizing.

'I mean,' said Chloë, keen to restore herself, 'are they abstract or figurative?'

Ronan smirked which unnerved her slightly. She marched on, pleased that he had to jig to catch up with her.

'Without consummate knowledge of the figurative there can be no abstraction,' he said with a flourish. Chloë waited for him to explain further and frowned slightly to hasten it.

'My work is an expression of my experience – and yet events or people are often portrayed in a non-figurative way, while my moods and emotions are frequently personified.' Chloë considered his words. They made sense and, though he spoke them soberly, it was without pretension.

'Which materials do you use?' she asked. 'Apart from Kilkenny limestone,' she added as an informed aside.

'I use materials best suited to each work – but I carve rather than model.'

'I see,' said Chloë, envisaging Moore over Rodin as she waited for more. Ronan stood still in the middle of the field, and the sheep lumbered away from him – in reverence, he believed; disinterest, decided Chloë. He gazed hard at a point beyond the horizon and obviously beyond Chloë's field of vision and comprehension.

'I'll hack at Purbeck as if it were timber,' he proclaimed, 'or I'll polish wood as if it were marble.'

Chloë watched a lamb give an involuntary buck before it trotted to its mother and demanded milk most impudently.

'I'll follow the vein in marble or work against it absolutely.'

'I see,' she said, 'dependent on the mood and subject?'

'Precisely!'

They walked towards the cottage.

'What'll you do with the Kilkenny limestone?' Chloë asked brightly as she fumbled for the key. Ronan gave a clipped and condescending chuckle. Chloë stared at him, expressionless.

'However can I know before I've seen the stone?' His smile was patronizing and Chloë did not like it. His smile was also rather attractive and it unnerved her that she'd noticed.

'How*ever* would *I* know?' she said flatly, unlocking the cottage and turning on her heels so that his 'Thanks, see you later' met nothing but her back.

'You showed him to the cottage?' asked Gus.

'Right to the door,' Chloë confirmed.

'And?'

Chloë frowned and cocked her head. Gus closed his eyes momentarily before fixing them on her.

'He's only Ireland's most promising sculptor! Did you *welcome* him? Settle him? *Chat* to him, for goodness sake?'

'Ah,' said Chloë, 'the Ballygorm welcome!' Her tiny note of sarcasm was lost on Gus who seemed pleased instead. '*I* certainly chattered,' said Chloë. 'I asked him about his work but found him to be rather intense, somewhat guarded.'

'Ronan Brady!' justified Gus, rolling his 'r's. 'I've asked him up to the house for lunch.'

'Lovely,' said Chloë, who always gave people a second chance.

Lunch was lively; Ronan quite opened out to Gus's informed questions and opinions, and ate much and fast. Chloë found herself heartened that Ronan gave Gus the same reply when he enquired about the limestone. With a careful glance at Ronan, and another at Gus, Chloë decided Ronan was merely the brooding artist type, of which she had heard much but hitherto never met. Nothing to be wary of, it seemed. She thought of the eccentric, foppish artists Jocelyn had known, but remembered too that they had worked with liberal daubs of bright colour and not immense blocks of blue-black rock.

'Chloë,' said Ronan, 'what do you like?'

I like laughter and affection. Simple things that give deep pleasure.

'Me?'

I like company and security. To feel wanted, useful and liked.

Gus and Ronan watched her enquiringly.

'I admit freely to knowing little about sculpture,' she confessed, laying her knife and fork neatly together on the plate, 'but I do know that I could stand in front of a Greek statue for days on end, regardless of its ruinous state.'

Ronan raised his glass of apple juice at her. Chloë surged and then told herself to stop it. Gus doffed his head in agreement. Chloë felt encouraged to continue.

'Pottery!' she declared with aplomb. The men raised their eyebrows to invite her to elaborate. 'Er, that it can stand by itself – artistically, I mean. That it is often much more than its function. What's the word – autonomous.'

'A vessel to explore and express?' suggested Ronan. Chloë nodded sagely.

'They're musical too, you know,' she said.

'Oh yes?' said Gus. Chloë nodded again, slowly and with conviction.

After lunch, while Gus walked Ronan to his workshop in the barn, Chloë phoned the South Bank Centre in London to request a brochure from the last Christmas exhibition. It arrived the next day.

'Do you like these?' she asked Gus, pointing to the

humming urns. He took the leaflet from her and observed it carefully and at length over the top of his glasses.

'Yes I do, Chloë. See if you can find out more about the artist. Have some photos sent here. Ask about prices. They'd look good on the terrace.'

Please, thought Chloë, *how about 'please'*.

* * *

Chloë takes an early night. She excuses herself from the dinner table even though it means forgoing the Bakewell tart for pudding. She explains that she has a headache but knows she could have said the pox, for all the interest that Gus shows.

'Good-night, then. Busy day tomorrow,' he says.

She walks tall from the dining-room but sighs heavily in the great hall; it seems to echo so she clears her throat loudly to cover it. That Gus might catch wind of her unhappiness unsettles her more than the emotion itself.

I'll get through it. Always have.

In her room, she peels off her clothing and runs a bath; she puts on the radio so that no one can hear her think, and no one can sense that there is anything remotely amiss.

I'm OK. I can cope.

Easing herself gingerly down into the too-hot water, she closes her eyes on the day and remains motionless until beads of perspiration trickle from her forehead to her chest via a run over her nose and cheeks and a tumble off her chin.

Carl. I'll think of Carl.

But she cannot conjure his face or recall his voice; distorting instead his accent into a vulgar caricature.

Remember! Fantasize!

She wonders why she did not give him her address at Ballygorm. She wonders why he did not ask for it. Why did she not ask for the appropriate *poste restante*? Why did he not ask her to write? She knows why and though she has been hitherto content with this knowledge, suddenly today she wishes it were not so; that she could contact him, see him, have him comfort and compliment her. She soaps her limbs carefully with her eyes shut, trying to remember how Carl's touch felt.

I do know that it felt nice. Good old Carl.

As Mrs Andrews had pointed out to her that morning, Carl had repaired Brett's damage and restored an element of fun and pleasure to Chloë's life. 'Life can suck,' Carl had told her, 'but if you suck at it for long enough it's sure to taste sweet!' He was uncomplicated, unpretentious and unthreatening, moreover he had a specific function. They had come together knowing full well that they would part. And when.

'Your three months were hermetic and precious,' Mrs Andrews illumined. 'The quarrels and other mundanities befalling relationships proper were banned by necessity.'

'So true,' Chloë responded mistily. 'We were happy enough to share a predilection for the common Mars bar and the smell of leather without feeling any obligation to discover more profound points of contact.'

No future rendezvous, no 'When will I see you again?', merely a metaphorical leg up for one another on to the next stages of their lives.

Good old Carl, a man for a very certain season. Though she had shared the winter months with him, when it had rained frequently and been very cold too, Chloë recalls Wales as a bright period of energy and laughter. Here she is in Ireland, where it is mild and the spring is maturing steadily, and yet a sombreness pervades. Here the landscape serves only as a view for Chloë to gaze upon, a backdrop against which she goes about each day. Despite its beauty, she does not feel a part of this terrain and cannot find its *genius loci*. Spring at Ballygorm is a contradiction of sorts for, save for the lambs, the pace is uniformly sedate and controlled. Nature's young colours and freshness are resolutely kept outside the front door to Ballygorm Manor. There is no hapless reshuffle. There is a point to everything.

And yet Jocelyn couldn't have known that there would be a Carl in Wales, just as she could not have foreseen Chloë's reception in Ireland. And Chloë can't quite see that Jocelyn would have been happy for Fate to colour and describe the route she had mapped out for her god-daughter. Chloë can't quite see it; not just yet.

Ronan Brady.

There must be a point to Ronan.

Chloë places her toe inside the bath tap and knows now, with some trepidation, why she cannot recall Carl's face.

Ronan's has taken its place. She can no longer hear Kiwi inflections for the Irish tongue is dominant.

And she kids herself that she wonders why.

Ronan is different. Behind his beauty lies an arrogance absent from, and anathema to, Carl. Brett was arrogant and, as such, repugnant. Ronan, however, wears his arrogance about himself like a rich velvet cloak braided with gold, and it is somehow compelling. Knowingly, he makes Chloë feel uneasy; small, insecure, unsure, and yet she feels drawn to him too. As happy-go-lucky as Carl was, Ronan is intense. Chloë shudders and then laughs aloud uneasily.

Ronan, it seems, can make her skin crawl, and tingle, simultaneously.

'Just the brooding artist type,' she declares to her distorted reflection in the tiles.

'Ego!' she says merrily, wondering where hers has gone.

'A new pair of shoes to try,' Chloë decides as she wraps herself up in a white cotton towel, 'to see if this pair might fit.'

* * *

30 April
Dear Mr Coombes,

We are setting up a commercial sculpture trail here at Ballygorm Manor. The emphasis is on young artists working in a variety of styles in any medium. We rather like your pots and wonder if you might like to exhibit them at Ballygorm? Perhaps you could send us photographs of any you think suitable.

I look forward to hearing from you and hope that you will wish to be a part of this exciting new project for Northern Ireland.

Yours sincerely,

C. Cadwallader

3 May

Dear Mr Cadwallader,

Thank you for your letter. I would indeed be interested – and delighted – to exhibit at Ballygorm Manor. I enclose photos of a selection of my work – I have chosen the large-scale pieces which I think would be more suitable for your purpose. They are all frost proof and mostly hand built.

I look forward to hearing from you again,

William Coombes

7 May

Dear Mr Coombes,

We were very pleased to receive your letter and the illustrations of your works. We would very much like to exhibit Large Coiled Urns nos. 1–5. Whilst we will insure the works while they are here, transport to and from is to be arranged by the artist.

Please advise when they are likely to arrive – and what price you would like to receive for each.

Best wishes,

Yours sincerely,

C. Cadwallader (Miss)

10 May

Dear Miss Cadwallader,

I am delighted for you to have the five pots on consignment and enclose my price-list for them. I am currently enquiring about transport costs and will inform you of delivery dates as soon as possible.

I have some smaller pieces too, mainly thrown – please let me know if you would like to see some examples.

Yours sincerely,

William Coombes

14 May

Dear Mr Coombes,

We look forward to taking delivery of your pieces at the end of the month and wait to be advised further.

Please could you send a CV for our catalogue?

Unfortunately, all works are to be exhibited out of doors so your smaller pots will probably not be suitable.

Best wishes,

Chloë Cadwallader

20 May

Dear Miss Cadwallader,

The pots are to arrive on 31 May and I will be delivering them myself. I am going to combine it with a short break in the 'emerald isle' as I have not had a holiday in three years and have never been to Ireland!

If it is possible, I would very much like to assist in the placing of my pieces – this would also afford me the opportunity to look around the Trail.

I look forward to meeting you at the end of the month.

Best wishes,

William Coombes

22 May

Dear William Coombes,

How lovely that you will deliver your pots in person. We will be happy to show you the Sculpture Trail at Ballygorm and give you lunch too.

Let us know of your time of arrival – and any dietary requests.

Best wishes until then,

Chloë

* * *

'Good morning, Ballygorm Sculpture Trail?'

'Hullo, may I speak to Miss Cadwallader?'

'Speaking.'

'Hullo there, good morning, this is William Coombes here. The, er, potter?'

'Mr Coombes! Hullo!'

'From Cornwall. About tomorrow –'

'Tomorrow indeed – we're looking forward to meeting you and seeing your pots in person, as it were. Do you know what time you'll be arriving? Do you need directions?'

'No.'

'Lovely! What time – ish?

'No, er – I mean, I can't *come*. Unfortunately. Hence the phone call. Hullo?'

'Oh *dear* –'

'My father's been taken ill. He lives in Wales. I've been summonsed.'

'I see, how ghastly. What a great shame.'

'Yes. Indeed. The pots are travelling by themselves and I've arranged for their collection at Belfast and delivery on to you. They'll arrive tomorrow. Lunch-time.'

'But you won't.'

'No.'

'Such a pity.'

'Yes.'

TWENTY-TWO

'How is he? I don't have a car. The train took an age.'

'We tried to call you.'

'Oh God!'

'No, no! To say that he's made a marvellous recovery! You'd already left – you needn't have come.'

William wanted to agree with the nurse wholeheartedly but bit back his bluntness.

'I wish I visited more,' he lied.

'Cornwall is a long way away – a different country,' the nurse said kindly, 'and your father's memory is poor. Very poor.'

William found his father pretty much where he had left him; just another figure in a long line of dementia, all slumped in chairs gazing listlessly out of the window deep into their pasts or at absolutely nothing. Mr Coombes was so motionless that, as William approached, his stomach wondered if his father were dead. He stood beside the old man's chair silently, waiting for a blink, a rise and fall of the chest, a twitch of a skeletal finger. William held his breath while his heart racketed. The air was singed with the sharp, acrid smell of urine and decay. And yet William was not prepared for his father to be dead, not ready for him to die.

Breathe!

An empty chair was close to hand so he retrieved it while his father's neighbour nodded and winked at him and chewed his tongue. He drew up the chair as noisily as he could but his father's mouth remained agape, his eyes fixed and unseeing. Gingerly, William proffered his hand and let it rest lightly on top of the old man's. It was not the hand of a dead man for, though cool and papery, a whisper of warmth wound its way through. Slowly, the old man turned towards him. He stared at him intently but William was not sure whether he saw him for there was no light in the eyes, no life behind them. The aperture of his mouth remained fixed. William smiled at him as widely as he could.

'Hullo!' he said cheerily.

Mr Coombes began a nod but had not the strength to lift his head to conclude it. His chin neared his chest, his gaze now resting near a drawing-pin by the skirting-board. William felt a stab of unwelcome tears, whose provenance he could not fathom. He sat a while longer, sharing in silence with his father the complexities of the bent drawing-pin.

He could have gone. It would have been easy; just jump to his feet, kiss the man cursorily and walk away. The nurses wouldn't judge. Mr Coombes wouldn't register. But William stayed for two hours, moving his thumb rhythmically over the tired landscape of his father's hand. He no longer noticed any smell. He felt most strongly that, inside the waning body, behind the gormless face, in spite of the drooling and wheezing, a brain and a soul were shouting but were unable to make themselves intelligible, let alone heard. Eyes that no longer saw, but had seen. And what they had seen had left an indelible imprint of sadness.

* * *

William worked voraciously. He was haunted by his father's loaded gawping. The man he had presumed to be catatonic, moronic even, he now believed to be otherwise. Behind the dull exterior, the wrinkled and puckered skin lying uselessly over brittle bones, a tiny light refused to go out. But it could not venture past the rancid, cavernous mouth to let itself be heard.

'I'll speak for him,' William said, sitting bolt upright in bed in the early hours.

'Life behind the seemingly lifeless,' he told Barbara as he rushed to the studio at the first hint of morning.

'Sound in the silent,' he mulled as he kneaded a batch of very cold raku clay.

'Emotion in the inanimate,' he whispered as he contemplated his memory and the raw material in front of him.

The project consumed him. He left Peregrine's Gully only once a week to cycle to St Ives and load his panniers with non-perishable goods. He excused himself in advance to Mac, whose delight that he was working once more with such verve far outweighed any disappointment that visits would be forfeited. William let the telephone go unanswered. He ignored Barbara and ate only when he remembered. Slowly the forms took shape. He slabbed and coiled great slumbering pebble shapes, each almost entirely enclosed but for a single small opening. These were round and dark and placed unexpectedly off centre, or at the side, or even towards the base of the form. The holes contradicted the fabric of the shapes. While he glazed the exteriors in the palest of crackles, the openings gave way into utter darkness. Though the forms were so obviously hollow, the holes heralded an interior that was opaque and thick. The pebbles lay peaceful and uniform from most viewpoints until disrupted entirely by the holes. Mouths open. Still and silent. But shouting out pain and panic. And secrets that could not be heard.

TWENTY-THREE

With the grand opening of the Ballygorm Sculpture Trail over a month away and all the plans going smoothly, Gus had become more generous with time off for Chloë and more receptive to her requests for the loan of a vehicle. Without actually being agreeable. He ensured that he was in control of such excursions by never suggesting them; he would offer Chloë simply an afternoon or morning off but never tendered transport. Even when won round, he resolutely sent Chloë on her way with a barrage of warnings to heed, and advice to take. Each occasion, therefore, that Chloë was rewarded with free time, she was also presented with the encumbrance of requesting formally the mechanical means to facilitate her expeditions. Her desire for space and a chance to explore, saw such requests become more reverential and polished. 'May I' was soon replaced by 'Would you mind if I', which in turn gave way to 'Please could I possibly' and, by her fourth excursion: 'Gus, if it isn't too much to ask, would you permit me to borrow a car as I'd dearly love to visit Bushmills?'

Invariably, Gus met her petitions with a loaded silence which forced them to hang, insecure and unanswered, in the oppressive air of the study while he gazed out of the window for dramatic effect. A simple and suitable request thus became a very great favour to which Chloë responded with effusive gratitude and barely disguised relief.

Chloë soon came to think on Ireland as the Land of Affable Polythene. Wherever she journeyed, small snags of plastic accompanied her. She was first aware of them on the Antrim coast road; caught on a jut of rock, trapped on a barb of fencing, knitted in branches, wrapped around the signs proclaiming each of the nine glens. Fluttering in the sea breeze, they appeared both to welcome Chloë and to wave her on; certainly she never conceived of them as mess or rubbish. Inland, the scraggy moorland barren apart from ragged sheep strewn like litter over the hills, Chloë was assured a wave from a jag of plastic caught on a thorn bush or impaled on a spear of rusting metal. She found, as she drove from glen to glen, that she drove from one drift of polythene to another. They had the same steadying effect as a compass, the same reassurance as a landmark.

If the furls of plastic seemed almost indigenous to the landscape, the mark of man, then, was a blemish. It horrified Chloë that, apart from the saving graces of Ballygorm and the very occasional medieval castle or early nineteenth-century hostelry, most of the buildings were modern, uninspiring and wholly unsympathetic to the lie of the land. Pastel coloured and stone-clad, lead-effect PVC windows, incongruous Corinthian columns and American soap-opera-style driveways heralded ugly bungalows whose gardens and discrepant rockeries were guarded by listless unicorns or lions of reconstituted stone. The structures sat awkwardly in their surroundings and yet the flourish of pride with which they were conceived of and built was far louder than the lack of taste they exhibited. Still, they hurt Chloë's eyes and disappointed her greatly. It was not as if she craved the picturesque, for the landscape was too rugged to permit it anyway. Nor was it roses and thatched roofs that she wished to see, but a historical Irish accent instead. Her woe, however, found approval with both Gus and Ronan.

'Aye,' brooded the sculptor, 'they bin rippin' down their daddies' homes, and with it, the spirit of the place.'

'The beauty of true vernacular architecture,' Gus qualified, 'is in its blend with the landscape. They *do* still exist, Chloë, but their survival is in their camouflage.'

And what of the Giant's Causeway where architecture and geology are inseparable; where Jocelyn would be with the fulmars and the mayweed? Why did Chloë not run there at the earliest opportunity? She did not want to talk to Jocelyn just yet. And anyway, after the Giant's Causeway, then what?

I use my little sorties, she explained by letter to Jasper and Peregrine, *to take stock of the situation. If Gus has been particularly unrestrained in his criticism, or if Mary has been bombarding me with her woes and those of all her family and friends, and if Ronan has been harping on in mixed metaphors about sculpture, then I usually find that the landscape and its people offer some solace.*

The land seems to mirror my emotions as well as offer respite when needed, it both mimics and empowers me. There are soft, lyrical passages and there are also great swathes of grandeur. It's a private place, discrete and independent. I always feel somehow more level when I return.

It was during a secret tête-à-tête with Mrs Andrews (her husband and Gainsborough were playing poker in Sudbury), that Chloë confided the sub-plot for such excursions.

'And you always go alone?' Mrs Andrews asked, genuinely interested and rather impressed.

'Always,' Chloë assured. 'I always go alone. Firstly, because I'm usually keen to be well away from all inhabitants at Ballygorm. Secondly, because I find I converse quite naturally with the people I come across. I'm not nearly as shy as I was.'

'And are there many?' gasped Mrs Andrews, imagining a swarthy race with raw knees.

'If I search them out,' Chloë explained, remembering the kindly old boy in a chemist at Cushendall with whom she had put the world to rights for a couple of hours the previous week.

'*Search?* Gracious!' Mrs Andrews clasped her breast. 'Where do they lurk? Are they terribly uncivilized?'

'Oh no!' Chloë laughed, thinking back to the two students with whom she had shared beer and crisps and reverential silence while listening hard to the waterfalls at Glenariff. 'They're friendly if you engage them – but it's as if they'd just as well be left to themselves.'

'Uneducated?'

'Not at all.'

'Ill-mannered?'

'Not in the slightest.'

'Insular, then?'

'Yes, insular – but in a proud, self-sufficient way. They're blunt and direct but with a smile and a kind tone. I like that.'

Mrs Andrews furtively removed her stockings and her shoes, stretched dainty toes out in front of her and into the embrace of a gentle breeze before burrowing them in the downy grass and burying the evidence with the skirts of her frock.

'What do you do, while you walk alone, Chloë my dear? Rarely can I walk off by myself without Mr A becoming all chivalrous and accompanying me. How I'd love to wear trousers and go for a great stomp, talk to birds or myself.'

Chloë laughed while quietly contemplating how it was *she* who had frequently envied Mrs Andrews the supposed security and grace of privileged eighteenth-century living.

'Ronan!' she whispered, suddenly and not a little coyly.

Mrs Andrews's toes reappeared from the hem of her skirt and wriggled with delight. 'Do tell!'

'I'm not sure how to,' Chloë confided, 'but it's something

along the lines of a little plan I have. I mulled over it in the study behind Gus's back a couple of weeks ago and have since developed and honed it during my occasional outings.'

Mrs Andrews's toes went apoplectic in anticipation.

'I thought,' explained Chloë, quietly but through a smile, 'it might be rather nice,' she furthered, rolling her words and glancing from her lap to her confidante, 'to be his muse!'

'Oh!' Mrs Andrews declared, hiccuping a little and nodding vigorously.

'His *muse*. I thought it might be fun,' Chloë continued, 'and half the fun has already been in the thinking about it.'

'I'll bet,' enthused Mrs Andrews.

'I mean, I'd never have *dared* contemplate such a thing before.'

'Before?'

'Before Wales. No, I mean before *all* of this. If I was still in London. With Brett. If Jocelyn was still alive.'

'And have you feelings for the sculptor?'

Chloë searched. 'He's, he's – be*guil*ing. He's occupying a great proportion of my late-night last thoughts.'

'Then why do you twist your face so? In this breeze, you'll stick like that, be warned!'

'Because, Mrs Andrews, I know full well that Ronan has not, and will not, touch the soft part of my soul in the way Carl did. I am attracted to him – fiercely, I might add – almost solely because of *what* he is. I've never met anyone like him but I've read about them, and seen them in films!'

'From what you've told me about him,' said Mrs Andrews, 'I'd say the merits of his personality are somewhat questionable for he seems undeniably imperious and moody.'

'Oh he is, he is,' agreed Chloë artlessly, 'he's a brooding sculptor whose cerebral and emotional millstone has to be sculpted away or else consume him!'

Mrs Andrews patted at her breast quickly and lightly.

‘And you see,’ Chloë declared, suddenly aware of how the standard of her speech improved greatly when conversing with Mrs Andrews, ‘once again it is the very confines of my seasonal sojourn which empower me. The notion that summer and Scotland are around the corner to offer respite or escape is immensely comforting.’

Mrs Andrews cocked her head and implored more. Chloë did not disappoint.

‘My sacred time with darling Carl has paved the way for an indecent interlude with Ronan Brady.’

‘Ah,’ colluded Mrs Andrews, ‘adolescent effervescence gives way to a burgeoning desire most carnal.’

‘Indeed. My first orgasm can’t possibly be my last!’

Though she was immensely proud of Chloë, Mrs Andrews also thought she really ought to raise her eyebrows, so she did. ‘It is not so much Ronan himself who causes your pupils to dilate and who has kindled certain fire deep within you,’ she declared triumphantly, ‘but the *idea* of him, Chloë dear.’

Chloë was too excited, too high, to speak more. She felt she had now been given a much respected seal of approval to bring her plan to fruition. The fact that it had been granted by a reproduction of a painted image of a long-dead eighteenth-century woman was of no significance to Chloë. She simply wanted Ronan the Sculptor to seduce her. And, from the glint and search in his eyes, the glances that frequently outstayed their intention, she was fairly sure that he wanted to.

And what would it be like?
How does a sculptor make love?
Could I ever, really, be anyone’s muse?
Me? Chloë?

* * *

‘Kilkenny limestone,’ announced Ronan, walking around

the great block as if he were a lecturer commencing his discourse, 'is a sedimentary rock indigenous to my home.'

Chloë perched herself on an upturned bucket in the workshop and looked about. Thick rope, a pulley, chisels and mallets and a scatter of gruesome-looking tools. And Ronan, in a boiler suit creased with dust and ripped by his labours. Cobwebs in the eaves. An old tractor half covered in the corner; a rusting pitchfork propped against it as if harvesting had come to a sudden end some years ago.

'Now isn't that a stroke a' luck,' Ronan laughed, 'that I should have always yearned to be a sculptor and there, on my doorstep, is one of the finest rocks to work with!'

Chloë regarded the clump and thought the grey-blue surface scattered with ash-coloured dints rather uninspiring but she didn't say so. The barn was cavernous and chilly but the sun was streaming in and it warmed her back so she was quite happy to stay put.

'What'll you make?' she asked in hushed tones. Ronan did not baulk at her question but held the crook of his finger beneath his nose and hummed and murmured as he paced around the stone. He knocked at his temple as if it were a heavy door.

'Bugger me – it's all up here,' he said, 'but I'm all clutey with these,' he explained, holding out clenched fists to Chloë who looked puzzled but understood him to mean either ham-fisted or having the equivalent of writer's block. She was tempted to go over to him, to cup his hands in hers, take them to her lips, kiss each knuckle. She stayed put; of course she did. She's in the here and now and Mrs Andrews is nowhere to be seen, or heard.

'Am I a distraction? Ought I to go?' she asked tentatively, hoping that he would protest.

'I've been up since the scrake and got nowhere by myself so you might as well stay. If you want.'

'OK,' said Chloë, 'if you'd like me to.'

Ronan grunted with a slight toss of his head and

continued his journey around the rock. He walked clockwise and then anticlockwise and stopped at practically all the points of an imaginary compass, squinting at the light, scrutinizing the great bulk before him. He sighed and heaved regularly and stood up and down on his tiptoes, a feat Chloë quite admired considering his caked, steel-capped workman's boots. She stayed awhile, hoping her presence might liberate the pent-up artistic genius still locked within the swaying, procrastinating, gorgeous Ronan. It seemed she made little difference and, after sitting silent and reverential for a good hour, she crept away.

Chloë visited Ronan daily for he rarely came to the house.

' 'Tis the dwelling of my patron and I have no place there,' he had said darkly. The sentiment Chloë understood; its vocabulary and delivery, however, she found affected and daft. She repeated it to Mr and Mrs Andrews.

'Silly bugger's a little too far up his own backside, I'd say,' considered Mr Andrews.

'Gracious!' added Mrs Andrews. 'It's trouble enough keeping Tom Gainsborough *out* of our house – to say nothing of the chambermaid's clothing!'

'I wish Ronan shared Gainsborough's predilection,' Chloë said to them, putting a hand forlornly to her breast. 'I sit on my bucket in his studio for an hour a day but all he does is sigh at his rock.'

'While you have your eye on his cock!'

'Mrs Andrews!' declared Chloë, blushing.

'Decorum, dear,' said Mr Andrews quietly.

It was true. Each day Chloë would visit Ronan and sit motionless with her ankles crossed daintily, trying hard to be alluring in her silence as well as in a slight parting of her lips any time Ronan should look at her. She stole cautious gazes at him as he paced and sighed. A glimpse of a tuft of chest hair at the dip of his neck made her quiver. Secretly, she would urge him to crouch, which afforded both of them refreshing viewpoints and a new, interesting perspective. If facing her, his boiler suit would cling to the muscles of his thighs; turned away from her and the material hugged his buttocks and stretched taut across the breadth of his shoulders.

When his brow furrowed with the effort of being a sculptor, Chloë observed a darkness cloud his eyes into velvet navy. When the sun caught them, or when inspiration alighted, she saw how their blueness reflected the sky and spoke of the sea. Sometimes he rolled his sleeves above his elbows. Chloë thought his elbows quite divine and his forearms worthy of Shakespearian depiction. On days when it was particularly warm, he unbuttoned his boiler suit and rolled it down, tying the sleeves around his hips. A T-shirt, meanwhile, delineated the muscles of his chest, proclaimed his trim stomach and afforded a good airing of his biceps, all of which delighted Chloë.

Spring was creeping into summer. She had arrived when the land breathed a pale, gentle green; now it was awash with emerald. The days were milder earlier and stayed warmer later, allowing Chloë to progress into softer, less substantial clothing. Once or twice she remarked to herself how Carl had desired her in spite of spattered jodhpurs, a prickly Fair Isle jumper and a grey thermal vest. Ronan, however, took no notice of her silk shirt tucked, as she thought, sexily into her jeans and unbuttoned a little on each journey from Gus's study to Ronan's studio.

Gus approved of her visits.

'Artists,' he justified, as if they were a different race, 'have low resistance against melancholia. A little chivvying is a very good idea. After all, the Trail opens in little over a month!'

So Chloë sits on her bucket and waits for signs and signals from Ronan. She is pleased that, over the course of a week or two, he has modified his grunt on her arrival, to a nod of the head, and now a relaxed 'Hi, there!' She says very little, certainly never interrupts him with a goodbye. The limestone is changing yet she is never there to witness it. Though Ronan broods on the fact that the form remains locked within the rock, that his tools are useless until his mind releases his hands, each day Chloë finds the stone has become smoother, a rhythm more pronounced. Has Ronan imposed this shape on to the rock, or did it exist already and he has merely uncovered it? She likes the way an inanimate object can change and grow. It has started to spiral, like a primeval mollusc, like a great python. It seems to live. Its surface is now smooth and often warm to the touch. And yet it is a lump of rock.

She remains silent though, for she believes that is what Ronan wishes, and anyway, she is still shy of her opinion.

TWENTY-FOUR

Gus was in a foul mood.

'Where the hell is Chloë?' he yelled in the empty study. 'Less than a fortnight to go until we're on the map and she announces she's leaving next week!' Tutting despairingly, he hammered on the window to dislodge the pigeons from their confabulation aboard the Antony Gormley bronze. Mary came scuttling in.

'Did you call, Mr Halloran?'

'No,' he said, reasserting his composure by rolling his head quickly. 'But have you seen Chloë?'

'Not since this morning,' Mary replied truthfully, hoping she would not be pressed further.

'Is she with Ronan?' he asked. Mary told him she really wouldn't know, but could she get back to the kitchen, her bread was ready.

'Ronan!'

'Mr Halloran, morning.'

'Seen Chloë?'

'Not this morning.'

'Damn!'

'Sorry?'

'We had, er, *words* last night.'

'God, and if we didn't have 'em yesterday afternoon too!'

The men were silent and gazed down at the blue-black sheen of the newly polished limestone.

'Have you decided where it should stand?' Gus asked.

'No, I can't seem to – half of me thinks the privacy of the wood, the other half craves pride of place right in the centre of the lawn! She's probably gone for a walk,' said Ronan.

'Hmm,' murmured Gus, turning on his heels and walking away.

'It's lunch-time, Mr Halloran,' said Mary, popping her head around the study door to find him standing by the window, hands in pockets and a pencil twizzling in his mouth.

'Chloë?' he said through his teeth while biting hard on the pencil to keep it in place.

'She said not to wait,' Mary trailed away, her mouth agape, suddenly horribly aware that her foot was firmly in it.

'What?' bellowed Gus, not sure where the pencil dropped and not bothered anyway.

'She said not to wait,' Mary repeated quietly but with no suggestion of timidity.

'*You* said you had not seen her!' Gus growled. 'What on earth is going on?'

Mary cleared her throat and held her head high.

'I said I had not seen her *since this morning*.'

'For heaven's sake, woman,' cried Gus, marching over to Mary who stood her ground.

'I saw Chloë this morning. Poor lass. Took the Land Rover and told me not to cook for her.' Gus's eyes zipped around Mary's face while his thoughts scrambled and his mouth dried completely.

'I reckon the girl's had enough of your barging,' called Mary over her shoulder as she left the study for the kitchen. 'Lunch is ready, Mr Halloran.'

* * *

When the world was moulded and fashioned out of formless chaos, this must have been the bit over – a remnant of chaos.

Thackeray

'Thackeray,' said Chloë to an inquisitive rock pipit, 'got it all wrong. The only chaos here,' she added to a boisterous guillemot, 'is that within me.'

Chloë had the Giant's Causeway all to herself. She had parked the Land Rover appallingly in the empty car park, skirted around the visitor centre and scurried down the winding path to the bottom of the cliff and slap bang into the middle of a well remembered O level geography lesson.

Her geography teacher had described it as a 'lunar' landscape. Thackeray, erroneously, thought it loony. Chloë thought it quite the most spectacular scene she had ever seen. The glum face she had worn on the journey, and all the previous day, at once opened out into an expansive smile. The gusts from the sea fortified her and the knowledge of Scotland just over the water was reassuring. The beauty and magnitude of the Giant's Causeway flung a neater perspective on her fraught little world. She was surrounded by the famous network of hexagonal basalt columns, some forty foot high, some a mere step; their regularity and longevity in some way giving structure to her thoughts.

Chloë searched for Jocelyn with her eyes alternately wide open and scrunched tight shut. She scoured the mayweed for her and listened hard to the fulmars and the pipits. She did not understand their language. Jocelyn, it appeared, would not be visiting today. And yet what was it that she had said in her Ireland letter?

I am there still because part of me never left.

Perhaps Chloë did not know where to look. Maybe she was not looking hard enough. Possibly, she was not quite ready to find Jocelyn. Not just yet. After all, what would she tell her? That she had given herself brazenly to a sculptor? Just because he was a sculptor, whatever that meant, and albeit one who was as pretentious as he was introverted? That she had realized her desire to become an artist's muse but in a way that appalled her? That yesterday she had insulted her host, her godmother's old friend? She'd confide in Jocelyn anon, once conclusions had been drawn, lessons learnt and decisions made.

For the first time, however, the landscape was not conspiring. It did not mirror her mood. It was, instead, an utter distraction; a sky-blue day with just the occasional vaporous cloud drifting across like a dream, the sea lapping lazily as if it were quite full but just wanted to taste the shore a little more, the sea birds carrying out their chores with chatter and aplomb. And no people. Chloë could not believe her luck for she had seen the ice-cream signs, the postcards furling forlornly in their rusting racks, she had seen the notice for the minibus to trundle the hordes down to the base of the cliff. Perhaps there was no ice-cream today and maybe the bus had broken down; no people to transport, no visitors to buy postcards.

'Am I complaining?' chanted Chloë as she tiptoed from stack to stack. 'I think not!'

She danced her way over those known as the Honeycomb and saluted the King and his Nobles. She laughed out loud and then giggled at hearing her own voice carried by the wind out to sea. She tried to traverse the columns solely step by precarious step but soon found that their differing heights and surfaces caused her to jig and stumble. She went in search of columns that were not hexagonal and, when she found one with eight sides and another with five, she was as thrilled as if they had been four-leaf clovers. Out of breath, she found the stacks which formed the Wishing Chair and sat awhile, breathing deeply and grinning. The sun streamed over her body and she allowed her eyes to close, to encourage memories of the previous fortnight to present themselves unhampered.

* * *

Ronan had kissed her furiously. He could not tolerate another unproductive day just pacing around his great rock and looking unconstructively at it. The form had started to swell as well as spiral, but its direction was uncertain and Ronan was damned if he knew where it was going. He knew where *he* was going to go, straight into the knickers of this affable young woman. This Chloë. Cadwallader. What a mouthful. Give me her mouth.

As she sits gazing out way beyond the sea, Chloë observes how she would have recalled her tryst with Ronan with more pleasure had not its consequence marred the memory.

Two weeks ago, Gus had gone to Belfast for a meeting with the Arts Council. He had most conveniently dropped Mary in Ballymena for a shop and an afternoon with her friends and had instructed Chloë to go directly to Ronan once she had finished the morning post.

'I fear he's a little off schedule, don't you? I think he works better under the watchful eye of the Ballygorm Sculpture Trail's administrative assistant, don't you?'

'Well,' faltered Chloë, not happy with the term 'assistant', 'he never seems to do that much while I'm actually *there* – though he has always pressed on by my next visit.'

'Which,' said Gus making no effort to mask the irritation in his voice, 'merely reworks my sentiments previously expressed.'

Chloë gave him a polite smile and shot daggers at him behind his back.

Gus straightened his tie, hollered for Mary and left

Ballygorm for the city, saying they would not be back until late afternoon.

The first thing Chloë did, once the drone of the Jaguar had died away, was to scamper up to her room to change. It was practically June and a most appropriate day for shorts; just gone nine in the morning and the sky was utterly cloudless, the scent of summer, though faint, came in wafts. She teamed her navy shorts with a white T-shirt that had shrunk slightly in the wash and stretched across her most becomingly. A soft woollen cardigan gave the outfit a practical touch and, as she perused the ensemble in front of the tall mirror on the landing, she thought she looked rather good. Her chunky socks and suede boots the colour of butter gave the impression that her legs were slightly more svelte than they actually were. She looked robustly feminine. And felt sexy. Mrs Andrews sent her on her way with her blessing. Mr Andrews pretended not to have seen her.

Chloë had rattled through the morning's post and dealt with all matters pressing. None pressed very hard and she found herself skipping over the lawn towards Ronan's workshop within half an hour. As usual, he was engrossed and unaware of her arrival, which afforded her the chance to gaze at him as he toiled. He must have been at it for some time, for the top of his boiler suit was down and his forearms were prickled with perspiration. Oh, how Chloë could have licked them! Instead, she stayed stock-still and silent. Ronan was on one knee with his back towards her, his buttocks delineated appetizingly beneath his blue overalls. With mallet and chisel, he chinked and chipped at the rock, exhaling loudly with the effort in much the same way as a tennis player in his final set. His hair was damp and nicked itself into little curls around his neck. His T-shirt was caught taut over his shoulder-blades and stuck damply between them. Still on one knee he laid his tools down and rested his head on his arm which was pressed against the rock. Sculptor had become sculpture and it made Chloë gasp. He turned slowly towards her, his eyes were slightly bloodshot from trickles of sweat. He had not shaved.

'Morning. Didn't see you – or hear you. Been there long?'

She shook her head and then cocked it. She nodded towards the sculpture.

'Nice work,' she said in a non-committal voice and with an almost imperceptible jut of her breasts.

'Coming along,' he responded, heaving himself upright while his knee joints cracked loudly in the process, 'finally.'

'Gus told me to cast a watchful eye over you,' said Chloë with a coy smile. 'He's gone to Belfast. And taken Mary to Ballymena. All day.' She took her hands from her pockets and slung them loosely on her hips.

'Yeah?' said Ronan, ruffling his hair and wiping his mouth.

'Indeed,' assured Chloë, lowering eyes ever so slightly.

Who made the first move? It was difficult to ascertain. They seemed to lunge for each other and soon Chloë found herself pressed against the rock while Ronan pushed his weight against her and sucked at her mouth as if he were starved. Fleetingly, Chloë praised the fact that Ronan's artistic style was undulating and curvaceous; had it been otherwise, the sculpture might not have been nearly so hospitable to her body. Its serpentines provided easy support for her and she soon let go so she could grab at Ronan's boiler suit and shove him closer. His buttocks were clenched and he moved against her, his erection defiant beneath the coarse material of his clothing. He cupped her breasts, pressing and kneading them, scratching at her nipples. She sucked in her stomach and elongated her trunk to enable him to slip his hand into the waist of her shorts and rip her T-shirt upwards and away. The movement was fluid and fast and, along with the trickle of a breeze whispering over her bare breasts, turned her on greatly. She looked at Ronan. His eyes were shut and his breathing was rasping and urgent.

Chloë grabbed at his arms and pulled her fingers over his flesh; the surface damp, slightly grimy, and she would not have had it any other way. He smelled strong but she filled her nostrils with it. They kissed and chewed at each other's mouths, chucking their tongues about until their faces were quite wet and Chloë's stung slightly from the abrasion of Ronan's bristles. Still his eyes were closed but Chloë did not mind, it meant she could ogle greedily, unchecked. As he sucked her neck hard and thrust his hand between her legs, she wondered why on earth she had chosen shorts over a skirt. He rubbed at her and she moved against him, the tufted fabric at the base of her zip catching fantastically on her clitoris now and then. He wrestled with her belt and fumbled with the button before snagging and tugging at the zip. She wriggled as he pulled but the zip had not finished its course and her shorts clamped themselves to the tops of her thighs. They pulled their mouths apart and Ronan took a step backwards. With a noise midway between grunt and growl he tore her shorts down with one violent swoop. The fabric burned at Chloë's skin but it felt only pleasurable. Ronan grunted again and smacked his hand up against the gusset of Chloë's knickers, pressing hard against the mound of her pubis while pinching the flats of his fingers against the soft flesh in between.

Don't let me come, don't let me come, willed Chloë, thinking of her own needs for perhaps the first time ever, while Ronan's fingers busied themselves with the elastic and then burrowed under it, directly into the folds of her sex. And all with his eyes closed.

I want to build my appetite. Savour. Like with Carl. Saviour. Like never with Brett.

Keen to enjoy an orgasm of penetrative making, Chloë wriggled away from Ronan's fingers and spun behind him so that he faced his sculpture alone and she pressed herself against his back, wrapping her arms around his stomach. She let her hands drop to the easy knot slung from the arms of his boiler suit. A far sight easier than a zip. The loose trousers fell about his ankles leaving him in his now sodden T-shirt and a pair of Y-fronts that Chloë instantly disliked but refused to dwell upon. She eased his T-shirt up as far as she could reach and he then crossed his arms and tore it over his head, affording Chloë a wonderful feast of his back muscles mixed with the heady scent of male sweat. She crouched and licked from the small of his back to between his shoulder-blades before resting her face against him and encircling his torso with her arms. Her hands made a lingering journey over his pectorals, his abdomen and down to his groin. She too had her eyes shut, for it enabled her to see him through the very feel of him. Particles of limestone dust clung to his body. Her face was pressed sideways against his back. Her mouth was open and a viscous drool of saliva crept its way out and down his back. She reached her hands lower while grazing his skin with her teeth. Lower. Lower. There. Y-fronts. Isn't there an opening somewhere?

Yes. Here it is. And here it is – heavens!

You haven't said a word but your gasps and groans say it all. Is it me, Ronan? Am I your muse?

Ronan grabbed her wrist and they rubbed him jointly for a few moments. Then he pulled her hand away from his cock and yanked hard at her arm so that she was hauled from behind him and they faced each other again. His eyes were open and locked on to her breasts. He dropped to one knee and pushed his tongue into her navel before travelling it upwards and over to each breast in turn. Chloë looked down on the top of his head, his shoulders, and tried to stop herself wondering if his prick had a dusting of limestone particles too. She couldn't quite see. Ronan was breathing heavily through his nose. As he sucked at each nipple, he closed his eyes and steadied himself with a hand on each of Chloë's buttocks. She bucked her groin forward and kept it pressed against his stomach. She could feel a pulse but was unsure whose it was. He gripped the tops of her arms tightly and pulled himself upright. Chloë removed her knickers from one leg and let them fall around the boot on the other.

Ronan put his hand to her throat and pushed, gently but insistently, until she yielded; letting her body tip back until it rested against the sculpture. He eased her legs apart and then, with his hands either side of her waist, lifted her slightly so that she was spread-eagled and supported by the sculpture. She stared at him, his gaze travelled between his cock and her sex. Chloë was holding on to a mound in the limestone with her right hand and grabbing at a deep dent in it with her left. Ronan loomed over her and, with his arms taut either side of her face, his hands catching sharply on her hair, pushed his cock deep and fast within her.

She came immediately and was sorely disappointed. He came soon after with a long and curiously high moan. It was the first true sound she had heard from him. His eyes, however, remained closed.

TWENTY-FIVE

'Dead or aloyve, aloyve-ho?'

Chloë flung her eyes wide open and blinked hard against the glare of the sun, wondering momentarily where she was. Ah! The Causeway. She could make out a silhouette but it acted as an eclipse and caused her to blink more to restore focus and vision.

'Pardon?' she said, still unsure to whom she said it.

'Aloyve,' said the voice, 'aloyve-ho!'

Chloë dropped her head a little and her gaze came to rest upon a pair of glinting eyes. They were very green and set deep into a ruddy face with ball-like cheeks and fizzy fair whiskers. Blush-red lips furled away from a haphazard set of large teeth; a tongue, unseen, clicked away behind them. A final blink from Chloë set the picture in focus and she saw that the features made up the face of a very small man who peered at her with his hands on his knees and a grin that was at once both lascivious and harmless.

'Hullo?' responded Chloë at last.

'B'jayz!' he responded. 'So ya'ar aloyve!'

'Indeed,' she assured, taking stock of his vehemently checked suit.

'Had my een on ya! Still as a doll, were ye!'

Chloë noticed that his tiny feet were laced to perfection in a pair of highly polished brogues.

'I'm fine,' Chloë declared with an embarrassed smile and fixed her eyes on the glinting shamrock on the man's tie-pin. The tie itself was green, woollen, and didn't surprise her.

'I was just miles away,' she explained, 'having a think.' She nodded at the man, and then out to sea, and then to herself.

'Down in the nyrps or up on the pig's back?' It seemed he could not speak without inflecting it as a song.

'The where on the what?' laughed Chloë who felt utterly at ease with him.

'The nyrps,' he moaned in a low, sad voice pulling an appropriate face of gloom, 'or the pig's back!' he cried, smiling inanely while flinging his arms about his head and skipping from foot to foot.

Chloë said 'Ah-ha' silently.

'Well,' she started, 'I came here because I had indeed a bad dose of your so-called nyrps but,' she stopped momentarily to solicit her senses with the sights and scents around her, 'but I suppose this place puts you firmly on the pig's back.'

The man stopped his gambolling and regarded her quizzically.

'And what'll I call ya?'

'I'm Chloë,' she said with an easy smile, 'Cadwallader.'

'Well, Cadwallydy, I'm Finn. McCool. But call me Finn if you please!'

Finn entranced Chloë with tales of the land. He pointed with conviction across the water to where the Scottish island of Staffa lay beyond the horizon, and spoke of the legend of the giant who built his causeway to reach his love living on Staffa.

'Of course!' said Chloë, playing Mendelssohn's *Hebrides Overture* in her mind whilst remembering more from her geography lesson about basalt columns at Staffa. 'What was the giant's name?' she asked Finn. He cocked his head this way and that, ruffled his whiskers and rubbed his eyes.

'Bugger me if I cannot recall!' he said exasperated.

'And was the lady at Staffa a giant too?' asked Chloë.

Finn snorted and sighed, wiped his brow and whistled, long and low.

'B'jayz,' he whispered, shaking his head incredulously, 'if she wasn't *huge*!'

They heard the impending visitors long before they saw them anting their way down the path. Finn hastily bade her farewell and scurried away, blending with the stacks and then the scraggy cliff. Chloë left the Wishing Chair to make room for the squeals of children and the chiding of parents, and to make some space for herself.

Off she goes. She takes the path past the Causeway which leads her to a cliff spliced in two with great basalt columns at either side like curtains to usher her through to the quiet bay beyond. When she turns, she half expects them to have draped closed behind her but of course they have not. The bay is a perfect horseshoe shape and as the waves saunter in, they seem to join hands in a perfect semicircle of spume. Chloë veers from the path to the water's edge and lays her hand gently on the surface of the foam. It fizzes against her skin and feels lovely. She takes her fingers to her mouth and tastes them. Salty. So salty that it surprises her though it really should not.

The sun is that of early summer, it catches her eyes without stinging them and sends a glow throughout her body. She turns back for the path and heads for the distant cliff. There she can see a patch of land peeled back to reveal an infrastructure of more basalt columns. It is the Organ. It is famous. She will have it all to herself. Close to, the columns soar upwards and again Mendelssohn booms out. Chloë knows she ought to reserve him until Scotland but as she does not know where she will be, she lets him ring out here. Just in case.

Unlike the stacks of the Causeway proper, these great towers are slightly segmented, mossed and lichened; they seem older, sad somehow. Chloë starts to feel contemplative. Ahead of her, the cliff head blooms rock of rose and terracotta. The gentle breeze fans the longer grass on the downy tussocks up and over like quiffs. She walks on. Planks of wood bar further entry with warnings of crumbling rocks. *Danger!* But Chloë can see a small, natural seat in the side of the cliff just a few yards on and feels strongly that she must reach it. She picks her way carefully under the barrier and treads cautiously onwards. She takes her time and makes it there on a lot of adrenalin. She concentrates on calming her breathing. When she has done so there is little else she can do with her mind than to cast it back again, into the heavy shadow of the consuming and depleting two weeks.

She watches the gannets hurtle and plunge into the sea. To the side of her, yellow birdsfoot trefoil smiles bravely from the tufted grass and herb Robert clambers out from behind a rock.

Sex with Ronan, she considers, was perhaps the most exciting she has ever had. And yet something so fundamental was lacking that, even if it hadn't later manifested itself in the ugly way it had, she doubts whether they would have had sex together again. From her experiences with Brett, she discovered that sex without love was possible though not pleasurable. It was all she had known. Until Carl. Only by having sex with Ronan has she realized that, in retrospect, the messy, noisy, laughter-strewn session in the insalubrious surroundings of the combie-van with Carl was lovemaking. Unequivocally.

'I think I did love Carl,' she says, under her breath to whoever will listen out on the cliffs, 'in a way.'

That silent, violent, self-absorbed morning she spent in the workshed with Ronan two weeks ago had been, initially, supremely erotic. But the lack of any reciprocal emotion to accompany it soon stripped any sensuality from the memory. They had fed themselves with no thought for the other's taste, or diet. Both had been starving. They had their fill and dissipated their hunger but they would not be going to that restaurant again. The menu was bland. Rather like *nouvelle cuisine* – the thought of it was exciting, it looked appetizing but was over quickly and forgotten even more so. And the price of it.

And yet she does not regret it. She thinks perhaps it is sometimes quite good to crush the mystique of something essentially inflated, overrated. Afterwards, Ronan and she managed fairly easily to restore their previous formal interaction. But she had rarely visited the workshop over the past fortnight. And Ronan had taken to working through the night. Or behind closed doors. Anyway, sculptures had been arriving daily and Chloë immersed herself in their siting. Abstract constructions in reclaimed timber and humorous pieces created from *objets trouvés*, shared the Ballygorm estate with more classical pieces and wholly figurative compositions. A giant snail carved from Purbeck marble nestled in the long grass while a totem pole stood proud in the woods. A small herd of red deer knitted and knotted out of wire, made their way into and out of the pond; their backs to the aluminium pyramid and sphere which lay enigmatically on the lawn. The five urns by the Cornish potter stood in a warm crowd of burnished hues, humming to themselves, while the sound of wind chimes trickled out from their camouflage in the horse chestnut trees. Chloë was busy, flat out, had too much to do to warrant lengthy periods in Ronan's workshop. And if she wasn't so busy, she soon found tasks to preoccupy her. Mary always welcomed assistance in the vegetable garden and Gus did not object to her reorganizing his library thematically and then alphabetically.

Then, yesterday, uncharacteristically, Ronan had called at the house with a percussive rap on the front door. Chloë was beavering away at final adjustments to the price-list, laying it out once more but in a different font and putting the titles in italics. Gus was on the phone to the *Irish Times*. Ronan hovered until they were ready for him.

'It's done,' he announced and led the way across the lawn, giving reverential berth to the Antony Gormley figure, walking in between the sphere and the pyramid and giving a quick spin to the bicycle wheel on the windmill construction along the way.

The great sliding door of the workshop was ominously drawn and Chloë and Gus stopped instinctively, allowing Ronan forward alone. He pushed the door across and it lumbered all too slowly, creaking. The sunlight entered immediately, a shard that illuminated only the back wall and the nose of the old tractor. As the door opened, light pervaded but the sheen on the polished limestone grabbed it entirely and the rest of the barn was muslin hung in soft grey hues. Gus hummed approvingly and walked into the workshop to circumnavigate the work.

Chloë gasped and stood immobilized.

It was her.

There she was.

Spread over the limestone.

Buck naked.

Splayed and prostrate.

'It's called *Her*,' announced Ronan, looking at no one.

TWENTY-SIX

Well, Chloë, you realized your aim. You became the artist's muse; immortalized, written in stone, both locked and released from the very fabric of the mineral. You were the inspiration for the piece, you were the solution for the sculptor's incarcerated creativity. Born of the rock. The reason for the stone. Conceived, carved, polished. How flattered you must feel!

'Ronan Brady!' Gus had declared once he had perused *Her* at length and from a variety of angles, 'truly magnificent!'

Chloë remained outside the workshop, clenching her nails into the palms of her hands until she could no longer feel the pain or her fingers. No one looked at her or invited her to cast her eyes and her compliments.

They don't need to, she thought, *they're having their eyeful right there.*

Gus made to leave and suddenly both he and Ronan were facing her, hands on hips.

'Chloë!' Gus declared.

'I can see it,' she shouted before tempering her voice, 'quite well enough, thank you. From here.'

'For heaven's sake, girl,' Gus retorted raising his eyebrows at Ronan, 'it's *sculp*-sure! You know – hands on! Come! Have a closer look. A feel.'

She ventured in and walked briskly around the sculpture. *There's my breast. That's my belly button. That crack. God.*

'Fascinating,' she said flatly. 'When the stone arrived I thought it rather dull – I never realized it had this incredible blue-blackness when polished.'

Indeed, this was her opinion, or part of it, and though Gus thought it flimsy he realized it would have to do. What was it worth anyway? The sculpture was worth a few thousand. He told her to discuss a suitable site with Ronan and left them, for a long-distance call to a wealthy Dubliner living in New York with a known predilection for sculpture and all things Irish. Ronan stood in the doorway, looking in. Chloë was round the other side of the sculpture with her back turned to it, facing the tractor and running her eyes up and down the prongs of the rusting pitchfork. She bit her lip hard, tears of anger welled painfully but she was determined that they should subside unseen. Ronan spoke in a voice that was soft and open and previously unheard.

'Well?' he asked.

Chloë spun on her heels and glowered at him. She could not speak so she narrowed her eyes and pierced him with them.

'Do you not like it?' His face creased with the search for approval. Still she could not respond but she snorted and stamped, thrust her hands on her hips and looked way beyond Ronan to the five urns on the lawn. They were so elegant and consummate. She wanted to run to them and sit between them; they had shoulders to lay one's arm about, they had music within.

'Do you not like it, Chloë?' Ronan repeated.

She sucked her cheeks in and stared at him directly.

'Cheap!' she hissed. He jumped a little and winced, as if her word coursed through him like poison.

* * *

Chloë knows that summer has arrived, not just because it is mid-June, but because she has sat on her natural bench on the forbidden cliff for almost an hour and no dampness has crept through her clothing. She is comfortable enough and her thoughts flow easily. The end of the month will see the beginning of Scotland and she feels already that her Irish sojourn has been and gone and she can wind down her business and pack up her things. She catches a drift of sweet coconut and thanks Jocelyn out loud for informing her that it is the scent of gorse. She cannot see it. Probably further along the path but she will not go in search of it. The path, after all, is dangerous. And she has too much to do here. She casts her mind away from the day in hand back to yesterday.

'What do you *mean* you didn't discuss a site for *Her*?' Gus's soup spoon hovered and shook, the liquid dribbled off it and back into the bowl. 'Where on earth have you been for the past few hours?'

'Walking,' Chloë said quietly, dabbing her mouth with the napkin though she had taken no soup.

'Walking!' bellowed Gus. 'But I asked you to help Ronan find a suitable spot for his sculpture!'

Chloë remained silent and twisted the napkin tight around one hand. She could hear Gus eating his soup and the rhythmic slurping irritated her supremely. She pulled the napkin taut until her hand throbbed and she knew, if she looked, that it would be quite purple.

I'm not your slave! she thought loudly to herself.

'What?' said Gus.

Out it came, unchecked.

'I am not your slave.'

'I beg your pardon!'

Chloë cleared her throat.

'Yes,' she spat, 'you may well have asked me to find a site

for Ronan's *thing*. But there was no "Please". There have been neither "p"s nor "q"s from you. Ever. Just orders and criticisms barked at me. Huge demands made of me. And woe betide if I flunk.'

Gus's spoon hovered again, his jaw had dropped. Chloë glanced away.

'I didn't come here to be treated like this,' she said in a calm, controlled voice, 'and I have done nothing to deserve such treatment.'

'Then why, might I ask, did you come?' said Gus, whose voice was quiet but pinched. Chloë found his eyes and held their gaze.

'I came,' she said coldly, 'because Jocelyn sent me.'

Gus lowered his eyes to his half-eaten soup. Was that pain she saw flicker over his brow?

Couldn't have been.

Gus? Feel anything? Surely not!

She waited until he ventured his eyes upwards and she caught them again before staring at his jugular.

'And what,' she said icily, 'would Jocelyn *think*, Mr Halloran? What do you think she'd have to say?'

The sweep and shift of power was intoxicating. Chloë's strength and conviction, the steadiness of her voice, had quite surprised her. And it pleased her too. A self-congratulatory smile was not, however, appropriate, so she bit it back. She scraped back her chair and rose, placing her hands with a smack on the table.

'Know what I think?' she laughed viciously. 'I think she'd be horrified – utterly appalled – at the pompous misogynist you are!'

Gus's spoon clattered into the bowl, a glob of pea soup splashed on to the tablecloth and slowly blotted. Gus's eyes were fixed to it, Chloë stared at the top of his head thinking that his yellowing hair must really be quite long under its slathering of wax.

'She'd be *writhing*,' whispered Chloë, 'writhing in her grave. Not that *you* give a damn!'

She walked across the room slowly and with her head held high. As she put her hand out to the brass handle of the door, she was amazed and delighted by its steadiness. Without turning, she delivered her *coup de grâce*.

'I'll be leaving,' she announced, 'a fortnight today. For Scotland. I believe you have an envelope for me.'

* * *

'Bout ye! If it isn't Cadwallydy!'

'Where on *earth* did you come from!' Chloë is delighted to see Finn McCool though the surprise of his sudden appearance threatens to dislodge her right from the cliff.

'Scapin' the crowds!'

'Me too,' she murmurs.

'Had your *tink*?' he asks without prying.

'Sort of,' says Chloë looking at her lap with a gentle sigh. 'I'm leaving for Scotland in a fortnight.'

She feels Finn catch his breath and, as he releases it, he sighs 'Scotland' mistily.

'It's just,' begins Chloë, 'I don't know. I felt so justified – but now I feel wretched. I suppose I don't know the full story. I suppose one never does.'

They sit in silence, the sun has slipped away unnoticed and the breeze has now a sharp edge to it.

'It's odd,' she continues to herself as much as to Finn, 'being strong, standing up for yourself – at last – seems only to carry a burden of responsibility with it too. In retrospect. Perhaps meek is easier after all.'

'Meek,' cautions Finn, 'be weak.'

'And I suppose shirking responsibility is weak too then,' ponders Chloë a little forlorn.

'More!' growls Finn. 'Bad. Very bad. Dangerous, even.'

Chloë's bottom is numb, her neck is stiffening and she is feeling tired. Finn stares intently across the sea at Scotland with an ambiguous half-smile that is semi-sad. Chloë claps her hands lightly on her thighs.

‘Oh well,’ she says in a jolly voice, ‘I’d better wend my way!’

‘Easy how you go, now,’ says Finn, without diverting his gaze.

‘It’s been lovely to talk to you,’ Chloë says warmly, crouching and extending her hand. He drags himself away from whatever is obsessing him and cups his hands around hers.

‘Pleasure was mine!’ He winks at her, gravely. Chloë makes a careful path back to the barrier alone.

‘Make your peace, Cadwallydy,’ she hears Finn call after her, ‘make your peace.’

When she has reached the safety of the path, she turns and waves. There is no longer anyone there to wave back.

She drives home with a trepidation which ensures that she motors at thirty miles an hour. Frequently, she stops to admire the view and take deep breaths. Up and over a steep hill, the road bisects a small lake. Really it is smaller than a pond, but it is a very deep navy and the wind breaks little crested waves upon it, which gives it the grandeur of a lake. There are Highland cattle grazing nearby.

‘All is pointing to Scotland,’ says Chloë, taking note of her worried, tired eyes in the rear-view mirror.

She is very near Ballygorm now but takes a minor road that will lead her back via three sides of a square. Dry-stone walls plot and piece the meagre fields of the wiry high ground; the rocks used in their construction are round and perched on top of each other in an apparently flimsy configuration. With the sky clearly visible through the spaces in between, the walls stretch across the land like lattice-work and seem most inappropriate for their purpose. It is a strange contradiction for, though they look weak, Chloë knows that she can push her weight against them and they will stay put. She stops the Land Rover and walks over to a section of wall and stares very hard at it; that she now shares its juxtaposition of fragility and strength does not escape her and she thinks on it awhile. She sits on her heels with her back resting lightly against the wall. A scrabble of sheep edge nearer and hear what she has to say.

'I've made myself plain. Said what I feel. Expressed my indignation. And yet, though I do feel cleansed in some way, I feel sad too. Remorseful, a little.' The sheep chew their cuds thoughtfully and Chloë mulls over her thoughts, running her fingers through the grass and pressing her back more firmly against the wall.

'Maybe I shouldn't have said anything. Taken it on the nose. Cried later.'

She wouldn't mind crying now, but she thinks better of it.

'Perhaps it's better – healthier – to feel sad rather than resentful.'

The sheep amble away. They seem to have faith in her. She's on the right track. So she drives on. She has not been along this road before. As it dips down towards the valley the stone walls are replaced by a hotchpotch of barbed wire fences and thorn hedges; a more vicious way of dividing a much gentler landscape. Just before she comes back on the main road, she passes a rusting grain silo in a field. It is redundant, battered and lying on its side. Graffitied.

'*Good luck Trevor + Julie*' it proclaims on its nozzle.

'*Loop loop, go home*' it reads in large white letters daubed along the side. Fleetingly, Chloë wonders what or who 'Loop loop' is, but the message strikes a graver chord.

'If someone told me to "go home",' she says aloud, 'where would that be? Where would I go?'

TWENTY-SEVEN

Chloë crept to her room. A tray had been laid with orange juice, sandwiches and biscuits. A small vase proffered a bunch of lilacs from the garden and propped against it was an envelope marked 'Scotland'. As she ate, she turned the envelope this way and that, holding it to the light, fingering the sealed edge. But she did not open it, nor did she give it to the Andrews for safe keeping. She did not even take it to her nose for a just-in-case. Instead, she popped it into her empty rucksack and went to bed. It was half-past eight but she did not want to have a bath or to think about anything. Sleep rescued her for a full twelve hours.

For the next few days, Finn's words, 'Make your peace', resounded in her mind on waking and on retiring. And yet the atmosphere was decidedly amicable so she saw no reason to undermine it by soliloquy or confrontation. Gus still found it difficult to infuse his requests with niceties, but his tone ensured that they were no longer demands or orders. Their contretemps thus went unmentioned, but the fact that Chloë now worked hard quite willingly, and that Gus neither barked at her nor criticized her, proved that all that had been said had been absorbed and reviewed.

She rarely saw Ronan; just from the window or across the other side of the lawn. He and Gus had chosen the site for *Her* while she had been at the Giant's Causeway and she was grateful that she could see it neither from the study nor from her bedroom. However, try as she did, with eyes closed or wide open, Chloë could not actually remember what the sculpture looked like. Or what it was specifically that she so loathed.

With a week to go, Chloë found she became restless and her sleep was fitful. Suddenly she was not so eager to embark for Scotland and yet she was primed to leave Ireland. She was tempted to call Skirrid End, to request a fortnight's respite, but she knew there was neither room nor reason for detours. Jocelyn knew what she was doing. Peregrine and Jasper had assured her of this, without actually shedding the light Chloë had requested on Gus.

It was Ronan's last day but he declined supper at the house. Chloë pretended she was utterly engrossed in her typing when he visited the study to make his farewells. She tapped whichever keys her fingers could travel to most swiftly while Gus thanked Ronan heartily and praised him to the hilt.

'Chloë, Ronan's going tomorrow. He's here to say goodbye – too busy packing his things to eat with us tonight!'

'Yes, yes,' said Chloë in a vague voice while adding a flurry of dollar signs, asterisks and sixes to the typing, 'bye then,' she called and turned her head towards Ronan but kept her eyes on the screen while her fingers worked furiously, 'best of luck!'

Something woke Chloë late that night. It was not a sound from outside but one from within.

'Shut *up*, Finn!' she grumbled, sandwiching her head between two pillows and begging sleep to envelop her again. It was no good. She was wide awake and lay in the dark for a while. Soon she realized it was not all that dark, for a full moon pressed a silver wave between the curtains and into the room. She observed the shadows for a moment and then went over to the window. It was a most beautiful night, with stars strewn liberally and the moon throwing platinum glints and glances over the trees and sculptures. Antony Gormley's bronze figure seemed to call to her and, though she felt momentarily daft, she raised her hand and waved to it.

Without considering her motive, she dressed herself, and crept downstairs and straight out into the night. She walked directly to the Gormley and put her hand on its arm, looking intensely at the face. Its eyes, despite their veneer of bronze, seemed to stare straight ahead. Chloë followed their gaze and alighted on the five urns. She touched the cheek of the statue and left for the pots. As she hummed softly into each, she detected that their echo seemed to come from the right. She turned in that direction and saw *Her* lying tranquil in the dip of the lawn that led to the pond. The moonlight blessed the limestone with a softness that defied its true fabric, and the stark blue-blackness under daylight was now washed a silken silvery grey.

The urns had stopped humming. There was not a sound.

Slowly, Chloë padded over to the sculpture and walked around it in her own time. She circled it four times and, on the fifth, ventured her hand out to its surface. That it was faintly warm surprised her. And yet it was a different sculpture from that which had so shocked and insulted her a week before.

It is me. I am Her. *And that's not a bad thing to be.*

'No one will know it's you,' called Ronan softly across the night. He strolled over to her from the urns. He was wearing jeans and a polo-neck and looked taller, lankier than in his boiler suit. Chloë turned towards him but did not speak. He approached without looking at her and ran his hands over the limestone.

'Funny how it is never cold,' he said.

'I thought the very same,' she answered quietly, with a meek and fleeting smile. They observed the stone together in a heavy silence. Ronan travelled his hands over the sculpture, letting them flow and slip into the dips and over the curves. Chloë realized she was holding her breath. There was something on the tip of her tongue but pride and embarrassment prevented its expression.

'A synthesis of Woman,' murmured Ronan, 'but no one will know that it's actually you, Chloë. Only you do. And I, of course!'

Though Chloë nodded, she was still a little uneasy. The work was neither crude nor shocking. Nor was it insulting, not really. Just blatant. Raw. Naked versus nude. Rather flattering, actually. The sculptor's muse – oh! how it was she who had tormented him. In carving her out of his system, he had immortalized her too. Set in stone and caught in time.

'It was a shock,' said Chloë flatly. 'I'd have appreciated a warning.' ('Chloë duck,' said Mrs Andrews later, 'surely that is why a muse is a muse – the artist is slave to her spell, whether or not she is aware of casting it. He cannot but press and mould and devote his art in and around her. Because of her.' Chloë thanked her effusively and gazed, rather proudly, at her own reflection awhile.)

'No one will know it is you,' Ronan reiterated. 'Some folk say that the secret is in the stone,' he continued much more warmly, 'but I like to think that the stone's secret is the prerogative of the sculptor.'

'I know,' started Chloë in a smaller voice before trailing off. 'I didn't mean to insult you. Well, yes I did, I suppose. But I wouldn't want to now. It's not half bad. It's me – this *Her* – after all.'

'I should have warned you,' Ronan conceded, 'but I want you to know that, er, when we – I mean, what happened – well, I had no ulterior motive. But afterwards, the passage of the piece suddenly became so clear. You were my inspiration. This is one of my best works and so I thank you, heartily.'

Chloë wondered whether her blush was discernible

under moonlight. She stood close to *Her* and laid her arm gently along it.

'Well,' she said after some time, 'I'm flattered then. So I must thank *you*, Ronan Brady.' They met each other's eyes and shook hands across *Her*, formally and firmly.

'Goodbye, then,' smiled Chloë, 'and the best of luck. Really. I'm glad that I've known you. A sculptor. And a very good one at that!'

Ronan lifted his head in recognition and acceptance.

'Bye,' said Chloë, taking her hand from his and raising it in a small wave.

'Fare ye well,' said Ronan once she was out of sight, 'Chloë Cadwallader.'

'Ahafta go nye,' choked Mary, dabbing her eyes and gulping, 'you take care of yous, ya hear me?'

'Of course I will,' said Chloë warmly, putting her hands on Mary's shoulders and coming close. They embraced.

'Thanks, comrade mine!' whispered Chloë.

'Wheeker of a gal,' sobbed Mary into her neck, 'wheeker of a gal.'

'I thought we could visit the shores of Neagh,' said Gus behind the wheel of his Jaguar while looking intently at the road ahead.

'Lovely!' said Chloë, gazing out of the window, eager to commit to memory the very hue of this verdant land.

'Mary packed a light picnic.'

'How nice,' said Chloë.

'Great that you can fly to Glasgow from Belfast,' remarked Gus.

'Most convenient,' agreed Chloë, 'my sea legs are dreadful.'

'So were Jocelyn's,' said Gus very quietly. Chloë rested her head against the window and decided not to comment.

Chloë had thought how Northern Ireland's great lake appeared disproportionate to its land mass on the map, but standing there on its shores she was content that it should be so. With the shore across the lough so distant, and no land visible either side of the water, Chloë could quite believe that it was a sea. Certainly the waves and busy ripples under the strong breeze compounded this impression, along with the pervading wafts of coconut from the gorse. The section of shore that Gus had taken her to was utterly unspoilt and they had strolled down fields to reach it. They walked along a small breakwater of great boulders smudged with rounds of lichen as yellow as egg yolk, to a small bench set conveniently and most picturesquely at the end.

Mary had packed hard-boiled eggs with the shells dented for ease of peeling, paste sandwiches, rock cakes, and apple juice decanted into a large jar. Chloë and Gus passed the food and drink between them affably.

'I've never had Mary's rock cakes before,' said Chloë, though their taste was certainly familiar.

'That's because she doesn't care for them herself,' explained Gus. 'I asked her to make them for me, according to a recipe I have.' He trailed off. 'I even make them myself sometimes, but unfortunately work dictated that I remain in the study and away from the kitchen yesterday.'

Chloë smiled and was about to ask polite questions concerning Gus's culinary hobby, when he started to speak again.

'We've not eaten paste sandwiches either, have we?'

Chloë thought the remark odd but she agreed that, indeed, they had not.

'You see, Chloë,' Gus said mistily, 'this picnic is a precise replica of the best meal of my life.' She was too baffled to respond but there was no need as Gus continued.

'I partook of it right here, where we sit today. But almost forty years ago. The view has changed little, Chloë – and apple juice from a jar still tastes just as it did then. That day was the best and worst of my life.'

Chloë put the rock cake in her lap. To hear Gus speak so freely demanded her unadulterated attention.

'When this picnic was packed the first time, Chloë, it was not Mary who prepared it,' he said, his eyes flitting across her face, 'but Jocelyn.'

You must be her great love! The one Gin alluded to!

Chloë ate no more and, automatically, she pushed herself closer to Gus.

O Jocelyn Jo, that's why I'm here!

As Gus spoke he looked at his lap mainly, sometimes out over the water, very occasionally to Chloë, scouring her face before darting his gaze away. Chloë learnt of a Jocelyn who had harvested elderberries into her skirt for Gus to make a cordial. She heard of a Jocelyn who had danced barefoot at the Giant's Causeway. She was told of her godmother's penchant for skimming pebbles into the sea at Ballygally. How she could envisage Jocelyn and Gus so clearly, wrapped around each other on the great sofa, reciting poetry, reading passages of Joyce, sharing silence. Being in love.

Chloë concentrated hard on Gus's words, soaking up a part of Jocelyn's life about which she had previously no inkling. He spoke of their courtship, of her rock cake recipe, that he still had the apron she wore, that it still hung on the hook in the larder and that Mary was not to touch it.

'And me?' Chloë enquired.

'You?'

'Did she – what did she say about me? How much did you know? Then, and before I came.'

'She said you were a "petal". She loved you intensely.'

'But why, Gus?'

'Why what, Chloë?'

'Why didn't I know of all this?'

He did not respond.

'Why didn't you say?'

Still he remained silent.

'Sooner?'

He looked away.

'And, most of all,' she asked forlornly, 'why did it not happen? You and Jocelyn?'

Gus sighed, picking the sultanas from the rock cake and flicking them into the water.

'I loved Jocelyn with every ounce of me,' he said quietly, 'but I knew she had loved and lost and would never tread the path again.'

You weren't Him?

All was as clear and yet as indistinct as the waters of Lough Neagh. At once, Gus's behaviour was justified and forgiven for it was dictated by pain rooted in goodness. Chloë allowed her heart to ache alongside his on the shores of Neagh and they shared silent thoughts of Jocelyn. When Gus raised his wrist to check the time, he found Chloë's hand tucked warmly round it. With his other hand, he held hers in place, just slipped it along his arm a little so he could see his watch.

'Well,' he exclaimed bravely, with a tender tap on her knee, 'we should make a move, I think.'

They packed away the remnants of the picnic and cast the crumbs of the rock cake on to the water. For the birds, you know, the fish.

'What an amazing place,' said Chloë, 'it's so vast!'

'Do you not know the story of the lough?' asked Gus.

'Is there one?' responded Chloë.

'Is there one!' he exclaimed. 'My dear, how do you think the Isle of Man came to be?'

'Sorry?' Chloë twitched her eyebrows and smiled back at Gus.

'Finn McCool, of course,' he said quite conclusively.

'Finn?' Chloë exclaimed. 'What's *he* got to do with it?'

'Well, soon after he built his causeway, he scooped up a handful of land and hurled it into the sea. The land became the Isle of Man; the space it left filled with water and became Lough Neagh.'

'Finn,' stammered Chloë, 'Mc*Cool*?' She frowned, trying to make sense of the nonsensical.

'Aye!' assured Gus. 'He was the giant. As legend has it. So people say.'

From the aeroplane window, Chloë is afforded a bird's-eye view of Lough Neagh. It proves to her that it is indeed land-locked. As if a great clod has been plucked away from the land. A few minutes later and she is looking down on the Isle of Man. It matters to her not in the slightest that its circumference bears little similarity to the lough's. She thinks to herself how deceptive appearances can be; how the smallest of men can be giants, that beauty often lies beneath that too hastily denounced as ugly.

'I mean, think of Kilkenny limestone!' she says to the air-hostess who smiles at her plastically.

TWENTY-EIGHT

Chloë Darling,

Scotland!

If you were wowed by Wales and bowled over by Ireland, brace yourself for this next land. I have travelled widely and seen many places that have quite taken my breath away; some which I've gazed down upon from up high, others that I have marvelled up at until my neck begged leniency. None, however, hold the allure of Scotland.

Just to be there! It is my favourite country. You shall see why.

The light here is invested with unique powers for it can entice colour and hue on the dullest of days. I have never been to any other country whose beauty remains constant despite the season or the time of day, and in spite of the weather. Nothing prepares you for Scotland's lofty grandeur though you may visit time and again.

The Welsh are a melancholy, perhaps justifiably bitter nation. The Northern Irish are private, provincial and decidedly mellow. The Scots have fire beneath their sporrans (I've seen it, my dear) – their pride is deep-

seated in their inherited passion for their country. Fraser Buchanan is everything a Scotsman should be.

You may never want to leave – but go onwards to England, my girl.

And then make your choice.

When death's dark stream I ferry o'er –
A time that surely shall come –
In heaven itself I'll ask no more
Than just a Highland welcome.
(Robbie B.)

Jocelyn

TWENTY-NINE

Chloë spent a night in Glasgow, partly because there was no reply at the Buchanans', partly because there was so much to see and do, partly because she wanted to carve a small space in which to chew over and digest Ireland. However, she found she could not do so in the confines of the luxury small hotel she had earmarked precisely for the purpose, for she allowed instead the mini bar and satellite television to enforce distraction. She had not seen a television, let alone watched one, since Christmas and, though she realized she had not missed it at all, she indulged in zapping between twenty channels whilst popping peanuts and sipping from whisky miniatures. She easily persuaded herself that, as she would undoubtedly be subsisting for the next three months on haggis, peaty water and only the occasional scone that Jocelyn's money might run to, room service was a justifiable must. Not least because it was her twenty-seventh birthday, a fact she had purposely kept from all at Ballygorm and was now bravely keeping from herself.

Just another year. No need to celebrate.

You mean, no one to celebrate with.

No cards. No candles. No Jocelyn. And as no one could

do birthdays quite like her godmother, what was the point? Jasper and Peregrine? They had sent her a card, of course they had; a padded, perfumed, musical extravaganza emblazoned with a glittery 'C' and swamped within with their idiosyncratic poetry in fine copperplate. Only it had arrived at Ballygorm after Chloë's departure.

So, cross-legged on a plump bed, she feasts alone on smoked salmon sandwiches and chocolate mousse, while keeping half an eye on the Scandinavian Snow Boarding Championships (in Swedish) and the other half on a film about open marriages (in Dutch).

Awaking the next morning, though her surroundings were strange, when Chloë cast her memory back to her room at Ballygorm and tried to envisage waking up there, it suddenly seemed so long ago and so far away. It had been warm, bright and open, that she remembered; the streets of Glasgow were dull and busy, and people were wearing jumpers. A small voice told Chloë that perhaps cities were simply not her thing. With coach ticket bought for that afternoon and rucksack deposited in the left luggage, she spent the morning at the Burrell Collection. There, she lost herself in the fine collection of French impressionism and thought herself quite honoured that Degas had a predilection for women with long, lush auburn hair. Often, with a slight shift of focus, she saw herself reflected from the glass in front of such canvases, and let down her locks or scooped them up into a bun accordingly.

Over a cup of very good coffee and a slab of shortbread, she gazed through the enormous wall-windows out over Pollok Park. Something moved. A deer. She held her breath. For a caught moment, the deer regarded her directly. In a blink, it moved off between the pines and was lost from sight. Chloë thought how lucky she was. And then she thought back to Ireland. Had she not been afforded a fleeting glimpse of Jocelyn? As she gazed at the parkland and trees, she realized that, though the deer had gone, its momentary presence had now left the view infinitely more beautiful than before its appearance.

The coach journey was a revelation and Chloë found herself already planning a life in Scotland. Scotland could be home, didn't Jocelyn say so? Or imply it? From being in the midst of the city, suddenly they were pacing through the most beautiful landscape and passing lovely villages with stone bridges and smoking chimneys. At every stop, Chloë was tempted to disembark but she was more inquisitive about meeting Fraser Buchanan and seeing just where she would be spending the summer. Before long, the waters of Loch Lomond lapped almost at the side of the road which edged its way along the contour of its shore. Road signs declared Crianlarich, Tyndrum, the bridges of Orchy and Awe and there were soon signposts for Rob Roy's house and cave. Chloë felt little waves of excitement; such romantic places were now hers for the exploring, could even be hers for the keeping. Unless, of course, Fraser Buchanan was opening a sculpture trail and intended to confine her to the grounds of the laird's lair. Chloë had decided to forbid her imagination from concocting Fraser Buchanan in her mind's eye, though she had a hunch that he would be portly and of not many teeth. She also prepared herself to be unable to decipher a word he said.

Loch Lomond went on and on; Chloë had no idea. It was not like Lough Neagh for its waters were stiller, its far shore nearer, the colour of the land surrounding it very different. In contrast to the bright, lime-emerald green of Ireland, here the shadow of Scots pine infused a blue-green tone over the land. The Scottish palette sang hauntingly in a minor key compared to Ireland's merry jig in a major. Eventually, the shores of the loch began to close in a little and Chloë knew her stop must be soon. She gathered her things about her, fiddled with her hair and then settled back into her seat with butterflies in her stomach; a desire to be on her way. Just after Tyndrum and before the Bridge of Orchy, the bus deposited Chloë and trundled off towards Glencoe. The driver had pointed down a small road off to the left so Chloë walked down it and into Glen Orchy. To one side a hill, smoked in shades of mauve and sienna, slithered down to the road; to the other the Orchy tumbled its course, intermittently hidden by dense pine. Ahead of her, a small clutch of buildings sat at the foot of a steeper hill, predominantly beige, within the sound of a waterfall. It was Drumfyn and she had arrived.

'What a perfect setting,' she gasped as she strolled towards the hamlet, 'and which one's Braer House?' she wondered. 'Which one's mine?'

The lady in the post office which also sold groceries, gardening implements and general chandlery, was helpful but less friendly than Chloë anticipated. The door had sprung a jolly peel of bells when she had entered and the lady had scuttled in from behind the bead curtain at the back. She was just as she should have been; about sixty, short and stocky, a good head of silver hair curled neatly about her face, pale blue winged glasses, a neat if thin mouth, arms loosely folded across a plain blouse and good bosom, an Aran-knit cardigan about her shoulders. Chloë brandished the name 'Fraser Buchanan' and asked directions with an eager smile, continuing to grin with her whole face as the lady told her where to go. Chloë bade her goodbye with effusive thanks and more smiling but the lady merely nodded her head and said 'Aye' before disappearing beyond the bead curtain.

Her directions, however, were excellent and made up for any lack of affability. The pavement became a small path which soon crept up and away from the road. After the lady's 'stone's throw', Chloë indeed came upon a sign proclaiming 'Braer House' and turned left up a steep drive, tree-lined and casting an eerie violet light. From far off, a trickle of laughter filtered through, though Chloë mistook it at first for the wind through pine needles. Soon, the trees stayed to the left and a neat lawn opened out to the right. A fine granite house stood straight ahead. And the lawn to the right was full of people. Wearing their finest; sipping what could only have been champagne. Talking fast in excitable laughs.

No one looked at Chloë as she clumped up the drive, weighed down by her rucksack, walking boots and bewilderment.

A hotel, perhaps?

The people moved aside when she said 'Excuse me' but still seemed not to notice her.

Am I to be a chambermaid?

She stepped between them and through the open door into the hallway of the house. The din inside was much louder but under it ran the scent of roasting chicken and baking bread and Chloë found she was relaxed and smiling. She spied a young man at the back of the hall refilling glasses from behind a small trestle table.

I don't want to be a barmaid.

She picked her way over to him.

'Hullo,' she said, 'I'm looking for Fraser Buchanan?'

He looked up at her, scanned her face momentarily and changed his startled look to one of relief and a short but expansive smile.

'Thank the sweet Lord!' he exclaimed in a highly intelligible but extremely Scottish accent. 'We thought you'd never arrive, girl! We thought you'd stood us up!'

'No, no!' assured Chloë, slightly bowed from the burden of her rucksack. 'I tried to phone last night but there was no answer.'

'Och,' he slammed his fist on to the table, 'not again! Telecommuni-compli-cations! Look, no time for that now, drop your stuff and take this tray out to the guests!'

I'm to be a waitress!

Too startled to ask why, Chloë deposited her rucksack under the trestle table and held out her hands for the tray. As he handed it to her, he looked her up and down swiftly and muttered something about jeans would have to do, at least they were black and her shirt was white. Chloë could see that he was in too much of a flurry to elaborate, and too preoccupied for her to ask again for Fraser Buchanan. He also called her Maggie but she made allowances for that.

'I'll ask again later,' she said to herself as she negotiated a clutch of chattering women in almost identical straw hats, 'there's time. Three months or so. But for now I'm needed out in the garden whether I'm Maggie or Chloë. In my jeans that are black, at least, and my shirt that is correctly white. How odd!' she exclaimed under her breath as a man in a beautiful waistcoat swooped a glass from her tray. 'What-*ever* is going on?

Chloë discovered what was going on when she spilt red wine down her front and went in search of a bathroom. The house was only two storeys high but it was long, and all the rooms upstairs to the right of the staircase appeared to be locked. The one directly ahead was a small single bedroom whose bed was stripped with the mattress up-ended. To her left ran another series of doors, all closed. She took pot luck, walked past two and grasped the handle of the third with conviction. It opened with ease. It was a bathroom. But there was somebody in it too. A bride. Sitting on the toilet, no less; looking out of the window at nothing in particular, muttering to herself.

'God, I am *so* sorry,' muttered Chloë, quickly closing the door and treating the empty corridor to her most pained expression.

'It's fine!' the bride called. 'Come back! Please!'

'Me?' asked Chloë with her face close to the door frame.

'Yes!' the bride called. 'Absolutely you!'

Chloë pushed the door open and edged her eyes and nose into the room. The bride was now sitting on the edge of the bath with one shoe off and an exultant smile on her face.

'Come in,' she beckoned, 'come!'

Chloë entered the room and the bride swished past,

closing and locking the door with a little giggle. She turned and held out her hand for Chloë, shaking it heartily.

'I'm Sally Lomax,' she explained and then gripped Chloë's hand hard while a look of joyous bewilderment skipped over her face. 'No I'm not!' she exclaimed. 'I'm Sally *Stonehill*, Gracious Good Lord!'

Chloë shared a small laugh with her.

'And I'm Chloë,' she said, 'Cadwallader.'

'An alliterative sister!' Sally declared with a whoop. 'You can save my wedding night!'

'I can?' asked Chloë, liking the girl enormously.

'I'm trying to get out of my bra,' Sally explained earnestly. 'I have no idea why I'm wearing one – I don't usually, you see.'

'I see,' said Chloë thinking her dress of ivory shot silk bedecked with intricate frogging quite divine.

'I was sort-of whipped up by this whole wedding palaver – I bought all the mags and went to all the shops,' she declared with her hand on Chloë's shoulder, '*every*one pushes lacy undies at you. So I bought some. In fact, I bought several pairs!'

'And they're uncomfortable?' asked Chloë. 'Itchy?'

'Fiendishly so, but that's not so much the point,' explained the bride. 'You see, I just craved to be *me* on my wedding day.' Chloë was unsure where the bra came in but let Sally continue. 'Some brides,' she explained while she and Chloë instinctively sat on the floor, backs to the bath and legs outstretched, 'pile their hair high and have make-up magicians reinvent them. Well, I can't think of anything more frightening for a groom than not to recognize his bride – so I did my own hair and my normal amount of face paint!'

'And the undies?' asked Chloë, who thought the bride's hair and make-up very fine.

'Well, Richie – he's my – oh gracious! My husband! Ha! He's my *hus*-band. Well, my *hus*band – Richard – would never recognize me all trussed up in a tit sling. It could very well disappoint him – sorely – and you know how awful that would be.'

'A disaster!' colluded Chloë, etching a look of abject horror on to the imagined face of Sally's groom in her mind's eye.

'But the dratted thing is press-studded to my dress – and with all these buttons up and down the back, there's no way I can get to it.'

'Which is where I come in?'

'Precisely!' the bride declared placing her hand on Chloë's knee and giving it a gentle squeeze. 'If you wouldn't mind!'

They knelt; Sally holding on to the bath chattering away nineteen to the dozen, Chloë unbuttoning the back of the dress carefully, admiring all the little details as she did. Sally told how they were from London but that Richard had proposed last spring very near Loch Lomond.

'We thought of marrying on Mull initially, where it all happened really. But Aunt Celia, who lives there, advised us to keep the isle our sacred, secret haven. Her friend owned this place, you see, so that's how we're here.'

'Fraser Buchanan,' Chloë marvelled.

'Aunt Celia's here, of course,' the bride was continuing, 'she's utterly wonderful. You must meet her – my mentor, my role model.'

'I had one too,' rued Chloë. Sally noted the past tense with sympathy.

As she felt her way along the bra strap for the press-studs, Chloë told her of Jocelyn's legacy, that she was now in Scotland, third stop, that she had been to Wales and Ireland and was going to England next. In the autumn. To who knows where.

'That's so exciting!' said the bride genuinely, drumming the edge of the bath lightly with her fists. 'I wonder where you'll choose to end up!'

'As yet,' confided Chloë, 'I have absolutely no idea. But Scotland's looking promising.'

'Ah,' laughed Sally, 'the spell of Scotland, cast over you and woven deep within you in just twenty-four hours!'

'Indeed,' agreed Chloë.

'Wait until it rains,' warned Sally warmly.

'I have a brolly,' countered Chloë, 'and I *did* live in Islington.'

'Well, wait for the midges!'

'I don't think I'm that tasty,' said Chloë.

With the offending bra gently removed, Chloë buttoned up the bride and they sat on the side of the bath and chatted.

'Had you known him for ages?' Chloë asked.

'Who?'

'Robert? No, *Richard* – your *hus*band.'

'Oh!' shrieked Sally. '*Him!* Actually no, not really! A few months in fact – rather turbulent too!'

'A whirlwind romance?' Chloë suggested.

'Actually,' confided Sally, nudging up close to Chloë, 'if I'd had my own way – and I'm eternally glad that I did not – there would not have been a scrap of romance in it at all!'

Chloë looked puzzled.

'It's a long story,' Sally assured.

'Oughtn't you to return to your guests?' said Chloë. 'To your *hus*band?'

'Gracious yes,' said Sally, 'I've been up here for ages. Tell me, is it fairly warm outside now?'

'It's lovely,' Chloë confirmed.

'Great!' said Sally, more to herself than anyone. Scooping up the skirt of her gown, she wriggled with determination. And removed her lacy knickers which she folded neatly with the bra.

'I may be Mrs Stonehill,' she said to Chloë, eyes dancing and cheeks blooming, 'but I'm still his same old Sal beneath it all!' Solemnly, she handed the underwear to Chloë. 'Would you mind hiding these for me?'

Chloë accepted them graciously and, after accompanying

the bride downstairs, ensured that they were tucked out of sight in her rucksack.

'Maggie, quick! I need the canapé plates washed and dried – we have to reuse them for the fresh fruit.' The young man's fawny hair was in disarray and flopped over his left eye and into the corner of his right. It made him blink a lot and, with his shirt now damp and clinging to his back and the tops of his arms, gave the impression that he had just performed a frenetic Highland fling.

'Sure, sure!' encouraged Chloë as she backed away into the kitchen to yet another round of washing-up. The light outside was hazing and she reckoned it was nearing six o'clock. The afternoon had scuttled past her while she tended to the guests and shared a private wink or smile with the bride. Her groom was most handsome, his speech poetic and honest. Chloë felt softly envious and somewhat wistful but, being unable to conjure up a suitable groom – or even the notion – for herself, she let her heart be warmed unconditionally as she delivered platters of fresh fruit to the tables.

'Coffee!' hissed the young man. Chloë winked gravely at him and was rewarded with an astonished smile. He was flustered and sweaty but it did not detract from his kind, open face and beseeching hazel eyes. Though he was of medium height and fairly muscular build, Chloë chanced upon his hands which were slender, smooth and decidedly dainty. She realized she did not know where the coffee was, or how it was to be made. And then she realized she did not even know his name but, as she could see that he was engrossed in the *petit fours*, she hurried back to the kitchen and methodically went through the cupboards saying 'It must be here somewhere' under her breath.

'Maggie,' he said, clapping his hands against his temples and sliding down the kitchen wall until he sat on his heels, 'what in the name of sweet Jesus!'

Making coffee for fifty with one *cafetière* was not feasible so Chloë had improvised with two large saucepans and a sieve.

'Don't worry,' she assured, 'all under control! I've tasted it too and it's absolutely fine.' With his mouth agape and a strangled squeak from his throat, he motioned to the side of the sink, and to a large steel urn. Chloë looked over to it and then down at her saucepans and the splashes of coffee on her shirt. She turned the gas off, walked over to the urn and placed her hands against it. Hot.

'Coffee?' she mouthed at the man.

He nodded, closed his mouth and gulped.

'Sorry,' she whispered though she could see he was not cross.

'Och! Maybe they'll have two cups apiece! Let's get pouring – here, let me have a taste.' He spooned himself a sip from the saucepan before kissing his fingers and throwing them to the air. 'Not half bad, Mags my girl, not bad at all – let's take from your saucepans first!'

The coffee was appreciated and most had refills. Evening was slipping into night and when Chloë stood on the doorstep for a breather, silence save the waterfall greeted her and told her that her stay would be good. Slowly, the guests filtered away, shooting a light show over the humpy field in which they had parked out of sight.

'I'll be a wee while,' the young man told her with a shake of a bunch of keys. 'I'm to take the bride and groom.'

'Take them where?' asked Chloë, scraping trifle from the curtain.

'To their hotel, their honeymoon suite!' he said in a matter-of-fact way. Chloë looked puzzled, having presumed that Braer House *was* a hotel.

'Not here?' she queried.

'Here!' he laughed heartily. 'This was a one-off! Sweet Jesus that Braer should be an hotel!'

With that he chuckled off out of the house. Just the bride and groom remained, Chloë could hear them laughing softly and scuffling in the hallway. She bade them a very good-night and the best of luck and was rewarded with the bride's posy and another conspiring wink. Chloë tipped her head in the direction of her rucksack and winked back. Sally beamed her a smile and gave her a quick kiss.

'Bye, Chloë,' she said. 'I'll think of you galivanting around Britain! You should write it all down – just the sort of story that us fusty old married women enjoy!'

'Goodbye, Mrs Stonehill,' smiled Chloë. She waved them off as the young man drove them away into the night.

Busying herself by tidying up, she felt suddenly too tired to analyse the day. Wiping the cutlery was far easier a task. The young man returned, smiled at Chloë, scowled at the roasting tins and donned apron and rubber gloves at once.

'Do you know it's nearly half-past ten!'

No, Chloë did not, though her aching back would have suggested it was a whole hour or two later. The phone rang but the young man was arm-deep in soapsuds and side plates.

'Could you?' he asked, cocking his head in the direction of the ringing.

'Hullo?' Chloë said to the handset.

'This is Maggie Campbell,' said the voice, 'is he there?'

Chloë presumed 'he' to be the man at the sink so she said, 'Certainly, please hold a moment.' Placing her hand over the mouthpiece, she whispered in the direction of the bubbles, 'Excuse me, it's for you.'

'Who is it?' he hissed over his shoulder.

'It's Maggie,' said Chloë.

'Maggie?' he uttered, dripping foam on to the floor and scanning Chloë's face in a futile attempt to make sense of the situation. He took the phone from her, not bothered that he still wore his rubber gloves.

'Yes!' he announced into the receiver before falling silent while an excuse was obviously given. 'Sorry? They did, did they?' He stamped and took a soapy, rubbered hand to his brow. 'And you left it until now to phone? Well!' he declared and it sounded like 'wheel' with the 'h', 'there's manners for you!' He tucked the receiver under his chin and raised his gloves and his eyebrows at Chloë. 'Thank you so much for calling!' he cooed with sarcasm spiking every word, 'and goodbye to you too!' he spat in the gentlest of voices.

Replacing the handset, he took off the rubber gloves, washed and wiped his hands thoroughly as if they were dirty, and then put the gloves back on.

'Bloody Campbells,' he hollered at the ceiling, 'always the traitors! Glencoe in the 1690s and now Braer in the 1990s!' He continued to glower at the ceiling a while longer before softening his expression and looking over at Chloë who stood at the door with one dishcloth over her shoulder, one over her arm and another in her hands, a concerned expression on her face.

'That,' he said, looking exasperated, 'was Maggie.'

Chloë nodded slowly and tried to look sympathetic.

He put his hands on his hips and regarded her quizzically.

'So who, if you please, are *you*?'

'I'm Chloë Cadwallader,' Chloë apologized, 'and I'm looking for Fraser Buchanan.'

THIRTY

'But I *am* Fraser!' the young man said, walking over to Chloë with his hand outstretched, 'Buchanan! 'Tis I! No other.'

Chloë backed away and looked suspicious. Of course he wasn't. How could he be? He was little older than she. He was lithe. He had good teeth. No whiskers. She understood what he said, though she could not comprehend a word of it.

'Are you *sure*?' was all she could think to say. 'Really?'

'I am quite sure,' he assured. 'I have my birth certificate upstairs if you wish!'

Chloë shook her head but still observed him cautiously.

'Come,' he declared, putting his hand gently on her shoulders, 'sit and have a wee dram with me.'

He took her back into the dining-room and they sat at the top table, sipping whisky and clinking glasses.

'Chloë Cadwallader,' he said rolling her name around with pleasure, 'of course!'

Chloë looked nonplussed but could think neither what to say nor ask.

'I am indeed Fraser Buchanan. But I am *junior*, if you see. My *da* was Fraser too; Buchanan as well, of course. Senior, if you like. He knew *all* about Chloë Cadwallader! Och! He told me last autumn that we may have a woman called Miss Cadwallader come to stay, though he could not say when. I presumed you to be a wee grey-haired lady with a carpet-bag and a small dog till he explained!'

'Where *is* your father?' asked Chloë, overlooking Fraser's past tense. The ensuing brief silence hung awkward for Fraser but innocent for Chloë.

'He died, Chloë,' he seemed to apologize, 'not two months ago.' He shook his head quickly with eyes closed, but placed a hand firmly over Chloë's to ensure her that it was OK, and not to be embarrassed.

'It was sudden,' he explained, 'a very good death – unlike your godmother's.'

'I'm so sorry,' Chloë muttered. 'I wish I'd known. Please forgive.'

Fraser tutted her unease away.

'As I say, it was a good death – and in life, surely that's what one hopes for?'

Chloë agreed readily and smiled back, accepting a second measure of whisky and raising her glass to the memory of Fraser senior.

'Did you know my godmother then?' she asked, the whisky catching her throat.

'Jocelyn?' exclaimed Fraser. 'Oh aye. And I knew she had an utterly cherished god-daughter but I never knew it was you, not until my da spelt it out last autumn. Carpet-bag and lap-dog indeed! Aye, I saw Jocelyn often when I was younger, but I had not seen her in recent years and I'm right sorry for that,' he rued, rotating the edge of his glass across his lips. 'Da continued to meet her for lunch in Glasgow every now and then but I merely sent my lazy love via him. My mother died when I was a bairn, you see – but your Jocelyn, why, when I was sixteen, seventeen, she was perhaps more important to me than anyone.'

He watched a smile of recognition light Chloë's face.

'She was?' she asked.

'Aye, she was that,' Fraser sighed and fell silent for a while. He gazed into his whisky, swirling the tawny liquid, but Chloë could tell he was not looking at it. She had the feeling he was assessing something of considerable weight and that it somehow concerned Jocelyn. Her eagerness to know more, however, encouraged her to maintain a supportive silence.

'You'll live alongside me?' asked Fraser quietly, keeping his eyes away.

'If I may,' said Chloë sweetly, 'for the summer. If you'll have me.'

Fraser regarded her quizzically, quietly acknowledging her link with Jocelyn. A distant cuckoo clock informed them that it was midnight and Fraser dipped his head slightly at each chirp. Chloë noticed how nicely his hair spun itself into whorls here and there. She pulled her fingers through her own locks in a patient but futile exercise in detangling.

'When I was sixteen, seventeen,' he explained, drawing breath and then taking a hearty gulp from the glass, 'I was right down there,' he pointed well beyond the floor. 'I was troubled and confused – and utterly alone. I could speak to no one for what I had to say I believed to be unutterable. Despicable.' Chloë kept quiet and sipped her whisky, running her eyes along Fraser's slender hands. He was obviously not a farmer. Or a sculptor.

'Jocelyn,' he continued, absent-mindedly twisting a spiral of Chloë's hair between his fingers, 'came on one of her visits – she'd come each season, you know?'

'Because "Scotland's beauty remains constant",' paraphrased Chloë mistily, 'despite season, time of day, the weather?'

'Aye!' laughed Fraser, giving Chloë's hair a gentle tug. 'You'll be her god-daughter all right!'

'I'm sorry, I interrupted you.'

'Not at all! Anyway, she could tell something was amiss – when I was sixteen, seventeen – that I needed to talk but was unable to ask. She took me out for the day on some pretext or another. We skimmed pebbles, talked idly, ate rock cakes she'd baked. My tongue was tied, there was lead in my belly. It was excruciating. It was when I said should we head back that she turned to me and put her hand on my cheek. Here,' he took Chloë's hand and placed it against his face, 'right here. She said to me – I remember it word for word – "Whatever you do, wherever you'll go, whoever you'll be, we will never cease to love you." How did she know? Hey?'

Chloë's eyes were wide. How did Jocelyn know indeed, she wondered, and what was it that she knew? Fraser scanned her face, Chloë searched back.

'Gay?' he suggested quietly.

Chloë's eyes did not widen but she nodded her head to say 'Ah ha! I see!' She let her hand stay against his cheek.

'I'm gay,' Fraser said openly and most mundanely, 'but however did she know? Back then?'

'Jocelyn had a gift,' said Chloë after a moment's reflection, 'an intuitive – I don't know – *feeling* for the soul, an innate understanding of the psyche – anyone's! She always knew when I was out of sorts – no matter how brave a face I pulled, how strong a voice I used.'

'Was it not just that!' Fraser agreed taking her hand from his face and holding it tightly between his. 'And you know, I think it was her unconditional acceptance that helped my father to embrace it too. She made sure I told him just before they went off for a day out together. When they returned, he held me – he rarely did – as if I were a wee one, and told me he was proud of his son.'

'I'm sure he was,' said Chloë warmly. They sat and sipped in an easy silence until the cuckoo announced one o'clock.

'You must be ex-*haust*-ed!' Fraser proclaimed, enunciating the 'h' again.

'I am a little sleepy,' conceded Chloë.

'Christ if I've not even made up your room!' wailed Fraser, clasping his brow.

'Don't worry,' said Chloë, 'I mean, you were hardly expecting me. Besides, I feel I could sleep anywhere!'

'With me?' Fraser asked logically with an open face. Chloë looked up to his amiable eyes glinting warmly, and down to his beautiful hands cupping the empty glass.

'Fine,' she declared before giggling an aside: 'It seems I'm destined to have a bedfellow in every country I visit. And you're hardly likely to jump me, are you!'

They unbuckled their tired bodies into Fraser's bed which was old, wooden and vast, and said good-night to each other. Just before sleep took her, Chloë found herself speaking abruptly and very loudly.

'Fraser!'

'Hmm?' he managed.

'The wedding,' she asked, suddenly envisaging bridal underwear in her rucksack, 'here? But Braer House is *not* a hotel?'

'Not a hotel,' confirmed Fraser woozily, 'but my inheritance. I was living in Glasgow up until my father died. An old friend of his – an aunt of the bride – asked if he wouldn't mind *hosting* the wedding – you know, opening the house. It was agreed months ago, you see. I could never have reneged.'

'Of course not!' said Chloë, realizing that she was quite thankful to have arrived on such a day.

They stopped talking and sleep hovered once more.

'Who's Maggie?' she asked suddenly, knowing sleep was impossible without an explanation. 'Fraser?'

'I put an advert in the local paper for a waitress to help with today,' he explained patiently, in a flat voice edged with slumber. 'She answered. In fact, she was the only respondent. I've not met her; she's away at school, you see.'

'Why didn't she turn up?'

'Because her parents got wind of where she was going.

Who she'd be helping. I don't know them – but they obviously know *me*. *Of* me. Of my despicable, *queer* type. My bent, faggoty *species*!'

'God, really?' said Chloë aghast. 'Do you seriously come up against such prejudice?'

Fraser sat up in the darkness for he knew he would have no peace from his bedmate just yet.

'It's funny,' he explained, 'I'm tolerated by some of the most unlikely people – and yet loathed by many I would have credited with open minds.'

'The lady,' exclaimed Chloë, a sudden clarity washing the furrows from her brow, 'in the multi-purpose post office?'

'Ho!' laughed Fraser. 'Molly! Now, Molly thinks I'm *diseased*,' he explained while Chloë winced, 'and yet she adored my father – deceased!' he smirked. 'Anyway, when she found out that the poor man's son was a "*you-know-what*, one of *those*", she never again charged him for his daily paper – as a perverted gesture of condolence! Oh, we laughed long about that one.' Chloë laughed alongside him. 'Now I have trouble even *buying* a paper from her. To say nothing of stamps!'

With pressing questions answered satisfactorily, further elaboration could well wait until morning. They bade each other good-night once more and Fraser wished Chloë sweet dreams. On waking the next morning, she could not remember if she had dreamt at all, never mind how sweet or otherwise they had been. She glanced over to Fraser who was still asleep. She was not surprised to see him and was happy that he was there. Noiselessly, she crept out of bed and tiptoed downstairs in search of her rucksack. She rescued the Andrews from the deluge of lacy lingerie which swamped them. Mr Andrews looked decidedly flushed from the ordeal and cleared his throat vociferously.

'Seems like a nice chap, that Fraser,' whispered Mrs Andrews, digging her husband sharply with her elbow for bristling slightly.

THIRTY–ONE

The Cornish summer blessed its visitors and its natives with consistently sunny, balmy weather. Skies of ultramarine were interrupted only in a most photogenic way by wisps of high cloud filtering across in the mid-morning and late afternoon. If it rained, it did so unobtrusively at night. The landscape remained verdant, the gorse dazzling and fragrant, the sea warm, and the cream clotted until it was positively brick-like. The sheep and dairy cows grew plump while the hotel owners and cream-tea sellers became quite fat from the rewards of tourism. William's summer was going spectacularly. He had finished a series of tall bottles with long, slender necks and tiny openings that made them ideal for single roses or vinaigrette. They were easy and satisfying to throw and the people who came to purchase his pebble pieces for their gardens often bought such bottles for their mantelpieces or kitchens too.

Living off the beaten track had its advantages, for caravan trails rarely blemished his view. Likewise, the dearth of fish and chips and fudge outlets in his vicinity allowed it to remain relatively unscathed by those holiday-makers dependent on such victuals. Though the popular National

Trust coastal trail passed within yards of the boundary of Peregrine's Gully, William saw this as a boon. He was quick to deduce that the calibre of visitors who preferred to stride the path from Zennor to St Ives, rather than pack themselves into the south beaches and broil, matched exactly potential patrons of his pottery. He had thus erected a small but enterprising, carefully calligraphed wooden sign on the edge of his land which proclaimed 'Ceramics' with an arrow, and had since welcomed a steady stream of inquisitive walkers with a penchant for pottery. Such people were rarely 'just looking' or, if they were initially, they soon found that they passed William their money most willingly. William would chat quite affably about glazing and the weather, while packaging the wares in wadges of bubble wrap bought in bulk on a whim the previous winter; keeping them safe for collection later, when his clients had traded walking boots for sundresses and sandals.

When they drove to pick up their purchases in the evenings, William surreptitiously arranged other complementary pieces to solicit their eyes and their purses; it was rare indeed for him not to hear 'Oh go on then! I'll have that small dish too!' While smiling pleasantly, he silently trebled an already excessive figure in his head, transferred it on to paper and then added a most courteous fifty-percent discount in red ink. The fact that he would elaborately discount his carefully inflated price tags, further aided sales. William was welding a new-found awareness of marketing with a recently uncovered trait of Cornish shrewdness. He even thought to send his CV with small, complimentary bowls to *Country Living* and *Crafts* magazines and was rewarded with short but illustrated listings for his effort.

After the last of the day's sales had been collected and William had exchanged pleasantries and shaken hands energetically, he added names and addresses to a somewhat haphazard mailing list. He thought he might send out cards at Christmas illustrating new works (with prices inclusive of postage and packing). It occurred to him that he marketed his wares just as well as Morwenna but remained thirty per cent richer at all times. Not to mention fathoms happier and more relaxed on both emotional and physical counts. At last he was catering for his public, and serving them well, without compromising his artistic needs. He still made mugs and teapots, bowls in sets of six, but he made them to his own specifications, and his anomalously healthy bank account was proof of their success.

Barbara found her master's countenance infectious and was pleased to play soppy nanny goat whenever be-rucksacked folk appeared at their gate. She even wore a bell on an embroidered collar so that William could hear precisely when to leave his studio, emerge into the garden and brandish his most welcoming smile from his clay-caked smock.

By early August, having confirmed that most pottery patrons walked and bought in the early afternoon, William could afford to take the odd morning off and would stroll to Mac's once a week for coffee and an animated exchange of their increasing fortunes.

'I'm clean out of medium bowls now and am selling as many bottles as an off-licence!'

'Well, I've been averaging twenty piskie mugs a day – sales that is – but only manage to make half that amount. Demand, you could say, is outweighing supply!'

The clientele of the local bed-and-breakfast establishments and holiday bungalows raved for Mac's pixie-embellished pottery, often buying a mug each for the whole family as well as other items that would do nicely as Christmas presents.

'Piskies see,' Mac would say with a burr and a wink that made tourists melt, 'are peculiarly Cornish!'

He was even in cahoots with a local fudge maker who piled squares of his confectionery into Mac's small bowls, doubled the price that each fetched separately and then halved the proceeds with Mac. They sold well, so well that

William reserved his kiln on Sundays as an overflow for Mac.

Mac was delighted to witness William's change of fortune and the resultant effect on the boy's psyche. He saw how the sun had streaked blond into William's hair, had tanned his skin nicely and deepened his eyes to conker brown. He also reflected on the strange irony that it appeared to be a certain deficit in the love department that had in fact reinstated the spring in William's step, the glint in his eyes and the enthusiasm infusing his days.

'Ever see that Saxby woman?' Mac enquired nonchalantly.

'Who?' smiled William, twitching his eyebrows most becomingly.

Mac found he could even ask quite openly after the health of William's father, and was informed that, once the deluge of tourists subsided, William would visit him again. Perhaps in a month or so.

An incident on the cliffs in mid-August hastened William's return to Wales.

Whilst walking to Mac's he came across his mother, or at least a carbon copy of her for she had been dead some six years. A young boy and his father were deeply involved in an intricate hybrid of volleyball and soccer using an old green tennis ball; their border collie acting as both goalie and referee. All three had concentration etched across their brows, their breathing short but elated. Every so often a peal of laughter accompanied by an abrupt bark rang out as a particularly skilful tackle or blinding goal was executed. They were playing on a perfect pitch provided by nature where the coastal path had climbed to the cliff head and spread out into a downy plateau.

William had fixed on them from far off. As he approached he heard the tight grunts and clipped laughter of excitement. Nearing, he saw flushed cheeks, watering eyes, hair sticking in shards to the back of the neck and forehead. He caught hold of their expressions of determined enjoyment and observed that the game was as important and satisfying to each of them – the father was not humouring the son and the dog was not a nuisance but an integral part of the game. It *was* a game, it was *play*, and yet the resolute effort of the players suggested it was something more as well.

A good few yards away, standing with arms folded and her back towards the sea, was a woman William deduced immediately to be the wife, mother and mistress. Her stance was at once familiar to him for it spoke of irritation, of patience drawing thin, of dissent about to be unleashed. He knew if he came closer he would see rage burgeoning behind narrowing eyes, screaming out from pursed lips. He reckoned her knuckles would be quite white and there would be marks on her arms from where her rigid fingers dug in. He wanted to go over, just to see, but found that a small voice of dread tinged with fear prevented him. He began a wide semicircle of avoidance but came to a halt when she spoke. Yelled.

'For heaven's *bloody* sake!'

The team froze. Even the ball ceased to roll and seemed to hide in a thatch of longer grass.

'Would you stop fooling around and come along. That ball is covered with dog drool. This is a *family* walk. Jee-*zus*!'

'Two minutes!' the father suggested in a small voice holding up two fingers gingerly.

'No!' she hollered.

'Muh-hum!' pleaded the boy, with one hand on his father's arm.

'For heaven's sake!' she stamped.

William watched the boy and father exchange fleeting looks of sympathy and dejection while the dog cowered with his head stretched low on the grass. As if he had just been beaten. As if he had done something very wrong. The troop shuffled slowly over to the cliff edge and William turned away, terrified he might call to them 'Push her off!'

And yet the pull to turn back to them again was magnetic. When he did, he saw the woman take the tennis ball from her husband and hold it aloft between her thumb and third finger with utter disdain. She let it drop over the cliff. The man's shoulders slumped, his hands rested loosely, hopelessly, on his hips. The boy hurled himself around the dog's neck for it was ready to leap and fetch the ball.

She led. They followed. She spoke incessantly in a clipped, forced voice ordering them to look at the sea and the beautiful landscape, to *appreciate*.

'Isn't nature just *mar*vellous! Well? Isn't it? For heaven's sake look up and about you! All this lovely fresh air!'

William had walked swiftly so he could remain in earshot though he was unsure why he so needed to be. It occurred to him that it was the men and the dog who had grasped the point and who were truly enjoying the gifts of the day and the land. *She* didn't seem to be having fun at all and, by forcing the family issue, she was in fact underlining that no unity existed at all. It was familiar to William and painful too, though he had rarely played with his father. And he had never had a dog.

'You seem a little –' Mac laboured over the most apposite word, '*out*.'

'Out?' asked William, pinching the pixie on his mug though he knew the fired clay would not yield.

'Yes,' mused Mac, '*out*. *Of* sorts. *Of* the window. Not *here*.' He allowed William his silence and aided it by pottering off to his kitchen to boil the kettle again. A few minutes later, he was aware that William was there, propping up the door frame and filling the small room with his physique and with his discomfort.

'Tea?'

'Just like her.'

William spoke the words as if they were three separate sentences.

'On the cliffs. I hardly think of her, Mac.'

William walked over to the sink and rested his lower back against it. Mac rocked gently against the counter looking out over his small, straggled garden.

'Mother,' William explained in a whisper lest she should hear. 'Mother,' he said slowly, even more quietly, in case Mac was mistaken. Mac nodded sagely without commenting.

'I think I resent Dad for not sticking up for me,' William said, his voice hollow, 'but I hate him more for not standing up for himself.'

Mac put his head to one side to say he understood, please continue.

'I can't understand why he did not,' William shouted. He looked at Mac. 'Why didn't he?' he implored. Mac cast his eyes away and back to the garden where the lavatera looked at him blankly and gave no advice.

'He was always nice to her. And to me,' William said. 'I do not under*stand*.'

'What,' asked Mac, 'what is it *precisely* that grieves you?'

'Why he was with *her*.'

'Because *she* was his wife,' Mac shrugged.

'She can't always have been like that!' William protested. 'Tell me my father had taste, had judgement!'

Mac fell silent but William was convinced that he was full of information.

'Mac!' he demanded.

'Your father was – is – a man of honour,' Mac said blankly.

'He's *feeble*,' William spat, knowing he should direct his anger at his mother but not knowing how to.

'No,' corrected Mac slowly, 'just too kind. Too selfless.'

'But if she loathed us so,' faltered William, 'why did she stay?'

Mac snorted lightly at the irony.

'Dog in a manger!' he sighed under his breath.

'Huh?' asked William.

Mac looked at him, scouring William's beseeching eyes,

and thought that ignorance, while not necessarily bliss, was perhaps for the best. After all, he had been given a secret to guard and guard it he must.

'Dog in a bloody *manger*?' William repeated, frowning and stamping.

Mac shrugged.

She hadn't wanted him – them – but there had been no way she would have let *her* have them either.

William returned to Crickhowell, the long train journey deciding him that, despite the earful he would no doubt receive from Mac, he would buy a car on his return. Something small, hardy and dependable, and as environmentally friendly as a second-hand car could be. He could afford one now, following the busy summer. He could visit Mac more often. Red perhaps? Maybe blue. Metallic grey is nice.

He found his father pretty much as he had left him, in the queue of senility. Now, however, they had been positioned out of doors, their backs to the long window, in front of which they had spent the colder months. William walked past the display of bulging ankles contained within chewing-gum-grey socks, of shrunken chests clearly delineated behind misshapen polyester sports shirts. Knitted, knotted feet strapped into big-buckled leatherette sandals; ear lobes that looked too large; knees to be ashamed of. Sore-looking shin bones glared out from behind papery, hairless legs; while flaps of crepe-paper skin hung listless from puny arms, gathering in folds around the neck like a turkey. Enough for a book on geriatric physiology, thought William, enough to illustrate a discourse on the merits of euthanasia. He hated himself for reviling them. He tried not to look.

'Hullo Dad!' he breezed, putting his hand on the old man's shoulder and squeezing it. It was warm. As if the sun had heated its surface alone, for his father's expression was quite lifeless. Slowly the old man turned to William and gaped at him, his eyes quite content to rest on his face with no element of recognition.

'Michael?' he croaked.

'Wi-lee-um!' William spelt patiently, sitting on his heels and tapping his father's hand with the syllables.

'Shall we stroll,' said the old man, 'over to the ladies?'

William looked about and saw no ladies. But his father had a glint in his eye and his face now had a light that came from behind and not from the sun.

'Sure!' said William, helping the old man out of the chair.

He was surprised that, despite his father's frame appearing so skeletal and brittle, there was a certain strength to it too. He walked faster than William anticipated and refused to take his arm though William hovered his hand close to his elbow.

'We'll go da-ha-ha-ncing,' the old man burst into song and executed a series of surprisingly nimble dance steps, 'and ro-mah-ha-ha-ncing!'

Without irritation, William allowed him to repeat the line, atonally, over and over. They strolled to an impressive cedar tree.

'Blast and bugger!' his father exclaimed. 'It appears we've been stood up, Michael old boy!' It dawned on William, with a certain discomfort, that his father thought him to be Mac. And he really did not want that, did not want to be mistaken for friend instead of son. Feared the old man might say or do something unbecoming for a father. Did not want to share in his father's bachelor flashbacks. It wasn't proper. It was a little disturbing. He led the old man over to the rose bushes and proffered the soft, fat heads to his nose. The old man closed his eyes and inhaled deeply.

'*My love is like a red, red rose,*' he quoted in a very matter-of-fact way and a very good Scottish accent.

'Is it now!' William laughed.

'*Like a melody that's sweetly played in tune!*' his father continued, having scanned the intervening lines to himself.

As William led him around the gravel path which snaked

neatly between lawn and flower beds, his father continued to recite Burns in exaggerated Scots.

'*Fare thee weel my only love!*'

William slowed his pace and tilted his head, listening for the next line though he knew it anyway.

'*And fare thee weel a while*!' his father obliged. '*And I will come again my love –*'

'*Though it were ten thousand mile,*' William interrupted quietly.

They had circumnavigated the garden and were back at his father's chair but he refused to sit. He stood instead with his hands clasped in front of his chest, taking elaborate snorts of the sweet summer day.

'Ah Scotland!' he cried, quite taking William aback.

'Wales,' William chided gently, taking a swift look about him to see if anyone had heard.

'Jostling in Scotland!' said his father, digging him in the ribs and winking slowly.

'You poor old sod,' said William quietly, knowing that his words did not register. 'You sad old thing. Lost it.'

His father winked back but allowed himself to be eased down into his chair.

William looked along the decrepit queue, some were nodding to themselves while others nodded quite involuntarily. Occasionally, someone laughed out loud but William doubted whether they knew at what they laughed. He observed the small pile of books and knick-knacks by each chair. He thought it most unlikely that his father read, let alone had any interest in *The All-Colour Book of Bicycles*, which lay underneath a mug by Mac. Or that he had much use for a road atlas of Great Britain which, on closer inspection, had pages missing anyway. William picked the mug up and placed it in his father's hands. His father sipped and sipped though it was quite empty while William flicked through the book on bicycles. It was badly bound and the resolution on the illustrations was appalling; overlapping purple outlines and green shadows, the type fuzzed in places. The front cover had almost come away but the back cover held on fast. Drawn on to the inside of it, over and over again, was a pattern William was sure he knew but could not quite place.

Curvilinear. Serpentine. Swirling arabesques.

He forced the page in front of his father who was reciting Burns again. William held the book steady until his father's eyes alighted on it. Something behind his eyes flickered sharply and then died, a light which came on and was then extinguished. His expression changed and became stony and troubled. His head stayed very still.

'Jer je je,' he dribbled, wrenching his eyes away from the book and into the midst of nowhere.

'I can't believe you've bought a car!' hollered Mac. 'A motor! Preposterous! You'd better take me for a spin this instant! Interesting shade of? Of?'

'Champagne,' clarified William, patting the bonnet of the little Renault, 'it was all the rage a few years ago.'

They drove to St Just and had toasted teacakes alongside scone-wolfing tourists before journeying on to a small beach known only to natives.

'How was Dad?' Mac asked, skimming his pebble two leaps further than William.

'Do-lally,' William replied, hurling a stone as far as he could. It went far enough for them not to hear it splash. They strolled by the water's edge.

'He called me Michael and suggested we went courting.'

The real Michael laughed but did not tell William why. For his part, William did not elaborate. And Mac did not ask him to.

'Then he started reciting Burns in a phoney Scottish accent.'

Mac continued to chuckle and asked which poem.

'Guess,' said William. Mac was right first time.

'I don't know,' William sighed, flopping down into the sand and resting his arms lightly on bent knees, 'I go there to visit and he has no idea who I am. There seems to be no purpose to my going. A waste of time. Exhausting. Upsetting. Really upsetting. Very little point.' He pulled his finger along the sand, spelt his name and then doodled.

'There *is* a point,' began Mac almost sternly, 'but you'll probably not see it for some while. Probably not till after you've buried him.'

William frowned at him but let it lie.

'It was odd,' he said lightly, changing the subject, 'he had this book and in the back was this pattern, over and over again.' William approximated it in the sand. Mac said nothing.

'Strange,' continued William, drawing it again, 'because I'm sure I know it.'

Though Mac remained standing to save his arthritic knees, he could see the pattern quite clearly. Not that William had even needed to draw it.

'It's a popular design,' suggested Mac, 'probably used for Liberty prints and the like.'

'Yes, probably,' conceded William. Then he raised a finger and cocked his head, frowning slightly. 'Hang on a tick: when I visited him in the early spring, I doodled on the condensation on the window-pane – you know, my initials, tracery at Tintern – and also this pattern which I'd just come across in the form of a brooch on my way to the Home.'

Mac did not comment.

'Maybe it's like the ability autistics have,' pondered William, 'you know, to draw from memory perfectly a building seen only once, or to solve great mathematical equations?'

'Maybe,' said Mac, nodding.

'So strange,' rued William, 'that he can seem so incapacitated and yet have drawn an intricate pattern having seen it only the once.'

'Only the once!' Mac exclaimed.

'Hey?' said William.

'Did he react when you drew it?' Mac asked.

'React!' scoffed William. 'Dad!' he chuckled cruelly. 'Only if you can call a chorus of je je je-ing a reaction!'

William stood up and walked slowly along the beach. Mac meandered over to the sea and gazed across it.

'Je je je for Jocelyn,' he said to himself sadly.

THIRTY-TWO

'Jasper? Jasper!'

'In the garden, darling!'

'Scottish epistle!'

'Ho! I'm coming in!'

Jocelyn had left her beloved garden in the best of hands and, though it nagged his back, Jasper spent most afternoons primping and tidying and annihilating imaginary weeds. The white Himalayan geranium had come out overnight but not even its gossamer petals threaded delicately with crimson could keep him away from a long overdue letter from Chloë.

'What does our wee lassie say?' he asked as he loped into the kitchen, a little out of breath and with soil clinging to his hair. 'Any Highland flings? And does she mention how Ireland ended?'

Peregrine scanned the letter.

'Yes she does,' he acknowledged. '*Could you not have told me about Gus and Jocelyn?* she asks, ah, and provides the answer immediately: *No, I understand perfectly why you could not. Anyway, I now feel a certain fondness for Gus – gratitude too – as if he afforded me a glimpse of a Jocelyn previously unseen.* Bless the girl!'

'What about the sculptor chappie?' asked Jasper, shaking his head over the sink and watching a centipede circumnavigate the plughole before delving down, past the point of no return. 'Conan or whatever!'

'Gracious me!' announced Peregrine, feigning abject horror. 'It says here: *Ronan did unmentionable things to me over a clump of Kilkenny limestone!*'

'The Barbarian! Can't have been comfortable,' rued Jasper shaking his head and causing more soil to spatter over yesterday's *Times*.

'Well, my dear, we wouldn't know now, would we? But Chloë assures us *the rock was warmer and more comfortable than one would have thought*. Good Lord! It appears the cad then carved the stone into a homage to her body! She says she was horrified and humiliated at first but now, her residing feeling is one of pride. Gracious! I hope she doesn't have any distinguishing birthmarks. Well, it seems they parted on good terms. What's this?'

'What's what?' said Jasper, quite content to forgo a direct recounting of the gory details of Chloë's sex life.

'The girl was in Ireland too long, that's what – says she saw a giant who was no taller than her shoulder!'

'Indeed?'

'Indeed,' said Peregrine, muttering 'Bloody paddies' under his breath.

'Where is she in Scotland? With Celia Lomax on Mull?'

'No, with Fraser Buchanan,' corrected Peregrine.

'But he's two months dead!' gasped Jasper.

'*Due*-nyar!' Peregrine stressed.

Jasper tapped his head and raised his eyebrows at himself.

'It seems they're both having a jolly time of it,' Peregrine continued: '*Neither of us have the foggiest what we want to do, what our purpose in life is to be*, she explains. *Fraser had been teaching in a Glasgow comprehensive which he found utterly soul-destroying. The kids taunted him too* – he's one of us, remember. *We are both lucky enough to have some money enabling us "time out" for a little while, and for this we are deeply indebted to our benefactors. So frustrating that we can't say so directly! Fraser senior sounded lovely and I wish I'd met him – do you remember him?* Do we! A sporran to bring tears to the eyes!'

Jasper's eyes watered. Peregrine flounced him a silk handkerchief.

'Enough!' Jasper chided. 'We're far too old to be so incorrigible. What is she doing with her time in Scottish Land?'

'It seems they've spent the month touring around the Highlands – Crianlarich, Bridge of Orchy, Spean Bridge; across to Oban, up to Fort William, over to watch salmon jumping at Pitlochry, a stroll through the estate at Blair Athol. *What unites this land*, she says here, *is this great dignity emanating over all. The beautiful hues of heather and bracken, the reflections cast and continually changing from all this inland water; the very lie of the land – the way the mountains simultaneously rise up from the lochs and seem to slip so gracefully, deep into them; the sweep of the glens extending over the land as a pianist's fingers over a keyboard – certainly Scotland is filled with music, from the song of the waterfalls to the lament of the bagpipes, and that Mendelssohn overture that I have stuck in my mind.* The girl really should use more full stops. Here she goes: *I hear, too, the plaintive mew of buzzards which seems to stretch to the horizon and I've also seen eagles for the first time in my life – nothing prepares you for their majesty; they ride the air with such consummate mastery, hovering effortlessly before tilting a feather tip and hurtling across the sky to spiral upwards, ever upwards, before plummeting like a bullet; their presence in the landscape imposing and yet so complementary too.* See how out of breath her sentences make me?'

'Scotland,' qualified Jasper, 'seems to be taking her breath away more!'

* * *

Fraser had swiftly become Chloë's confidante and she his. They were the siblings their parents had never given them; Fraser, because his mother had died when he was three and his father never remarried; Chloë, because Torica and Owen quickly discovered at her birth a supreme deficit of parental proclivity. Chloë found she had indeed a brother; Fraser, a sister. Both now had a best friend for whom they could show unconditional and easily platonic love.

Scotland suited Chloë very well and though she was not Scottish, she would have been proud to be so. Indeed, many presumed that she was, and she did not correct them. At last she felt utterly at ease with her luscious auburn hair. It no longer seemed out of place and people did not comment as they were prone to do in other countries: 'Look at that hair! Is it a bind? Are you Scottish?' Despite Fraser's initial anxiety, the small community around them warmed to Chloë immediately and those who had previously blanked Fraser now granted him a degree of cordiality, albeit at a safe distance. Some easily persuaded themselves that och, the lad had found a lass and all is well again. Whatever their reasoning, nods were now given when passing the pair and pleasantries exchanged when newspapers, or pints of milk or bitter, were bought.

Fraser and Chloë became steadfast house-mates and Chloë soon confided to Mrs Andrews that she could even envisage Braer becoming her home.

'Rather ramshackle, dear,' Mrs Andrews had said, trying not to wrinkle her nose.

'Bit cut off – and rather grave, all that granite,' agreed Mr Andrews. 'Anyway, you've England next on the agenda.'

'Braer's not ramshackle,' protested Chloë, wondering if Jocelyn's itinerary was really set in stone, 'it just rambles in a somewhat unkempt way.'

'I.e. *ramshackle*,' Mrs Andrews declared, rolling her 'r' triumphantly.

'Look,' Chloë said, 'we can't all have acres of parkland in Suffolk. Indeed, we don't all want that! Anyway, I like everything a little out of sync. I loved the antiques in the tack room at Skirrid End and the horse rugs on the bed – and I felt rather clumsy amongst all the order and control at Ballygorm, remember. Just because half the rooms here are empty, and the others are filled with incongruous items of furniture doesn't make Braer less of a home than yours. I feel at home here, that's what counts. And anyway, Fraser and I take it in turns to hoover and dust. And we wash up immediately after every meal.'

Mr and Mrs Andrews regarded each other with a small shrug of the shoulders before taking their leave of Chloë. They had ordered a mahogany library table by Gillows of Lancaster and it was due to arrive that morning, as were two dozen quails for a small dinner party they were having that evening.

Chloë and Fraser did not eat quail but they cooked together and concocted great stews and substantial soups over which they congratulated themselves heartily. They kept house and shared a home; having heart-to-hearts, reading quietly, laughing frequently or nattering into the small hours.

'Come blether with your brother,' Fraser would invite, patting the sofa, or drawing up a chair in the kitchen, or holding out his hand as they strolled along the Orchy. Whilst they were delighted to share, they also gave each other space and silence instinctively. If Chloë's door was shut, Fraser would stroll past it and then call to her later from the bottom of the stairs. Chloë seemed to know, too, when to chat and when to let him be, gazing out of windows or immersed in book or thought.

Her room was far more cosy than the Victorian austerity at Braer initially suggested. On her first morning, Fraser had busied himself making sure the room was ready and decorous. He glossed the window-sills and gave a lick to the single bed with the remaining paint. He took down the frayed blind whose sides curled like a stale sandwich, and disappeared into the attic to emerge some time later with a pair of lined curtains in maroon and gold Madras check.

'Jocelyn made these,' he told Chloë, 'she came to stay directly after a long trip to India where she bought the fabric. A "thinking trip" she called it, for some reason!'

Chloë was delighted and took the curtains from Fraser, hugging them close to her and burying her nose deep. Musty, not Mitsuko. But heavenly.

'Jocelyn must have known that I'd find these,' she announced to Fraser, 'that they'd keep me safe and snug. Made for the Buchanans and now made use of by me.'

'She liked it here,' Fraser assured her. Chloë nodded vigorously and wrapped her arms about Fraser, embracing him fully but gently.

'This house and its inhabitants meant something – much – to her,' she said, 'and thereby all the more to me.'

Once Fraser had extricated himself from Chloë's arms which were obviously quite happy to stay put all day, he set a little terracotta amphora over a saucer on the bedside table and added a few drops of lily-of-the-valley essence. Then he bunched together a clutch of flowers and interesting twigs from the garden and placed them in a jug on the chair by the window.

'The sills aren't dry,' he explained when he finally presented the room to Chloë, 'but you can move the flowers there later.'

'Actually,' said Chloë, 'I rather like them there, on the chair.'

'Then I'll fetch another,' Fraser said.

'No, no,' protested Chloë, already quite overwhelmed, 'it's fine!'

But Fraser brought in an old loom chair that had a quicksand effect and was dangerously comfortable. Everything was. And Chloë refused to heed Mr Andrews's warning that she would have to pack up and go once the bracken had turned and the hills were shot through with deep violet and brown. At the moment the hills were green and gold and blushed with pink; a whole spectrum away.

Neither Chloë nor Fraser knew what they wanted to do in the long term, so it seemed a very sound idea to spend the meantime pondering such matters at length against the conducive backdrop of the Highlands. For perhaps the first time, Chloë found true purpose in Jocelyn's stratagem. She believed her godmother knew this country as well as she knew her god-daughter, that she had prophesied the impact of the place and trusted the clarity of light to filter right through to Chloë's soul and sense.

Scotland itself will tell me what to do. Where to go. What to be.

Yes?

Do you still not believe that you can fathom it for yourself, all by yourself?

No?

Not just yet?

'What do you want to be when you're big?' asks Fraser at Mallaig as they gaze over the Sound of Sleat to Skye. Chloë hums 'Speed Bonny Boat' all the way through, twice, while she racks her brains.

'When I grow up,' she labours, until she bumps her mind against the dark wall of no idea, 'er, I shall be a princess! And you?' She stands up and pulls Fraser to his feet. They face the water and close their eyes while the warmth of the sun licks their faces and the breeze blesses their lungs.

'Well,' Fraser proclaims in a childish voice, 'I'd like to be a lustman, I mean a dustman!' Chloë digs him in the ribs. 'Or maybe,' he laughs, 'Spiderman!' and he chases Chloë to the water's edge, contorting his fingers in arachnoid approximation.

'Perhaps I'll be a salmon farmer,' he mused as he and Chloë played Pooh-sticks over an unstable bridge at Pitlochry. But they spoke no more of it because it was too tempting to see who could spot the most salmon jumping instead. Chloë won; she saw fourteen. She had never seen fish leaping before. Oh, to catch one. Make a wish.

'I'll bet you were a brilliant teacher,' Chloë announced on waking from a doze in the heather in a glen near Oban. Fraser accepted her compliment silently and then mulled over it.

'Only if the children wanted to learn,' he clarified. 'I could teach them, aye, until the answers were right every time. But if they did not want to *learn*, my purpose and *enjoyment* were nothing.'

'Did they really *tease* you,' Chloë asked tentatively, 'did they really *know*?' She scoured Fraser's face and was relieved to see no hurt traverse its prettiness. He smirked.

'I neither denied nor confirmed – and I never gave them aught, of that I was right careful. Och, but the gossip! "Ho *mo*! I've left my *homo*-work behind!" ' he mimicked in falsetto, ' "and my pencil's *bent*, sir!" '

'I need to go to the sickbay, I feel queer!' Chloë interrupted merrily in plausible Glaswegian. 'I think it was the faggots at lunch-time, sir.'

' "It's such a gay day, Mr Buchanan, can we not pick us some pansies?" ' cried Fraser, enjoying the last laugh.

They take a day-trip over to Mull and Chloë spends the ferry crossing explaining to Fraser the pointless intricacies of working with students at an inner-city college.

'Sorry, have I been bending your ear?' she asks when he interrupts to point out Duart Castle on the headland of the isle.

'Och, I wouldn't fret,' he assures her, 'it was bent already!'

Taking photos of Fraser by the candy-coloured buildings of Tobermory harbour with a disposable camera, Chloë knows she will never return to that job, or to one remotely similar. As Fraser photographs her on the return crossing, the light still more than adequate though it is nearing ten o'clock, she knows too that she will never return to the city. Any city. She knows now what she does *not* want; but realizes as well that she still has no idea what it is that she actually does want to do. Jocelyn's money will not last forever. And it occurs to Chloë now, that she would not have wanted it to anyway.

Fraser and Chloë walked through Glencoe but it was far too awesome for anything but reverential silence and the occasional stunned gasp at the sheer beauty and enduring melancholy that permeated.

'What do you want?' Chloë asks Fraser as they sit in the kitchen scalding their tongues on piping hot flapjacks. 'Fraser?'

'A blob of ice-cream?' he suggests. Chloë pulls a face at him that says 'No! but really?' Fraser goes to the freezer and returns with a tub of vanilla ice-cream. It is very yellow and glistens with tiny shards of ice. It is also frozen solid. Fraser hammers a spoon down into it but it takes a stance like Excalibur. Dejected, he takes the tub by the spoon over to the stove.

'I don't know, my Chlo,' he says with honesty, 'a good life, a loving partner?'

'Has there ever been one?' she asks. 'Someone?'

Fraser returns to the table and munches on a now pleasingly chewy flapjack.

'Only lust,' he bemoans, contorting his lips to dislodge oat flakes from his gums, 'and a fair bit of it,' he sighs and seems to chide himself, 'I always initially mistake it for the love that it invariably never turns into!'

Chloë understands without actually being able to share the sentiment or predicament. They chew on.

'But no,' Fraser rues, 'never a someone.'

'Not yet,' Chloë says warmly. Fraser nods. 'But that's what you'd like,' she clarifies. Fraser nods.

'You?' he demands.

'Me?' Chloë responds.

'Aye,' he says sternly, 'and you?'

'Well,' Chloë starts while her finger is in her mouth, searching out clogs of flapjack from her molars, 'there was Brett who was a selfish, sexist pig but it took me an age and a half, and Jocelyn's death, to realize! And then, in Wales, there was this darling boy called Carl.'

'Carl,' rolls Fraser approvingly.

'Mm,' confirms Chloë, 'he was lovely – a Kiwi, you know, from New Zealand?'

'Aye! Down there! Fruity!'

'We had a lot of fun!'

'Down *there*!' suggests Fraser with a lascivious wink. Chloë can't help but blush.

'Details?' Fraser says slyly. 'Please?'

'He was a "rum 'un", as you'd say!' chuckles Chloë. 'He provided all the fun that Brett had deemed unnecessary. A healthy mixture of kindness, honesty and lots of sweaty fumblings too!'

'Ooh!' Fraser writhes.

'Ultimately,' proclaims Chloë, laying her arm over Fraser's and giving it a squeeze, 'a terrific bonk in the back of an orange van!'

'An orange van!' cries Fraser with awe and respect.

'Very orange!' confirms Chloë. 'It was fun – happy sex. I didn't know you could have such a thing. Brett was silent but for unpleasant grunts and a horrendous phoney American accent which was not funny at all.'

'I'll bet!' sympathizes Fraser. 'So where is he now?'

'Who?'

'Well, I'll not give a toss for Brett's whereabouts,' Fraser spits before purring, 'Carl – where's he?'

Chloë falls silent and wonders suddenly why she has no idea where he is. How stupid of her. Of them.

No, not really.

'Somewhere in Europe,' she says warmly, 'I don't know

where. I'll never see him again, you see. We came – and we went.'

Fraser looks puzzled.

'It was like lining each other's pockets with gold,' Chloë says wistfully, 'giving each other the wherewithal to go forward. To go on.'

'Leaving a lovely taste?' suggests Fraser.

'Indeed.'

Suddenly Fraser leaps up and the chair clatters to the floor.

'Oh no!' he weeps, staggering across the room to the stove. 'Damnation and buggery!' he wails, holding aloft the ice-cream tub. Excalibur has disappeared from view. Fraser makes a most funereal procession back to the table, holding out the tub in front of him forlornly, pain etched across his face. Chloë stifles the giggles and pulls a very serious face of condolence. He places the tub on the table and they peer in. Pale buttercup soup slops back at them. Slowly, Chloë dips in a finger and takes it to her mouth. Fraser scans her face, his own as downtrodden as a bloodhound's. Her eyes light up and she coos while she sucks her finger.

'Gorgeous,' she whispers, 'abso-bloody-lutely gor-jesus!' she says, smacking her lips and dipping the same finger back in.

Fraser fetches two spoons.

'Och,' he moans in ecstasy, slurping spoonfuls in quick succession, 'vanilla velvet mousse!'

'Clouds *de Crème Anglaise*!' Chloë elaborates with closed eyes, her spoon clinking on the drowned Excalibur. Eventually it surfaces, as Fraser and Chloë do away with the goop surrounding it. They fight over who shall lick it clean. Chloë pats her thighs and her stomach sensibly and says Fraser must have it.

'These thighs, this stomach,' Chloë proclaims when he has quite finished, patting them again, 'have been immortalized!'

'Oh aye?' says Fraser, licking up a trickle of canary yellow that has coursed its way down the side of his hand to his wrist.

'Ronan!' whispers Chloë.

'Who he?'

'He be Oy-rush!'

'Begorra be-jayz!' laughs Fraser. 'A leprechaun?'

'Pah!' Chloë exclaims. 'A strapping lad of statuesque physique!' Fraser wriggles. 'Broad shoulders, chiselled jaw,' she continues while his eyes dance, 'jet-black hair and piercing blue eyes and,' she says with a wink, 'a tight peach of a bum!'

Fraser slithers down his chair with his tongue lolling and begs her to stop.

'And a dick to die for?' he conjectures in a hoarse whisper.

Chloë pauses for dramatic impact before twisting her face and shaking her head quickly, wrinkling her nose. 'Actually,' she concedes, 'not really!'

'Not in Carl's league?' asks Fraser, looking sorely disappointed. Chloë shakes her head sadly.

'But way out of Brett's,' nods Fraser. Chloë pulls a grimace in reply. She tells him about the ensuing sculpture and he asks her to describe it, to draw it. She tells him to use his imagination. He says he can't. She says that's his bad luck. He asks Chloë if she thinks there's any chance he'd be able to entice Ronan to do a piece called *Him*. Chloë's reply sorely disappoints him. They sit awhile, quiet, quite still, lest the melted ice-cream should curdle within. Fraser is tinged green. The cuckoo chirps out that it is eleven o'clock and Chloë yawns spontaneously. Fraser sighs, cups his head in his hands and then throws Chloë an exasperated expression.

'We have to find you a man!' he declares, grabbing her hand and squeezing it.

'Pardon?' Chloë replies, fighting to have her hand back.

'I can't be outdone by Wales, by the Oy-rush!' Fraser explains, gripping her wrist. 'And as I am unable to assist personally in such matters, God only knows what might befall you in England!'

Chloë laughs and says that he's daft. He hisses 'Sassenachs' very seriously.

'The interludes in the other two countries were merely by the by,' she says lightly, 'anyway, I'm in love with Scotland utterly and no earth-moving, multiple orgasm can possibly improve on that!'

Fraser regards her suspiciously and pokes her in the ribs.

'I'm not *look*ing!' she laughs. 'Nothing is *lack*ing!' she assures. 'I'm happy enough as I am,' she concludes confidently and very loudly, suddenly wondering very quietly to herself if she'll ever have sex again.

And if so, when. And with whom, for heaven's sake!

Fraser puts his head back into his hands and sighs even more sonorously. The face he then turns to Chloë is criss-crossed with theatrical angst and his eyes flicker with carefully contrived despair. He swipes his brow in an enormous gesture.

'Well then,' he wails, 'I have to find *me* a man!'

THIRTY-THREE

August was drawing to a close and Chloë was delighted when Fraser suggested a few days in Edinburgh to catch the last of the city's famous Festival. Only he went manhunting with a verve and vigour that quite threatened to come between him and Chloë. When his ulterior motives surfaced, she was both irritated and hurt, and a little lonely too. Mr and Mrs Andrews were guarding Braer and Chloë missed them supremely.

The search for a bed-and-breakfast was hampered by Fraser's new-found ability to pivot his head through three hundred and sixty degrees. No reasonably good-looking man escaped his attention, even if he had his arms about a woman or was dressed in a traffic warden's uniform. Fraser sought Chloë's response and approval constantly.

'Him! Did you see? Chlo?'

'Yes, dear, very nice – but he was with his wife and two children!'

'Aye, but he may be *latent* – he may not know what he's missing! Och, but would you look at the arse on that now!'

'Fray-*zer*!'

'What I'd give for a man in uniform! What I'd *pay*!'

'Fray!'

'I know, I'm sorry – but it's like being let loose in a sweetie shop. So much to lick and gobble!'

'Zer! You'll get ill.'

'I'd die happy!'

Eventually, once Fraser had had mental sex with at least thirty passers-by (most of them unwitting, all of them unsuitable) they found themselves strolling past Murrayfield stadium. Fraser was fantasizing out loud about being reincarnated as the soap in the communal bath for the First Fifteen when Chloë saw a street to the right with bed-and-breakfast signs strung along its length like bunting. She grabbed his hand and held on tight with both of hers, dragging him down the street while he cooed about lather and cauliflower ears.

'I could be the scrum's hooker!'

'Frr!'

'OK, OK. Spoilsport!'

She was still holding on tight when, four houses later, they came across the first 'vacancies' sign.

'Knock!' she hissed, not daring to let go. 'Ring!' With his free hand, Fraser did both, pouting all the while.

Mrs MacAdam saw a very nice young couple standing, hand in hand, on her doorstep and welcomed them in. They saw a lounge bedecked in every conceivable shade of pink in fabrics of every possible synthetic persuasion. She had only the one vacancy, she explained, a last-minute cancellation for which she had kept the deposit.

'Do you think that unreasonable?' she asked, twitching fussy net curtains to check on goings-on outside.

'Och no,' said Chloë in a very passable Scots accent that made Fraser raise his eyebrows, 'you can't be having that. Well within your rights, I'd say!'

Mrs MacAdam offered them humbugs from a dish that formed the skirts (pink) of a china figurine of Cinderella. Fraser and Chloë tried not to notice the dust caught stickily in the creases of cellophane, nor that the sweets had a certain mustiness that overpowered any vestige of mintiness. After lengthy calculations which involved much muttering, eyes scrunched shut and the pummelling of her pudgy fingers into her pink tracksuit-clad thighs, Mrs MacAdam arrived at a four-night rate for them. This they accepted and were offered another humbug to seal the deal. The three of them sat and sucked in silence for a while, smiling awkwardly every now and then.

'Deary deary dear!' Mrs MacAdam exclaimed once she'd crunched the last of her sweet, her cheeks flushing the same shade as her tracksuit. She shook her head and slapped each of her own wrists in turn. 'You'll want to be seeing your room, silly me. Come!'

Fraser and Chloë exchanged raised eyebrows as the landlady bustled them out. Their room. Singular. Or, rather, double. They hadn't thought of that.

Decorated in every possible hue of gold and yellow, the room would have been huge had not the most enormous bed taken up most of it. It was swamped by a very shiny satin-look eiderdown and a mound of frilled cushions in various tones of poor gold.

'This is your side,' dictated Mrs MacAdam to Chloë, patting the left side of the bed, above which a painting of a gypsy girl with disproportionately large eyes and a sorrowful kitten hung. 'And this side is for you!' she proclaimed to Fraser, circumnavigating the bed and plumping the cushions on the right side of the bed which lay under the gaze of a bug-eyed gypsy boy with a forlorn puppy at his heels.

'Suits me down to the ground!' announced Fraser, winking at Chloë who stifled giggles by sucking in her cheeks and biting on them.

'Right!' Mrs MacAdam said with no intention of leaving. It was only after Chloë and Fraser professed ample appreciation and heaped praise that she left, telling them that breakfast was served between seven and nine.

In the Green Room.

Chloë and Fraser could hardly wait to launch themselves

on to the bed and thrust their faces deep into the cushions so they could release the laughter that had been so hard to keep at bay. Had Mrs MacAdam heard their muffled shrieks and snorts, she would have interpreted them as the effect the Gold Room had on young lovers. The effect on Chloë was a sneezing fit of staggering length which she attributed to the synthetic lavender room spray that had obviously doused all the furnishings. When she had ceased her sneezing and Fraser his sniggers, they lay side by side on the bed, out of breath, enjoying an intermittent titter.

'Bathroom!' whispered Chloë and they scrambled off the bed to search for it. They found it behind a clapboard partition they had previously presumed to be the end of the room. The suite was yellow plastic and rather stained, the surrounding tiles a mustard colour bedecked every now and then with a marigold motif that proved to be stick-on; most were furling at the edges and Fraser could not resist peeling one off completely. He presented it to Chloë most solemnly and she accepted it graciously, taking it to her nose and finding that even the sticker smelt of lavender. She sneezed accordingly.

On their way out, they came across Mrs MacAdam twitching her curtains. She had changed into another tracksuit, this time violet and a little too small for her. Just as they were about to leave she called after them.

'Mr and Mrs, er?' she began with raised eyebrows.

'Buchanan?' Chloë suggested, not daring to catch Fraser's eye.

'Aye,' Mrs MacAdam said with detectable relief, 'Buchanan! You won't mind taking your shoes off and leaving them on the mat when you return?' Chloë and Fraser regarded their shoes automatically. 'The carpets!' Mrs MacAdam explained in an unnecessary whisper. 'I have slippers I can lend you,' she furthered.

'Slippers won't be necessary,' Fraser assured her, imagining something pink and feathery, 'and it will be no problem to take our shoes off.'

As Fraser and Chloë walked away, they heard tapping. They turned back and saw the net curtains twitching. More tapping. And then the net curtains were thrown over her head like a bride casting off her veil and Mrs MacAdam stood at the window waving expansively. Chloë and Fraser waved back while Fraser said 'Mrs Mac*Mad*-am!' between his teeth. They continued. And so did the tapping. If they did not stop, turn and wave every four strides or so, they were challenged by indignant rapping.

'You forgot your Scots!' reprimanded Fraser when they had turned the corner and he could feast his eyes on Murrayfield stadium and the hidden fantasies it promised him. 'You said "Buchanan" in English. That'll not do, girl! If you're to be my Mrs, you must talk like a Buchanan at all times!'

'Righty ho!' trilled Chloë, rolling her 'r' and sounding not unlike Mrs MacAdam.

Chloë adored Edinburgh and thanked Jocelyn often, out loud and to herself.

'If it wasn't for Jocelyn, I'd not be here,' she said to Fraser, both of them wearing moustaches from their cappuccinos. They raised their cups to her. 'I'd probably never have seen Edinburgh at Festival time.'

'And you'd have never set up with me,' Fraser said. Chloë marvelled at her good fortune.

A whole year. All for me. Treats and surprises. So much to discover, to search for, to find.

Fleetingly, Chloë even thought that if she had to live in a city, this was one she could tolerate quite happily.

But do you really want to live in a city?

Actually, no.

And what could you do here?

A job in student welfare at the University?

I hardly think so.

Perhaps just a simple waitressing job in New Town?

You were tired enough at the wedding at Braer. And

spilled enough, too. And mightn't the granite depress you after a while?

Might it?

The long, cold and wet winters?

Spoilsport!

Just now, though, the city in the summer is treating Chloë very well. And so, at the moment, is Fraser.

Their first two days have been spent with every possible moment filled and sleep a low priority. They've chased the events of the Festival all over the city to watch, listen and be thoroughly entertained. From increasingly inventive mime artists, to acrobats from the Ukraine (Fraser gawped throughout and was speechless for a good hour afterwards); from children's orchestras to octogenarian one-man-bands; from the obligatory Peruvian pan-pipe ensembles, to tap-dancing Australian scaffolders (Fraser needed to go out for fresh air); from a girl called Kate with a cello that seemed human, to a man called Louis who performed madrigals on a toilet. Some acts made them laugh until it hurt, others were so painful that their toes curled involuntarily. An opera in Russian made them weep but so too did the lamentable efforts of a small Belgian with a flute.

Their mouths watered as they swooned their way around a sculpture exhibition constructed entirely from chocolate, and their mouths dried at the gut-wrenching but mind-blowing readings by a Bosnian poet. Every street corner, every café, every little passageway leading to the Royal Mile, to Grassmarket, Lawnmarket, Fruitmarket, to the Gardens – every square inch of Edinburgh – had been appropriated as a stage, and the whole world, it seemed, was represented. Though the Mexican cabaret singer was consistently half a tone out, she sang with such aplomb and with such determination that Fraser and Chloë leapt to their feet in standing ovation with the entire audience. Her passion for her craft, and her pluck, epitomized the spirit of the Festival.

Best of all were the acts that came out after dark, after

midnight. Comedy that scraped the edge of bad taste, satire that made one wince, drag acts that made one blush. It was at Sharon Gri-la's show (a transvestite whose legs Chloë would quite happily have killed for) that Fraser fell hopelessly, utterly and selfishly in love. Or, rather, his version of it.

At first, Chloë thought someone was eyeing her up. Absorbed as she was in Sharon's rendition of 'How Much is that Doggy in the Window', she could detect, too, the heat of another's gaze. She located the eyes but saw that they burned past her and straight at Fraser, just catching her cheek on their way. She nudged Fraser.

'I know, I know,' he hissed, agitated, 'don't go on! Don't make a scene! Can't have him getting the wrong idea about me, about us!'

In the interval, Fraser asked Chloë to excuse him. Chloë sent him on his way with a wink and a grin. He was obviously anxious and excited.

He never returned.

Chloë's cheek remained cold throughout the second half, for there was nobody's gaze grazing the side of it. The seat next to her was empty and, she believed, conspicuously so. She felt slightly uncomfortable but persuaded herself that it was not because she was prudish, but because she felt a little left out. When the show had finished she made her way, as casually as possible, to the foyer. Neither Fraser nor his mustachioed suitor were to be seen. As the audience dispersed, Chloë hung around wearing a deceptively nonchalant half-smile until only she remained and her facial contortion was unnecessary. She felt uneasy. What was she to do? Wait? Search? She decided to wait on the steps until two-thirty but only a Burns-reciting drunk passed by before passing out on the corner. Chloë's stomach turned, her spirit was low.

Suddenly, she went quite cold and yelped involuntarily.

'He has the key!' she wailed to the night. 'Fraser has the key.'

Chloë had money for a cab but black taxis in Edinburgh are a rare and restricted commodity, and during the Festival they are gold-dust indeed. She did not feel like hunting down a minicab but felt even less like walking. She could hear drunken revelry, raucous singing, a row, and she did not want to come across any of the perpetrators. She hated the city, hated Edinburgh, she did not feel at home, at ease here. She wanted to cry but she hadn't for months so why do it now? The last time she had cried had been for Jocelyn; by comparison, to cry for oneself seemed profane.

Jocelyn, Jocelyn, why am I here? What should I do and where should I go? What should I be? And where? How soon? And will I know? And how will I know?

Jocelyn wouldn't be answering her tonight but, ten minutes later, she sent a black cab.

Chloë hovered outside Mrs MacAdam's, willing the lace curtains to twitch. All was still. And hideously quiet. It was half-three in the morning. With butterflies in her stomach and a hard, painful tightness to her throat, Chloë rapped on the door as merrily as she could. And waited. And rapped again. And rang. And waited. Lights came on and in the silence of the street she could make out the muffled thuds of stairs being descended. All went quiet. Chloë knew the spyhole was being consulted. A chain rattled.

'Mrs Buchanan!'

'No key,' said Chloë forlornly, her eyes cast away from Mrs MacAdam, her Scots accent forgotten, 'very sorry.' The door was opened and Chloë taken under Mrs MacAdam's arm. The landlady did not ask, she did not have to. She'd been a landlady long enough. She'd seen it before, been through it before. Men!

'Tiff?' she suggested at the top of the stairs. Chloë nodded. 'I'll go down and chain the door then!' she said in a kind, conspiratorial way. 'Off with you to beddy-byes!' Chloë could not even manage a meek smile but she twitched one corner of her lip and it seemed to satisfy Mrs MacAdam.

Mr and Mrs A, can you hear me? I can't do all this by myself.

You might have to, Chloë.

THIRTY-FOUR

Fraser did not show up for breakfast, Chloë did not feel like it. Mrs MacAdam made no comment. Chloë left the house and waved every four steps to the corner. She felt supremely irritated and desperately hurt, rather as she had with Gus, so she reacted in a similar way by taking herself off for a little excursion. The three late nights were taking their toll so she ventured no further than the Mound and the welcoming portal of the National Gallery. There, she ignored time and travelled the day away. She went to a peasant fête in the seventeenth century, gossiped with the court ladies in the eighteenth, and stood alongside a handsome duke from the nineteenth. One of the court ladies knew Mr and Mrs Andrews and instructed Chloë to send them her heartiest regards.

'He was quite a catch!' she said ambiguously behind her fan, glazed eyes peeping coyly over the top of it.

'I'm sure,' replied Chloë, adding that he seemed very happy and settled. The lady raised her eyebrow but said no more. Chloë decided not to dwell on it. Historically, it seemed that men, of whatever sexual persuasion, were weak-willed and far too fickle.

She lazed on the comfortable leather couches and

allowed the reverential quiet of the gallery to soothe her. The invigilators were discreet and she did not notice them. She spent much time in each room, alternately walking and then sitting, peering close at the works and observing them from afar. She was lost and quite happy. Their worlds felt safe and preferable. She didn't have to acknowledge the here and now. She needn't even have been in Scotland.

Oh, but if not Scotland, where then?

She perused another room of paintings.

The wonderful thing about art is that these painted characters seem so at ease with their lot within the canvas.

We all paint our own pictures. It is knowing when to lay down the brush and be content with the result.

When Chloë met William after lunch, in a small anteroom before the grandiose display of Victorian painting, her heart was captured for the whole afternoon.

He was beautiful in an unassuming way; almond eyes set either side of a plain nose; a sensible, sensitive mouth, and softly waved hair parted slightly off-centre. He seemed older than his twenty-eight years, a strong chin and smooth brow suggested a kind but guarded man, a gentle disposition tinged perhaps by a certain sadness. For a while, they just gazed at each other, not speaking, not really needing to. Chloë did not want to. William could not. William Stuart, Earl of Dunreath, had died in Naples in 1862 of scarlet fever but the marble of his commemorative bust and the incisiveness of the sculptor's touch brought him to life with little need for imagination or persuasion at all.

Chloë touched her fingertips along his cheek and let them journey down, over and under his jaw to his neck. Closing her eyes, she let her whole hand travel down his neck to the dip at its base and stroke there awhile. When she opened her eyes he was gazing at her intently. He did not have to ask. Chloë stood on her tiptoes and came even closer to him, her eyelids dropping slightly with the weight of emotion. She kissed him very slowly, softly, on the side of his mouth and then travelled to the centre of it with her tongue tip. Slightly salty. She pressed her lips full against his, first cupping his lower lip, then his upper. Marble, it seemed, was far more luxurious than skin, and just as smooth and warm.

Encroaching footsteps prevented Chloë from lingering and brought her back to the present. William now stared beyond her and way past the young gallery guard who had sat down quietly. And though Chloë stood directly in front of him and fought hard against blinking, William's eyes, which appeared to have seen so much, now saw nothing. Chloë thought how Brett's stare had often been thoroughly stony, yet William's eyes, though stone, had just penetrated her more deeply than those of any other man. She could not bear the injustice that the centuries kept them apart, that William had died so young, that the presence of the young invigilator now prevented one final, vital kiss. She left the room with a soft, light step and did not turn to look back. In the gallery shop there was a postcard of William Stuart, Earl of Dunreath. But it was not him at all, merely a photograph of his marble portrait bust.

'Chloë! Oh, my sweet, sweet girl!'

Fraser was pelting along Princes Street towards her. For some reason, she turned to check that she was the Chloë of his attentions. A daft half of her hoped it might be otherwise, for he was still hollering, running, getting closer and causing much attention.

'Chloë!' He was quite breathless and wore a moustache of tiny beads of sweat. 'Chloë!' he panted, dropping his hands on his knees and allowing his back to heave until it started to steady. 'Chloë!' he murmured, scouring her face and twitching his brow in as imploring a way as possible. Gently, he put his hands on her shoulders and sought her eyes. Even when he had them, she refused to unclench her pursed lips. 'Chloë!' he whimpered in a dejected, small voice, eyes cast down, shuffling slightly.

'Where on earth are your shoes?' Chloë asked. 'Why are you in your socks?'

She continued to walk and he followed a respectful step behind her, jigging and skipping to avoid the footfalls of the passers-by and the noxious deposits of their dogs. Initially, Fraser babbled an effusive and long-winded apology omitting any true explanation. Soon, though, he fell silent; relieved and grateful that Chloë had neither made a scene nor reprimanded him publicly. The fact that she was walking his way, or at least tolerating his accompanying her, was good news. A very good sign. Good luck.

As they walked beyond the hub of shoppers, Chloë kept up her pace and her silence, Fraser trotting at her heels compliantly.

'Shoes?' she asked eventually over her shoulder. 'Socks?'

'Och, Chloë!' Fraser cried earnestly, taking her elbow and giving it a sharp tug to make her stop. She did so reluctantly, still refusing to look at him. 'MacWallader, will you not just hear me?' She cocked her head and regarded him through slanted eyes, raising an eyebrow to suggest he commence what had better be a convincing soliloquy.

'My sweet girl, I've been looking all over for you. I did wrong – majorly – and I know it and I feel wretched. I feel wretched because an apology is not enough, but more I feel wretched because I know I've hurt you. I cannot quantify the value of your friendship. I realize now that I need it far more than I thought I needed the passion last night. Tell me I can still have it? Earn it back?'

'Why the socks?' Chloë repeated because, though she had easily forgiven him, as was her wont, she also did not want him to know that just yet.

'I returned this morning – late morning. With *him*. We were in the bedroom. Mrs MacMad knocked and entered.'

'Oh, God!' Chloë gasped horrified, a gamut of lewd images cavorting across her mind's eye.

'No!' Fraser exclaimed. 'We were not – well, we were just talking. On the bed. Clothed – but on the bed. Mrs MacMad said, "Mrs Buchanan has gone out." And then *he* said, "you told me *I* was Mrs Buchanan!" Really camping it up, he was. The tart. Anyway, we both started laughing uncontrollably – exacerbated by illegal substances, I'm ashamed to add. So she threw us out. I did not have time to collect my shoes which were, of course, by the front door. I've been pacing the streets ever since. Look, my toe! Look at the time, it's nearly six.'

'And where, might I ask, is *he*?' asked Chloë so she could bite back a smile. Fraser, however, saw it. He put his arm gently around her shoulder and touched her ear lobe with the tip of his nose.

'There's only one Mrs Buchanan,' he said fondly. '*He* was an aberration. A*na*thema! Anath-a-my-mistakes! I thought it was love last night. But found it only to be lust – and limited – this morning. Surprise bloody surprise. And he? Where's he? *He* was so scared of Mrs MacMad that he practically shat his troos! Certainly, he was last seen scampering down the street in a very strange way! The poof!'

Chloë laughed a little and then fixed Fraser an uncompromising and searching stare.

'You hurt me, you did.'

'I know,' he nodded gravely.

'You're the first person whom I've actually really cared for who has done so.'

'I am?' he said quietly.

'You are,' Chloë confirmed, looking away and then looking at him, 'and it hurt.'

Fraser looked at Chloë's shoes and then up at her face. Pale, she looked tired and pale and he hated himself. She looked as fragile as porcelain, certainly she was as precious as it. He sighed, touched her cheek and slipped his hand down to cup the back of her neck. He drew her face towards his and placed his forehead against hers. One of her ringlets tickled his nose. He ignored it.

'I'm sorry,' he said, 'MacWallader.'

'Please don't do it again.'
'Oh, I won't.'

Chloë returned to Mrs MacAdam's while Fraser hid around the corner, revving the engine and giggling to himself.

'Hello, my deary deary dear!' Mrs MacAdam chirped from the midst of maroon velour.

'Mr Buchanan?' asked Chloë, batting her eyelashes. She watched Mrs MacAdam falter but pretended not to notice. Mrs MacAdam shrugged her shoulders and ushered her to the plump settee and the offer of the mintless humbugs. They sucked in silence, Mrs MacAdam's dilemma almost deafening. Chloë crunched her sweet first.

'I'd better pack,' she said in English before clearing her voice and infusing her Scottish lilt, 'take everything with me. I'll not be going home. I'll go to my mother's in Aberdeen. Should he return, please tell him nothing.'

Mrs MacAdam pulled her thumb and finger across an imaginary zip over her lips. Chloë packed and sneezed.

'How much do I owe you?' she asked Mrs MacAdam. Knowing her penchant for deposits, Chloë was most surprised when Mrs MacAdam gave the air a quick wave and mouthed 'He'll pay'. Chloë mouthed back 'You sure?' 'Oh aye!' moved Mrs MacAdam's mouth. Chloë gave her a smile which she hoped was meek and not guilty and offered her hand for a firm, farewell shake. On their way to the front door, the women stopped and regarded Fraser's shoes for a long moment. Finally, Chloë turned her head away from them and walked past. Neither spoke; both had their reasons.

'Goodbye, and thank you,' Chloë said to Mrs MacAdam from the doorstep.

'Don't you worry about waving, Mrs Buchanan,' said Mrs MacAdam, 'your hands are full and you've enough on your plate.'

'Shoes?' Fraser enquired.

'Heavans!' Chloë exclaimed, wide-eyed and winsome. 'I quite forgot. Silly, silly me!'

That night, Mrs MacAdam stripped the bed in the Gold Room. The next morning, she burned the sheets. A week later, she put Fraser's shoes on the bonfire and burned them too.

THIRTY-FIVE

By mid-September, Chloë was convinced that Scotland was at its most beautiful. The midges had gone, and so had most of the tourists. The streams and waterfalls remained energetic and the hills sighed with colour. The heather shimmered purple and brown, the bracken shone auburn and russet and so did Chloë. The days for the most part were dry and, though still long, they were now tinged by a breeze that was essentially gentle but sang of the proximity of autumn. Buzzards wheeled lazily in the afternoons while red deer welcomed the camouflage of autumn and to spy one was a gift indeed. Most treasured, though, were the eagles. Irrationally, Chloë would often pray that a distant buzzard hugging the hills or skimming the sky just might be an eagle. 'You'll know when it's an eagle,' Fraser assured her nodding sagely. 'You'll not doubt it. You won't think to wonder if it might be a buzzard.'

She came across an eagle at close range one afternoon, sitting somewhat incongruously on a short telegraph post in the field behind the garden at Braer. It regarded her directly but remained quite still, its neck feathers lifted and lowered by the constant breeze. Chloë stopped and sat, hugging her knees, on a boulder. It was an eagle all right, not just because its size so dwarfed that of a buzzard, but because its poise and its stare contained such authority and presence, its estimation of its spectator undoubtedly supercilious. Chloë wondered whether to call for Fraser but decided to keep the moment all for herself. It was unlikely there would be another. She watched the bird but never saw it blink. Something caught its attention and it craned its neck, the feathers following the movement like chain-mail. Oh, to reach out and touch it, sneak a feather perhaps! The bird returned its uncompromising stare to Chloë and she found herself smiling warmly at it.

'Hullo, Mr Eagle!' she said softly, raising her hand in a meek salute. It continued to observe her as if she were very strange indeed and then, with a slight shift and a practice wing flap, it took to the air calling, calling. *Wee! Chlo-wee!*

Chloë scrambled to her feet and shielded her brow with her hands so she could follow the bird. It alighted on a distant branch. She raised her hand and waved expansively. The eagle remained motionless and it occurred to Chloë that, unless she had known where to look, she would never have noticed an eagle there at all. How many times had she missed one, she wondered. How often had they been watching her? What did they make of her? Was she recognized? Acknowledged? She waved again and was charmed and delighted that the eagle took to the air. The bird seemed to skirt the very edge of the sky and then suddenly he was amongst the clouds, circling and assessing and enjoying himself very much. Down he swooped and then soared again. Down he came and skimmed across the treetops fast. *Wee! Chlo-wee!* With a tilt of his wing-tip he commanded the wind to take him up again and, riding the thermals, he wheeled and hung and seemed to be flying for the sheer hell of it. And then he was gone. Chloë was not sure when she lost him but though she scoured the skies and prayed and pleaded, he was nowhere to be seen.

'I'd like to be an eagle,' she said to Fraser later over a humble supper of oatcakes and crumbly cheese.

'And I'd like to be a bus driver!' responded Fraser, pulling a face.

'No,' Chloë insisted, 'I'd like to be an eagle – or at least, like one. They seem to have such control and they seem to be so self-sufficient.' Fraser conceded defeat. Chloë continued, 'Eagles seem to have a consummate understanding of the purpose of their lives, don't you think? They do what they do so very well; they learn how to ride the thermals and how to use the wind to their advantage. They blend in with their surroundings and yet they add to them too.'

'Aye,' agreed Fraser earnestly.

'I guess that's what I crave,' said Chloë, a little forlornly, 'to really fit in somewhere, to feel so utterly at ease, in control and strong. That my surroundings should nourish me so.'

Fraser fell silent and dabbed at crumbs on his plate, eventually looking up at Chloë with dull, drawn eyes.

'September'll be gone afore long,' he said quietly. Chloë nodded. 'Could you be an eagle here, do you think?' he asked. She shrugged and tipped her head. 'Will you not stay a wee while longer, Chloë MacWallader? Build a nest?' Chloë did not respond. 'Just test out your wings some more before you fly on? Fly away?' Fraser implored.

Chloë smiled at him and stroked his cheek. 'I cannot start to build my nest until I've found the bough. It may be here, but I can't know that unless I've flown on – I'll never fly away, Fraser, never from you. I'm probably more of a homing pigeon than I'll ever be an eagle! But pigeon or raptor, I now know that I have to see just how far my wings can take me. They don't feel very strong at the moment, that I can tell you, but they do feel like they need a stretch, an airing. If I fly free, I can fly true. As yet, I've been neither high enough nor far enough.'

'When'll you go, my girl, lassie mine?'

'End of the month. October.'

Fraser scrunched his eyes tight. When he opened them, they were quite wet.

I feel so loved, Chloë marvelled to herself later, *for the first time perhaps, someone actually needs me. Cares if I go. Wants me to stay. Maybe I ought to, for a little while longer.*

The feeling of well-being, of strength, which she experienced on a solitary walk through the dew to the waterfall the next morning, decided Chloë that she would journey on at the end of the month. Not because she had been told to. She found she actually wanted to.

Jocelyn would be proud.

Yes, she would indeed. So are we. And you should be too, Cadwallader. No advice sought from Jasper and Peregrine. Didn't even consult the Andrews. Fait accompli.

Fate.

I can't wait.

Fraser wanted to ensure that the remainder of Chloë's stay would be filled to the brim with quality time. He woke her at the first mention of dawn each morning and kept her with him until the cuckoo yawned its protest from the wooden clock face in the early hours. He dreaded her leaving, he abhorred the idea of Braer without her. Of being without her. On his own. He did not want Chloë to go to England. It was far away. It was England. He wondered whether to pretend that he did not know of an envelope marked 'Chloë: England'; that the one so titled in the bureau drawer wasn't for her after all but for someone else. Didn't she know, he had a *cousin* called Chloë. I mean a sister. Friend. No, a colleague. Ultimately, he did tell her of the envelope but she said she didn't want it just yet.

While walking alongside Loch Lomond one morning, an idea came to Chloë practically out of the blue.

'Fraser?' she started, slowing her pace and holding her head at an acute angle.

'MacWallader?' he responded, ruffling her hair.

'I think I have an idea,' she continued.

'Oh aye,' he said, 'you *think* so, do you? Either you do or you don't, surely?'

'Hush up and listen! You know Braer?'

'Aye, I think that'll be the house in which I live.'

'It has, what, six bedrooms?'

'Well, seven officially – the room with my windsurfing gear and the piano.'

'Even better.'

'Put it on the market, you mean?'

'Gracious no!' cried Chloë, stopping dead. She looked over the mirror surface of the water. No one was about. Something rippled the surface. A fly, perhaps. A buzzard could be heard but not seen. Ahead of them, the fingers of the glens dipped into the loch along its length. Was it the clarity of the water that brushed them blue and violet? Or was it the hues of the land, cloaked in bracken and smothered with heather, that spun colour and definition across the loch?

'Fraser?'

'MacWallader!'

'Look!'

'Goats?'

'Yes. Wild?'

'Oh aye! They may graze for free and it is forbidden to kill them. They kept Robert the Bruce warm while he hid in the cave – later Rob Roy's cave. Did you not know?'

'No! Really?'

'Oh aye – why shouldnae be?'

'Indeed – Robert the Bruce hey!'

'The Bruce, Chloë, him indeed.'

The fragrant scent of pine surrounded them. Ahead, Ben Lomond soared.

'Fraser?' Chloë started again.

'Yes, MacWallader, I be he.'

'Remember Edinburgh? Mrs MacAdam? The pink and the gold and the green? Shoes by the front door?'

'How,' bemoaned Fraser, performing a quick tap-dance, 'could I forget!'

'Braer!' declared Chloë before walking on ahead in silence but with purpose.

'Tell me if I'm being unreasonable,' Fraser started, 'but would it be at all possible for you to elaborate just a little so that I may get a drift, just an inkling, of what on earth it is you're driving at?'

Chloë twisted her nose and dug him hard in the ribs until he yelped with indignation. She chased him to the water's edge and rugby-tackled him to the soft ground. They let their laughter subside and their breath come back.

'Remember Mrs MacMad's abhorrence of your – er, deviant sexuality?' asked Chloë theatrically. Fraser regarded her slyly, knowing she meant no offence and yet still unable to grasp her allusion.

'Aye,' he said slowly. He watched Chloë's lips come together. 'You're going to say "Braer" again, aren't you?' he chided; Chloë nodded enthusiastically.

'Braer!' she declared.

'I thought so,' said Fraser despondently. 'You may as well say it again, for I'm no nearer understanding you!'

'Braer,' complied Chloë, 'turn Braer into a weekend retreat for nancy boys!'

Slowly, very slowly, Fraser's brow softened, his eyes spun shards of light and a smile of prodigious proportions criss-crossed his face. He pounced on Chloë and pinned her to the ground, spreading himself over her in the missionary position. He kissed her square on the lips. And again. And again. But soon he smiled so emphatically that he could not pucker his lips and his teeth grazed hers. Then he jumped up, pulled her to her feet and danced a perversion of the polka and the tango before steadying her and hugging her tight.

'You bloody genius girl!' he marvelled, and it sounded like 'guh-rrl' in his enthusiasm. She shrugged her shoulders and said it was just an idea. 'Just an idea!' cried Fraser.

'MacWallader, it's a veritable brainwave. It's the answer to my prayers and to my bank manager's probings!' He twirled her about again. 'Shall we go back and talk colour schemes?'

'Let's!' said Chloë, twirling around with her arms outstretched. The loch scumbled over a tumble of rocks, the secrets of Time its very own.

Fraser and Chloë scrutinized each room at Braer, sucking hard on pencils and filling reams of notebooks. With deference to Mrs MacAdam, they decided on colour themes for the rooms though they forsook gold, pink and green for Magenta Divine, Mellow Yellow, In the Navy (Fraser's room), Blush (Chloë's), Cream Dream, Indigo Jones and Calamity Brown. They spent a hectic day in Glasgow, choosing knick-knacks that looked more expensive than they were; buying paint, overalls and rollers; ordering beds and blinds, and swathes of muslin and calico to 'drape around'. They bought plain china and simple glasses in bulk and fought over whether cloth or paper napkins were more suitable. Chloë said, 'Cloth! Or I'll take my idea back and leave tomorrow!' Fraser obligingly bought forty gingham napkins and said his guests could always wear them as neckerchiefs if they so wished. They bounced their heads against a variety of pillows before plumping for polyester which were half the price of duck down and, the assistant assured them, fire retardant, allergy free and guaranteed to hold their shape.

'Furniture!' wailed Chloë as they sat in the garden on their return, exchanging the fumes of the city for the fresh, sweet air of Drumfyn. 'You can't have a room with only a bed!' Fraser brushed her worries away and took her up into the attic.

'Should I have a full house,' he explained, 'I'll have to sleep up here. To do that, I must clear it first. And, as you can plainly see, there's enough furniture lying around up here to bedeck – well, a guest house!'

The attic became their den, their snug, and they clambered up there at all times of the day and night, sometimes with coffee, sometimes with whisky, once with a bumper bag of marshmallows. They came across Fraser's English essays book and found much hilarity in reading the stories out loud. They found a box of Lego and Stickle-Bricks and whiled away a whole day absorbed in their recreation of the Manhattan skyline. They snuggled up on a brown, corduroy beanbag, spoke of the past and postulated on the future.

'Well, I'm sorted, I'm going to be a landlady,' Fraser declared, finding a box of kitchen utensils and placing a sieve on his head, 'but what about you, Chloë? What'll you be if you'll not be my cherished chambermaid?'

'At the mo', I really have no idea,' Chloë replied earnestly, checking Fraser's knee-jerk reflex with a rolling-pin, 'but I *will* know. And you'll be the first I tell.'

'Promise?'

'Cross my heart.'

In between times spent Up the Attic, the pair were embroiled in a decorating frenzy. But, as the Blush and In the Navy rooms were already done, it was not too difficult a task to see to the remaining five.

'Especially,' qualified Fraser through a mask of Creamy Dreamy freckles, 'as paint effects and the "distressed" look are so in vogue!'

'Just as long as the *effect* of the marbling in Magenta Divine does not cause migraines – and guests in Indigo Jones do not find it *distressingly* cobbled together!'

They assaulted the walls and each other with paint-sodden rags and rollers, brushes and sponges and a floor mop that created a wonderful effect. The bride's underwear, which Chloë had continued to guard much to Fraser's amusement, proved excellent for more detailed mottling around window frames. Doused with Mellow Yellow warpaint, Chloë went to the post office to buy up all the onions that Molly had. Molly eyed her suspiciously, her arms locked around her bosom.

'Onions!' she muttered in I-know-what-you're-doing undertones.

'Yes,' said Chloë openly, 'we're decorating the house and if you keep sliced onions around, they absorb the fumes of the paint.'

'Oh aye,' said Molly not believing a word, 'we'll say nothing about *para-gliding* then.'

Chloë was puzzled. The old woman continued, 'Come girl! That politician! Trussing himself up and putting an onion in his mouth for a – For Indecent Personal Pleasure!' she spat. 'Was he not a para-glider?'

Chloë tried not to laugh.

'Pa-ra-phil-ia,' she said very slowly in a calm voice, 'and it was oranges, not onions!'

Molly regarded her sternly as if to say, well, did they not both begin with 'p' and surely that was the point?

'Actually,' continued Chloë slyly, 'that reminds me, Fraser *did* want oranges, didn't he. I'll take a dozen. And a couple of metres of that cord.'

On Chloë's last night, Fraser presented her with the envelope marked 'England'. They regarded it together, handed it back and forth but said nothing and left it unopened, propped against the ketchup bottle while they had their last supper.

'Will you make coffee?' Fraser asked her. 'In a saucepan, like on your first day?'

Of course she would. Should they melt a tub of ice-cream too? Absolutely. Abso-bloody-lutely gor-jesus! The combination was wonderful; the ice-cream adding symbolic and necessary sweetness to the evening, the coffee strong enough to tide them through to the early hours.

'Fraser?'

'MacWallader Fair?'

'Your dad,' Chloë faltered. Fraser tipped his head and regarded her. A question had been welling within her for days, weeks even, and now it burned lest it should go unanswered before she left. And yet she was suddenly in a dilemma whether to ask at all, and how to phrase it.

'MacDoubleYou – what is it? My da, you were saying.'

'Your da,' Chloë repeated distractedly. 'Jocelyn?' she furthered. 'Were they –?' she wondered only half aloud. 'Did they –?'

Fraser laughed softly through his nose and shook his head, smiling and sorrowful simultaneously.

'No, Chlo,' he said with audible regret, 'they never did. My da let that part of his heart slip into the grave with Mam. And I believe Jocelyn's heart was dedicated elsewhere too. I canna be sure. I never did ask. Perhaps that's why they were so close. They both appeared resolute in their fidelity.'

'And why she felt so safe here,' said Chloë, 'so at home.'

Chloë was somewhat sad. She'd half envisaged Fraser senior being the suitor of Jocelyn to whom Gus had lost. She'd half hoped he might have been, because Fraser senior must have been at least as lovely as his son. And Jocelyn, of course, was incomparable. And it would have tied her closer to Fraser, made him almost a real brother.

'My da remained in love with Mam till his dying day.'

Chloë gave a resigned sigh after a few minutes' silence and respect. 'It's time,' she said, regarding her knees sternly as the cuckoo protested that it was three in the morning. Fraser placed the envelope marked 'England' on a cushion, knelt at Chloë's side and presented it to her ceremoniously. They examined the envelope in turn and, instinctively, took it to their noses. No Mitsuko. No reason not to open it. No, please don't go. I have to. You can come and stay. I'll visit. Me too. I'll write. Don't phone. I'll write too.

'Don't open it!' shrieked Fraser as Chloë took her thumb to the corner of the envelope. 'Say it says "Birmingham"! Or "Croydon"! Then you'll not go, Chlo, and yet you *must* – wherever it might take you. Otherwise it'll be like breaking the chain, a circle left incomplete, the last page of a book missing.' He touched her chin and tilted his head, big eyes soft and sad, 'An unfinished symphony,' he declared, patting Chloë's knee bravely but casting his eyes away.

As Chloë tucked down in Blush for her last night, or what was left of it, she reached for her rucksack which was on the chair at the foot of the bed, the flowers moved temporarily to the window-sill. She patted it fondly, stroked the straps and laid her hand firmly against its side. To Chloë, it was more animate than its red canvas exterior might suggest; though it was she who carried it, did it not contain and transport so much of her too?

'Here we go,' she whispered, 'last stop.' The rucksack, however, never answered her. Chloë sat back on the bed and regarded it with a nod and smile. She reached over to the bedside table and retrieved the envelope marked 'England', still unopened. She lodged it behind the straps of the rucksack and then slipped down into the bed, pulling the sheets up to her chin. But she did not switch off the light. She listened hard to the silence and closed her eyes to absorb it for posterity. The early hours in Scotland, she decided, were wholly unique and as unlike those in Ireland as the Welsh nights had been. What were English nights like? Could she remember? Well, she'd find out soon enough. Did Islington count? Not any more.

She was indeed ready to leave Scotland though she loved it so. She must complete the circle, add the last link to the chain, finish the book, though she debated whether her sojourn could be defined a symphony in need of completion.

'I'd settle for a small tune,' she said quietly, 'a ditty. Something plain and simple.'

Around the chair hung her jacket; Jocelyn's brooch glinting softly in the light squeezing in through the crack in the Madras curtains. There on the chair was her rucksack. Behind the straps, the envelope marked 'England'.

'Open it, child!'

'Mr A, I'm sleepy. It can wait.'

'Tush, do you imagine we're not *burning* to know where we might be going!'

'So you want me to open it now? Right now? This minute?'

'Well, how will you know which train to board? Which direction to head? Where on earth to go? Of course open it right now, this minute!'

Chloë took the envelope under the bed covers because paper tearing seemed twice as loud in the small hours.

'Oh! Before I forget, I met some friends of yours – acquaintances – at the gallery in Edinburgh.'

'Indeed?'

'Mrs A,' said Chloë with a wink, 'they say he was quite a catch!'

'I think, my dear,' said Mrs Andrews, drawing back her shoulders, smoothing her skirts primly and sidling away from her husband ever so slightly, 'they rather said "cad".'

Chloë, however, was scrutinizing the fourth map torn, of course, from the same source as the others. This last letter, however, she decided to leave for the long train journey tomorrow.

THIRTY-SIX

Chloë my girl,

Bay View Guest House
St Ives
Cornwall

Call them first to confirm the reservation.

See you there!

Jocelyn

THIRTY-SEVEN

The room is small and narrow. A riot of pink flowers papers the walls up to the picture rail before rampaging over the ceiling, with a brief interlude for a cornice the colour of strawberry ice-cream. The curtains are also floral and very pink, but of a different hue and pattern to the wallpaper. The lampshades and bedlinen, in shades of anaemic raspberry and limp fuchsia, are strewn with flowers too. There is a tapestry picture of a bouquet but it is crooked. A china posy, whose petals are for the most part chipped, teeters on the window-sill. The carpet is swirled with eddies of cerise, blotches of salmon and streaks of a colour close to raw bacon. Pink, pink, to make the boys *wince*!

The room is filled, gorged, with flowers yet none are real or even remotely like true flora. Some have uniform, rounded petals, but are certainly not impatiens; others have petals perfect for love-me-love-me-not plucking, but are definitely not daisies; some look vaguely like pansies but oversize thorns curtail the illusion. Most inappropriate, most unbecoming. The overall impression of the room neither evokes summer, nor the countryside, nor even an overstocked florist. Its enduring effect, rather, is to bestow on its inhabitant a headache of ponderous proportions.

Pink, pink. Chloë shuts her eyes tight against the barrage and the confusion and the botanical inaccuracies of her surroundings. Her heavy head, aching from a long journey and further pained by these pretend posies and all this pinkness, rests gingerly against a bedstead of padded velvet the colour of well-chewed bubble gum. She is fully clothed and though her brown jeans and bottle-green jumper clash with the room, she is too tired to rectify it, too tired to change. And anyway, she does not own one piece of clothing that is remotely pink. ('Pink,' Jocelyn had warned her at a very young age, 'would be the ultimate insult to your intelligence – and to your hair!')

Chloë lies stiffly on the bed, with hands loosely clasped beneath her breasts; she is very pale and her hair, a little lank and damson dark today, accentuates her wanness. She could very well be an alabaster effigy in a chantry chapel of some lesser cathedral, save for her chunky, lace-up boots which tap and twitch every now and then.

It had been a long, tiring journey to the pink room, traversing England on an intrepid train called the *Cornish Scot*. Knowing both races to be fiercely patriotic, Chloë denounced the name a contradiction in terms. Surely, you were either Scottish or Cornish; Land's End or John O' Groat's, one extreme or the other, north or south, top of the land or base of it – and she should know, she was stuck on a train bumbling along its length. As the train moseyed from Lancaster to Crewe, she rued her own lack of identity.

Could I not be Scottish, with my red hair and passable accent?

Sorry Chloë, you've had the misfortune not to be born one.

Should I search for the place first? And then something to do. Or should I find my métier *– and then a suitable location to practise it?*

Can't tell you that.

With the Midlands uninspiringly upon her and the train glued to the track two minutes out of Birmingham New Street, she knew she had no desire to be a Brummy. Cheltenham Spa, however, looked rather promising; she could teach young ladies. Taunton even more so; she could set up a cider works. By Newton Abbot she was asleep; awake with a cricked neck at Bodmin and feeling quite beastly. Her legs desperately needed a stretch but her queasiness forced her to stay as still as possible. She fixed her gaze out of the window without really observing the landscape, her temple juddering against the pane every now and then. Raining. Just great.

Chloë opens her left eye but the flowers appear to be closing in on her so she shuts them out again. Fraser appears in her mind's eye, his open, boyish face creased into the smile which wrinkles his nose and makes his eyes water. So clear. So lovely. Brother mine. He's slipping, he's fading fast and if Chloë tries to force him to stay his face changes into that of a total stranger.

Who are you? Where am I? Jasper! Peregrine!

They sashay across and decorate the blank screen on the inside of her eyelids. They say it's time to go, see you later, write soon. Clasping each other theatrically, they waltz out of sight. Good-night, ladies, good-night. Sweet ladies, good-night, good-night!

Come back!

Chloë unbuckles her eyelashes enough to enable the tears caught in the corners to ease and ooze out. A pink blur confronts and nauseates her. She returns to the dark purple safety of shut eye and waits for company. No one comes. She calls for Carl but he is so long ago, now too far away; a different country then, a different country now. She cannot recall the colour of his eyes and is thus denied the armature around which she might have constructed a reasonable likeness. It dawns on her that she most probably will never see him again, certainly not in the flesh and maybe not in her mind's eye either. She will never forget him though, she remembers all about him. Remembers him well.

She wonders whether to summon Ronan instead. Though his startling eyes are certainly unforgettable, ice-piercing icy blue, Chloë finds that she does not wish to grant them too much space in her memory. She files Ronan away from the forefront, to a mental drawer labelled 'Antrim: Summer'.

'A man in each season,' she says aloud, the pastel profusion bedecking the ceiling causing her eyes to spiral involuntarily, 'and yet no man for all seasons.' She sits up and regards her hands as they are easier to contemplate than the shortcomings of her romantic history so far. She takes her fingers to her nose and finds they smell faintly of toast, which is strange as she has not eaten toast. A packet of crisps and an apple, while she read a report in the paper proclaiming that the former contains more vitamin C than the latter. Nothing, then, since this meagre snack on the platform at St Erth waiting for the local shuttle to take her to St Ives. The Bay View Guest House, St Ives. She shuffles over to the window and pushes it open. It is almost dark but she knows anyway that she would not be able to see the sea, and the only bay in view is this bay window which faces the road and a petrol station. She curses and throws her blackest look around the room.

'Jocelyn said "See you there",' she growls under her breath. 'But in a room with a monopoly on pink kitsch? I hardly think so!' Angry tears, hot and oily, sting her cheeks. 'I don't understand!'

She will leave tomorrow. Just leave. Jocelyn has been dead for almost a year and, though she is remembered often and fondly, she did *not* appear in Wales, or in Ireland. She did not visit Chloë in her supposedly beloved Scotland, so surely she is even less likely to surface here. Too artificial, far too pink.

The next morning, Chloë gathered her jacket and her wits about her and left the room with a spiteful smirk at the ceramic sign on the door which was decorated with small flowers pretending to be forget-me-nots and inscribed 'The Pink Parlour'. She snatched the key from the lock. Jocelyn would not be seen dead in a pink parlour. Certainly she would not be resurrecting herself in one.

The pleasant autumn morning and the gifts of St Ives soon soothed her sulk and she browsed the cobbled streets and dipped into craft shops. As a perverse protest at their interior decorating, Chloë had churlishly refused the guest house's breakfast and took instead a full cream tea at elevenses time at a café with a bona fide bay view. A stroll along the length of Carbis Bay, all but deserted, truly unwound her and the brisk breeze fortified her. She skimmed stones for a while and turned her face full on to the sun's gentle autumnal embrace. She found herself smiling without effort. What a beach! Wasn't Cornwall meant to be overcrowded? Commercialized and spoilt? Perhaps she would not leave today, maybe not even tomorrow, perhaps she'd be a tourist for a week or two. Maybe hire a bicycle and visit tin mines, visit the Tate; stay long enough and do just enough to warrant postcards to Wales and Ireland, to Scotland and London. Whatever would they think of her otherwise!

Though Chloë thought it odd that Jocelyn should send her to such a place as the Bay View Guest House, she thought it far stranger that no one there seemed to know her godmother. Jocelyn had sent a letter and a cheque some eighteen months before, the landlord explained before apologizing that rising costs and the council tax meant the cheque would now only stretch to seven days and not the ten Jocelyn had requested. This suited Chloë, who prophesied all that pink turning her slightly mad if she stayed more than a week anyway.

Then what? she wondered as she filled her pockets with pebbles perfect for skimming. As she skimmed in earnest to beat her previous score of five, she wondered why Jocelyn had sent her to a place to which she seemingly had no connection, and why for only ten days? She scanned the horizon and scoured her memory but could find no instance of Jocelyn talking about Cornwall and could remember no friends of hers who were Cornish. Gin Trap, Gus, Fraser senior – it was obvious why Chloë had been sent to them. But Cornwall? The Bay View Guest House? It was a mystery and, as Chloë crouched at the water's edge and drew her fingertips across the spume, she realized she could not possibly leave until she had made sense of it. And even if and when she solved it, she still could not leave until she knew to where it was she intended to go. Gwent, Antrim and Drumfyn were vivid in her mind's eye and strongly placed in her heart. They were there for her. Yet none beckoned.

'You'd need to be awfully rugged to live in the lie of the Black Hill,' Jasper had said on a rare phone call from Chloë towards the end of her stay in Scotland. 'I shudder at the consequences of a life of pitchforks and bridles and interminable winters on your slender hands and fair complexion.'

'And I rather think you're too foreign to ever feel at home amongst the shamrocks,' connived Peregrine, on another receiver. Their voices spoke of desperately serious expressions.

'Scotland?' she asked tentatively. She could practically hear them shaking their heads.

'You're English,' rued Jasper in a whisper, 'Ing-*lish*!'

'Sassenach!' growled Peregrine. 'The Scots would never have you!'

'Or if they did,' warned Jasper, terror edging his words and no doubt streaming across his face, 'it would be with haggis and Irn Bru for their tea!'

Chloë's demeanour was utterly restored by a lazy day spent within the call of the ocean; a sense of calm and capability returning with the evening tide. Where sky met sea was hazed by the smudge of the slumbering sun and a whisper of its fading warmth kissed Chloë's face with a promise to return. Well-being coursed through her veins; strengthening trust in Jocelyn's reasons, and gratitude for her generosity, were reinstated. Chloë was traversing Jocelyn's kingdom and she knew that something far greater than another's sovereignty united it. She'd find out what. When Jocelyn was ready for her to. Maybe Jocelyn *was* here, perhaps she just had to be found.

When Chloë returned to the guest house, the Pink Parlour was no longer an affront, just twee and not really to her taste. After a relaxing bath (although it was some trek to the end of the corridor and up to the next landing), she lounged on the bed, swaddled by a vast towel that was luxurious if thoroughly pink. Only Mr and Mrs Andrews could witness how violently her hair clashed with it, but they hardly looked refined themselves, lodged as they were against the frame of the floral tapestry.

THIRTY-EIGHT

It was all very well deciding to allow herself a fortnight as a tourist, but Chloë gave up after a week. Her prepaid time at the Bay View Guest House was finished and the bottom of Jocelyn's purse was now visible. Though she enjoyed exploring and visiting and treating herself to cream teas, she also knew full well that she wanted to feel useful. Admittedly, she'd been worked to the bone by Gus but had made up for it with a relatively leisurely stay with Fraser. Though still unsure of the reason for Cornwall, Chloë could now afford neither the time nor the money just waiting for its purpose to transpire. She contemplated how she had been gainfully employed in Wales, in Ireland, in Scotland too but only because the people there had been instructed to oversee her welfare. On pain of death, no less; for who could refuse a dying woman's behest? In all three countries and the people therein, the bond with Jocelyn had been a unifying factor; reciprocal and fundamental. Cornwall, however, seemed to have no link to Jocelyn. Had she ever even been here? Did she not know anyone?

Did she just think I'd need a holiday?

And now I've had one, what on earth am I going to do?

Get up, get a grip and get a job?

Mr and Mrs Andrews expounded the merits of paid labour, saying her finances and her spirit would both benefit. It came as some surprise to Chloë that she landed a job effortlessly, and was even able to pick and choose. There was one going in Penzance, in a ceramics gallery owned by a woman called something-or-other Saxby, but the bustle of the town and the somewhat supercilious attitude of the gallery's proprietor made waitressing at a wholefood café with friendly staff and a sea view in St Ives far more attractive. She stayed on an extra week at the Bay View Guest House and though they offered her a larger room for the duration, she assured them she was quite settled in the Pink Parlour. They gave her a discounted rate and little extras like sandwiches or cocoa late at night; seeming to care for her welfare, despite not knowing Jocelyn. The reduced rate still consumed too large a percentage of her salary but Chloë would never have thought how to counter that, had the landlord not presented an idea, quite literally, on a plate.

'Why not rent a room, dear?' he said, with a burr to his words as delicious as the toast he proffered. 'Plenty going at this time of year. A nice *peed a dare* for you near the sea!'

'Really?' Chloë exclaimed, quite astonished. 'Do you think I should?'

'Well,' the man said, 'it's not for me to say, dear. I can't make up your mind now, can I. But it would seem more economical, wouldn't it? If you're deciding to stay, that is.'

Chloë pondered over such a huge notion while her toast went quite cold. The landlord replaced it with a fresh batch and a copy of the previous week's local paper which he had fished out of the kindling pile, not that Chloë needed to know or would have minded. With only a little snatch absent-mindedly eaten from two slices of toast, Chloë pored over the paper with the landlord.

'I'll just have a little look,' she said, circling a few details with a red pen and searching her landlord's face for approval, 'just to see. I don't need to take anything immediately. I'll just see what's around. Then make a decision.'

'You do that, my dear,' he burred, pointing to an interesting-looking notice that she had overlooked.

Chloë liked the first place she visited enough to write a cheque for a month's rent without thinking twice. Without really thinking at all.

If I had've, I'd never've.

You're telling us!

She felt quite exhilarated on walking back to the Bay View.

'It's lovely and I can afford it!' she justified to the landlord, suddenly a little worried about her haste. That he gave her his best wishes with a further reduction from her bill, decided Chloë that she had done the right thing.

'I've found us a nice place to live,' she announced to the Andrews.

'You speak for yourself,' Mr Andrews countered, utterly sick of the Pink Parlour. He took his wife's arm and they promenaded back to their own lovely home while Chloë packed and praised her nous and nerve to the hilt.

The bedsit was one large, odd-shaped room spanning the top floor of a pretty terrace house above Porthmeor beach, near the artists' studios at Downalong. The ceilings were slanted and a stripped pine floor ran throughout. The furniture was sparse but nice; an old iron bed, a sofa that was still plump despite the upholstery having seen better days, a cheap cane chair and two matching bedside cabinets, an old chest of drawers with hints and glints of the layers of paint it had worn in its lifetime. The galley kitchen was minute but functional and the drawers contained a sensible selection of well-worn utensils. Mrs Stokes, the landlady, was plump and rosy and had cheeks like little crab apples. She let Chloë be, but was always around to share company and her incomparable baking.

She had known Barbara Hepworth and happily regaled Chloë with unashamedly embellished tales of the artists and goings-on in St Ives in the 1950s. But she did not know Jocelyn. Still Chloë could find no one who did, though she made sure to mention her name often.

A second-hand bicycle with more gears than Chloë could ever need, and bought against her next week's wages, completed her picture. Shift work kept her time varied; providing free days for exploring while occupying evenings she would otherwise have spent alone. And she *is* on her own, with no point of contact, yet she is neither lonely nor being conscientiously brave.

The temperate climate helped, as did the pleasing landscape, alternately picturesque and stark; lush pasture suddenly becoming moorland, the shafts of the old tin mines punctuating the landscape as aesthetically as the standing stones, the twisted thorns. Contrast: like the way that artists and potters coexisted quite happily alongside the old fishermen and the plump ladies keeping safe the institution of cream teas; that the people were unsurprised by her, that they neither probed nor ignored, allowed her to feel safe and, with that, settled. She liked the spiky mess of the gorse, the thatches of scurvy grass, just as much as the late batches of pale toadflax; clusters of pretty lilac flowers like plump lips imploring her to stop and stoop. 'Pig's Chops!' she could hear Jocelyn declare in awe though still she cannot find hint of her anywhere.

Though Chloë feels that she is well on the way to being accepted, that she is no longer side-glanced as a tourist, that there could be the making of a good friendship with Jane at the café, she just needs to ascertain whether she accepts Cornwall. Certainly, she no longer feels a tourist. But does Cornwall make her feel at home? Is there enough here for her?

Where can I slot in?

Could she become part of its fabric, a stitch that

contributes to the strength of the whole but has an autonomous role as well?

Would I want that?

Need we answer!

But where?

Here?

Not sure.

* * *

William loved to witness autumn give way to the first signs of winter. All around him, nature shut shop for the next season. The bracken turned, and then turned again from colour to texture; the gorse became brittle and the grass pale. Here and there, tormentil scurried over the ground in a late flourish of tiny, brave yellow flowers. The summer-soft breeze, however, was churned into hurling, buffeting blasts while the sea carried away the last of its warm waters and blueness in exchange for a darker sea; heavier somehow, slate cold throughout. You could walk some distance from its edge but still have your breath caught and captured momentarily by a maverick gust. You could stand high on a cliff, lick your lips and taste salt.

Barbara grew her beard long and traded her summer sleekness for a more appropriate coat, coarser and slightly greasy. She took to spending long periods standing with her back to the wind while it splayed a parting in her coat and played it into whorls. Her bell was put away, as was William's striped deck-chair. The portable gas heater was brought out and put in the studio, its centre section taking the chill off early October, its full force required by the end of the month.

The acquisition of a motor car, however, denied William his customary excuse to hibernate and, to Mac's unspoken relief, there was now no reason not to remain mobile. His weekly visits to Mac continued and obliged William to carry on shaving. The previous winter, the more Morwenna had nagged, the longer he had left it and he had derived a perverse satisfaction from the allusion to Barbara as well as a certain relief that he was deemed and denounced unkissable. To shave clean for the trip to London last year had been almost as burdensome as the excursion itself and, in protest, he had remained defiantly bristled over Christmas. Now, as he worked on a series of pitchers with plump bodies and furling lips for this year's display at the South Bank, he laughed at the irony that he was alone at last, yet as smooth as a baby's bottom.

Mac, though he thought William's face and bone structure far too fine to hide behind hair, would have preferred him to be bearded but not alone. The ghastly Saxby woman was gone and William's countenance was restored; surely it was time now.

'Time for *what*?' William teased.

'To move on,' Mac said cautiously.

'And go where?' feigned William.

'Where you will let people come to you,' replied Mac, punching William's heart with a force that vanquished ambiguity. William laughed loud and sharp, shook his head and regarded the old man.

'I'm a *pot*ter,' he explained as if to a child.

'Precisely!' Mac proclaimed. 'You live in clay on a cliff with a goat.'

'And,' qualified William, 'I am very happy with it!'

'But,' cautioned Mac, holding his index finger aloft before pointing it directly at William and poking him on the biceps, 'for how long?'

'For the foreseeable future,' William proclaimed sternly, smacking his knees and trying to close the conversation. 'And if, Mac, I find I'm lonesome, I'll find me a wife and breed me a chile!'

His Texan accent served only to rile Mac who responded with the thickest of Cornish burrs.

'And who'll have the cliffclay manan gohte?

William paused.

'Heidi?' he asked while his smile spread. Mac hurled a cushion at him.

'Just keep your peepers open,' he winked at William, 'and should someone knock,' he continued, tapping at his chest again, 'let 'em in.'

William leapt to his feet, eyes narrow above a wry smile. He peered under Mac's chair, under the table; he removed books and looked behind them, he hurried to the kitchen and then back again.

'I can't see anyone *here*!' he sang a little too sarcastically.

'That,' said Mac, his look piercing straight through William, 'is because no one knocked.'

'And yet you're a clay-caked, content old potter!' said William triumphantly. Mac wore a half-smile that made William shift and shumble and hold on to the armchair while darting his gaze to and from Mac with a meek grin.

'Content, yes,' said Mac, rising. He came very close to William, thrust his hands into his trouser pockets and rocked on his heels, observing him reprovingly. Then he stood absolutely still and grabbed William's chin in his left hand, pinching at the flesh not wholly inadvertently. He placed his right hand over William's heart and gave his chest another uncompromising shove.

'Content, yes,' he whispered while the stillness of the room hung to his words. He held on to William's desperate-to-dart eyes, dropped his own and then raised them again, staunchly. 'But I'd love to have been blissfully happy.'

William drove back slowly, at a pace safe enough for him to gaze from the window and ignore Mac's words. And forget Mac's tone. At Peregrine's Gully, he walked in and out of the rooms, trailing a hand gently along the window-sills and walls; letting fingers dab at the soil around the house-plants, dip in and out of his bowls and vases which were on display and not for sale. He pulled his hands quickly and lightly over the tightly packed spines on the bookshelf wall, like a pianist sweeping over a vast keyboard. Only there was silence. But William did not observe it for long. He sprang up the carpet-bare staircase in a dissonant dance of sorts and tried not to be disconcerted by certain creaks that were suddenly unfamiliar. He went into the spare bedroom and strummed his old guitar badly while trying to guess how much the small change half filling the oversize whisky bottle amounted to. Enough, he reckoned, for a whole round of whiskies. Only, William never stood a round because he rarely went to a pub. And when he did, it was for a bitter shandy and solitary supping well away from the bar.

He caught sight of himself in the large mirror propped against the wall and immediately diverted his gaze to its flamboyant driftwood frame. Slowly, however, his eyes inched their way back and soon, William shuffled over on his knees to have a closer look. He grabbed his chin the same way Mac had, clamping and closing his grasp until his lips puckered and he looked quite silly. He scrutinized his face and noticed for the first time that his eyebrows were not symmetrical. He saw that his forehead was lined and that none of the furrows traversed his brow unbroken. As if he had suddenly thought better of the worries that had caused them. As if the lines had been broken off mid-thought.

His hair needed a cut.

I'll go to St Ives, tomorrow.

He glowered at a blackhead on the side of his nose and pinched it hard, unsuccessfully. Further along, another two taunted him but he decided to leave them alone and eat more fruit instead. He found an ingrowing hair on his throat so he jutted his chin to stretch the skin while scraping his nail persistently until the offending hair sprang released; far longer, darker, than the surrounding bristles. Like the solitary oak amongst the scrub at the boundary of Peregrine's Gully.

I'll have a proper, cutthroat shave at the barber's. St Ives tomorrow.

There was now nowhere left to look but at his eyes and his first glance presented him with the spectacle of his pupils shrinking. Because it was far easier to look *at* his eyes rather than into them and beyond, he sat cross-legged and, placing a hand over each eye in turn, spent quite some time observing the antics of his pupils instead. On his way to have another peer at the lines on his brow, he caught full sight of himself. He looked swiftly away, unbuckled his legs and got to his feet, wincing at the sound of his creaking bones more than at the sensation itself.

I'm getting old!

You are!

He walked out of the room avoiding the mirror, making a note to take the whisky bottle to the bank in St Ives the next day. There was bound to be enough for a haircut *and* some potions and lotions to banish blackheads and furrows.

He went through to his bedroom and its bareness after the clutter quite startled him. He stood against the radiator, scorching the palms of his hands, while gazing out and over the cliffs to way beyond the sea. Though he rocked against the heat and felt it course a path from the base of his spine right up between his shoulder-blades, he shuddered with a chill that was not physical but affected him totally.

'I am not *unhappy*,' he stated out loud, his eyes tracing the curl of the iron window lock over and over. 'And I am *perfectly* content,' he reasoned as he walked over to the window to check the lock and see if there was perhaps a draught which had made him shiver. The old windows, however, appeared to be in excellent order. William returned to the radiator. He looked at his shoes and decided he could do with a new pair. He could afford them now, too, whether or not the funds from the whisky jar stretched that far.

St Ives, tomorrow.

'I am not *lonely*,' he laughed briefly, 'and am quite content to be on my own. Alone.' Through the window, he could see that the afternoon had turned windy and grey. He kicked his shoes off and let his socked feet slide in little semicircles over the floorboards in front of him.

'If you can happily be alone without being lonely,' he said quietly, 'does it necessarily follow that if you are not unhappy, you are thus happy?'

The room was silent. The question hung unanswered. A sudden gust from outside threw a small twig against the window but William could find neither meaning, nor an answer, in this.

'Is it not *preferable* just to be content? I rather think I'd be a happy man if I remained content the rest of my days.' Still caught in a pocket of breeze, the twig jittered against the window. 'And I doubt whether I'd die bitter for having never tasted blissful happiness!'

After all, just how mind-blowing and life-enriching, just how sweet, can Mac's hallowed 'blissful happiness' be? wondered William as he skated across the floorboards, over to the window. Carefully, he opened it and retrieved the dancing twig. In was safer in his hands. But its life was gone instantly, and it lay still, brittle, and somewhat forlorn in his hands. Suddenly, the bedroom was too bare, too stark. He looked at his bed and wondered whether, ever, someone might share it with him. Not once had he invited Morwenna to stay. Sex had always been conducted at her place. William had kept Peregrine's Gully secret and sacred. He had kept Morwenna out. There had never been a woman at Peregrine's Gully during his residence, though what difference this had made, or would have made if otherwise, he was unsure. William looked at the bed again. Would there ever be?

'I'm just wondering,' he said loudly, grabbing his genitals defiantly, 'not bemoaning!'

For the time being, he was still more than happy to have the metaphorical bed back to himself, and his own bed all for himself.

But will you remain so?

And are you blissfully happy that you sleep alone?

He placed the twig carefully on the pillow, the side of the bed he did not sleep in. As he wandered through to the bathroom and made a note to buy toothpaste and cream cleaner tomorrow in St Ives, he understood that blissful happiness most probably eluded people on their own. A small and almost unwelcome voice deep inside pointed out that it was undoubtedly a sublime state created within oneself by another.

'And I don't need anyone. Certainly not "another".'

To be sure, William. But might you not, quite simply, *want* someone?

'Not *any*one.'

No. Not *any* old person. But perhaps, at some time, a *some*one?

'There's Barbara and Mac. They are very important to me.'

But have they ever made you blissfully happy?

'Blissful happiness has not been noticeable for its presence in my life. I wouldn't know.'

But a taste of it might be very nice indeed?

'God, this place needs a good dust,' says William very loudly as he runs his fingers along the window-sill while walking quickly down the stairs; too quickly to hear the creaks. 'I'll buy polish and new dusters in St Ives, tomorrow.'

If you make it, William; usually you think of umpteen excuses not to go.

As Chloë cycles to work, she passes a man walking purposefully in front of her with a large whisky bottle half filled with coins. She estimates that there is probably enough to buy a high-tech gel saddle and a bell for her bicycle. As she free-wheels down into town, she wonders where one acquires such bottles. It would be a good idea to start a collection of her own; Jocelyn's inheritance is now dwindling proper and waitressing does not pay much.

William has left the car some way out of St Ives. He resents pay-and-display parking but a sly ten minutes on a yellow line last month taught him an expensive lesson he'd rather not repeat. As he walks down into the town, the weight of his bottle of change suggests that a good lunch might very well be purchased from its proceeds too. A bicycle swishes past him, picks up speed and disappears from view over the hill.

But not before he has caught a glimpse of the rider; hair in deep red twists and twirls ribboning out behind her, catching the light of the November morning and adding its own luminescence to the day.

William catches his breath. And he is not sure why.

THIRTY-NINE

Well, they have to meet, don't they – it was practically decreed in Chapter One. And, though we realize there is an aged army of Jocelyn's compatriots standing in the wings to assist, how are William and Chloë ultimately to come together? Will they even like each other? And will she stay? Oh, the disappointment of it if they don't and she doesn't. Chloë's year, however, has been more than just a journey leading to this lovely man; it's been a quest for home, a search for strength and for herself. It won't be wasted time if she doesn't find William.

But wouldn't it be good if she did. . . .

'Ho! Our piskie sends missive!'

'About time, I'll say.'

Peregrine peered at the letter through Jasper's spectacles held at arm's length. They went through to the drawing-room and Jasper silenced *Gardeners' Question Time* because not even clematis chrysocoma took precedence over Chloë Cadwallader. Peregrine found his own spectacles under the *Radio Times* and returned Jasper's, placing them daintily on the tip of his beau's nose. He settled himself into the old armchair and rested his slippered feet on the pouffe for which Jocelyn had exchanged a jar of Branston Pickle on a trip to Algiers in the 1960s.

'Now, let's see,' he muttered, scanning the letter while a be-thimbled Jasper darned socks patiently, observing him over his spectacles every now and then. 'Oh!' Peregrine exclaimed, pushing the letter on to his lap, tutting and grimacing, and then picking it up and reading on. 'Dear!' he continued, pulling his lips into a pained contortion. 'Buggery buggerdome!' he fulminated quietly, rubbing his eyebrows and shaking his head. Jasper remained silent but for a momentary wince when the needle went wayward. Peregrine held the letter aloft, cleared his throat and read, with no need for a warning against bla bla-ing.

'She says she had an enjoyable week's holiday, has spent an interesting month waitressing and living in pleasant digs, but can't see the point of staying on so please could she come back to stay with us until she decides what to do and where.'

'Just like that?' gasped Jasper, pricking himself again. 'No punctuation?'

'Not in the opening line,' affirmed Peregrine, remarking that the rest of the letter appeared to be punctuated appropriately. 'She says here, *I can't see why Jocelyn sent me here – apart from it being one more place I previously did not know. I do like it here, quite a lot actually, but as I can find no link here with Jocelyn, there seems little true purpose to my staying. I worry that just liking the place isn't reason enough – Jocelyn must have had something up her sleeve, but I can find no indication of what it is.*'

Jasper finished the socks, held them to the light, rolled them into correct pairs and threw them at Peregrine. 'Continue!' he implored, turning his attention to a tapestry cushion he had started the week before.

Peregrine gathered the socks and lodged them between the small of his back and the chair.

'She goes on to say, *I know I'm not what you'd call a socialite, but I'm getting a little bored of my own company.*

Why does she use "getting" when she could very well say "I have become" or "I am now"?'

'She's lonesome,' said Jasper, 'leave her be!'

'She says she is *not* lonely, that she does not mind being on her own,' clarified Peregrine.

'Ah,' responded Jasper, 'but does she say she is *happy* to be so?'

Peregrine conceded that he could not find mention of the word in the letter, but then nor does he see 'unhappy'. 'She says she misses Wales: *But in a wistful way; neither Scrabble nor Monopoly are possible by oneself and reminiscing requires a minimum of two participants. I had my solitude in Ireland but, in retrospect, though I was often lonelier there than here, it was a good time, good for me – and ultimately for Gus too, I think. Here, though people are friendly, no one knows Jocelyn so I question why I am here. I miss my Fraser and he misses me too, but we do not long for each other and I know I could not really live with him permanently. Anyway, he wrote to say how Braer has thrived in its first month as a guest house and I know he does not now need me. I couldn't go back anyway, not so soon. It would be going backwards.*

'I'm sure I gave as much in the other countries visited as I received. Was I not a great help to Gin? Ultimately, so much more than just an administrator to Gus? Wasn't it I who enabled Fraser to find the direction and confidence previously eluding him? So what's my function here? I miss all three countries in some way or other; each gave me something precious and unique. But such gifts I was able to take away with me. I have them with me here – but I'm just not sure Cornwall is where I should set up a mantelpiece on which to put them. I'm having fun as a waitress, I've met a really nice girl there much my own age, but I can't be doing this for the rest of my life. Only what else could I do? And down here? I think I should come back for a while, don't you? Would you mind? Perhaps we could look at the map together.'

Peregrine and Jasper looked over to a photograph of Jocelyn and raised their eyebrows in unison.

'Chloë's almost there,' Peregrine considered, 'at least she likes the place and has gone ahead and organized herself.'

'Perhaps she just needs that little prod now – as we all prophesied she might,' said Jasper after a while.

'Time for the phone call?'

'I think so.'

Mac walked slowly around the ground floor of his cottage muttering, 'Good Lord! Good Lord!' to himself, to his plants and to a confederation of pixies gathered on yesterday's newspaper spread over the kitchen table. Later, William asked him what it was that the Lord had done to warrant such repeated praise. Mac said 'Oh, nothing! Nothing!' in an exceptionally breezy way. Puzzled but not overly curious, William left him preaching to the pixies and spent the afternoon glazing jugs instead.

FORTY

'Have you heard of somebody called Michael Mount?' Chloë asked Mrs Stokes, waving Peregrine's letter at her.

'Mount? Mount,' mused Mrs Stokes, 'Michael Mount,' she laughed heartily, 'you mean St Michael's Mount!' and she laboured the word into 'sunt' to make her point.

'No no no!' sang Chloë trying not to sound rude. 'A *Mister* Michael Mount.' She scanned the letter. 'Lives in Carn *Tregen*?' She repeated it twice, with the 'e' soft and then hard.

Mrs Stokes twitched her top lip and pulled her eyebrows together, humming into the crook of a finger. 'Tregen,' she confirmed with a soft 'e'. 'Any more?' she asked, determined that she did indeed know everyone between St Ives and St Just.

'Doesn't say much,' Chloë said forlornly, wafting the single-page letter again. She read from it verbatim: '*Clodders dear, it really wouldn't do to leave Cornwall before you've given it a chance. We think it a very nice county. Remember, Jocelyn only ever had your best interest at heart, and you've said that you do like the place and the folk you've met. Jocelyn trusted you'd be happy there so don't let her down by giving up. She knew you well, did she not? You seem to have carved a little niche for yourself too, even if it seems a little unglamorous just now. Do you not think it could lead on to something? You could be running the restaurant soon – or even setting up on your own. Don't be defeatist or too proud.*

'Oh, we quite forgot about Michael Mount, an old friend of Jocelyn's. He used to live in Carn Tregen and we have some vague recollection that he has something for you. Neither of us can remember what, though we have racked our brains and wrung our memories! We rather think he is known locally as Mac – to differentiate him from some Cornish castle or other! He is, or was, a potter. Good luck, pixie. Pecker up. Do write. JP.'

'Justice of the Peace!' murmured Mrs Stokes with left eyebrow raised approvingly.

'Hardly,' chortled Chloë, 'Jasper and Peregrine – my, um, uncles, I suppose. Or aunts, rather.'

'Indeed!' exclaimed Mrs Stokes, rising her right eyebrow to meet the left and trying not to let her inquisitiveness contort them too obviously.

'Do you know him? Mac?'

'*Of* him,' Mrs Stokes qualified, 'indeed I do. Getting on a bit now – but alive, I do assure you.'

'A potter?'

'Yes, a potter he be.'

A fleeting image of the five urns standing serene and timeless at Ballygorm weaves across Chloë's mind and leaves her smiling gently, and humming softly. With a shake of her head she is back in Cornwall, asking Mrs Stokes if she might make a phone call.

When the phone rang out at Mac's cottage, he was busy in the kitchen brewing tea and laying out morning biscuits neatly on a plate.

'Would you mind?' he called through to William.

'Hullo?' said William into the Bakelite receiver which smelt strong but not unpleasant.

'May I speak to Michael Mount, please?' said a female voice.

'Michael Mount?' was all William could think to say.

'Mac?' the voice furthered.

'Oh,' breezed William, 'Mac! Sure!'

'Are you Mac?' asked the voice, tinged now with suspicion.

'No! Gracious!' hastened William. 'I'll just call for him. Who shall I say it is?'

'Jocelyn's god-daughter,' the caller declared.

William asked the voice to hold for a moment and he laid the receiver gently on the occasional table, next to Mac's pipe and *The Times*. He walked quietly through to the kitchen and observed Mac interspersing rich tea biscuits with chocolate bourbons. Saliva shot through his mouth. Though he had no particular penchant for biscuits, he had quite forgotten about breakfast that day and now found himself ravenous.

'Who was that?' asked Mac, dunking tea bags held between two forks in and out of the pot.

'Hmm?' murmured William, tearing his eyes away from the biscuits.

'On the phone?' asked Mac. 'Any message?'

'Blimey!' exclaimed William, slapping his temples. 'Still there! Holding for you!'

'Who?' laughed Mac.

'Josephine's niece?' suggested William, head cocked, knowing the details were inaccurate but unable to remember them precisely. Mac's smile vanished and yet his expression remained chipper. He glanced swiftly at the phone mounted to the kitchen wall but ignored it. Instead, he hurried through to the sitting-room, pulling the door ajar discreetly behind him.

Having delivered the message, William returned his gaze to the biscuits. In the kitchen alone, he perched on a stool and held a bourbon biscuit aloft, daintily between thumb and index finger. He took it to his nose, closed his eyes, and breathed in the nostalgic scent of baked chocolate. He dabbed his tongue gently against the sugar crystals on the surface. One or two detached themselves and dissolved deliciously in his mouth. Tiny, and yet their sharp sweetness sent a stab of pleasure along William's jaw. He was famished. He could easily have wolfed the biscuit in a single mouthful. Instead, he carefully prised the top layer away and regarded the two parts. The bottom layer, with its velvety fillet of chocolate cream, he inverted and scraped along his lower teeth, furrowing the soft chocolate on to his tongue and pressing it up on to the roof of his mouth. He sucked away, in a small heaven. It was so sweet and soft, so comforting and delicious, so nourishing and pleasurable, he could have wept. Instead, he ate three more.

'Hullo? Mount speaking!' announced Mac, addressing himself as such for the first, and probably only, time in his life.

'Hullo!' sang a soft voice. 'This is Chloë. Cadwallader. Jocelyn's god-daughter?'

Mac was silent. Why should the voice sound so familiar? Previously unheard. No true genetic link. And yet it struck him deeply and he smiled fondly while gazing glazed at the middle distance.

'Jocelyn?' she implored. 'Jocelyn March?'

Mac cleared his throat.

'Hullo,' he said quietly, 'I'm so glad you've called. I knew you would.' He paused. 'I've been waiting.' He paused again. 'Chloë!' he mused gently, mainly to himself.

* * *

'Well?' asked Mrs Stokes who had hovered out of sight but not out of earshot behind the door to her part of the house.

'I'm going round there tomorrow morning,' said Chloë,

her eyes dancing. 'He *did* know my godmother! He sounds very nice indeed. I like potters!'

Mrs Stokes asked Chloë whether she thought she might stay another month. Only the rent was due and she needed to know in advance.

'Probably,' considered Chloë, feeling brave and quite proud of it, 'but could I let you know for sure tomorrow? Afterwards? In the afternoon?'

Chloë sets off at a good pace by bicycle for Carn Tregen. She decides Mac will be a dapper man with slick white hair and sharp blue eyes. His hands will be long and refined with tell-tale squints of clay caught under his fingernails. His voice will have a soft burr which will suit his general deportment and he will offer her sherry and peanuts. His house is to be Victorian, hung throughout with velvet curtains the colour of port and original William Morris wallpaper in many of the rooms. An old cat called Tompkins will be part of the furniture. Up in the eaves there is to be a suite of rooms that Mac will offer Chloë in return for a peppercorn rent and some company. She will accept with great surprise and humility, and she will tell Mrs Stokes this afternoon that she will not be signing for another month.

Chloë dismounts from her bicycle. The approach to Carn Tregen is far too pretty to free-wheel past. The road sweeps up and over in a straight line to the village, rather like the train on a bridal gown. After yards of this tarmac satin, a frill of small buildings pans out to either side. Smoke streams like chiffon from a few of the chimneys and, as Chloë nears, a bouquet of painted front doors presents itself. A church steeple stands daintily above all. Herring gulls wheel and rejoice overhead and car horns toot conversationally.

'Sexy! Sexy!'

That was not the gulls.

'Show us your pants!'

Nor was that.

The calls come from a parade of small schoolboys, clasping on to the green mesh fencing of their playground and scampering along its length like monkeys. Chloë is startled, but amused and just a little flattered too. She tries not to grin, to encourage, and then tries hard to ignore the impudence of eight pairs of eight-year-old eyes undressing her.

'Phoarr!' gurgles one.

'Ooh er, look-at-her!' chants another.

'Miss Sexy!' hisses a further child.

'What colour are your pants?' asks the smallest of the gang in a most conversational way. Chloë regards him directly.

'They're blue and white,' she informs him, 'stripy.'

For some reason, this information makes the boys scurry away, laughing hysterically and whooping with delight and embarrassment. As Chloë reaches the perimeter of the playground, the boys stampede back but say nothing, just panting in awe of the sexy Miss who has accepted their compliments so graciously.

'Let's see!' they cry, but their request for a flash from Chloë is swallowed by her laughter and a sudden gust from the sea driving salt to the back of her mouth and making her eyes water.

As she winds her way down into Carn Tregen, Chloë realizes that the gulls are actually bickering, that car horns are being sounded indignantly and that most of the houses to the left of the road are modern and nondescript. However, those to the right and those lining the steep street down to the harbour are overwhelmingly picturesque and sit, pastel pretty and patient amidst the scamper and bustle of the harbour. A boat has just come in, crates are hurled from the deck, scuttling over the wet cobbles, and grabbed by thickset men in rubber trousers and huge boots who are wearing T-shirts despite the chill. The gulls are beside themselves with greed, swooping and cursing and coming as near to the crates and the men as they dare. A cursory sifting takes place right here on the harbour side, with anything obviously small, damaged or inedible being discarded. The gulls shriek as they hover, and yell as they dive for the scrap heap. The men curse and laugh and shout and belch.

Chloë regards the catch; the reason for the noise, the bounty for the fisherfolk, the swag for the gulls, the life-stuff of man and bird alike. Quite dead, still the fish slither as their oily little bodies sort themselves out and finally settle against each other. Quite dead, light continues to dance and glint off their scales. Glimpses of silver, glances of gold; mercury shooting, rust rolling. Pieces of hake!

There is something vaguely traumatic about it all. Chloë walks away gladly, sadly, and concentrates on Mac's precise directions instead.

Something about their eyes, she contemplates as she leaves the village and the noise and the action.

So glassy and still. And yet so expressive.

Unsuspecting at the time of death. A look of remorse; that they should be but the money of man, the carrion of gulls.

Dead and unseeing. Yet seeming to see so much.

She shudders sharply. Her eyes alight on a rotting fish, its body torn and now forsaken, its eyes withered but still intact, staring still, just dulled. A stillness, a grace superseding the indignity of this last resting place – half on tarmac, half on grass, beside a hedge and far from the sea. Chloë walks on and shudders again, greatly perturbed that she should wonder and imagine how Jocelyn's body must look now. A year on. Heavens, a year today.

Jocelyn. Have you still flesh? Have you been stripped to a rattle of old bones? Can you speak if your tongue has gone? Can you be with me if you are six feet under? Have you any idea?

Dead and unseeing. Yet seeming to see so much.

Mac slept badly. He was excited and nervous. Chloë, of

course, would look nothing like Jocelyn and yet he did not doubt that glimpses of the old girl would shine through and invest his cottage once more with the warmth and colour she had conveyed in abundance. He was frightened too; of being helplessly emotional, of saying too much. He wanted to work but November was crueller than true winter for though the cold was not as severe, the pervasive dankness seeped into his joints and rendered them painful and useless. Such pain would he have tolerated gladly, taken more even; only that his fingers, his wrists, his knees, might oblige and bend in spite of it. How could he be so upright and lithe one day, so brittle and incapacitated the next? When his doorbell rang out, he called 'Coming!' in a loud, cheery voice because he knew it would take him some time to creak and crack his way out of the chair and over to his visitor.

And wasn't she lovely! A pre-Raphaelite muse but peppered with freckles and a winsome expression that made her seem artless and all the more attractive.

'Chloë!'

'Mr Mount?'

'Mac – won't you come in?'

He gave her tea in a mug whose handle was a vine over which a pixie clambered. Just like the one Jasper kept his gardening twine in. She marvelled at the coincidence, and then declared it marvellous that it was not a coincidence at all. When Mac informed her that he made such mugs, she was charmed; when he gave her one of her own, she was utterly delighted.

'Do you remember this brooch,' she asked him, proffering a chunk of her jumper towards him.

'Like I saw it yesterday,' he assured her.

Here was a man she had never met before, had hitherto not even heard of, and yet there was already a tangible exchange of great warmth and empathy between them, congenial and comforting. They talked the morning away and Chloë gave Mac a colourful account of her travels. It did not worry her that he knew neither the Gin Trap, nor Gus, nor the senior or junior Buchanans. It was enough that he had a friend living in South Wales, shared Jocelyn's love of Scotland and expressed a desire to visit the landscape of Northern Ireland.

'When did you meet Jocelyn?' she asks.

'Moons ago, my love, *moons*!' he replies.

'She's been gone a year. Exactly.'

'I know.'

'I miss her still.'

'I do as well.'

'It seems impossible that someone so full of life – and who lived it to the full – should ever be denied it.'

'But don't you think that makes her immortal in some way?'

'I do. I suppose. But that's not enough. I want her back.'

'You don't mourn alone, Chloë. It follows that those who loved Jocelyn have great affection for each other too.'

'How did you meet?' asks Chloë, comforted as much by Mac's words as by his arm, which she finds around her shoulder.

'Mutual friend,' replies Mac nonchalantly. He unbuckles himself from his chair, declining politely Chloë's offer of assistance, and fetches an old leather book from the overstocked bookcase. Chloë stands up and they both rest against the long arm of the old chair as he flips through the pages.

'What book is it?' Chloë enquires.

'Oh the book is not the point,' Mac assures her, 'it merely protects something – where is the blighter? – precious. It's *Gulliver's Travels*, by the way.'

The blighter turned out to be his only remaining photograph of Jocelyn. She was very young and a little blurred. Younger than Chloë had seen her in any other photograph, even those Peregrine carefully hinged and annotated in white, in thick black albums. Mac could not remember the date though he scoured the card for a clue. Pre-war, for sure. Her hair was oddly platinum, bobbed and furled to perfection; her lips dark and delineated into a careful Cupid's bow.

And her brooch! Look there! Look here!

And who is that by her side?

'That's not you?' Chloë half asked, knowing that, though wrinkled and stooped, the man next to her could never have been that tall; his face too comfortably round and suiting his persona too well to have ever been any other shape. Certainly not the handsome face with the well-defined jaw and clean cheekbones of the man in the photo.

'No, not me!' agreed Mac, a little wistfully, a little remorsefully.

'Who is he?' wondered Chloë aloud, gazing at the photo as though it might fade any moment.

'Our mutual friend,' explained Mac, placing the photograph carefully back in the book, between pages 111 and 112.

'What's his name?' Chloë asked, wondering if she had ever met him. This friend. There had been so many.

As Mac put the book back into its precise position, he chose not to hear her. Relieved that she did not repeat the question, he turned from the bookcase, rubbed his hands and gave her an inviting smile.

'Now!' he declared. 'I must fulfil my duty and give to you what Jocelyn entrusted to me!'

Chloë tried not to bounce on the seat but failed.

'What is it, what is it?' she all but squeaked. 'And how on earth did she know I'd actually find you!'

Mac raised his eyebrow and his index finger as if to say 'Wait, you lovely young thing, you!'

Images of silk shawls, fine oil paintings, exquisite jewellery and antique china sprang to Chloë's mind though she had no preference.

'Please,' she implored, knowing full well that doleful

eyes would win this old man around, 'just tell me! I can't bear it.'

'A key,' announced Mac, head cocked, knees creaking.

With Mac disappeared to retrieve this heirloom, Chloë settles back into the chair and wonders what the key might unlock. Maybe this was the point of Cornwall, hidden treasure!

Maybe I had to be on the verge of leaving before this could have happened.

Chloë reckons that the key will be dainty, filigree; perhaps tied to an old brown card scrawled with something ambiguous and only half legible. She gazes over to the spine of *Gulliver's Travels* but, though she wants more time with the photograph, she feels strongly that she should await Mac's invitation. For the while, she is content that it is there. It makes her feel safe. Another friend of Jocelyn's. As she lets the coarse velvet of the upholstery catch soothingly under her fingernails, she decides that she really does like Cornwall. And there is a link with Jocelyn and thereby a very good reason to stay on. Maybe she could run the café. Even have one of her own.

Chloë realizes, with some disappointment, that Mac's cottage is far too small to accommodate her. No eaves. No cat called Tompkins. Mac does, however, have a seductive burr to his voice and Chloë is content that he should offer her tea and biscuits in place of sherry and peanuts.

'So I'll book in for another month with Mrs Stokes,' she says quietly as she stokes the fire, 'while I'm treasure hunting!'

Mac peers into the depths of his 'odds 'n' sods' drawer and a careful chaos confronts him which he understands at once. He removes the bundle of waxy green string, the candle stubs, the secateurs still in their box and two right-hand rubber gloves. He pushes the clothes pegs, broken but useful, to one side, and lodges a packet of petunia seeds, a tape-measure and a fuseless plug against them. Taking the carefully folded plastic bags from the floor of the drawer, he wriggles his wrist to the furthest end. No, not the strapless digital watch, not today. Nor the pewter hip-flask. Ah! That's where his pocket knife disappeared to! No, none of these. Here! An envelope; the brown paper now furred, the 'JM' faded, the adhesive long absent from the lip. Its contents; ah yes, safely within.

Mac feels the shape of the iron key through the paper while a multitude of memories flit across his mind; a host of images, a barrage of voices from long ago, way back then, clamber about his head. He opens the envelope and has a peek. It has not rusted at all. Nor have the memories. As fresh and significant as a lovely day just gone.

'Can I help?' calls a voice from the here and now.

'Can she?' Mac asks quietly.

'She could –' muses a voice from a long time ago, 'but maybe we ought to help her on her way.'

'Jocelyn?' says Mac softly.

'Mackerel!' she chides.

'That you?' he whispers, not daring to turn around, not needing to.

'It is me,' she answers.

Mac lays the envelope on the tabletop and smooths it with his weathered old hands.

'I found it for her,' he says.

'I think I've changed my mind. Maybe I'd rather she found it for herself.'

'Can I help?' came the voice again, from the sitting-room.

'No, no!' called back Mac, breezily. 'Be with you in a tick-tock!' He pushed the envelope into the furthest corner of the drawer and laid the folded carrier bags over it for good measure. Carefully, he reinstated the jumble into precisely the harmonious disorder in which he found it, and closed the drawer boldly.

'OK,' he nodded quietly, 'okey dokey, Jocelyn Jo. Circumstances have provided the opportunity you hoped for. Him and her. Young, free and so near. Just needing a gentle shove in the right direction. And then it's up to them.'

He returned to Chloë who looked pretty relaxed and very pretty in the simpering light of the afternoon. Her eyes widened as he came into the room, and scanned first his hands, then his pockets, finally his eyes; imploring.

'My dear,' he said, tapping at his temples as if he was losing his mind, 'it is not where I thought it would be.'

Panic and disappointment streamed over Chloë's face and altered her countenance visibly, sinking her body deep into the chair as if she had been winded, stripping her eyes of any glint, pulling the corners of her mouth downwards dolefully.

'Have you lost it?' she asked forlornly.

'Gracious no!' encouraged Mac, shuffling over to her and laying a hand on the top of her head. She batted her eyes up at him: 'Mislaid it?' she suggested.

'Good Lord forgive you!' he remonstrated, patting her head and letting his hand slip down through her hair, his fingers catching on her ringlets; it felt lovely for them both.

'Is it not here?' she enquired, twisting her neck this way and that as he continued to play with her hair.

'No,' he conceded, 'it isn't.'

Chloë nodded reluctantly.

'But I know precisely where it is,' triumphed Mac, levering himself away from the arm of the chair. Chloë stood up, her eyes shining once more. He took her chin in his hand and squeezed it, while winking at her.

'Where?' she whispered, putting her hand gently on his wrist.

'It's in my old studio,' he explained, his open face and soft smile hiding the whitest of lies convincingly, 'not far from here. Near Zennor. Last house off the cliff lane. Meet me there tomorrow, at elevenses. We'll rummage together and see what we come across.'

FORTY-ONE

The next morning, Chloë went directly to the café and asked if she could swap her shift. Yes, of course, no problem at all with it being so quiet and all, but would she mind just doing the egg mayonnaise quickly before she went. Yes, of course, no problem.

William thought he'd take lunch to Mac and made a trip to the wholefood café in St Ives which did a lovely line in filled granary rolls and fudge brownies that were to die for. He loved the place; the smell of warmth, of baking, of goodness, that solicited him whenever he visited. He hadn't been for ages and, as soon as he entered, he wondered why on earth not. The scent was intoxicating, and he stood very still with his eyes closed for a few moments. There was nobody serving anyway; just somebody humming out the back.

'Hullo?' he called but the humming overrode his voice. He listened awhile, gazing out to the sea through the window at the back of the café. A very peaceful scene. He closed his eyes again and breathed in deep. Egg. Very fresh.

'Hullo?' he called again.

Chloë had bits of eggshell clinging to her arms, mayonnaise over her fingers and butter swiped across her cheek when she heard the call of a customer.

'Hullo?' she called back, unwilling to leave the task she was hurrying to complete.

'Any chance of a sandwich this side of tea-time?' laughed the voice. Chloë looked at the clock. Nine-thirty. She laughed too.

'In a mo',' she called back. 'I'll send someone out. Jane! Jay-In! Customer, please!'

Jane appeared from the storeroom with a clutch of bananas and was immediately thankful that the customer had been spared the sight of the condiment-daubed Cadwallader.

'Can I help you?'

'Yes please,' said William.

Jane called back to Chloë for two rounds of egg-mayonnaise sandwiches on granary and fetched them when Chloë sang 'Yoo-hoo!' a minute or two later.

'And two pieces of fudge brownie,' William said, adding, 'make that three – I'll *have* to have one now,' with a guilty smile. His order was wrapped in greaseproof paper and placed tidily in a small, recycled brown paper bag with handles and the café's insignia. He thanked the sales assistant he deduced to be Jane profusely and loudly.

'No problem,' Jane smiled, 'enjoy!'

'Thanks a lot,' called the egg-mayonnaise girl from somewhere in the kitchen.

'Bye now,' smiled William, brandishing his bag of delicacies.

'Crumbs,' says Jane, handing Chloë a great swathe of paper towels.

'Where?' Chloë cries, brushing herself down vigorously.

'No,' Jane laughs, 'not where but *who*! He was ten times more scrumptious than our egg-mayonnaise granary sandwiches. In fact, make that fif*teen*!'

Chloë nudges her friend. 'Ah,' she says, 'but was he as divine as the fudge brownies?'

'Easily,' Jane assures.

Mac kept both his front and back doors locked. When William rapped at the door, at first light-heartedly and then more insistently, Mac stood stock-still in an upstairs room, biting on his lip to ensure silence. He glimpsed William scratching distractedly at the sandy flop of his hair, saw he had come prepared with a customary little feast, heard him knock again and call through the letter-box and then watched him wandering away.

'Oh Jocelyn,' Mac murmured some minutes later, retrieving the bag William had left on the doorstep. 'I've done as decreed. "*If Fate has it that they're both young and free,*" you said, "*give 'em a gentle shove.*"'

Mac rifled through the treasures in the bag. 'We all thought it contrived,' he theorized with a mouthful of fudge brownie, 'but now that they *are* so near, I concede indeed the merits of a helping hand.'

Placing the wrapped sandwiches in the fridge until lunch-time, and making a futile resolution to save the other brownie till tea, Mac returned to his piskies. They assured him he had acted with Jocelyn's best intentions, and with those of Chloë and William too, in his heart.

'It's up to them, now.'

The fronts of Chloë's thighs hollered for mercy and though her bicycle chinked and skittered over the divots and dunks of the lane, she pedalled on; albeit through clenched teeth. This was the cliff lane and gusts from the sea alternately gave her a helpful propelling, or smacked her in the face so suddenly that she could neither pedal nor breathe. And this was the last house. Up that stony path. Look at this pothole.

Chloë dismounted and pushed her bike the last few yards, ringing her bell merrily to tell Mac she had arrived. The cottage at the end of the path was called 'Peregrine's Gully'. It did not ring a bell. She said 'Jasper's Gully' out loud and was sorry for him that it did not scan so well. By the garden gate was a sign pointing 'Studio'.

'Mac!' she called, her bicycle bell trilling feebly against the insistent breeze. 'Mac!'

Barbara knew her name was not Mac, but someone was calling so imploringly that she left the small patch of sweet grass she had recently discovered and sauntered over to inspect the stranger. She was about to bleat a welcome but decided instead to creep up behind the visitor first. Just to surprise her. Just to make her entrance. Softly, she ambled over; her cloven hooves, the colour of apricot, scuffling noiselessly through the grass. The stranger was still calling, somewhat sorrowfully, standing on tiptoes and peering through cupped hands into the darkened studio. Barbara nuzzled the backs of her knees boldly in a combined gesture of welcome and comfort. Chloë leapt, gulping down her shriek with shock. Barbara bleated triumphantly and butted Chloë's thigh with her horny forehead in an effusive display of affection.

'Heavens!' gasped Chloë, repeating it many times while her hand clasped her heart and she fought to catch her breath. Then she giggled.

'Hullo goat!' she laughed heartily, twisting the milky white ears and rubbing the damp little nose. 'Aren't you lovely!'

Chloë chattered to the goat who, unfortunately, was unable to tell her where Mac was and what time he would be back. She was, however, extremely good company and they snuggled up on the steps to the studio which was locked and too dim to make out much other than the general position of the workbench, the potter's wheel and some shelving carrying ceramics which were swallowed from definition by pervasive shadow. Chloë looked at her watch. Way past elevenses. Well, Mac was elderly and she was now on the evening shift. She could wait, she was warm now and the goat both jollied and relaxed her. Chloë tried to remember out loud the story of the Billy Goats Gruff but Barbara found this somewhat tasteless and wandered off until Chloë coaxed her back by humming 'Greensleeves' softly and melodically. Barbara gruffled and bleated at opportune moments. They were still making music when William returned at noon.

That's Greensleeves! he thought. *That's Barbara. And that isn't.*

He made his way to the back of the house as noiselessly as he could, cocking his head to the strange duet. It was comical and yet it was melodious. Barbara's voice was familiar; strident and rasping. But this other voice – plaintive and tuneful? Familiar, somehow. He creaked the garden gate. The music died at once. Barbara bleated and defecated simultaneously in welcome and delight, skipping over to him, butting and stamping and tugging at the knees of his jeans with her hard, blunt teeth. He made his way over to the shadowy figure who had scrambled up from the studio steps. It was a woman. Barbara trotted back to her. William followed.

'Je-zus!' he exclaimed quietly, his mouth agape, his eyes dancing, his brow twisting, his heart thundering. His senses were alight and allowed the lack of sense in the situation to be utterly irrelevant.

'Jesus Aitch!' he murmured, not taking his eyes off her. 'It's the humming girl!'

'The humming girl?' questioned Chloë, not waiting for an answer. 'You're not Mac!' she said crossly, stamping from foot to foot to thaw them. The young man had remained motionless but for closing his mouth and drawing it into an expansive smile of generous warmth. To Chloë, it was an odd smile to expend on a stranger, appearing to brim with the affection usually reserved for those known well. Mind you, it was a very nice smile too, and she was pleased to be the recipient.

'You're not Mac,' she repeated a little shyly, now not

knowing quite where to look and so fixing on Barbara's quivering tail instead.

'No,' the man conceded, smiling even more brazenly, 'I'm William. Won't you come in?'

He took her through to the kitchen. Barbara begged to be allowed in too and hollered furiously at the closed door before stamping off in a sulk which William knew he would pay for later.

'Tea?' he suggested, scouring the humming girl's face with scarcely hidden delight.

'OK,' agreed Chloë cautiously, darting away from his intense eye contact to blow on her chilled fingers.

'You want *Mac*?' he asked over his shoulder while retrieving mugs and tea bags. Chloë, however, did not quite hear him; momentarily distracted by his broad shoulders tapering to a neat bottom, and athletic legs hinted at behind nicely hanging jeans.

'Mac?' he said again.

'Yes!' she cried, banishing her meanderings and praying she was not blushing. 'This is his old studio and he has something for me,' she informed him. William turned around and regarded her quizzically.

'No it's not!' he chided gently.

'Yes,' assured Chloë, 'it is. Actually. He's meeting me here, we're going to rummage together, you see.'

'Rummage!' laughed William. *God, her skin really is like porcelain.* 'Indeed?' He brought over two mugs of strong tea and heaped a spoonful of sugar into both. Chloë thought it rude to inform him that she took her tea weak and unsweetened but was pleasantly surprised at how quickly his brew warmed and revived her. And she didn't want to offend him; not least because he was friendly and open. And rather attractive too. She'd stay awhile, wait for Mac here with him. They sipped in silence, smiling occasionally over the rims of their mugs.

'So,' said William once he had drained his, 'who, exactly, are *you*?'

The humming girl did not answer; she was miles away. She was gazing full force at the corner of the room and, as he watched, the colour slipped from her face and faded away.

'Hullo?' he said. She did not hear. His gaze followed hers and alighted on his tall coiled urn, presently home to an umbrella and the raffia mat on which he had sunbathed away many a summer afternoon. She looked quite shocked; a tiny, lovely dent in her brow spoke of it; her eyes, fixed and wide, proclaimed it; her silence and sudden deafness emphasized it. Tentatively, he walked his fingers over the table and touched her knuckles lightly.

'Hey?' he said.

She looked at him, her face giving nothing away. She caught hold of his eyes and refused to let them go, burrowing into them, trying to make sense of it all.

Could it be? Could it really be? Him? This chap? Was it? Now? How come?

What lovely eyes, she thought.

What did I think he'd look like!

Fresh and handsome, she observed.

I never stopped to think!

This couldn't be happening, this couldn't be real. Blink, girl!

Slowly, Chloë's flat expression softened and the corners of her mouth lifted easily.

'Hey!' he welcomed.

'Hey!' she replied.

'Who are *you*?' he asked again.

'I'm Jocelyn's god-daughter,' she informed him with a spirited smile, 'and you,' she proclaimed, squeezing his wrist quickly, firmly, '*you* are William Coombes!'

William's face was wide open, his lips parted and his eyes would not keep still.

She knows me*?*

Oh yes!

She knows *me*!

She does indeed.
The humming girl?
The very same.
With the freckles and the porcelain skin, the beautiful neck and eyes of mahogany?
And the tresses of burnished auburn that have lingered with you so.
In my kitchen?
Right here.
And she *knows* me?
'You *are* William Coombes,' pleaded Chloë, her brow twitching and magnetizing William's senses, 'aren't you?'
Suddenly she so wanted it to be him that she found herself terrified that perhaps it was not. He had said his name was William. Don't let coincidence ruin the possibility.
'I am he,' he declared softly.
'Hey,' said Chloë through her smile, 'I'm Chloë. Cadwallader?'

After the penny had dropped, they dissolved all formality in a round of unfettered laughter and Good-Lording.
'Would you like to see the studio?' William asked, still shaking his head slightly.
'Would I!' Chloë grinned, offering her mug for a refill.
There in the studio, his heaven and hers, he stood back while she inspected. Traversing the room in a world of her own, she ran her eyes and her fingers over all that greeted her; she smelt the clay, spun the banding wheel, examined the tools and held little pots of glaze pigment up to the light. She flipped through books and dipped her fingers gingerly, before dunking them entirely, into a small bowl of *terra sigillata* that had the entire workbench to itself. She sat quietly astride William's wheel. Motionless, she gazed out to the cliffs and beyond.
William watched her all the while. Here was the humming girl, right here, whom he had known so well for

almost a year yet never met. Reality had not let the day-dream down and the flesh was as enchanting as the fantasy. The very stuff of his late-night last thoughts was now rummaging about his studio in front of him. She was lovely and real and ingenuous.

Might she? William wondered silently, hoping that she would. Commanding all powers of telepathy, he implored her to do it; hum.

Don't!

Do!

Chloë didn't need to be asked, aloud or otherwise. He watched her gather her hair back, dip her face in and out of the vessels, trailing her hands over them, brushing her forearm against one surface, pressing her cheek against another, making small music all the while. She declared that this piece sounded so much lower than the range of the Ballygorm urns, that one there just a tone or two higher. She told him of the tune they had made, of the comfort and pleasure they had given her in Ireland. That they looked beautiful in the luminescent Antrim spring, that she still thought of them; standing intimate, united and timeless. But William was too overcome with the luck of it all even to take the compliments on board, let alone graciously. He just nodded and said 'Oh' and did not think to tell her that they had been sold as a set and that he had been commissioned for more.

Chloë understood it as modesty and liked him all the more for it. He sat in the slip-splashed Windsor chair while she perched neatly on the end of the trestle; they chatted and smiled and marvelled to themselves that they should have met. The humming girl and the lone potter.

It was late afternoon. Chloë was just recounting the story of Mrs MacAdam and Fraser's shoes to William, when the prefix of the landlady's surname reminded her why she was at Peregrine's Gully and put a temporary hold on her train of thought.

'Mac,' she murmured, a little alarmed, her eyes searching William's for the course of action.

'He said to meet him *here*?' asked William. 'For a *rummage*?'

'At elevenses,' confirmed Chloë to stress the authenticity of the arrangement and the urgency of the situation.

'What were you to rummage for?' William enquired, keeping his own curiosity at bay lest it should unnerve her.

'The key!' announced Chloë.

'To what?' asked William.

Chloë sighed and squeezed a lump of terracotta clay. 'I have absolutely no idea.'

William phoned Mac who claimed to have had a funny turn, deary me. Whatever could he have been thinking? Gracious, please forgive – damned dementia! The key? But of course, right here in the cutlery drawer. Of course. Where else? Come and get it. No, not now. Tomorrow, a cup of tea? For two? Ah! For three! See you then. Oh, and lovely sandwiches, thank you.

William walked Chloë to her bicycle. The afternoon had been treated to a glorious burst of sunshine; the sun itself a distant pink lozenge that proffered little warmth but invested the land with a clear, crystalline light. He heard himself suggesting they could walk together to Mac's the next day.

'I mean, if you like. Er, if you'd like some company.'

'Heavens yes! I mean, thank you.'

Although impressed by Chloë's conscientious acquaintance with much of the north coastal path, this would be a section she would not have explored and William found himself keen that she should not tread it alone. Or at least, not without him.

'So much nicer to share,' said William, not actually to Chloë but out loud, none the less.

'Tomorrow, then,' said Chloë, suddenly unable to regard William directly though she knew she'd curse herself later for forgoing such an opportunity.

'Yup,' William affirmed, kicking a clod of grass and grinning at Barbara.

FORTY-TWO

Chloë cycled appallingly to Peregrine's Gully, her knees as much a-quiver as her senses.

I wonder if he'll be as handsome today!

She very nearly parted company with her bicycle twice but her desire to arrive in one piece, unflustered, and with her hair almost in place, was far stronger and she arrived at William's late but unscathed.

Heavens, he is. What am I thinking! He's a stranger – and he's probably utterly psychotic or else madly in love with someone else anyway.

William, whom thankfully we at least know to be single and sensible, sat Chloë at his table with a mug of sweet tea. Worrying that she might chill, he disappeared to fetch a thick jumper. He took the stairs two at a time and wondered why his heart was racing when he was actually rather fit.

I'm probably falling for something. The flu. A cold.

He walked back down to the kitchen measuredly, bundled the pullover into her arms self-consciously, and blew his nose sonorously. On their way out, he introduced Chloë formally to Barbara, reading and then ridiculing any significance in the goat's acceptance of and apparent affection for her.

'Where are you from, Chloë Cadwallader?' he asked as he guided her to the far end of the garden and straight out towards the cliffs under a scatter of kittiwakes. 'Where do you live?'

'I'm not sure really,' pondered Chloë, hoping it did not matter. 'How long have you lived out here at Peregrine's Gully?' she digressed half presuming him either to say he was xenophobic or that he would be moving in with some girlfriend soon.

Girlfriend?

Well, look at him! Isn't he bound to have one? And I suppose it'll make things easier if he does.

William, however, informed Chloë that he and Barbara had lived there for almost seven years.

As they walked past Pendour and Porthglaze coves, William regaled her with shamelessly embellished tales of smuggling days and was charmed by the way she marvelled and said 'Really? Heavens!' with such wide eyes. He cupped her small shoulders in his hands and turned her gently inland to face the mountains of West Penwith, pointing out the rocky hills of Hannibal's Carn and Carn Galver, explaining that unfortunately the latter obliterated the lonely chimney of Ding Dong Mine from view.

'Maybe you'd like to visit it one day?'

'Yes, I would.'

'Maybe I could take you?'

'Oh! I'd like that. Thank you.'

'Not at all. Soon, perhaps?'

'Soon as you like – shifts permitting.'

'Oh? Where do you work?'

'The Good Life – in St Ives, it's a wholefood café.'

'You don't!'

'I do!'

'A-bloody-mazing.'

Tramping onwards, slaloming through the gorse, Chloë

told William about Skirrid End, about Table Mountain and the Sugar Loaf and she remarked that though these Cornish hills were undeniably lower, they were certainly not lesser. She declared them to retain the quintessential grasp of mountains; a remoteness, a stillness, a solemnity and grandeur.

'Do you know, they remind me of Wales, of Scotland – an irrefutable Celtic tone, I think, underlining and uniting.'

Heavens, am I prattling? Does he even find me interesting?

While Chloë racked her brains, accordingly, for another topic of conversation, William interjected: 'Actually, my father lives in Gwent, quite near Crickhowell.' William liked very much the way Chloë spoke of the land with such reverence. Wasn't that rare for a woman? Or those he had known at any rate.

'Crick?' Chloë murmured. 'That was just around the corner.'

'Before your sojourn in Northern Ireland?' William reminded himself out loud, chancing too upon the image of the pony-trekker with Chloë's hair, of the brooch in the fruit bowl at the farmhouse.

It couldn't have been! Could it?

'Yes,' confirmed Chloë, 'before Antrim and most recently, bonny Scotland.'

'And which place did you like the best?' asked William, wondering where he had put the letters she had written him from Ballygorm. 'Which is your favourite and to which will you return?'

'I loved them all,' she sighed a little sadly, 'and hope to go back to each some day. For a visit. A holiday.'

'To live?' furthered William, presuming that she'd say 'Scotland'.

Probably has some bloke waiting for her, kilt and all.

An image of 'Loop Loop Go Home' daubed on the redundant grain silo near Ballygorm shot across Chloë's mind. Home? Where? She shook her head and shrugged her shoulders. William was surprised by his relief and hoped it was not audible.

'And Cornwall?' he said softly after a quiet moment, not wishing to press, not wanting to pry, but oddly keen to know everything right now.

'Cornwall is last on Jocelyn's itinerary,' Chloë explained.

'And do you like it here?' he asked, gazing over the sea as if her answer would not matter. He did not like the ensuing silence. And the fact that he did not like it alarmed him rather.

'Yes,' replied Chloë, glancing at William's cheek and repressing a startling urge to touch him. 'I do like it here. I think. So far.'

William strode on ahead, walking backwards and grinning at Chloë.

'Do you believe in fairies, Cadwallader?' he called, thrusting his hands into his pockets and springing lightly on the spot. 'In pixies and the little folk?'

Chloë caught up with him and wiped her nose briskly on the borrowed jumper, squeezing her thumb and forefinger into the corners of her eyes to pinch away the tears elicited by the wind.

'Why yes,' she said gravely while the sunlight spun copper from her hair and brushed gold and pink over the right side of her face, glinting in the rivulet coursing down her cheek, 'I rather think I do.'

'Good,' declared William, who would have liked to kiss her but walked on staunchly instead, forwards this time and in the right direction, 'Mac *will* be pleased.'

'Do you believe in giants?' she asked some time later and once they had caught their breath back from an arduous climb. 'William?'

'I don't see why not,' he reasoned, 'though I've never had the pleasure.'

Chloë waited a few seconds, wondering whether it was wise to confide.

'I have,' she said furtively; and her tales of Finn McCool

took them right to Mac's door and on into his sitting-room. On their arrival, she spied *Gulliver's Travels* lying now on the occasional table, on top of *The Times* and underneath Mac's spectacles. She watched carefully as William fanned the pages and admired the binding. The photograph, it appeared, was gone.

The key was a clumsy iron piece with simple teeth and a plain punched end. To Chloë's delight, it *was* tied to a brown tag but the message was hardly ambiguous. 'No. 3 Penbeagle Street, St Ives' was all it read. Mac could elaborate no further.

'Did Jocelyn not say *any*thing else?' Chloë implored.

'Not that this tired old brain can remember,' apologized Mac.

'So you actually knew her godmother then?' William asked.

'Oh yes,' said Mac, 'in our glory days.'

'What a coincidence,' marvelled William.

'Isn't it just,' agreed Chloë.

'It is indeed,' Mac confirmed.

'Tell me tales, please, from the glory days,' Chloë begged, snuggling deep into a chair while Mac nodded sagely and flipped through the memories as if leafing through a vast photo album.

'Sounds as if she was a special character,' was all William could contribute.

'You'd have loved her,' said Mac to William.

'She'd have loved you,' furthered Chloë, half aloud but loud enough.

Number Three Penbeagle Street. Chloë repeated the four words to herself frequently during her shift that evening. *Number three.* What a lovely day she had had. *Penbeagle Street.* He's called William, Jane, and he was just as nice on second viewing. On a par with the fudge brownies. *No. 3.* Two cappuccinos for the window table. *Penbeagle St.* Measly tip!

'Night-night! See you tomorrow. Oh? Well I'm on an early so I'll see you the day after, then.'

Number Three Penbeagle Street. Where was it? What did it mean?

But I'm exhausted and cold. It's too dark. Don't want to go on my own in the dark. I have the key, the key to Number Three.

Wonder what Number Three might be the key to?

Chloë went to sleep in William's jumper even though she was quite warm enough. She woke, however, very early and sweltering, and wriggled free from it. Sleep, it soon transpired, was to elude her until the next night-time. She padded over to the window and looked out over Porthmeor, cradling William's jumper in her arms. She buried her nose in deep. It did not smell of William, not that Chloë knew his scent just yet, but it smelled lovely; clean, of someone else's choice of fabric conditioner. She folded it neatly and placed it on top of her chest of drawers. Half an hour later, she decided she had cooled down sufficiently to slip it on again.

Later, when it was morning proper and a decorous time to greet the day, Chloë scolded her reflection before and after brushing her teeth.

'Why oh why did I witter on about fairies and giants and heavens knows what else?'

I've blown it.

William had also woken with the dawn but he had risen with it. As he kneaded and wedged a batch of particularly uncompliant clay, he cursed himself with every push.

'Why on earth did I bring pixies and the like into the conversation?' he chastised under his breath. 'She'll think me quite soft.'

I ought to be more formal, Chloë decided over her breakfast cereal, *appropriately reserved, I think.*

'I think I should be just a little aloof,' William announced to Barbara, 'guarded,' he furthered, 'hold back somewhat.

I'll call her tomorrow, then. The day after, perhaps. Probably.'

Chloë, it transpired, had cycled down Penbeagle Street on most days, having never known its name. It was narrow but bright and led straight to the front after dog-legging half-way down. Cobbled, there was no pavement, and a gully that started at the left coursed its way over to the right by the end of the street. It played havoc with the ball-bearings on Chloë's bicycle. She passed two Tea Shoppes with pastel shutters at the windows, a bookshop, a butcher's shop guarded by a plaster model of a chipped but cheery cleaver-brandishing butcher, a small shop selling prints and art books, another which stocked everything a fisherman might require. The buildings jigsawed into a lopsided terrace, formed over the years because of spacial necessity rather than during a specific building epoch or according to a particular architectural style. Penbeagle Street was pretty and quintessentially Cornish.

Number Three was the penultimate house on the west side. A single-storey building, its door was a dusty mustard colour, the paint clinging on in a precarious mosaic of cracks. The number '3' itself was delineated by a darker and uncracked mustard; an imprint of the number plate, long gone. There seemed to be no windows, just an expanse of chipboard emblazoned with a warning against bill stickers and declaring 'Tamsin loves Jake' in small, neat letters, in the bottom right corner. Otherwise it was bare and gave no clue to the interior.

The notion that there was indeed an interior, was huge and daunting. Chloë regarded the key, then the keyhole, and decided she would be late for work if she stayed, even though she would arrive early if she left. She arrived early at the café and stayed on past her time. She cycled back via a longer route which bypassed Penbeagle Street. When she returned to her room, she slipped on William's jumper, said

'Hullo, back in a mo' ' to Mrs Andrews and went directly to Mrs Stokes to ask if she might make a phone call.

'Hullo?'

Lovely voice.

'Will-iam? Chloë here. Cadwallader.'

Lovely voice.

'Hey! I was going to call you. Not today, but tomorrow rather. Or the day after. Well, probably today actually!'

Laughter. Short, clipped, slightly embarrassed.

Silence. A little too long.

'Well, anyway,' said Chloë, clearing her throat, 'I was wondering if I could ask you a favour?'

'Shoot!'

'I couldn't quite do it, you see.'

'What?'

'Go in all by myself. To Number Three Penbeagle Street.'

'Ah.'

'I stood there for a while. It's all boarded up. The key fits. But I don't want to turn it alone, you see.'

'I do see. Not sure what you might find?'

'Exactly.'

'Spiders? Mice?'

'Exactly.'

'I could do tomorrow morning.'

'Brilliant. I'll see if I can change shifts. Thank you already, William. What time? Thank you. Look forward to it.'

'Me too.'

Despite all her intentions, when Chloë heard the doorbell ring the next morning, she skipped down the stairs and flung open the door, greeting William with a radiant smile and an effervescent 'Hullo there!' For his part, William forgot to suck in his cheeks and creased his face instead into an enormous grin which caused dimples like great crevasses and furled his lips right away from his teeth. There they stood, slightly breathless, sparkling away at each other. Mrs Stokes hovered out of sight but observed it all through a crack in the door.

'Nice-looking couple,' she said to the saucepan with a wink as she heard animated laughter line the pathway and disappear only with the chug of a car engine.

FORTY-THREE

Hitherto, of course, Chloë had not expected to come across a rather attractive man in Cornwall. Certainly not one who could cause an almost forgotten flutter deep within her. But there again, she had not foreseen Cornwall providing her with a friend in the making, in Jane. Nor presenting her with a lifestyle that evidently suited her, and a landscape which provided such a decorous backdrop to it all.

While William dragged his heels to the bank, Chloë reorganized her shifts.

'A-*gain*!' Jane exclaimed, feigning shock and unable to conceal excitement. A local boy for Chloë? Good; perhaps she'd stay. 'Still on a par with the brownies?'

'Over par,' Chloë illumined.

'But how does he rank with the banoffee pie?' Jane asked suspiciously.

'Say, one and a half times as nice,' Chloë decided after much carefully contrived deliberation, 'that is, at this point in the proceedings.'

Jane nodded and said 'Proceedings, hey!' with a mouth full of biscuit mixture. 'So what does he look like? Come on, come on!'

Chloë twisted her face as if she had to think hard. 'Not bad,' she reasoned slowly, wondering whether William's hair was tawny, as in owl, or wicker, as in basket.

'Not *bad*?' Jane mulled, pleasantly exasperated. She offered the bowl of biscuit mixture to Chloë who tunnelled her finger in.

'More chocolate chips,' she suggested. Jane agreed and then sent Chloë on her way with a wink and 'Be careful! Enjoy!'

'He's just a nice bloke,' Chloë reasoned at Jane's raised eyebrow, 'and he likes walking.'

Chloë tried the key tentatively, as if it could not possibly fit. She was surprised, almost a little disappointed, when it turned easily. William stood discreetly on the other side of the street, busying himself by half-heartedly reconciling his cheque-book; but as Chloë pressed persuasively against the door, she looked over her shoulder and beckoned him with her eyes. Inside, they stood in silence, in darkness and in dust. It was not long before they cleared their throats and declared 'Heavens, let's get some air in here!'

Accustomed to the gloom, they made out a narrow door at the back of the room and found that the key worked this lock too. As they creaked the door open, a glance of light swung into the room; a long, gossamer triangle in which dust particles danced with relief. They saw chipboard on the inside of the back wall and, with a short plank which lay at his feet, William levered it away. An arched window, whose fanlight was a garland of stained glass, was revealed. They took stock of the room. It was utterly bare. But its proportions were pleasing and Chloë felt her smile broaden. Without speaking and without being asked, William went back outside the building and prised away the chipboard from the front. Another window was uncovered, no stained glass but a fine double sash all the same. Only one pane was cracked.

'Nice space!' encouraged William, catching Chloë's eye

for a little too long before swiftly returning his attention to the room.

'Isn't it just!' agreed Chloë, turning away to examine a wall and hide her blush.

William pointed to a corner. Chloë followed his direction and alighted on a long white envelope that, on closer inspection, had yellowed all around the edges and curled at the corners most forlornly.

'I'll be outside,' said William tactfully.

'Don't!' pleaded Chloë reaching out for his arm, but taking her hand back self-consciously before it made contact. 'Please?'

He stood by her. Her hair smelt of lemons and he inched his face just a little closer to the back of her head. She drew the contents from the envelope. They were the deeds to Number Three Penbeagle Street. Chloë's name had been typed by a land agent's secretary and Jocelyn's signature, though bold and familiar, had undoubtedly faded. Neither the paper, nor the envelope, smelled of Mitsuko.

'It's yours!' William congratulated, flicking the paper between thumb and forefinger.

'It is, isn't it!' Chloë marvelled, kissing the deeds quickly and clutching them to her breast.

They spent the morning examining the building. The back door and arched window looked out over a walled, small sunken garden that was currently obscured by rubble and chickweed, beer cans and a dead gull. Inside, apart from the useful plank and a dusty but unused polystyrene cup, the room was totally bare. And large. William paced it out and declared it to be a good thirty-five feet by almost the same. He pointed out the original coving and crouched on his knees to inspect the skirting-boards which he declared a find. As Chloë sat on her heels beside him to inspect it, she rested her hand on his shoulder. Naturally, lightly; both to steady herself and because she just wanted to.

'I've never thought much about skirting-boards before,' she confided, hoping he would not judge her because of it.

They grinned at each other and touched foreheads gently, just for a moment.

'You smell lemony.'

The bareness of Number Three Penbeagle Street gave Chloë a headache. The building was empty and yet stuffed full of possibility. The building, after all, was hers. Hitherto, the most valuable item she had owned was the mountain bike she had bought the previous month; the most precious, Jocelyn's brooch. Now Jocelyn had bequeathed her an empty building to do with as she liked, and for which she had so many glimpsed ideas that they ricocheted around her mind in an indecipherable and unfathomable tangle. Chloë's head was thrumming. William said that he knew a cure. Chloë remarked to herself, as casually as she could, that he very well might *be* the cure.

They drove up the coast to Portreath where they ate baked potatoes oozing with dark yellow butter. Then they atoned for the cholesterol with a bracing walk along the cliff, on a stretch of coastal path as spectacular and unique as anywhere else on the north coast. The cliffs, soaring up from the sea and plummeting down deep into it, were buffed brown and beige, streaked through with pink and grey, striated with ivory. William gave a theatrical discourse about granite intruding into the surface rock, about metalliferous veins. He explained that the resultant natural beauty that Chloë so admired had solicited the mining industry which had so scarred the landscape with man's greedy mark.

'Mines,' he propounded, 'are but the hallmarks of cupidity for which the devastation of the cliffs was justified.'

His carefully measured grandiloquence caused much hilarity.

'But I *like* the impact of the derelict mines on the landscape,' Chloë protested through her laughter while William decided her eyes were more conker than mahogany, 'the characteristic chimney stacks, the ghostly shafts – in their ruinous state they're actually picturesque.'

William snorted softly and smiled generously.

'Well,' Chloë continued aboard her soapbox, 'I'd say that they're an established and integral feature of the landscape, and quintessentially Cornish.'

'Yes, Chloë,' conceded William, cocking his head and looking up at her, 'I agree with you. I was just playing the devil's avocado!'

Feeling no need to check her actions, Chloë pinched him smartly on the back of his neck, which was warm. She could well have lingered, but she chased him to the cliff edge instead. It was like being with Fraser. No it wasn't. It was different. New. Even better.

They flopped down on to the downy grass; out of breath, cheeks rosy, ear lobes cold, noses noisy. The stunning rocks of Ralph's Cupboard hushed them into reverential silence. But it was temporary. Soon they were spinning elaborate yarns about who Ralph was. And just what it was he kept in his cupboard.

FORTY-FOUR

Chloë had never had tuna-fish casserole with salt-and-vinegar crisps topping. William had never made it before. It was a resounding success; she liked it just as much as he swooned for her bean-and-leftovers soup. One day, they chatted so hard that Chloë was still holding her handlebars and William still had an open tin of sweetcorn in his hands an hour later; the steps to the kitchen separating them and yet not keeping them apart at all. An afternoon soon after, hardly a sentence passed between the two of them; William threw an assortment of teapot spouts while Chloë nestled against the studio steps with Barbara, reading *Lorna Doone* rather noisily.

Shifts permitting, Chloë and William continued their excursions together. If Chloë's work was uncompliant, William would invariably visit the Good Life and try hard not to distract her. His presence, however, she found an utter distraction.

And I wouldn't have it any other way.

William was not Cornwall's only promise, though his continuing gentle courtship was an added pleasure Chloë could never have prophesied. There was Jane too, and their steady friendship now exceeded the boundaries of the café and was developing at a nice pace over shared lunch-hours and shopping trips to Penzance. A close girlfriend her own age was a new concept, and one which she embraced readily.

Jane gave Chloë her seal of approval; for what it's worth, she said. Chloë found she valued it quite highly. And she told her so. Jane remarked wasn't that what mates were for, and would Chloë mind doing her shift the next day. Chloë said she'd do it with pleasure and that was what friends were for.

So life in Cornwall, it transpired, was turning out to be not too bad at all. Chloë realized, with some triumph, that not only was she coping all on her own, she was actually enjoying it too. That her enjoyment was of her own making, not laid on and ready organized for her, was a concept new and pleasing. It was not a fact that she dwelt upon, but it did enable her to get on with daily life, and sleep nourished and happy. She was on her own and yet she wasn't alone. Perhaps for the first time in her life, she had befriended people with whom she had no previous connection. None of the 'Chloë, you must meet so and so', or 'This is Chloë Cadwallader, Jocelyn's god-daughter'; now it was merely 'Hullo, I'm Chloë. Yup, I work in St Ives.'

People liked Chloë Cadwallader for the affable girl that she was. And she liked them, for they were uncomplicated and generous. They did not know her late godmother, and it mattered neither to them nor, now, to Chloë. Cornwall, it seemed, had invited her to stay a while longer. And, for the moment and perhaps beyond, she had accepted.

Locals now greeted her daily and by her name. Mrs Stokes reduced her rent in return for a spot of decorating, a task Chloë undertook gladly. She felt useful, comfortable and trusted, and she was happy to put her own little mark on the place. Cornwall's gifts, however, lay only partly with the folk who resided there; they were also deep sown into the very lie of the land itself. Chloë's affinity with the landscape was unforeseen; how could she have known that living within the sight and scent of the sea would instil daily a sense of well-being she was now not prepared to go without?

Jocelyn can't have known it either. And yet I feel she would have been pleased and proud of me. Cornwall, it appears, may very well be to me as Scotland was to her.

Accordingly, she finally arranged an oddment of things on the mantelpiece: a little dolphin made from shells that was so kitsch it was cute, a smooth pebble William was about to skim out to sea at Portreath, a greening reproduction of a Picasso portrait which made the Andrews wince. And a collection of William's pots, some unglazed, that, much to Chloë's bewilderment, he had rejected as seconds. It felt neither presumptuous nor premature. It was time.

There were thus many good reasons to stay on in Cornwall, but perhaps none so great as Number Three Penbeagle Street. Chloë had shown it now to Jane who had hugged her, called her a 'lucky beggar' and then begged her to turn it into an aerobics studio. Chloë had told Mrs Stokes about it, who vaguely remembered the place before it was boarded up but, infuriatingly, had no recollection of its previous use. Chloë also invited Mac, having asked William if he wouldn't mind fetching him. Not at all. Enthusiasm was universal and they all admired the skirting and the coving which Chloë was keen to point out. She brought people to Number Three that they might rub their chins alongside her for ideas of what she could do with the place. And, though they furrowed their brows diligently, no one alighted on anything plausible. Not that Chloë minded; the ultimate decision, she realized, would only ever come from her. For Chloë, for the time being, though it was bare and a little musty, it was enough that Number Three Penbeagle Street was all her very own. She went there often to just sit and gaze and think, for she felt safe and strong there.

Chloë felt rather good that she was now happy to take each day for its own. She hadn't written to Jasper and

Peregrine for weeks. Fraser owed her a letter but she was only vaguely aware of it.

Though Chloë was unsure how to read her emotions concerning William, she realized too that she craved neither approval nor advice. Jane's supportive winks and nudges sufficed.

This carefree headiness, however, was infused soon enough with a more sober resonance when Chloë and William almost held hands as they explored around Godrevy.

Their fingers brushed inadvertently as they set off for their walk; spontaneously they knotted them together. But only for an instant before snatching them back to themselves, with an awkward smile apiece. They lay flat on their stomachs and marvelled down at Hell's Mouth and Dead Man's Cove. Their shoulders pressed against each other.

For warmth.

For safety.

She could have kissed him. He could have held her. Instead, William told Chloë that Red River got its name in the eighteenth century after the Gwealavellan slaughter but, on seeing her face crease in horror, he confessed that Gwealavellan was a small hamlet of untroubled history, and the river was named Red after the coloured mining spoil coming down from Camborne.

His hair is the colour of a wicker basket, she thought triumphantly as she jabbed him in the ribs and held her head high, pursing her lips and wrinkling her nose at him. Only the sparkle in her eye told that she was not cross at all.

'Oh, Chlo!' William suddenly heard his voice, detached, declaring. Chloë turned to him, then looked away as she realized it was not a prelude but an autonomous sentence and she was a little bashful of its possible meaning. Quietly, they propped themselves up on their elbows and, with faces cupped in their hands, allowed the sea to share their private thoughts. Chloë was still having hers when William turned to her. Gently, he proffered his little finger while holding on tight to her eyes.

They're back to mahogany again.

Slowly, he eased his finger up into one of her ringlets. The spiral was strong yet supremely soft. He gave a little tug and released it; the lock sprang back as it had been before. He did the same to another. And another. Holding Chloë's gaze all the while. She regarded him, at first a little startled, then somewhat bashful, soon unashamedly desirous. Her heart threatened to burst right through her ribs and she was aware how immensely turned on she was. And simultaneously perplexed, yet relieved, that she was rendered immobile because of it.

'Sorry,' William said, coiling a lock between two fingers, 'I just had to.'

'Do it again,' allowed Chloë, 'it's nice.'

Where has this tenderness come from – surprisingly soon, for them both, and yet so naturally? It is neither forced nor premature; not expected yet it is not a surprise. They are thoroughly at ease and yet their senses are on fire. Their souls are filled and thrilled with the portent of it all; while simple contentment flows through their veins as well.

They both believe in Fate but they credit Coincidence too.

Fate, though, must be neither hastened nor tempted; of this William and Chloë are acutely aware. Lying on her stomach on a cliff's edge with William's hand cupping the back of her head, Chloë realizes that the simple first kiss she had so desired from Carl can wait this time. William, she has a feeling, will not be going anywhere. And nor, for the time being, will she. She feels comfortable. In Cornwall. On the cliff. William's hand. Her head resting lightly against it. The embrace of winter's tired sun and heaven's scent.

With some trepidation, William wonders if he is teetering on the edge of – no! Impossible. Or is it? Maybe she could push him right over the edge with one small gesture. Right here. This afternoon.

Do it!

No, don't!

I'm just teetering on the edge of this cliff, that's all.

Yes, William.

FORTY-FIVE

How tall is he? About six foot? A little taller than Fraser. Yes, about six foot. Thirty years old. Why does that seem a nice, safe age? *What* colour is his hair? Tawny, as in owl.

But does he like me in the way I like him?

Does he find me attractive?

Might we get it together? How might that happen? What do I have to do towards it?

Slowly, William began to occupy a great deal of Chloë's precious day-dreaming time, and a great proportion of her night-time thoughts too. Such secret meanderings were sometimes supremely erotic; mostly, though, they were decidedly romantic. The more brazen she became in her mind's eye, however, the more shy she became in his company. And, though she cursed herself sternly, it appeared that she was unable to rectify this. Moreover, because she presumed the strong character in her fantasies to be preferable, she felt compelled to keep the more timid version from William's view. Thus she took on extra shifts, spent more of her spare time with Jane and, once or twice, even asked Mrs Stokes to say she was out should William phone. And yet still William accosted her thoughts. Of course he did. In desperation, after a disturbed night of highly lustful dreams and subsequent self-reproval, she phoned Fraser at the tiniest mention of dawn the next morning.

'MacWallader! Good God, I thought you were phone-bic!'

'I am, usually.'

'What's up? My letter's in the post – I promise, I swear. Chloë? You still there?'

'Can I come back? To Braer?'

'What's up?'

'A man. I think.'

'Hussy! I like it!'

'Fraser?'

'Sorry, bunny. What's happened?'

'Nothing. Yet.'

'Oh? Well, is he nice?'

'Lovely.'

'Is he a looker?'

'He's pretty gorgeous. Well, *I* think so.'

'Ooh! Well muscled? Tell me he bulges – oh, tell me he does!'

'He's fit, Fraser; athletic looking. You know, lovely in Levi's?'

'Wow, Chlo! I need to sit. More!'

'He's a potter. He lives in a picture-perfect cottage on a cliff with a goat called Barbara.'

'MacDoubleYou. I'm gasping. Marry him. Or else I will.'

'Can I come back, then?'

'What? Why!'

'Because I don't know what to *do*.'

'Do you think he rather likes you too?'

'Hmm.'

'Would that be an affirmative mumble?'

'I think so.'

'Well then, you most definitely *can't* come back here. Well, you can – but not without *him* – there!'

'Fray-zer! I need you. I *don't* know what to do.'

'I think you rather do.'

* * *

'What do you think, Barbara?'

She's a goat, William, and even if she does hold opinions on the matter, she is unable to tell you – or, rather, you are incapable of understanding her.

William has suddenly decided that he probably ought not to get involved with Chloë. He tries to reason that his freedom and privacy are of supreme importance in his life. He also considers whether she hasn't become a little more guarded, somewhat cooler of late. Certainly, he hasn't seen her so often recently. Not as often as he'd like.

Not that I've missed her.

Not that much.

Not much!

He tries not to acknowledge that he fears Chloë leaving Cornwall, and the chance of it, for some other country. Where there may be someone else. It is not as if there was a space in William's life before, which Chloë has now actively filled, but he is in no doubt that if she were to go, a dull void would take her place.

And then he would be afforded only glimpses of memory. And what use would those be?

A glance of her porcelain neck.

Her incomparably soft twirls and curls, so rich and red that they radiate light. Oh, the feel of them!

Eyes mahogany, sometimes conker, lately a rich chocolate too.

The sight of her, yes, but the sound of her more so; the sound of her. She makes funny noises while she reads. She sings under her breath as she walks. And she hums with his pottery, caressing his senses *and* affirming his merits as a ceramicist too. But he hasn't heard her for a while.

'Oh God, Barbara, isn't to actually *hear*, more preferable than merely to *recall*, to remember?'

Barbara regards him as if he is a fool.

'Of course it is, damn it.'

* * *

Ridiculously early one morning, after mulling over more possible uses for Number Three Penbeagle Street, Chloë sits cross-legged on the bed, swaddled in William's jumper which she has consistently neglected to return. The post-card reproduction of *Mr and Mrs Andrews* by Thomas Gainsborough (1727–1788) lies, a little dog-eared, in her lap. Sixty-one years old when he died – what an injustice! She decides swiftly not to let the Andrews know, let alone the artist himself. She comes across Mr Andrews on his customary early morning 'blow through'.

'Where's your wife?' she asks.

'Charming!' he exclaims. 'Will I not do?'

'I don't know,' Chloë says honestly. 'I think it's Women's Things.'

'Hmm,' he contemplates, 'biological er, disturbances?'

'No!' Chloë cries. 'Well, I suppose it could be – all because of a man I've met.'

'Now that's not like you, Chloë dear,' says Mr Andrews, very interested, 'not like you at all. Sit down on the bench and we'll have a chin-wag. Rex! Heel! Good dog.'

'I've met a chap.'

'You've met a chap.'

'Yes.'

'And his name, girl?'

'William Coombes.'

'And has he a respectable trade?'

'He's a potter.'

Mr Andrews considers this, and then considers it good.

'Remember the urns at Ballygorm?' Chloë continues. 'They're his. Not only that – the ceramics I so loved at the South Bank last year too; which I remembered even when I was in Antrim. Isn't that weird?'

'Actually,' Mr Andrews counters, 'I'd think it rather comforting in some small way myself. This huge world full of people revolving around their own minor worlds and yet you two, it seems, destined to meet.'

'Yes,' Chloë agrees, 'because if it hadn't been in London, or even in Ireland, it would still have been here.'

'So why is it my wife whom you seek?'

'Oh,' mumbles Chloë, 'I don't know. You know? Just a chat, some advice. I think.'

'Advice, hey?'

'A cure for a stomach full of butterflies?' Chloë suggests meekly.

'Gone off your food?' Mr Andrews asks, and it sounds like 'orf'. Chloë nods. 'Can't sleep a peep?' he furthers. She nods vigorously. 'Mind wanders and dances around in circles?' Chloë agrees. 'Not altogether unpleasant a sensation, is it!' he declares.

'No,' Chloë concedes, 'but strange.'

'And would you be happier if it were to subside, disappear even?'

'No,' declares Chloë, suddenly alarmed, 'absolutely not.'

'Well then,' Mr Andrews declares.

'But,' falters Chloë, 'is it *safe*?'

'It's safe,' he winks, 'dear, dear girl.'

She feels slightly easier, though she's not sure why, and thanks Mr Andrews accordingly. She takes off William's jumper, folds it and places it on the chest of drawers. She would, of course, be forgetting it accidentally on purpose when she next saw him.

Mr Andrews woke his wife rudely.

'Mr A!' she declared. 'Gracious me! Put that thing away. And put me down at once.'

'Cadwallader,' he declared, wrestling with his garters, 'is in love.'

The last Tuesday in November was when, finally, William, watching Chloë climb and wriggle her way through the ancient holed stone of Men-an-Tol, realized he was running up the one-way street of being in love with her. He did not tell her so just then, as the emotion itself was too raw and unexplored; the notion simultaneously baffling and intoxicating, uninvited and yet not unwelcome.

Chloë had, in fact, found herself in much the same place the day before. Two pages from the end of *Rebecca*, she suddenly stopped reading. Reaching for the closest thing to hand that would serve as a bookmark, she slipped a National Gallery postcard of a Gainsborough double portrait between the pages and put the book down. She walked over to the window, juddered the sash up and thrust her face full on against the spiky chill of November.

'Heavens,' she said, smiling and frowning, 'I wonder if I'm falling in, you know, love?'

She knew her feelings to be as strong as the wind and as fresh as the air, and if that was how being in love felt, then it was a condition to be welcomed.

FORTY-SIX

Chloë could not sleep. She rose soundlessly at two in the morning, dressed without a fuss and stepped out into the cold. The familiar cycle route soon warmed her and the sound of the sea made her feel safe.

Number Three Penbeagle Street was no more gloomy at night than it was during the day, the other buildings, however, now seemed lonely and forsaken without their daytime activity. The key turned easily as she knew it would and Chloë pushed her bicycle through first and followed it, closing the door behind her with an unobtrusive click. The lamp on her bicycle spun a soft light on the interior but cast no shadows for there was nothing in the room to produce them. Just the walls. The windows. The two doors. The original coving. The fine skirting. And the unused polystyrene cup it had seemed rash to throw away.

'Are you there?'

'Yes, I am here.'

'*Is* it you?'

'Yes, it is me.'

'Jocelyn?'

'Sweet Chloë.'

Chloë did not need to see her to know she was there. She felt her; a warmth enveloping, comfort seeping. Jocelyn was very near. As close as ever she had been. Mitsuko. For a while, Chloë stood very still and said nothing. She feared the lump in her throat might make her voice falter; break, even. And that would upset Jocelyn who had decreed no tears. Now that she was here at last, finally with her once again, Chloë could not spoil her visit. So she just stood, resting her back lightly against the wall, the backs of her knees nudging the back wheel of her bicycle, one hand on a warmed tyre, the other in her pocket. She gazed over to the arch window and caught a glint of ruby, a glance of emerald picked out from the fanlight by her cycle lamp. Beyond, the neglected garden emerged as two sombre humps, like an old hippo, patient and camouflaged in a drying water-hole. She closed her eyes and prophesied a flourish of small flowers instead, whites and mauves and perhaps forget-me-not blue. No pink, that was for sure. She envisaged variegated ivy, perhaps Virginia creeper clambering up the wall, and she went over to the window and peered through. She saw clematis stampeding. A small table or two. Perhaps the sound of a trickle of water. Endless. So possible. How exciting.

'Isn't it!' Jocelyn declared. 'I *knew* you'd find it so!'

'Can't wait,' said Chloë gratefully, turning back into the room and leaning against the window-sill. 'The key unlocks more than Number Three Penbeagle Street, doesn't it?' she mused.

'Flinging open the doorway to the rest of your life, my duck!' declared Jocelyn.

'A great, big open space,' exclaimed Chloë. 'A little frightening,' she added quietly.

'Challenging!' corrected Jocelyn kindly. 'Do you think I'd send you anywhere where you would not be safe?'

'No, Jo,' said Chloë, 'you never would.'

They shared an audible smile and sighed each other's name.

'Cornwall,' started Chloë cautiously.

'Cornwall!' agreed Jocelyn.

'Why no introduction? Like you gave for the other places? Jocelyn?'

'Because, my dear, it needs no explanation. I did not need to expound its beauty for I knew you could find it by yourself. I know you very well. I knew it would suit you. I believed it might provide the solace for you which Scotland gave to me. After all, is it not here that you found me?'

'Heavens, yes it is,' marvelled Chloë.

'And so,' said Jocelyn, 'it is here that I can now leave you, for you can let me go.'

'I can't!'

'You *can*, darling.'

'I don't want to.'

'But I'd like you to.'

Chloë bit back tears.

'I need you to,' said Jocelyn.

'And I – Need – You,' whispered Chloë.

'I think you'll find you just *think* you do, my darling.'

Chloë considered this. 'I *want* to keep needing you.'

'Why is that?'

'I suppose it makes me feel safe.'

'Safety,' said Jocelyn, 'is ultimately of one's own making. And I rather think you now have an inkling of that fact.'

'I do?' said Chloë somewhat incredulously. 'I suppose I do,' she said forlornly.

'Built up and developed over your year away?'

'*Your* year away!' countered Chloë.

'No,' said Jocelyn firmly, 'your own.'

'Yes,' said Chloë quietly after a moment's reflection, 'mine.'

'Doesn't it feel good to say so?'

'Not sure,' Chloë wavered, 'it feels strange, new.'

'I think,' Jocelyn declared, 'that you'll develop a taste for it.'

'*Do* you?' whispered her god-daughter, who held implicit trust in Jocelyn and believed everything she said.

'Oh yes,' said Chloë's godmother, 'I do.'

Chloë said 'Heavens' to herself and then sighed contentedly out loud.

'Do you think you might be happy here, Chloë? In Cornwall? Because you could always sell Number Three if you like; take the proceeds to wherever you decide to settle.'

'No!' Chloë exclaimed, surprised at the brevity of her reaction. 'It's mine! And yes,' she said, chewing the notion and finding it appetizing, 'I think I could be happy here. Funnily enough.'

'*Bliss*fully happy?' goaded Jocelyn gently. Chloë turned and faced the garden again. 'Why don't you answer?' asked Jocelyn, 'Chlo?'

'Possibly,' was all she muttered after a while.

'Now girl!' laughed Jocelyn, who could always tell when Chloë was blushing, even if her back was towards her, even over the telephone, even between the lines of a letter. 'What have I told you about ambiguity? Is it not an affectation that is neither witty nor necessary?'

'I don't mean to be ambiguous,' hurried Chloë, missing the warmth in Jocelyn's voice. 'I was just wondering.'

''Bout what?'

'About the acceptable speed for love to appear and root itself.'

''Bout time!'

'But *is* it?' whispered Chloë, incredulous, as if, without Jocelyn's go-ahead, the whole concept could so easily have remained untenable, implausible. 'Really?'

'Isn't it!' Jocelyn declared. 'Oh Chloë! If you detect even an inkling of happiness, a tiny glimpse of love, a mere hint of contentment, for heaven's sake grab it and don't let go. Don't, ever, think twice.'

Her words hung in the velvet brown of the room and when she spoke again, her voice was low and shot through with wisdom, with experience, tinged with sadness: 'Don't lose it, my duck. It comes but once. Do not question it. Do not forsake it. It cannot be retrieved.'

Chloë cycled back; slow, sad but somehow exhilarated too. Jocelyn's voice filled her head and images of William solicited her mind's eye. The knowledge of both was immensely soothing. Later, as she pushed her face into the pillow to stifle her sobbing, she laughed as she cried.

Oh Jocelyn Jo, don't go.

Oh William!

Stay!

FORTY-SEVEN

And so to the kiss that seals their fate and our story.

William's intention was that Chloë should see Carn Galver. He offered the Good Life his voluntary services as a washer-upper if only they would excuse Chloë her shift.

'Fine by me,' said Jane, eyeing November's dwindling clients dawdling over herbal tea refills. The proprietor released Chloë but demanded that William honour his debt the next Saturday night. Chloë whispered to Jane that she would gladly do her shift on that night.

It was a piercingly clear day and William knew that a walk to the summit of Carn Galver would afford them priceless views over both coasts and justify a hearty tea too. They did not make it. In fact, they would not make it to the top until late January, though they went there often. The pull of the ancient landscape was too strong in other directions, and it seemed to lure them invariably to places not on their itinerary. But always for a reason: a particularly beautiful sky, a peregrine falcon just yards away, sunlight turning the standing stones to gold. They were quite happy for chance to lead the way and were rewarded with the secrets and gifts such detours provided.

When William told Chloë that a journey through the pierced stone of Men-an-Tol would bring her luck and health, she bundled her jacket into his arms and wished her way through the rock. As he helped her through, a shot of sunlight, pink and warm, alighted on her face and kissed it before William could. It spun the stone soft, it pulled flame from her hair, it sank deep into her eyes and turned her skin truly into porcelain. She could have been the mermaid of Zennor and, just at that moment, William thought she very probably was.

As she came through the stone, the sunlight clung to her and caught on something shiny, shooting liquid silver into William's eyes. Her brooch. Familiar. Why not! But he didn't have time to think on it now. Chloë pressed her back against the stone and closed her eyes so that the sun could embrace her face fully. It defied the pervasive scent of winter and brought with it the reminder of summer, the promise of spring. She could feel just a whisper of breeze breathe over her cheek, lifting a lock of hair and gently laying it down again. She felt beautiful.

Do I look beautiful too? Does he find me so?

She opened her right eye and saw William.

He does. And he is lovely himself.

He came close to her, his gaze swallowing her whole.

He is now going to kiss me.

Cautiously, William stretched out his hand until his fingertips rested lightly on her shoulder. He came a step nearer and moved his hand to course the curve between collar-bone and breast. Closer still; with his forefinger, he traced the lines of her brooch. Lightly, quickly and deftly. He stepped towards Chloë once more, until his feet stood either side of hers. His heart seemed to be pounding in his throat but he had forgotten how to swallow. Then he let his hand drop further until it quite covered her left breast and he left it there for a tender, delicious moment. Chloë's soul surged and she could discern her heartbeat deep between her legs. William could feel it too, but under his hand, through her clothes, beneath her breast.

The instant he eased his hand, he saw her eyebrows twitch almost imperceptibly. They told him: please, leave your hand, touch me still, touch me there!

I want to.

I want you to.

He knew then that she wanted to be touched as much as he wanted to touch her. Her lips were parted, his eyes were glassy and burning.

Kiss me, William.

I am going to kiss you, Chloë.

Now.

Right now.

The gesture was as spontaneous as it was long awaited; a moment's desire that was momentous, an instinct that was far-reaching.

William's face nears Chloë's, the sun is blocked yet her beauty is not compromised. Eyes are open; they press their lips against each other and the relief that courses through William mixes with the delight that fills Chloë. They are saturated with emotion and share it at once. Soft lips lightly against each other, the sensation of another's breath on the skin, eyes so close that focus goes, cold noses touching. Instinctively, the kiss changes from one of tenderness to one of passion and, opening their mouths, they gorge themselves on each other's taste.

Chloë knots her fingers around the belt loops of William's jeans and guides him close against her. She feels abandoned and comfortable. Oh, how he fits! William places one hand on her neck, the other is enmeshed in her hair and holds her as close to him as he can. His erection presses against the seam of his trousers, and against Chloë's stomach; the sensation is fantastic for them both. Their tastes are distinctive and they find each other delicious.

They hear sounds, involuntary expressions of warmth and desire. They are hungry and they have never been so full. The rock supports them and the sun allows them to kiss on, despite the diminishing afternoon. Deserted November affords them the privacy; the spirituality of the place, the prayer. One kiss against an ancient rock will give shape to their foreseeable futures. They knew it to be so before it happened. And after, they are content that it should be.

FORTY-EIGHT

William blamed Barbara. And then he blamed Mac. If Barbara had only shown her customary distaste and accompanying aggression, he could have denounced Chloë as just-another-woman. And if Mac had not propounded the theory of blissful happiness, William could have remained blissfully unaware of its existence and all the panoply that went with it. And though he blamed them both and cursed them liberally, he did so with an easy smile and a glint to his eye.

It was all their fault, bless them.

Their fault entirely and oh! was he grateful.

Only, he couldn't work under such pressure, with such a distraction, and it wasn't long before this nagged him.

'You can't *work*? Dear boy, that's not like you,' exclaimed a startled Mac on seeing William at his doorstep three days in a row; offering, predictably, a bag of Good Life goodies.

'I know,' William growled, flouncing down in a chair and holding his head in his hands.

'How's that Chloë girl?' Mac asked with a carefully contrived edge of innocence, not telling William that she'd visited him the day before. William's face shone and his eyes danced. Much in the same way as Chloë's had, Mac observed.

'She's fine.'

'Lovely girl.'

'Mmm.'

'Might she not be the reason for your lack of motivation? Subconsciously at any rate?'

'Mac!' William exclaimed, off his guard and suddenly wanting to be back on it.

'Forgive me,' Mac declared, 'but she *is* your girlfriend, isn't she? And aren't you, er, rather more than just *fond* of her?'

What? Girlfriend? Who?

William felt suddenly rather compromised; half wondering how Mac knew, half doubting whether he wanted it to be public knowledge. After a careful silence though, he confided in Mac that he was pretty happy. Mac slapped him on the shoulder and ruffled his hair.

'Good,' he declared, 'jolly good.'

As he watched William walk – no, that was more of a swagger – to his car, Mac remarked to himself that it would not be long before the boy was using a far stronger adjective.

Girlfriend? thought William later, mesmerized by a winter sunset. *What sort of a word is that!*

A rather descriptive one, surely.

'Girlfriend,' he said tentatively, seeing if it fitted his tongue. How it tasted. He laughed sheepishly. It tasted sweet.

'But it sounds so corny!'

The surface of the water way below swelled and glinted. A gull bobbed along.

'Bird!' he said.

'Babe!' he said.

'Chick,' he cried sarcastically.

Better than 'lover', William, isn't it?

'If I have a girlfriend,' he reasoned later with Barbara,

thawing his hands under her coat, 'if she is known to others as my girlfriend, it means that I'm having a relationship. A proper one.'

So?

'Am I ready?'

The thought of not being ready, of losing what was coming into focus the more he saw of Chloë, made him shudder and decide he was more than ready. He went directly to his studio and decided to make her a teapot.

William and Chloë, however, did not acknowledge between themselves that they were now a couple, an item, that they were seeing each other, dating, that they were in a relationship, going steady. They were taking things very steady indeed; just spending time together, enjoying simply kissing. There was a newness for both of them, a beam of light magic they had not experienced in their previous entanglements. Neither wanted to rush through this stage. There was so much to talk about, so much to find out. So much to savour. It was fun to grow.

I'm not going to waste too much time on bloody Morwenna.

I don't think it's necessary to tell him about Ronan's sculpture.

Chloë and William had taken to settling into the kitchen chairs at Peregrine's Gully, taking sips from great mugs of scalding, sweetened tea in between telling each other more about themselves; listening without prejudice to one another and imparting unchecked. Such sessions invariably started with them sitting upright and conversing animatedly, mugs cupped in their laps and ears peeled. They usually ended with Chloë resting her head on the table in the crook of her arm, while William propped his face in his hands though it squashed his features and slurred his speech.

'Morwenna really wasn't a big deal to me – I was a bigger deal to her, she and her thirty per cent.'

'You toy boy, you! Is this teapot *really* for me, William? It's gorgeous. Ronan made a sculpture for me, well, for Ballygorm; rather funny actually, in retrospect.'

'Yes?'

'Mmm.'

Chloë, however, always returned to her digs, whatever the time and usually by bicycle. William invariably accompanied her by car; little toots and the full beam from his headlamps lining and lighting the way. She did not speak to the Andrews as regularly; Gainsborough had finished the portrait and November saw the couple spending more time indoors in front of the fire in the library. Similarly, her letters to Jasper and Peregrine became shorter and fewer. Not that they minded.

'Must fit in with her life now,' Jasper commented.

'Now that she has such a full one down in Cornwall,' Peregrine furthered, holding a single page of paper with writing only on the one side.

'She doesn't say much about her *boyfriend*,' Jasper rued, 'just that he's a "tremendously nice fellow".'

'She doesn't have to – and with this much space left in her letters,' Peregrine declared, brandishing the piece of paper again, 'we can read all we wish between the lines with ease.'

Back in her bedsit, Chloë would gaze out over the sea, ebony and silver, and ask it what to do next.

I adore him, I do. And I desire him. I want to sleep with him, heavens I do, but I know I'm holding back. Why is that? I can't seem to let go. Why can't I? Is it that the slip-road from Cornwall might disappear if I do?

The sea never spoke to her. But it was always there for her, swelling and moving, in and out, high tide and low. Consistently, constantly. Lovely; how she loved it.

FORTY-NINE

'Chloë!'

'Mrs Andrews – it's been an age. How *are* you?'

'Freezing, my dear. We've – I mean, I've been getting intimate with the fire in the study – I can't bear to be apart from him. Er, *it*. Tell me your news – how's the potter fellow?'

'He's well. I – Mrs Andrews, I'd love to talk, truly I would. Only I'm late as it is. I'm on my way to see him, William. My potter fellow. We're going to have a quick bowl of the soup we made yesterday and then we're off on a walk. Can I catch up with you later?'

'Oh please do. I'm dying to know. I crave details, my dear, you know how I crave details.'

Chloë Cadwallader's bicycle, hitherto her metaphorical trusty steed, today let her down. Not gently, but with a rather uncompromising lurch and crash. With all those gears, and those sturdy tyres, she had decided to cycle cross-country. It was against National Trust rules. She should have known. In fact, she did; so it served her right.

Why? she chastised herself as she found herself in a heap, precariously close to a large thatch of gorse, her cycle on its side a few feet away, its front wheel spinning futilely.

Why? It was hardly much of a short cut anyway.

Perhaps you just wanted to get to Peregrine's Gully as quickly as was logistically possible?

Possibly. But now look at me. I've torn my jeans and scratched my knee.

And you've got bits in your hair too. Never mind, it won't matter to William.

William caught sight of Chloë trudging up the path. He left the soup burbling away and walked briskly towards her, Barbara in tow.

'Oh Chloë! Crikey – you OK?'

'I'm fine,' Chloë said clearly, brushing away William's concern and Barbara's inquisitive nose.

'You're late,' he said, taking the handlebars from her and gently pulling a leaf from her hair. 'I was worried.'

'I had to walk the last two miles,' she explained, slipping her hand into the back pocket of his trousers.

'Are you hurt?' he asked, scouring her face and laying the back of his warm hand against her chilled cheek.

'No, just cross,' she assured. 'Bloody bike. Silly me.'

William propped the errant cycle against the side of the cottage.

'Oh bugger,' he said, 'the soup! Listen, you pop upstairs and put yourself back together. There's TCP in the cupboard under the sink, plasters too – or there should be.' He sent Chloë on her way with a gentle pat to the bottom, returning his attention to their soup, whistling merrily.

The TCP stung but there was no need for plasters. Not that there were any; Chloë had a good rummage. She was hot, but no longer bothered, and flung off her jumper and T-shirt while she ran a basin of water. She plunged her arms into the warm water. And then stood very still. And somehow knew she should just stay there. Just as she was. And wait.

Downstairs, William stopped his whistling. He looked

into the saucepan and gazed at the surface of the soup phut-phutting without really seeing or hearing it. He felt as if something, some force, was pulling him; he was drawn out of himself though his head was clear and he knew himself very well. He left the soup, left the wooden spoon in it too. Almost in a daze, he left it, still simmering, and made his way measuredly to the bathroom.

Chloë in a vest. Her face hidden by her hair. Stooping over the basin, sponging her neck while the water trickles over her arms like tiny rivers running their course. Chloë in a vest. Nipples defined. Jeans cinched in at the waist. Water on her arms. Her face hidden. Arms slender, pale. Porcelain? Perhaps.

The sound of William clearing his throat. Chloë turns. His handsome, brawny face; hair tousled. Wicker basket. Her hair falls away from her face, one or two auburn swirls catch and remain there. The sight of her. And of him.

Chloë and William observe each other. In silence, rock steady, intently. The only movement comes from a rivulet of water coursing from Chloë's neck, across her shoulder, over her chest and under her vest. Has it stopped? Where? Between her breasts? More than likely. Let me see. Come and check.

William steps towards her, she turns her gaze back to the basin. Slowly, he approaches. Her breathing is fast but silent. She gazes at her hands underwater, distorted a little, at the base of the sink. He's here. Behind her, William presses his body very gently against hers, encircling her waist with his dream-worthy forearms, brushing the side of her neck with his nose, tasting the tip of her ear lobe with his tongue. He unwraps his arms and, while he kisses her more fervently on her neck which she has now instinctively thrown back, he runs his fingertips up and down her bare, damp arms. Up and down. She has goose-bumps. Her fast breathing is audible. She can't reach any part of him to kiss so she presses her neck strongly against his face. While he murmurs his lips against her neck, he feels down the length of her slender arms, from shoulder to wrist, until both sets of hands are deep in the basin. His fingers are distorted too, but they are also interleaved with Chloë's in the warm, limpid water.

She makes a little gasp, involuntary, unaware of how seductive it sounds. William takes his hands from the sink and swiftly to her breasts. Sudden sound and movement. The drag and splash of water. Chloë wet but hardly breathing. William twirling her towards him. He brings his face in line and takes her mouth first with his eyes and then with his lips. He is holding her wrists and she is kissing him back. She frees an arm and grasps the back of his head so that she can kiss him more deeply and taste him better. She finds she is starving. Never has she been so hungry. He has swooped her tight close to him.

They stop a moment to regard each other. Her pupils are huge, her cheeks are rosy and her sweet, short breathing whispers over him. Her arms are still damp, her chest rises and falls. She cannot know how alluring she is in her damp, funny, sensible vest which both hides and heralds her breasts. William places his hand softly on her shoulder and then lets it slip down in a simple, fluid movement. The journey to her breasts may be short but it is exquisite. He feels her body pitch as he cups his hand over one, a perfect pip of a nipple pushing through cotton to be at the centre of his palm.

A small smile at one corner of her mouth accompanies her swift removal of the garment. And so Chloë stands before him, semi-naked, her upper body slim and milky in comparison to her lower half, jean-clad and enticing. William sweeps his hands over her torso, so lightly, all over. He watches her close her eyes and swoon. Another dusting of goose-bumps prickles over her arms. Lips part imploring to be kissed. Nipples stand to attention and crave it.

My pleasure.

Mine too.

As William encircles Chloë in his arms, she brings her hands to her breastbone, as if in prayer. No, not in prayer but to unbutton William's shirt. His chest immediately. No T-shirt. No vest. Isn't it smooth! A bloom of hair over his stomach and down into his trousers. So masculine. Never seen; only imagined. William runs his hands from her neck, down her arms to her fingers; lightly, he pulls her towards him while he steps backwards. He is sitting on the edge of the bath and gathers her to him, between his legs. His hands at her buttocks. Her hands either side of his neck. Again she kisses him; letting him have her tongue, then taking it away so she can graze the side of his mouth. She has a hand enmeshed in his hair, the other unbuckles her belt. William unzips her jeans and pushes them down.

Chloë is wearing blue-and-white stripy knickers. Never seen; never imagined. They turn him on. Her stomach is flat but her waist dips and her hips curve. Everything about her is sinuous and beautiful, his desirous eyes tell her so. She looks at him, sitting on the edge of the bath, his leg muscles clearly defined under his trousers, his chest wide, his stomach rippled, no ounce of fat. A bulge in his lap. It excites her. She reaches her hand out tentatively but stops midway; he grasps it and they complete its course together. They feel his hardness and desire through the fabric; their breathing quickens and gazes glaze. William stands up.

He's so much bigger than me.

She's so small and precious.

Chloë helps him unbuckle his belt, not that he needs assistance but just because she wants to knit fingers again. As he bends to remove his trousers, she does the same. She leaves her knickers on because he stands before her resplendent in his. Boxer shorts. Thank heavens! Plain, crisp and white. They fold into each other again, her skin has cooled and he is lovely and warm. She can feel his cock pressing against her and she opens her legs a little so she can push her crotch against his thigh. All the while, they kiss. They can hear the noise it makes and it increases the fervour they feel. Now Chloë is sitting on the edge of the bath and William notices how her stomach curves a little. Like a beautiful vase; porcelain. Or perhaps she is carved from marble. No, she is too warm and soft to the touch. She is drawing him towards her. She is easing down his boxer shorts. He sees his cock spring out into the air and it excites him. And her. She bends her face over his groin. He is unsure where her mouth is, behind all her hair, but he hopes it is near. He cradles her head against his stomach and sees the tip of his cock appear through a tangle of russet ringlets. He steps away a little. She is looking up at him. He holds her face in his hands and strokes her, from her forehead, over her cheeks, down to her chin. She takes his hands away and holds them. She holds on to his gaze too, until her head is too low. She kisses his cock tenderly and lightly. Licks a little, here and there. He gasps and groans softly. The sound of him emboldens her. She sucks more deeply, more of it. He grasps her shoulders and lifts her away, pulls her up from the bath and bites the apple of her cheek gently.

'I want you,' he murmurs. She can't reply. She is near delirious with lust and too full of excitement. William leads the way from bathroom to bedroom. Bare and clean, uncluttered and conducive. Chloë can see the sea. Oh, what a room! She goes to the window and gazes away, hearing William throw back bed covers somewhere in the distance.

'Chloë.'

His voice is soft, low. She turns. He sees her silhouetted, her contours classical and more beautiful than ever he had imagined. More perfect and flowing than he could ever hope to throw in clay. He slips down between the sheets and holds a corner open for her. She walks over to him. He steadies her arm as she removes her blue-and-white stripy knickers. He rummages under the covers and presents her with his boxer shorts, white and crisp, warm too. She places them with care, together, on the bedside table and sidles into the bed, next to him. She's home.

FIFTY

The soup burned. The pot was ruined. The kitchen smelled strangely of caramel. Toast and marmite was nice enough, fortifying too. As timetabled, they ventured once more to Carn Galver, just a little later than they had planned. Once again, they didn't quite reach it. They strolled back with apologetic glances to the mountain. A brave entourage of pony-trekkers snaked into the distant hillside. Chloë pointed and said nothing.

'Wish you were in Wales?' asked William, moving his hand in from her shoulder so that his thumb touched the corner of her mouth.

She shook her head adamantly but clasped his hand against her face as she did so. The memories were sweet to her, but old. Past.

'Rather be on horseback?' he suggested, stroking her cheek with the back of his hand before returning it to her shoulder.

Chloë smiled and shook her head again. They walked on quietly.

'And Men-an-Tol more than suffices,' she said suddenly but only half aloud, concluding a long conversation she had just had with herself.

'Hey?' asked William, making her stop.

'Sculpture!' she declared, wide-eyed and artless. 'No need for Ireland and sculpture trails – Cornwall seems to be one vast sculpture park! From the granite boulders lining the way from Zennor to St Ives, to the standing stones. From the forsaken mines to the giant masonry of the cliffs –'

'Wicca Pinnacle!' interrupted William.

'Zennor Quoit!' agreed Chloë.

'The Tate at St Ives,' reasoned William.

'Hepworth's garden!' settled Chloë.

She walks on, holding out her hand that he might take it. He slips his hand into hers and her fingers fold around his, like daisy petals at dusk.

'So,' he summarizes, 'no to Wales and to horses; no need for Ireland and no call for sculpture gardens.'

'No,' says Chloë.

'Scotland?' he asks.

'Scotland!' she sighs mistily. He falls silent and they walk on. He daren't press her. He needn't.

'Too far,' she says kindly. He looks puzzled. 'From you,' she whispers while her eyes dance and she touches his lips with her gloved hands.

'From others?' he pumps.

'Others?' she asks.

'Nearest and dearest?'

'*You* are but two feet away from me!' she laughs, a little embarrassed. His smile and his sparkle tell her she needn't be.

'Those dear are not near,' she explains, 'but they could not be dearer were they nearer. They live in the four corners of a kingdom united by Jocelyn. Even if they were all in one place –' she hovers, 'and if that place was not here – still would I stay.'

Chloë breathed in the coconut scent of the gorse and implored William to do the same. She ruffled his hair and stroked his back as he bent tentatively to the flowers.

'You see,' she said, 'I had to stand up straight and all by myself here – possibly for the first time ever. I'm not overconfident, or very ambitious, certainly I'm not that sociable. I've always quite *liked* to be told what to do, where to go. Oh my Jocelyn! And to an extent, she did just that – right up until Cornwall. She sent me to the Gin Trap, who asked me to accompany small children on horseback. She told me to go to Gus, and he ordered me to phone these people, type this letter, order this, organize that. Then she sent me to Fraser, and he told me to take drinks out to the wedding party in the garden; then what colour to paint which room! And though I feel I began then to see a way to express myself, I'd invariably turn to Mr and Mrs Andrews for guidance in moments of even the slightest doubt.'

'Mr and Mrs Who?'

'Andrews,' said Chloë in a matter-of-fact way.

'The only couple I know by that name are a pair of Gainsborough toffs residing on a wall at the National Gallery!'

Chloë smiled to herself and then over to William. 'I thought you might,' she said fondly, 'and they are the very same.'

William interrupted her with a kiss.

'Chloë-Chloë-Chloë!' he chanted like a sea bird. 'The Girl Cadwallader!' he declared. He shook his head in amazement and gave a little snort, as if crediting some great coincidence or remarkable revelation. She was so sincere, and that she spoke from her heart solicited his own even more. He slipped his hand into the back pocket of her jeans and gave a little squeeze.

'What?' she laughed, skipping in front of him and then walking on, backwards.

'That you should have an eighteenth-century couple, albeit painted, as your confidantes,' he caught up with her and touched her nose with his, 'and that I should have a goat as mine!' They walked on, marvelling at their eccentricity, their affinity.

'Anyway,' she recapped easily over the interlude of goat and Gainsborough, 'Cornwall and no one. Nothing to do! But I found a little job, all by myself. My comfortable digs. All on my own. I began to make friends with strangers; making my own introduction. And then I found that I had Number Three. The kaleidoscope was still for once, and presented me with a lovely pattern that I really liked.'

She kissed William. He kissed her back. She raised her eyebrow and he winked at her.

'And what'll you do with Number Three? Any ideas?'

'Loads,' she laughed, 'but only one that I think is really feasible.'

'And what's that?'

'To enable people to venerate the coving and admire the skirting-boards, of course.'

'And how'll they do that?'

'In a comfortable chair with a mug of coffee or a cup of sweetened tea!'

'What? Just sit there and stare at the walls?'

'No, silly! Well yes, if they want! I thought, in the true tradition of St Ives, that Number Three should share its pleasing proportions with people who will be nourished by them. I'll do the garden too, so they can sit outside in the summer. And have a think. Or a day-dream. Whatever!'

'So, a Tea Shoppe,' said William, unable not to sound disappointed.

'Heavens no!' scolded Chloë, 'just Number Three. I'll sell coffee and books, tea and tables.'

'Tables?'

'To write on – poetry, letters, music, fiction – whatever their calling!'

'A space conducive to those of artistic sensibilities!' William mused, delighted.

'Precisely,' said Chloë.

'Rather than to those in search of fat scones and clotted cream!' William continued, grasping the idea and not wanting to let go.

'Exactly.'

'Niche in the market,' he congratulated, his beam telling her he thought her quite brilliant.

'But,' said Chloë slyly, 'they *can* buy the mugs from which they drink!'

'Don't tell me,' William groaned jovially, 'bedecked with pixies and glazed in Cornish sludge.'

'But of course,' she defended, 'anyway, Mac's behind me all the way.'

'I bet he is,' laughed William, 'and what's his cut?' Chloë wrinkled her nose and her eyes sparkled. William pressed her nose gently with his thumb. Inside, she danced.

'New books?' he asked, plucking some marram grass and tucking it behind her pretty ear where it became as beautiful as any flower might have been.

'Not practical,' she reasoned, 'coffee blotches and tea stains would render them second-hand before they were even bought first time around.'

'Perhaps discounts for customers who bring a book!' enthused William.

'Perhaps,' Chloë said.

'We'd better get cracking,' he declared, 'if you want to be up and running for the season.'

'I'd planned to do some measuring and a spot of painting tomorrow. Want to come? I mean, join me?'

'Readily, Chloë, will I do both.'

Chloë and William met at Number Three the next morning. Along with a tape-measure and a clutch of paintbrushes and rollers, Chloë arrived with Mr and Mrs Andrews and introduced them cordially to William. They explained to him that they were only temporarily housed in the postcard and that once Chloë had primed and painted the long wall, they would move from their lodgings at Jocelyn's house to take residence on it. For the time being, William made two slits in the rim of the polystyrene cup and tucked Mr and Mrs Andrews into it.

Suitably mounted and positioned on the back window-sill, Mr and Mrs Andrews oversaw the lackeys and remarked to themselves that the job would be done quicker if the labourers did not kiss each other quite so much. Chloë turned Mr and Mrs Andrews around so that they faced the garden and she could no longer hear them.

Back at Peregrine's Gully at tea-time, William suggested they rummage in his spare room.

'Look at all this stuff – there's plenty you might find useful at Number Three. I *thought* you'd like the driftwood mirror – of course you can have it. We can take it there and experiment with positioning.'

Experiment with positioning. The words hung loaded. Chloë cursed herself for a short but unmistakable giggle and turned her attention to the whisky bottle.

'It was *you*!' she cooed, remembering when she had seen it. Not so long ago, really. Seems an age, actually.

She dug in her pockets and trickled a clutch of coppers into the bottle.

'Pennies for my potter,' she said sweetly. William was standing at the other end of the room, holding the guitar and striking a spontaneous chord.

'You're lovely, Chloë,' he said, quite unabashed.

'Am I?' she responded, embarrassed and reddening. 'Heavens.'

'Very,' he assured her, 'heavenly.'

'I think you're really rather nice too,' she said softly, eyes wide and smile likewise.

'Does that make us a pair?' William laughed. Chloë considered this.

'Yes,' she declared, nodding and clutching her hands in triumph, 'we match.'

'Does that mean we're a couple, then?' asked William quietly, walking over to her and taking her hands in his.

'Yes,' Chloë proclaimed, squeezing his fingers and taking them to her lips, 'it does.'

William lunged for her with a barrage of kisses. She

retaliated with a deluge of her own. They stopped, slightly breathless, their eyes hazed, their senses ablaze.

'I –' William began, stroking her neck and then kissing it. Chloë did not mind that his sentence remained unfinished. She touched his ear lobe very gently and then stood on her tiptoes to kiss it.

'Make love to me,' she whispered aloud for the first time ever, her words coming as naturally to her as the notion.

They wriggled each other out of their clothing, the guitar knocked to the floor with an atonal crash that they hardly heard.

'Chloë,' William murmured hoarsely. She held her head to one side, admiring the curve of his neck, the dip of his cheek, the amazing light emanating from his eyes. No sculpture was ever so beautiful. Such beauty could not be sculpted, or painted, for its reality was surely too vast to capture and contain. But it had caught her and she felt absorbed right into it.

Both the feel of William's body and the sight of it gave her untold pleasure. Here, at last, was a man with whom she could be both passionate and tender; for whom her surging feelings of love and desire had blended. She needn't be restricted to one or the other, for William had enabled the release of both impulses in her. Thus they laughed as much as they sighed and their eyes were open as often as they were closed involuntarily with the pleasure of it all. Chloë both stroked and grabbed him, kissed him lightly and sucked him greedily. She looked deep into his eyes with tenderness, and eyed his cock with unabashed desire. Love and lust merged, and the combination was unimaginably beautiful and intoxicating.

As William pushed his cock deep inside her, he swore involuntarily and apologized beseechingly. Chloë laughed at him sweetly and then let herself gasp and moan at the feel of him moving deep within her, her eyes locked on to his all the while. They found their rhythm in intense silence but when William came, he called her name, holding her face and watching her with incredulity and ardour.

'Oh Chloë, oh God, Chloë, Chloë.'

But he chanted in his own voice; the lilt of his Cornish accent, as much as his touch, precipitating her own orgasm.

As he stroked her in that precious, lazy, post-orgasm non-time, he realized how a woman's body was indeed more malleable than clay and, at last, he deemed it preferable. He was still the clay-caked cliff man with goat, but he had now tidied a space for one other. And she filled it perfectly. And filled it gladly. This russet-headed humming girl who talked to paintings.

'Stay?' asks William.

'I'll stay,' says Chloë.

Later, when it's bedtime for them both at William's home, she finds a small twig on the pillow.

'Dancing twig for my humming girl,' William explains, clambering into bed swaddled in a T-shirt, boxer shorts and socks. She smiles at him and places the twig carefully on the upturned tea chest, next to her brooch and on top of a copy of *Poldark*. She's wearing leggings, a sweatshirt and William's socks too.

It is freezing.

It is winter.

'I dreamt about your brooch,' he told her the next morning as she brewed tea and measured out Quaker's oats and milk from a beaker into a saucepan. 'You weren't in it, though. There was a tall lady wearing it, very elegant and graceful, but kind too. I'm sure I know her, I'm sure I do, but I just can't place her. Strange. Probably an actress, or something. Maybe the character from a book.'

'Maybe,' murmured Chloë, who was only half listening. Though the porridge resembled wallpaper paste and clods were forming before her eyes, she was utterly absorbed in the choice of William's gorgeous handmade breakfast bowls.

Chloë knew then that she had first fallen for the potter through his pots. Their creator could only be as beautiful as they were, and William's ceramics were quite the most lovely things she had ever seen. Genuine, secret and so very strong; quiet and serene until the music was released. Here indeed was a man for all seasons, for did he not encapsulate the romance of Carl, the passion of Ronan, the companionship of Fraser? If he was this dazzling in winter, what could he be like in spring! And summer. Ah, autumn too!

FIFTY-ONE

'William?'

'Yes, Chloë, what d'you want?'

'Pardon!'

'You *do* want something, don't you!'

'How do you *know*?'

'Because you put a "y" in my name?'

'Hey?'

'You call me "Willi-yum".'

'Do I?'

'You do!'

'How do I say it when I'm not after something?'

'You say "William" – although latterly, you've taken to calling me "Double You", which I actually rather like!'

'You do?'

'I do!'

'Guess what?'

'What?'

'I rather like it that you call me "Clop" and "Cadders". And that, at the height of passion, you chug my name out and then elongate it – like you're on a roller-coaster!'

'Sorry?'

'*Chlo, chlo, chlo – weee*!'

'And you don't mind?'

'Not at all – no need to blush!'

'Am I?'

'You are indeed. Anyway, Willi-yum with a "y", can I ask you something?'

'Shoot!'

'I was wondering, do you not feel you'd like a practice run in the car before we go to London for your show?'

'Pardon? A practice?'

'Dummy run? You know, a long journey: plenty of pit-stops, lots of mirror-signal-manoeuvre practice!'

'I *do* know. What you mean is, either you don't trust my driving, or you want to go somewhere and would I mind chauffeuring you!'

'Actually, well, yes!'

'Which?'

'The latter.'

'Well, that's fine then – had it been the former, I'd have told you to take the train! Well, where then?'

'Wales – Gin wrote to tell me that the greyhound died and she's just as sad as she was when Jocelyn passed away. I thought I might visit. I'd love her to meet you. And, er, I thought we might call in and see your father. I'd love to meet him.'

'Hmm.'

'*Hmm?*'

'I'm thinking! Hmm.'

'Have you thought?'

'Yes.'

'And?'

'Yes, I'll drive to Wales; I'll meet Sherry or whoever, and you shall meet my pa.'

'William?'

'What do you want now!'

'Sorry, was there a "y" in there?'

'Loud and clear!'

'Say "Mars bar", please?'

'Mars bar?'

'Yes.'

'OK, Mars bar! There! Mars bloody bar! Why are you smiling? Why are you looking at me like that?'

'Because you say it just like me!'

Chloë was stricken with *déjà vu* just as soon as they'd crossed the Severn. It was but a month off a year since she had arrived in Wales with her rucksack heavy, her mind full and her confidence low. How young she had seemed! Troubled, small – a wholly different Chloë; one still choked by a film of Islington and subservience. Now her rucksack was tucked into a corner of William's spare room. And much of its contents decorated accommodating areas of her bedsit, as well as Peregrine's Gully and Jasper's Studio, as Chloë had decided to call it. William did not mind. (Nor did Barbara, who had discovered Chloë's trainers just inside the kitchen door and thought them quite the tastiest things ever.)

Mac was joining them on the trip.

'I'd like to see the old boy, wish him Merry Christmas and say goodbye – who knows which one of us will pop their clogs first but I'd say I'm odds-on favourite!' he had proclaimed to William, in a disconcertingly chipper way.

Mac sat in the back of the car and watched Chloë trying hard not to fidget. He observed William tap her knee and turn it into a gentle caress. He saw Chloë take her fingers over his and stroke his knuckles. He heard them chat animatedly; finishing sentences for each other, or leaving them half spoken but utterly understood. He saw Chloë shoot William glances that were unseen, and he watched William's cheekbones rise with the potency of a private smile. Mac was not a gooseberry; he was superfluous, and it delighted him. He sat quietly and absorbed the scene, nodding sagely at all the details.

'Here,' Chloë pipped, 'up this lane! A few yards on the left. Oh God, I mean right!'

It was all strangely familiar to William and when he saw the fruit bowl on the kitchen table he gave Chloë's pony-tail a loving tug.

So it was *you!*

'Chloë!'

'Gin!'

They embraced warmly and Gin told her she had quite changed: 'You have colour in your cheeks I'll attribute to Ireland, strength in your bones I'll say comes from Scotland, and a glint in your eye that's pure Cornish!'

Chloë looked over to William who grinned openly, and then she looked down at her boots while smiling proudly.

'How do you do, William!' Gin boomed, thrusting her hand towards him and wiping it on her jodhpurs when she saw it was clogged with sugar beet. 'How's your father?'

'My father?' queried William.

'Have you not visited him? Or are you going tomorrow? Don't tell me I'm the *raison d'être* for your trip?' she said, covering the potential *faux pas* with a loud voice and a lunge for the kettle. 'Mac! How are you?'

'Dandy, Gin, just dandy!'

Both caught a drift of the immediate bewilderment racking Chloë and William so Gin fiddled with tea bags and Mac tried to coax Yap from the chair.

'Do – do you know each other? Have you met?' flummoxed Chloë.

Gin and Mac stared at each other.

'Don't know him from Adam!' Gin declared with a hint of a wink that only Mac saw.

'Wouldn't know her from Eve!' colluded Mac, twitching his nose in code.

Chloë took William on a guided tour. Mac declined to join them. And declined from telling them he knew Skirrid End as well as his own cottage. Gin then took them all to visit the final resting place of the greyhound. She had been buried under a crab-apple tree. With all the remaining Scrabble pieces. Gin vowed she would never play again.

In some ways, Chloë was glad that they refused Gin's offer to stay the night at the farm. Skirrid End was sacred to her and to the memory of Carl, for without Carl there would certainly have been no William. They readily accepted the offer of a hearty supper. However, before they had taken a mouthful, they were victims of a hapless reshuffle of absolutely no point whatsoever.

But perhaps it has a very particular point, thought Chloë later as she listened to William sleeping, gazing out of a small window over the velvet-cloaked dingle to the lumbering hills asleep beyond. *While I'm in Cornwall, getting on with living, Gin and her gang are still reshuffling merrily, if haplessly, in the shadow of the black hill. Meanwhile, Gus sups port in the drawing-room, while sculptures surround him, serene and silent. On the shores of the loch, Fraser melts ice-cream over the Aga, and primps and pampers and lusts after his guests. In Notting Hill, Jasper is knitting and Peregrine is most probably doing* The Times *crossword. Everyone – and that includes me, yes it does – is in their true home. And the world can turn. And the seasons can change.*

An owl haunted the valley with his call. Chloë inched open the window and seared her nose with the scent of mid-winter. The Usk was babbling busily, despite the hour.

'That everyone is where they should be makes me feel safe. Safe, confident and eager to continue in Cornwall. Because I know now that the *genius loci* – the spirit of the place – is found not just in the lie of the land but through the contentment and commitment of those who dwell there.'

'I spy,' enthused Chloë, today in the back seat, 'with my little eye, something beginning with, um, "h"!'

'Hedgerow!' Mac triumphed. ' "Little lines of sportive wood run wild"!'

'Wordsworth!' exclaimed Chloë quietly, catching Mac wink at her from the rear-view mirror.

Jocelyn! thought Chloë, remembering how her godmother had quoted great Wordsworth in her letter for Wales. She touched her brooch subconsciously for reassurance and then found she needed none. How *was* that?

A year on. A year full on.

How easily she could have remained the Chloë that Jocelyn's first letter had found – seemingly trapped in a hostile city, locked into an unfulfilling job and smothered by totally the wrong man. Chloë gazed at the back of William's head. Tawny-wicker-basket-owl. She widened her gaze and took in the back of Mac's head too. Two men so dear to her now, and yet unknown this time last year.

I was living in a city which so sapped me, too good for a truly lousy job, and I was *too precious for awful Brett. But how did I come to be here, today? How in heavens did I do it? How did you get me here, Jocelyn?*

I could easily not have gone.

And though in some ways I've been cushioned by my travels, my inheritance – a year out, as it were – I reckon I've learnt far more than ever I could, snared in London. A year on. I've grown. Up.

She looked out of the window. Gwent, Wales. Previously unknown, now familiar. Remembered always for introducing Chloë to fun, frolics and unconditional acceptance.

Across the water, Antrim, Northern Ireland.

Where I learnt to express myself, stick up for myself, and found that I'm actually quite strong.

Way, way ahead, Loch Lomond and the Trossachs, Scotland.

Where I discovered a brother and learnt how to fly, up and onwards; strong enough to decide to continue on my own.

Underneath them all, Cornwall, England.

Where I alighted with all that I'd experienced. And where, at last, I have found my home, my métier *and the man I think I'll love forever.*

Heavens! How the notion of those three concepts had previously unnerved me.

Chloë accepted a boiled sweet from Mac and sucked it while her head juddered against the window. She saw her hazy reflection in the glass; swallowed sweetness.

Hullo, I'm Chloë Cadwallader. I'm happy that I am.

' "M", "m" – "m" for Mountain,' William said, inadvertently interrupting Chloë's thoughts. She was pleased though, the here and now were fine. This trip back to Wales was suddenly so much more than just an enjoyable jaunt; it was affirming, proving to Chloë just how far she'd come, how happy she was with the place she had found, the space she had carved.

'Are we there yet?' she cleared her throat and asked William, brushing away a tear that no one saw.

'Nearly. Your go, Mac.'

'I spy, bla bla, something beginning with "J"!'

'J?' laughed Chloë. 'You may as well have said "q"! What on earth begins with "j" in Wales – apart from Jones-the-Thingummy!'

'J,' pondered William.

'J,' mused Chloë, 'je, je, je –'

'Here we are!' announced William, crunching up the deep gravel drive of the nursing home.

'J for *what*?' demanded Chloë as she helped Mac from the car.

'Je-jar of je-juniper je-jelly!' Mac announced, pointing to the curious home-made condiment Gin had foisted on them.

'Ah!' laughed Chloë, wondering why Mac was regarding her so quizzically.

William was quite shocked to see that the customary early

winter demise of a proportion of the residents had not been made up for. The remaining rattle of old bones now made a hollow echo in the vacuous room. He was slightly anxious and walked ahead of Chloë and Mac. How he wished his father would stride over and say 'Chloë! Delighted to meet you. Heard so much about you from William.' How he would love his father's approval, whatever it was worth.

He saw him immediately, now not so far down the dwindling line of window gazers, sitting still and listless. The old face, nearly transparent, cracking into a semblance of life with a gentle tap to the shoulder.

'Benedict?'

'No, Dad.'

'William!'

The recognition lasted but a moment, but in that time William saw his father's eyes glisten and felt a lump knot itself in his own throat. There was too much to say and no time to say it. But a strong squeeze from his father's hand and a full smile from William spoke silent reams. By the time Chloë and Mac arrived, William had turned into Benedict, and his father into any old Alzheimer's victim.

His eyes lit up with a lively sparkle when Chloë's face came close and smiled at him.

'Hullo!' he said shyly, holding out his hand that Chloë might take it.

'Hullo!' she cooed, holding his hand between both of hers and perching on the footstool. She asked how he was and he said he was as fit as a fiddle, thanking her very much. Lovely day, she declared. Lovely jubbly, he replied. They continued to converse happily about their health and the weather. Chloë removed her jacket and laid it neatly over her knee, remarking that wasn't it warm for the time of year. Balmy, he said, only it sounded inescapably like 'barmy'. She tried not to notice that he was staring at her breasts but it was difficult to ignore as he had started to drool; moistened lips, saliva slipping. A bony finger trembled its way towards her. She held her breath. Mac and William were talking quietly and were unaware of her discomfort. His finger neared her as the dribble reached his chin. However, he touched only the brooch; lightly, tracing the pattern with ease and confidence, and with no hint of a shake. She unpinned it and wrapped his hands around it. He clasped his hands very tight and looked Chloë full on while tears filmed over his eyes.

'Je, je, je,' he whispered, bedraggled.

'Juniper jelly jar?' asked Chloë kindly.

Unexpectedly, he gave her a most reproachful look.

'Is he je, je, je-ing?' whispered William gently in her ear. She nodded. 'Let's get a cuppa,' he suggested, laying his hand gently first on Chloë's head and then on his father's brittle shoulder.

'Hullo, old thing!' says Mac, easing his stiff frame into a plastic chair and taking a share in the footstool with William's father.

'Hullo!' he booms back.

'Well,' Mac declares, 'some welcome!'

They sit in affable silence. William's father unbuckles his hands just enough for Mac to peep at their precious contents.

'Je,' he starts.

'Je,' Mac responds with sincerity. His patience gives his friend the impetus to try and finish the word; searching for his tongue and his strength, sifting through memories that are just too beautiful and sad.

'Jocelyn!' he declares at last in a hoarse whisper, breathing the word out as if it could well be one of his last. He sighs with relief, as if only the scourge of a stammer prevented him from saying it sooner.

'Jocelyn!' Mac confirms. Their eyes light up and a smile is shared. 'And all is well, old thing,' says Mac, coaxing the brooch from him, 'very well indeed. Amazing what a gentle shove can achieve.'

He kisses the old man on the forehead and they hold

hands and share their past silently until William and Chloë return with sweetened tea for everyone.

'Perers!' Jasper fumbled in his pockets for his spectacles, tapping his chest, thighs and buttocks extensively. 'Peregrine!'

'On the lav!' came the distant reply.

'Letter from her ladyship,' Jasper bellowed, 'and I am in want of spectacles!'

'I'll just do the paperwork and then I'll be with you!' shouted Peregrine.

Jasper took the envelope through to the drawing-room and sat himself down, tapping the letter against his knee to the tune of *Mission Impossible.*

'Not so impossible after all!' He winked at a photograph of Jocelyn. Peregrine floated in and sashayed over to him, curling himself neatly on the arm of the chair.

'Darling,' he declared, 'you'll find your glasses on top of your head! But oh, 'tis too late! I'm here and be-spectacled, so I shall read. Hand it over – now – young man!'

Pushing his bottom lip out and batting his eyelids, Jasper gave Peregrine the envelope.

'Let's see what grammatical atrocities the girl presents today, shall we!'

'Even if they're utterly appalling,' said Jasper, pulling up his silk socks and wincing at his scaly shins, 'I'd like it in full. No bla bla-ing, if you please.'

'Yes, master!' lauded Peregrine, using a pencil to open the envelope. They rejoiced in discovering three pages written on both sides. Peregrine scanned through quickly. 'Ha!' he cried. 'Ho!' he boomed. He laid the letter flat on his knees and fixed Jasper with a smile and a twinkle not seen for some time. 'They're coming to stay!'

'Read,' Jasper hollered, 'verbatim!'

'*Darling Ladies, it's me and I brandish apologies for the tardy gap between letters. I've been very busy and most preoccupied.* She underlines "most". *William is still a tremendously nice fellow but he is now much more too.* Oh, do listen to this Jasp! *I have fallen irrevocably in love with him and want to be with him always.* Irrevocably! Ah, the poppet! Cliché Cadwallader continues: *He is music and light, colour and depth and I do love him so. I sleep safe and happy and I awake content and grateful. We travel to the dark side of the moon and back, and stand at the still point of the turning world.* Have we not warned her of plagiarism?'

'Hush, Peregrine, you're far too hard! This is a first for Chloë. We were there too, remember!'

'Where?'

'The dark side of the moon, of course. Now stop taking the mickey and read the bloody letter, would you?'

'Were we on a package tour? Ouch! That hurt! She says that Number Three is taking shape. She's painted the walls a mottled damson she claims would make Fraser proud. Picked out the skirting and cornicing, sanded and varnished the floor entirely herself, and stripped the front door down. *If it's this satisfying before I've even opened for business, my career looks rosy indeed.* Ah! *Jasper*, she asks, *I'd so love you to cast your eye over the garden. We've cleared out the rubble and, though small, the space is crying out for the touch and vision of a true horticulturalist. I'd like it to be aromatic – William reckons it will be a sun trap during the summer. Any ideas? Perhaps you and Peregrine might like to come and stay? Fraser is coming in February, which is his off-season, to do adventurous things with calico and muslin. How about late January?* How about it indeed?'

'I'm counting the days!'

'Little minx – listen here! *You see, we'd love to return the hospitality – which is a somewhat presumptuous way of asking if William and I could stay with you in a fortnight. He's having a show of his ceramics at the South Bank again – they're to die for but for heaven's sake don't take that literally when you do see them! Please say we can, and say you will!*'

'You can!' sang Jasper.

'We will!' cried Peregrine.

'That it?'

'Gracious no! Another page to go! *I see now*, she says, *why Jocelyn sent me here. It is not so much her link with the place, I don't think, as her intuition that it would suit me unconditionally. She was right, clever lady. I longed for her in Wales, I craved her in Ireland and I searched hard for her in Scotland. But I found her here in Cornwall. How I love her and all I have learnt from her. I've felt closer to her here than in any of the other locations and yet I don't need to talk to her so much and I seek her approval less often. How strange!*'

'No, Chlo, not really.'

'Not at all! *And so*, she concludes, *my days are full with my recent finds! There was buried treasure here in Cornwall but it took me a year and a journey to learn how to look for it. Now that I have found it, I am going to hold on tight and cherish all that I have. In that way I will be doing Jocelyn proud and keeping her memory alive, don't you think? I've struck gold in William, but the jewel that I found is that Cornwall is my home. And it's heaven. There's no place like it – I never knew. William told me this morning that I make him "blissfully happy". Me! Can you imagine! Do I really have that power? That gift? I always thought true happiness was solely of one's own making – but William makes me far happier than I could ever have made myself. And did I tell you how beautiful his pots are?*'

'That it?'

'Yes. Can you believe she began her last sentence with an "and"?'

'That's our Chloë!'

'Our Clodders indeed. What fun it shall be to see her.'

'And him!'

'Together. Clever old Jocelyn!'

'Wily old thing!'

Peregrine went over to the mantelpiece, bowed to Sẽnor and Señora Andrews, and then brought back a photograph of Jocelyn taken a few months before she died. Swathed in velvet; wrapped in her bright countenance. There was something going on in her eyes that could only be read in retrospect.

'Ah well,' sighed Jasper, winking at Jocelyn, 'the circle is now complete; the tale told; the picture perfect.'

'Indeed,' agreed Peregrine, 'the old girl can finally turn in her grave and go to sleep, settled and content.' He took the frame and buffed it lovingly against his cashmere pullover.

EPILOGUE

Mr Andrews unfurled a cream silk stocking up and over his leg, admiring his shapely calf muscles in the driftwood mirror as he did so. He procrastinated over which pair of calfskin shoes he would wear and, by the time his wife gave her melodious rap to his door, he had whittled it down to any of three pairs.

'Which oh which?' he implored her, fret and worry etched persuasively across his brow.

'The black. With the plain buckle I think.'

'You are a doll,' he sighed, 'but which cravat, in heaven's name?'

'White damask,' she exclaimed as if it were a very simple question.

'And the tricorn edged in gold?'

'Well, what do *you* think?'

'I want to look dandy for our girl Cadwallader. After all, it is her generosity that has seen us so comfortably ensconced in this delightful abode.'

'And away from those bloody Latino counterparts in bloody Notting Hill,' Mrs Andrews furthered with a little shudder.

'Language, dear,' chided her husband.

They looked around them. All was neat, tidy and comfortable. And deserted. It was nice to have the place and some peace to themselves, having arrived late the day before when nearly every chair was taken and all the muffins had gone. The silence now was welcome. Soon enough, the healthy din which had surrounded them the previous day would no doubt be upon them again; conversations in earnest, letters spoken out loud whilst being penned, poetry being recited quietly in a corner. Not that they minded, they were quite looking forward to it. Colourful. Friendly. Ambient.

Mrs Andrews straightened the lace panel on her sky-blue frock and fluffed the frill of her sleeves.

'Oh, you look divine!' enthused her husband in a gruff voice laced with desire. 'Come here, wench!'

They embraced tenderly, Mr Andrews bucking gently up against the skirts of his wife's dress while she wriggled daintily against him.

'Mr Andrews,' she declared, quite breathless, 'per-lease!'

She walked over to the driftwood mirror and straightened her straw hat before pulling it jauntily to one side. Running a finger over the oddment of tables and chairs, she held it up for her husband to inspect. It was perfectly clean.

'Good old Chloë!'

'Quite the house-proud hussy,' Mr Andrews declared.

'Oh, she doesn't *live* here at Number Three,' Mrs Andrews informed him, 'she's still in those funny digs near the beach and the artists.'

'Not building a love nest with her potter chappie?'

'No. Or "not yet awhile" as Chloë herself said to me yesterday. They are, however, building their love on very firm foundations. They are taking their time and luxuriating in all the various stages of finding one's true fellow.'

'Sensible and sweet,' said Mr Andrews.

'That's our girl,' his wife replied. She went over to the window which looked out to the small sunken garden at the back. An ivy had started to clamber up a trellis. Snowdrops peeped out here and there, and small green shoots stuck their heads above good soil to see if it was a good time to grow. It was.

'Come, my love,' Mrs Andrews called to her husband, 'see the magic woven by old Queen Jasper.'

'Dinky!' rolled Mr Andrews. 'Isn't that grand!' They admired a large, burnished terracotta urn out of which a healthy pieris was beginning to blaze.

'Is that one of his?' asked Mr Andrews.

'Need you ask!' his wife retorted, sweeping her arm in a wide arc to direct attention to the large consignment of William's ceramics elsewhere in the room. She sat herself down demurely in a small, comfortable sofa festooned with cushions. He stood beside her, his leg cocked, his hand in his pocket. She took a paperback book from a small, rickety table at her side and placed it in her lap.

'From Chloë's selection here,' she explained, 'I wanted a nice introduction to modern literature so she suggested this, it's called *Middlemarch*, by George Eliot. Rather good, actually.'

'Never heard of 'im!'

'Her,' Mrs Andrews corrected witheringly.

'How you women now get up and go!' Mr Andrews marvelled. 'Look at this place, a credit to Cadwallader, don't you think?'

'Certainly,' enthused his wife, looking about her and noting all the details. Tables and chairs. Plants and pottery. Two hat-and-cloak stands either side of the door; one antique and in oak, the other contemporary and in steel. Etchings clamouring for space in between the bookshelves. Finally, the Andrews estate, pride of place, above the counter behind which Chloë surveyed her kingdom while pouring coffee into pixie-clad mugs.

'She's found her feet and her home,' Mr Andrews declared, perusing the scene and nodding sagely.

'*And*, my duck, her clitoris,' added Mrs Andrews, 'via dear Mr Coombes.'

Mr Andrews, speechless momentarily, was about to admonish his wife's impropriety when the front door opened and the wind-chimes rang out.

'Morning you two!' greeted Chloë, carrier bags heaving and hanging from her bicycle handlebars.

'A very good morning to you, Cadwallader dear,' said Mr Andrews concentrating hard on his corn stooks.

'Morning, dear,' called Mrs Andrews from her bench, winking.

'Right!' said Chloë, unpacking cartons of milk and a clutch of books. 'To work.'

[illegible]
and Mr [illegible].
Mr Andrews, [illegible] his [illegible]
[illegible] when the [illegible]
[illegible]
[illegible] 'Cut' [illegible]
[illegible]
[illegible]
Andrews [illegible]
[illegible] Mr Andrews [illegible]
[illegible]
[illegible]
[illegible]